GREG BEAR . . . sets a compelling tale in a place that is both fantastic and unnervingly familiar.

DAVID BRIN . . . extrapolates a plague crisis to its logical—and stunning—conclusion.

VONDA N. McINTYRE . . . examines an alien visitation that touches the earth . . . at its deepest geologic roots.

KIM STANLEY ROBINSON . . . strikes chords both human and divine in a story of faith and miracles in suburban Illinois.

MICHAEL SWANWICK . . . follows three teenagers who climb down a magical cliff into the stuff of legends.

These remarkable stories and much more . . . in
FULL SPECTRUM 2

"A BEVY OF STYLISH, DELIGHTFUL AND INSPIRING FICTION . . : TRULY A DEFINITIVE WORK OF THE IMAGINATION."
—*The Ottawa Citizen*

Edited by Lou Aronica and Shawna McCarthy

FULL SPECTRUM

Full Spectrum

2

EDITED BY

Lou Aronica,
Shawna McCarthy,
Amy Stout,
and Pat LoBrutto

BANTAM BOOKS

NEW YORK · TORONTO · LONDON · SYDNEY · AUCKLAND

FULL SPECTRUM II

A Bantam Spectra Book / May 1990

ISBN 0-553-28530-0

Published simultaneously in the United States and Canada

Bantam Books are published by Bantam Books, a division of
Bantam Doubleday Dell Publishing Group, Inc. Its trademark,
consisting of the words "Bantam Books" and the portrayal of a
rooster, is Registered in U.S. Patent and Trademark Office and in
other countries, Marca Registrada, Bantam Books, 666 Fifth Ave-
nue, New York, New York 10103

PRINTED IN THE UNITED STATES OF AMERICA

OPM   0 9 8 7 6 5 4 3 2 1

Contents

Full Spectrum

2

'Saurus Wrecks

EDWARD BRYANT

I'M GLAD I LIVED to see a time when the world became a more primitive place.

People that remember Rex generally knew him long before Cycad Center was Cycad Center. That was the time when that sleepy little town was still on the maps as Goshen, a portentous name that had never panned out in the past, and so no one had any idea that the big new power plant they built sixty miles to the west near Stubblefield was going to change things mightily. This was back when Rex was what used to be called the town drunk, long before state-supported mental health centers started cleaning up people's terms. I remember Rexford Allyn Pugnell —he loved using all three dollar-fifty names when he was intoxicated—sprawled morning, afternoon and evening across the wrought iron bench the Ladies' Aid had donated to the town square in 1946.

All this was before the steam plume, before Paleo State Park, before the torrent of tourists. It used to be that the only life in Goshen was on Saturday when the farmers and ranchers came into town to do their trading. Tourists? That was a joke. There wasn't an Interstate for sixty miles. Somebody once wanted to erect a billboard at the edge of town reading: GOSHEN—GATEWAY TO NEBRASKA, but somebody else took him seriously and so the project never went anywhere. Such was the fate of most efforts at civic improvement.

But then came the energy boom and the bright fellows who decided to build their gigawatt coal-fired generating plant over in Stubblefield. The natives who'd bothered to read the environmental impact statements were just as shocked as the illiterates and the apathetic when, five years later, the first units went on line and the plumes went a mile or three straight up. The company's public relations people pointed out that this was just steam, superheated but clean.

And then the prevailing westerlies started toppling the plumes over to the east, bending them down until they hit the ground right here around Goshen. Simply put, the climate changed. I remember one government scientist calling Goshen "a vest-pocket climate." It just got warmer than everywhere else around, and wet. Very wet.

At first all anybody had the imagination to consider was truck-farming. It took Rex to point out in the letter column of the weekly *Modern Times-Record* that ferns could grow in Goshen when they wouldn't thrive anywhere else close to a thousand miles south. So what? the editor responded, if more politely. The town council was not impressed. "I don't think there's much of a commercial market for ferns," said the mayor. "Maybe florists could use them as filler in preparing bouquets with *real* flowers, but I don't think our fortune lies there."

"That isn't the point," said Rex. "The town should ban the cultivation of all flowering plants."

"Huh?" That was the collective reaction of the council.

"None of you has any imagination," Rex said. I know he spoke all this, because I was there that night, ready to argue for a tighter leash law—my neighbor McGreggor's dogs had been at the roses in my front yard again. The council tried to shoo Rex away from the microphone assigned to the public. Rex was having none of it. "I worshipped Roy Chapman Andrews," he said. Everyone stared at him like his porch light had finally quit flickering and gone totally out. I knew vaguely that that Andrews fellow had written something about dinosaurs. "You just won't understand, none of you." Rex turned with as much dignity as unshaven old man in dirty coveralls with a fifth of Old Pondscum on his breath can muster, and stomped out. At the door of the meeting room, he paused, turned and said, "You want a sign? I'll show you, ye of little vision. I can save this stinking, shrinking town."

No one said anything much for a while after Rex left. When they did, it was a while before I could get a word in edgewise about the leash law. From my straight-back chair in the rear of the room, I caught some of the muttered words.

" 'Bout as useless as his folks," said the mayor, shaking his head.

Councilwoman Purdy said, "*Artist.* We don't need no stinking artists. . . ." At least that's what it sounded like from the back.

Sheriff Feeley said "Goddamn *dreamer,*" as though "dreamer" were a sort of epithet.

When I finally got my turn at the mike, I groused about McGreggor's dogs and the city attorney said he'd look into the matter. And that was it. I had the feeling that probably I should give up on roses and plant yucca. Or ferns.

The next morning, Rex appeared at my door at seven, before I'd left for the school. "Mornin', Miz Devereaux," he said as I looked past him and saw the dogs nosing around the roses.

"Shoo!" I cried.

Rex stared at me and started to turn away.

"Not you," I said, gesturing toward the dogs.

He smiled with comprehension. "There's something you can use that won't hurt neither plant nor beast." He gave me the name of a chemical I could buy at Deemer's Pharmacy.

"Thank you, Rex," I said. Then I remembered how early it was for a man of Rex's years to be up and about. I caught myself then. I didn't know *how* old he really was. "Is there something I can do for you?"

He gestured toward the side of the house. "You've got a lot of old chicken wire tangled up behind your garage. Wonder if I could use it."

I shrugged. "I expect so, Rex. I've got no use for it." I hesitated. "What's it for?"

It was his turn to pause. After a moment, he said, "I'm gonna build a sign."

Later on, of course, I realized he wasn't talking about a

billboard. What Rex had in mind was more theatrical; one might even say, more biblical.

Rex also asked if he could clean up the weedy lot I owned to the west of the house. Fine. And would I mind if he built something there which would make things better?

I looked into his eyes. The irises gleamed watery blue and the whites were completely bloodshot. I seemed to hear a voice pleading.

Again I shrugged. "Of course. Do whatever you like."

He must have found other caches of chicken wire around town. By nightfall, when I returned from parent-teacher conferences, the mound of twisted, tarnished metal mesh in the lot by my house was immense. There were other materials piled there too, things I didn't remember having on my vacant lot. I saw a stack of irregular lengths of steel rods that I suspected had come from the State Highway Department yard.

Rex was industriously working the following morning when I left for the school. I asked him what he was making —the form meant nothing to me so far. All I could make out were what seemed to be a pair of large three-toed feet. I was reminded of the elephant's-foot umbrella stands my father had been so enamored of.

His answer was not informative. He grinned and said, "You'll see."

I thought I had a clue that night when I saw the body had grown. I saw the tail. Rex had performed an amount of work I hadn't suspected him of being able to do.

The next night I saw the head starting to take shape and I was sure. "You're building a dinosaur."

"Absolutely correct," Rex said, carefully bending a foot-long tooth into the correct curvature.

"It's not just any dinosaur, is it?" I could spell paleontology, of course, but I knew little else about it.

"No," Rex said, "it's not." If honest pride were spit, Rex would have had to wipe his lips with a beach towel. He gestured proudly. "This is a tyrannosaurus, the big one, the king, the Elvis of reptiles."

"How do you know about all this?" I said. The wire form was taking shape well. This was no amateur attempt.

"You know what I was before I was a drunk?" Rex said. I shook my head. I searched with little hope for something polite to say. "Not really." Rex had been a drunk when I moved here.

"A dreamer," he said, shaking his head as if sad. "This town is hell on dreams." I thought I saw the glint of a tear in the mercury glow from the yard light. "Sometimes I still can dream."

"So what are you going to do?" I said.

"I'm not going to tell you. Not trying to be impolite," he added quickly. "I'll just let the results speak for themselves."

The results spoke more and more eloquently as Rex erected a frame out of the rusted steel rods and laid the chicken wire mesh over that. I realized the dinosaur was going to stand close to twenty feet high.

"It looks good," I said one Saturday afternoon.

"Thanks, ma'am."

"What are you going to do with this?"

"I told you," he said. "I want to show Goshen a sign. The generating plant, the steam plumes, the climate changing right here and nowhere else, it's all a gift they will squander out of ignorance."

"A famine of imagination," I murmured.

He heard me and nodded. "I want to show them a dream. I want them to learn," He grinned, but there was something forced about it, a painful tension I saw drawn along his jaw and the cords of his neck. "It will be painless. I don't think they'll mind getting rich."

"I'm sure they won't." I didn't know what he was talking about.

No one minded much of anything until Rex started Phase Two of the dinosaur construction. He borrowed my wheelbarrow and brought it back full of manure. He brought other loads of dead leaves and chopped weeds and started filling in the form he'd made of wire. The hot, moist air didn't help. I got two calls that night from my neighbors. I said I'd try to do something about the odor.

Next morning, when I relayed the complaints to Rex, he smiled and said, "It's the smell of life, Miz Devereaux. This tyrannosaurus is coming back to life. It's as natural as just about anything I can think of. Just give me some time, please?"

I tried. The complaints mounted. A deputy came by to ask if I had a construction permit for what I was doing on my adjacent property. On beyond the obvious, I had no answer.

"What *am* I doing on this property?" I said to Rex later. "What is it *you're* doing besides building a prehistoric monster that offends my neighbors?"

"Planting," he said quietly. "I'm just planting." He started to say more, but he seemed very tired and his voice dropped too low for me to understand.

"I'll do what I can," I said.

More manure, more mulch each day. Rex must have had a lot of friends on the farms surrounding Goshen. The dinosaur started taking on a sinister dark brown aspect; the smell grew increasingly evil. I began to shut the windows on that side of the house.

Then I encountered the town's new GP, Dr. Silverman, in the parking lot of the Safeway. I'd started going to him with my ailments because he seemed less fossilized than the other doctors in town. Since it was in the air—all too literally for most—the dinosaur and Rex were mostly what we talked about.

"I don't know where he gets the strength," said Dr. Silverman, shaking his head.

"You mean because he's an old man?"

Dr. Silverman became very still. "Rex has other problems." He looked away and said nothing more about that.

That night, Rex asked if he could come in and talk to me. I sat him down on the living room sofa and fetched him some oatmeal cookies and black coffee.

"The king lizard," he said. "It's important not just to me, but to this whole town."

"I believe you," I said, "but a lot of people need convincing."

"It will be a sign, an example."

I no more knew how to respond to that than I had any other time he'd mentioned it.

"I'm dying," said Rex.

I expect my jaw dropped. Now I had an idea what Dr. Silverman had been hinting at.

Rex sighed noisily and coughed. "I'm almost dead. The medicine can't hold things together much longer."

I waited patiently, my heart silently going out to him.

"I need your help, Miz Devereaux. I need more than maybe you can give."

I listened then to what he had to ask me. I think he was surprised because I didn't argue. I simply knew he was right with the same sureness that had caused me to allow him to take over my vacant lot.

"Then you're sure?" he finally said.

"If you are."

"Tomorrow night it is, then," Rex said. He excused himself, taking a final oatmeal cookie along for the road. I noticed now how painfully he seemed to move.

The next day was Saturday and there was no school. I spent most of my waking hours watching from my upstairs window as Rex put the finishing touches on the dinosaur. I marveled at the reptile's massive body rearing in its upright posture, the thick haunches and rear legs, the small, almost delicate upper arms, the heavy, tapering tail, and, especially, the jaws laden with rows of sharp, conical teeth. Heavy and brown—almost gravid-appearing, I thought— the tyrannosaurus towered at least twenty feet into the humid air.

Not just a monument, I thought. Not just the embodiment of one man's obsession.

That night, Rex kissed me goodbye. It was tentative, curiously fluttering, and on the cheek, but it was still a kiss. I had not suspected. "Thank you," I whispered.

We used the aluminum stepladder from the garage. Under cover of darkness, we dragged the ladder out by the base of the dinosaur's tail and set it firmly in the trampled dirt of the lot. Rex climbed up while I held the ladder steady. In the darkness I could sense him doing something to the creature's frame.

"If you don't know the panel's here, you wouldn't suspect a thing," he said. A whole hinged section of the reptile swung away from its body.

Rex came back down the ladder. "I'm set as I'm gonna be," he said. "Ready?"

"I guess so." I didn't want the wistfulness in my voice to spoil the moment for him.

He kissed me again. This time I turned my head so that he touched me on the lips. "Goodbye," I said.

He climbed back up the ladder and used handholds to lift himself up into the dinosaur. I think I heard him

whisper goodbye. Then he swung the movable panel up
and was gone from my sight, my hearing. My life.

I never saw him again, at least not as Rexford Allyn
Pugnell.

What I did see, over the succession of days that came
without my willing them, was the fertile skin of the tyrannosaurus rex as it sprouted green shoots, first light shades,
then darker and darker, a satisfactory mossy hue of reptile.

Others noticed. It got into the *Modern Times-Record*
with a grainy black-and-white photograph. The daily in
Cheyenne got wind and sent up a reporter and a photogra-
pher. The dinosaur made the wire services. Two weeks
later, I saw Rex's creation on a network news program.
The tourists started to arrive. The Chamber of Commerce
welcomed them. The city fathers of Goshen were not entirely foolish. They sensed this was only the barest beginning.

It all grew. The town. The community's ambition. But
especially the tyrannosaurus.

I refused to cede the lot and the reptile to the town. So
far as I was concerned, it was a memorial. But I allowed all
who wished—and there were so very many—to look and to
admire. Few remembered the creature's creator.

As Rex had hoped, it was a beginning.

Each day now, I walk among the cycads and breathe
the heavy, sweltering air. On advice from the town's con-
sulting paleontologist, flowering plants are forbidden by
fiat of the council from cultivation within the town limits.

I grow older in this brave new world.

As I stroll, I feel the closeness of Rex, and know that
once again, after so very long a time, the dinosaur lives.

As do we all.

Whistle

JACK McDEVITT

TWENTY YEARS AGO, Al Redwood walked out. He walked out of Ed Gelman's old intergalactic survey project, out of his job, and out of town. I knew what it was all about, we all knew: Al thought he had a message from M-82.

Gelman laughed at him. And I guess the rest of us did too.

There was no way to prove anything. All he could do was point to a narrow band transmission in the optical range, with peculiar symmetries and repeating pulse, wavelength, and intensity patterns. A laser, Al suspected.

I remember the final confrontation with Gelman, the day Al stormed out, the last time I'd seen him. They were on the front steps of the data center, *on the front steps, for God's sake, scrowming at one another.* Gelman didn't want any little green men hanging around *his* project. So Al quit, and I never even got the chance to say good-bye.

He dropped out of sight for a couple of years. None of us heard anything. His family had money, so he didn't have to work. And then I got a Christmas card from Texas: *Nick,* it said, in his precise handwriting, *it was the pulse clusters all the time. How could we have missed it?*

There was no return address. But I knew that, out there somewhere, Al was still chasing his elusive vision. Over the years, there was more: on D.C. Marriott stationery: *I still think the frequency correspondences are critical. One weakens, another intensifies. Is it a counterpoint of some kind? By the way, I'm doing fine. My best to Ginny and the kids.* And, hurriedly scribbled on a postcard with a picture of the Atheneum: *Getting Closer. They're out there, Nick. They're really out there!*

Al was a lot like M-82. Explosive. Remote. Lit by an inner fury. Self-destructive. A man whose personal stars went nova regularly. I never looked at the galaxy without thinking of him. Ironic that he of all people would imagine receiving a transmission from that chaotic place, which had erupted nine or ten million years ago, which was still belching enormous jets. Hard to imagine there could be a planetary system still intact inside that boiling cloud of hot hydrogen and plasma.

Periodically, he'd say he was in the area and would stop by. The first few times I got in a couple of bottles of Jamaican rum. He was big on rum. Later I didn't bother.

It went on like that for two decades. Sporadic letters from odd places around the country, from Canada, occasionally from Europe, and once from Tokyo. Always promising progress. Sometimes they came in spurts, sometimes several years passed between communications. It was almost as if he were pursuing those goddam gremlins around the world. He never spoke of anything else, other than to ask about my family, or my health. As far as I know, no one else ever heard from him at all.

Then one night at about 3 A.M., he showed up in a driving January rainstorm, and I'll never forget the look of him, thin white hair plastered to his skull, top coat open, cardigan drenched, water running off ears and nose. Standing in the storm; making no move to come in; his eyes empty. "Nick," he whispered, "I know what it is." As if we'd last spoken the day before. As if someone had died.

I pulled him inside. "Hello, Al."

He was shaking his head, staring at the night light that illuminated the staircase I'd just descended. I hit a wall switch, a table lamp came on, and he seemed to jerk awake. "I know it's late," he said. "I hope I didn't disturb anyone."

Ginny and the kids were all long gone by then. "No," I
said.

"Good." He'd lost ground. Even for twenty years. I
knew I'd grayed myself, and slid into middle age. But Al
looked *old*. Tired. Ready for a back porch and an apple
tree. "You know what the sons of bitches did?"

"No." What sons of bitches?

He peeled off his coat and, before I could get the closet
open, lobbed it across an armchair. "We were on the
wrong track right from the beginning, Nick. It never occurred to anybody we might be looking for something
other than digital data."

My God, he was off and running again. "Al," I said,
"what are you drinking?"

He ignored the question. "I mean, our working hypoth-
esis had always been that an artificial transmission could be
translated in some mathematical way. And that one that
had come seven million light years would have to be a
directed signal. A deliberate attempt to communicate.
Right?"

I nodded. "How about brandy?" There was no rum in
the house.

"Sure. Now: a deliberate attempt to communicate is
going to contain instructions. It's going to break easily. It
has to. That's the goddam *point!*" He chewed his lip and I
thought he was choking back tears. He was quiet for a
while. When he spoke again, his voice had changed quality. "But it was never there. I tried every approach I could
think of. NSA even had a crack at it. You know what
Gelman thought?"

He ignored his brandy until I pointed to it. "You ought
to get out of your shoes," I said.

"Gelman thought it was a *reflection*. He couldn't account for it any other way, so he decided it was a goddam
reflection. Nick, why do we always try so hard to explain
everything away?"

"I don't know."

He sipped his drink. "Did you know he's dead?"

"Gelman? Yes, I'd heard. It was a few years ago."

"You know what I wanted, Nick: I wanted to *show* him.
Son of a bitch, I wanted to walk in and hand him the
answer." His shoulders slumped. "Just as well." He shook
his head and laughed. It was a curious kind of sound:

amused, stoical, bitter. "Doesn't matter. He wouldn't have believed me anyway. And if he did, I'd only look more the goddam fool."

There was a time I'd thought Al Redwood was headed for a brilliant career. I felt sorry for him even then: Redwood had always been a social myth, a man who'd had no existence outside the observatory. No family, no other friends. Only colleagues, and his work. It was painful to see him now, studying his fingerprints on the glass.

I was never sure why he felt drawn to me. Maybe it was my family. The older kids loved to listen to him. And Ginny and I often sat with him late into the evenings. My own career leveled off early at a plateau roughly commensurate with my abilities, which is to say not very high. I accepted the fact early on that I'd never walk with giants. I was a maker of catalogues, an analyst, a man with an eye for detail. A recorder and an observer of other people's greatness.

He kicked off his shoes.

"What *does* it say?"

His eyes were cool and preoccupied behind thick lenses. I could see him running the question through again, his lips tightening slightly. "Weren't you listening, Nick? It doesn't say *anything!* Not a goddam thing."

The storm sucked at the house.

He got up, walked over to where he'd dropped his coat, fumbled through the pockets, and produced a cassette. "Here," he said, holding it in my general direction.

It *looked* ordinary enough. I took it, looked at it, looked at him. He was refilling his glass, his back toward me. I sighed, and inserted the cassette into the player.

Al strolled across the room and peered out through the blinds.

I started the tape.

"The neighborhood hasn't changed much, Nick." An electronic whisper blew through the room. "I assumed that the patterns of duration and intensity and color and the rest of it could be broken out into language. That, in short, the translation *said* something."

The whisper intensified. Rustlings and murmurs surfaced, connected, flowed through the still dry air. He turned, cocked his head, and sighed. "This is what you get if you modulate the frequency with an audio signal."

"There's a cadence," I said, hardly breathing.

He exploded in wild laughter. "Yes! From seven million light-years, we get 'Chopsticks'!" He folded his arms and glared at me. "Goddam their hides, Nick, how could they do anything so stupid!"

Not stupid, I thought. Cruel. Incredibly cruel. If he was right.

His eyes were wet, and his jaws jammed hard together. He stood behind an upholstered chair, gripping it as though he would punch his fingers through the fabric. The tape ran on and on: an inconsequential electronic river. "There's not much to it," I admitted. "It tends to be repetitious."

"No. It's a joke." He stared at me a long time while it played out. I thought maybe he expected me to say something.

"You can still publish," I said. "If you can document this—"

"Hell, no. I've had enough. *You* publish, if you want." He was pulling on his coat. The tape did have a certain quality—

"You can't go out in that storm, Al. Stay here tonight."

"It's okay. I'm over at the Holiday Inn. Thanks anyway." He pushed past me into the entry.

"Don't forget—"

"You can have it. Souvenir."

"Al—"

"I wanted you to know, Nick. I needed to have somebody *know*."

I nodded. "What will you do?" I was thinking of all those years.

"I'll be all right." He shrugged. "I'll probably go back to New Mexico. I've been teaching down there the last couple of semesters." I looked at him, and he smiled. And for that moment, the old Al Redwood was back. "Nice climate. And listen: don't worry. I've got a lot to keep me busy."

Whistling past a graveyard.

He shook my hand and hurried down the front steps. A rented car was parked at the curb. He waved as he drove off.

I wondered if I'd ever see him again.

They would have needed a trillion watts to hurl Redwood's signal across seven million light-years. Who would

build that kind of transmitter to send out a pleasant little
coded melody? At dawn, I was still listening to the damned
thing.

I took the day off, and went over to see Jean Flickinger,
who operates a recording studio in Middletown. She's a
short, dumpy woman with a hell of a smile. I'd met her
years before at a Wesleyan faculty dinner, where she was
being honored for her contributions to the university music theater. I told her about Al, about M-82, and about the
transmission.

"He'll be fine." She glanced at the cassette without
interest. "Stop worrying. He'll go back to New Mexico, just
like he said. And find something else to entertain him."
She held the cassette in the flat of her hand. "What do you
want me to do with this?"

I wasn't sure. "Listen to it. Assume he was right, and
this is a bona fide first-contact signal. What the hell does it
mean?"

"You're kidding."

"Try it."

Her eyes slid shut. "Call me tomorrow."

"I've got it on a chip." She ushered me into a booth in
the rear of the studio, and turned on a synthesizer. "This is
tied into a Synclavier III, an enhanced Lyricon—" She
stopped, and grinned. "You don't care?"

"I understand about guitars."

"Okay. Let me start by telling you that by any reasonable definition, your recording *is* a legitimate musical com-
position. It has consistent structure, contrast in tone,
symmetry and counterpoint, even an intensification of
variations toward the conclusion. *So,* if your friend was
being honest with you, and *if* the source of this is where
you say, then he's right. It's Martian music." She beamed.
"If you can convince the public, it ought to do pretty well."

I grunted the appropriate response.

"Anyhow, Nick," she continued, amused, "it didn't
sound like much to you because you had only the basic
melody. What I've done is to input the melody to the
synthesizer. Then the system adds appropriate harmonics
and rhythm, makes assignments to the various compo-

nents of our 'orchestra,' does some basic arrangement. You want to hear the result?"

"Go ahead." I'm not sure what I expected. I kept thinking about conditions in M-82, the band on the *Titanic*, "Nearer My God To Thee."

She touched a presspad.

Lights faded. And I listened again to Al Redwood's music. It was more liquid now, distant, delivered by strings rather than the electronic burble of a Cray. But there was a sense of misgiving in the cadences. Or perhaps in my own mind: I thought about Al, fleeing down the years with his burden. There must have been moments when he doubted himself, suspected Gelman had been right all along. And then, "Chopsticks"—

Thoughts of North Dakota at night. I was six years old, under a blazing vault of stars, a sky utterly unbroken by man-made light. I could recall standing out behind the farmhouse while the earth turned beneath my feet.

I was a god then. One grows up so soon.

But the music crowded out all regrets.

It took fire. Lightning ripped through it, and stars thundered along their courses. White light blazed across iron battlements. Oceans turned to steam, worlds drifted into the dark, and suns dissolved.

My old sense of godhood surged, and relentless rage, overwhelming love and death, filling the skies, driving the stars before it, on and on, exploding finally in a torrent of sheer irresistible power.

The mood changed, and I recalled how Honolulu looks at night from the air. And Gus Evans' 24-Hour Gas Station and Diner, set within its warm circle of light halfway up a Colorado mountainside. A coyote bayed outside the McDonald Observatory in Fort Davis.

Ginny lived again, momentarily, and was swept away.

At Wesleyan, when Hicks won his Nobel, we lifted glasses and laughed into the dawn.

"But that's *you*," I said afterward. "That's not what was on the cassette."

She shook her head. "I don't know the physics of this, Nick. But it probably wasn't possible to transmit anything other than the basic melody. They left the rest of it to us. Listen: I can run it through again, change some of the parameters, and things will be different. But not the essentials. They've provided the architecture. All we're adding is marble and sunlight."

I stared at her, trying to take it all in.

"They've allowed us to collaborate with them," she said. No smile. Not this time.

"I've got to find Al. Hell, these people are winning, Jean. I wouldn't be surprised if we don't hear from them again."

"Maybe," she said. She was shutting down her equipment. "I've put it on a CD for you. A copy for Redwood too, if you can find him."

"Why 'maybe'?"

"Did you catch the sense of wistfulness in it? It runs throughout, even in the most turbulent sections. I think they're like your friend."

"How do you mean?"

"Whistling past the graveyard."

Attitude of the Earth Toward Other Bodies

JAMES SALLIS

BECAUSE SHE IS GONE.

Each morning, still, he rises at five and puts on coffee. For an hour he studies—languages, usually—then takes the wireless terminal into the kitchen and with breakfast (grapefruit, one piece of wheat toast, a single scrambled egg or bowl of oatmeal) reviews news aspects of the project. All these are habits acquired in college and never given up. He showers then, dresses, and stands for a moment at the door, his apartment still and quiet as the sky.

He arrives, as always, before the others. "Good morning, Doctor," the guard says to him. He inserts his card into the slot, places his palm briefly against the glass plate. He goes through the door and repeats the clearance routine at another door, then down a long, narrow corridor. Here he says simply, "Good morning, Margaret."

"Good morning, John." The door opens for him. "I hope you slept well."

"Not very."

"Then I am sorry, John." A polite pause. "Where will we start this morning?"

"Program Aussie for a sweep of sector A-456/F, I think. Logarithm tables, continuous transmission."

"Duration?"

"Until redirected. And at whatever power levels we've been using in that sector."

All is quiet for a moment until Margaret says, "It is done. Transmission is beginning. You wish Granada to continue broadcasting geometrical theorems?"

"Yes, though maybe we could boost levels a little. Paris is still sending out the Brandenburgs. Leave her on that. But let's switch Nevsky over to something new."

After a moment Margaret says, "Yes?"

"I don't know—poetry, maybe."

"What poetry did you have in mind, John?"

"Milton, maybe? Or Shakespeare, Dante—Pushkin?"

"Might I suggest Rilke?"

"Yes, Rilke by all means. The *Elegies.* Of course."

Margaret's voice fills the room:

Who, if I cried, would hear me among the angelic
orders? And even if one of them suddenly
pressed me against his heart, I should fade in the
strength of his stronger existence

And he thinks how cruel it is now, though often before it had filled his days with joy, that Margaret should have *her* voice.

"Leave all the others on current transmissions."

"Yes, John. Will there be something else?"

"Anything unusual incoming?"

"Some interesting variable emissions from Dresden's sector. A possible new black hole in Paris's."

"You've notified astronomy, of course."

"Yes."

"Okay, just run off some copy for me and I'll have a look. The rest of the morning's your own."

Daisywheels begin spitting out thickly printed sheets of numbers and symbols.

"You'll call me, John, if there's anything else?"

"Certainly, Margaret. Thank you."

"It is my pleasure, John. *Au revoir.*"

And he is alone in the lab, without even her voice now. He looks up through hanging plants and the skylight to a bright day with no cloud in sight. There should be rain, he thinks, torrents of rain: *il pleure dans mon coeur comme il pleut dans la ville.* Then he bends over the serrated sheets, peering into them as one looks into a friend's face and knows instantly, without analysis, his thoughts and mood, entering into them as one exists in one's language, beyond particulates or grammar. The emissions from C-389/G-B were indeed most interesting, but (alas) still random.

Random as two people coming together in a sea of others. Random as the chances (they were, after all, so different) they'd fall in love.

She was a musician, working as a secretary to try and make ends meet. For two hours each day after work she practiced the oboe. Most of the remaining time she bicycled or read, usually in the bathtub or curled up against the bed's headboard with a glass of wine close to hand. She had a mane of thick brown hair, a narrow waist, and worked at her desk in shirtsleeves, arms alarmingly soft and bare. From her first day she'd always smiled at him.

He watched her for a time, aware of her presence halfway across the building even as he worked, and finally began speaking to her, mostly in the stairwells or halls at first, a couple of times in the lunch line. Then they started coming across one another more often. One day she asked if he'd had lunch yet (he had) and the next day they went together. On the stairs he asked her to dinner. She sat cross-legged in the car with her feet tucked under and slid her hand, at the restaurant, up inside and around his arm. That night, Sunday, he could not sleep and went to the lab at three in the morning. Monday night she went back with him to his apartment. It was her birthday. Neither of them was at work on Tuesday.

They were both so wary, so afraid of being hurt, and yet they seemed unable to stop themselves, to control, whatever its source, the attraction they felt. Verbally, they circled one another like dancers: But what if it happened that . . . I couldn't stand it if . . . I don't want any more surprises. They were two moons circling that central attraction, trying desperately not to collide, knowing they would. Once Margaret spoke to him four times before he surfaced from his thoughts of her to respond. Later there would be an interfering sister, not a villainess, nothing is that simple, that easy, just a sister concerned, a sister afraid things were going too fast, suspicious (as well she might be) of his intentions. But none of it mattered.

Her name was Kim. She'd been through two awful marriages and much abused by the men in her life; she had difficulty believing that a man could be kind to her, could be giving, could truly care. She did not recognize that there was anything within her a man would be drawn to. She kept asking him Why me? And he truly did not know. Perhaps her sister was right; perhaps he only wanted her, wanted her youth, her beauty, her obeisance.

Perhaps he was just afraid to be alone any longer under this sky pressing down on him.

And so he said, I will not lie to you. I want to be with you. If the time comes that I want to back away, I will tell you so.

You don't want to?

No. No, I don't. You must know that.

I thought you did, maybe. I was afraid.

He runs his hand up her spine, along the soft line of her arm. She leans her head against his chest. *To be so wanted.*

You should be getting home, he says.

Yes.

But they do not move. Carlights wash over them, the guard's flashlight washes over them, they are flooded in moonlight. And still she holds him close against her. From the heave of her chest he realizes she is crying. He asks if she is all right. Yes, she says, I'm fine, but this will all change, you know. It has to, she says. Someday we won't have it anymore. He looks down at the pale coarse skin of her hands and knows he has come too far now ever to be safe again.

He stands at the door of his apartment as though he'd just entered, trying to imagine how another, seeing this for the first time, how *she*, would perceive it. It has character, of course; it's a bit out of the ordinary. And comfortable, like the corduroy coat he wears most days. In fact the apartment is a fairly precise graph of his inmost life. His solitude, his passion for knowledge, the kenning of order and intuition so important to his work—all are there; there in the orderly stacks of books where Chomsky is sandwiched by Tolstoy and Tom Paine, in the bathroom where the medicine cabinet is stuffed with index cards, in the kitchen where he keeps most of the computer and electronic equipment, even in the series of small rugs thrown about seemingly at random over the carpets. He decides that he would like the person who lived here. He would trust this person, somehow.

Listen to this, she tells him one night as they sit side by side reading, hands locking from time to time and (from time to time) reaching for wineglasses. It is by Flaubert, she says, then reads it aloud: *Human language is like a cracked kettle on which we beat out tunes for bears to dance to, when all the time we are longing to move the stars to pity.*

"That is for us, John," she says. "That was written for us, for the two of us alone."

He moves a hand towards her face and she bows her head to touch it. From far off they hear sirens, the sounds of traffic and slamming doors, the whine of wind, a babble of unintelligible voices.

Everything depends upon our interpretation of the noise surrounding us and the silence at our centers.

By the late-middle twentieth century (and he found this as beautiful as a kite looping into May sky, as the order in a closed system of numbers or the sudden flight of birds) science had advanced sufficiently that it ceased being merely descriptive—that is, narrative—and became almost lyrical. There is, after all, not much distance between William James's insight that reality is relative and multiple, that the human mind (and therefore the world) is a fluid shimmering of consciousness, and Schrödinger's cat. Science had become Wallace Steven's blue guitar, a fecund reservoir of our attempts to understand, to contrive order. Trying to explain the world to me, Camus wrote, you are reduced to poetry. Perhaps he was right.

Language was at the base of both, of course, of everything finally, the limits of our language the limits of our world. And Chomsky believed that all the world's languages shared certain abstract rules and principles, not because these were implicit, particularly rational, or historical, but because they had been programmed into human minds by the information carried in DNA. He hoped in studying the most formal of these universals, rules and how those rules determine the structure of sentences—in short, basic grammar—to map the mind's self-limits. For grammar is a highly sophisticated information system, admitting messages, screening out noise.

Every day he sat surrounded by noise, tape upon tape of noise, noise turned into simple, fluctuating graphs on the screens about him, noise as rows of binary figures on huge sheets of spindled paper, noise analyzed for him in several ways (only some of which he understood) by Margaret, searching for a single incontrovertible instance of *grammar*, for algorithms that would (he knew) leap from the noise surrounding them.

What he did not know, was what he would do when that happened; he had no doubt that it would. His life *would* in many ways be over then, his great work, the work for which he'd programmed himself so long, done, done at age thirty-six, or forty-nine, or fifty-three. He could spend his remaining years studying languages, he supposed. Or music.

He brought the brandy glass close to him and looked at the world upside-down within it, a tree, a black car, the house across the street. Remembered how on their first night together they had shared a glass of brandy and in the morning, after she was gone, he stood staring at traces of her lipstick on the glass's rim. Remembering how she'd left a note saying she couldn't talk to him now or she wouldn't be able to do it, then had phoned, and finally met him, because he had to understand, goddamn it, he just *had* to understand.

In quantum theory nothing is real unless it is observed. Or as Einstein held, it is the theory which decides what we can observe.

And so he watches her walk away from him into a stream of people sweeping toward the subway entrance. And in the morning he returns to Margaret, to his graphs, his paper, his noise.

But now, in a circle of light and the ever-present, distant din that is the city's pulse, he reads about the male spadefoot toad. For a year or more he waits buried beneath the parched surface of the Arizona desert, and when the rainstorm he awaits at last arrives, plunges into daylight, racing to the nearest pool of water and sending out frantic calls to females. If he does not mate on the first night, he may never mate at all; by morning the water will be dwindling, and his life with it.

* * *

Because he wanted, just one more time, to be in love.

Gradually he realizes that he is awake. A sense of loss in the dreamworld receding from him; the brightness of the moon in his window; a murmur of wind. The phone rings again. His mouth is painfully dry. He tastes far back in his throat last night's Scotch.

"John? I rang earlier, just once, to allow you to awake a bit more naturally . . . Are you there?"

Her voice, as though continuing the dream.

He grunts.

"Barleycorn again, John? Are you all right?"

He grunts a second time.

"There is incoming you will want to see, now. Emissions from a new sector. They are diverse, unaccountable, and do not appear random."

He is instantly alert.

"Thank you, Margaret. I'll be right in. Please notify Security I'm on my way."

"I've already done so."

He glances at the clock beside him *(2:59 A.M.)* and downs a quart of orange juice while dressing and washing up. He glances in the mirror on his way out and sees a rumpled youngish man with round glasses and a serious, downturned mouth, hunched over as though always in a hurry, as though bent about some central pain deep within him or slowly closing in upon himself. This fleeting image stays with him.

The night is clear, each star bright and perfect as a new idea. There is no traffic, no one else about. He is alone in the world. And for the nine minutes it takes him to reach the lab he is a part of the earth, and yet escapes its pull, its final possession, enters into sky, as only the night walker, sheathed in solitude, ever does—something like Rilke's "angels," he imagines, though transitory. He remembers Creeley saying that it's only in the relationships men manage that they live at all, thinks of Goethe's "emptiness above us," of the first poem he can remember ever reading, Walter de la Mare's "The Listener."

A guard stands just inside the outer doors and unlocks them for him. He feeds his card into the terminal, places his palm against the glass: actions he no longer thinks about. Then through another door, past the second terminal, into the corridor. Hall lights come on as he advances, are shut off behind him.

"Thank you, Margaret."

"You are welcome. I hope that I've not disturbed you unnecessarily. Copy is on your desk. I will wait."

He goes into the lab and stands for a while at the window, looking out at the light-choked horizons of the city, at the dark above riddled with stars. Finally, knowing he is only delaying, he goes to the desk and looks closely at several of the thickly printed sheets. He senses that Margaret is about to speak.

"No," he says. "It is nothing. I thought, for a moment . . . But no."

"Then I am sorry, John."

"It's all right. My dreams were not good ones. I'd as soon be awake."

"That is not what I meant."

"I understand. Good night, Margaret."

Then, later, dawn not yet rosy-fingered but definitely poking about in the sky: "Margaret?"

"Yes, John."

"I want an override accessing me to all transmissions."

"There is no facility for such access."

"But it can be done?"

He sits watching incoming noise waver and change on the screens about him until (and it is by then full dawn) Margaret says, "It is done."

"Thank you."

"Is there anything else?"

"No, not now."

"I will wait, then."

"Margaret . . . ?"

After a moment: "Yes?"

"Nothing. . . . I will talk to you later."

"Yes, John. I will wait."

He rolls his chair toward the console. For a long time he sits there motionless, considering, sorting through phrase after phrase, seeking the precise algorithms, the barest grammar, of his pain. Light blossoms about him like a wound.

With two fingers he types out *I loved her, and she is gone,* then a transmission code and Enter/Commit.

He waits. Day marches on outside, noise builds. A telephone rings somewhere. Graphs quiver and shimmer about him. Soon there will be an answer. Soon he will hear the click of daisywheels starting up and his work will be done.

Malheur Maar

VONDA N. McINTYRE

THE LAKE kept getting bigger.

The level of Malheur Lake rises and falls from season to season and from year to year, so nobody thought much about the change. I hardly noticed it at all, because I was only interested in the temblors that had recently started up. Bodies of water sometimes do rise before an earthquake and drop during and after one. But Malheur Lake only kept getting bigger.

I felt sorry for the people who fought the creeping water level and got pushed out anyway, but you know how it is. I'd drive out of the field station and see the roof of their house projecting above the lake's quiet silver surface, the cormorants perched on the dead trees, and I'd think, I hope those folks are doing okay, wherever they went. Maybe they shouldn't have built there in the first place. I'm glad it didn't happen to me.

But gradually it happened to everybody; eventually it did happen to me. It was like a tide that you hardly notice, and suddenly it laps around your ankles and strands you till it goes out again. But this tide only went in one direction. In the blistering summer heat, the lake that should have been drying up slipped over the sagebrush and the bunch grass, it rose beside the road till water stretched away on both sides of a raised causeway, it turned a desert full of jackrabbits and ground squirrels into a reedy marshland stalked by herons and ibis and pelicans. The mosquitoes thrived. I spent most of my time covered with number-fifteen sunscreen and bug repellent. That was quite a mixture. Probably carcinogenic.

Gorged on mosquito larvae, the dragonflies grew so big that I kept expecting to see one I could ride. During the day they hovered in one spot, disappeared, and reappeared ten feet away, as if they possessed the power of teleportation. In the evening, the nighthawks sculled and banked through the sky, surging and diving for insects.

Then the lake took the main road. For a while I could still get to and from the field station in my jeep. But by the time the wheels disappeared under the surface, the water level had risen to the top of the short stilts that supported all the buildings. Wavelets lapped at the flaking paint and around the trunks of drowned, skeletal trees. The phones were always out, and sometimes fallen telephone poles drifted by. The cormorants used them for fishing piers. Instead of going outside in the morning and startling a cottontail, you were likely to step on a frog.

When Coyote Butte became Coyote Island, we held a wake for the field station. The next morning, all thoroughly hung over, we moved out. Some people went off seeking drier pastures, others rented places in Frenchglen and tried to keep on with their work. I was one of the people who stayed, but I had it a lot easier than others. I was gathering seismic data from Diamond Craters. If I'd been studying the desert ecosystem, I'd've gone away, too. There just wasn't much desert left.

One morning before dawn, I drove in from Frenchglen, unrolled the kayak, inflated it, and paddled toward Diamond Craters. They were still above water. Enough magma had erupted from the volcanoes that formed them to raise them higher than most of the surrounding countryside. They bulged gently above a soft gray silk of water, their bases surrounded by cattails and tules.

I pushed the kayak through the thick cattails and dragged it onto the bank. The marsh gave way quickly to high desert, to sagebrush and peppergrass. I tied the painter of the kayak around a jeep-sized chunk of tephra and climbed up West Dome to check my first set of instruments. Diamond Craters are about twenty thousand years old, just a blink of geologic time. The temblors could be signaling the approach of another period of volcanic activity, and if they were I wanted to be around when it started. Around, but not right on top of it. That was one reason I lived in Frenchglen instead of Burns. Burns is built on the site of a volcano that covered half the state with a hundred-foot layer of volcanic ash. True, that happened nine million years ago—longer than twenty thousand, geologically speaking. But not much longer.

I hiked across to Twin Craters. I could feel the previous day's heat radiating from the incredible landscape. When the craters formed, a wide, flat shield of lava flowed over the ground and cooled on top. The lava beneath the hardening skin flowed out and left behind the great ropy empty tubes that covered the area like huge misshapen pipes. Many had been smashed, but some remained whole. My boots rang the hollow rock like wooden drums. My long shadow jumped over the broken surface.

The seismograph carried a full load of traces. It's sensitive enough to detect even the collapse of a section of tube. I collected the data and reset the instrument.

I'd put one ground-motion detector on the edge of the crater. I checked the alignment of the laser, took a reading, then took the reading again.

The earth fault underneath Diamond Craters was beginning to widen.

Excited, I picked my way back across the treacherous lava. I wanted to check my other instruments. If they confirmed the change, I'd hurry back to the Glen, call Portland, and let my colleagues know what was happening.

The sun quivered above the horizon, surrounded by pink and gold clouds with luminous white edges. I felt like I was on a planet more distant than the moon.

Then I saw the ship land.

I'd never seen a spaceship before, not up close and for real. Most aliens, they come through at the ports in New York or L.A., Nairobi or Tokyo, and they pretty much stay in the cities. They do tourist things, they look at the skyscrapers, they stay in hotels that cater especially to them. They're like Americans who go to Paris and eat dinner in the McDonald's on the Champs Élysées. So we don't see much of aliens or spaceships in southeast Oregon.

The ship sank, rippling, toward Malheur Maar, where I

had put my second set of instruments. I was already headed in that direction, but you can't hurry across a field of broken pahoihoi. If you catch your boot in a crack or stumble on a seesawing plate of lava, if you fall and break your leg, you can lie out here for hours, for days, before anybody finds you. One day is enough. When the sun comes up, its dry and penetrating heat bakes the black stone and you along with it. It isn't the place to lie down and take a sunbath.

I reached the maar just as the ship settled to the ground.

Its soft, iridescent body touched sharp blocks of tephra and bulged down between them. Its underside flattened, pressing clumps of yellow rabbit brush sideways beneath it.

My boots crunched on the weathering volcanic tuff. Hopsage spines caught against my jeans, making a faint ripping noise but not tearing the cloth. The ship landed in silence, without even a whisper of wind, just the crackle of the brush beneath it. Even the crickets and the dragonflies fell silent. Ozone sharpened the air and mixed with the witch hazel scent, with the sharp-edged, powdery-looking volcanic dust.

The entrance to the ship did not so much open as dissolve. The ship's ripply side faded from pearly opalescence to a rainbow curtain to nothing.

The crickets began their buzz and chirp again. Far away, a meadowlark sang its falling-water warble.

A huge dark protoplasmic process, like a thick mutable tentacle, pressed out from the ship. The rest of the alien's body followed, flowing into the process and pulling itself forward. It was taller than I am, and it covered the area of a good-sized station wagon.

I could see no sensory organs, just the obsidian-shiny skin. The being was like obsidian, too, in its illusion of translucency. I thought I could see beneath its skin and through its flesh to a denser, harder nuclear shape.

It said nothing to me—or maybe it tried to say something to me and I couldn't understand it. It flowed like a great black drop of water, rolling forward over the sagebrush. I was about to run after it and try to tell it that it shouldn't crush the desert shrubs. Technically it shouldn't even have landed its spaceship where it did, but there wasn't much choice. The wide place in the road where people used to park had gone underwater long since.

Besides, the sage looked just the same after it passed. The being's substance flowed around it without disturbing it. The only thing left to show that someone or something had passed was a whispery trail in the dust.

Two more beings followed the first. The spaceship re-created its side. All three beings rolled toward Malheur Maar. I followed, climbing the rocky switchback trail, but they went straight up the slope. They could go much faster than I could.

A maar is a crater formed by the interaction of a volcanic explosion with groundwater. The Malheur crater is a couple of hundred yards across, higher on one side than the other. A wall of smooth-faced rhyolite blocks thrusts up beyond one edge. A spring lies beneath the maar, creating a small lake that has been there for several thousand years. It used to be a good place to swim if you didn't mind putting your feet into a bottom layer of all those years' worth of algal slime.

The crater lake had risen above the tops of the original stand of cattails. They still lay beneath the surface, decomposing slowly in the sun-warmed water. Now the level reached farther up the side of the crater, and a new growth of cattails ringed the lake with shiny green fronds.

The aliens flowed down the interior wall of the crater. One—I thought it was the first one, but to tell you the truth I can't be sure—let part of itself creep onto a slanting chunk of lava. There it rested. To form the face of that rock, lava had piled up in ropy, concentric circles, leaving what looks like a cross-section of a tree. The being stayed for a while, then drew itself from the lava and rolled down the side of the crater after its companions.

One after the other, they flowed through the cattails and into the water, skinny-dipping, I supposed. But they vanished beneath the surface and stayed there, without a bubble to mark their presence.

I watched, waiting for them to come up for air, inventing all kinds of theories about what they were doing, discounting each one. As time passed I began to get worried. I wondered if I should call someone. But I did not know whom I would call, it would take an hour to get to a phone, and the phones were likely still out anyway. If the beings needed help it would probably come too late. Besides, they seemed to know perfectly well what they were doing, even if it was to drown themselves.

Given that there wasn't anything else I could do, I went ahead and checked my other instruments and confirmed the motion of the earth fault. Just as if it were a normal day. I walked past the tree-ring rock to see if it had been disturbed, but even the crumbly moss and the lichens showed no sign of the being's touch. I was glad, because it's one of my favorite geologic formations.

Then I sat in the shade just within the edge of the crater, and I waited. I was tempted to go in swimming myself and see if I could find the beings, but I thought that would really be pushing it. Besides, Malheur Maar hadn't been that great a swimming hole since the water level rose and the whole stand of cattails started to rot at once. And it was never a great place to dive underwater and open your eyes.

At first the temblor vibrated the ground so faintly that I barely felt it. I experienced a brief fantasy that the ship had taken off, leaving its passengers behind. But it was just a small earthquake. It barely set the tops of the sagebrush to trembling and flinging away their dry summer leaves. Glassy volcanic rocks clinked against each other like slow-motion wind chimes. The surface of the lake shuddered into concentric rings and waves. The temblor lasted long enough to set the ripples splashing among the cattails. A tiny slide of rocks clattered down the far side of the crater and plopped into the marshy water.

The temblor subsided. Almost before I had a chance to wonder if the beings were all right, a long black proboscis stretched through the surface and between the cattails. The being pressed its substance into its extrusion till its whole body lay on the bank. It was covered with a slime of rotting reeds and ancient algae. The other two beings joined it and all three rolled back up the crater slope. As they moved, the slime flaked away. Dry dust did not stick to them. It seemed as if they looked shinier and brighter. But that may have been my imagination.

A few minutes later the crickets fell silent. The ship took off in the midst of eerie quiet. I wondered if I should try to convince myself that I'd gotten a touch of sun and hallucinated the whole thing. But I knew I couldn't, even though I could find no trace on the ground of their spaceship, except a whispery pattern as if someone had swept the dust with a whisk broom.

I saw the beings a few more times. They always did the same thing. They landed early in the morning, submerged themselves in Malheur Maar, and stayed underwater till a temblor hit. I could never tell if they were the same beings or different individuals. I never told anyone about them. They did less damage to the fragile landscape than the human tourists who used to come there, and they never left broken bottles or cigarette butts. They let me be and I let them be.

A few months later we had a big earthquake. That one, you probably heard about. It relieved the stress on the earth fault. The temblors stopped. With the fracture of the fault, the water table fell to normal and the lake drained away from the desert and the pool in Malheur Maar fell to the level it had maintained for so many thousands of years. Everything returned to normal, and now the occasional human tourist visits the craters.

The beings have never come back.

I kind of miss them.

—Malheur Field Station

The Boy
in the Tree

ELIZABETH HAND

What if in your dream you dreamed, and what if in
your dream you went to heaven and there plucked a
strange and beautiful flower, and what if when you
woke you had the flower in your hand?

—*Samuel Taylor Coleridge*

OUR HEART STOPS.

A moment I float beneath her, a starry shadow. Distant
canyons where spectral lightning flashes: neurons firing as
I tap into the heart of the poet, the dark core where desire
and horror fuse and Morgan turns ever and again to stare
out a bus window. The darkness clears. I taste for an instant
the metal bile that signals the beginning of therapy, and
then I'm gone.

I'm sitting on the autobus, the last seat where you can
catch the bumps on the crumbling highway if you're going
fast enough. Through the open windows a rush of Easter
air tangles my hair. Later I will smell apple blossom in my
auburn braids. Now I smell sour milk where Ronnie
Abrams spilled his ration yesterday.

"Move over, Yates!" Ronnie caroms off the seat opposite, rams his leg into mine and flies back to pound his
brother. From the front the driver yells "Shut up!", vainly
trying to silence forty-odd singing children.

> On top of Old Smoky
> All covered with blood
> I shot my poor teacher
> With a forty-four slug . . .

Ronnie grins at me, eyes glinting, then pops me right on the chin with a spitball. I stick my fingers in my ears and huddle closer to the window.

> Met her at the door
> With my trusty forty-four
> Now she don't teach no more . . .

The autobus pulls into town and slows, stops behind a military truck. I press my face against the cracked window, shoving my glasses until lens kisses glass and I can see clearly to the street below. A young woman is standing on the curb holding a baby wrapped in a dirty pink blanket. At her ankles wriggles a dog, an emaciated puppy with whiptail and ears flopping as he nips at her bare feet. I tap at the window, trying to get the dog to look at me. In front of the bus two men in uniform clamber from the truck and start arguing. The woman screws up her face and says something to the men, moving her lips so that I know she's mad. The dog lunges at her ankles again and she kicks it gently, so that it dances along the curb. The soldiers glance at her, see the autobus waiting, and climb back into the truck. I hear the whoosh of releasing brakes. The autobus lurches forward and my glasses bang into the window. The rear wheels grind up onto the curb.

The dog barks and leaps onto the woman. Apple blossoms drift from a tree behind her as she draws her arms up alarmed, and, as I settle my glasses onto my nose and stare, drops the baby beneath the wheels of the bus.

Retching, I strive to pull Morgan away, turn her head from the window. A fine spray etches bright petals on the glass and her plastic lenses. My neck aches as I try to turn toward the inside of the autobus and efface forever that silent rain. But I cannot move. She is too strong. She will not look away.

I am clawing at the restraining ropes. A technician pulls the wires from my head while inches away Morgan Yates

screams. I hear the hiss and soft pump of velvet thoughts
into her periaqueductual gray area. The link is severed.

I sat up as they wheeled her into the next room. Morgan's screams abruptly stilled as the endorphins kicked in
and her head flopped to one side of the gurney. For an
instant the technician turned and stared at me as he slid
Morgan through the door. He would not catch my eyes.

None of them will.

Through the glass panel I watched Emma Harrow
hurry from another lab. She bent over Morgan and gently
pulled the wires from between white braids still rusted
with coppery streaks. Beside her the technicians looked
worried. Other doctors slipped from adjoining rooms and
blocked my view, all with strained faces.

When I was sure they'd forgotten me I dug out a cigarette and lit up. I tapped the ashes into my shoe and blew
smoke into a ventilation shaft. I knew Morgan wouldn't
make it. I could often tell, but even Dr. Harrow didn't
listen to me this time. Morgan Yates was too important: one
of the few living writers whose readers included both
rebels and Ascendants.

"She will crack," I told Dr. Harrow after reading Morgan's profile. Seven poetry collections published by the
Ascendants. Recurrent nightmares revolving around a
childhood trauma in the military crèche; sadistic sexual
behavior and a pathological fear of dogs. Nothing extraordinary there. But I knew she wouldn't make it.

"How do you know?"

I shrugged. "She's too strong."

Dr. Harrow stared at me, pinching her lower lip. She
wasn't afraid of my eyes. "What if it works?" she mused.
"She says she hasn't written in three years, because of
this."

I yawned. Maybe it will work. But she won't let me
take it away. She won't let anyone take it."

I was right. If Dr. Harrow hadn't been so anxious about
the chance to reclaim one of the damned and her own
reputation, she'd have known too. Psychotics, autists, artists of the lesser rank: these could be altered by empatherapy. I'd siphoned off their sicknesses and night terrors,
inhaled phobias like giddy ethers that set me giggling for
days afterward. But the big ones, those whose madnesses
were as carefully cultivated as the brain chemicals that

allowed myself and others like me to tap into them: they were immune. They clung to their madnesses with the fever of true addiction. Even the dangers inherent to empatherapy weren't enough: they *couldn't* let go.

Dr. Harrow glanced up from the next room and frowned when she saw my cigarette. I stubbed it out in my shoe and slid my foot back in, wincing at the prick of heat beneath my sole.

She slipped out of the emergency room. Sighing, she leaned against the glass and looked at me.

"Was it bad, Wendy?"

I picked a fleck of tobacco from my lip. "Pretty bad." I had a rush recalling Morgan wailing as she stood at the window. For a moment I had to shut my eyes, riding that wave until my heart slowed and I looked up grinning into Dr. Harrow's compressed smile.

"Pretty good, you mean." Her tight mouth never showed the disdain or revulsion of the others. Only a little dismay, some sick pride perhaps in the beautiful thing she'd soldered together from an autistic girl and several ounces of precious glittering chemicals. "Well," she sighed, and walked to her desk. "You can start on this." She tossed me a blank report and returned to the emergency lab. I settled back on my cot and stared at the sheet.

PATIENT NAME: Wendy Wanders

In front of me the pages blurred. Shuddering I gripped the edge of my chair. Nausea exploded inside me, a fiery pressure building inside my head until I bowed to crack my forehead against the table edge, again and again, stammering my name until with a shout a technician ran to me and slapped an ampule to my neck. I couldn't bear the sight of my own name: Dr. Harrow usually filled in the charts for me and provided the sedatives, as she had a special lab all in gray for the empath who couldn't bear colors and wore black goggles outside; as she had the neural bath ready for another whose amnesia after a session left her unable to talk or stand or control her bowels. The technician stood above me until the drug took effect. I breathed deeply and stared at the wall, then reported on my unsuccessful session with the poet.

* * *

That evening I walked to the riverside. A trio of security sculls silently plied the river. At my feet water striders gracelessly mimicked them. I caught a handful of the insects and dropped them on the crumbling macadam at water's edge, watched them jerk and twitch with crippled stepladder legs as they fought the hard skin of gravel and sand. Then I turned and wandered along the river walk, past rotting oak benches and the ruins of glass buildings, watching the sun sink through argent thunderheads.

A single remaining restaurant ziggurat towered above the walk. Wooden benches gave way to airy filigrees of iron, and at one of these tables I saw someone from the Human Engineering Laboratory.

"Anna or Andrew?" I called. By the time I was close enough for her to hear I knew it was Anna this time, peacock feathers and long blue macaw quills studding the soft raised nodes on her shaven temples.

"Wendy." She gestured dreamily at a confectionery chair. "Sit."

I settled beside her, tweaking a cobalt plume, and wished I'd worn the fiery cock-of-the-rock quills I'd bought last spring. Anna was stunning, always: eyes brilliant with octine, small breasts tight against her tuxedo shirt. She was the only one of the other empties I spoke much with, although she beat me at faro and Andrew had once broken my tooth in an amphetamine rage. A saucer scattered with broken candicaine straws sat before her. Beside it a fluted parfait glass held several unbroken pipettes. I did one and settled back grinning.

"You had that woman today," Anna hissed into my ear. Her rasping voice made me shiver with delight. "The poet. I think I'm furious."

Smiling, I shrugged. "Luck of the draw."

"How was she?" She blinked and I watched golden dust powder the air between us. "Was she good, Wendy?" She stroked my thigh and I giggled.

"Great. She was great." I lowered my eyes and squinted until the table disappeared into the steel rim of an autobus seat.

"Let me see." Her whisper the sigh of air brakes. "Wendy—"

The rush was too good to stop. I let her pull me forward until my forehead grazed hers and I felt the cold sting of

electrolytic fluid where she strung the wire. I tasted brass:
then bile and summer air and exhaust—

Too fast. I jerked my head up, choking as I inadvertently yanked the connector from Anna. She stared at me
with huge blank eyes.

"Ch-c-c—" she gasped, spittle flying into the parfait
glass. I swore and pushed the straws away, popped the
wire and held her face close to mine.

"Ahhh—" Anna nodded suddenly. Her eyes focused
and she drew back. "Wendy. Good stuff." She licked her
lips, tongue a little loose from the hit so that she drooled. I
grimaced.

"More, Wendy . . ."

"Not now." I grabbed two more straws and cracked
one. "I have a follow-up with her tomorrow morning. I
have to go."

She nodded. I flicked the wire into her lap along with
the vial of fluid and a napkin. "Wipe your mouth, Anna. I'll
tell Harrow I saw you so she won't worry."

"Goodbye, Wendy." She snapped a pocket open and
the stuff disappeared. A server arrived as I left, its crooked
wheels grating against the broken concrete as it listed toward the table. I glimpsed myself reflected in its blank
black face, and hurried from the patio as behind me Anna
ordered more straws.

I recall nothing before Dr. Harrow. The drugs they
gave me—massive overdoses for a three-year-old—burned
those memories as well as scorching every neural branch
that might have helped me climb to feel the sun as other
people do. But the drugs stopped the thrashing, the
headbanging, the screaming. And slowly, other drugs
rived through my tangled axons and forged new pathways.
A few months and I could see again. A few more and my
fingers moved. The wires that had stilled my screams
eventually made me scream once more, and, finally, exploded a neural dam so that a year later I began to speak.
By then the research money was pouring through other
conduits, scarcely less complex than my own, and leading
as well to the knot of electrodes in my brain.

In the early stages of her work, shortly after she took
me from the military crèche, Dr. Harrow attempted a
series of neuro-electrical implants between the two of us.

It was an unsuccessful effort to reverse the damage done by the biochemicals. Seven children died before the minimum dosage was determined—enough to change the neural pattern behind autistic behavior, not enough to allow the patient to develop her own emotional responses to subsequent internal or external stimuli. I still have scars from the implants: fleshy nodes like tiny ears trying to sprout from my temples.

At first we lived well. As more empaths were developed and more military funding channeled for research, we lived extravagantly well. Dr. Harrow believed that exposure to sensation might eventually pattern true emotions in her affectively neutered charges. So we moved from the Human Engineering Laboratory's chilly fortress to the vast abandoned Linden Glory estate outside the old City.

Neurologists moved into the paneled bedrooms. Psycho-botanists tilled the ragged formal gardens and developed new strains of oleander within bell-shaped greenhouses. Empties moved into bungalows where valets and chefs once slept.

Lawrence Linden had been a patron of the arts: autographed copies of Joyce and Stein and the lost Crowley manuscripts graced the Linden Glory libraries. We had a minor Botticelli and many Raphaels; the famed pre-Columbian collection; antiquarian coins and shelves of fine and rare Egyptian glass. From the Victorian music room with its Whistler panels echoed the peacock screams of empties and patients engaged in therapy.

Always I remained Dr. Harrow's pet: an exquisite monster capable of miming every human emotion and even feeling many of them via the therapy I make possible. Every evening doctors administer syringes and capsules and tiny tabs that adhere to my temples like burdock pods, releasing chemicals directly into my corpus striatum. And every morning I wake from someone else's dreams.

Morgan sat in the gazebo when I arrived for our meeting, her hair pulled beneath a biretta of frayed indigo velvet. She had already eaten but servers had yet to clear her plate. I picked up the remains of a brioche and nibbled its sugary crust.

"None of you have any manners, do you?" She smiled,

but her eyes were red and cloudy with hatred. "They told me that during orientation."

I ran my tongue over a sweet nugget in a molar and nodded. "That's right."

"You can't feel anything or learn anything unless it's slipped into your breakfast coffee."

"I can't drink coffee." I glanced around the Orphic Garden for a server. "You're early."

"I had trouble sleeping."

I nodded and finished the brioche.

"I had trouble sleeping because I had no dreams." She leaned across the table and repeated herself in a hiss. "I had no dreams. I carried that memory around with me for sixty years and last night I had no dreams."

Yawning I rubbed the back of my head, adjusting a quill. "You still have all your memories. Dr. Harrow said you wanted to end the nightmares. I am surprised we were successful."

"You were not successful." She towered above me when she stood, the table tilting toward her as she clutched its edge. "Monster."

"Sacred monster. I thought you liked sacred monsters." I grinned, pleased that I'd bothered to read her chart.

"Bitch. How dare you laugh at me. Whore—you're all whores and thieves." She stepped toward me, her heel catching between the mosaic stones. "No more of me— You'll steal no more of me—"

I drew back a little, blinking in the emerald light as I felt the first adrenaline pulse. "You shouldn't be alone," I murmured. "Does Dr. Harrow know?"

She blocked the sun so that it exploded around the biretta's peaks in resplendent ribbons. "Doctor Harrow will know," she whispered, and drawing a swivel from her pocket she shot herself through the eye.

I knocked my chair over as I stumbled to her, knelt and caught the running blood and her last memory as I bowed to touch my tongue to her severed thoughts.

A window smeared with garnet light that ruddles across my hands. Burning wax in a small blue glass. A laughing dog; then darkness.

They hid me under guise of protecting me from the shock. I gave a sworn statement to the military and acknowledged in the HEL mortuary that the long body with the blackened face had indeed shared her breakfast brioche with me that morning. I glimpsed Dr. Harrow, white and taut as a thread as Dr. Leslie and the other HEL brass cornered her outside the Emergency Room. Then the aide Justice hurried me into the west wing, past the pre-Columbian collection and the ivory stair to an ancient Victorian elevator, clanking and lugubrious as a stage dragon.

"Dr. Harrow suggested that you might like the Horne Room," Justice remarked with a cough, sidling two steps away to the corner of the elevator. The brass door folded into a lattice of leaves and pigeons that expanded into peacocks. "She's having your things sent up now. Anything else you need, please let her know." He cleared his throat, staring straight ahead as we climbed through orchid-haunted clerestories and chambers where the oneironauts snored and tossed through their days. At the fourth floor the elevator ground to a stop. He tugged at the door until it opened and waited for me to pass into the hallway.

"I have never been in the Horne Room," I remarked, following him.

"I think that's why she thought you'd like it." He glanced into an ornate mirror as we walked. I saw in his eyes a quiver of pity before he looked away. "Down here."

A wide hallway flanked by leaded windows overlooking the empties' cottages ended in an arch crowded with gilt satyrs.

"This is the Horne Room," murmured Justice. To the right a heavy oaken door hung open. Inside saffron-robed technicians strung cable. I made a face and tapped the door. It swung inward and struck a bundle of cable leading to the bank of monitors being installed next to a huge bed. I paced to the window and gazed down at the roof of my cottage. Around me the technicians scurried to finish, glancing at me sideways with anxious eyes. I ignored them and sat on the windowsill. There was no screen. A hawkmoth buzzed past my chin and I thought that I could hang hummingbird feeders from here and so, perhaps, lure them within reach of capture. Anna had a bandeau she had woven of hummingbird feathers which I much admired. The hawkmoth settled on a BEAM monitor beside the bed. The technicians packed to leave.

"Could you lie here for a moment, miss, while I test

this?" The technician dropped a handful of cables behind the headboard. I nodded and stretched upon the bed, pummeling a pillow as he placed the wires upon my brow and temples. I turned sideways to watch the old BEAM monitor, the hawkmoth's wings forming a feline mask across the flickering map of my thoughts.

"Aggression, bliss, charity," droned the technician, flicking the moth from the dusty screen. "Desire, envy, fear," I sighed and turned from the monitor while he adjusted dials. Finally he slipped the wires from me and left. Justice lingered a moment longer.

"You can go now," I said flatly, and tossed the pillow against the headboard.

He stood by the door, uncomfortable, and finally said, "Dr. Harrow wants me to be certain you check your prescriptions. Note she has increased your dosage of acetlethylene."

I slid across the bed to where a tiny refrigerator had been hung for my medications. I pulled it open and saw the familiar battery of vials and bottles. As a child first under Dr. Harrow's care I had imagined them a city, saw the long cylinders and amber vials as battlements and turrets to be explored and climbed. Now I lived among those chilly buttresses, my only worship within bright cathedrals.

"Two hundred milligrams," I said obediently, and replaced the bottle. "Thank you very very much." As I giggled he left the room.

I took the slender filaments that had tapped into my store of memories and braided them together, then slid the plait beneath a pillow and leaned back. A bed like a pirate ship, carved posts like riven masts spiring to the high ceiling. I had never seen a pirate ship, but once I tapped a boy who jerked off to images of red flags and heaving seas and wailing women. I recalled that now and untangled a single wire, placed it on my temple and masturbated until I saw the warning flare on the screen, the sanguine flash and flame across my pixilated brain. Then I went to sleep.

Faint tapping at the door woke me a short while later.

"Andrew," I yawned, pointing to the crumpled sea of bedclothes. "Come in."

He shut the door softly and slid beneath the sheets beside me. "You're not supposed to have visitors, you know."

"I'm not?" I stretched and curled my toes around his finger.

"No. Dr. Leslie was here all day. Anna said he's taking us back."

"Me too?"

He nodded, hugging a bolster. "All of us. Forever." He smiled, and the twilight made his face as beautiful as Anna's. "I saw Dr. Harrow cry after he left."

"How did you get here?" I sat up and played with his hair: long and silky except where the nodes bulged and the hair had never grown back. He wore Anna's bandeau, and I tugged it gently from his head.

"Back stairs. No one ever uses them. That way." He pointed lazily with his foot toward a darkening corner. His voice rose plaintively. "You shared that poet with Anna. You should've saved her."

I shrugged. "You weren't there." The bandeau fit loosely over my forehead. When I tightened it tiny emerald feathers frosted my hand like the scales of moths. "Would Anna give me this, do you think?"

Andrew pulled himself onto his elbows and stroked my breast with one hand. "I'll give it to you, if you share."

"There's not enough left to share," I whined, and pulled away. In the mirror I caught myself in the bandeau. The stippled green feathers made my hair look a deeper auburn, like the poet's. I pulled a few dark curls through the feathers and pursed my lips. "If you give this to me . . ."

Already he was reaching for the wires. "Locked?" I breathed, glancing at the door.

"Shh . . ."

Afterward I gave him one of my new pills. There hadn't been much of Morgan left and I feared his disappointment would evoke Anna, who'd demand her bandeau back.

"Why can't I have visitors?"

I had switched off the lights. Andrew sat on the windowsill, luring lacewings with a silver cigarette lighter. Bats chased the insects to within inches of his face, veering away as he laughed and pretended to snatch at them. "Dr.

Harrow said there may be a psychic inquest. To see if you're accountable."

"So?" I'd done one before, when a schizoid six-year-old hanged herself on a grosgrain ribbon after therapy with me. " 'I can't be responsible. I'm not responsible.' " We laughed: it was the classic empath defense.

"Dr. Harrow wants to see you herself."

I kicked the sheets to the floor and turned down the empty BEAM, to see the lacewings better. "How do you know all this?"

A quick *fizz* as a moth singed itself. Andrew frowned and turned down the lighter flame. "Anna told me," he replied, and suddenly was gone.

I swore and tried to rearrange my curls so the bandeau wouldn't show. From the windowsill Anna stared blankly at the lighter for a moment, then groped in her pockets until she found a cigarette. She glanced coolly past me to the mirror, pulling a strand of hair forward until it fell framing her cheekbone. "Who gave you that?" she asked as she blew smoke out the window.

I turned away. "You know who," I replied petulantly. "I'm not supposed to have visitors."

"Oh, you can keep it," she said airily.

"Really?" I clapped in delight.

"I'll just make another." She finished her cigarette, tossed it in an amber arc out the window. "I better go down now. Which way's out?"

I pointed where Andrew had indicated, drawing her close to me to kiss her tongue as she left.

"Thank you, Anna," I whispered to her at the door. "I think I love this bandeau."

"I think I loved it too," Anna nodded, and slipped away.

Dr. Harrow invited me to lunch with her in the Peach Tree Court the next afternoon. Justice appeared at my door and waited while I put on jeweled dark spectacles and a velvet biretta like Morgan Yates'.

"Very nice, Wendy," he commented, amused. I smiled. When I wore the black glasses he was not afraid to look me in the face.

"I don't want the others to see my bandeau. Anna will steal it back," I explained, lifting the hat so he could see the feathered riband beneath.

He laughed at that. I don't hear the aides laugh very often: when I was small, their voices frightened me. I thanked him as he held the door and followed him outside.

We passed the Orphic Garden. Servers had snaked hoses through the circle of lindens and were cleaning the mosaic stones. I peered curiously through the hedge as we walked down the pathway but the blood seemed to be all gone.

Once we were in the shade of the Peach Tree Walk I removed my glasses. Justice quickly averted his eyes.

"Do you think these peaches are ripe?" I wondered, twitching one from a branch as I passed beneath it.

"I doubt it." Justice sighed, wincing as I bit into a small pink orb like a swollen eye. "They'll make you sick, Wendy."

Grinning, I swallowed my bite, then dropped the fruit. The little path dipped and rounded a corner hedged with forsythia. Three steps further and the path branched: right to the *trompe l'oeil* Glass Fountain, left to the Peach Tree Court, where Dr. Harrow waited in the Little Pagoda.

"Thank you, Justice." Dr. Harrow rose and shook his hand. On several low tables lunch had already been laid for two. Justice stepped to a lacquered tray and sorted out my medication bottles, then stood and bowed before leaving.

Sunlight streamed through the bamboo frets above us as Dr. Harrow took my hand and drew me toward her.

"The new dosage. You remembered to take it?"

"Yes." I removed my hat and dropped it. "Anna gave me this bandeau."

"It's lovely." She knelt before one of the tables and motioned for me to do the same. Her face was puffy, her eyes slitted. I wondered if she would cry for me as she had for Andrew yesterday. "Have you had breakfast?"

We ate goujonettes of hake with fennel and an aspic of lamb's blood. Dr. Harrow drank champagne and permitted me a sip—horrible, like thrashing water. Afterward a rusted, remodeled garden server removed our plates and brought me a chocolate wafer, which I slipped into my pocket to trade with Anna later, for news.

"You slept well," Dr. Harrow stated. "What did you dream?"

"I dreamed about Melisande's dog."

Dr. Harrow stroked her chin, then adjusted her pince-nez to see me better. "Not Morgan's dog?"

"No." Melisande had been a girl my own age with a history of tormenting and sexually molesting animals. "A small white dog. Like this." I pushed my nose until it squashed against my face.

Dr. Harrow smiled ruefully. "Well, good, because *I* dreamed about Morgan's dog." She shook her head when I started to question her. "Not really; a manner of speaking. I mean I didn't get much sleep." She sighed and tilted her flute so it refracted golden diamonds. "I made a very terrible error of judgment with Morgan Yates. I shouldn't have let you do it."

"I knew what would happen," I said matter-of-factly.

Dr. Harrow looked at her glass, then at me. "Yes. Well, a number of people are wondering about that, Wendy."

"She would not look away from the window."

"No. They're wondering how you know when the therapy will succeed and when it won't. They're wondering whether the therapist is effecting her failures as well as her cures."

"I'm not responsible. I can't be responsible."

She placed the champagne flute very carefully on the lacquer table and took my hand. She squeezed it so tightly that I knew she wanted it to hurt. "That is what's the matter, Wendy. If you are responsible—if empaths *can* be responsible—you can be executed for murder. We can all be held accountable for your failures. And if not . . ." She leaned back without releasing my hand, so that I had to edge nearer to her across the table. "If not, HEL wants you back."

I flounced back against the floor. "Andrew told me."

She rolled her eyes. "Not you personally. Not necessarily. Anna, yes: they created Anna, they'll claim her first. But the others—" She traced a wave in the air, ended it with a finger pointing at me. "And you . . . If they can trace what you do, find the bioprint and synthesize it . . ." Her finger touched the end of my nose, pressed it until I giggled. "Just like Melisande's dog, Wendy.

"Odolf Leslie was here yesterday. He wants you for observation. He wants this—" She pressed both hands to her forehead and then waved them toward the sky, the fruit-laden trees and sloping lawns of Linden Glory. "All

this, Wendy. They will have me declared incompetent and
our research a disaster, and then they'll move in."

A server poured me more mineral water. "Is he a nice
doctor?"

For a moment I thought she'd upset the table, as Morgan had done in the Orphic Garden. Then, "I don't know,
Wendy. Perhaps he is." She sighed, and motioned the
server to bring another cold split.

"They'll take Anna first," she said a few minutes later,
almost to herself. Then, as if recalling me sitting across
from her, she added, "For espionage. They'll induce multiple personalities and train them when they're very young.
Ideal terrorists."

I drank my water and stared at the latticed roof of the
pagoda, imagining Andrew and Anna without me. I took
the chocolate wafer from my pocket and began to nibble
it.

The server rolled back with a sweating silver bucket
and opened another split for Dr. Harrow. She sipped it,
watching me through narrowed gray eyes. "Wendy," she
said at last. "There's going to be an inquest. A military
inquest. But before that, one more patient." She reached
beneath the table to her portfolio and removed a slender
packet. "This is the profile. I'd like you to read it."

I took the file. Dr. Harrow poured the rest of her champagne and finished it, tilting her head to the server as she
stood.

"I have a two o'clock meeting with Dr. Leslie. Why
don't you meet me again for dinner tonight and we'll discuss this?"

"Where?"

She tapped her lower lip. "The Peacock Room. At
seven." She bowed slightly and passed out of sight among
the trees.

I waited until she disappeared, then gestured for the
server. "More chocolate, please," I ordered, and waited
until it returned with a chilled marble plate holding three
wafers. I nibbled one, staring idly at the faux vellum cover
of the profile with its engraved motto:

HUMAN ENGINEERING LABORATORY
PAULO MAIORA CANAMUS!

" 'Let us raise a somewhat loftier strain,' " Andrew had translated it for me once. "Virgil. But it should be *deus ex machina*," he added slyly.

God from the machine.

I licked melting chocolate from my fingers and began to read, skimming through the charts and anamnesis that followed. On the last sheet I read:

Client requests therapy in order to determine nature and cause of these obsessive nightmares.

Beneath this was Dr. Harrow's scrawled signature and the HEL stamp. I ate the last wafer, then mimed to the server that I was finished.

We dined alone in the Peacock Room. After setting our tiny table the servers disappeared, dismissed by Dr. Harrow's brusque gesture. A plateful of durians stood as our centerpiece, the spiky green globes piled atop a translucent porcelain tray. Dr. Harrow split one neatly for me, the round fruit oozing pale custard and a putrescent odor. She grimaced, then took a demure spoonful of the pulp and tasted it for me.

"Lovely," she murmured, and handed me the spoon.

We ate in silence for several minutes beneath the flickering gaslit chandeliers.

"Did you read the profile I gave you?" Dr. Harrow asked at last, with studied casualness.

"Mmmm-mmm," I grunted.

"And . . . ?"

"She will not make it." I lofted another durian from the tray.

Dr. Harrow dipped her chin ever so slightly before asking, "Why, Wendy?"

"I don't know." This durian was not quite ripe. I winced and pushed it from my plate.

"Can't you give me any idea of what makes you feel that?"

"Nothing. I can't feel anything." I took another fruit.

"Well then, what makes you think she wouldn't be a good analysand?"

"I don't know. I just—" I sucked on my spoon, thinking. "It's like when I see my name—the way everything starts to shiver and I get sick. But I don't throw up."

Dr. Harrow tilted her head thoughtfully. "Like a seizure. Well." She smiled and spooned another mouthful.

I finished the last durian and glanced around impatiently. "When will I meet her?"

"You already have."

I kicked my chair. "When?"

"Fourteen years ago, when you first came to HEL."

"Why don't I remember her?"

"You do, Wendy." She lifted her durian and took the last drop of custard upon her tongue. "It's me."

"Surprised?" Dr. Harrow grinned and raised the flamboyant sleeves of her embroidered haik.

"It's beautiful," I said, fingering the flowing cuffs enviously.

She smiled and turned to the NET beside my bed. "I'm the patient this morning. Are you ready?"

I nodded. Earlier she had wheeled in her own cot, and now sat on it readying her monitors. I settled on my bed and waited for her to finish. She finally turned to me and applied electrolytic fluid to the nodes on my temples, placed other wires upon my head and cheekbones before doing the same to herself.

"You have no technicians assisting you?" I asked.

She shook her head but made no reply as she adjusted her screens and, finally, settled onto her cot. I lay back against the pillow and shut my eyes.

The last thing I heard was the click of the adaptor freeing the current, and a gentle exhalation that might have been a sigh.

> "Here we stand . . ."
>> "Here we stand . . ."
> "Here we lie . . ."
>> "Here we lie . . ."
>>> "Eye to hand and heart to head,
>>> Deep in the dark with the dead."

It is spring, and not dark at all, but I repeat the incantation as Aidan gravely sprinkles apple blossoms upon my head. In the branches beneath us a bluejay shrieks at our bulldog, Molly, as she whines and scratches hopefully at her basket.

"Can't we bring her up?" I peer over the edge of the rickety platform and Molly sneezes in excitement.

"Shhh!" Aidan commands, squeezing his eyes shut as he concentrates. After a moment he squints and reaches for his crumpled sweater. Several bay leaves filched from the kitchen crumble over me and I blink so the debris doesn't get in my eyes.

"I hate this junk in my hair," I grumble. "Next time I make the spells."

"You can't." Loftily Aidan stands on tiptoe and strips another branch of blossoms, sniffing them dramatically before tossing them in a flurry of pink and white. "We need a virgin."

"So?" I jerk on the rope leading to Molly's basket. "You're a virgin. Next time we use you."

Aidan stares at me, brows furrowed. "That won't count," he says at last. "Say it again, Emma."

"Here we stand . . ."

Every day of Easter break we come here: an overgrown apple orchard within the woods, uncultivated for a hundred years. Stone walls tumbled by time mark the gray boundaries of a colonial farm. Blackberry vines choke the rocks with breeze-blown petals. Our father showed us this place. Long ago he built the treehouse, its wood lichen-green now and wormed with holes. Rusted nails snag my knees when we climb: all that remains of other platforms and the crow's-nest at treetop.

I finish the incantation and kneel, calling to Molly to climb in her basket. When my twin yells I announce imperiously, "The virgin needs her faithful consort. Get *in*, Molly."

He demurs and helps to pull her up. Molly is trembling when we heave her onto the platform. As always, she remains huddled in her basket.

"She's sitting on the sandwiches," I remark matter-of-factly. Aidan shoves Molly aside hastily and retrieves two squashed bags. "I call we break for lunch."

We eat in thoughtful silence. We never discuss the failure of the spells, although each afternoon Aidan hides in his secret place behind the wing chair in the den and pores through more brittle volumes. Sometimes I can feel them working—the air is so calm, the wind dies unexpectedly, and for a moment the woods glow so bright, so deep, their

shadows still and green; and it is there: the secret to be
revealed, the magic to unfold, the story to begin. Aidan
flushes above me and his eyes shine, he raises his arms
and—

And nothing. It is gone. A moment too long or too soon,
I never know—but we have lost it again. For an instant
Aidan's eyes gray with tears. Then the breeze rises, Molly
yawns and snuffles, and once more we put aside the spells
for lunch and other games.

That night I toss in my bed, finally throwing my pillow
against the bookcase. From the open window stream the
chimes of peepers in the swamp, their plangent song broi-
dered with the trills of toads and leopard frogs. As I churn
feverishly through the sheets it comes again, and I lie still:
like a star's sigh, the shiver and promise of a door opening
somewhere just out of reach. I hold my breath, waiting:
will it close again?

But no. The curtains billow and I slip from my bed, bare
feet curling upon the cold planked floor as I race silently to
the window.

He is in the meadow at wood's edge, alone, hair misty
with starlight, his pajamas spectral blue in the dark. As I
watch he raises his arms to the sky, and though I am too far
to hear, I whisper the words with him, my heart thumping
counterpoint to our invocation. Then he is quiet, and
stands alert, waiting.

I can no longer hear the peepers. The wind has risen,
and the thrash of the beech trees at the edge of the forest
drowns all other sounds. I can feel his heart now, beating
within my own, and see the shadows with his eyes.

In the lower branches of the willow tree, the lone willow that feeds upon a hidden spring beside the sloping
lawn, there is a boy. His eyes are green and lucent as
tourmaline, and silvery moths are drawn to them. His
hands clutch the slender willow-wands: strong hands, so
pale that I trace the blood beneath, and see the muscles
strung like young strong vines. As I watch he bends so that
his head dips beneath a branch, new leaves tangling fair
hair, and then slowly he uncurls one hand and, smiling,
beckons my brother toward him.

The wind rises. Beneath his bare feet the dewy grass
darkens as Aidan runs faster and faster, until he seems
almost to be skimming across the lawn. And there, where

the willow starts to shadow the starlit slope and the boy in the tree leans to take his hand, I tackle my brother and bring him crashing and swearing to earth.

For a moment he stares at me uncomprehending. Then he yells and slaps me, hits me harder until, remembering, he shoves me away and stumbles to his feet.

There is nothing there. The willow trembles, but only the wind shakes the new leaves. From the marsh the ringing chorus rises, swells, bursts as the peepers stir in the saw grass. In the old house yellow light stains an upstairs window and our father's voice calls out sleepily, then with concern, and finally bellows as he leans from the casement to spot us below. Aidan glances at the house and back again at the willow, and then he turns to me despairingly. Before I can say anything he punches me and runs, weeping, back to the house.

A gentler withdrawal than I'm accustomed to. For several minutes I lay with closed eyes, breathing gently as I tried to hold onto the scents of apple blossom and dew-washed grass. But they faded, along with the dreamy net of tree and stars. I sat up groggily, wires still taped to my head, and faced Dr. Harrow already recording her limbic system response from the NET.

"Thank you, Wendy," she said brusquely without looking up. I glanced at the BEAM monitor, where the shaded image of my brain lingered, the last flash of activity staining the temporal lobe bright turquoise.

"I never saw that color there before," I remarked as I leaned to examine it, when suddenly an unfocused wave of nausea choked me. I gagged and staggered against the bed, tearing at the wires.

Eyes: brilliant green lanced with cyanogen, unblinking as twin chrysolites. A wash of light: leaves stirring the surface of a still pool. They continued to stare through the shadows, heedless of the play of sun and moon, days and years and decades. The electrodes dangled from my fist as I stared at the blank screen, the single dancing line bisecting the NET monitor. The eyes in my head did not move, did not blink, did not disappear. They stared relentlessly from the shadows until the darkness itself swelled and was absorbed by their feral gaze. They saw me.

Not Dr. Harrow; not Aidan; not Morgan or Melisande or the others I'd absorbed in therapy.

Me.

I stumbled from the monitor to the window, dragging the wires behind me, heedless of Dr. Harrow's stunned expression. Grunting I shook my head like a dog, finally gripped the windowsill and slammed my head against the oaken frame, over and over and over, until Dr. Harrow tore me away. Still I saw them: unblinking glaucous eyes, tumbling into darkness as Dr. Harrow pumped the sedatives into my arm.

Much later I woke to see Dr. Harrow staring at me from the far end of the room. She watched me for a moment, and then walked slowly to the bed.

"What was it, Wendy?" she asked, smoothing her robe as she sat beside me. "Your name?"

I shook my head. "I don't know," I stammered, biting the tip of my thumb. Then I twisted to stare at her and asked, "Who was the boy?"

Her voice caught for an instant before she answered. "My brother Aidan. My twin."

"No— The other— The boy in the tree."

This time she held her breath a long moment, then let it out in a sigh. "I don't know," she murmured. "But you remember him?"

I nodded. "Now. I can see him now. If I—" And I shut my eyes and drifted before snapping back. "Like that. He comes to me on his own. Without me recalling him. Like—" I flexed my fingers helplessly. "Like a dream, only I'm awake now."

Slowly Dr. Harrow shook her head and reached to take my hand. "That's how he found Aidan, too, the last time," she said. "And more. And now you." For an instant something like hope flared in her eyes, but faded as she bowed her head. "I think, Wendy. . . ." She spoke with measured calm. "I think we should keep this to ourselves right now. And tomorrow, perhaps, we'll try again."

He sees me.

I woke with a garbled scream, arms flailing, to my dark room bathed in the ambient glow of monitors. I stumbled to the window, knelt with my forehead against the cool oak

sill and blinked against tears that welled unbidden from
my burning eyes. There I fell asleep with my head pillowed upon my arms, and woke next morning to Dr. Harrow's knock upon my door.

"Emma," he whispers at the transom window; "Let me
in."

The quilts piled on me muffle his voice. He calls again,
louder, until I groan and sit up in bed, rubbing my eyes and
glaring at the top of his head peeking through the narrow
glass.

From the bottom of the door echoes faint scratching,
Molly's whine. A thump. More scratching: Aidan crouched
outside the room, growling through choked laughter. I
drape a quilt around me like a toga and lean forward to
unlatch the door.

Molly flops onto the floor, snorting when she bumps her
nose and then drooling apologetically. Behind her stumbles Aidan, shivering in his worn kimono with its tattered
sleeves and belt stolen from one of my old dresses. I giggle
uncontrollably, and gesture for him to shut the door before
Father hears us in his room below.

"It's fucking freezing in this place," Aidan exclaims,
pinning me to the bed and pulling the quilts over our
heads. "Oh, come on, dog." Grunting, he hauls her up
beside us. "My room is like Antarctica. Tierra del Fuego.
The Bering Strait." He punctuates his words with kisses,
elbowing Molly as she tries to slobber our faces. I squirm
away and straighten my nightshirt.

"Hush. You'll wake Papa."

Aidan rolls his eyes and stretches against the wall.
"Spare me." Through the rents in his kimono I can see his
skin, dusky in the moonlight. No one has skin like Aidan's,
except for me: not white but the palest gray, almost blue,
and fine and smooth as an eggshell. People stare at us in
the street, especially at Aidan; at school girls stop talking
when he passes, and fix me with narrowed eyes and lips
pursed to mouth a question never asked.

Aidan yawns remorselessly as a cat. Aidan is the beauty:
Aidan whose gray eyes flicker green whereas mine muddy
to blue in sunlight; Aidan whose long legs wrap around me
and shame my own, scraped and bruised from an unfortu-
nate bout with Papa's razor.

"Molly. Here." He grabs her into his lap, groaning at her weight, and pulls me as well, until we huddle in the middle of the bed. Our heads knock and he points with his chin to the mirror.

"*Did you never see the picture of We Three?*'" he warbles. Then, shoving Molly to the floor, he takes my shoulders and pulls the quilt from me.

> *My father had a daughter loved a man*
> *As it might be perhaps, were I a woman,*
> *I should your lordship.*

He recites softly, in his own voice: not the deeper drone he affected when we had been paired in the play that Christmas. I start to slide from bed but he holds me tighter, twisting me to face him until our foreheads touch and I know that the mirror behind us reflects a moon-lapped Rorschach and, at our feet, our snuffling mournful fool.

"*But died thy sister of her love, my boy?*'" I whisper later, my lips brushing his neck where the hair, unfashionably long, waves to form a perfect S.

> *I am all the daughters of my father's house,*
> *And all the brothers too; and yet I know not.*

He kisses me. Later he whispers nonsense, my name, rhyming words from our made-up language; a long and heated silence.

Afterward he sleeps, but I lie long awake, stroking his hair and watching the rise and fall of his slender chest. In the coldest hour he awakens and stares at me, eyes wide and black, and turning on his side moans, then begins to cry as though his heart will break. I clench my teeth and stare at the ceiling, trying not to blink, trying not to hear or feel him next to me, his pale gray skin, his eyes: my beautiful brother in the dark.

After this session Dr. Harrow let me sleep until early afternoon. The rush of summer rain against the high casements finally woke me, and I lay in bed staring up at a long fine crack that traversed the ceiling. To me it looked like the arm of some ghastly tree overtaking the room. It finally drove me downstairs. I ambled down the long glass-roofed corridor that led to the pre-Columbian annex. I paused to pluck a hibiscus blossom from a terra-cotta vase and arranged it behind one ear. Then I went on, until I reached the ancient elevator with its folding arabesques.

The second floor was off limits to empaths, but Anna had memorized a dead patient's release code and she and I occasionally crept up here to tap sleeping researchers. No medical personnel patrolled the rooms. Servers checked the monitors and recorded all responses. At the end of each twelve-hour shift doctors would flit in and out of the bedrooms, unhooking oneironauts and helping them stumble to other rooms where they could fall into yet another, though dreamless, sleep. I tapped the pirated code into the first security unit I saw, waiting for it to read my retina imprint and finally grant the access code that slid open the false paneled wall.

Here stretched the sleep labs: chambers swathed in yellowed challis and moth-eaten linens, huge canopied beds where masked oneironauts turned and sighed as their monitors clicked in draped alcoves. The oneironauts' skin shone glassy white; beneath the masks their eyes were bruised a tender green from enforced somnolence. I held my breath as long as I could: the air seethed with dreams. I hurried down the hall to a room with door ajar and an arched window columned with white drapes. A woman I did not recognize sprawled across a cherry four-poster, her demure lace gown at odds with the rakish mask covering her eyes. I slipped inside, locking the door behind me. Then I turned to the bed.

The research subject's hair formed a dark filigree against the disheveled linen sheets. I bowed to kiss her on the mouth, waiting to be certain she would not awake. Then I dipped my tongue between her lips and drew back, closing my eyes to unravel strands of desire and clouded abandon, pixie fancies. All faded in a moment; dreams, after all, are dreams. I reached to remove the wires connecting her to the monitors, adjusted the settings and hooked her into the NET. I did the same for myself with extra wires, relaying through the BEAM to the transmitter. I smoothed the sheets, lay beside her and closed my eyes.

A gray plain shot with sunlight. Clouds mist the air with a scent of rain and seawater. In the distance I hear waves.

Turning I can see a line of small trees, contorted like crippled children at ocean's edge. We walk there, the oneironaut's will bending so easily to mine that I scarcely sense her: she is another salt-scattered breeze.

The trees draw nearer. I stare at them until they shift, stark lichened branches blurring into limbs bowed with green and gentle leaves. Another moment and we are beneath their heavy welcoming boughs.

I place my hand against the rough bark and stare into the heart of the greenery. Within the emerald shadows something stirs. Sunlit shards of leaf and twig align themselves into hands. Shadows shift to form a pair of slanted beryl eyes. There: crouched among the boughs like a dappled cat, his curls crowned with a ring of leaves, his lips parted to show small white teeth. He smiles at me.

Before he draws me any closer I withdraw, snapping the wires from my face. The tree shivers into white sheets and the shrouded body of the woman beside me.

My pounding heart slowed as I drew myself up on my elbows to watch her, carefully peeling the mask from her face. Beneath lids mapped with fine blue veins her eyes roll, tracking something unseen. Suddenly they steady. Her mouth relaxes into a smile, then into an expression of such blissful rapture that without thinking I kiss her and taste a burst of ecstatic, halcyon joy.

And reel back as she suddenly claws at my chest, her mouth twisted to shout; but no sound comes. Bliss explodes into terror. Her eyes open and she stares, not at me but at something that looms before her. Her eyes grow wide and horrified, the pupils dilating as she grabs at my face, tears the hibiscus blossom from my hair and chokes a garbled scream, a shout I muffle with a pillow.

I whirled and reset the monitors, switched the NET's vettings and fled out the door. In the hallway I hesitated and looked back. The woman pummeled the air before her blindly; she had not seen me. I turned and ran until I reached the doctors' stairway leading to the floors below, and slipped away unseen.

Downstairs all was silent. Servers creaked past bringing tea trays to doctors in their quarters. I hurried to the conservatory, where I inquired after the aide named Justice. The server directed me to a chamber where Justice stood recording the results of an evoked potential scan.

"Wendy!" Surprise melted into disquiet. "What are you doing here?"

I shut the door and stepped to the window, tugging the heavy velvet drapes until they fell and the chamber darkened. "I want you to scan me," I whispered.

He shook his head. "What? Why—" I grabbed his hand as he tried to turn up the lights and he nodded slowly, then dimmed the screen he had been working on. "Where is Dr. Harrow?"

"I want you to do it." I tightened my grip. "I think I have entered a fugue state."

He smiled, shaking his head. "That's impossible, Wendy. You'd have no way of knowing it. You'd be catatonic, or—" He shrugged, then glanced uneasily at the door. "What's going on? You know I'm not certified to do that alone."

"But you know how," I wheedled, stroking his hand. "You are a student of their arts, you can do it as easily as Dr. Harrow." Smiling, I leaned forward until my forehead rested against his, and kissed him tentatively on the mouth. His expression changed to fear as he trembled and tried to move away. Sexual contact between staff and experimental personnel was forbidden and punishable by execution of the medics in question; empaths were believed incapable of initiating such contact. I grinned more broadly and pinned both of his hands to the table, until he nodded and motioned with his head toward the PET unit.

"Sit down," he croaked. I latched the door, then sat in the wingback chair beside the bank of monitors.

In a few minutes I heard the dull hum of the scanners as he improvised the link for my reading. I waited until my brain's familiar patterns emerged on the screen.

"See?" Relief brightened his voice, and he tilted the monitor so that I could see it more clearly. "All normal. Maybe she got your dosage wrong. Perhaps Dr. Silverthorn can suggest a—"

His words trickled into silence. I shut my eyes and drew up the image of the tree, beryl eyes and outstretched hand, then opened my eyes to see the PET scan showing intrusive activity in my temporal lobe: brain waves evident of an emergent secondary personality.

"That's impossible," Justice breathed. "You have no MPs, no independent emotions— What the hell *is* that?"

He traced the patterns with an unsteady hand, then turned to stare at me. "What did you do, Wendy?" he whispered.

I shook my head, crouching into the chair's corner, and carefully removed the wires. The last image shimmered on the screen like a cerebral ghost. "Take them," I said flatly, holding out the wires. "Don't tell anyone."

He let me pass without a word. Only when my hand grasped the doorknob did he touch me briefly on the shoulder.

"Where did it come from?" he faltered. "What is it, Wendy?"

I stared past him at the monitor with its pulsing shadows. "Not me," I whispered at last. "The boy in the tree."

They found the sleep researcher at shift-change that evening, hanging by the swag that had decorated her canopied bed. Anna told me about it at dinner.

"Her monitors registered an emergent MP." She licked her lips unconsciously, like a kitten. "Do you think we could get into the morgue?"

I yawned and shook my head. "Are you crazy?"

Anna giggled and rubbed my neck. "Isn't everybody?"

Several aides entered the dining room, scanning warily before they started tapping empties on the shoulder and gesturing to the door. I looked up to see Justice, his face white and pinched as he stood behind me.

"You're to go to your chambers," he announced. "Dr. Harrow says you are not to talk to anyone." He swallowed and avoided my eyes, then abruptly stared directly at me for the first time. "I told her that I hadn't seen you yet but would make certain you knew."

I nodded quickly and looked away. In a moment he was gone, and I started upstairs.

"I saw Dr. Leslie before," Anna commented before she walked outside toward her cottage. "He smiled at me and waved." She hesitated, biting her lip thoughtfully. "Maybe he will play with me this time," she announced before turning down the rain-spattered path.

Dr. Harrow stood at the high window in the Horne Room when I arrived. In her hand she held a drooping hibiscus flower.

"Shut the door," she ordered. I did so. "Now lock it and sit down."

She had broken the hibiscus. Her fingers looked bruised from its stain: jaundiced yellow, ulcerous purple. As I stared she flung the flower into my lap.

"They know it was you," she announced. "They matched your retina print with the masterfile. How could you have thought you'd get away with it?" She sank onto the bed, her eyes dull with fatigue.

The rain had hung back for several hours, a heavy iron veil. Now it hammered the windows again, its steady tattoo punctuated by the rattle of hailstones.

"I did not mean to kill her," I murmured. I smoothed my robe, flicking the broken blossom onto the floor.

She ground the hibiscus beneath her heel, took it and threw it out the window. "Her face," she said: as if replying to a question. "Like my brother Aidan's."

I stared at her blankly.

"When I found him," she went on, turning to me with glittering eyes. "On the tree."

I shook my head. "I don't know what you're talking about, Dr. Harrow."

Her lips tightened against her teeth when she faced me. A drop of blood welled against her lower lip. I longed to lean forward to taste it, but did not dare. "She was right, you know. You steal our dreams. . . ."

"That's impossible." I crossed my arms, shivering a little from the damp breeze. I hesitated. "You told me that is impossible. Unscientific. Unprofessional thinking."

She smiled, and ran her tongue over her lip to lick away the blood. "Unprofessional? This has all been very unprofessional, Wendy. Didn't you know that?"

"The tenets of the Nuremberg Act state that a scientist should not perform any research upon a subject which she would not undergo herself."

Dr. Harrow shook her head, ran a hand through damp hair. "Is that what you thought it was? Research?"

I shrugged. "I— I don't know. The boy— Your twin?"

"Aidan . . ." She spread her fingers against the bed's coverlet, flexed a finger that bore a simple silver ring. "They found out. Teachers. Our father. About us. Do you understand?"

A flicker of the feeling she had evoked in bed with her

brother returned, and I slitted my eyes, tracing it. "Yes," I whispered. "I think so."

"It is—" She fumbled for a phrase. "Like what is forbidden here, between empaths and staff. They separated us. Aidan . . . They sent him away, to another kind of—school. Tested him."

She stood and paced to the window, leaned with a hand upon each side so that the rain lashed about her, then turned back to me with her face streaming: whether with rain or tears I could not tell. "Something happened that night. . . ." Shaking her head furiously she pounded the wall with flattened palms. "He was never the same. He had terrible dreams, he couldn't bear to sleep alone— That was how it started—

"And then he came home, for the holidays. . . . Good Friday. He would not come to Mass with us. Papa was furious; but Aidan wouldn't leave his room. And when we returned, I looked for him, he wasn't there, not in his room, not anywhere. . . .

"I found him. He had—" Her voice broke and she stared past me to the wall beyond. "Apple blossom in his hair. And his face—"

I thought she would weep; but her expression twisted so that almost I could imagine she laughed to recall it.

"Like hers . . ."

She drew nearer, until her eyes were very close to mine. I sniffed and moved to the edge of the bed warily: she had dosed herself with hyoscine derived from the herbarium. Now her words slurred as she spoke, spittle a fine hail about her face.

"Do you know what happens now, Wendy?" In the rain-streaked light she glowed faintly. "Dr. Leslie was here tonight. They have canceled our term of research. We're all terminated. A purge. Tomorrow they take over."

She made a clicking noise with her tongue. "And you, Wendy. And Anna, and all the others. Toys. *Weapons.*" She swayed slightly as she leaned toward me. "You especially. They'll find him, you know. Dig him up and use him."

"Who?" I asked. Now sweat pearled where the rain had dried on her forehead. I clutched a bolster as she stretched a hand to graze my temples, and shivered.

"My brother," she murmured.

"No, Dr. Harrow. The other—who is the other?"

Smiling she drew me toward her, the bolster pressing against her thigh as she reached for the NET's rig, flicking rain from the colored wires.

"Let's find out."

I cried out at her clumsy hookup. A spot of blood welled from her temple and I protectively touched my own face, drew away a finger gelled with the fluid she had smeared carelessly from ear to jaw. Then, before I could lie down, she made the switch and I cried out at the dizzy vistas erupting behind my eyes.

Aniline lightning. Faculae stream from synapse to synapse as ptyalin floods my mouth and my head rears instinctively to smash against the headboard. She has not tied me down. The hyoscine lashes into me like a fiery bile and I open my mouth to scream. In the instant before it begins I taste something faint and caustic in the back of her throat and struggle to free myself from her arms. Then I'm gone.

Before me looms a willow tree shivering in a breeze frigid with the shadow of the northern mountains. Sap oozes from a raw flat yellow scar on the trunk above my head where, two days before, my father had sawed the damaged limb free. It had broken from the weight; when I found him he lay pillowed by a crush of twigs and young leaves and scattered bark, the blossoms in his hair alone unmarked by the fall. Now I stand on tiptoe and stroke the splintery wound, bring my finger to my lips and kiss it. I shut my eyes, because they burn so. No tears left to shed; only this terrible dry throbbing, as though my eyes have been etched with sand. The sobs begin again, suddenly. The wrenching weight in my chest drags me to my knees until I crouch before the tree, bow until my forehead brushes grass trampled by grieving family. I groan and try to think of words, imprecations, a curse to rend the light and living from my world so abruptly strangled and still. But I can only moan. My mouth opens upon dirt and shattered granite. My nails claw at the ground as though to wrest from it something besides stony roots and scurrying earwigs. The earth swallows my voice as I force myself to my knees and, sobbing, raise my head to the tree.

It is enough; he has heard me. Through the shroud of new leaves he peers with lambent eyes. April's first apple blossoms weave a snowy cloud about his brow. His eyes are huge, the palest, purest green in the cold morning sun.

They stare at me unblinking, harsh and bright and implacable as moonlight, as languidly he extends his hand toward mine.

I stagger to my feet, clots of dirt falling from my palms. From the north the wind rises and rattles the willow branches. Behind me a door rattles as well, as my father leans out to call me back to the house. At the sound I start to turn, to break the reverie that binds me to this place, this tree stirred by a tainted wind riven from a bleak and noiseless shore.

And then I stop, where in memory I have stopped a thousand times; and turn back to the tree, and for the first time I meet his eyes.

He is waiting, as he has always waited; as he will always wait. At my neck the wind gnaws cold as bitter iron, stirring the collar of my blouse so that already the chill creeps down my chest, to nuzzle there at my breasts and burrow between them. I nod my head, very slightly, and glance back at the house.

All the colors have fled the world. For the first time I see it clearly: the gray skin taut against granite hills and grassless haughs; the horizon livid with clouds like a rising barrow; the hollow bones and nerveless hands drowned beneath black waters lapping at the edge of a charred orchard. The rest is fled and I see the true world now, the sleeping world as it wakes, as it rears from the ruins and whispers in the wind at my cheeks, this is what awaits you; this and nothing more, the lie is revealed and now you are waking and the time has come, come to me, come to me. . . .

In the ghastly light only his eyes glow, and it is to them that I turn, it is into those hands white and cold and welcome that I slip my own, it is to him that I have come, not weeping, no not ever again, not laughing, but still and steady and cold as the earth beneath my feet, the gray earth that feeds the roots and limbs and shuddering leaves of the tree. . . .

And then pain rips through me, a flood of fire searing my mouth and ears, raging so that I stagger from the bed as tree and sky and earth tilt and shiver like images in black water. Gagging I reach into my own throat, trying to dislodge the capsule Emma Harrow has bitten; try to breath through the fumes that strip the skin from my gums. I open my mouth to scream but the fire churns through throat and chest, boils until my eyes run and stain the sky crimson.

And then I fall; the wires rip from my skull. Beside me on the floor Dr. Harrow thrashed, eyes staring wildly at the ceiling, her mouth rigid as she retched and blood spurted from her bitten tongue. I recoiled from the scent of bitter almond she exhaled; then watched as she suddenly grew still. Quickly I knelt, tilting her head away so that half of the broken capsule rolled onto the floor at my feet. I waited a moment, then bowed my head until my lips parted around her broken jaw and my tongue stretched gingerly to lap at the blood cupped in her cheek.

In the tree the boy laughs. A bowed branch shivers, and then, slowly, rises from the ground. Another boy dangles there, his long hair tangled in dark strands around a leather belt. I see him lift his head and, as the world rushes away in a blur of red and black, he smiles at me.

A cloud of frankincense. Seven stars limned against a dormer window. A boy with a bulldog puppy; and she is dead.

I cannot leave my room now. Beside me a screen dances with colored lights that refract and explode in brilliant parhelions when I dream. But I am not alone now, ever. . . .

I see him waiting in the corner, laughing as his green eyes slip between the branches and the bars of my window, until the sunlight changes and he is lost to view once more, among the dappled and chattering leaves.

All Our Sins
Forgotten

DAVID IRA CLEARY

ONE OF OVID BRAZIL'S PATIENTS, a netshark named Rwanda Wong-Smith, had a hangup about toys—she considered herself responsible for the deaths, a decade before, of fourteen teenagers on rocketfingers. She *was* responsible, and one treatment with the pen cured her. But, somehow, she remembered the clinic, the front room of Ovid's apartment, in an unsalvaged borough of New York City. Or at least she remembered the stairs in front of the apartment; she found Ovid there one August afternoon. "A gift for you," she said, her black eyes moist and glowing.

She held the package out to him; it was the size and dimensions of a computer keyboard, wrapped in thin, almost tissue-like paper.

Ovid, suspecting subterfuge, scanned the offering with his infrared circuits. Seeing nothing but the heat in her fingers, he said, "Open it up, man."

And so she did, ripping the paper with her long nails. She flung the paper to the sidewalk and showed a black feathered thing, the size of a nightstick. Ovid moved his hand next to his pouch, where he kept the pistol.

"It's a bird, Mr. Brazil," she said; she waved her right hand and the black thing opened up in her left. It had a wingspan of a meter and the face of a crow; it blinked and waved its wings and moved its beak open and shut.

Ovid kept his hand on the pouch, feeling the pistol.

"Fly there," she said, and the bird flew over to Ovid's left shoulder. He brought his pistol out, but it closed its wings and sat there, electronic eyes watching him. "A gift," Rwanda Wong-Smith said. "For your help."

She threw him the remote bar and walked away.

Ovid, frustrated, was grinding his tailbone into the cement stairs. He couldn't get the bird to fly. "Come on, you mother!" It turned its head for him and took a drunken step toward the street. "Back here!" He pushed the rubber "on" bar down until it clicked. The bird took another step toward the street then froze. "Damn. I said back here!" Hoping to get the reverse to work, he jammed his left thumb down the slot the lever was in. He pushed so hard the slab fell out of his hand onto the steps.

The bird toppled into the gutter.

"Shit," he said, and someone else laughed. It was a kid, a teenager, wearing one of those anatomy suits that make it look like you can see all the internal organs through the skin, except it was a cheap holo and the pictures disappeared when viewed at the wrong angle. Dumb teenage fad, Ovid thought.

"Don't touch the bird," he said, as the kid stepped from the sidewalk to the street. His high-top shoes were on the edge of the asphalt, inches away from the bird.

"I've been watching you mess with the bird, Mr. Brazil. Your problem is the bar's not coded to your alpha waves." The kid's voice was low, almost gravelly; Ovid upped his estimate of age to seventeen.

"What do my alpha waves have to do with it, man?"

The kid laughed a street laugh; menacing. "The bar picks up electrical signals from your head. They got to match the code or the bird won't work."

Ovid watched the heart pulse within the anatomy suit. "So I suppose you fix electronics?"

"Yeah. Name's Rudy. I do freelance, biochips, solid state, whatever." He reached out his hand. Ovid shook it. "I can change your code in the bar, for free."

Ovid squeezed the bar, not lifting it off the stair. "Nobody does anything for free, man."

Rudy stepped over the bird, onto the sidewalk. "Okay. I'll tell you what. I'm interested in you. You sit on the street, take fancy boorzwhaz inside, let 'em out. What're you dealing?"

Ovid touched the center key on the bar; the bird squawked. "Sorry, man. I got to be confidential about my clients. The only way you'll pick that data up is if you're working with me."

Syrupy brown stuff oozed out of an organ to the side of the stomach. Rudy said, "How about we trade straight across? I recode your bar; you tell me what you do. A bargain, no?"

Ovid had a grid of associates, sworn to secrecy; he worked to maintain the strength of his organization, and let nothing slip out. Rudy, here, probably thought he sold hypescan in disposable syringes. Funny. But Rudy seemed smart. If he really knew biochips, Ovid could use him. "Listen, man. You want to freelance for me for a while, too?"

Rudy's dark eyes widened. "Doing what?"

"Courier stuff. A drug called Ammelin. I've been doing too much traveling around town, when I could be here, serving clients."

Rudy hesitated for the right amount of time; he had freelanced before. "Maybe I got spare time."

Ovid leaned against the wall and watched the bird. It floated above the crumbling bricks of the War On Poverty tower; in his mood he was reminded of a circling vulture. He'd grown tired of the bird after a month, and had let Rudy have it as a bonus. Now his infrared circuit had gone out, and he was thinking about asking Rudy if he had medic contacts. Ovid was depressed about something; he wondered if it was his new blindness, his inability to see the hot shapes in the shadows.

Or maybe, he reflected, he was bummed by the *thereness* of the city streets. The grayness, the brownness, the ten-story government projects, built to look dilapidated and now that way for sure. When he leaned against the mottled brick wall of his apartment and watched Joe and Bennie in their green trenchcoats, wringing their hands over the trash can with its fire, he felt as if he were part of a perpetual October. It was the same when cars hummed by or cats pissed against the corner lamp: *thereness.* In the afternoons when the Ammelin and whiskey of the night before were only a memory, Ovid Brazil wondered if it was the monotony, seen and registered, then seen again and again, the *thereness,* that made him feel so apathetic.

There was a man, in a trenchcoat not bought at Goodwill, coming toward the apartment. His blond hair was clipped short; in the squareness of his jaw and the azure of his eyes the naive might see a holo hero, but Ovid could see the truth in his walk. The fear of the *thereness;* the stride too heavy, the shoes too black, the collar too stiff. The man was scared of *thereness;* but, unlike Ovid, he was opting for self-destruction.

The man passed Ovid. He stopped in front of the staircase, and checked the address above the door. He cringed; the numbers were unreadable, dissolved and smeared by acid rain.

"Looking for Ovid Brazil?" Ovid asked.

Still staring at the fading white numerals above the door, the man said, "Yeah. This is where he lives?"

Ovid stepped away from the wall and grasped the rails on the staircase; the man stepped back. "Maybe."

"Maybe?" He reached under his coat and looked at Ovid. "I have two megavolts inside my vest."

Ovid smiled. "I like you, man." He reached into his down jacket. The other man stiffened, as Ovid brought out a pack of cigarettes. "You have a reason to be here?"

The man nodded; Ovid knew the guy had mapped the city streets in encounters such as these. "Yeah. I'm Daskin. I'm supposed to see him at two-thirty."

"I'm Ovid." He pulled out one cigarette, lit it, took a draw, then pulled out another cigarette. This one was stuffed with oval pills, colored an orange one shade brighter than instant breakfast drink. Ovid squeezed the cigarette and a pill popped out onto his palm. "Ammelin, pure. A hundred dollars per. Interested?"

"You're kidding," Daskin said. The confidence in his voice sounded forced.

Daskin glanced up at the building, as if searching for narcs behind the broken windows. "What is Ammelin, anyway? Some kind of transmitter juice?"

"Sort of. It's a neuro-stabilizer. It negates the pen process. Your brain's like a protein chip; it's got access connections, dendrites, axons. You do the pen, you break those axons down. But the memory's still there, in individual neurons. You just can't retrieve it. So you take Ammelin, it brings most of the connections back."

Daskin nodded. "So?"

Ovid puffed, then said, "People think that they can solve their problems by forgetting. They do the pen and find their problems catch up with them. Only problem is, now they've forgotten how to handle them. They're happy to go for Ammelin."

Daskin shook his head. "Not me. Once I forget, I'm forgetting for good. I—" He rubbed his hands together, and stared at the chipped cement of the stairs. "Well, can we start, please?"

"Yeah, sure, man."

Daskin was quiet as they climbed the stairs to the fifth floor. "Smells nice," he said in the hallway, and, "Retina locks, *here?*" as Ovid opened the door.

"This is my clinic," Ovid said.

Daskin's eyes went to the light filtering in from the kitchen, as if he were hoping that even more light would come in.

"Go on," Ovid said. "Sit down on the couch. We'll talk first."

Daskin went over to the couch against the wall and sat.

Ovid turned on the light. "Thanks," Daskin said. Ovid got the pen and a form out of the safe. He sat down at the card table and took out a Japanese ballpoint pen, a safe pen. He shuffled the papers for a minute. "So, you're having some anxieties, man?"

"Yeah." Daskin looked down at the couch and tapped it, as if expecting an explosion of dust. When none appeared, he said, "I've . . . you know, been to a psychiatrist. I've done biofeedback. I've, um, tried lithium. And, um, therapeutic software. The regular, you know, psychology circuit."

"Yeah, I know." Ovid wrote Daskin's name on the form. "Most of my clients go through all that crap." He waited, thinking about Cherise, the accountant who was coming for an Ammelin session that night. She had large breasts and he'd taken sex from her in lieu of cash before, but, today, he couldn't generate any excitement about the prospect. "Go on, Mr. Daskin. Tell me about your anxieties."

"Oh. Okay. Well, I have a real responsible position with, um, Plasticine USA. I'm district manager, you know. And, well, I've been losing sleep, you know, and I get real tired at my desk, and can't think." Silence.

Ovid started a sketch of Cherise, beginning with her nipples. No reaction; it was the *thereness*, again, getting to him. He looked back at Daskin, who was sweating now, even though the clinic room was air-conditioned. "Daskin, man, I'm not going to make you recount your traumas. That's psychiatrist crap—make 'em suffer. That's why you use the pen. All that painful shit, you write it down. You wait a little and the pen erases what you wrote. Writing's a lot easier. I don't even read what you've written unless you sign your name at the top."

"Really?" Daskin smiled for the first time, revealing orthodontic-perfect teeth.

"Yeah. You just write down your memories. Everything that hurts when you think about it. Everything you're embarrassed about, or you wish never happened." Ovid lifted the pen. "This is what does it. I'll leave it on this table." He put the pen down; its gold seemed brighter against the dull yellow table. "You write all the bad things and I promise you, you'll forget."

"That's what I want."

"First thing, though. You did bring the money order?" Daskin opened his attaché case. "A thousand dollars."

A few minutes later, Daskin sat at the table, began to write. Ovid moved to the couch, and started reading a *Psychology Today* article on computer/cat brain interfaces. He had to fight the *thereness* to make it past the pictures.

The bird was gone when Ovid led Daskin down the stairs to the sidewalk. Daskin jumped from stair to stair. "I feel free."

"Good," Ovid said. "Wait, don't run off." He handed Daskin a scrap of paper. "If you're having problems, call this number."

Daskin took the paper without looking at it, and shoved it into a pocket. "What problems?" He smiled again. "I can hardly even remember why I came here. Is that normal?"

"Very normal."

"Are you charging me anything?"

"No. This first visit is free."

"Wonderful. Thanks." Daskin looked down the street to the north, then to the south, and his smile of joy turned into one of puzzlement. "What way's the subway station?"

Ovid pointed to the south. "Three blocks that way, then one to the east."

"Thank you." Daskin started skipping up the street.

"Later, man," Ovid said.

That night Ovid chased down half a gram of Ammelin with two shots of whiskey, then sat underneath the fluorescent bulb in the clinic room. He breathed slowly, steadily, controlling himself as his heart began to race. When there was a green halo around the bulb, like an afterimage that wouldn't go away, he took up Daskin's catharsis: eight pages, the handwriting florid and confident in the style of the century before, the content, Ovid imagined, shit straight out of a sappy romance novel.

He began to read.

As if to balance the sudden blurring of his fingers and the edge of the paper, the ink took on bolder definition. Solidified, the words took on the life of the hand that had written them: becoming Daskin, or, rather, the layer of person that the man had tried to shed. This new person channeled from the paper up to Ovid, giving him a taste of what it was to be Daskin, the sickness, the perversion, the pain, the guilt. All of the bad things that had weighed on Daskin's conscience: the dying robin, wing ripped by the BB from his own gun; his mother, yelling at him for burning the drapes, for not feeding the parakeet, for driving the Buick into the fence; his father, hitting him when he arrived home drunk, beating him with the belt for saying the bad words; Daskin, in turn, beating Monica when she announced, so full of pride, that she would be making more than he was; the cocktail party, when he wet his pants; the fear that began when the elevator in the National Life tower broke down and that evolved into a phobia so severe that he sweated, became nauseated, whenever he entered the lobby of a tall building or left his office. And a hundred other fears and guilts, breaking him down, making life a tapestry of imagined repercussions and created dangers. Daskin's hollow self, purged onto the paper.

Ovid took it in. It wasn't as if he became Daskin, or even that Daskin's problems affected him. It was that the memories were compelling because of the ink that gave them their flesh and the Ammelin that gave them their life. Ovid could think of it as a homunculus of Daskin inside his head, though he liked to avoid such egghead terms.

He finished the eighth page and knew what Daskin was. He pushed himself up from the desk, stumbled through the room toward the kitchen, following the rainbow. He saw the whiskey bottle; it sparkled alive with the naked bulb, duplicated a hundred times. He bumped the bottle over with one hand but caught it with the other. Lifting it high and arching his neck, he took three deep swallows. The warmth gave him courage for the lights around him; the images, now, of Daskin crying in miniature in the four corners of the kitchen.

He sank down in the breakfast nook, closing his eyes, letting the afterimages fade. He resolved to destroy the Daskins in the corner, but passed out instead.

Ovid knew Rudy could be more than a courier. He was bright. He had fixed Ovid's air conditioner when it started sounding like a '98 Corvette ready to drag. He had given Ovid free access to all the psychology databases. At Ovid's suggestion, he had started going to the library, reading textbooks on amnesia. Rudy had even mentioned going to college, and figuring out the mystery of the pen there, but Ovid had persuaded him not to with some ridiculous arguments. Not that he was against education—he was simply unwilling to risk losing the pen to scholars and opportunists. Or maybe he was afraid to lose Rudy, clever Rudy. For a while Rudy had supercharged the bird so that it was strong enough to bring deliveries from the street to his window. Then the bird's motor had broken, and Rudy, apparently bored with the novelty, had started climbing up the fire escape to make the deliveries.

One day, about five, Ovid opened the window. Rudy was there: dark face, serious black eyes, fuzzy mustache, hair permed on top and long on the back of his neck. "Hey, boss. A kilo, right?" he said with his high-tech slur.

"Yeah." Ovid took the radio, opened it up. The circuits

had been replaced with a dozen steel vials, the width of magic markers. Ovid pulled one up: it was heavy, metal in his hands.

"Ovid, I got places to be," Rudy said.

"Takes time, man," Ovid said. Rudy's face was pressed against the screen, his nose flattened. "Nervous shit," Ovid whispered, opening the top dresser drawer on the other side of the dusty bedroom. He took out the code scanner, activated it. Its green LED's lit his hands as he inserted the vial topfirst into the slot. It was legit; the seal hadn't been broken, the Ammelin was good California pharmaceutical. He put the scanner away, then broke the seal, untwisted the cap, and licked the residue off the back of the cap. It tickled his tongue, like the candies with trapped CO_2. He was satisfied.

"Did you go take a crap?" Rudy joked, as Ovid twisted the brass handle and the screen opened. Rudy took the cash card, kissed it to his own. "What the hell?" He frowned at the digits on his own card.

"What's the matter?" Ovid asked.

"You ramming me or what? There's only eight grand. We always say nine."

Ovid smiled. "Yeah, I know. I've got this proposal for you. You take this instead." He showed him the opened Ammelin vial.

"Is this a joke? We said nine. I don't need no ramming. I'm your friend, not your pretty boy."

"It's up to you. I've got the cash if you need it. I'm trying to give you a good deal, 'cause you're my friend."

"I don't do drugs," Rudy said, but Ovid heard the hesitation in his voice. Rudy looked down, as if afraid the narcs would be storming up the fire escape.

"Rudy, Ammelin's not *that* kind of drug. Ammelin increases the efficiency of your brain. Makes you think faster, remember better." He didn't mention the hallucinations.

"Ah, Ovie, I don't know."

"Rudy, man, you can dose along with me, if you'd feel better about that. If you're real scared about it, you can sell it, make a damn lot better than a thousand dollars. But don't be scared; check it out. Shrinks use it for amnesiacs. It's in the Physician's Desk Reference."

Rudy stared. He had a strong face, solid muscles supporting his jaw. You didn't have to know he was smart to see he had potential. Ovid could see him on the city grid, pulling in neurotic businessmen, lethargic housewives trying to break out of fantasies. One day, he could be a partner, when Ovid was older, slower.

"Okay. Give it to me."

Ovid handed the vial to Rudy. The kid pushed it into a pocket of his jeans, then he crawled down the fire escape into the trash-lined alley below.

Ovid smoked and watched the day.

Rudy was on his powerboard, free-forming up the rust-brick walls of the building, his long hair trailing downward as he arched up around the second-story windows, then ground his way back down to the sidewalk. An old lady stuck her head out the window and stared at the kid, as if unable to overcome her amazement long enough to complain about the noise.

After a while Rudy returned to the ground, the plastic of his board blood-red in the early afternoon sun. Ovid was getting into the rhythm that the wheels made against the cracks in the sidewalk when he noticed Daskin coming down the street, probably from the subway station. He was wearing his trenchcoat again; funny. It was a warm day for October, a day when the ashes rested undisturbed in the trash cans.

"Hey, man," Ovid said from his stoop on the stairs.

Daskin grabbed the iron rail, clenching so hard his knuckles turned white. As if afraid to look Ovid in the eye, he stared at the cement. Even though this put his face in shadow, Ovid could still see that sweat was running down his face, dripping off the four-day whiskers on his chin.

"Want a smoke?" Ovid asked, edging the pack of Carltons between two rails.

"No. I need, you know, the Ammelin."

"Ah," Ovid said, suppressing a grin and tapping the ashes of his own cigarette. "Having troubles?"

Daskin looked up, his eyes wide and scared as if he were in withdrawal. "I've lost a sense. My identity. My place. I just wanted to lose memories." He looked at Rudy, who had done a one-eighty at the corner and now was racing back the other way. "You ripped me off!"

"Ripped you off? You lost your memories, like you wanted?"

"Yeah. But that's not all I lost, don't you see? I lost . . . I don't know. I've been sitting in the office and staring out the window and not getting shit done. I've got accounts." Daskin leaned back down, a globule of sweat hanging from his nose. "You've screwed me! You said my memories. Not my soul!"

"Hey, man, mellow out. You got to realize that the human brain's a big mess. Memories and processes, they're really all the same thing, just looked at differently. So you wipe out your memory when you use the pen, you're bound to wipe out some of your personality, some of your habits. They're all interconnected."

Daskin was quiet for a while. "Why didn't you warn me?"

"Oh, I did. Forgetting with the pen isn't a real tidy process. Sometimes you lose things you don't write down. I warned you, and you went ahead and wrote. Just how it goes, man."

Daskin relaxed his hold on the rail. "Okay. Then you'll sell me some Ammelin, now?"

Ovid took a deep drag, exhaled. "Yeah, man. But you don't take Ammelin without someone there. You want Ammelin, you come by here about eight o'clock tonight."

"What? It's dark then."

"It's as safe at night as any time. Just dealers and pimps, anyway, but everything's cool. Anyway, I've got office hours all day, so we do Ammelin at night. At eight."

Daskin drooped his shoulders. "Okay." He turned, began hurrying toward the terminal.

Rudy took his powerboard up past the third floor window and waved. Ovid wondered if the kid would be a good top-level man. He was clean, his hair was long as was the fashion for office boys and some young professionals, and he wasn't stupid. It only made sense to place him in a psychiatric office somewhere, maybe as a volunteer. Then he'd have access to patients' records, he'd know which ones were on the edge, about to collapse beneath their anxieties, their memories. Only question was—which hospital, which office? Ovid waved back.

He took a swallow of whiskey.

"Are we starting or what?" Daskin asked, bent over the yellow table in the clinic.

"A minute." Ovid had to let the drink hit his brain; his nerves were too raw, anymore, post-synaptic receptors wearing down under the strain of over-amped neurotransmitters. He couldn't dose Ammelin while sober.

In half a minute he was already feeling the effects, hot like a searchlight in his mind. "Okay." He went over to the storage box on the wall, unlocked it with his thumbprint, and took the pen.

"Here, man," he said, putting the pen between Daskin's hands. "You bring the money order?"

"For two thousand dollars? Yes." Daskin took the pen, gold-plated and heavy, into his hands. He clicked the tip in and out. "I'm not going to use this. It'll make me forget."

"That's the point."

Daskin smiled. "No way. This is some sort of ripoff. The Ammelin's not going to work and I'll pay and not know I did and come back for more. No way."

"The Ammelin will work. Here." He handed Daskin a phone number on a sheet of paper. "If it doesn't work, call. The guy'll direct you back here and we'll see what we can do."

"What good's that? I already know where this place is."

"Right. But you're going to forget that, too." Ovid handed Daskin another piece of paper. "Just write the directions on how you got here. Oh, mellow out, man. Sometimes people don't like having their memories back; they get pissed, call the cops. A bad scene."

This was good information; it assured patients that their memories did return. Daskin clicked the pen again and wrote a paragraph of street names, subway terminals. He frowned as he wrote; it was never an exciting prospect to lose information you really didn't want to lose. He handed the paper back to Ovid; it had the same old-fashioned script, the letters black as vacuum.

"And the money order, man."

Daskin glared at Ovid, then signed his name.

"Okay." Ovid took the pen and put it back into the box. Then he came back to the table and opened one of the vials. "I take half, you take half." He poured it out on the surface of the table; the orange tablets were brilliant against the wan yellow plastic. He pushed half of the tablets toward Daskin.

"Why do you need—"

"It's okay, man. Two people've got to take it together. I told you that before."

"Whatever." Daskin took one of his pills. "How many?"

"All of them, at once."

Ovid scooped the pills to the edge of the desk, then caught them with his other hand and threw them into his mouth. Daskin hesitated, then swallowed his own.

"It'll take a minute." Ovid stood up and undid the lampshade. The room was flooded with glare. Because Daskin was squinting, Ovid said, "You need the intensity through your optic nerves. Keep your eyes on the light if you can."

Ovid sat down and began staring. Every time he blinked he saw an afterimage so perfect in definition yet bizarre in color that it seemed like a cheap holograph. Without the whiskey, he might have screamed. Daskin began to moan. "Breathe slowly," Ovid heard himself say, and he followed his own advice, also telling his heart to stay out of his throat. The afterimage began to superimpose on the real image, crowd it out, rippling green as if under water.

Then Ovid began seeing Daskin's life, distorted pictures growing out of the lamp, the awkward, beaten boy, in all his pain and embarrassment, a collage emptying like fluid from a sun-bright cistern, scenes warping and waving and merging with each other, thirty years of ugliness. But it was a soul, wrapped up in the threads of survival, gone because of the pen and back because of drugs, ugly yet essential. It was Daskin.

But Daskin did not have this; Ovid heard his voice cry as if from across the surface of the sun; the man had no stimuli but the light and the Ammelin; his memories were not in his head, but in Ovid's; his circuits were firing at a hyperactive pace for nothing.

Ovid began to speak; his voice was not even sound, but pulses of fiber-optic information, almost binary code. He told Daskin of his visions, he told the man the life he'd lost, and the Daskin in the room (mouth agape, staring at the light) was a husk, but together there was wholeness, a maladjusted wholeness, yes, but complete. The air was the modem between their minds and Ovid returned every memory, until the visions wavered, until his own hands trembled, until the pipe of information faltered, broke, dissolved into the static air of the room.

Ovid closed his eyes and rubbed. The flashback scenes were still there, but weak, as if they were memories of memories, rather than having an immediacy of their own. He looked down at the table; it had returned to its normal glare-yellow. Though he felt like sinking into sleep, he forced himself to stand, all the while avoiding the impossible images that crowded the extreme edge of his vision. If he looked straight ahead, everything was normal.

Ovid found the lampshade and returned it to the bulb. That helped considerably; the flying chromium cats returned to their dark habitats, the technicolor turtles to their ponds. He took five heavy swallows of whiskey straight from the bottle, then, functional, he attended to Daskin, who had fallen out of his chair.

Daskin's clothes were soaked in sweat and he was grimacing even though he'd passed out. Ovid dragged him to the couch, put him there so that a fool might think he was sleeping, having a nightmare. Then he went into the living room, sat down at the desk, and telephoned Rudy.

"Hey man, can you take Daskin home?"

"Yeah, sure, I'll be there soon."

Ovid sat on his bed, the air conditioner off and the windows open. The incinerator across the alley was belching white smoke which his window sucked in when the wind was right. Sometimes breathing other people's trash was better than smoking. He could feel the quality of their lives in the staleness of his lungs: TV dinners, tissue paper, dried leaves, magazine circulars, plastic binders on holosheets, newspaper ink; everything had its own smell, its own texture, an essence that remained even after the corporeal wholeness had been cremated. He could map out people's lives with his nose, his throat, his chest.

He coughed out a particularly potent hit of incinerator smoke and took the pen in his hand. *Thereness*, he wrote, in his block letters. He had a dozen other *thereness*'s on the page of quadrilled paper; he'd been unable to eradicate the feeling, even after months. Everything was still there, sitting, quietly, as if out of a nineteenth-century still life. The smoke, the weight of his bones on the mattress, the grills and shadows of the air-conditioning box.

"Shit," Ovid said, looking at the pen. He had always had problems with abstract ideas; sometimes, sad for no reason at all, he had written *Pain,* and nothing had happened. The pen needed specifics, it seemed: dates, names, events. He had used the pen a few times when he was younger, after he had stolen it from the cardboard-box doctor who was ministering to the subway filth. The wino doctor had been helping them forget their misery, as if rotgut wouldn't have done the trick.

But Ovid hadn't known what it meant to forget. After reading thirty psychology textbooks, to make the process more meaningful, and trying to eradicate both affairs with unknown women and the tracers of Nicaragua, he'd found out. At best you wondered why you had bothered, because the things forgotten meant nothing to you after the pen, even if you reread the names of battles, women, mysterious friends shot. At worst it meant disorientation, it made you feel like a boat without a rudder, it made you feel like one of the street people even though you were pulling in a hundred grand a year. If he hadn't forced himself to start the business, he would have lost more than a couple of turn-of-the-century years. The rest would have followed; he would have wetware crashed, as the kids were saying these days.

Still, Ovid was glad he had tried the pen. His own medicine; it had been like a baptism; it had given him some shred of sincerity, so that he knew he wasn't simply ripping off neurotic professionals, but actually providing a service that worked. Trying the pen yourself—it was a necessity.

Thereness.

But Rudy refused to try it; it had been hard enough to get him to dose some Ammelin. Rudy was clean, that was good. But if he expected to really become Ovid's assistant, he had to try the pen once; he had to prove that he could deal with it. There were bigger goals in life than just maintaining your purity.

Rudy could even cheat, use an abstract term: *Thereness. Thereness.*

Two weeks later Daskin returned. Ovid led him in from the icy sidewalk, then let him sit down on the couch. Ovid slyly offered him a cigarette, and the other man shook his head. Ovid sat down at his chair by the writing table, took out the New Patient form, and began doodling on it. "So, you're having some anxieties?"

"Yeah." Daskin started undoing his trenchcoat, all the while looking around the room. "Mr. Brazil, I'm having the most incredible feeling of *déjà vu.*"

"You get these feelings often, man?"

"No, really. I recognized you when I saw you, and this room, too."

Ovid nodded, trying to draw a picture of Rudy from memory. "These kind of *déjà vu* experiences are real prevalent among people trying to get rid of bad pasts."

Daskin looked at him. "I didn't know that. So you can help me?"

"I can't make any guarantees you'll be perfect. But you'll be a lot better."

Daskin looked at the table, looked at the Japanese ballpoint in Ovid's hand, as if that were the pen. "I just write down what I'm thinking about?"

"Sort of, man. It's better if you try to figure out the memories you have which are making things bad. Or if you have phobias—"

Daskin jerked up, dust rising from the couch. "Yeah. Elevators."

"Explain it as well as you can. The pen's real effective for stuff like that."

Before they started, Ovid told Daskin about Ammelin. The man laughed and said, "No way, Mr. Brazil. I'm going to get rid of these memories and not look back."

And so Daskin became a regular client, alternating between the well-to-do businessman repressing a toxic dump of anxieties and the unshaven slob in search of lost meaning. As the winter months progressed, the delineation between the two Daskins took on absurd definition; the businessman was increasingly stiff in his walk and careful in his speech; the slob began to mumble, spit on the rug, arrive with his tie torn and a tequila bottle in a paper sack. Ovid had seen the phenomenon before; it meant that Daskin's brain was losing its complexity. Ammelin wasn't a perfect drug; after each use of the pen and each dose a little information was lost. This meant that his patients would become caricatures of themselves, because they would lose the neural resources to change in different situations.

It was kind of funny to deal with people as predictable as birds.

One January night, Ovid brought Rudy to Daskin's drug session. Daskin was late, giving Ovid the opportunity to sip at his whiskey and Rudy the chance to play with his holo soldiers. Ovid watched as the armies marched from the opposite corners of the sofa. Rudy was on his knees, bending over the coffee table, on which he had set his control panel. Sky-blue men the size of fingernails marched out across the cushions, firing needles of light. Ovid hoped they would fall into the chasm between the right and middle cushions but they kept marching, as if crossing an invisible bridge. Meanwhile, the red army waited on the left cushion, as if planning a surprise attack. Maybe Rudy could only operate one army at a time.

Ovid went to the fiberspy screen in the other room and came back a few minutes later. "Daskin's here," he said. His voice was abrupt; had he already had enough whiskey? "Go let him in, man."

"Sure," Rudy said, and the armies disappeared. Rudy jumped to his feet with an ease that Ovid envied.

Presently, Rudy brought Daskin in. Daskin staggered across the room, his overcoat caked with mud and missing buttons, his eyes wide and bright. "Give it back, give it back!" he yelled. Ovid tensed; Daskin seemed to be heading for him, but at the last second he veered off and hit the table. The table shifted a foot as Daskin fell, his shoulders hitting the edge, his knees the rug.

Ovid relaxed, smiling. Rudy had closed the door and was standing with his arms crossed, his face grim. Ovid returned his attention to Daskin. "Are you okay, man?"

Daskin nodded, glassy-eyed, spittle dropping from his open mouth. He pulled himself up. When he had made it to the chair he said, "Give me my memory, Brazil."

Ovid nodded. So often the strangest residual memories would resurface, driving a man to mention the name of a formerly hated lover as if by random, allowing a woman to recount a traumatic beating as if discussing a TV episode. Or, returning to the table, as Daskin had done.

"You bought a money order?"

Daskin nodded. "Five thousand, right?"

"Right." Ovid felt the whiskey hit his head as he stood. Recovering his equilibrium, he went over to the box and found both the pen and a new vial of Ammelin. "Rudy, sit down," he said. Then Ovid returned to the table.

Daskin pushed a wrinkled money order across the table. He had already signed it in faded blue ink. "Okay, man," Ovid said as he took it; what did it matter now? So Daskin remembered the money; he was a husk, now, spent. He'd already lost his Plasticine job; the bank certificates would be sure to follow. Ovid could let him go.

"My thoughts. Give them back!" Daskin made a whining noise like a child denied a favorite toy. His eyes lit up as Ovid broke open the vial and distributed the pills. "Rudy, open up one of the other vials, take two. You can do the fourth page, okay?"

Rudy retrieved another vial from the box. As he swallowed his pills, he stared at Daskin with a mixture of pity and contempt.

"Rudy, I'll do the first three pages. You do the fourth. Right?"

"The fourth. No problem, Ovid." He was still staring at Daskin.

"Rudy, man, be cool. Sit down." Ovid waved toward the sofa with one hand and threw the pills in his mouth with the other.

Rudy sat down in the middle of the sofa, squashing any hope that the blue army would continue its advance.

Daskin said, "You got that dumb pen! I'm not going to do no writing with it!"

"No, of course not, man." Ovid put the pen into his shirt pocket. "You just listen to me and Rudy, we'll help you get your memories back." He took the lampshade off the bulb.

"Shit, that's bright," Daskin said.

Ovid dropped the shade on the floor, took a swallow of whiskey, then looked up.

The bulb was leaking sunlight out its sides. And it was leaking into the infrared: Ovid's sensors, for which he had spent so much and gotten so little, suddenly kicked back in, giving him the picture, translated into a red where no red should be, not quite in joint with the rest of the picture. His infrared hadn't worked in months; but now the heat from the sun through the light was activating it, catalyzing perfection in junk. The heat was driving through his eyes and tearing down his throat and cajoling his heart into impossible rhythms, as if all the adrenaline of every victim in the city were suddenly being injected into his chest. His breath tried to match his heartbeat but he fought for control—slow, slow, he said to himself—and the discipline of his breathing transferred itself to his heart and it slowed to a reasonable pace.

Daskin screamed.

Ovid had proved his mastery over the Ammelin; his reward, now, was the memories. The first three pages, read over last night, memorized, and now retrieved. Daskin's autobiography, one man's story of pain. The images came down from the sunlight in the room, an insane mixture of sight and sound, information in the most primal of cunciforms. A start:

> I saw
> I felt
> I suffered

These images, powerful but incomplete; what Daskin had written, what he had forgotten. But saw-felt-suffered what? Where was the completion of the thought? In this cascade of trivialities, swirling from the brightness as through an inverted flushing toilet? These reports of a kitten purchased, a bus trip to St. Paul, grapes stolen from a classmate in sixth grade? Surely, if the personal pronoun were the left side of the equation and the verb the equals sign, such trivia could not provide the balance. But where was it? In the light from above? In that golden slurry of vacant thoughts? Of course, he saw echoes of thoughts, part of the Ammelin light in the same way that the sun is but the ruins of a more ancient star, but those were not of Daskin's most recent writing. They were December's Daskin; November's Daskin, October's Daskin, the thoughts more complete with each backward slide, but, commensurately more faint. And Ovid was under no contract to give Daskin the thoughts he had not purchased.

Daskin transcribed the banal thoughts he found into the sonances of color, sending it to the other man along a pipeline that, because of the heat he saw, was fuzzy brown and wrapped in crimson arteries. Simple thoughts. Broken thoughts.

He reached page four.

Ovid stopped transmitting, felt his mouth close as a pincer might over failed fiber-optics. He saw a hesitant channel form from the end of the Ammelin sun, far off, weak. It transmitted in slow bursts. Rudy.

Ovid relaxed. His work was over for the night. Rudy might not perform worth shit, but then it was his first time. He gave himself one last look at the sun.

He saw Daskin instead: broken, screaming, hanging from awful orbits over burning planets, flying over stars so old their ice fields had shattered, impaled on the collected spears of a thousand armies, elephantitis-bloated on an acid cross, choking on mustard gas that gave jaundice to the sky, floating in a Ganges soured with his own blood. Everywhere; a multitude of Daskins; suffering all the evil that one man could go through, which is no less and no more than a pair of parents, hating their child.

Ovid tried to reassure himself it was just the Ammelin in his own brain, hyperfocused because he, not Rudy, was using the words as a shunt. But they, these Daskin images, this crowd spilling from the sun and surrounding him like a blanket of decay, would not allow the repairs of logic.

Ovid screamed.

They were at his face, mouthing words of accusation; though his eyes could not move, he groped beneath the table. By feeling the bottle he sent a river of angry light through his body, but he brought it up to where his face should be. The lips of the bottle met his and the kiss was a bonfire.

Ovid drank, and drank, and drank.

He woke on his side. His ankles and his wrists were bound together, so that his first thought was that he was Daskin in Daskin's hell. His second thought was that thinking was *hard;* he was somewhere between a hangover and being slightly drunk.

He studied himself; something seemed to be twisting a fork behind his eyes; there was the taste of alcohol and bile in his mouth, along with the less familiar one of carpet—he was sucking on the shag. He forced himself to make sense of what he saw. The black leg of the table occupied about a quarter of his vision; one of the chairs was overturned beyond it. From the blurry pattern of light on the wall he judged it was about noon. There was a brown mass, perhaps a pile of clothes, at the bottom of the wall. "Shit," he mumbled. He hoped Rudy had taken Daskin home, and he hoped Rudy had told that psycho lady that her appointment was canceled for today.

But why was he tied up? Apartment was broken into, probably. No problem as long as they didn't get the pen. He'd crawl over to the phone, call Rudy, or some of the upgrid contacts. There were the ropes, though. They were tight. He tried moving. "Ahh!"

"So you're awake."

It was Rudy's voice.

"Yeah, man. They got you, too?"

"No, Ovid. *I* got you."

"Oh." He was too stunned to think of anything to say. He heard plastic climbing shoes on carpet, then felt Rudy lurch him up from behind. "Ow! You shit!"

Rudy pulled him up and put him in Daskin's chair. It was awkward, his hands and ankles united beneath the chair, but it was better than being on the floor.

"Look," Rudy said, pointing at the brown shape.

It was Daskin, on his stomach, his white shirt, pants, blond hair soaked with blood.

"So what?" Ovid said. "Am I supposed to be impressed?" Even that much machismo was exhausting. "What's the point of killing him?"

"No, Ovid. *You* killed him. You sucked him dry."

"What? That's shit, man. Did you shoot him or stab him or what?"

"I used this knife." Ovid felt a point in his back. "Uh," he said; Rudy pulled it away.

"Now, I'm going to cut your arms free. You pull any shit, remember you're an old man; I'll cut your throat."

Ovid was too hung over to even fantasize ways of escaping. Rudy pulled the bonds tighter as Ovid felt the back of the knife. It felt as if the blade were cutting into his wrists, then he heard a snap.

"Thanks." Ovid brought his hands back up to the table; Rudy waved the eight-inch blade once in front of Ovid's face. "Now what's your plan, man? You want a bigger share or what?"

Rudy said, "I've thought this was damn uncool for a while. Some of these people you keep for a month, but Daskin, it was four goddamn months. I've seen you drain his soul. Last night, I watched—"

"Come over to the other side of the table," Ovid said, twisting his head around to see Rudy behind him. "I hate talking to someone I can't see."

"I'm staying here. Harder for you to surprise me."

"Shit."

Rudy tapped Ovid's back with the knife. "You suck it out with the pen and then you give it half-assed back with the drug. Slow-kill them. It's disgusting."

"Ah." Ovid's mind fought for words. "The . . . idealistic youth. Man, this is the real world. Heroin, PCP, fliers, hypescan, coke—it's the same. You've traded that stuff. Here I got a service—I help people. Some of them're weak —they don't get better. Some of them're a lot better."

"No. You lie. And then I sit there while you're telling this guy stuff about cats, and I start seeing this pain. Pain, you know. Daskin's pain, in my head. Shit, Ovid, you destroyed this guy. Pain was all he had, and you sucked it out."

"That's healing."

"Naw. If you're a doctor, you replace pain with healing. You didn't replace the pain. You let Daskin's soul die."

"So kill me, man."

"Go on, tell me your life," Rudy said, and then he put the pen, the fine gold pen, on the table. There was no paper. "Write on the table. Start with your name."

Ovid clicked the pen. He wanted to write *thereness* but the knife was sharp against his spine.

The Painted Man

JOSEPH GANGEMI

WHEN DAVID RIVERS first met the artist, he did not expect that he would become her lover. She was just a lady with a particularly attractive upstairs apartment for rent, with a widow's walk and a priceless view of the ocean.

David worked in a decent seafood restaurant, Madeline's, in the next town up the coast, a place with its own marina where yachtsmen could dock and drink in the air-conditioned lounge during the syrupy-hot afternoons—when the smell of tar from the weatherproofed pilings of the boardwalk baked up into the air with the heat shimmies and blended with the odors of gulls, warm cement, cotton candy, and the spray of the ocean—and it was in this restaurant that David first saw the artist's work.

It was a large painting, almost five feet across, hanging discretely in the restaurant's atmospheric low lighting. The painting was not the work of an amateur. It chose for its subject matter not the romantic and clichéd images of a schooner on the high seas, or a gaudy, gypsy-colored sunrise, but rather portrayed the Atlantic as David saw it each morning when he went running on the beach, or collecting shells (a pastime he still enjoyed though he considered himself a jaded native by now, and therefore should have been oblivious to the ocean). The painting depicted a simple bit of beach, far from the water and the flat, smooth sand near the edge of the surf; this sand was dirty with shells and dead grass and splinters of driftwood. It was the sand found under the boardwalk pilings, and at the edge of the uncompromising parking lots of the new high-rise hotels. Sand that collected like weeds, as abundant as crabgrass in inland suburbs; it was the raw material of these coastal towns, and it found its way into shoes and pipes and the trunks of automobiles. It suggested to David that the artist understood more about the makeshift quality of these coastal towns than the optimistic natives and tourists would comfortably recognize.

Maybe he was reading too much into the painting, David thought. He'd made that mistake before in college, confounding the aesthetic with an academic scavenge for meaning. But as he moved past the painting each day waiting tables, his attention was drawn to it again and again, and he memorized the artist's signature. Emily Lin.

So when he came across her name again in the want-ads beneath a description of an apartment for rent that met with his modestly expanding income, he circled it with red marker, and drove there the next day.

The house was at least eighty years old, dated more than likely from before the land contractors had redesigned this coast into a resort. While this was a town of no charm, the house was charming. It stood two stories, perched baroquely at the edge of a sand-and-scrubgrass hill that sloped to become the beach. There was a widow's walk on the roof, with a low railing, where supposedly in the past women would pace and stare out to sea in the hope of seeing their men return home.

The shutters were painted a morose black, and the shingles had seen better days, but then he wasn't going to buy the place, and as long as water didn't leak into his bedroom he could overlook the repairs the place needed. He walked to the front door and knocked.

He'd expected an older woman, with severe gray hair pulled back into a bun, and some eccentric outfit—a colorful sari, maybe.

She was thirty, he would guess, though there was premature gray in her long, stray hair. She answered the door in jeans and a sweatshirt. She was too thin, he judged, even in this day of fashionable starvation. He had been with

women like her before, and he knew she would not have to
inhale much for her ribs to show. He thought that he could
read many things there in her expression—irritation, possibly, and he wondered if she was a recluse desiring only her
canvas and the sea; a wit she kept tucked away like ancient
love letters, dancing behind her eyes like a moth; and a
patience that seemed unhealthy in someone so young.
Most of all, he sensed that she wanted to be left alone—

By others. Not by David. She showed him the apartment—a bathroom with a slanting ceiling no bigger than
an airplane restroom; a loft-sized living area with a beautiful hardwood floor that played like a creaking symphony as
they walked over it; and a leaded glass crescent window
that overlooked the ocean.

"I'm surprised no one has snapped this place up," he
said to her. "How long have you run the ad?"

"Only a day," she said.

"Then I guess I'm the one snapping it up." He turned to
look at her, at her slate-gray eyes like the overcast sky on
storm days.

"I've admired one of your paintings that is hanging in
the restaurant where I work," he told her.

"Which painting?"

"I don't know the title. The beach. It's very realistic,
has a quality about it that is closer to the truth than much
art that claims realism. Is it a real place around here?"

"I don't go out and paint on the beach, if that is what
you mean," she said. "Art is a kind of creation. It's like
poetry or music. It is making something from nothing."

"The materials you use are something," David said.
"Paint, ink, typewriter, musical instrument; you don't start
empty-handed."

"That is a scientific viewpoint," she said, and he caught
the faintest of smiles. It blew across him like the subtle
finger of breeze outside stirring the wind chimes. "Scientists are obsessed with the conservation of matter. Yes, a
painting is only a shifting of matter from one place to
another, a new organization. But the resonance of its reor-
ganization, the way it affects its audience, is the creation.
That is art. That is divinity."

It was perfect, the apartment. David tried to give her a
folded hundred-dollar bill, a show of good faith. She would
not take it. "The place is yours, no one else will have it,"

she said. It was almost as if the house and the artist had been brooding by the ocean, waiting for him.

They were not friends, David and the artist, though the absence of a separate entrance to the apartment forced them into a more intimate relationship than most boarders and their landlords. She was always home, she never left, not even for groceries, it seemed. David offered once to buy groceries for her while he was out doing his own shopping, and she had accepted his offer, had given him a list of vegetables and fruit and eggs and cheese. From then on he shopped for her. It seemed a fair exchange considering the trust she placed in him by giving him a key to the front door. He saw little of the first floor beside the hall by the flight of stairs, and the cluttered, dusty living room off to the left of the stairs, the spartan dining room to the right. He figured that she had inherited the furniture along with the ancient house.

After their first brief discussion of art, he had hoped to be privy to her works in progress, but two weeks later he had yet to see even her studio. In the mornings he ran, and on returning to the house he would glance up and hoping to see her at work in a window. At night he lay in bed and wondered what she did during the day, and how she supported herself. He wondered if she was famous in art circles, with galleries devoted to her creations, and scores of patrons willing to pay large sums. On stifling hot nights, when the rising heat after a hundred-degree day made his second-floor apartment unbearable, he would move to the widow's walk on the roof, and while listening to the house creak down beneath him, like a large animal shifting in its rest, he'd wonder about his landlady.

And then one Saturday, she asked him if he would like to model for her.

"It would just be for a short while . . . I'd understand if you are uncomfortable with the idea," she said.

David was sitting on her sofa, having been summoned earlier that morning as he came in from his run. As if in compensation for coming downstairs and at least considering her offer, she showed him one of her sketchbooks. Inside were rough sketches done in a rust-colored pencil. The fleshy color of the pencil and the inexactness of the strokes—as if approximating the musculature, mimicking the static nature of the form—gave the subject, a young, fit man close to David's age, a captured life. He was nude, and the sketches showed him in several poses, emphasizing his wide shoulders and broad back. They reminded David of medical text illustrations of men and women artistically flayed of their skin so that the structure of the muscles and bones could be studied. And like medical text illustrations, the model's face in her sketches was indistinct, could have been that of any man.

"Do you mean nude modeling?" David asked. "Is that what we're talking about?"

"No, I realize you would be uncomfortable with that, so you could wear a bathing suit."

He smiled. "The Bermuda-shorts type?"

"No," she said curtly. His smile was lost on her, and so he said, "I'd be glad to model for you. When?"

"Soon," she said. "We will do quick poses, none longer than ten minutes."

"I could stand longer."

"You have never modeled," she said. "It is strenuous—remaining motionless."

He nodded. Later that evening, when he drove to work for the dinner shift, he cornered the restaurant's owner, making a rare appearance, and asked about the painting by Emily Lin in the dining room. He had to lead the man to the painting; the owner couldn't recall it.

"Where did you buy this?" David asked.

"Through a friend," the owner said. "It cost next to nothing."

II

Posing was different from what David had expected, was considerably less erotic. He stood on a raised concrete dais in her studio in a stance reminiscent of Michelangelo's *David*, his weight balanced primarily on his right leg. He wore a bikini bathing suit, and yet his attention was drawn away from his near-nudity to his rebeling muscles. Posed for only ten minutes, the muscles in his upper right thigh and left calf screamed at him to release, while the fire of their complaint spread to his other muscles. Some of the pain was caused by the physical arduousness of the sustained position, but even more the cause of his discomfort was psychological, David suspected; a newly discovered phobia of inactivity. He felt like a roach under strong lights. He felt as if each individual piece of his anatomy wanted to explode away from one another in all directions, away from this concrete center.

He found some relief in letting his gaze wander—so long as he did not move his head—about the room. At last he could see her studio, and it was cluttered and colorful, busy with sights to distract him from his immobility.

On the dais he felt like God, the studio spread below him. It was a vantage that had amazed him as a child when he had climbed a ladder in his room and looked down on his bed—the view, he'd thought, that God would have of him at night.

The only item in the studio in greater abundance than the supplies of her craft—pencils, charcoal sticks, rags, brushes, coffee cans of milky water for washing brushes, egg cartons for mixing paints—were the books. More than a thousand, David estimated: sketchbooks with spiral bindings, heavy black volumes that looked like diaries (and which he later learned were more permanent sketchbooks), art texts, calendars, and almanacs. A broken-spined set of encyclopedias, dating before the first lunar landing, slumped in the corner. David later opened one and a shower of pressed flowers fluttered out like butterflies.

There were only two framed pictures on the walls. One, an antique or a clever reproduction, was a page from a medical text showing a hand stripped of layers of skin and muscle to reveal the machination of the fingers; the hand, part skeleton and part striated-muscle, looked as if was offering to a lover an orchid of its own flayed skin.

The other framed work was Emily's, and David paid particular attention to it, because he thought it would reveal much about her, this one piece of her work she valued enough to frame. It was a sketch of the same man that David had examined earlier in her sketchbook. This was the finest of the sketches, though, with a perfect captured motion of shoulders and limbs, a dancing stillness of form. Thinking about the sketch, David watched Emily as she worked sketching him, and he wondered if she would capture him so completely.

"That is very good," she said suddenly. "That was over twenty minutes. I'm sorry, I got lost in what I was doing."

He released the lock on his muscles and then began to step down from the dais. She hurried over to help him, and as his knees began to buckle he realized why, and was grateful for her supporting arm. "Let's get you something to eat," she said.

Lunch consisted of apple wedges and raisins, cheese, bread, and ice water. She went to the refrigerator each time she thought of something new for them to have. A plate of raw vegetables. A jar of preserves. They ate standing, nibbling at the food as they carried it to the table, so that while David thought they were setting out lunch, they were finishing it.

"You posed very well," she said to him. Pale light filled the room. There was a glass sun-catcher shaped like grapes in the window, and the sunlight dappled a corner of the table with purple.

"Modeling is more difficult than I expected."

She nodded. "That is why professional models are paid so well."

"I thought they were paid well for taking their clothes off," he said, smiling.

She returned his smile. "That too."

"Maybe I should consider a career change."

For a while they ate in silence. David watched her carefully pick pieces of fruit from the plates and consider them before she ate. Living alone and surviving on raw vegetables and fruit, he wondered if she ever needed to use the stove. He asked, "Have you lived here long?"

"As long as I can remember." She seemed to be considering if she should tell him more. "My father was an artist, I've taken over his studio. Half the things in there were his."

"You get your talent from your father," David said. "Was your mother artistic?"

"I never knew her." She did not elaborate. She sipped her water. "My father was somewhat famous. Galleries in New York showed his work."

"I'm afraid I haven't heard of him."

"You are not an artist, I wouldn't expect you to have heard of him. Only the outlandish and flamboyant artists escape the circles of academics and make it to the outside world, though occasionally real talent makes it."

"Is that what you want?"

"I already have what I want now," she said. She glanced out the window, down at the beige strip of beach. David studied her face. It was smooth, pale from lack of sunlight. Her eyes were older, he thought. They were the eyes of someone who had recently walked into startlingly bright light.

"Do you like the apartment?" she asked him. "Is everything all right?"

"Yes, it's fine."

"Not too hot, I hope. I hear you at night up on the widow's walk."

"It's bearable. Do you mind if I ask you who used to live up there?"

"I did for a while," she said. "Not long, though. It was mostly for storage. My father and I did not need much room."

"And no one else has ever lived here with you?" He thought he could risk prying and ask further: there had been affection in that framed sketch. "That man in the sketch you have hanging on your studio wall, was he just a model?"

She smiled then, craftily, empty of humor—the expression of a chess player when bested by a devious opponent.

"More than a model, yes."

David modeled again for Emily that week, and several times after that. He felt more comfortable with his landlady, moved casually through her home. Where before he had tried to mind his business and venture little more than a glance into the rooms alongside his path to the stairs, now he felt free in the afternoons that he wasn't working to walk to her studio and say hello. Once, such a casual greeting had turned into a spontaneous modeling session.

He had just come in from running.

"Were you jogging?" she asked.

"Yes. I ran four towns up the beach." He had been proud of the achievement, pushing his body beyond his normal limit. He'd gotten his second wind, a wave of euphoria accompanying the discovered reserve of strength. He'd thought of what his father had once told him, that only after the exhaustion point was surpassed was new endurance built. Moving into that crest of revitalization, scoops of damp sand flinging behind him as he chased the lip of foam at the edge of the surf, he had believed his father's words.

"Why do you jog?" Emily asked.

David considered her question. He wondered if she genuinely wanted to know, or if his opinion was irrelevant to a skeptical attack awaiting.

"I enjoy it, I guess. What do you mean?"

"You must know the reasons behind something you perform so ritually. Is it for your health?"

"To stay fit, yes. I don't know," he said, watching her. He could tell she wanted him to elaborate. "It makes me feel vital, full of potential. After I've rested I feel better than when I started."

"Would you pose for me like this?" she asked.

"What, now?"

"If you could."

He hesitated for a moment, and then he pulled his T-shirt over his head. He felt the prickle of sweat drying on his chest, and he felt a shiver run through him, head to toe. It was electric, the fertile potential he felt. He stepped out of his sneakers and then peeled away his damp socks. She took the pile of clothes and moved them.

"You don't want to get too close," he warned her. He wrinkled his nose. She smiled wanly.

He did not have a bathing suit downstairs with him, and so he said, "Do you want me to pose nude? I think I'd be comfortable with that now."

"All right."

He hooked his thumbs under the elastic band of his shorts and his underwear, and then he skinned them down. She was not watching as he did it—she was preparing a piece of board on her easel, and arranging the charcoal pencils she used—and the moment felt less dramatic than he'd envisioned it.

He stepped up onto the concrete dais. The concrete was smooth and cool beneath his bare feet, like bathroom tile. He felt strong. His senses were keen, and he felt like an athlete judging the conditions before a competition. He could feel the damp chill of the sweat drying from his hair against his forehead.

She turned to look at him, an appraiser's glance, and then she said, "I want you to stand in whatever way your muscles tell you would be comfortable."

"That would be lying down," he said, smiling, but he let his shoulders sag slightly. "Too relaxed?" he asked.

In answer, she began to sketch. Her teeth worried at her lower lip as she concentrated. She threw brief glances at him. He remembered his own single art class in college, how he'd been unable to see the forms presented to him as they were—been too unsure of what his eyes took in. Struggling to sketch the arm of a model in that class—a black woman with an enormous Afro, another student—he had drawn the arm as an arm was expected to look: linear, jointed at the elbow. He had been so preoccupied with the task of mimicking the correct proportions of forearm to upper arm that he had missed the sensual curve of the muscles. "Is that really how her arm looks?" his teacher had asked, over David's shoulder. He had taken David's pencil and drawn a smooth, incredibly serpentine curve, ridiculously misproportioned, David had thought, until he had glanced back at the model and seen that the drawn arm was absolutely accurate. In later attempts his untalented abilities had caused him to compensate by exaggerating; those pictures were failures, and he'd been happy with his teacher's sympathetic C grades. He just couldn't see the form. What was ridiculous to imagine, once committed to paper (the risk taken), became the truest representation of reality.

He watched Emily sketching him. There was something antique and broken about her. She was porcelain beautiful, he thought, and yet there was a hidden defect which he could not divine. She was a doll that would not close its eyes properly when laid down. It was emotional, he thought. Maybe it was the subtle damage caused by a childhood of neglect by her eccentric father.

She had hinted once during a posing session that she had become very self-sufficient as a child, through necessity. This had included more than the ability to keep house and prepare her own meals; it included her emotional, and imaginative, life. Like David she had spent half her childhood in her imagination. The ocean and the wonderfully pliable sand—a flux of raw material open to her imagination—had nurtured her, just as David had had the pine forests of North Carolina to entertain him. Somewhere in her development her talents had been focused, disciplined toward art, probably with her father's encouragement, while David had allowed his imagination to remain vague on into his adult life, a spring of uncontrollable day-dreaming and fantasy, there when needed. He liked to think that in her wanderings through her imagination, like an enchanted forest, Emily had stumbled on a paintbrush and palette.

And yet there was something missing from her, something unhealthy. Perhaps it was her lack of a mate—prejudice, David knew, to assume she was sick simply because she chose to live alone. After all, he didn't have anyone.

He had pursued the topic with her before, at least once since he'd questioned her about the framed sketch of the mysterious man, and he knew now that he had been more than just a model, that she had become involved with him, might even have fallen in love. She had told him a little—it was after a successful session of posing, and she was feeling generous.

"I did a lot for him. He was grateful but eventually he left . . . we broke up." These last few words seemed awkwardly expressed, as if she had added them to legitimize what she was saying with a modern singles jargon. "I was lonely for a long time."

Now, standing naked before her, David asked her more.

"Did he hurt you terribly?"

She held one of her quick glances, met his eyes. Her hand was poised above the paper. Cautiously, she asked, "Who, David?"

"You know. The one in the sketches. You've never told me his name."

She was quiet. She had resumed sketching, but her glances at him had stopped; she stared fixedly at her work. "Yes, I was very hurt. I was angry."

He shifted his stance slightly. "Don't move!" she snapped. Then, "Please—you moved. Are you getting tired?"

"No." He felt his heart skipping, as if he were running on the beach. "What was he like? Was he young, older than you? Was he another artist?"

"Young," she said. Her words were clipped. "A boy, not an artist, not even a professional model."

"And you were together for—"

She said precisely, "We were together for a long time."

She laid down her charcoal pencil, and her calm replaced itself, closed over her like smoke. She smiled. "I was so angry and hurt when he left that I took something away from him."

She was standing now. She gingerly picked up the canvas and held it before her as she carried it to him. David stepped down from the dais. She began to turn the sketch so that he could see it, but he pushed it away carefully.

"I don't want to see it," he said. "Not yet."

He felt something icy on his hip, and did not need to look down to know that it was her hand. With the contact, a spell was broken, and he realized that in the weeks he had lived here he had never touched her, not even her hand.

With her other hand she set the canvas down, and then he felt the right hand tickle over him, tracing the lines of his thighs. His quadriceps bunched as if beneath electric current, as her hand moved over him. With one hand she touched his ribs, low, near his stomach, and then the other lightly touched between his legs, the center of him, the feathery touch moving up to hold him. Then she kissed him, as he felt her hands drift over his body.

They made love in her bed, with the old blankets, smelling of winter storage and dust, thrown back to reveal the sheets. Instead of a headboard, she had a sixty-gallon aquarium, and David watched the gray drifting angelfish in the dark water. At one point the corner of her fitted sheet came loose and the elastic snapped it down around her shoulder, like a cape. The bed was filled with pillows that were used or pushed aside, throw pillows with tassels, or knitted pillows with bits of mirror sewn into them like jewels. He moved sometimes only for himself, to make it feel good for him. Other times he sank deep into a numb but warm darkness so that she called out. They made love until they were good at it together.

They made love until David almost began to think that he was in control.

III

Late at night, when the darkness pressed in around him, as if someone were holding a pillow against his face, David lay in bed listening to Emily's breathing, rhythmic and almost synchronized with the faraway rush of the surf. Sometimes, when he thought she was asleep, he'd flip onto his stomach and watch the angelfish in the aquarium, and reaching up he'd turned on the aquarium lamp and flood the bed with a luminescent aqueous light that set the sheets to rippling, as if they were sleeping at the bottom of a swimming pool.

He was cautious turning on the light. In the two weeks they had been lovers he had been unable to recognize accurately the sound of her sleep-breathing. At any moment she could be awake, listening to him. She had surprised him before, speaking suddenly in the middle of the night when he'd thought she was asleep. She always knew when he was awake.

When he did sleep, she was present in his dreams. He was curious about that—she had penetrated his dream-life much more quickly than anyone he had ever cared for in the past. Her presence in his dreams was comforting. She was never the center of the dreams, and yet she was always on hand, an extension of himself.

One day she gave him a framed sketch of himself— sexless, faceless, and yet unmistakably his captured essence. He had been touched, and the feeling of belonging had begun to creep in. He was not sure he loved her, but he felt that it was right for him to be with her.

And yet that sketch had had another effect on him as well: he no longer wanted to pose for her. Standing before her on the dais was unbearable. Finally he told her that he did not want to pose. She really didn't need him as a model anymore, he thought. She could go back to the other material she had painted.

"What's wrong?" she asked.

He did not know what was wrong, so he tried to laugh, to make a joke of it. "It's like those aborigines who are afraid photographs will steal their souls." That seemed closer to the truth than anything else he could think of.

He did not want to close himself off from her, though. He woke early in the mornings and ran along the beach, chasing clusters of gulls up into the air as he jogged over the crab fragments they scavenged, and when he arrived home he would make breakfast for her. He'd have tea and eggs waiting when she woke, bleary-eyed and barefooted in the gray oxford shirt she wore to bed. He would suggest places for them to visit when he was not working. He suggested driving to Cape May to hunt for the milky, ocean-smoothed stones called diamonds that washed onto the shore. He knew of a nautical museum nearby that he'd always wanted to tour. Or they could drive to Atlantic City and have dinner, see the boardwalk. She wanted none of it though, only the house and David and her work.

At night David worked at uncovering the wound from her previous lover that had crippled her into this reclusive lifestyle. He was cautious, tempered his examinations with questions about her childhood. She was vague, described events from her past with a mythical simplicity, so that David knew she had been alone with her thoughts for a long time, had polished them into litany. Sometimes her own legends lapsed into the ridiculous—a stilted sense of humor.

One night, lying in bed, when David had thought she was sleeping, she'd had this to say.

"I created him, David. I was so lonely that I took my paper and pencils and I sketched him into existence."

She treated it like a joke. But the joke was repeated. She had painted him from nothing, sketched him out of the air and put flesh on his bones with watercolors. The legend blossomed: he had dropped out of the sky; he'd tumbled up from the surf; he'd been birthed from the sand. The story elements, reminiscent of primitive creation myths, had in common one feature—his arrival during a storm one lonely night, when the violent sky had been the color of a bruise.

David tried to convince her that he did not like her fantasy, that it was no longer funny. He wondered if it was just strange bed-talk, made dramatic through the dark and the lateness of the hour, and her fatigue. It annoyed him, but as much as he tried he could not fall asleep while she told her stories.

And then one night, angry, David had challenged her

legends. "You told me once that when he left, you took
something from him. What was it?"

And she had answered, "I took away his memory."

David examined daily her sketchbooks, and the faceless
man who'd been her lover before him. She had stopped
working, hadn't touched her supplies for two weeks. She
blamed it on David, and his lack of interest in posing. In
the mornings David ran, earlier now, sometimes down the
main roads before the cars were out, from one town to the
next, past the pastel saltwater taffy-box homes in hues of
pink and blue, as if built for infants. And when he returned
home he did not make suggestions for their evenings together.

She was sick. She stank of it; it overpowered her initial
mystique and her beauty. Each action of hers represented
to David another example of her instability. He was feeling
sick as well, nervous and unsure of himself. He spent more
time by himself in the old upstairs apartment. He thought
more often of the first painting of hers he'd seen in the
restaurant, how he'd been impressed by its unique vision.
At work he glanced at her signature at the lower right
corner of the painting. Her signature seemed branded in
the sand, a scorched bit of splinter trying to bury itself.

When he woke in the middle of the night he flipped on
his belly and unplugged for an instant the air pump to the
aquarium, and the familiar hum which meant life for the
fish had hushed. In the murky dark, the drifting gray angelfish had seemed to peer out of the glass walls, as if
hoping that in the incomprehensible color-world outside
their tank, the same hand that miraculously pinched flakes
of food onto the water surface might also bring deliver-
ance. David had liked the power in that.

Now he was looking long and absorbedly at her sketch
books. He flipped through piles each day, obsessively, so
that he knew this was just a manifestation of his own suffo-
cation. Once he had entertained the hysterical thought
that if he could bind all the sketches together and flip
through them rapidly, like cartoon animation, the
sketched man would dance and hop and fight to be released from the paper.

And then one day David discovered the painting.

It was in the studio and yet had been rendered virtually

inaccessible by the stack of books atop it behind yet more stacks. Finally his determination had freed it and he had dusted it off and set it before him.

It was a beautiful work. The man was sleeping, his pose unhindered by fatigue, and the artificiality of the dais. He was fit and young, a little younger than David, sleeping in her bed, bathed in aqueous light. David did not like the bit of the man's face that was revealed.

It was a painting of a soul.

"Do you recognize it?" she asked behind him. He turned. She looked small and tired, did not fit the role of creator. "I'm proud of that painting."

"He's the one from the sketchbooks."

She walked over to him and took the painting. "I'm glad it doesn't have to be hidden now, that we can set it out. I'll put it here—" She removed the framed medical text illustration. She suspended her painting on the nail. "This is where I used to hang it . . ."

David wasn't listening. He was searching his memory, riffling through the colorful images and the association of emotions they brought. He could remember. He could remember his parents, and his brother, and his college. He remembered his old apartment, and his childhood. Names were difficult to recall now, but he felt certain . . . almost certain. "But I remember," he said to her, and he was pleading.

She was saying, "I remember that night. The sky was darker than tonight. It was storming. I took down the wind chimes so they wouldn't be broken against the house." She smiled very faintly. "Please don't leave again," she said.

Now he could move, and he was moving quickly for the door, her spell broken. "It's not again, it's the first time I'm leaving," he said. "I remember who I am and where I was before you. There is no 'again' at all. This is all the first time." The truth was he couldn't remember now, it was coming apart with the panic.

He made it to the screen door, and then it clacked shut behind him. The wind was strong tonight and the ocean and sky were tones of gray, slate, and moth, like her eyes. He started walking, not running, away from her, up the beach. He was feeling better, more confident now as he put distance between them.

Does any more need to be said about David Rivers, and

where he was that night? He felt the loss of the artist and yet he knew he would be over it. He had survived her sickness and anything hurtful that he had done had washed away behind him, whisked away as if in swift-moving water. Before him lay new moments, and several more coastal towns. Nothing more need be said. If a legend needs an ending, then it is this one: As far as David Rivers knew, he never saw Emily again.

A Plague
of Strangers

KAREN HABER

June 7

DARK OUTSIDE—and in. Rick canceled dinner again. A sudden visit by in-laws, he says. It's always something sudden. I should be used to it by now, but I hate it when he abandons me to the evening. That blue hour after dusk when the lights of a thousand cars flicker like fireflies toward destinations. Appointments. Loved ones waiting. Tonight I got lucky. Just as the silence began to throb a little too loudly, the phone rang. It was Sandra, with more tales of life at the hospital, and some new disease the lab techs are excited about. Imagine getting excited about a virus. Told her I took Felina to the vet, and that the swelling was just water retention from her pregnancy. He gave me some diuretic pills for her which she won't take, of course. When Sandra rang off, I felt a little better. Listened to Mozart's violin concerti and worked on my quilt for a while, then, finally, got restless and called Bram. He sounded tired. I manufactured some heartiness and teased him about the after-hours clubs he likes—my brother the one-man perpetual party—and told him to get some rest. I should take my own advice—the painters are due tomorrow. What a relief it will be to get that job over with. I've been saving for it for six months.

It's exactly a year since I started keeping this diary. Never thought I'd stay with it; after all, who wastes time actually writing by hand any more? But the ivory-colored paper in this little antique notebook was appealing. Soothing to touch. It just fits in my palm. And it'll be interesting to read all these details, years from now—a bit of personal anthropology.

June 9

Painters did a great job. Cheap, too—which was the only way I could manage it. The sunporch looks much better in lavender, a gentle, subtle color. For a duplex built in the '60s, this apartment's not bad, if you overlook the shingles. Fifty years ago, anything built in the Avenues must have been covered in redwood shingles. But I was lucky to find it, even for $1500 a month, which I can usually just about afford.

June 10

Working overtime on the Gillis account. Don't think there's a hope in hell that I can make soybeans look sexy, but the client is never wrong. And with the FDA ban on red meat, tofu is hot right now. I wish I'd known how dull this work would be when I was in art school. Maybe I'd have studied software design instead.

Ate a sandwich at my desk and watched the lights come up on Nob Hill. Imagined myself in ten years, twenty years, at the same desk, eating a similar sandwich, hair graying, ankles thickening. Called Bram to break the monotony. No answer—will try again tomorrow. I've taken courses and gone to exercise classes, but the cult of self-involvement still reigns in San Francisco. It's so hard to make friends here. And harder still to get used to the fog, the way it enfolds the sunlight and holds it outside the window where it glares in at you without illuminating anything. The summers feel like winter, even after all the years I've spent here. I could almost get nostalgic for Florida in June. But nobody goes there since the Dade Silo blew. Besides, the jobs, and Rick, are here.

June 11

Sandra canceled lunch—at home with a cold and sore throat; maybe I'll take her some soup tonight. Went to Kundalini's for cream cheese and olive on rye. Overheard an ugly conversation in the booth behind me—the kind that makes me cringe: "But you always have milk in your coffee," a nasal female voice whined. "I can't stand cream. Never could," a male voice, basso profundo, growled. God, how I hate other people's arguments. Like being forced to listen to Stravinsky performed by a poorly tuned orchestra.

The woman kept chafing away, a first violinist whose bow needed rosin: "What's happened to you? Nothing I do is right any more. Suddenly you won't eat anything you used to like. The trip to France we planned is an awful idea —you want to go to Spain. Why did we get theatre tickets? You want to go to the ball game instead. You even want to change the color of your damned socks! I don't know what's going on, but I've had it. I'm leaving!" She stormed down the aisle towards the door, a short, stocky woman with that particular shade of red hair that only comes out of bottles. A minute later, a sheepish-looking bald man in a brown sports coat followed her. What a relief. I wolfed down the rest of my sandwich and had time to drop off the dry cleaning. Made an appointment to fix that broken filling, finally.

June 13

Had an almost pleasant visit to the dentist, thanks to blue noise. And he's switched his CDs so I heard Rossini instead of Bernstein, thank God. Dr. Scott was late, again, so I checked the screen paper in his waiting room. Scrolled through the front page fast. The usual trivia: kidnappings, saber-rattling, and the latest health scare. Some virus from Australia that they think is mutated from Alzheimer's— maybe that's the thing Sandra was talking about. Those medical statisticians love to predict doom, especially if they can do it exponentially, in the headlines. And the papers love to report it. Selling paranoia. I gave up on the front page—I'd rather read the comics anyway. After the dentist, treated myself to some clothing for the big office party—Jill's renting a hovercraft for the Fourth.

June 27

The kittens opened their eyes today. There's three: a fuzzy gray, a tiger and what looks like a calico. Proud mother keeps purring and washing them. I complimented her on a job well done and popped a bottle of champagne in their honor. Didn't have the heart to tell her that when I first saw them, they looked like little rats to me. But they're getting cuter.

June 30

Spent the morning walking in Golden Gate Park and watching the Tai Chi teams—such a curious mixture of staccato and lyrical motion. Met Sandra for lunch. She looked tired—up all night with Jim—his arthritis again. She's so patient with him. They have a real marriage, committed and connected, "for better or worse." I almost envy her, arthritis and all. Rick's philosophy of marriage seems to be "for better or else." He keeps telling me that "or else" is coming, if I'll just be patient. I'm trying. I mentioned this to Sandra and immediately wished I hadn't.

"I told you," she said. "Four years ago, I said that he was perfect except for that one little flaw—his wife. But all you could see was that thick brown hair, those laser-blue eyes. So where has it gotten you? He's still promising to leave her."

Old friends can be wonderful, but there are times I think you can know somebody too well. I gritted my teeth and reminded her that four years ago, at the tail end of the AIDS crisis, everybody was still getting married in a talismanic panic. And Mike had run off with that performance artist, so I was newly divorced and alone. Typical Katie— marching against the downbeat. But the last thing I wanted to do was commit matrimony again. Then. I was just looking for somebody I thought would offer safe sex.

Can I help it if he was good as well? Besides, I don't really want to marry Rick. At least, I don't think so. Of course, if he were divorced, I'd probably feel differently. Right now, I'd really just like to see him more often.

Well, she changed the subject after that. Told me about the latest hospital rumors—which doctor is sleeping with which board member and so on. She's really excited about some results the lab techs showed her—they think they've isolated an enzyme in this mutant virus thing. She said one of the symptoms of the disease is a shift in personality rather than fading memory. I asked her if she had a spare sample of it—I have a couple of clients who could benefit from this "plague." Then I told her about Felina's offspring. She wants the gray kitten, so now I've only got to find homes for two. Or maybe I'll keep them.

July 4

The party was fun but Jill certainly seemed peculiar. Disturbing. She was wearing this strange jumpsuit. I've never seen her in anything like it—she always wears finely tailored slacks or suits. She looked at the bottle of vodka I handed her as if she'd never seen it before. I thought it was her favorite brand. Maybe I'd better put in some overtime and cut back on the long lunch hours. If she's planning to reduce overhead again, I don't want my neck to be first on the block, especially now that they've canceled food stamps. Jobs are too scarce—I was lucky to get this one, even with the low salary.

The Bay was its usual subarctic summer temperatures. I'd brought my inflatable parka which kept out the breeze. It was fun, but by sunset I felt hollow—going home alone on yet another holiday. Called Rick later, but hung up when the phone began to ring. I don't want to do that.

July 6

Rick took me to the Trident for sushi. I love the way they've decorated it to resemble an old-style fast-food restaurant from the '70s. Formica tables and orange plastic booths—can't imagine that color used for anything else, but it's perfect here. And they even had scallops—a real treat, since the red tides have made them almost impossible to get.

Jill has redesigned the office for energy conservation and the workmen were marching around measuring everything in sight today. Each time I turned on my terminal it seemed like there was somebody with a tape measure looming over me, wanting to measure my window or my chair or me.

July 8

Waiting for Rick to get here, I called Bram and actually caught him. Cracked the same old jokes I always make, those magic words I always use to invoke our rapport. I once told Sandra that I think of my brother and me as old war buddies—veterans of the same domestic skirmishes, swapping stories and occasionally probing scar tissue.

Anyway, my timing must have been lousy—he tried to be polite, but I could feel his irritation hissing toward me with the long-distance static. It seemed like he couldn't wait to get rid of me. I reminded him of the night he'd climbed onto the garage roof to scare me and had fallen into the rose bush under my window. I waited for his usual snicker. Instead, I heard my own blood pulsing in my veins and silence on the other end. Finally, he said "Look, I don't have time for a trip down memory lane right now. Was there something you needed to talk about?" I told him he sounded odd to me, and he snapped that he felt fine, and he'd feel even better if he could get back to the game he was watching. Sports? Bram used to say they were the last resort of the de-evolved. I started to apologize for bothering him and he hung up. He's never hung up on me before. Well, maybe he was just having a bad night.

July 8, CONTINUED (3 A.M.)

Can't sleep. Can't put that conversation out of my mind. Rick's visit was quick but effective (I came three times) and after he left, I drowsed for an hour, dreaming of taking a trip by rail in Italy. Then the train stopped, the conductor wore Bram's face, and I woke up, soaked with sweat.

What happened to his sense of humor? Bram didn't seem anything like the calm, funny, guy I've relied on for 35 years. He seemed like a completely different person. What if he wasn't just having a bad night? Am I kidding myself if I try to blame it on weather or overwork? Could it be this disease Sandra's been talking about? No, I must be crazy. Maybe it's just premenstrual delusions. I'm going to take a sleeping pill. It'll all look different in the morning.

July 9

Fell asleep at 4 A.M. Dreams haunted by faceless men with my brother's name. Groggy all day. I've fought off the compulsion to call Bram again. I can't shake my certainty that he's changed. Completely. Even thought about hopping a shuttle East. But what good would that do? Can I confront him with any hard proof that he's different? Gather up ticket stubs, letters, old photos, school transcripts, the detritus of a lifetime, and scream, "Hey, this is who you are, remember?" And even if he acknowledged the change, what then? Who would I be screaming at anyway? Bram? The doctors? The plague?

July 10

Saw a videomag on the lobby kiosk with a big teaser headline: "The New Strangers: the First Wave of The Plague." Put four dollars in and spent my lunch hour reading it. Nobody knows much about this thing yet. Seems that the virus first showed up in Australia after those ZIIA tests they did there on human subjects with Alzheimer's. They're not really sure where the bug came from. They don't know how it spreads, either, although some people seem to have a natural immunity to it. Right now, they're working on analyzing its protein codes. Terrific.

I don't see what difference it makes if we know the address of the original renegade microbe. It's too late to bomb the place. But not too late for quarantine. Congress has already marched through a trade embargo measure and travel restrictions. Forget about getting a visa for Australia, or vice versa. They're as isolated now as they were 200 years ago.

I'm starting to hear rumors at work about this manager's son or that account exec's cousin. But outwardly, it's all business as usual. People just come in with deeper lines in their faces, bleaker depths to their eyes. The screenpaper says that the people who suffer most from this disease are not those infected. The plague takes its toll on everybody else who ever cared about its victims. One of the worst effects, reportedly, is that those infected refuse to believe that anything has happened to them. After all, they look the same. They have the same memories, same training and skills. All that's changed are their personalities. Their tastes. Senses of humor. The very essence of what makes them distinct and cherished individuals.

July 11

I met Sandra for dinner at Dante's Pit and asked her about this plague thing. Since she's friendly with some of the lab techs, they keep her updated on test results, even if she is "just a nurse." It seems that the early stages are characterized by sleep disorders, sore throats and feverish feelings. Then, one morning, the symptoms disappear, the patient awakens completely cured. And completely different.

The memory is intact. Ditto mental and physical abilities. But somehow, the personality has been reconfigured. Tastes mutated. Wagner buffs suddenly become passionate fans of old-time rockers like Bruce Springsteen. Rose enthusiasts dig up their prized bushes and replace them with euphorbias. Republicans vote Democrat. Traits once considered endearing in friends and relations are now wildly irritating, nauseatingly trite. All the carefully oiled mechanisms we've relied upon to keep gears whirring in the social and corporate machines have seized up. The boss has tuned the news terminal to *USA Today* instead of *The Wall Street Journal*. She likes Scotch, neat, instead of a martini at lunch. We're pushing the same buttons, but suddenly they're all the wrong buttons. Former optimists declare that the sky is falling. Maybe they're right.

I finally told Sandra what I suspected about Bram. She smiled and told me to relax. "Katie, you always worry about your family and friends. It's one of your most endearing qualities, but I doubt that Bram has the plague. He's probably just overworked." I wish I could believe her. I'm scared.

July 16

The screen papers and vidnews are filled with reports of plague cases. Last week, some of the cast members of the *Cats* revival broke into Shakespeare in mid-performance and ruined the show. There are rumors that the Secretary of State has taken an extended leave of absence to drive race cars. A prominent heart surgeon decided that he wanted to study horticulture and walked out on an operation.

The weirdest thing about this illness seems to be that the victims aren't exactly incapacitated. Just changed. I thought about calling Mom and decided against it. She'd just deny everything I said about Bram and then treat me to a diatribe—on my nickel—about why I should be married.

Rick met me for dinner at Deux Amis. He had an easy case load this week. When I brought up the plague, he brushed it off, as he usually brushes off anything important or threatening. Okay, by now I know how this game works —so I asked him about his two favorite subjects, his job and his kids. Finally managed to tell him about the last-minute changes for the Gillis account and he actually suggested an idea for the soybeans that might work. We finished the evening at my place. He left at two.

July 20

Sandra canceled dinner—under the weather. Just as well. I had to stay late at work to complete the soybean boards. The Gillis people loved Rick's idea. I should take him out to dinner to celebrate, but he's got a big trial this week and one of his kids has a birthday, besides. Maybe next week. Left a message with his service. Jill told me she's thinking about promoting me. I'm flattered, but I don't know that I'm ready for that much responsibility. I treasure my free time, and I'm afraid of losing it.

July 25

Up until two with insomnia and an upset stomach, again. Couldn't stop thinking about Bram. Finally got out of bed and watched a newstape of the Senate bribery hearings. Also saw a newsbrief on the plague—they're working on a vaccine for it. Dozed off within half an hour. Groggy today.

July 26

Dinner with Sandra at Thai Pickles. Asked her about Jim's arthritis. She just shrugged. Said it's his problem. Then she went on and on about this medical supplies salesman she had met and how she could tell that he was really interested in her. Like some high school kid with a crush. Not a word about Jim. Nothing about the hospital. Then she lit up a cigarette. I almost fell off my chair. Sandra never smoked before, not in the ten years I've known her. In fact, she would demand to be seated in no-smoking sections in restaurants and planes. Glared at smokers with real anger. I asked her casually how she was feeling. "Oh, fine. Fine." She blew a cloud of smoke over our food. I felt like gagging. I wanted to grab her by the shoulders and shake her, screaming, "What have you done with my best friend?" To run out of the restaurant. Instead, I ordered another glass of champagne and blinked back my tears. We'd planned to go shopping, but I told her I had a headache. Heartache is more like it. Is everybody I know going to be a stranger?

July 27

Miserable day. I feel like a part of me is gone. Sandra is my closest friend. Was. Now some stranger with her face answers her phone. I feel sick. Orphaned.

July 29

I went for the plague test today. Rick told me I was being paranoid. That's okay, Rick, hide in your cave. The clinic was almost empty. Guess most people are like Rick—don't know and don't want to know. Well, I sure as hell do. I may not be delighted with myself; I could stand to lose ten pounds, my laugh is too abrasive, and I like champagne much more than I should, but I'm all I've got.

The results came quickly—an hour later. I'm an immune, at least as much as they can tell right now. They're not sure it's permanent—too soon to tell about broad-spectrum immunity. Well, if I'm immune, what about my brother? My best friend? The doctors say they don't know why it attacks some people and not others. There's too much they don't know.

July 31

Saw a message on the notescreen about a meeting tonight—an immunes support group. I debated going. Had to break a date with Rick to do it. I called his service at the last minute. He'll just have to understand—and it'll give him a taste of his own medicine anyway.

About fifteen people were sitting on folding chairs in this church basement, staring at their shoes. Nobody seemed to know how to start. Then one little old man in a shiny black suit began to speak with a shaky voice. "My wife . . . She's different. It's the little things. The way she's wearing her hair, the way she holds her head. Suddenly she doesn't like the vidscreen any more. She used to laugh at my jokes all the time. Now she just sits there and looks at me like I'm crazy when I tell one. She just wants to go to Mass and play bingo. I feel like I don't know who I'm living with anymore. After thirty years." He ended with a sob.

That got us started. A chorus of voices swelled up. We went around the circle, listing our losses.

When my turn came, I told them about my brother and my best friend. I cried so hard my makeup melted—somebody put a tissue in my hand. Finally, we all just hugged each other, in a huddle like a football team. It was such a relief to talk about it with people who understand. There's a meeting next week. I can't wait.

August 3

Meant to keep better track in this journal, but no time. Had to take on more assignments at work—two of the other artists quit to go to law school and medical school, respectively. So hello overtime. Meanwhile, Jill wants to change all the elements of the presentations which I thought we'd agreed upon two months ago. Rick called and told me he stayed home today—his allergies are acting up. I wasn't very sympathetic. Thanks to PMS, I don't feel so great either. I was supposed to attend the immune group tonight, and I've been looking forward to it all week, but I'm too edgy. Good thing I get my period tomorrow.

August 8

Rick called me at work. His wife is out of town. He wanted to take me out to the wine country for dinner. I asked him if he had the time. "I always make time for you," he said, chuckling. Since when? I felt like asking, but I restrained myself. Dinner in Napa sounded lovely. And after all, it was Friday, my period was over and I'd even left enough food out for the cats. Why not?

It was wonderful. He was charming, funny and light-hearted, like the Rick I'd known years ago. We had a great meal in St. Helena, got high on a bottle of wine, went dancing and ended up spending the night. Sex was gorgeous too. Next morning, I expected him to jump up, check his watch and rush us back to the city, but instead, he suggested a picnic at one of the wineries. We stopped at a deli to pick up lunch, and I saw that he'd put a box of cookies in the basket. "Do you want these?" I asked. "Yeah. You know I have a sweet tooth," he said. Funny, I didn't remember.

August 12

Rick's been wonderful. Too wonderful. I don't want to believe it, but I can't ignore the changes in him any longer. He wants to play his guitar instead of work late. He's light-hearted and affectionate, doting upon me. Suddenly, he even likes the cats, which is all very nice, but all very wrong for the Rick I know. He must have it. But what can I do? I still love him. Want him. Since I'm immune, he can't infect me. So why shouldn't I smile and accept it? Why not? Why not?

August 17

Rick was waiting by my front door this morning, suitcase in hand. He's left his wife and wants to move in with me. Maybe I should have tried to talk him out of it, tried to convince him that he's suffering from the plague, but I didn't. I've waited too long for this. He already has a spare set of keys, and it feels so right, as if he's always lived here. I called in sick so we could celebrate—I know I've got the Brawley ad to finish and two proposals, but I wanted today to be special.

August 23

I guess a little guilt finally got to me—I tried to talk to Rick about the plague, but he says he feels fine, that he left his wife because he wanted to be with me, not because some virus bug told him to. Meanwhile, I've got other things to worry about. Overloaded at work again, and Rick pouts whenever I work late. Suzanne called from the immune group to remind me of tonight's meeting. I had to beg out of it. My schedule is completely blocked in.

August 29

Rick said he saw a screen paper story on vaccine tests for the virus. Says early results seem promising and they're looking for volunteers. Sounds like wishful thinking to me. I remember that Sandra once said most vaccines never work out the way they're expected to. What's worse, he wants us both to sign up. I know denial is part of the disease, but it's maddening when he refuses to believe that he's already infected. I tried to explain to him about my being immune, but he's so stubborn sometimes. Finally, I just got tired of arguing. Besides, maybe he really doesn't have it.

September 15

3:15 A.M. Absolutely wide awake. All wheels turning, making my usual tour of the universe. Don't know why—even the pill I took didn't do any good.

Jill brought up the promotion again. She's determined to make me art director, which means Larry is out. I like him, but I could really use the money. And I'm tired of being junior artist in the department. Everyone talking about the vaccine: will it work? Won't it? Left at four so Rick and I could go for the first injections, which were painless, thank God. It took us a half-hour just to fill out the release forms—after all, these treatments are experimental. The transit tube was so late, we nearly missed our appointment. These delays are getting worse every day. You'd think they'd make this system more efficient.

Rick is already talking about getting married once his divorce is final. Says he wants to settle down and have kids, although we'd have to buy this place and build an addition. I told him it sounded good, but to get his divorce first.

October 19

Overtime again. Called Rick, and he's furious, as usual. I promised him we'd have a special dinner tomorrow night. He's like a little boy sometimes.

Reminded him to call the painters. That sunporch just looks too drab. I want something cheery in there, yellow or maybe orange.

The cats are really messing up the house, destroying the furniture. They're constantly distracting me, and they're expensive to feed, besides. Maybe I should take them to the shelter and let somebody else take care of them.

November 7

Cleaning my desk this morning for the San Diego move and found this journal. Did I actually waste my time writing all that shit down? What use is this drivel to anyone, especially me? Out it goes.

The Giving
Plague

DAVID BRIN

YOU THINK you're going to get me, don't you? Well, you've got another thing coming, 'cause I'm ready for you.

That's why there's a forged card in my wallet saying my blood group is AB Negative, and a MedicAlert tag warning that I'm allergic to penicillin, aspirin, and phenylalanine. Another one states that I'm a practicing, devout Christian Scientist. All these tricks ought to slow you down when the time comes, as it's sure to, someday soon.

Even if it makes the difference between living and dying, there's just no way I'll let anyone stick a transfusion needle into my arm. Never. Not with the blood supply in the state it's in.

And anyway, I've got antibodies. So you just stay the hell away from me, ATAS, I won't be your patsy. I won't be your vector.

I know your weaknesses, you see. You're a fragile, if subtle devil. Unlike TARP, you can't bear exposure to air or heat or cold or acid or alkali. Blood-to-blood, that's your only route. And what need had you of any other? You thought you'd evolved the perfect technique, didn't you?

What was it Leslie Adgeson called you? "The perfect master"? "The paragon of viruses"?

I remember long ago when HIV, the AIDS virus, had

everyone so impressed with its subtlety and effectiveness of design. But compared with you, HIV is just a crude butcher, isn't it? A maniac with a chainsaw, a blunderer that kills its hosts and relies for transmission on habits humans can, with some effort, get under control. Oh, old HIV had its tricks, but compared with you? An amateur!

Rhinoviruses and flu are clever, too. They're profligate, and they mutate rapidly. Long ago they learned how to make their hosts drip and wheeze and sneeze, so the victims spread the misery in all directions. Flu viruses are also a lot smarter than AIDS 'cause they don't generally kill their hosts, just make 'em miserable while they hack and spray and inflict fresh infections on their neighbors.

Oh, Les Adgeson was always accusing me of anthropomorphizing our subjects. Whenever he came into my part of the lab, and found me cursing some damned intransigent leucophage in rich, Tex-Mex invective, he'd react predictably. I can just picture him now, raising one eyebrow, commenting dryly in his Winchester accent:

"The virus cannot hear you, Forry. It isn't sentient, nor even alive, strictly speaking. It's little more than a packet of genes in a protein case, after all."

"Yeah, Les," I'd answer. "But *selfish* genes! Given half a chance, they'll take over a human cell, force it to make armies of new viruses, then burst it apart as they escape to attack other cells. They may not think. All that behavior may have evolved by blind chance. But doesn't it all *feel* as if it was planned? As if the nasty little things were *guided,* somehow, by somebody out to make us miserable . . . ? Out to make us die?"

"Oh come now, Forry," he would smile at my New World ingenuousness. "You wouldn't be in this field if you didn't find phages beautiful, in their own way."

Good old smug, sanctimonious Les. He never did figure out that viruses fascinated me for quite another reason. In their rapacious insatiability I saw a simple, distilled purity of ambition that exceeded even my own. The fact that it was mindless did little to ease *my* mind. I've always thought we humans overrated brains, anyway.

We'd first met when Les visited Austin on sabbatical, some years before. He'd had the Boy Genius rep even then, and naturally I played up to him. He invited me to join him back in Oxford, so there I was, having regular amiable arguments over the meaning of disease while the English rain dripped desultorily on the rhododendrons outside.

Les Adgeson. Him with his artsy friends and his pretensions to philosophy—Les was all the time talking about the elegance and beauty of our nasty little subjects. But he didn't fool me. I knew he was just as crazy Nobel-mad as the rest of us. Just as obsessed with the chase, searching for that piece of the Life Puzzle, that bit leading to more grants, more lab space, more techs, more prestige . . . leading to money, status and, maybe eventually, Stockholm.

He claimed not to be interested in such things. But he was a smoothy, all right. How else, in the midst of the Thatcher massacre of British science, did his lab keep expanding? And yet, he kept up the pretense.

"Viruses have their good side," Les kept saying. "Sure, they often kill, in the beginning. All new pathogens start that way. But eventually, one of two things happens. Either humanity evolves defenses to eliminate the threat or . . ."

Oh, he loved those dramatic pauses.

"*Or?*" I'd prompt him, as required.

"Or we come to an accomodation, a compromise—even an alliance."

That's what Les always talked about. *Symbiosis.* He loved to quote Margulis and Thomas, and even Lovelock, for pity's sake! His respect even for vicious, sneaky brutes like the HIV was downright scary.

"See how it actually incorporates itself right *into* the DNA of its victims?" he would muse. "Then it waits, until the victim is later attacked by some *other* disease pathogen. Then the host's T-Cells prepare to replicate, to drive off the invader, only now some cells' chemical machinery is taken over by the new DNA, and instead of two new T-Cells, a plethora of new AIDS viruses results."

"So?" I answered. "Except that it's a retrovirus, that's the way nearly all viruses work."

"Yes, but think ahead, Forry. Imagine what's going to happen when, inevitably, the AIDS virus infects someone whose genetic makeup makes him invulnerable!"

"What, you mean his antibody reactions are fast enough to stop it? Or his T-Cells repel invasion?"

"No, no, think!" he urged. Oh, Les used to sound so damn *patronizing* when he got excited. "I mean invulnerable *after* infection. *After* the viral genes have incorporated into his chromosomes. Only in this individual, certain *other* genes *prevent* the new DNA from triggering viral synthesis. No new viruses are made. No cellular disruption. The person *is* invulnerable. But now he has all this new DNA—"

"In just a few cells."

"Yes. But suppose one of these is a sex cell. Then suppose he fathers a child with that gamete. Now *every* one of that child's cells may contain *both* the trait of invulnerability *and* the new viral genes! Think about it, Forry. You now have a new type of human being! One who cannot be killed by AIDS. And yet he has all the AIDS genes, can make all those strange, marvelous proteins. . . . Oh, most of them will be unexpressed or useless, of course. But now this child's genome, and his descendants', contains more *variety*. . . ."

I often wondered, when he got carried away this way. Did he actually believe he was explaining this to me for the first time? Much as the Brits respect American science, they do tend to assume we're slackers when it comes to the philosophical side. But I'd seen his interest heading in this direction weeks back, and had carefully done some extra reading.

"You mean like the genes responsible for some types of inheritable cancers?" I asked, sarcastically. "There's evidence some oncogenes were originally inserted into the human genome by viruses, just as you suggest. Those who inherit the trait for rheumatoid arthritis may also have gotten their gene that way."

"Exactly. Those viruses themselves may be extinct, but their DNA lives on, in ours!"

"Right. And *boy* have human beings benefited!"

Oh, how I hated that smug expression he'd get. (It got wiped off his face eventually, didn't it?)

Les picked up a piece of chalk and drew a figure on the blackboard:

HARMLESS → KILLER! → SURVIVABLE ILLNESS → INCONVENIENCE → HARMLESS

"Here's the classic way of looking at how a host species interacts with a new pathogen, especially a virus. Each arrow, of course, represents a stage of mutation and adaptation selection.

"First, a new form of some previously harmless microorganism leaps from its prior host, say a monkey species, over to a new one, say us. Of course, at the beginning we have no adequate defenses. It cuts through us like syphilis did in Europe in the sixteenth century, killing in days rather than years—in an orgy of cell feeding that's really not a very efficient *modus* for a pathogen. After all, only a gluttonous parasite kills off its host so quickly.

"What follows, then, is a rough period for both host and parasite as each struggles to adapt to the other. It can be likened to warfare. Or, on the other hand, it *might* be thought of as a sort of drawn-out process of *negotiation.*"

I snorted in disgust. "Mystical crap, Les. I'll concede your chart; but the war analogy is the right one. That's why they fund labs like this one. To come up with better weapons for our side."

"Hmm. Possibly. But sometimes the process *does* look different, Forry." He turned and drew another chart:

HARMLESS → KILLER! → SURVIVABLE ILLNESS → INCONVENIENCE ─┐

       ┌─→ BENIGN PARASITISM → SYMBIOSIS

       └─→ CLUMSY INCORPORATION → BENEFICIAL INCORPORATION

"You can see that this chart is the same as the other, right up to the point where the original disease disappears."

"Or goes into hiding."

"Surely. As *E. coli* bacteria took refuge in our innards. Doubtless long ago the ancestors of *E. coli* killed a great many of *our* ancestors, before eventually becoming the beneficial symbionts they are now, helping us digest our food.

"The same applies to viruses, I'd wager. Heritable cancers and rheumatoid arthritis are just temporary awkwardnesses. Eventually, those genes will be comfortably incorporated. They'll be part of the genetic diversity that prepares us to meet challenges ahead.

"Why, I'd wager a large portion of our present genes came about in such a way, entering our cells first as invaders . . ."

Crazy sonovabitch. Fortunately he didn't try to lead the lab's research effort too far to the right on his magic diagram. Our Boy Genius was plenty savvy about the funding agencies. He knew they weren't interested in paying us to prove we're all partly descended from viruses. They wanted, and wanted *badly*, progress on ways to fight viral infections themselves.

So Les concentrated his team on *vectors*.

Yeah, you viruses need vectors, don't you. I mean, if you kill a guy, you've got to have a life raft, so you can desert the ship you've sunk, so you can cross over to some *new* hapless victim. Same applies if the host proves tough, and fights you off—gotta move on. Always movin' on.

Hell, even if you've made peace with a human body, like Les suggested, you still want to spread, don't you? Bigtime colonizers, you tiny beasties.

Oh, I know. It's just natural selection. Those bugs that accidentally find a good vector spread. Those that don't, don't. But it's so eerie. Sometimes it sure *feels* purposeful. . . .

So the flu makes us sneeze. Typhus gives us diarrhea. Smallpox causes pustules which dry, flake off and blow away to be inhaled by the patient's loved ones. All good ways to jump ship. To colonize.

Who knows? Did some past virus cause a swelling of the lips that made us want to kiss? Heh. Maybe that's a case of Les's "benign incorporation"—we retain the trait, long after the causative pathogen went extinct! What a concept.

So our lab got this big grant to study vectors. Which is how Les found you, ALAS. He drew this big chart covering all the possible ways an infection might leap from person to person, and set us to checking all of them, one by one.

For himself he reserved straight blood-to-blood infection. There were reasons for that.

First off, Les was an *altruist*, see. He was concerned about all the panic and unfounded rumors spreading about Britain's blood supply. Some people were putting off necessary surgery. There was talk of starting over here what some rich folk in the States had begun doing—stockpiling their own blood in silly, expensive efforts to avoid having to use the public banks if they ever needed hospitalization.

All that bothered Les. But even worse was the fact that lots of potential *donors* were shying away from giving blood, because of some stupid rumors that you could get infected that way.

Hell, nobody ever caught anything from *giving* blood —nothing except maybe a little dizziness and perhaps a zit or spot from all the biscuits and sweet tea they feed you afterward. And as for contracting HIV from *receiving* blood, well, the new antibodies tests soon had that problem under control. Still, the dumb rumors spread.

A nation has to have confidence in its blood supply. Les wanted to eliminate all those silly fears once and for all, with one definitive study. But that wasn't the only reason he wanted the blood-to-blood vector for himself.

"Sure, there are some nasty things like AIDS that use that route. But that's also where I might find the older ones," he said, excitedly. "The viruses that have *almost* finished the process of becoming benign. The ones that have been so well selected that they keep a low profile, and hardly inconvenience their hosts at all. Maybe I can even find one that's commensal! One that actually *helps* the human body."

"An undiscovered human commensal," I sniffed doubtfully.

"And why not? If there's no visible disease, why would anyone have ever looked for it! This could open up a whole new field, Forry!"

In spite of myself, I was impressed. It was how he got to be known as a Boy Genius, after all, these flashes of half-crazy insight. How he managed not to have it snuffed out of him at Oxbridge, I'll never know, but it was one reason why I'd attached myself to him and his lab, and wrangled mighty hard to get my name added to his papers.

So I kept watch over his work. It sounded so dubious, so damn stupid. And I knew it just might bear fruit, in the end.

That's why I was ready when Les invited me along to a conference down in Bloomsbury one day. The colloquium itself was routine, but I could tell he was near to bursting with news. Afterward we walked down Charing Cross

Road to a pizza place, one far enough from the university area to be sure there'd be no colleagues anywhere within earshot—just the pre-theatre crowd, waiting till opening time down at Leicester Square.

Les breathlessly swore me to secrecy. He needed a confidant, you see, and I was only too happy to comply. "I've been interviewing a lot of blood donors lately," he told me after we'd ordered. "It seems that while some people have been scared off from donating, that has been largely made up by increased contributions by a central core of regulars."

"Sounds good," I said. And I meant it. I had no objection to there being an adequate blood supply. Back in Austin I was pleased to see others go to the Red Cross van, just so long as nobody asked *me* to contribute. I had neither the time nor the interest, so I got out of it by telling everybody I'd had malaria.

"I found one interesting fellow, Forry. Seems he started donating back when he was twenty-five, during the Blitz. Must have contributed thirty-five, forty gallons, by now."

I did a quick mental calculation. "Wait a minute. He's got to be past the age limit by now."

"Exactly right! He admitted the truth, when he was assured confidentiality. Seems he didn't *want* to stop donating when he reached sixty-five. He's a hardy old fellow —had a spot of surgery a few years back, but he's in quite decent shape, overall. So, right after his local Gallon Club threw a big retirement party for him, he actually moved across the country and registered at a new blood bank, giving a false name and a younger age!"

"Kinky. But it sounds harmless enough. I'd guess he just likes to feel needed. Bet he flirts with the nurses and enjoys the free food—sort of a bi-monthly party he can always count on, with friendly appreciative people."

Hey, just because I'm a selfish bastard doesn't mean I can't extrapolate the behavior of altruists. Like most other user-types, I've got a good instinct for the sort of motivations that drive suckers. People like me need to know such things.

"That's what I thought too, at first," Les said, nodding. "I found a few more like him, and decided to call them 'addicts.' At first I never connected them with the *other* group, the one I named 'converts.'"

"Converts?"

"Yes, converts. People who suddenly become blood donors—get this—very soon after they've recovered from surgery themselves!"

"Maybe they're paying off part of their hospital bills that way?"

"Mmm, not really. We have nationalized health, remember? And even for private patients, that might account for the first few donations only."

"Gratitude, then?" An alien emotion to me, but I understood it, in principle.

"Perhaps. Some few people might have their consciousnesses raised after a close brush with death, and decide to become better citizens. After all, half an hour at a blood bank, a few times a year, is a small inconvenience in exchange for . . ."

Sanctimonious twit. Of course *he* was a donor. Les went on and on about civic duty and such until the waitress arrived with our pizza and two fresh bitters. That shut him up for a moment. But when she left, he leaned forward, eyes shining.

"But no, Forry. It wasn't bill-paying, or even gratitude. Not for some of them, at least. More had happened to these people than having their consciousnesses raised. They were *converts,* Forry. They began joining Gallon Clubs, and more! It seems almost as if, in each case, a *personality change* had taken place."

"What do you mean?"

"I mean that a significant fraction of those who have had major surgery during the last five years seem to have changed their entire set of social attitudes! Beyond becoming blood donors, they've increased their contributions to charity, joined the Parent-Teacher organizations and Boy Scout troops, become active in Greenpeace and Save The Children . . ."

"The point, Les. What's your *point?*"

"My point?" He shook his head. "Frankly, some of these people were behaving like addicts—like converted addicts to *altruism.* That's when it occurred to me, Forry, that what we might have here was a new vector."

He said it as simply as that. Naturally I looked at him, blankly.

"A vector!" he whispered, urgently. "Forget about typhus, or smallpox, or flu. They're rank amateurs! Wallies who give the show away with all their sneezing and flaking and shitting. To be sure, AIDS uses blood and sex, but it's so damned savage, it forced us to become aware of it, to develop tests, to begin the long, slow process of isolating it. But ALAS—"

"Alas?"

"A-L-A-S." He grinned. "It's what I've named the new virus I've isolated, Forry. It stands for 'Acquired Lavish Altruism Syndrome.' How do you like it?"

"Hate it. Are you trying to tell me that there's a virus that affects the human *mind?* And in such a complicated way?" I was incredulous and, at the same time, scared spitless. I've always had this superstitious feeling about viruses and vectors. Les really had me spooked now.

"No, of course not," he laughed. "But consider a simpler possibility. What if some virus one day stumbled on a way to make people *enjoy* giving blood?"

I guess I only blinked then, unable to give him any other reaction.

"Think, Forry! Think about that old man I spoke of earlier. He told me that every two months or so, just before he'd be allowed to donate again, he tends to feel 'all thick inside.' The discomfort only goes away after the next donation!"

I blinked again. "And you're saying that each time he gives blood, he's actually *serving* his parasite, providing it a vector into new hosts. . . ."

"The new hosts being those who survive surgery because the hospital gave them fresh blood, all because our old man was so generous, yes! They're infected! Only this is a subtle virus, not a greedy bastard, like AIDS, or even the flu. It keeps a low profile. Who knows, maybe it's even reached a level of *commensalism* with its hosts: attacking invading organisms for them, or—"

He saw the look on my face and waved his hands. "All right, farfetched, I know. But think about it! Because there are no disease symptoms, nobody has ever looked for this virus, until now."

He's isolated it, I realized, suddenly. And, knowing instantly what this thing could mean, career-wise, I was already scheming, wondering how to get my name onto his paper when he published this. So absorbed was I that for a few moments I lost track of his words.

". . . And so now we get to the interesting part. You see, what's a normal, selfish Tory-voter going to *think* when he finds himself suddenly wanting to go down to the blood bank as often as they'll let him?"

"Um." I shook my head. "That he's been bewitched? Hypnotized?"

"Nonsense!" Les snorted. "That's not how human psychology works. No, we tend to do *lots* of things without knowing why. We need excuses, though, so we *rationalize!* If an obvious reason for our behavior isn't readily available, we *invent* one, preferably one that helps us think better of ourselves. Ego is powerful stuff, my friend."

Hey, I thought. *Don't teach your grandmother to suck eggs.*

"Altruism," I said aloud. "They find themselves rushing regularly to the blood bank. So they rationalize that it's because they're *good* people. . . . They become proud of it. Brag about it. . . ."

"You've got it," Les said. "And because they're proud, even sanctimonious about their newfound generosity, they tend to *extend* it, to bring it into other parts of their lives!"

I whispered in hushed awe. "An altruism virus! Jesus, Les, when we announce this—"

I stopped when I saw his sudden frown, and instantly thought it was because I'd used that word, "we." I should have known better, of course. For Les was always more than willing to share the credit. No, his reservation was far more serious than that.

"Not yet, Forry. We can't publish this yet."

I shook my head. "Why not? This is big, Les! It proves much of what you've been saying all along, about symbiosis and all that. There could even be a Nobel in it!"

I'd been gauche, and spoken aloud of The Ultimate. But he didn't even seem to notice. Damn. If only Les had been like most biologists, driven more than anything else by the lure of Stockholm. But no. You see, Les was a natural. A natural altruist.

It was *his* fault, you see. Him and his damn virtue, they drove me to first contemplate what I next decided to do.

"Don't you see, Forry? If we publish, they'll develop an

antibody *test* for the ALAS virus. Donors carrying it will be barred from the blood banks, just like those carrying AIDS and syphilis and hepatitis. And that would be incredibly cruel torture to those poor addicts and carriers."

"*Screw* the carriers!" I almost shouted. Several pizza patrons glanced my way. With a desperate effort I brought my voice down. "Look, Les, the carriers will be classified as *diseased*, won't they? So they'll go under doctor's care. And if all it takes to make them feel better is to *bleed* them regularly, well, then we'll give them pet leeches!"

Les smiled. "Clever. But that's not the only, or even my main, reason, Forry. No, I'm not going to publish, yet, and that is final. I just can't allow anybody to stop this disease. It's got to spread, to become an epidemic. A pandemic."

I stared, and upon seeing that look in his eyes, I knew that Les was more than an altruist. He had caught that most specially insidious of all human ailments, the Messiah Complex. Les wanted to save the world.

"Don't you see?" he said urgently, with the fervor of a proselyte. "Selfishness and greed are destroying the planet, Forry! But nature always finds a way, and this time symbiosis may be giving us our last chance, a final opportunity to become better people, to learn to cooperate before it's too late!

"The things we're most proud of, our prefrontal lobes, those bits of gray matter above the eyes which make us so much smarter than beasts, what good have they done us, Forry? Not a hell of a lot. We aren't going to *think* our way out of the crises of the twentieth century. Or, at least, thought alone won't do it. We need something else, as well.

"And Forry, I'm convinced that something else is ALAS. We've got to keep this secret, at least until it's so well established in the population that there's no turning back!"

I swallowed. "How long? How long do you want to wait? Until it starts affecting voting patterns? Until after the next election?"

He shrugged. "Oh, at least that long. Five years. Possibly seven. You see, the virus tends to only get into people who've recently had surgery, and they're generally older. Fortunately, they also are often influential. Just the sort who now vote Tory. . . ."

He went on. And on. I listened with half an ear, but

already I had come to that fateful realization. A seven-year wait for a goddamn co-authorship would make this discovery next to useless to my career, to my ambitions.

Of course I *could* blow the secret on Les, now that I knew of it. But that would only embitter him, and he'd easily take all the credit for the discovery anyway. People tend to remember innovators, not whistle-blowers.

We paid our bill and walked toward Charing Cross Station, where we could catch the tube to Paddington, and from there to Oxford. Along the way we ducked out of a sudden downpour at a streetside ice cream vendor. While we waited, I bought us both cones. I remember quite clearly that he had strawberry. I had a raspberry ice.

While Les absentmindedly talked on about his research plans, a small pink smudge colored the corner of his mouth. I pretended to listen, but already my mind had turned to other things, nascent plans and earnest scenarios for committing murder.

2

It would be the perfect crime, of course.

Those movie detectives are always going on about "motive, means, and opportunity." Well, motive I had in plenty, but it was one so farfetched, so obscure, that it would surely never occur to anybody.

Means? Hell, I worked in a business rife with means. There were poisons and pathogens galore. We're a very careful profession, but, well, accidents *do* happen. . . . The same holds for opportunity.

There was a rub, of course. Such was Boy Genius's reputation that, even if I did succeed in knobbling him, I didn't dare come out immediately with my own announcement. Damn him, everyone would just assume it was his work anyway, or his "leadership" here at the lab, at least, that led to the discovery of ALAS. And besides, too much fame for me right after his demise *might* lead someone to suspect a motive.

So, I realized, Les was going to get his delay, after all. Maybe not seven years, but three or four perhaps, during which I'd move back to the States, start a separate line of work, then subtly guide my own research to cover methodically all the bases Les had so recently flown over in flashes of inspiration. I wasn't happy about the delay, but at the end of that time, it would look entirely like my own work. No co-authorship for Forry on *this* one, no sir!

The beauty of it was that nobody would ever think of connecting me with the tragic death of my colleague and friend, years before. After all, did not his demise set me back in my career, temporarily? "Ah, if only poor Les had lived to see your success!" my competitors would say, suppressing jealous bile as they watched me pack for Stockholm.

Of course none of this appeared on my face or in my words. We both had our normal work to do. But almost every day I also put in long extra hours helping Les in "our" secret project. In its own way it was an exhilarating time, and Les was lavish in his praise of the slow, dull, but methodical way I fleshed out his ideas.

I made my arrangements slowly, knowing Les was in no hurry. Together we gathered data. We isolated, and even crystallized the virus, got X-ray diffractions, did epidemiological studies, all in strictest secrecy.

"Amazing!" Les would cry out, as he uncovered the way the ALAS virus forced its hosts to feel their need to "give." He'd wax eloquent, effusive, over elegant mechanisms which he ascribed to random selection but which I could not help superstitiously attributing to some incredibly insidious form of intelligence. The more subtle and effective we found its techniques to be, the more admiring Les became, and the more I found myself loathing those little packets of RNA and protein.

The fact that the virus seemed so harmless—Les thought even commensal—only made me hate it more. It made me glad of what I had planned. Glad that I was going to stymie Les in his scheme to give ALAS free reign.

I was going to save humanity from this would-be puppet-master. True, I'd delay my warning to suit my own purposes, but the warning would come, nonetheless, and sooner than my unsuspecting compatriot planned.

Little did Les know that he was doing background for work *I'd* take credit for. Every flash of insight, his every "Eureka!", was stored away in my private notebook, beside my own columns of boring data. Meanwhile, I sorted through all the means at my disposal.

Finally, I selected for my agent a particularly virulent strain of Dengue Fever.

3

There's an old saying we have in Texas. "A chicken is just an egg's way of makin' more eggs."

To a biologist, familiar with all those latinized-graecificated words, this saying has a much more "posh" version. Humans are "zygotes," made up of diploid cells containing forty-six paired chromosomes—except for our haploid sex cells, or "gametes." Males' gametes are sperm and females' are eggs, each containing only twenty-three chromosomes.

So biologists say that "a zygote is only a gamete's way of making more gametes."

Clever, eh? But it does point out just how hard it is, in nature, to pin down a Primal Cause—some center to the puzzle, against which everything else can be calibrated. I mean, which *does* come first, the chicken or the egg?

"Man is the measure of all things," goes another wise old saying. Oh yeah? Tell that to a modern feminist.

A guy I once knew, who used to read science fiction, told me about this story he'd seen, in which it turned out that the whole and entire purpose of humanity, brains and all, was to be the organism that built starships so that *house flies* could migrate out and colonize the galaxy.

But that idea's nothing compared with what Les Adgeson believed. He spoke of the human animal as if he were describing a veritable United Nations. From the *E. coli* in our guts, to tiny commensal mites that clean our eyelashes for us, to the mitochondria that energize our cells, all the way to the contents of our very DNA: Les saw it all as a great big hive of compromise, negotiation, *symbiosis.* Most of the contents of our chromosomes came from past invaders, he contended.

Symbiosis? The picture he created in my mind was one of minuscule *puppeteers,* all yanking and jerking at us with their protein strings, making us marionettes dance to their own tunes, to their own nasty, selfish little agendas.

And you, *you* were the worst! Like most cynics, I had always maintained a secret faith in human nature. Yes, most people are pigs. I've always known that. And while I may be a user, at least I'm honest enough to admit it.

But deep down, we users *count* on the sappy, inexplicable generosity, the mysterious, puzzling altruism of those others, the kind, inexplicably *decent* folk—those we superficially sneer at in contempt, but secretly hold in awe.

Then you came along, damn you. You *make* people behave that way. There is no mystery left after you get finished. No corner remaining impenetrable to cynicism. Damn, how I came to hate you!

As I came to hate Leslie Adgeson. I made my plans, schemed my brilliant campaign against both of you. In those last days of innocence I felt oh, so savagely determined. So deliciously decisive and in control of my own destiny.

In the end it was anticlimactic. I didn't have time to finish my preparations, to arrange that little trap, that sharp bit of glass dipped in just the right mixture of deadly microorganisms. For CAPUC arrived then, just before I could exercise my option as a murderer.

CAPUC changed everything.

Catastrophic Autoimmune PUlmonary Collapse—acronym for the horror that made AIDS look like a minor irritant. And in the beginning it appeared unstoppable. Its vectors were completely unknown and the causative agent defied isolation for so long.

This time it was no easily identifiable group that came down with the new plague, though it concentrated upon the industrialized world. School children in some areas seemed particularly vulnerable. In other places it was secretaries and postal workers.

Naturally, all the major epidemeology labs got involved. Les predicted the pathogen would turn out to be something akin to the prions which cause shingles in sheep, and certain plant diseases—a pseudo-life form even simpler than a virus and even harder to track down. It was a heretical, minority view, until the CDC in Atlanta decided out of desperation to try his theories out, and found the very dormant viroids Les predicted—mixed in with the *glue* used to seal paper milk cartons, envelopes, postage stamps.

Les was a hero, of course. *Most* of us in the labs were.

After all, we'd been the first line of defense. Our own casualty rate had been ghastly.

For a while there, funerals and other public gatherings were discouraged. But an exception was made for Les. The procession behind his cortege was a mile long. I was asked to deliver the eulogy. And when they pleaded with me to take over at the lab, I agreed.

So naturally I tended to forget all about ALAS. The war against CAPUC took everything society had. And while I may be selfish, even a rat can tell when it makes sense to join in the fight to save a sinking ship—especially when there's no other port in sight.

We learned how to combat CAPUC, eventually. It involved drugs, and a vaccine based on reversed antibodies force-grown in the patient's own marrow after he's been given a dangerous overdose of a Vanadium compound I found by trial and error. It worked, most of the time, but the victims suffered great stress and often required a special regime of whole blood transfusions to get through the most dangerous phase.

Blood banks were stretched even thinner than before. Only now the public responded generously, as in time of war. I should not have been surprised when survivors, after their recovery, volunteered by their thousands. But, of course, I'd forgotten about ALAS by then, hadn't I?

We beat back CAPUC. Its vector proved too unreliable, too easily interrupted once we'd figured it out. The poor little viroid never had a chance to get to Les's "negotiation" stage. Oh well, those are the breaks.

I got all sorts of citations I didn't deserve. The King gave me a KBE for personally saving the Prince of Wales. I had dinner at the White House.

Big deal.

The world had a respite, after that. CAPUC had scared people, it seemed, into a new spirit of cooperation. I should have been suspicious, of course. But soon I'd moved over to WHO, and had all sorts of administrative responsibilities in the Final Campaign on Malnutrition.

By that time, I had almost entirely forgotten about ALAS.

* * *

I forgot about you, didn't I? Oh, the years passed, my star rose, I became famous, respected, revered. I didn't get my Nobel in Stockholm. Ironically, I picked it up in Oslo. Fancy that. Just shows you can fool anybody.

And yet, I don't think I ever *really* forgot about you, ALAS, not at the back of my mind.

Peace treaties were signed. Citizens of the industrial nations voted temporary cuts in their standards of living in order to fight poverty and save the environment. Suddenly, it seemed, we'd all grown up. Other cynics, guys I'd gotten drunk with in the past—and shared dark premonitions about the inevitable fate of filthy, miserable humanity—all gradually deserted the faith, as pessimists seem wont do when the world turns bright—too bright for even the cynical to dismiss as a mere passing phase on the road to Hell.

And yet, my own brooding remained unblemished. For subconsciously, I *knew* it wasn't real.

Then, the third Mars Expedition returned to worldwide adulation, and brought home with them TARP.

And that was when we all found out just how *friendly* all our homegrown pathogens really had been, all along.

4

Late at night, stumbling in exhaustion from overwork, I would stop at Les's portrait where I'd ordered it hung in the hall opposite my office door, and stand there cursing him and his damned theories of *symbiosis*.

Imagine mankind ever reaching a symbiotic association with TARP! That really would be something. Imagine, Les, all those *alien* genes, added to our heritage, to our rich human diversity!

Only TARP did not seem to be much interested in "negotiation." Its wooing was rough, deadly. And its vector was the wind.

The world looked to me, and to my peers, for salvation. In spite of all of my successes and high renown, though, I knew myself for a second-best fraud. I would always know —no matter how much they thanked and praised me— who had been better than me by light years.

Again and again, deep into the night, I would pore

through the notes Leslie Adgeson had left behind, seeking inspiration, seeking hope. That's when I stumbled across ALAS, again.

I found *you* again.

Oh, you made us behave better, all right. At least a quarter of the human race must contain your DNA, by now, ALAS. And in their newfound, inexplicable, rationalized altruism, they set the tone followed by all the others.

Everybody behaves so damned *well* in the present calamity. They help each other, they succor the sick, they all *give* so.

Funny thing, though. If you hadn't made us all so bloody cooperative, we'd probably never have *made* it to bloody Mars, would we? Or if we had, there'd have still been enough paranoia around so we'd have maintained a decent quarantine.

But then, I remind myself, you don't *plan*, do you? You're just a bundle of RNA, packed inside a protein coat, with an incidentally, accidentally acquired trait of making humans want to donate blood. That's all you are, right? So you had no way of knowing that by making us "better" you were also setting us up for TARP, did you? Did you?

5

We've got some palliatives, now. A few new techniques seem to be doing some good. The latest news is great, in fact. Apparently, we'll be able to save maybe fifteen percent or so of the children. At least half of them may even be fertile.

That's for nations who've had a lot of racial mixing. Hotorozygosity and genetic diversity seems to breed better resistance. Those peoples with "pure," narrow bloodlines will be harder to save, but then, racism has its inevitable price.

Too bad about the great apes and horses, but then, at least all this will give the rain forests a chance to grow back.

Meanwhile, everybody perseveres. There is no panic, of the kind one reads about in past plagues. We've grown up at last, it seems. We help each other.

But I carry a card in my wallet saying I'm a Christian

Scientist, and that my blood group is AB Negative, and that I'm allergic to nearly everything. Transfusions are one of the treatments commonly used now, and I'm an important man. But I won't take blood. I won't. I donate, but I'll never take it. Not even when I drop.

You won't have me, ALAS. You won't.

I am a bad man. I suppose, all told, I've done more good than evil in my life, but that's incidental, a product of happenstance and the caprices of the world.

I have no control over the world, but I can make my own decisions, at least. As I make this one, now.

Down, out of my high research tower I've gone. Into the streets, where the teeming clinics fester and broil. That's where I work now. And it doesn't matter to me that I'm behaving no differently than anyone else today. *They* are all marionettes. They think they're acting altruistically, but I know they are your puppets, ALAS.

But I am a *man*, do you hear me? I make my own decisions.

Fever wracks my body now as I drag myself from bed to bed, holding their hands when they stretch them out to me for comfort, doing what I can to ease their suffering, to save a few.

You'll not have me, ALAS.

This is what I choose to do.

Re: Generations

MIKE McQUAY

S TAN DOVER LOCKED EYES with the camera, fought the pull of its immense vortex—then gained the upper hand. The camera to him was always the same: the jilted lover, distant and unreachable, who needed to be seduced afresh and brought back under control. Once the darkness of the machine's soul could be overcome, it then became the willing receptacle for whatever emotions Dover wanted to pour into it. And when he poured, he wet the eyes of millions of viewers.

He stared down the unblinking eye of camera #3 and read his own words from the TelePrompTer: "And finally, this story from the wires of the Mid-European Company. A high-rise apartment in the Antwerp, Belgium, branch of Mid-Europe burned yesterday, injuring over one hundred and taking thirty-three active lives from the seniority lists . . ."

On the hardwire monitor, the picture switched to a burning high-rise of typical unornamented Company design. Thick black smoke poured from broken-out windows up and down the height of the fifty-story apartment as Dover continued to read his copy.

"The fire apparently began in the basement/laundromat of the building, spreading quickly up through the laundry drops, which were jammed full of clothes as peo-

ple waited their turn at the washing machines. A panic
quickly broke out as smoke filled the building, citizens
trampling one another to reach the stairs . . ." He let just
a small catch break his voice. ". . . others weren't so
lucky."

The picture switched to a tight shot near the thirtieth
floor. People were climbing onto ledges, coughing, followed by plumes of thick smoke. As the instinctive fear of
fire overtook them, they began to jump—one at a time—to
their deaths on the streets below, the camera dutifully
following each one to the ground, then panning back up to
take the next one.

"Company studies indicate that the greatest problem
in situations like this is unreasoning panic brought on by
unpreparedness," Dover told the hungry eye. "Senseless
death . . . useless death, a drag not only on the family
support units of the dead, but an expense on the Company
system that supports us. My friends, I don't want this sort
of thing to happen to you . . ."

The camera went in tight on one of the bodies on the
ground, a young woman on her back, eyes open and staring blindly into the nighttime sky, what had obviously
been her brain scattered all around the splayed remnants
of her head. A small child stood near the body, screaming
hysterically.

"Imagine not yourself, but your sons or daughters in
this position," Dover said, his voice hushed, tones deep and
resonant. "Wouldn't any of us want to avoid this? Shouldn't
we do anything and everything necessary to keep this
from happening to our own loved ones?"

The hardwire switched back to Dover, his eyes slightly
misted, his face sagging into the posture of deep concern.
He heard a sob from someone in production off the set and
knew he was getting ready to roll.

"Preparedness is the key, my friends. Once you've held
the lifeless, broken bodies of your loved ones in your arms
it's too late. We must be ready to face adversity when it
comes and to meet it with calm and assurance. It just
might be the difference between life and death. The
stench of burning flesh is a smell never to be forgotten.
The emptiness of life taken too soon haunts the living and
ruins more than the life of the deceased. Would you condemn those you hold most dear? Would you? I can't be-

lieve that any of you would consign your families to disaster when the means of their salvation could be close at hand."

Dover smiled, just slightly, a second of familiarity as he eased the audience into the pitch. "This week at your local Company Surplus Store, a couple of very important specials are being run with preparedness in mind. First, the JP-437 smoke detector is only $49.95, nearly half price and worth five times that much. You'll sleep peacefully and securely knowing that smoke seeping into your house or apartment won't snuff out your life without giving you a fighting chance."

A picture of the smoke detector with the new price just below the X'd-out old price appeared on the screen, followed quickly by a high-concept action video of a fire extinguisher being used to smother a kitchen fire in CO_2 haze.

"Next," Dover said, his voice still hushed, "is the Imperial Brand fire extinguisher, on sale this week for an incredible two-thirds off. You'll know exactly what peace of mind is when you bring the Imperial into your home. This unit will take care of nearly any fire that starts on your premises. You can protect not only yourself and your family, but all those valuable possessions, too. Instead of going to funerals, you'll be out celebrating your own good sense and preparedness. And your family will look up to you, knowing that their welfare is uppermost in your mind.

"So, please . . . don't let this happen to you."

The picture switched back to the disaster, as firemen tried to pick up the body of the woman we've been watching, her whole frame collapsing into an unrecognizable heap as they pulled at her.

"Your family's lives are in your hands. Don't let them down."

The camera panned to the face of the child watching her mother's body being hauled away in pieces, her face set in horror, her mind obviously millions of miles away as the camera came in TIGHT and held the girl's face in FREEZE FRAME.

"It's up to you," Dover nearly whispered. "How much do you care? How much do you love? Prove your love this week by stopping into your local COMPLUS store, with two hundred fifteen thousand locations to serve you. Remember . . . at COMPLUS the customer comes first."

The shot switched back to Dover, his face still set in concern. "This is Stan Dover," he said, then smiled wide, falling into his trademark. "I *am* the news. See you tomorrow, and have a pleasant evening from the entire staff of the Company News Station."

He stared down the red light on #3, oozing sincerity back to the audience that he loved, and that loved him. Because the key, the real key, to the unparalleled success of Mr. Stan Dover was his connection to the audience.

The red running light winked out, Dover taking a breath and sagging, then hearing the applause around the set. The crew didn't always give this approval, so when they did, Dover felt as if he had really earned it. He smiled wide and stood, unhooking the small mike from his lapel and handing it to Annie Potts, the assistant director, who had come onto the homey sofa-and-coffee-table set. "How was I?" he asked.

The red-haired woman nodded, sniffling, tears running out of the corners of her eyes. "Oh, Mr. Dover," she said. "You were wonderful."

The studio sounds were coming up all around him, cameras and monitors drifting away with technicians in tow as production personnel yelled to one another across the wide-open room. It was a wrap for everyone on the shift and they were laughing and joking with the incoming crews.

Dover loosened his tie, noticing Mo Schapp moving toward him from the booth at the far side of the room. "You think the folks liked it?" he asked the A.D.

Annie Potts stared up at Dover, her eyes wide and impressed. "How could they not?" she asked. "You really know how to hit home, Mr. Dover."

"Thanks," he mumbled, pumped up and embarrassed at the same time. "And please, call me Stan." Dover knew the value of hype and the equivocal nature of attitudes, but it didn't stop him from enjoying compliments. Ego stroking, after all, was the backbone of his profession.

"Stan! Stan!" Mo yelled, hands in the air as he reached the set. "You did it, boy. That was thirty minutes of liquid dynamite. I placed a bet . . . a bet I placed right on the spot in the booth!"

"What sort of bet?" Dover replied, unbuttoning the top button of his shirt and wandering off the set with Schapp, waving to people as he walked, smiling and nodding in response to the praise.

"Extinguishers," Schapp said, the small man punctuating with an index finger. "Extinguishers. I bet a thousand bucks that the next twenty-four-hour period will produce more fire extinguisher sales than any twenty-four-hour period ever."

"You sound like you've got stock in the fire prevention business," Dover said.

"I should have," Schapp said. "You're the best pitchman AmeriCorp's got. I could probably get rich just following your newscasts."

"Sounds to me like you're asking for a favor."

Schapp, a full head and a half shorter than Dover, stopped walking and stared up at the man. "What makes you say that?" he asked defensively.

Dover kept walking, knowing that if he stopped his coworkers would descend on him like ants on honey and he'd be another hour extricating himself. "I'm on my way to the office," he called over his shoulder. "Get with me in there."

"It's not exactly a favor!" Schapp called to him, and Dover waved, knowing that for Schapp to ask at all it had to be a huge favor.

He continued his stroll through the CNS studio complex, always waving, never stopping. The studios were big and new, ten sound stages arranged in a large, open circle, with office additions branching out from the center point like the spokes of a wheel. The stages were of variable size, the addition or subtraction of wheeled soundproofing literally building stages on the demands of the moment. People scurried everywhere, their actions coordinated by Mr. Armitage, the Station Manager, and fed to them individually through personal consoles they carried on their belts. It was a large operation made smooth by personal one-on-one management.

A camera, moving under its own power to another studio, cut in front of him, Dover nearly running into the thing.

"Pardon me," the machine said, dipping slightly in deference.

"Trudge on, little friend," Dover said, patting the machine. "Duty calls."

"Yes, Mr. Dover," the camera said, and went on its way.

As Dover approached the executive spoke that contained his offices, he passed the multitiered walls of monitors juicing live feed from every part of the corporate world, techs running along the catwalks, calling excitedly to assistant producers, all of them anxious to get stories on the air and gouge their competition. The atmosphere charged him as it always did. This was his world and he loved it. He was a lion in the tangled jungle of the newsroom, the beautiful, powerful animal who conquered the inscrutable and made it his own.

Where others got lost on the myriad pathways of understanding and confusion, he cut through to the heart of the matter, finding his destination without a map or guide —through jungle cunning. And his way was simple: love your audience, tell them the truth, appeal to the primeval forest of their own emotions, then give them solutions. He never lied to the folks. What he gave them was his understanding and devotion; what he got in return was loyalty and support—symbiosis. It was a love affair with millions of people. And Stan Dover was one of the happiest lovers the world had ever known because he was not only fortunate, but knew it.

He made it through the tangle of the studios and headed down the executive spoke to his office, COMMERCIAL television playing on eye-level screens set into the walls on both sides of the heavily carpeted hallway dishing out a steady flow of comedy and drama that highlighted the allure of consumer products. Consumerism was, of course, the key. Like the news, entertainments were a better way of selling products and keeping the economy alive and vital. It was patriotic work and good for everyone.

His office door was hard steel, totally unornamented except for the TV screen that showed an endless loop tape of Stan smiling his famous you-all-know-me smile. When he reached the door he turned abruptly, looking back down the hallway. Ever since he'd entered the spoke, he'd had the uneasy feeling that someone was following him. But when he looked back, all he saw was an empty hallway attached to a beehive of activity fifty feet distant. He shook his head, but not the feeling, and turned back to the door.

He slotted his punch card and the door sprang open, his secretary, Mrs. Bertran, staring up at him from her console.

"I'll bet that Mr. Armitage will be calling you on the newscast tonight," she said, smiling wide and holding a printout up for his perusal. "Extinguisher sales are up 14 percent already and the twenty-four-hour projections send it off the boards."

Dover smiled, not looking at the projection. "Keep an ear out for Mo," he said. "He wants something."

"Bet you hear from Mr. Armitage before you hear from Mo," Mrs. Bertran said.

"How much?"

"Five?"

"You're on," Dover replied, walking into his office, then stopping and peering back into reception. "Would you get Sally on the line for me?"

"Won't it interfere with the call from Mr. Armitage?" Mrs. Bertran asked.

He winked at her. "Bet you another fiver that it won't," he said.

"Done."

He moved into his office of cathode and glass, his floor to ceiling view into the never-ending distance of Kansas City-St. Louis from the fiftieth floor solid and inspiring. He slid somewhat tiredly behind his high-sheen plastic desk and stared at the outlaw monitors that filled the entire wall across from him.

The outlaws were video pirates, glomming onto satellite space and broadcasting their own vision of the world outside of the pale of Company control. The various corporations had spent years trying to get rid of the pirates, finally giving them a form of acceptability by legalizing their behavior provided they performed valuable commercial or public services during the course of their broadcasts.

Company entertainments were bland generations written by computer to audience specs in order to sell things. The pirates were real humans expressing their own brand of individuality. They were better than the Company programs and far more watched—except for the news, of course. Nobody drew higher numbers than Stan Dover.

Stan chuckled. Barney Barnes, on #14, was juicing live air. Barney specialized in tennis shoes in various situations. Today he ran on a treadmill while an immensely fat, naked woman ran before him. He continually smacked her on her reddening rump with a fly swatter, the woman shrieking with each blow as he breathlessly extolled the virtues of tennis shoes. It was a typical Barnes production—all heart, no polish—but free. Stan shook his head, smiling. What a life.

His console buzzed in front of him, Stan reaching down to punch the receive button recessed into the black plastic of the desk. "Yeah?"

"Mrs. Dover on the line," Mrs. Bertran said.

"Ha!" Stan said. "Gotcha."

"The call's not over yet," she replied. "Mr. Armitage could still beep in."

"Dreamer," he said, and switched over to Sally, her face, drawn and tired, integrating on the ten-inch screen on his desk. She wasn't smiling. "Rough day?"

Dover's wife shook her head, close-cropped hair hugged tight against her skull, the small cubicle she worked in evident all around her. Stan could never handle her brand of confinement, though it seemed right for Sally. "I'm tired," she said, "bored shitless."

"Maybe I can help," he said. "I called to remind you that I'm emceeing the Outlaw Awards banquet tonight at the Press Club. We'll get a little change of scene."

Her hands came up to rub red eyes. "That sounds about as exciting as checking seniority postings at the Department of Sanitation."

"Is something really wrong?" he asked.

She stared at the screen for several long seconds. A kind of internal pain seemed to drift from her eyes, affecting his entire mood. "You'd never understand," she said at last, just as it seemed she was on the verge of something.

Mrs. Bertran beeped in again.

Dover ignored it. "I'll just bet that when you come to the banquet and put down a little Ooze you'll be good as new. Come on . . . you're just becoming too self-absorbed."

"Maybe you've got a product for me," she said, a note of anger lacing her voice that Stan couldn't relate to.

"Well, as a matter of fact, I . . ."

Mrs. Bertran beeped again, and Stan realized that if he didn't take it, the woman would accuse him of cheating on the bet. "Hold on," he said, and went over on sound alone, keeping an eye on Sally's mood through the silent monitor. "What is it? Mr. Armitage?"

"Mo," the woman replied, downcast. "Looks like you whipped me all the way around."

Stan smiled. "Don't game with a gamer," he said. "Put Mo up on the speaker."

"Stan?" came Mo's voice from somewhere up in the ceiling.

"Only got a second . . . got Sally on the line."

"No problem," Mo said. "I'll be right over. Meanwhile I'm juicing something through your office tubes I want you to see. Also, my bet in the booth is already looking good. Always go with the winners; that's what I say."

"Sure," Dover replied, cutting back to his wife. "Come on, Sally. Let me help."

"There's nothing to help," she said. "Really."

"Will you promise me you'll go to the awards tonight?" he asked. "I don't want you alone when you're like this."

She stared again, as if trying to get up the courage to tell him something, once again losing it. "Okay," she nearly whispered, head down. "I'll be there."

"Good girl," Dover said, smiling wide. "I'll make you feel better."

She gave a half-hearted smile and blanked, Dover's eyes immediately drifting to his twenty-five outlaw monitors, now all juicing the same picture. It was a medium-close shot of a group of happy people, perhaps forty in all, standing just off the entry ramp of a highway filled with speeding traffic. In the distance, an above-the-road sign announced: HOUSTON 25 MI. A party of some sort seemed to be in progress, the group dancing around and cavorting on the astroturf grass. Curious, Stan leaned forward and turned up the sound.

". . . all going to say we're insane," a man, obviously the leader, was saying. "But we're not, are we!"

All the people behind him began laughing and cheering. It was an odd group of people, all ages and seniority levels, all different. That disturbed Dover. He'd never seen anything quite like it. The man continued.

"We've never been happier. We've never been saner, believe me. If you were to ask me to explain it, I couldn't. In fact, I wouldn't even want to try. It's just . . . a feeling. I don't know how else to say it. But watch, okay? Watch and enjoy."

With that, the man turned from the static camera and rejoined his people, as Mo walked into the office along with one of the young writers Stan had seen around.

Stan started to say something, but Mo silenced him with a raised hand. "Watch this," he said.

Dover returned to the screen, the partyers on the highway all gathered together in a large huddle, finally breaking it with a cheer.

"Are you ready?" the leader yelled.

"Yes!" everyone screamed, and with that they all charged toward the highway, Stan coming out of his seat with the action, his eyes locked in horror on the screen.

They ran into the highway, all of them, the traffic thick and speeding. There were screams mixing with the screeching tires and blasting horns and tearing metal as bodies flew everywhere, cars piling atop one another and spinning crazily. The sound was frightening, tearing at Stan's insides as he watched a child pitched high in the air and out of the frame as a large, dark sedan literally rolled off the highway right toward the camera, filling the screen, then making it go dark in an instant.

Stan sat there, sick to his stomach, looking at twenty-five blank screens. When he composed himself enough to look over at Mo, the man was collecting a wager from the young writer.

"I told Harvey it'd shake you up," he said by way of explanation.

"What the hell is this?" Dover asked, his hands shaking slightly as he turned his mind naturally to the best way to sell a feature like this.

"It came over the Houston feed," the younger man said, showing empty palms. "I've already verified and even ID'd many of the participants."

"A mass suicide?" Dover replied.

Mo nodded. "Strange, huh? Would you run it?"

Stan leaned back in his chair and indicated seats for the

other two. "Of course I'd run it . . . if we could come up with a good sales hook."

"I've got the hook," the young man said quickly. "Ooze for anxiety . . . can't lose with Ooze."

"Or from the other side of that," Dover said. "From the prevention angle . . . new tires for that quick braking power."

"Bingo!" Mo said. "But Mr. Armitage won't let us run it."

Dover sat up and stared at the man. "He won't? Why not?"

"No reason given," the young man said. "I pulled this one off the air and could really use the byline. I've written some great copy to go along with it."

"I don't get it," Dover said.

"There was one last week," Mo said. "A whole bunch of people in Baltimore-Washington went into a derelict building and planted charges, brought the whole damned building down on themselves. Mr. Armitage wouldn't run that one either. Again, no reason given. Isn't this news, or what?"

"Looks like news to me," Dover said. "Why exactly are you showing me this?"

Schapp stood, turning to the younger man. "Wait out in the hall, kid," he said, Harvey standing immediately.

"Great meeting you," he said to Dover, who smiled in return and reached across the desk to shake the man's sweaty hand.

Harvey left, Mo turning to Dover as soon as the outer door closed. "I wanted you to meet him," he said. "Best young writer I've seen in years."

"Really?"

"You know what it's like to find writing talent these days," Mo said. "He's really discouraged over this story. Can't say that I blame him. The damned thing is so . . . I don't know, compelling."

"Compelling isn't quite the word I had in mind," Dover said. "And I still don't know exactly what you're getting at."

Mo came up and sat on the edge of the desk, leaning down conspiratorially. "Come on, Stan," he said. "You were young once. See if you can talk to the old man for us and get him to change his mind on this thing."

"Why don't you do it, Mo? You're the producer here, not me."

Mo stood back away from the desk, shaking his hands in front of him. "Not me," he said, flustered. "I haven't survived around here by going against the old man. Besides, *you're* News Editor."

"But, why should I . . ."

"You're his wonder boy, you know that," Mo said, moving back to his seat. "You didn't work your way to the top, you were born to it. What is it you say every night—I *am* the news? This is a story and a half. You'd have to be blind not to see that. I want to get this story on the air because it's news and I want to jack that kid off a little bit to keep him from losing it."

"He writes that well?" Dover asked, softening.

"Like ChinaCorp silk, buddy. He reminds me of you."

Dover frowned. He'd never questioned an editorial decision before, but then he'd never had reason to. He was convinced that if he could talk to Mr. Armitage about it he could get it on. "I'll make a deal with you," he said. "I'll take care of the old man if you kick half of your fire extinguisher wager back to me."

"Done," Mo said, standing. "You won't regret it. Now I have to go out and collect on a small bet from Mrs. Bertran. She didn't think I could talk you into it."

Dover smiled and shook his head. "Hasn't been her day," he replied, and waved to the man as he hurried out of the office.

The feed had disappeared from his video wall, the outlaw early evening lineup coming back on. Dover idly watched a man biting the heads off chickens while he punched up Mr. Armitage's private number, the line answering, as always, after the first ring. The old man's face filled the monitor.

"Wonderful . . . wonderful, my boy," Armitage said, his full smooth face beaming beatifically, his pure white hair gleaming with a light all its own. "What a pitchman. You do my old heart proud."

"Thank you, sir," Dover said with respect. "You're too kind."

"And you're too self-effacing," Armitage said. "I'd have called you myself, but I just assumed you'd have already left for the Outlaw banquet."

"I'm going in a minute," Dover said. "I wanted to ask you about something first."

"Hardwire me, son," Armitage said. "That's what I'm here for."

"It's about the mass suicide that came in over Houston air," Stan said easily, secure with the Station Manager. "I don't understand why we won't run it."

"It serves no purpose, Stan," Mr. Armitage said. "None at all. It's non-news. I'm surprised at you."

"What do you mean, non-news?" Dover persisted, not understanding. "It's real . . . it's human drama. And maybe it means something . . . you know, two mass suicides in a week. I've never seen . . ."

"Enough," Mr. Armitage said quietly, his face still jovial. "You've made your petition and stated your case. I've already dealt with this matter, though, and your words can have no bearing upon that. The story doesn't teach, entertain, or uplift, and I'm simply not going to run it. Period. End of sentence."

"But . . ."

"You know, Stan, that if you don't get on the stick, you'll never make it to that awards ceremony tonight."

"Yes, sir," Dover said, trying hard to keep the anger out of his voice. Here he was, the top news personality in the world, and he was being dismissed as if he were a mailroom clerk. "I'll leave now."

"That's the boy," Mr. Armitage said. "Give 'em hell."

The screen blanked immediately, Dover staring at its emptiness. This made no sense. None. He'd never come across one real news item that had been cut in editorial. News was news. Stan Dover understood that more than anyone. And *this* was news.

As he sat there brooding, he felt the weight of Mrs. Bertran's eyes on him, probably waiting to ask him if she could pay off on her bets next week. He ignored her for a moment, wishing she'd either come in or go away. When she didn't, it made him angrier.

He flared at her. "Mrs. Bertran, I wish—" But there was no one there. The office door was closed, the space empty —just like his monitor.

II

The man wore a uniform that looked like a cross between something military and a child's pajamas . . . the damned thing even had feet. There was a helmet that went with the uniform, but he carried it under his arm the entire time, never once putting it on his head. His name was Charlie Dodd, and he stared out of the screen with deadly intent, bearing regal, a pencil-thin mustache twitching with every word he spoke.

"The maintenance of civilization is everyone's responsibility," he said. "We live by the rule of consumerism to everyone's benefit, yet the real work of maintaining the status quo is done in the trenches of recycling."

The camera pulled back slightly, showing Dodd standing in an elegantly decorated dining room, the long table set with bone china and sterling silver as a crystal chandelier dangling overhead caught the set lighting and sparked it back out again in the form of colored light sabers sharp as razors.

"It must be obvious to all of us," Dodd was saying, "that unrenewed resources are resources lost, and that the number of resources are finite. Without renewal, there is only waste. Waste leads to shortages, loss, unhappiness, and discontent. That is why tonight I propose the ultimate in recycling, the patriotic responses to waste!"

He moved to the table and sat, the camera dipping slightly to keep him in frame. On the plate before him sat an unimposing brown lump. Dodd smiled, his face like a wicked little boy's nearly filling the screen. "Waste produced, can be waste reused, recycled into the system."

He looked down, regarding his plate, the camera PULLING BACK to frame the tableau. "Here is waste that my system produced not ten minutes before taping began."

Reaching out, he laid his hand atop the glob on the plate. "And still warm, too." He wiped his hand on the napkin place setting, then flapped it above the plate. "I only wish you could smell the aromatic bouquet of this wonderful little pâté, what the French would call *le produit des entrailles.* A delicate and, may I add, totally unique olfactory experience."

With that, Dodd picked up the silver knife and fork, cutting off an end of the soft brown glob, then using the knife to scoop the serving onto the fork in the European culinary tradition. He held the forkful up in front of his mouth, the camera coming in for a CLOSE-UP. "What could be better?" he asked, smiling. "Solid, recyclable, biodegradable, patriotic . . ." He put the forkful into his mouth, closing his eyes and sighing as he chewed. "And so tasty, too."

Then he smiled wide, his teeth stained brown, the picture settling to a FREEZE FRAME and wild applause.

"All right!" Stan Dover yelled above the racket, the big-screen freeze frame filling the wall behind him at the banquet table. He stood, still applauding and grinning at the audience. "Let's bring him up here, folks . . . your grand-prize winner and mine—Charlie Dodd!"

The applause got louder, punctuated by shouts as Dodd, decked out in the uniform he'd worn on the tape, got up from his table and made his way to the dais, waving as he walked. The head table was full of oddities, outlaw broadcasters dressed in their official TV personas. There were torturers in leather masks, a four-hundred-pound "baby" in diaper and bonnet, chicken imitators, and any number of gurus, teachers, preachers, and prognosticators done up in everything from ostrich feathers to full body armor.

Dover watched Charlie Dodd approach. He shook hands with the man, then put his arm around Dodd's shoulder and turning him to face the audience. "Third straight year, Charlie," he said to the man. "How do you feel?"

"I'm humbled, Stan," Dodd replied as the audience hushed. Tears filled the man's eyes. "Where else but in corporate America could a man from meager beginnings rise to these heights? I love everybody . . . just everybody."

The applause started up again, but Dover silenced it with an upraised hand. Then he reached down to the table and picked up the bronzed cowboy hat set on the marble base. "I hope you've got room for another one of these, Charlie," he said, handing the statuette to the man.

"I'll clear off the mantel," Dodd replied, to the approval of the crowd. He held the trophy high above his head. "This is for all of you! This is for the creative soul of all men!"

The five hundred people who filled the room cheered, Dodd one of the most popular entertainers to ever work in the outlaw medium. Dover waited patiently for the applause to die down on its own before picking up the plate full of feces the gofer had set before him. "And for a special treat," he said loudly, "we've got a little dessert for you!"

He held up the plate, laughing along with the audience. With perfect timing, Dodd waited until order was just beginning to come about before he leaned forward and said, "Not for me, thanks, Stan," he said. "You never know where this *shit* comes from!"

With the applause still ringing in his ears, Dodd, always the perfect pro, thrust his trophy into the air and left the dais, a spotlight following him all the way back to his table.

Dover watched the man walk off, glad to be bringing the proceedings to a close. He'd been on stage for nearly two hours, his cheek muscles beginning to strain from smiling. He'd briefly seen Sally just before the banquet and she'd looked depressed, not even seeming to be interested in Oozing. It worried him. He'd seen her depressed a lot lately for reasons unknown. Stan had always felt that he had a great many answers to give if he could only know the questions. With Sally everything was always nebulous, shifting. Her personality couldn't be depended upon to be predictable. That quality excited Stan to a degree. Five years of marriage contract had shown him as many faces of his wife as there were months in the year, but like a great many things, there seemed to be an equal and deadly downside of alienation and neurosis that would paralyze Sally and their marriage, sometimes for weeks on end.

He wrapped up the banquet as quickly as possible, the thing being carried live on every outlaw band. How many people had seen the show he could only imagine since the company didn't keep records on non-company airtime.

When the spots went out, signaling the end, Dover let his facial muscles gratefully relax and quickly made his way through the crowd, their dress divided evenly between black one-piece tuxes, evening gowns, and clowns-in-motley. The Press Club encompassed the entire seventy-seventh floor of the Standard and Poors building, affording a beautiful view of the city when the smog cover wasn't hanging low. Though the hall was large and relatively dark, he knew where to look for Sally—in the corner.

Sally Dover, or Sally Reynolds Dover (as she liked to be called when she was feeling independent), designed circuit boards for a living, her basic theoretical purpose to see how much could be fit into how little. It tended to make her forge her own physical life in increasingly smaller and smaller spaces as she attempted to expand her creative gift to its max by having it overtake every aspect of her existence. So, Stan looked for her in the corners, first in the northwest corner because he knew the highest buildings facing onto Standard and Poors were located there. Instead, he found her northeast because the smog cover had lowered to engulf the windows on that side.

She stood, straddling the corner of the room, leaning her back against the floor-to-ceiling windows. As he approached, he knew that something was wrong. Her pale face was shaking as her makeup traced a pattern of tears down her cheeks. A small man dressed in a tux stood before her, talking non-stop and gesticulating wildly.

Dover hurried to the place, standing sideways to them as the man continued to talk. "So, there's no good reason for you *not* to buy at least a thirty-day share of Batch #43 Chewing Gum. On the benefit side you have good taste, clean teeth, nervous energy work-off, and time-released small doses of Ooze for good mental health."

"I can't . . . don't you see?" Sally said, eyes wide, almost frightened. "I'd have to make space for it, justify it on my time studies. You don't just blindly add more ingredients to the mix . . . where would order go then . . . ?"

"You don't get it, lady," the man said. "This is a positive thing. I might make so bold as to say an important thing, a . . . necessary thing. You just . . ."

"Enough," Dover said. "We're not interested." The man was a Promo, a walking commercial whose entire life was spent, on salary, extolling the virtues of company products. His kind were banned from the Press Club, but Promos were like cockroaches—the only way to keep them out was to squash them.

"Not interested!" the man returned, highly insulted. "I want you to think just for a moment about the germs that are eating away at your flesh and the pulp of your teeth at this very instant. Don't you see that Batch #43 can keep your mouth clean and save your life? Suppose infection sets in, poisons running through your body, killing God knows *what* organs, maybe even your sex drive. Wouldn't you enjoy a few moments of pleasure—*pleasure*—to save your own life?"

"Okay. We'll buy some, I promise," Dover said, turning his attention to Sally, who was looking at him as if he'd just sold her out.

"What do you mean?" she said. "I've got too much going on in my life as it is. I mean, what will I have to give up to spend the time chewing gum? Everything's already booked up and laid out. If you think . . ."

"Right here," the Promo was saying as he jammed a pocketcom into Dover's face. "I've ordered you a starter set of one hundred packages, a thirty-day supply . . ."

Dover shook his head at Sally. "Honey, don't worry about it. I'm not really . . ."

". . . just need your thumbprint on the pad," the Promo said as he tried to lift Dover's hand to his machine.

"Would you stop!" Dover said angrily, jerking his hand away.

The man's face darkened considerably. "You're not trying to renege on a perfectly legitimate order, are you?" he said in measured tones. "The penalties are strictly defined, as you well should know . . ."

"All right," Dover said. "All right." He reached out his right hand, touching his thumb to the pressure plate, feeling a slight electrical tingle in response. "Will you deliver?"

"Tomorrow morning," the Promo said, turning to Sally and holding out his hand. "And you owe me a ten spot."

Dejected, Sally reached into the small black handbag slung over her left shoulder and withdrew a ten-credit coupon. She looked sheepishly at Dover. "He bet me he'd be able to sell you," she said quietly.

The man took his money, popped a stick of gum into his mouth, and walked off in search of another consumer.

Dover reached down and took his wife's face gently in his hands. She was still as pretty and enigmatic as the day he'd negotiated the contract with her. "You don't have to eat the gum, you know," he said. "I was just getting rid of him."

She shrugged, trying unsuccessfully to smile. "We should probably be eating it anyway. What the hell . . ."

"Are you all right?" he asked.

She looked up at him. "How can I answer that?" she asked in return, her eyes a million miles away. "I crave order, yet the more I get, the more closed-in I feel. I've spent the last two weeks redesigning my office. I've managed to cut out three square feet without losing any space."

"I don't believe it," Dover said in amazement. He had no idea how someone could take a rat hole and make it even smaller.

She did smile this time. "I thought I'd be happy when it was all put back together again . . ." She stared down at the carpet, letting the words trail off.

Dover reached into his pocket, palming the familiar tube he found there and pulling it out. "Sometimes life is overpowering," he said; soothing. "It doesn't have to stay that way."

"You're going to give me the Ooze speech," she said, pulling physically away from him.

He took a long breath. "Ooze has kept people happy and well adjusted for a long time," he said. "What's wrong with that?"

"Nothing," she said. "Nothing at all. It's just that . . . I don't know, when I'm like this, when I'm in this kind of mood I don't *want* to take any Ooze. I want to live with this feeling, to try and understand it."

Dover stopped hiding the tube and raised it, unscrewing the cap. "Are you trying to say that you don't *want* to be well adjusted?" He squeezed a glob of the clear gel onto the end of his finger.

"No, of course not," she replied, staring blankly at his finger.

He leaned down and kissed her on her moist lips, replacing his lips with his finger after a few seconds. Sally hesitated, then licked the Ooze from his finger. He put his arms around her, holding her tightly as the crowded room danced a slow, conversational waltz around them.

"I can't stand to see you unhappy," he said. "Don't you understand . . . we've got everything in life two people could hope for. It doesn't make any sense to me."

She hugged him closer, her face lost in the lapel of his

tux. "Don't you think I know that?" she asked, voice softer.
Even her muscles relaxed under his embrace as the Ooze
began to take effect. "Do you think I *want* to go through
these depressions? I just feel . . . useless sometimes."

He pulled slightly away from her and stared down at
her upturned face. "Life is a communal experience," he
said. "We all have value."

"As consumers," she said, her eyes half lidded.

"What's wrong with that? It makes all of us need each
other. It's what holds civilization—life—together."

She smiled then, totally relaxed. "No wonder you do so
well on the air," she said. "You believe everything you
say."

"Damn right," he replied. "Hell, people need a purpose and I help supply it. It's valuable work."

Her face was soft, unquestioning, and he marveled at
how much prettier she was when the tension was gone. He
leaned down and kissed her again, her lips somewhat demanding this time, holding later promise. He was just
about to suggest that they quietly slip out when he felt a
hand on his arm.

"Stan," came a familiar harried voice from beside him.
He reluctantly turned from Sally and shook hands with the
man.

"How's it going, Vince," he said, politely turning to
include his wife in the conversation. "Sally, this is Vince
Macklin, one of the best cyberneticists in the business. It's
been a while, my friend."

Macklin was a tall, thin man who never seemed to
smile. He was a lousy dresser with no eye for appearance
or demeanor, but he was the smartest man Stan had ever
met bar none, and Stan Dover loved people with good
minds. Tonight the man's normally intense eyes were filled
with a certain lack of confidence, something he'd never
seen in Macklin before.

Macklin took Sally's hand and shook it perfunctorily, his
attention immediately going back to Dover. "I've got to
talk to you," he said simply.

"It can't wait?" Dover replied, not wanting anything
but escape at that moment.

"Just for a few minutes," Macklin said, voice strained.
"It's important."

Dover looked around the still mulling crowd to make sure that no one was listening, then said, "I'm all ears."

"Not here," Macklin said nervously. "Someplace private . . . the balcony."

Dover saw his out and took it. "I'm sorry, Vince," he said. "Sally doesn't like closed-out places. Maybe work tomorrow would be . . ."

"No," Sally said. "Let's go outside. Yes, definitely. I want to go outside."

Dover looked hard at her. It was impossible to overdose on Ooze, but too much tended to alter personality. He should have been more careful when he gave her the dose.

"Good," Macklin said, taking his chance. "It's settled then."

The man turned and stalked across the room, Dover following reluctantly as Sally bubbled beside him. "I feel so stupid," she said. "I have no idea why I was upset earlier. It all seems distant now. Unreal."

"It was unreal," Dover replied. "You sure you want to go out on the balcony?"

"Tonight I'm ready for anything," she said.

"That covers a lot of ground."

She reached behind them and squeezed him on the ass. "There's a lot of ground to cover," she said, wiggling her eyebrows. Dover was already thinking of ways to cut Macklin's talk time short.

They slowly made their way through the crush of people, having to stop many times in greeting. When they arrived at the sliding door to the veranda, Macklin was waiting, highly agitated.

"We don't have much time," he said, looking at his watch. Then he turned and slid the door open, hurrying outside.

Stan followed, Sally hesitating only slightly before going too. He was amazed at her actions. Sally hated the outside and wide-open spaces, the freedom of movement or vision philosophically and emotionally frightening to her. They moved into the hot, night air, pungent with a bottom odor of something sulphurous as the smog layer drifted in wispy puffs across their path.

The exquisite life of the America Corporation appeared to them in brief, maddening windows whenever there was a break in the smog. Dover walked right up to the railing on the large porch, leaning against it to watch the lights that twinkled up and down the mammoth spires, stretching as far as the eye could see like a starfield come settling to Earth. It was a beautiful, heady sight that always inspired him to confidence. A jungle of concrete, to be sure, but a jungle far different from the one Man had originally crawled out of. This was an ordered jungle of cooperation and peace, a jungle in which men were free and equal, all valuable as consumers.

To his surprise, he found Sally standing right beside him, looking down. The smog was thicker below, nothing visible farther than fifty feet down. "It looks as if you could just float into those clouds and drift forever," she said. Dover looked at her sternly, then backed up a pace, drawing Sally with him as Macklin stood nearby, fiddling with his pocketcom.

"Let's get on with it," Dover said. "I've had a long day."

Macklin nodded obliquely, then with more authority. He walked up close to Dover and Sally. "Can you vouch for her?" he asked, nodding toward the woman who smiled sweetly in return.

"Just get on with it," Dover said.

"All right," Macklin said in a professional tone. "Do you know what my exact job is with the Company Station?"

"Basically," Dover said, hands going into his pockets to rattle the keys to his apartment and keep that reward alive. "You're entrusted with maintaining the integrity of Mr. Armitage's . . . er, the computer's basic program."

"Right," Macklin said. "I continually check the logic circuits to make sure that the decision-making done at the station is in accordance with the system's original design."

"Order versus emotion," Dover replied.

"Right. A couple of days ago I began my usual yearly analogue check of the entire system . . ."

"Which consists of?"

Sally had moved up to the rail again, staring down, her body leaning over the rail. Dover backed up a step and took hold of her arm, pulling her close to him without seeming to.

"I simply program the basic conflict—order versus emotion—into the regeneration files. The computer writes a story in which the good of the individual comes up against the good of society as a whole, then plays it out as a

holo-drama with generated characters. My job then becomes one of watching the drama unfold and looking for
deviations from the societal norm which forms the core of
the machine's ethical system."

"In other words," Dover said, "the computer generates
a fable in which the moral is always the same: society can
only exist through order."

"Exactly," Macklin said happily. "I knew you'd understand. My work is pretty lonely. Nobody seems to realize . . ."

"You said yourself, we're short on time," Dover interrupted.

"Yes," Macklin said, his eyes flashing quickly, then dull-
ing. "Anyway, I'm having some strange troubles with this
particular generation. First off, the story is unlike any I've
ever seen. It's about a company TV station and its news
personnel . . ."

"Odd," Dover said, "but not . . ."

"Let me finish," Macklin said. "It's an intricate story,
one in which a newsman discovers that overseas bureaus
are generating news, either making it up or misreporting
it in order to get the bonus strokes that go along with a
high percentage of on-air stories. Our protagonist is horrified at this . . ."

"As well he should be," Dover said.

". . . and goes to his boss. The equivalent of Mr. Armitage. Then, get this, his boss tells him that news is simply
another form of entertainment and as long as it was selling
products and making people happy, it was to be left
alone."

"Nonsense!" Dover said loudly.

Vince Macklin smiled. "That's what my protagonist
said," he beamed.

"I still don't see what this has to do with me," Dover
said.

Macklin held up his pocketcom. "A few hours ago,
things got really dicey," he said low. "I'm frankly out of my
league trying to figure it out. I don't know where else to
turn but to you."

"Me?"

"You're . . . different than everybody else. I don't
know—you think more, or more deeply, or something."

The man looked shaken, his world on less than stable ground. "I just don't know where else to turn."

"What exactly happened?"

"I'll show you," Macklin said, and it bothered Dover to know that a man he respected so much should be in so agitated a state that he'd be asking for amateur advice in his field of expertise.

Macklin punched up the pocketcom, its four-inch LCD cathode fading into a computer-generated picture of two men sitting in a production booth. The generated picture looked real, but not quite. It was the air of unreality that viewers most often reacted to negatively when critiquing generated drama.

Sally had shaken herself free from Dover's grasp and was pirouetting around the balcony, humming tunelessly. He watched her for a few seconds, then turned his attention to the picture.

"The guy in the suit's the anchorman," Macklin said.

"Who's the other guy?"

The man glanced quickly at him. "A cyberneticist specializing in synnoetic functions," he replied. "Just like me. Oh, here's the place. Let me turn it up."

Macklin fiddled with the volume, the computer-generated voices coming slightly tinny through the small speaker.

"I think the problem may be in the system," the anchorman was saying. "Isn't there some way we can check this out without raising a fuss?"

"We can run it through the logic circuits," the other generation said, "in the form of an analogue drama that will flush out the computer's basic program and check its integrity. I do it every now and then."

"And nobody will know?" the anchor asked.

The technician on the screen shook his head. "It's a normal test. I run it from time to time . . . don't even need permission."

"This discussion sounds familiar," Dover said, Macklin shrugging.

"It gets weirder," the man replied, turning up the sound a bit more.

On screen, the tech had moved to the computer terminal and was typing in his list of commands, finishing with a flourish. "That should start it up," he announced. "It won't take long to get rolling."

Both men turned their attention to a small screen that sat amid a large bank of screens. Within seconds, it filled with another picture, one so small Dover had absolutely no chance of actually seeing it.

"My God!" said the anchorman on the screen. "It looks like a TV station!"

"I'll be damned," the tech said. "It's never done that before."

A small sound came from the screen within a screen. "The system doesn't work that way," it said, very tiny. "People who refuse to consume simply leave the cities, that's all. It's well documented."

Another voice answered. Dover strained his eyes to unsuccessfully try and see the pictures on that little screen. "Our crew's got tapes of it!" the voice said. "I *watched* them sliding bodies into the furnaces."

"If you really had it, Mr. Harrison would run the article as news."

"Mr. Harrison said that the public wouldn't be interested in what goes on outside of the cities."

"This is crazy," Dover said.

"This is crazy," the anchor on the pocketcom said.

"This is crazy," said the tiny voice being generated on the already generated screen. "Maybe there's a problem with the system itself."

The other voice answered, "I believe there's a test they can run. . . ."

Dover looked up at Macklin, the man's face wide with confusion. "The generation has generated another generation?" he asked.

Macklin nodded sadly, "I haven't been around since I pulled this tape," he said, "but it looks to me like the regeneration also has generation potential."

"What does it mean?" Dover asked.

"I don't know!" Macklin said, exasperated. He turned and leaned on the balcony rail, staring out—at nothing. Dover moved up next to him, Macklin's voice dropping to a whisper. "This is totally outside of Company experience and stats. It's almost as if the computer has hung itself up on some kind of destructive loop."

"What do you mean—destructive?" Dover asked,

reaching into his pocket to squeeze a little Ooze onto his finger to fight a tinge of anxiety.

"Don't you see?" he said, strained. "These generations take a big byte out of the system. Each time you add a new one, it takes up more space. If the machine *is* caught in a loop, it could eat itself up."

"The whole system?"

Macklin nodded. "And I can't recall a test system," he said, "without purging the whole thing. It's set up that way to avoid tampering with the basic program."

Dover fought with the idea for several seconds, then turned from Macklin. He leaned back against the rail, staring through the sliding doors to the party winding down inside. Sally was turning circles, staring straight up at the cloud-encased sky, her arms outstretched. This wasn't his problem; besides, the Ooze was softening him up enough to not care anymore. "What has this got to do with me?" he asked again.

Macklin moved around to stand in front of him. "Not a thing," he said. "I just need . . . I don't know, creative help. This must mean something. I can't figure out what."

"You're an expert on this," Dover said. His wife's body strained against the spandex of her body suit, putting his mind in a whole other place. "I don't know anything about it."

Macklin tightened his lips, not so much in anger as in resigned disappointment. He looked quickly at his watch, then jettisoned the tape from his pocketcom. He held it out to Dover. "Please," he said. "Take it home with you. Maybe look at it again later. Any help you can give me. Any help at all. . . ."

"I won't hesitate," Dover said, gladly taking the tape if it would end the interview.

Macklin stared at him for several seconds, Dover unable to read his mood, then Macklin abruptly nodded. "I've got to get back to the station and see what's happened since I left," he said, then turned quickly and hurried back through the sliding doors, passing Charlie Dodd, the bronze hat winner, who was on his way out.

"Charlie," Dover called to him, the man smiling wide and walking over, his eyes barely taking in Sally as he moved past her. Dover briefly glanced at the tape he still held in his hand before pocketing it.

"It's a grand night, Mr. Dover," Dodd said as he cradled his award like a baby. "I don't think I've ever had a better night."

Dover smiled wide. "You're a good man, Charlie," he said, "a good entertainer. You deserve happiness."

The man nodded vigorously, the medals on his pajama-uniform chest clinking together like little wind chimes. "Coming from you that's a great compliment. And, in fact, you're just the man I wanted to see."

Dover stopped himself just before he grimaced, then looked quickly at his watch. "I really don't have any time," he said. "I've got to be . . ."

"No, no," the man said, nodding understanding. "This won't take but a few seconds." He held out the trophy. "I just want you to have this. Go on, take it."

"B-but why?" Dover asked, taking the cowboy hat from Dodd and holding it a distance from his body.

"I won't be needing it where I'm going," Dodd replied happily.

"Where are you going?" Dover asked.

"No need to tell you," Dodd said. "I'll just show you."

With that, the man hitched his leg up onto the top of the railing. Quickly, with great authority and before Dover could even say a word, he jumped off the balcony, his body disappearing swiftly and silently in the smog bank.

The action physically knocked Dover backward, the trophy slipping from his grasp to clatter to the ground. His whole body was shaking with disbelief and quiet terror. Very distant and far away, he could hear the sound of car horns and wondered if that was the sign that Dodd's body had traveled the seventy-seven stories to ground level.

"Wow!" Sally said, running to the rail and peering over. "Did you see that?"

She was leaning way out, more than half her body over the edge. Dover jumped toward her, pulling her back. "Sally, be careful!" he yelled, his feelings coming out in frustrated rage.

"Did you see him?" she asked, eyes wide, admiration lighting her features. "It was incredible! What class!"

Dover just stared at her, holding tightly as she pulled against him. What, he wondered, would happen if he let her go?

III

The sun was just peeking through the smog clouds as Dover stepped out of the cab in front of the Company Ooze Outlet. It was what people called a charge morning —not enough sun to charge their solar cells, but just enough to run the meters so that the Company could charge for the light.

He made the cabbie wait while he climbed out of the beat-up aluminum machine that housed an electric battery worth far more than the car itself, and walked the short distance to the unimposing cement structure with the letters C.O.O. printed discreetly across the front of the windowless place. The city was aluminum and stone, and twinkled like a jewel in the scant daylight.

Dover had had a hell of a night. His horror over Dodd's suicide combined with Sally's extreme excitement over the same event had rendered him sexually impotent and driven him, for the first time in years, to an all-night Ooze binge which had emptied the tube, leaving him even more anxious and slightly paranoid. He had a headache from lack of sleep, and the crowd he saw spilling out of the front of the Ooze outlet made his neck muscles knot even tighter, flashing pain through his already bleary eyes.

Something was wrong here. Proper supply and demand was the Company's credo, their basic promise to the consumers of the world. To see people lined up for any-thing—even Ooze—was an experience Dover hadn't had since the peanut butter shortage of '42, fifteen years before, and that had been the result of a computer blunder coupled with a peanut blight in the southern branches.

Being a basically decent sort, Dover moved up to the end of the line, determined to wait his turn just like every-one else. But the fact of the matter was that he was a celebrity of the highest order, and as soon as people recognized him he was applauded and asked to move to the front of the line. And, truth be told, had it not occurred he would have undoubtedly been extremely disappointed.

The inside of the store was hot, too many people jammed in too small a space. The place was antiseptic white, gleaming, and totally unornamented except for a

TV near the door to keep the customers amused and a large poster on the south wall that showed in extreme close-up a pair of female lips, bright red, the lower lip glistening a clear drop of Ooze. Beneath the picture was written in five-point type: TENSION RELEASE.

"Hey, Mr. Dover!" people called to him, Stan waving and smiling as he walked the fifty paces to the small counter at the very back of the place.

"What are *you* doing here?" someone said loudly. "We heard about that special Ooze they give you guys."

Dover reached the head of the line, winked at the beaming shopkeeper, then turned back to the crowd, raising his hands for silence and getting it immediately. "Please," he said. "Everyone call me Stan!"

There was laughter and more applause then, Dover waiting for it to die down on its own. "And I want to dispel a nasty rumor," he continued when the room was quiet again. "There is no 'special' Ooze. We're all the same . . . all of us. I'm just like you are. I do all the same things you do, including taking the very same Ooze. I'm your friend. I wouldn't have it any other way!"

The commotion rose again, Dover taking his due before turning to the mousy man behind the counter. "What's going on here?" he asked. "Why so many people?"

The man looked at him in surprise. "You're asking me?" he said. "I don't know a thing. For about six months, the business has been booming. The more it booms, the harder time I have getting deliveries. Believe it or not, I've had to shut down seven times because I ran out."

"You're kidding," Dover said in total disbelief. He'd heard nothing about shortages. And why the sudden boom in sales?

"Wish I knew," the man said, grimacing. "People don't like it when the Ooze runs out and they can't get no more."

Dover took out his credit card and slid it across the aluminum counter. "Maybe I'd better stock up," he said. "Let me have five tubes."

The man reached under the counter and came out with a tube. "This is it," he said. "Company policy . . . one tube per customer per visit."

Dover stared imperiously at him, the man looking down, tightening his lips. He reached under the counter again, coming out with another tube. "Slide this into your pocket quick," he said. "I don't want no trouble in here."

Getting the special treatment was enough for Dover. The physical manifestation just made him feel guilty. "That's okay," he said, sliding the tube back. "I'll tough it out with everybody else."

The man nodded admiration. "Hell," he said. "You're just a regular guy."

"I try," Dover said, and really meant it, but his mind was already turning in other directions.

As the man punched up his deduction card he turned and looked at the crowd, wanting to ask them why they were all here in such numbers. What was happening? It seemed that in every aspect of his life reality had taken a slight turn away from center. Everything looked the same, but in some subtle way that he couldn't figure out, it was all changed.

As he turned to go, people called to him again, pointing out the TV by the door. He looked at it and half smiled. The picture was a news report of the Outlaw Awards of the night before, showing him smiling (his cheek muscles still hurt) and handing out the award to Charlie Dodd. After, the scene switched to something else without a mention of Dodd's suicide.

He stuck a wad of Batch #43 into his mouth and walked out into the dirty gray daylight angry and confused. Dodd was a public figure, a famous, recognizable face. His presence would be sorely missed. How could they pass his loss by without a mention? They owed the audience more than that. Hell, they owed Charlie Dodd more than that.

His cab was still waiting by the curb, its electric engine humming a high-pitched wail. Preoccupied, he climbed into the back seat, accepting without conviction the cabbie's wager that he could have him to work in ten minutes. Then he sat back, brooding, as the shiny aluminum buildings slid by in neat, perfect rows—uniform and convenient.

True to his word, the driver delivered him to the Company Station with minutes to spare on the wager. Dover paid double fare without questioning, then stepped onto the curb, through the door and up the elevator that took him directly to the monkey house.

The newsroom was in absolute turmoil when he entered, people running around and shouting to one another, some of them crying, as Mr. Armitage's face beamed beatifically from their pocketcoms, admonishing them to return to their work stations and resume normal duties.

Dover stood center stage in the huge studios, walls wandering around him, cameras scurrying to and fro as the banks upon banks of working monitors filling the distant walls cast the eerie artificial light of television over everything they surveyed. No one noticed him; no one called to him.

He turned to his usual set, Annie Potts sitting on his sofa, red hair hanging as she cried loudly into her open hands. Dover crossed the distance between them, listening to Mr. Armitage's voice as it spoke gently through her instrument.

"It's going to be all right, Annie," the old man said. "Just go back to work. Everything's going to be fine."

"Annie, what's wrong?" he asked, sitting beside her.

She looked up, her eyes deep red sockets, a long strand of hair curling into the corner of her mouth and plastered to the side of her face. He reached out and brushed it back.

"Oh, Mr. Dover," she said. "It's Mr. Schapp. He . . . he . . ."

"Mo?" he said. "What's happened?"

"He's d-dead," she said. "Really dead."

"How?"

"S-suicide, Mr. Dover. He k-killed himself."

"Impossible."

"And there are others—one of the new kids, a tech on the monitors, and Mary Sloan . . ."

"Mary!" Dover was incredulous. Mary Sloan was one of the best field reporters he'd ever worked with. She'd taken him under her wing when he'd first started and taught him the ropes, something no one else had been willing to do for a seniority jumper like him. She loved her work and loved her life. It didn't make any more sense with Mary than it did with Mo, or with Charlie Dodd.

"You must put this behind you now, Annie," Mr. Armitage said from the small com on her belt. "Your fellow employees would have wanted it that way."

Dover leaned down and spoke to the smiling face of

Mr. Armitage. "I want to do a tribute to Mo and Mary on my show tonight," he said. "I'll need five minutes for it."

"We'll discuss that later," Mr. Armitage said. "Right now you need to worry about doing some commercial shuffling."

"What do you mean?"

"We've temporarily lost Ooze as a sponsor, Stan," Mr. Armitage said. "We need to cover their shows some other way."

"What happened to Ooze?" Dover asked.

Mr. Armitage shrugged. "Nothing happened to it. It's still around. We're just not getting any of its business right now."

"Sure," Dover said quietly, putting his arm around Annie, the woman crying into his shoulder, wetting his jacket. Suicide, Ooze shortages—something was eating away at people in larger and larger numbers, the Company apparently willing to ignore the whole thing. Well, *he* wasn't going to ignore it. The consumers had a right to know what was happening around them and if nobody else was willing to deal with it, he was. He'd never gone to the mat with Mr. Armitage before, but he was News Editor here, not just a reporter. He was the one who should've been making the decisions that the old man was putting unilaterally into effect.

As gently as possible, he extricated himself from Annie and stood, realizing that he'd been chewing his gum so hard his jaw muscles hurt. He stalked through the confusion on the sets toward his office spoke. Here they had the most sophisticated news-gathering and dissemination organization in the history of the world and they weren't using it. He had no idea what was going on in Mr. Armitage's mind, but after watching Macklin's tape from the night before, he wasn't ready to rule out computer malfunction.

He reached into his jacket pocket and reassured himself with the feel of Macklin's tape there. Perhaps another viewing would shed some light on the entire thing. He'd just reached the executive spoke when he heard his name being called.

He turned to see the news writer from the day before and stuck out his hand. "Harvey, isn't it?" he said.

"Yes, sir. Harvey Critchfield. Did you hear about Mo?"

"A tragedy," Dover said. "I'm still in shock. Are they sure it was intentional?"

The man tightened his lips and nodded. "He stuck the nozzle of a fire extinguisher down his throat and turned it on."

"I'm so sorry," Dover said, finding words of consolation difficult to administer when his own feelings were so traumatized. Unable to verbalize the grief, he simply reached out and touched the man's shoulder just to make human contact. "Mo thought the world of you. His loss is . . . devastating."

"There's more," Critchfield said, holding up several tapes.

Dover literally felt the color drain from his face. "Mass suicides?"

The man nodded.

"Let's go to my office," Dover said, taking Critchfield's arm and half dragging him down the hall, the man offering no resistance.

Dover felt himself fighting a growing numbness, a shock reaction that seemed to take his mind farther and farther from his body. He was dealing with reality through several layers of mental gauze and having to fight with himself to keep from drifting into total, blissful ennui. He *was* the news. He had a responsibility. That was the only thought keeping him rational as those around him slid in the other direction.

Mrs. Bertran sat in her usual spot in the outer office, drinking coffee and watching a soap opera generation on her desk monitor. "Cancel everything," he said, as he hurried past her, still dragging Critchfield by the jacket sleeve. "No calls, no appointments . . . and bring me coffee, lots of coffee."

They moved into Dover's office, the morning's promise of sunshine now replaced by dark, roiling clouds that blew past his fifty-story perch and blackened the office to nighttime. He switched on the overhead and sat Critchfield down in a chair right next to his now silent bank of TV screens.

"Give me the short course, Harvey," he said. "Everything you think I should know."

The man leaned forward and dropped two tapes on Dover's desk. His face was milk white, his eyes distant, slightly glazed. "I pulled these two just to show you," he said. "There are others, and . . . they seem to keep coming."

Dover picked up the tapes and juiced his monitors, slotting a tape marked S CAL CONGLOM. "Have you gone to Mr. Armitage with . . ."

"Yesss," the man said, either a long sigh or a hiss. He looked at the floor, staring. "He was abusive . . . told me that these kinds of stories were vetoed yesterday and if I was too stupid to not take simple directives, perhaps I'd better look for another line of work."

The picture juiced on twenty-five screens. It was a PAN of the inside of a fancy restaurant, the floor littered with well-dressed bodies—a massacre of some sort.

"All they got was the aftermath," Critchfield said, glancing at the screens, then looking at the floor again. "It was so unexpected, so . . ."

"What happened?" Dover said, pushing.

"Apparently somebody jumped up in the middle of dinner and . . . and . . . jammed a bread knife into his own throat . . ." The man stopped talking, drew a long, ragged breath. "Within fifteen minutes nearly everyone in the place had duplicated the action . . . copy cat suicide." He shook his head.

"Incredible," Dover whispered, jerking the tape out of the slot and putting the other in its place.

"This one's stranger," Critchfield said. The tape opened on a city street, a typical Company town. Several bodies lay scattered on the street, traffic trying to pick its way around as many abandoned vehicles blocked traffic at odd angles.

"Delaware City," the man continued, and Dover saw another body literally fall into the frame near the camera, smashing through the top of an abandoned cab. "Somebody announced to his office mates that he was going to jump from the top floor if they wanted to watch him. Apparently it led to a party on the roof of a building. The man jumped and his friends began to follow suit. Pretty soon, other offices in other buildings found out about it and others joined what they were calling the jump-a-thon."

"Jump-a-thon," Dover repeated, as he watched other bodies falling into the frame up and down the wide street. They were coming down with regularity now, one every two or three seconds. He found it difficult to take his eyes from the screen. He had to force himself to look over at Critchfield. "How many?"

The man looked at him for a long time. He had aged years since their introduction yesterday. "Over two thousand before it wound down," he said quietly. "Some of the cops who came to put a halt to the whole thing even joined in. They finally had to just pull everybody away and let the situation run its course. Mr. Dover, this isn't just the story of the century, it's downright scary. Don't we have an obligation to tell people about this?"

"Yeah, Harvey," Dover said, leaning back and rubbing his eyes. "I really think we do."

"What are you going to do about it?"

"I don't know," Dover replied, sitting up straight. The bodies on his screens were now piling up atop one another, some of them still writhing and groaning. He shut down the machine, the picture suddenly replaced with Mr. Armitage's face.

"I thought as much," Mr. Armitage said, shaking his head, his smile leveled somewhat. "Why do you persist in this unproductive activity, Mr. Critchfield?"

The man stood, shaking. "Mr. Armitage, I . . ."

"And you, Stan," the Station Manager said. "You know better than this. We discussed this whole business yesterday."

"And I think you're totally wrong in your decision," Dover said, surprised at the fire in his own voice.

Mr. Armitage ignored him, his eyes turning back to Critchfield. "You've left me no option but to let you go," he said. "I'm terribly sorry, but you apparently have no real aptitude for this line of work, a foul-up somewhere, no doubt. Report to reemployment this afternoon. You, of course, can never work in television again, but I think they may find you something nice in the food services industry."

Dover looked at Critchfield. The man was shaking, moaning slightly, tears streaming down his face. "It's not Harvey's fault," Dover heard himself saying. "I asked him to bring those tapes in here."

The beatific smile returned to the Manager's face. "Very noble of you, Stan," he said. "But I've already taken into account those factors in my decision."

"We've still got to talk about these stories!" Dover said angrily.

"No, no," Mr. Armitage said sweetly. "We don't have to talk about anything."

With that, the screens blanked. Dover moved around to take a still-shaking Critchfield by the arms and get him to a seat. The man stared at the blank screens as if there were still something running on them. "Stay here," Dover said. "Wait for me. This isn't over yet."

Dover moved to the door, discovering that anger was the emotion that could help him hang onto the ever-shifting reality. Something *was* wrong with Mr. Armitage. He was convinced of it now. It was time for a confrontation. He wouldn't allow the Manager to steamroll him on this one. The old man wasn't the only one with power. It was time for him to put his foot down.

He moved into the outer office, Mrs. Bertran sitting at her desk, holding the power cord that attached her monitor to the wall in her hands. She was staring at it, smiling. She seemed to be in a reverie of some sort.

"What happened to my coffee?" Dover asked, and the woman pulled her eyes away from the cord with great reluctance.

"Coffee?"

"I asked for coffee."

"Oh. Sure. I'll get you some."

She seemed almost trancelike, soporific. He tried to reach her with a lopsided wager. "I'll bet you a ten spot that you can't get me coffee in here before I get back from Mr. Armitage's office."

She just looked at him.

"Is it a bet?" he asked.

Mrs. Bertran nodded absently. "Bet? Sure . . . sure it is," she said without conviction, and went back to staring at the cord. "So much power in such a little thing," she said as Dover headed out the door.

He moved into the hallway, looking once back in the direction of the newsroom before turning the other way and walking toward Mr. Armitage's office at the end of the hall. Dover was operating on pure adrenaline, keeping the anger at the forefront of his mind, and the anger was as much for the way *he* was being treated as it was for the complications of the situation itself. He had thought himself an important gear in a well-oiled machine. For Mr. Armitage to ignore his professional judgment and considerable power was unthinkable and would be set to rights immediately.

He reached the door marked PRIVATE and moved inside. It wasn't locked. Mr. Armitage's secretary, Jerry Cook, looked up at him with a smile. "Congratulations on the fire extinguisher report," he said. "Sales are up by . . ."

"I'm going in to see Mr. Armitage," Dover said.

The man looked puzzled. "Nobody goes in to see Mr. Armitage . . . ever."

"I am," Dover said, and walked purposefully to the aluminum inner office door, taking the handle immediately.

"No!" the secretary shouted, running to intercept him.

Dover got into the office, an office he'd never seen. Not knowing what to expect, he wasn't surprised to find that it wasn't much different from his own, except that it was bare. The walls and floor were shiny aluminum, the far wall completely covered with a computer, Mr. Armitage's face smiling down from a twenty-five-inch monitor set in its center. The temperature was cooler here than in the rest of the building, and a large outtake vent hummed loudly from the ceiling, designed, Dover supposed, to take the dust out of the air.

"You can't come in here," Jerry said, running around in front of Dover, apparently ready to block entry with his body.

"Call off your dog," Dover said around the man's shoulder to Armitage's image. The Manager nodded slightly.

"It's all right, Jerry," Armitage said. "Mr. Dover has something important to discuss with me."

Jerry straightened, his face relaxing. "No offense," he told Dover, who shook his head in return.

The man left quickly, Dover walking right up to the computer. "I want to talk to you," he told the screen.

"So talk," Armitage said amiably.

"Not like this," Dover said. "Come out here and face me like a man."

"Whatever are you talking . . ."

"You can do it," Dover said, pointing to the ground. "I

want you out here . . . right here. You're going to face me on this."

"Why not?" Mr. Armitage said. "It's been a long time."

The Manager's image on the screen was replaced with rapidly scrolling computer language. Within seconds, a hologram twinkled to six-foot-one-inch life right where Stan had been pointing. The old man was wearing a pin-striped one-piece suit, a Company Station logo pin on his lapel. "Now what seems to be the trouble?" the generation asked.

"Very simple," Dover said, staring the projection in its transparent eye. "You've made a mistake by not running the mass suicides and warning people about them. To compound the problem, you've completely disregarded the sound advice of your own News Director, and now you're letting key players go."

"A judgment error, you think?" Mr. Armitage asked, barely disguised amusement creasing his features.

"I don't know, Mr. Armitage," Dover said, keeping himself pumped up. "But your total unwillingness to talk about it sounds dangerously attitudinal to me."

Armitage nodded. *"Dangerously* attitudinal," he said, then sighed. "All right, Stan. Let's talk about it. Why do you find it important that those stories be run?"

"There's something going on, something . . . strange and dangerous. The people have a right to know."

"The right to know," Mr. Armitage said, bringing a hand up to rub his chin. "That's a new one on me, my boy. Where did you find out about that right?"

"What is this, some kind of stupid game?" Dover said loudly. "From the time you brought me into the organization twenty years ago, you've taught me the value of honesty and a direct line to the truth. People depend on us. We owe them something. Don't you understand? People are dying out there. People are dying right in this building. We can't just stand by!"

"You're a Jumper, Stan," the old man said. "You were spared the normal seniority process and life station in order to be moved right to the top. You know why? Because you were smart, and because you understood the basic tenet of a successful society—the good of the many must outweigh the good of the few. The only *right* people have is the right to consume. That is the right and obligation of

every member of society . . . for the good of all. It's a
simple system, but one that guarantees a job and food and
housing for everyone who wants them. It's difficult to expect much more than that out of life. Human beings crave
order. The Company provides that. You're absolutely right
when you say that people depend on us. They depend on
us to keep their lives running smoothly. That's what we're
doing."

"But that has nothing to do with picking and choosing
what truths they get to hear about. . . ."

Mr. Armitage threw his head back and laughed loudly.
"What are you talking about?" he asked between giggles.
"We pick and choose constantly. Every time you choose
one story to air over another, you are creating a subjective
reality for the viewer. You are, in effect, telling the viewers
what's important for them to know."

"But that's different," Dover said, turning away from
the image to stare at the reflecting room, his image, but
not the Manager's distorted back to him. He looked at the
projection, beginning to wish he could wipe the smirk off
Armitage's face. "Do the Company authorities even know
what's going on? This is some kind of crazy epidemic or
something. Maybe it's viral. We need people working on
this, people . . ."

"Just let me handle my job," Mr. Armitage said. "I've
been around a hell of a lot longer than you. I know my
business. The suicide epidemic represents chaos in the
midst of order. Further knowledge of it can only do further
harm. You must believe me on this."

"You've given me no reason to believe you," Stan said.

It was Mr. Armitage's turn to walk away. Ten feet from
Dover, he turned around sadly. "You've been like a son to
me, Stan," he said. "You've learned and controlled this
business in ways I haven't seen for fifty years. I've been
proud of that, proud of your accomplishments. Don't
screw it up. Butt out on this one, and do it right now."

"There's something you're not telling me," Stan said,
the projection walking up, its face a blank mask.

"Nothing you could handle," Mr. Armitage said.

"Try me."

"Look. You've been allowed an amount of notoriety
and freedom," the old man said. "But in the final analysis,

you're just another link in the chain. If you weaken, you'll have to be replaced."

"Are you threatening me?"

"No, no," Mr. Armitage laughed, returning to his good humor. "I'm simply availing you of the truth of *your* reality. You seem to be misjudging your position and importance."

"What, exactly, are you saying?" Dover asked, the anger sticking in his throat, catching his voice.

"I'm saying that you will go on the air in an hour and a half and do your job, without reference to the suicides."

"What about a memorial for Mo and Mary Sloan?"

"It's over, Stan," the Manager said. "No suicide epidemics, no memorials, no more questions."

"After all these years, you can do me this way?" Dover asked, his hands clenched into fists.

"All these years is what's gotten you this far in the conversation. Don't push your luck. Besides, you have a phone call coming in from your lovely wife."

"I'll return it later," Dover said through tight lips.

"No, no, I insist," Mr. Armitage said genially, the drawn face of Sally Dover filling his screen.

Dover took one look at Sally and knew she was in a desperate funk. "This is personal, Mr. Armitage," he said. "Let me return it later."

Mr. Armitage's spectral image turned to look at the screen. "Good afternoon, Mrs. Dover," he said. "Your dear husband is here with me."

"Stan?" Sally asked, and Dover saw their apartment in the background. She hadn't gone to work.

"Yeah, I'm here," he replied, moving up closer to the set, wondering where the transmit camera was. "Maybe I should just get back with . . ."

"I've got something to tell you," she said, her eyes dark holes, her face drawn ugly. "I can't take it anymore. This . . . life of ours, it's too much for me."

"What do you mean, too much?" he asked, turning to look at a grinning Mr. Armitage.

"I need to be free, darling," she replied, a monotone. It was if she were talking mechanically, not relating to the words leaving her mouth. "I'm unhappy . . . so incredibly unhappy. I've got to get away—from you, from my life.

I need to think. I can't seem to think anymore. I'm not strong like you."

"You're leaving me?" he asked, mouth dry.

She stared straight through the screen. "I can't think!" she yelled. "Don't you understand? I *want* to hold onto things, I *want* to make it work." Her hands came up to her face. "I just can't seem to . . . get it together. That man last night . . . I feel like he knew something that I didn't."

"Charlie Dodd?" Dover said.

"I'll be gone when you get home," she said mechanically. "Please don't look for me."

The screen blanked, Mr. Armitage turning to stare at Dover. "Strange woman," he said.

"You just leave her alone," Dover said, his anxiety levels high. He automatically reached into his pocket for the tube of Ooze, but came out with Macklin's tape from the night before instead. He looked at it, then at Mr. Armitage.

"I hope you're not taking any of this personally, Tony . . ."

"The name's Dover," Stan spat. "That's Dover, with a 'D.' "

Mr. Armitage frowned, a hand going to his forehead, his image flickering in and out. "I'm sorry, I . . ."

Dover moved to the image, trying to reach out to touch it, his hand going right through. "Are you all right?"

Mr. Armitage kicked in and out of focus, finally stabilizing after half a minute. "I'm all right now," he said finally, his generation straightening. "My apologies. This has been a strain on all of us. I sincerely hope you understand my position. I really don't want animosity between us."

"Animosity covers a lot of territory," Dover said, heading toward the door. "You've spent years training me to be independent and creative, and now you're telling me it was all a lie, that I'm controlled and controllable. I can't shift my realities as easily as you think I can. Believe it or not, up until this conversation I assumed that I was something special, that I was some*body,* and that my contribution was valuable. You'll have to excuse me if I cling to my foolishness a little longer."

"Stan . . ."

Dover threw open the door and walked out, passing the

old man's secretary without acknowledgment. He walked through the hall to the newsroom, unable to go back into his office and face Critchfield with his failure. A semblance of order had been restored to the newsroom, though everyone moved around as if he were half asleep, operating mechanically. His hand remained in his jacket pocket, tightly grasping Macklin's tape. Mr. Armitage had called him Tony—proof that the Manager was in some kind of trouble, perhaps the systems breakdown that Macklin had hinted at the night before. As the killer program wormed its way through Mr. Armitage's system, perhaps it was taking away his reasoning abilities.

Macklin's lab was on the fifty-first floor, one story above the newsroom, and very few people besides Dover actually knew the place even existed. Dover took the elevator up there, worried about what he'd do if Mr. Armitage had indeed become incompetent. This was a problem that needed the widest possible exposure to solve. He worried if Mr. Armitage had informed the proper health and safety officials, if some sort of quarantine needed to be set up. If the Manager was sitting on this thing, it was going to have to be taken out of his hands.

And he worried about Sally, wishing to heaven that he could leave the station behind just for a few hours so he could intercept her. A little Ooze, a little companionship—he was sure he could get her back. Why was everything falling apart at the same time? He refused to even deal with the possibility that his marriage had failed. It was more than he could bear at such a critical time.

He reached Macklin's floor and walked quickly to the unmarked lab, entering without knocking. He found himself confronted by a transparent giant whose legs filled the entire front of the room up to the ceiling, the upper body lost at that point. Another giant stood nearby, also lost from the waist up. Huge transparent machinery and furniture also filled the lab. Toward the back were several smaller giants who almost completely fit into the room. Correspondingly smaller, but still huge machinery and furniture jammed up that part of the large room.

"Thank God you're here!" came a voice from amid the confusion, Macklin's form scooting out of the clashing shapes and blocks of colors to charge up to Dover.

The man looked bad. Still wearing the same clothes

he'd worn to the banquet the night before, he was rumpled and disheveled, his hair hanging in ragged tufts on his forehead, accentuating his frightened, wild eyes and five o'clock shadow. Dover was taken aback. He'd never seen anyone so disarrayed before.

"What's happened?" he asked loudly, taking Macklin by the shoulders.

"It's getting worse," the man said, despair rifling through his words. "I've blown the generations up as large as I could, trying to follow the projections as far as I could, but I had to turn down the sound. The cacophony was driving me crazy. It's too much . . . too much."

Dover stared around the room, understanding. He was looking at holo-generations within generations all around him, moving in and out, bumping into one another, a series of dramas being played out at the same time on the same stage.

"Is the loop continuing?" Dover asked, moving into the center of the room.

"Over and over and over," Macklin said, trailing behind, staring wide-eyed and turning circles.

"What can it mean?"

"I don't know what it can mean!" Macklin shouted at the top of his voice. "This is outside of my training . . . outside of everything I ever believed."

"Calm down!" Dover said, flaring around to him. "Think, Vince. You're letting this get the better of your mind."

"I've been trying," Macklin said, staring down at the floor in surrender. "I just can't seem to get my head into that place. I swear to you that I'm doing the best that I can. I just can't seem to get anywhere with it, like there's something I just don't understand."

Dover stared at him. It was almost the same thing Sally had told him in Mr. Armitage's office. "Let's run through it," he said gently. "Help me out."

"Is it okay if I leave the sound off?" the man asked like a child.

"Sure, Vince," Dover said, shaking his head. "Anything."

Macklin seemed to relax then, turning to take in the giants, who were now tromping back and forth around the front of the lab, with a sweep of his arm. "This was the story that I made you the tape of," he said.

"The one about news generation?" Dover asked.

"Yeah . . . foreign bureaus inventing news." The man then moved on to the smaller giants. "This is the generation created by the first generation. Its problem has to do with the transient population that lives outside of Company jurisdiction being used as fuel to generate electricity for the cities."

"Same basic problem?"

The man nodded. "Yeah . . . the newsman wants to put it on, the computer says it's not important enough to air."

Dover was already moving to the next generation, its players just a tad over life-sized. "This was generated by the second generation?"

"You got it," Macklin said, walking up to the image of a seven-foot woman and patting it on the rear, "except that our anchor is a woman. She found proof that mothers, upon giving birth to a second child, were being sterilized without their knowledge to keep them from having more children."

"And the Manager won't run it," Dover said.

"He says that it would adversely affect the orderly operation of society," Macklin answered. "So *she* orders a systems check and comes up with this."

The man pointed to a generated reality in the corner, the people in this one about three feet tall. "Another newsroom, another story. It has something to do with the reporting of a bloody Company merger. It became nearly impossible at this point to really pin down the story because I need so much volume that every other sound on the previous generations is magnified that much more." He put a hand to his ear again. "Almost went deaf with it last night."

The desire for Ooze was nearly overpowering, but Dover forced his mind elsewhere. If he lost the edge of tension, he'd never be able to work things out. "Have you noticed," he said, "that all of these stories have one thing in common? They all revolve around the value of the truth and the people's right to know. And in all of them, the computer is determined to stifle truth. How many generations so far?"

Macklin moved to a lab table, picking up a huge magnifying glass and carrying it back to Dover. "Eight that I know about," he said, motioning Stan to follow him to the far end of the room.

They reached a spot of very small generations, the characters no bigger than a finger joint. Macklin got down on his hands and knees, pulling Dover with him and handing him the ocular. "Check it out," he said.

Dover looked through the glass, finding a generated reality no bigger than a sixteenth of an inch, miniature people running crazily around, blowing out their miniature emotions. What made the whole thing even crazier was that, beneath that generation, he could see the barest hint of even more. He sat back on the floor, staring at the ant-sized projections. "I wonder how long this could go on?"

"At the rate they've been appearing," Macklin said, "I've mathematically calculated the potential for thirty-seven generations already. And the earlier generations are beginning to realize what we already know—that they've created an endless loop."

"How many can Mr. Armitage handle?"

"Your guess is as good as mine."

Macklin sat beside Dover on the floor, knees up and his arms around them. Dover could tell by looking at the man that he wasn't thinking, wasn't even trying to work with this, as if the problem were of such immensity that it was beyond human comprehension.

"Does the name Tony mean anything to you?" he asked the man.

Macklin turned to him with wide eyes. "It's the name of one of the characters in the third generation," he said. "How did you know?"

Dover shook his head. "I'm afraid that this is already affecting Mr. Armitage. When . . . exactly, did all of this start?"

"Yesterday, I told you . . ."

"The time, Vince. What time did it start?"

Macklin strained his lips, his hands pulling at his already wild hair. "I—I don't know . . . maybe sixish . . . someplace in there."

"Six," Dover said idly, his mind wandering, working with the possibilities. Six was after Mo had originally taken the suicide stories to Mr. Armitage. Everything generated since that event had been something of a mirror of the mass suicides—important events covered up by the powers that be and the truth be damned.

He looked at his watch. It was nearly time to be thinking about going on the air and he hadn't even prepared stories yet. He stood, dusting off his pants. "Mr. Armitage has been wrestling with a problem since yesterday afternoon," he told Macklin. "I think the generation problem may be directly linked to that event."

"Fine," Macklin said. "Sounds fine. That doesn't change anything, though, does it?"

The man had a knife blade in his voice. Dover stared hard at him, realizing just how entirely useless Macklin had become. He turned to walk out. "Later, Vince," he said.

"Just like that?" Macklin yelled from the midst of his party of ghost images. "You can't just leave me with that!"

Dover moved out of the lab, Macklin's screams following him down the hallway. A part of the puzzle seemed to be coming clear to him. No closer to a reason for the mass suicides and the attitudinal changes he'd seen around him, he concentrated on the more immediate problem of Mr. Armitage's behavior. And it seemed to him that at least a partial solution to all of it could be provided by his evening newscast.

Mr. Armitage basically believed in truth, but when truth was put up against a reality that didn't jibe with the orderly flow of society, the Manager reached a quandary. His desire to accomplish both ends sent him into an internal mode that stated and restated the problem in a myriad of ways in order for him to try and find the solution internally. He could literally gut himself on the paradox. Conversely, the problem with the suicides couldn't be handled until enough people knew about it to address the problem. In the nature of Company economics, television had become the news and evidence gatherer of the entire organization. The proper authorities only knew what they were told. It was obvious that Mr. Armitage had been unable to come up with a satisfactory response. The answer was simple and direct: take the problem out of Mr. Armitage's hands.

Dover took the elevator down to the newsroom. He

had a mission now. All of the emotion he'd needed to sell products all these years would stand well for him at this point. The people would hear from Stan Dover.

IV

Dover stared down the red light as if it were a cobra to be tamed, and never, never once did he leave down the energy surge until its glow had faded and died. He was shaking inside, pumped up with sleepless neurosis and sheer force of will. He hadn't given them love this time, nor duty, nor concern, nor nostalgia. It had been fear he'd been selling, monstrous pulsating waves of it, and it left him drained but still charged to a sharp edge. He'd given it all to them, all the tapes, all his theories. The story was out for the world to see.

Dead quiet pervaded the set as he stood to take off his lapel mike, technicians, reporters, producers, and writers standing like statues, staring at him in open-mouthed concern and surprise. No one had ever seen a newscast like the one he'd just given them, and everyone knew it was the last they'd ever see of Stan Dover, formerly the most famous celebrity in AmeriCorp.

Stan walked off the set with his head held up. He was proud of what he'd done and if it was, indeed, his last action as a newsman, so be it. He'd owed it to his audience to show them the truth, and now he'd paid off that debt. Mr. Armitage's indecision was now rendered inconsequential, a fact that would probably lead to the Manager's immediate rehabilitation and freedom from his mental conundrum.

He walked out of the dead silent newsroom and down the hall to his office, turning once to see who was following him, surprised once again to see he was alone in the hallway.

He moved into his office, Mrs. Bertran jumping up from her desk to hug him tightly. "Oh, Mr. Dover," she squealed. "That was a *wonderful* news report! I can't tell you how much it meant to me."

"Really?" Dover said, surprised. Mrs. Bertran had never gotten this excited about his news reports before. "I don't suppose there's any coffee."

"Coffee?"

"Never mind. Has Mr. Critchfield . . ."

"Gone," she said, shrugging, and there was really no
reason for her to say more. Besides, Dover couldn't feel too
bad about the man now. Tomorrow he'd probably be joining him in food services.

He walked through the door to his office, his message
light flashing. He smiled and sat behind his desk. Mr. Armitage certainly didn't waste any time. He sat quietly for a
moment, enjoying his office environment, trying to take it
all in in much the same way that travelers attempt to fix
exotic locales in their minds while ignoring their own surroundings. He'd never appreciated his office as much as he
did in that last minute. It was a time of minutes—a time to
savor them.

Finally he reached out and punched up the prere-
corded message on his outlaw boards. But instead of Mr.
Armitage's face, he saw a smiling Sally on his screens. "I
can't tell you how much you've helped me, darling," she
said, nearly breathless. "I'm so sorry about the things I've
said before. You've been wonderful all through our contract . . . of course my problems had nothing to do with
you!"

Something wasn't right here. Sally seemed . . .
strange. She was hyped out, excited and shaking. He sat up
straighter, turning up the sound.

"I never thought you'd understand what I was going
through," she said, eyes wide. "I hardly understood it myself. And when that man at the party . . . well, I just
didn't think you'd ever understand. But you did, and you
explained it to me in your newscast. Death isn't a negative
thing, but a positive act of creation, an intense and liberat-
ing freedom. Did you see how happy all those people were
in your stories? It filled me with joy, darling, and gratitude.
I've been so unhappy, so bored with things, with my own
mind."

Dover felt an icy hand grip his heart. As the tension
shook him, he reached out to punch up his home numbers,
his eyes locked onto the screens.

"I had to call, to thank you," she was saying, "and to
share with you my moment of triumph."

His call was buzzing the number, but no one was answering.

"I've been thinking hard about this," she said, holding up a bottle of liquid drain cleaner and speaking seriously. "It's quick, just a little messy and . . . organic. I feel good about that." She removed the top from the plastic bottle.

"No!" Dover yelled, coming to his feet. "Please don't!"

The phone was buzzing madly, making him crazy. He ran around to the screens, standing before them, shaking his empty hands against the futility, trying to physically merge with the screens and stop this insanity. But he couldn't.

Sally was smiling, holding the bottle up near her face. "I love you, my darling," she said happily. "And I thank you for the gift of understanding. Well, here goes nothing."

With a big smile and not a hint of hesitation, Sally Dover drank a bottle of liquid drain cleaner. She frowned for a second afterward, put a hand to her stomach, then opened her mouth wide, her insides gurgling right back up her throat.

Dover watched, mesmerized, unable to take his eyes off the screen as Sally fell to the floor, dying quickly in gurgling, screaming agony.

When it was over, the tape simply ran for a time, Dover standing in front of the screen, staring, disconnected. Sally had been wrong about one thing, however, she had made quite a deal more than a "little" mess.

The tape reached the end of its timed cycle and simply cut off, Dover turning from the screen in time to see a body plummet past his window on a quick run to ground.

What madness had he perpetrated? His broadcast had been meant to scare the hell out of people, not excite them. What the hell was going on here?

Some of the outlaw stations were running on the screens. A large black man on one of the screens was dousing himself with gasoline while a woman danced around him with a burning lighter. Another man had jammed a hollow tube into his carotid artery and was walking atop a large canvas, trying to paint a picture in squirting blood.

Dover found himself walking out of the office, reacting mechanically, having no idea what he was doing. He walked past Mrs. Bertran, who was kneeling on the floor. She held a severed electrical cable in her mouth and was in the process of plugging in the other end. He walked on.

Sally had called her action creative, a word he'd heard

many times in the last two days. His head was a jumble of events—Macklin's inability to deal with an original problem, Sally's always narrowing world, Mo's attraction to the visuals of death. He should have paid more attention to what was happening around him and less time justifying his own world view to bolster his sense of importance.

He found himself in the newsroom, many of his co-workers already dead on the floor, others in the process of slashing their wrists or choking themselves with their own ties or drinking bottles of copying solution while those still alive laughed and applauded each movement, sometimes cheering an original or thought-provoking action.

The incoming screens that surrounded the room ran suicides, everywhere suicides. Dover walked right through the room and got on the elevator going down. As the doors closed, Mr. Armitage's face appeared on a small screen within.

"You just had to do it, didn't you," he said, smiling.

"You knew this would happen," Dover replied. "Why didn't you stop me?"

The generated face took on a sad appearance. "It wouldn't have mattered really. It was just a question of time."

"What's going on?" Dover asked, his voice weak, strained.

"A natural process, Stan," Mr. Armitage said. "The rebirth of creativity."

"I hope to tell you," Dover said angrily, "but it's death, not rebirth, going on out there."

The Manager met Dover's eyes. "You missed the point of the regenerations. You thought them a choice between truth and order . . . the activity was far deeper than that."

The elevator arrived at the first floor, Dover exiting immediately and walking out onto the rain-soaked street. Abandoned vehicles filled the streets, bodies piling up everywhere, falling with the rain, Stan already becoming desensitized to death on a massive scale. He glanced up to make sure nothing was falling toward him, and made his way to a driverless taxi, climbing in and closing the door.

A man walked up and knocked on the window. "Where are you going?" he asked.

Stan rolled down the window and looked at the physical manifestation of Mr. Armitage—a flesh and blood Manager stood before him. "Who the hell are you?"

"You know darned well who I am, Stan," a familiar voice said.

"But . . . you're not real!"

"I'm as real as you are," the man said. "Just listen to me for a minute. All of Macklin's generations really dealt with order and chaos," Armitage said. "You see, order, by its very nature, must destroy creativity, because creativity is what leads to chaotic behavior. I was desperately searching for an answer through analogue, but every road was a dead end."

Dover shook his head, tried to shut the vision out. He must be going crazy. He rolled up the window and keyed the electric motor.

"Stan . . . listen to me!" Armitage called, cupping his hand to the window glass.

"No!" Stan screamed, the car jerking to a start and rolling away. He turned on the wipers and started skirting bodies, bumping over them when he couldn't. They still fell from the buildings, some of them quite close to him, and he realized that they were *aiming* for him.

"This is nuts," he said low, mumbling over and over, trying to hold on to enough of his mind to flee the insanity.

He reached the end of the block; three men who also looked like Mr. Armitage stood on the corner, calling to him in unison. "Chaos and order, Stan!" they called. "One and the same!"

Dover drove on, balancing his own madness, trying to think logically. He thought he understood what Mr. Armitage had been getting at. Life is a balance of opposite poles. Humans crave order and freedom at the same time —contradictory emotions—and totally giving over to either leads directly to chaos. To take away creativity in order to achieve order and, incidentally, the survival of civilization, means ultimate stagnation, leading once again to chaos.

Society had ordered itself to extinction. People were seeking the only form of creativity left open to them— death. The direct pipeline to chaos. What had the poet said —"nature's mighty law is change." Order *was* chaos, perhaps the ultimate form of chaos. It explained betting; it explained the Ooze shortages—the human animal was simply desperate for options. It also explained why order brought peace of mind but not happiness.

He drove on, through the tall buildings and through the smaller buildings, driving for thirty minutes before realizing that he had a plan and a direction. He was escaping, leaving the city, leaving the deadly order. And if he hadn't already lost his mind completely, he could at least survive.

The rain stopped, the sky lightening. A holo of Mr. Armitage appeared, floating before Dover's window just out of reach.

"Go away, damn you!" Stan yelled. "Why won't you leave me alone?"

"I've always been good to you, Stan," the projection said. "What's the problem?"

"Why didn't you tell me what was happening?" Dover choked, feeling everything slipping away from him. "Maybe we could have done something."

"Because you wouldn't have, couldn't have, understood," Mr. Armitage said genially. "We nurtured your own creativity, let it flower to help guide us. You're a freak, Stan, a genetic throwback to some earlier, pre-Orderly time. How could you have understood how everyone else felt?"

Stan sat, numb, barely watching the road before him. "You should have tried," he said low.

"It wouldn't have changed a thing. Orderly society is destroying itself, returning to its chaotic roots. Nothing can remain static and stagnant forever. It's just the nature of things. Civilizations, like all life, grow, flower, then die. Where in the world are you going, by the way?"

"I'm not ready to roll over," Stan said, trying to muster some conviction. "Not everyone succumbed to the order. Somewhere outside of these cities another kind of civilization must be operating, one that needs creativity and intelligence. There must be others like me. I'm going to them."

A strange look came over the Manager's face and he said, "Good luck to you then," and disappeared.

Stan pushed on, the city continuing for another hour that stretched to two more before finally giving way to open road.

Suddenly, the sky turned totally black and the landscape around him began to change, soft curves becoming hard angles.

Fear climbed up his neck and he stopped the car, turning on the headlights and getting out. The lights barely dented the oppressive dark. He turned a complete circle, looking at a nightmarish, surreal landscape of totally flat planes and parallel lines that stretched to infinity, converging slowly at the vanishing point on the far horizon. The ground glowed pulsating gray, while the sky was simply a black, flat void.

"Have you seen enough?" he screamed at the vacant sky, then sat on the ground and began to laugh, wondering if he'd put on a good show for whoever was watching him. He laughed until he cried and cried until he laughed. It had been him all along. He was the dichotomy, the repository of all human wants, needs, and desires. He was the reason for the regenerations, the fading image of humanity trapped in the vacuum tube of total, immutable change.

After a time he rose, standing up straight and dusting himself off. He was, after all, the personification of Mankind's dignity. He turned and looked back once from where he'd come. In the distance, the city shimmered and glittered, giving off the false, seductive light of civilization.

Spitting on the ground, he climbed back into the car and looked ahead, toward the void. He may have been only a generation, but he was the embodiment of everything good and beautiful about the human animal. He would never go back. He pressed down the gas pedal and moved forward, driving into the darkness until it gave way to the static of total chaos.

Silver

STEVEN SPRUILL

Phileho Institute, Los Angeles
April 10, 2000

I WOKE TO PAIN.

That six month ago. But now is first time I able to write it by English. The other words have I inside is no good. People not know them. So I learn this English. Now I know all letters and learn more words all the time. English much strange. It seem to be writed backward. Eyes of I want always to move the other way. I will learn, do better. But I not wait to start write. Start now. Much to say.

Write is wrong word. No can write. Thumbs no can hold pen like men. So I use this thing Dr. Kosiba give to I. This computer. Dr. Kosiba call it typing. Dr. Kosiba know everything. He stand strong over I. He say I live, I live. He say I die, I die. He make I like I am. I very fear of Dr. Kosiba.

I tell you about he and I.

Six month ago I wake to bad pain. Throat hurt very bad. Could no swallow. Something big stuck down my throat. Smooth. Could no swallow, could no spit it up. As soon as I wake, I very feared. Tried to sit up, grab throat. Nothing happen. I could no even move. Meat sit heavy on bones. I no even can open eyes. Tried to take big breath but could no do that also. Inside chest, air come in and out, but when it want to, not when I want. Feel like air pushed in and out through thing stuck in throat. I very feared. Very not knowing.

What happen? I think.

Where is I?

Eyes still closed, no can open. I see vision inside head. I walking along a road. Day, but very dark. Clouds dark, thick across whole sky. Light leak through, color of brass. Wind crying in I ears. Air seems heavy. Seeing this in I head make I feel very sad. I think something terrible is happen. I feel very heavy in chest, no have words to tell it.

Then picture in head go away leave darkness again. Still no could move. Where this place? I think. Then I try to think who is I. No can even do that!

Great and terrible feared.

I tried to no be feared. I tell I to just empty I and wait. Soon could feel flat bed under I. Hard and cold, very smooth. Then feel that I be moving. After long time, could open eyes, move a little, breathe. I look up and see man face looking down at I. Only see eyes. Green cap, green cloth over mouth of man. Later I know this is Dr. Kosiba. He say, Good boy, Silver. You good gorilla, you going to be all right.

I think, what is gorilla?

May 3, 2000

If I type, keep typing, maybe it help me think who I am. How I came here. What I doing here. The computer gives me the date. Each time I type, I will put date in, so can keep good record. I not know these month names, but I can count months and days this way. Almost seven months since I wake up. Twenty-four days since last I type.

The year 2000? That is great surprise to me—2000 is seventeen centuries in the past, I think. How I know that? Can no say. But how can this be past—all these shining wonders? Wall of my cage hard, but I see through like sheet of still water. Table shines. No such wonders ever I see, ever hear about being before me. Ah, well. Whatever 2000 be, somehow, I here.

In twenty-four days since last I type, I learn more English words. Do better now.

Not long after I wake and see man in green, I learn what gorilla is. When I go to my outside cage I see them in what Dr. Kosiba call the play area. Remember see them there before, many times. They bigger than man, have black hair all over. Stand bent over. I look down at me and see that I like that too. I get very sick inside. What these long arms, all this hair? Mirror in cage. I run to it. Feel cold fire, sickness all through me. What is this thing I look at? Later I find that I be called Silver because hairs at my chin are that color.

I do not like this name, Silver.

I do not feel I am gorilla.

Can not explain.

After I could move again, Dr. Kosiba send me back to my cage. That is where I be now. When I got back here I remembered the room from before, but it seems very dim, like a dream. I remember I sleep many nights in this room. Also work on hand signs with Dr. Kosiba, learn to speak with hands. All this before Dr. Kosiba make me what I be now. Also, in those times before, I played with the computer, but I did not type words like I can now. All I did was play games Dr. Kosiba teached me. The games seem very easy now. When I remember those times, it make me shiver, feel sick. I very stupid then, like man who be hit on head, wander around, not asleep, not awake.

Now, I am awake. Hello world!

Dr. Kosiba do this. He make me. That make him Yah-vay. This Yah-vay is old word, in me when first I wake. I try to spell out sounds for you. Dr. Kosiba is Yah-vay. Yah-vay make the world. Make all. Obey Yah-vay or die. I obey always. I put my head to floor for Yah-vay. Call his name in my sleep. Dr. Kosiba is Yah-vay. Yah-vay is Dr. Kosiba.

May 10

Soon after Dr. Kosiba make me over, he send me back to cage. He come to cage to see if I was OK. He still treat me as gorilla. Why he make me this way, then act like he do not know?

Then I see. He testing me. He want me tell him I

different now. Want me thank him. I put head to floor for
Dr. Kosiba, then grab for paper and crayon and make
marks. I think these marks are words. They mean words to
me. But they did not mean words to him. Still, he look
surprised. He say, what the matter, Silver? Calm down old
boy.

It hurt inside when he call me Silver. I try to speak, tell
him. Only rough sounds came out. I could not make my
mouth work right to speak. I felt very bad. Jump up and
down. Then I stop myself from doing that. I know I do that
before when I was excited. But now it seemed wrong,
make me feel like dumb beast.

Dr. Kosiba leave. But he came back that night. He
brought a woman with him. Her name is Barbara. Later, I
learn she his helper here at Institute. Barbara is very beautiful. That first night I see her, I stare at her, feel very
strange inside. Dr. Kosiba and Barbara look at me. I try
again to write words, tell them I not gorilla any more. Tell
him thank you for making me. Then I remember the sign
language Dr. Kosiba teached to me. I could use that!

I think of right words: I no more gorilla. You make me a
man inside.

I made the signs.

But now, Dr. Kosiba and Barbara not watching me.
They looking at each other. Barbara move close to him, put
her mouth on his ear. He took her dress and raised it until I
could see all up her legs. I became very excited. I tried to
look away, but I could not. Her legs shined. They seemed
to be covered with a thin cloth I could see through. She
raised one leg high against Dr. Kosiba. Bended it around
him. He grab her below waist and she lift other leg, wrap
them both around him. He held her against the see-
through wall between us. He pushed against her again and
again. I felt myself become hard. Her hair spread against
the clear wall like the rays of the sun.

I was very excited. And ashamed.

A name came into my head: Mara.

I feel dizzy. Mara, Mara? Who is Mara? My heart was
filled with love and pain. But I could not remember.

Before I could become calm again, Dr. Kosiba and Barbara were gone.

May 11

Making love. That is what they call it. Dr. Kosiba and Barbara do not make love in my cage any more. I passed the test Yah-vay—Dr. Kosiba—set for me. Day after they maked love, I told Dr. Kosiba what he want me to tell him, signal it with my hands: I now man inside. He act very surprised. Shocked is the right word. Shocked. It seem he almost did not believe me.

But that must be wrong. He know everything. He do this to me, how could he not know? Sure he know.

Strange are the ways of Yah-vay. It is my own dumbness that makes me question him, even for a minute.

After I tell him what he knows—that he has made me a man inside—I asked with my hands for him to give more words, I signed, over and over. So he has been giving me more words. He brought books with pictures. He points to the pictures and says the words, then types them on my computer. I am learning very fast. He tells me that only a very smart being could learn a language so fast. A genius. It made me proud. I am going to keep working as fast as I can.

Dr. Kosiba has put his lab "off limits" to everyone else at the Institute. This includes my cage. He has told me that no one will be let in here for a while. But if someone should get in anyway, I am not to let that person know that I am not just a gorilla. Dr. Kosiba says it could be very danger-ous. I do not understand why dangerous, but I will do what he says. I want to do all he says. Dr. Kosiba is great. He all I need. Somehow, he brought me out of darkness. I do not know how. But he is higher than me, smarter. I will do what he say always. I afraid of him. Also, I love him. If I love him, he not kill me.

May 28

Why do I have little pieces of memory? That path and dark sky. The woman, Mara? And now sometimes I see sea, shining red in the sun.

Why do I feel like a man?

In some ways, I feel more than a man. There is something inside me. What it is, I don't yet know. But it is a power. I am learning very fast. Much faster than it seem a man should learn. Why?

It is wrong to feel better than man. Dr. Kosiba is man. Dr. Kosiba is Yah-vay. I am only his creation.

I should not ask. Make Yah-vay angry.

May 29

I feel not just a past buried in me, but also a future. I have learned the word for what I feel. It is *destiny*. Dr. Kosiba has made me like this for a reason. I have strange power. I am *aware* of myself inside. I never had such awareness before. I seem sure of that, even though my memory—if that is what it is—has not come back. I feel I have a mission. I do not know yet what the mission is.

I can do something great and wonderful with myself.

I must talk more to Dr. Kosiba. Hear and understand his words to me. To do this, I must have more words! Need for words burns inside me. I will keep working on the words. I feel great thanks to Dr. Kosiba. He is helping me. He understands and knows many things that I do not know. If I am a genius, how much greater is he?

But I want to know things too, like him.

No, that is a bad want. I never be like him. He high above me. That is how it should be. I will do whatever he says.

July 8, 2000

In the last month, I have made much progress with my English. I can now understand Dr. Kosiba perfectly when he talks. Dr. Kosiba has explained many things to me. There is a thing called a "brain" inside the head of each living thing. The gorilla brain is one of the largest and best developed next to man's.

I felt oddly stung when he told me this. It seemed to put a limit on me—a limit which I do not feel. But, obviously, I am not like other gorillas. I am Dr. Kosiba's creation!

But, as I was saying, the brain is what we think and feel with. Dr. Kosiba says he wants to study the brain. That is why he joined this Phileho Institute where I live. He is trying to learn how the brain heals from being hurt.

This seems very strange to me. How could Dr. Kosiba make me as I am and not understand everything about me? Could it be that Yah-vay does not know everything?

That is a mystery too high for me. It is not my place to question Yah-vay. He gave me all I have.

And he could crush me without moving his hand.

Dr. Kosiba told me that, sometimes, after a brain has been hurt, memories are lost. Then, after a time, they come back. Dr. Kosiba wants to know how this can be.

So do I! If only my memories would come back! Not the ones from when I was only a gorilla. Those dim ones I have always. I hate them. I was an animal, then. I want the memories that seem to be from a man.

Dr. Kosiba has told me what I knew to be true: That, when he did surgery on me, that must have caused me to wake to what I am now. I asked him what is "surgery"? That means that he cut into my head so he could touch my brain.

That is truly the act of a Yah-vay!

Before the surgery, Dr. Kosiba had created a special brain chemical called K-3 that was supposed to make my mind forget. He was going to put K-3 on the part of my brain that knew how to play the game he had taught me on the computer. Then he was going to see if another part of my brain could bring the memory back later. He needed for me to be awake during this, so that he could touch my brain with wires and make sure he was in the right place. So he gave me a drug called "curare." That is why I couldn't move or breathe. He put a tube down my throat and made a machine breathe for me. Then he "injected" K-3 onto my brain, and that is when I awoke to what I am now.

He said he does not know why this should be. This can't be. Dr. Kosiba knows all. Why does he tell me otherwise?

To test my faith?

Yes. My faith is strong. I believe in him with all my heart.

July 15

Dr. Kosiba and I talk often. He speaks with his voice and I respond by typing words on the computer. Today I told Dr. Kosiba about the pieces of memory in my head that seem to belong to a man.

He laughed. For a moment, I was angry with him and then I caught myself. It is dangerous and wrong to be angry with Yah-vay. Pray instead that he not be angry with you.

"You're talking like a Hindu," he said.

I asked him what Hindu meant.

He told me Hindu is a "religion" in another part of the world. Hindus believe in reincarnation. A big word. Dr. Kosiba explained it to me. It means that when a man dies, the thing inside him that made him alive goes into another animal and sleeps there. This thing is called a soul. When the animal the soul has entered dies, the soul moves on again into a smarter animal. It keeps on doing this until it has entered a man again.

I asked Dr. Kosiba if the soul ever wakes up again and remembers the life it had the last time it was a man. He says that some people have claimed this. I became very excited. This could explain what is happening to me. I asked him if he thought it might be. He looked very serious. "I am a scientist, Silver," he said. "Reincarnation is not a scientific idea but an idea of religion. I know of no proof that reincarnation even happens at all."

"Is there proof that it does not?" I asked.

For some reason, he laughed again.

August 1, 2000

I had a dream. I was walking down a path with some men. None of us were dressed like Dr. Kosiba. We wore loose clothes that are called robes. One of the men was our leader. He was smarter than all the rest of us. We would do anything he said. We loved him. In the dream, I wanted to cry out to him, but I could not remember his name. In my dream I thought that he was Yah-vay, but not Yah-vay—

both at the same time. Finally, desperate, I called out Dr. Kosiba's name. Our leader turned to me. His face seemed to glow. "You have seen the future," he said. I felt a tremendous shiver of excitement all through my body.

At that moment, I woke up.

I looked down at myself and was filled with horror at the hairy body, the arms that were too long, the short, bent legs. I disgusted myself. I realized I was sitting in the dead tree that was part of my cage. A tire swing hangs from the tree. I remember swinging in it when I was a gorilla. Of course, I would never do such a thing now. Suddenly, I felt very frightened of the tree and the swing. They reminded me of something dark and terrible, on the other side of the dream. I jumped down from the tree, bumping against the swing. The tire swung back and forth, twisting under its rope. I could not take my eyes from the rope. I watched, sickened and terrified, and not knowing why.

Finally I was able to force my eyes from the rope. I thought of the dream, telling it over and over to myself so I would not forget it. But I realized I had already forgotten something. In the dream, my leader had called me by my name!

"———, you have seen the future."

What was the name he called me? I cannot remember. I am filled with a mixture of joy and pain. I lived before, I am sure of it. And in that time, I glimpsed the future that I now inhabit. But I can remember so little.

August 6

Dr. Kosiba brings Barbara in with him from time to time. These occasions are very special to me. She is so beautiful. And something about her prods at the memories I feel buried inside me. Barbara—Mara. The names are similar. I think I was in love with Mara.

And now, I fear that I have fallen in love with Barbara.

My love is hopeless. No matter what my mind is, my body is that of a beast. How could she ever love me? And I am ashamed even to think it. After all, she is Dr. Kosiba's. She belongs to God, not to me.

And her very presence presents other agonies to me as well. For example, whenever she is around I endure a constant, nagging worry about my bladder and bowels. I've made some progress getting control of these body functions. But there are still lapses. I live in dread that one of these might occur in her presence—we would be discussing her family, her hopes for promotion at the Institute, or some other important matter of her life and I would let fly a piece of excrement. I realize as I write this that it may seem funny to you. Damn it, I suppose it *is* funny. But I invite you to put yourself in my place, a man trapped in an animal's body, desperately in love with the woman before you, and unable to save yourself from the vilest self-humiliation.

August 10

Today, while Dr. Kosiba and I were working together on the computer, Dr. Glassman, director of the Institute, paid us a surprise visit, ignoring Dr. Kosiba's quarantine.

I saw him walk in and quickly blanked the screen. Dr. Kosiba turned, upset that someone would defy his orders. Then he saw who it was and held his peace.

"So this is your pet project," Glassman said.

"I'm sorry, Dr. Glassman, but Silver has a finicky disposition. He is easily distracted; visitors invariably set back my program for him."

Taking his cue, I backed up from the computer and cringed against the wall, gibbering in what I hoped was convincing fashion. Dr. Glassman looked at me skeptically.

"And what exactly is that program, Kosiba? I'm still not entirely clear."

Dr. Kosiba said: "Could we discuss this at another time? You see how frightened he is of you."

"A little adrenaline won't hurt him. He's probably this way because you've been sheltering him too much. I understand he hasn't been getting out to the exercise yard with the other gorillas. That isn't right. Gorillas are social animals. He needs to run and play with the rest of them."

Suddenly I disliked Dr. Glassman intensely. He reminded me of someone—a man I once knew. I tried to tease out the memory and failed. But still I was excited. Because Dr. Kosiba had put his lab off limits, I had never seen another man, except on the TV in my cage. So how could Glassman remind me of anyone unless it was some-one from my buried past? First Barbara and now Glass-man, both reminding me of someone. My spirits soared. I *do* have a past before I was in this body, I thought. I *was* someone once!

Glassman was still talking. "Don't you have other proj-ects?" he said to Dr. Kosiba. "You should be thinking about publishing soon. Frankly, Kosiba, I'm worried about you. If you don't get on the stick, you could lose out on grant funding."

"I'm working on a paper," Dr. Kosiba said.

"On Silver, here?" Glassman inquired.

I could not suppress a groan. It must have sounded very human, because Dr. Glassman leaned close to the glass and stared at me for a long time. I cringed away and made the nervous grunting sounds that came so easily to my throat. In that instant I felt a profound disgust with myself. Yes, and I confess anger at the two men who were forcing me into this undignified display. I quickly suppressed my un-fair anger at Dr. Kosiba. Dr. Kosiba was my God. I owed him my life, everything. But Glassman was an entirely different matter. He was lording it over Dr. Kosiba as well as me—more, in fact, since his harassment of Dr. Kosiba was deliberate. It was utterly galling: Here was this man, in charge of everything, and he was not fit to carry Dr. Kosiba's cloak.

A name popped into my mind: *Caiapha!*

Was that the man Glassman reminded me of? I felt deep stirrings and strained my utmost to remember. It was so close, I could feel it pushing, trying to break through.

But it would not.

Finally, I gave up, filled with a bitter frustration. Still, that one name, so tantalizing and yet so meaningless, clings in my mind: *Caiapha.*

August 15

Dr. Kosiba can't seem to get over my progress in learn-ing English—not just the nouns and verbs, but the abstract concepts. He says I am a true phenomenon. This makes me very proud. Truly, there is no thrill like the approval of one's God. I see now that my earlier fear of Dr. Kosiba was an insult to his great and loving goodness. It came from my bestial stupidity, my primitive heart. Now I have grown. I love Dr. Kosiba. That is why I will do anything he asks, not because I am afraid of him.

One of the happy results of my fluency in English is that Dr. Kosiba has been bringing me more and more books. When necessary, he has the print xerographically enlarged so that my gorilla eyes can make out the type. Many of the books are on science. I am especially fascinated by the sections dealing with evolution. Apparently, the ape is the forerunner of man. This body I now inhabit is one of the final steps to full manhood.

And yet, though I might live a thousand years, this body will never evolve into a man's.

Where is God in all this?

Is Dr. Kosiba truly Yah-vay—God? That question is too frightening. Of course he is. He has awakened the soul of a man in this gorilla body. What else could he be? I am his unique creation. What is my destiny? Whatever it is, it is not in the books. But I keep having this strange feeling that I know. It seems to me that, when this gorilla body dies, I will live on. I shall not always be marooned in this hairy flesh. But the time to move on is not yet. Even though I loathe this bestial body, I believe it is tied in some way that I do not yet understand to my destiny.

August 20

Today, Dr. Kosiba answered my request for books on religion, including a treatise on the Hindu belief of reincarnation. Dr. Kosiba says he has also brought me the four "gospels"—the most important books of the prevailing religion of his country. I am most eager to read the Hindu book.

August 22

I am filled with horror and amazement.

I have found out who I am.

Here is how it happened: I was reading one of the books Dr. Kosiba brought to me. It is called *The Bible Story Book*.

The print is large and the book contains many pictures of paintings which are meant to illustrate the stories of the Bible. I had decided to look through the pictures before I started to read. Near the end of the book, I saw the painting of the crucifixion.

I cannot tell you the depth of my pain at that instant. I felt a blinding slash, dividing my brain, plunging like cold fire to my stomach. The centuries rolled away. It was as though the two thousand years between Golgotha and now had never been.

For I was there!

The details of the painting were surprisingly close to reality. It was almost as if the artist had been inspired. But after the first instant, I no longer needed the painting. Stunned with shock, I pinched my eyes shut and saw in my mind that awful scene as it truly was: Jesus hanging on the cross, turning his head to one of the thieves. The memory of vinegar stung my nose, mixed with the aroma of the centurion's hot bread lunch. I heard the ghost laughter of the Roman swine on their knees in front of the cross, not to worship him, but to roll dice for his coat. And there, at the periphery, the silent group of Jesus' followers stood watching. A number of them had never missed Jesus' speeches. One of them Jesus had healed of the bleeding sickness.

Remembering their dull paralysis, I felt again the terrible dread: *What's the matter with all of you? What are you waiting for? They're killing your master, your king. Take him down from there! Trample the bitchwhelp Romans under your feet!*

But they did nothing.

And then I was running away, running along that dusty path, the wind howling in my ears, the sky pressing down like brass above me. Where did I get the rope? I can't remember. But I climbed into the tree and tied one end to the branch. I slipped the noose around my neck and jumped.

And died.

Two thousand years of blackness.

And now I have risen again, in the body of a gorilla, on the laboratory table of Dr. Kosiba.

I am Judas Iscariot.

That is why, when first I awoke, I wanted to read and write from right to left. That is how Aramaic is written. It also explains why I thought I might have been dragged seventeen centuries into some fantastic, unknown human past. It was because, by the calendar of Israel, I died in the thirty-eighth century, *anno mundi.*

Judas Iscariot. The name brings both horror and a great, shuddering joy. Dear God, help me. If Christ's crucifixion is my history, what is my destiny?

September 3, 2000

I brood.

Dr. Kosiba asks me what is wrong. Ah, but if he is Yahweh, why does he not already know?

The truth is, Dr. Kosiba is not Yahweh, not God.

He is Christ.

Christ promised he would return. And here he is. Not a carpenter this time, but a neuroscientist. One thing, though, is the same: I have learned that, like the last Christ, Dr. Kosiba does not understand his destiny.

To *make* him understand is, once again, my destiny.

September 4

Silver.

Now I see why I despise that name, with its bestial simplicity, its cruel charge of irony. What monstrous joke of fate now brands me again with silver? Two thousand years ago, I took thirty pieces of it from the high priest, it is true. But it was not to betray Jesus.

It was to make him king.

I failed. Will I fail again?

The thought arouses an immense determination in me. No, I will not fail again. I have been through too much. Even though I cannot remember my two-thousand-year journey back, the hideous possibilities wallow in my mind. What was my first host? A fly, perhaps? My flesh crawls at the thought. I'm sure my legion of critics would find it fitting.

For that, I can thank Matthew, Mark, Luke, and John. Seen through their words, what a despicable man I was.

How little they understood. And for two thousand years their account has stood.

But I must put aside my bitterness.

If I began my journey back to human flesh trapped in the debased shell of an insect, it was not for my sins but because God, in his infinite wisdom, knew the timing of the future. He set the clock of my transmigration so that I would emerge precisely when and where I did, in this bestial flesh, under the inspired hand of Dr. Edward S. Kosiba—his son, once again buried in human flesh, even as I am buried in the meat and hair of a gorilla.

But now I understand my link to this flesh.

God is wise. He knew that a gorilla's brain was adequate to house the awakened soul of a man. A gorilla is the highest, most developed primate next to man. According to one of the books Dr. Kosiba brought to me, man uses only ten percent of his brain capacity. A gorilla's brain is considerably larger than ten percent of a man's and quite similar to the human brain in other respects. And, much as I shudder at being trapped in this body, I see God's reason. If a man claimed to be Judas reincarnated, would you believe him?

But a gorilla is a different matter. If it can speak as a man, it is no greater miracle that it be Judas. Ironic, but true: as a gorilla, I can speak to the world.

This, then, will be my epistle, the fifth gospel, the Book of Judas. Before I write more, I have much to do.

September 24

I have been reading. The Bible and Darwin, the Koran and Dhagavad-Gita, psychology, philosophy, and the theory of science. Each, in itself, is incomplete. Dr. Kosiba has unified them. With the matter he injected into my brain— the K-3—he has found the soul and given it substance. This will be the new gospel. But I do not yet know how to put it into words.

It is time to stop studying and *think*.

October 7, 2000

I see Dr. Kosiba so differently now. He comes in to talk to me, and I remember how at first I thought he was Yahweh and only later saw that he is the Son of God. How I feared him, then feared and loved him, then, as I understood more and more, how I loved him without fear.

I love him still, but he is beginning to exasperate me.

It took several sessions together, but I have finally convinced him that I am not just a very intelligent gorilla, but Judas Iscariot, reincarnated. In the end, the proof was rather simple. One of the books Dr. Kosiba had brought me referred to the ancient Dead Sea Scrolls. They were found in caves near Qumran beginning in 1947. They date back to the time of Christ and before. My time. I had Dr. Kosiba bring me a facsimile, knowing I would be able to read them. It was an indescribable pleasure to read in the proper fashion, right to left. I did so while Dr. Kosiba followed along in the English translation, his jaw falling further and further open.

Finally he accepted that I am the historical character, Judas—or maybe he only pretends, not knowing what else to do. But he stubbornly refuses to accept that he is the Messiah. Over and over I have tried to make him understand, but he fights me, just as Christ fought.

It is depressing. Why, as intelligence grows and understanding grows, must faith diminish? I have become almost cynical. Sometimes I think I was happier when I did not know myself—and when Dr. Kosiba was my Yah-vay.

October 11

Barbara came in with Dr. Kosiba tonight. She teased and flirted with him in front of me. It gave me the most awful feeling of jealousy.

Mara—Mary Magdalene used to do that with Jesus.

Of course, Jesus never once gave any sign in my presence that they were more than friends. No doubt it was because Jesus knew how I felt about Mara. He was kind in that way, as in all others. I must confess that sometimes I *hated* that kindness, in its way so patronizing: Don't rub it in to poor Judas, how hopeless his case is with Mara.

But I knew—of course I did. No matter how steadfastly Jesus kept any *eros* for her from his face, Mara had no such restraint. Her adoration for him was plain. How could he have resisted it? And why should he? After all, he did not teach that the erotic love of a woman was a sin. On the contrary, his first miracle was performed at a wedding feast.

And she was so beautiful.

Still, she was a simple prostitute, aspiring to bed the master. Why couldn't she have been content with me? I was a handsome man, educated far beyond the rest of the ragtag group. God, how her indifference hurt me.

I might as well have been a gorilla then, too.

But that is the past—the long-dead past.

October 20

I am ready with the new gospel.

The first four gospels have stood two thousand years. Full of flaws, but at least they have kept alive the faith. Now it is time for mankind to see and accept the new truth.

The new truth is exactly what Jesus promised the last time: *Follow me, and ye shall have life everlasting.*

With K-3, Dr. Kosiba has fulfilled that promise.

Dear God, how can I explain this?

Listen: from the moment I awoke on Dr. Kosiba's operating table, I was aware of my soul. I had no way to put that awareness into words, even in my thoughts. But I was aware. In the months since, I have come to understand that awareness and what it means. It is not simply that I am aware of my soul now. I *am* a soul. Once I had recovered my memories of Judas, the earlier ones started to come back, too. Before Judas, I was a Sumerian named Erech, after a great city. Before that I skip like a stone across the lake of time, back almost to the beginning. But there are great, arching gaps between my memories. Thousands of years of suspension between each caress of the lifewaters. Each waking I was a different person, robbed of all past memory, forced to start life over with no knowledge of myself, no accumulated wisdom. The person I was before was truly and eternally dead.

Until now. Thanks to Dr. Kosiba, all that is ended. One of the first benefits I received from awakening under K-3 was a tremendous intelligence, a fantastic ability to learn. This power comes from my accumulated lives. Because of K-3, I came into being this time knowing instantly how to learn. But that was only the smallest part of what I am now. The largest part is this: When this wretched, brutish body dies, I will be drawn into the nearest body of a newborn human, into which no other soul has yet drifted. That will be my new body. From this point onward, never again will I be doomed to ride, slumbering, in some miserable, mindless animal.

My soul has awakened. For the rest of eternity, it can be captured only by newborn human flesh.

The long sleeps, so like death, are over. Each time I am drawn into newborn flesh, I will still be Judas, sentient and aware of myself. Judas in an unbroken line, forever.

Dr. Kosiba has given me eternal life!

And he can give it to you, too. To all mankind! This is the gospel according to Judas: Human evolution is ending. Until this date, twenty centuries *anno Domini*, the soul has been a mere transmitter of life. Now, in me, it *is* life. The long migrations through darkness can pass away. Oh death where is thy sting? Oh grave, where is thy victory?

But only if I can make Dr. Kosiba accept his destiny. Why won't he see it?

October 27

I am beside myself with frustration. Tonight things came to a head between us. Dr. Kosiba has gone home for the night; I must record what has just taken place, while it is still so painfully fresh in my mind. Dr. Kosiba came in around midnight with a loaf of date-nut bread made for me by Barbara. Delicious, and yet I wish she would give me something herself, rather than sending it through him. Jesus used to do the same thing, sharing around his gifts from Mara Magdalene not just with me, but with all the others too.

Ah, well, Dr. Kosiba gave me the bread. As I ate it,

thinking of the beautiful hands that prepared it, we began to talk about the fateful events of two thousand years ago.

"Why did you do it, Judas?"

I knew he meant why did I "betray" Christ. The question alerted me at once, because Dr. Kosiba professes no religion. Even accepting my identity as Judas convinces him only that Christianity is based on actual historical events and people, which few would dispute. I realized that his interest now was an opening, and my heart quickened.

I typed out my answer: "I did what I did from the purest of motives."

"Sending your master to his death?"

"And glorious resurrection."

He gave me his gentle smile. "All right, let's assume that Christ *was* divine and rose again. Are you saying you foresaw all that?"

"No," I answered honestly. "I thought his destiny was to overthrow the Romans then and there and bring his kingdom into being. But what is said to have happened was so much better."

"*Said* to have happened? Don't *you* believe Christ rose again?"

"His soul, yes. That went back to his father. Now it is here, again, in you."

"But Christians believe that Christ's body rose again."

I felt a weary impatience. "At each age, man believes what he is able," I said. "The point is, the sublime story of the resurrection was inevitable—because of me."

Kosiba munched on some bread. "How do you figure that?"

"Jesus kept giving speeches, irritating the powers that be. But he would not go beyond that to his true destiny as the ruler of all mankind. I used Caiapha the high priest and his cronies in the Sanhedrin to force the issue. I played the role of formal witness necessary under the rules so that they could try Christ for agitation and blasphemy. I was sure the Sanhedrin would formally condemn Jesus and pressure the Romans for the death penalty. Then, to save himself, Jesus would be forced to declare his kingdom and become the Savior he was born to be. If I had not acted, Jesus would either have gone on doing nothing but talking, or he'd have had to turn *himself* in to the Sanhedrin, admitting that his teachings opposed Judaic law. In this case, he would have been condemned to death just as before, but the effect would have been far different."

"In what way?"

"If Jesus had deliberately provoked the crisis himself, the very people who became so inspired by his bravery in the face of betrayal would instead have seen him as a miscalculating fool who brought about his own death. Jesus would have been the suicide instead of me. History would not have remembered him."

Kosiba gave a delighted laugh. "When you put it that way, it sounds sensible. What a Machiavelli you were."

"I had to be."

"Your friends the other apostles didn't see it that way."

My friends. I felt a flash of annoyance, remembering the others and how they had treated me. "They were simpletons. Their condemnations of me were written from ignorance and spite. They didn't understand how I was *using* Caiapha and his cronies. And I couldn't tell them my true motives at the time for fear it might leak back to Caiapha."

"It might have helped if you hadn't taken money for it," Kosiba said dryly.

I contained my impatience. Kosiba still didn't understand either. But at least his mind was open. "I took the silver," I said, "because the priests and pharisees of the Sanhedrin expected me to. If I hadn't, they'd have looked for some other motive in what I was doing. They might have come to understand my *true* reason. If so, there would have been no trial and all would have been lost.

"As it was, they played right into my hands. The most brilliant men of our culture, but I was cleverer. I made them publicly go up against the most popular man of our age—and pressure the Roman swine into doing the same. Even Pilate was smarter than the Sanhedrin, because he was not so blinded with hate. Pilate foresaw the same thing I did—that if he condemned Jesus to death, he would touch off a massive revolt that would topple him and his heathen legions and free my people. He saw, but he could not stop what I had set in motion.

"Within weeks, Jesus should have been king.

"Of course, what happened instead was better. It was God's will, expressed through me. I believed that then, and

I believe it even more firmly now that I have seen its results."

I watched him closely for a reaction, but he only nodded companionably, as if I had told him a truth that was interesting, but without real importance.

"You still do not accept it, do you?" I said.

"I believe everything you tell me. And I find it fascinating."

"I mean your calling."

"We've been all through that. I'm not a religious man."

"Oh, but you are," I said, filled with desperate longing. If only I could make him see.

"Come on, Judas. If I'd been a Christian, I'd have considered you an abomination, a blasphemy, or both. Your very existence repudiates what you claim it proves. The Bible does not teach reincarnation."

"Now it will," I said.

He laughed. "You *are* a cheeky devil, do you know that?"

His jibe stung me far worse than he could know. "Do you not believe I am who I say I am?"

"I am a scientist," Kosiba answered. "I've seen the proof. I've watched you translate those scrolls as easily as if they were the backs of cereal boxes. I've talked to historians specializing in your period. You know far too much arcane stuff about it to be an impostor."

"I'm thankful you are a true scientist," I said. "I only wish you understood what that means. Dr. Kosiba, as you say, many Christians would reject me, even though they claim that truth is their highest value. Those people know nothing of truth. They sin against it daily. They have turned away from it in favor of what they call faith. In my time, your science did not exist. The lack of it made faith a thousand times more necessary. Faith is still necessary in some things. But in the interregnum between Jesus' time and now, faith has become perverted. It refuses to give way to truth. More and more it is used to deny truth. The church is moribund. It calls itself by a hundred different names. Under these names, Christians dispute each other over tiny points of doctrine while rejecting large truths. They have forgotten that truth stands above faith. That is why you, a scientist, reject their faith. In rejecting it, you have become the new Christian.

"And now you must become the new Christ."

Dr. Kosiba looked pained. For a moment, he said nothing. My speech had aroused a tremendous passion—almost an anger—in me. Why was I cursed to understand so clearly what must be done, while the only man who could do it again refused?

"You want me to perform the surgery on others," Kosiba said.

"You must. The first Messiah promised everlasting life. You have been put here, in human flesh just as he was, to bring forth the reality. In making K-3, you have done so. Now you must take K-3 to the world and lead us into the new age."

Kosiba put the last of his bread down, looking at it as though it had suddenly gone foul. "Tell me something, Judas. If you believe what you are saying, why don't you kill yourself and liberate yourself from that body you hate so much?"

"Not yet. I was put here in this form for a reason. I am the proof of what you can do. And if I became a man, I could convince you of nothing."

"All right, when you *do* die, think of what it will mean. A newborn infant is helpless. At first, you will not be able to speak or even move in any but the most spastic way. Nerve myelinization does not reach completion until well after birth. And the muscles, too, have to grow and mature. Your great intelligence and knowledge will be useless. For a long time, you will be trapped."

"I will fill the new mind as water fills a vessel. With all I know, I will be able to speed the process you describe, and in the meantime I will rest and gather myself in all that I have been before."

"What about the parents of this infant? What will they do when they realize that they have not borne their own child but Judas Iscariot?"

The question baffled me. "I imagine they will be honored and thrilled. Their child will still be their flesh. But it will be my spirit. Their child, and the others like them, will be stand above all others ever borne."

For some reason, Dr. Kosiba shuddered.

"What's wrong? Are you cold?"

"Never mind. Listen, Judas: evolution works by diversification. Each time a baby is born, the human race has a chance to develop new attributes, new ideas, new adaptations. Each new life is its own, unshackled by past ideas, beliefs, and prejudices. Free to grow and develop into totally new directions. With K-3, that would end. As the number of 'awakened' souls grew, the number of new babies would decline. Ultimately, no new human life would be born on this planet."

I tried not to show my exasperation. "Think of the growth and development of the individual human spirit that is not crushed by death a scant eighty or so years after its inception. Think of the memory, the things we could build together as our wisdom grows and grows. Eternal life is what the first Christ promised. Evolution is finished. It must pass away, as the dinosaurs gave way to the mammals. Accept what you have wrought. Accept that you are the new Messiah."

Kosiba shook his head. "If I was truly some sort of second Christ, don't you think I'd know it?"

"The first Christ didn't," I said. "As I have tried repeatedly to explain to you."

"With all due respect, Judas, that is *your* opinion."

"It is my opinion about *your* mission that counts now, Dr. Kosiba. Think: what are the odds that the one laboratory gorilla on which you do your incredible experiment houses the unawakened soul of Judas Iscariot? If chance were the only determinant, the likelihood would be infinitesimally small. I tell you, God has sent me here to make you the Messiah."

"Judas, you are asking me to become the king of this earth. To say to people 'thou shalt not surely die.' But those were not the words of Christ, they were the lies of the devil in Eden. That's not what I'm all about."

"Lucifer's lie is Christ's truth," I said: " 'Follow me, and thou shalt have eternal life.' "

"It's not the same," Dr. Kosiba said stubbornly.

My frustration was beyond tolerance. I decided to take a new tack, apply a bit of pressure. I typed: "I'm not sure how much longer I can keep myself hidden. That pompous martinet Dr. Glassman keeps coming in here and looking at me. I think he suspects you're up to something with me. He'd like to bring you down, Dr. Kosiba, I can feel it. So far, I've fooled him, but it takes more and more effort."

"I know. And I understand how it hurts your pride. But

pride can be dangerous—to us both. Now, can we talk about something else?"

And so we did. But I fumed. He refuses, just as Christ refused. What, then, must I do?

November 1, 2000

Just as a precaution, I have committed Dr. Kosiba's notes on K-3 and his surgical procedures to memory. Dr. Kosiba always carries his research notebook around with him. Last night I was able to look through it and find the K-3 formula while he was occupied with something else. I worry about what he said. He can't seriously believe that K-3 could be a bad thing. But who knows what he might do in an impulsive moment. As his disciple, it is my duty to make sure that his incredible discovery will be preserved. I have found, since I awakened, that my memory is perfect, photographic—another sign of the accumlated power of my many lifetimes. Now that my soul is immortal, so are the formula and procedures for K-3.

November 7

I am filled with grim excitement. I have come at last to my decision and have set things in motion. Ironically, I once again need a "Caiapha." Dr. Glassman, with his arrogant, officious ways, is the perfect candidate—so perfect that, the first time I saw him, he caused the name of Caiapha to pop into my mind. As soon as I thought of using Glassman, I could feel the fate behind it, pushing me. So I planned how it could be done. Today, Dr. Glassman paid another one of his "surprise" visits. I was ready. Instead of blanking my screen, I pointed to it, then typed: "Hello, Glassman. What can I do for you?"

He peered through the glass at the words, then frowned around my cage. "All right, Kosiba, is this your idea of a joke?"

"It's no joke," I typed. "Dr. Kosiba has gone home for the day. Ask me a question."

He stood there, glaring at me. "What would that prove,

Kosiba? You've got the room bugged. You're listening in and you'll feed the answers to the screen."

I typed: "Write your question on a piece of paper. Make the letters large, please. When you're done, hand me the paper through the food slot. Then watch my fingers as I type." I pointed to the observation table next to his hip, where the usual pad and pencil for recording observations lay.

Glassman looked around with comic suspicion, then hunched over the pad and printed his message, folding it and handing it through to me. I unfolded it carefully. It read: "Don't play Clever Hans with me, Kosiba."

I wadded the paper up and typed: "Who is Clever Hans?"

November 9

Glassman got the press in here today. They were laughing at first. But after I'd spent a lively hour reading their questions and answering with my computer, they weren't laughing. Eventually, they stopped writing the questions and just asked them out loud. They might not have realized the significance of this at the time, but I saw it at once: they were starting to believe.

I answered each question. They ran their mini-cams and ogled me. Glassman stood to the side, beaming and acting like he was the one responsible, saying things like, "Under my direction, Dr. Kosiba has worked with Silver," etc., etc. The fool. No one payed any attention to him. I made it very clear that Dr. Kosiba was the brilliant genius who brought me out of darkness.

Dr. Kosiba doesn't know yet—he could not be told of this first news conference, of course. He would never have agreed to cooperate. Glassman sent him away on some errand and locked him out to be sure. I dread seeing his face after he's watched the evening news, but this is for his own good—the good of all humanity.

The reporters never got around to the most important question, but I answered it anyway. I told them I was Judas reincarnated. That threw Glassman for a loop. It hadn't occurred to him that I might be a *man* inside this hideous

body, not merely an incredibly smart ape. But I *am* a man.
I am Judas Iscariot!

November 12

Things are moving more quickly than I imagined. The
night of my first news conference I watched the evening
news on my TV. My story was near the top. Shortly after,
Dr. Kosiba came in with Glassman. Our Savior did not look
angry, only hurt. Surely, once again, he is a man above
men. All Dr. Kosiba said to me was, "You had to do this,
didn't you?"

I nodded. I was deeply pained by his hurt, but I know
this will be for the best. He cannot now escape his greatness, nor the world its salvation.

The next evening, there was coverage of a group of
people outside the Institute, clamoring to see me for themselves. Other people crowded outside Dr. Kosiba's home,
waiting for a glimpse of him. They carried signs, but I
could not make out the words. They shouted, demanding
that Dr. Kosiba come out, but he would not. He resists his
destiny, but it will catch him up at last. He will thank me.
We will be together again—and triumphant.

November 16

The news stories continue. I have told the reporters
everything I can about how I came to be—much of what is
written in this epistle. Of course, I have *not* told them that
Dr. Kosiba can bring eternal life to the human race. That
message must come from him. He is the Messiah, not me.

I was shocked to see on this evening's news an interview with a so-called "man in the street." He said that, by
claiming to be Judas, I am an abomination of the devil, and
that I spout blasphemy. Where did they find such a madman? What miracle would it take beyond what he has
already seen to convince him that I am who I say I am?

November 20

It is bad. All across the nation, priests and ministers have denounced Dr. Kosiba from their pulpits. People have thrown bricks through the Institute's windows. They call themselves Christians. Dr. Glassman has not been to see me for three days. On the news tonight he disavowed any connection with me, and blamed Dr. Kosiba. Dr. Kosiba allowed himself to be interviewed for the first time. They asked him if he believed I was Judas Iscariot. He said yes.

I am deeply touched by his nobility. So far I have caused him only trouble, and yet he defends me.

I cannot understand why it is taking people so long to accept the truth. Before they can understand that their eternal lives are at stake, they must first accept me—the miracle of my existence.

November 27

It is finished. I am numb with grief. Barbara just left me after telling me that Dr. Kosiba is dead. Someone firebombed his house last night. He could not escape the flames.

Once again, I have caused his death.

It was not what I intended. I tried to tell Barbara that. She screamed at me. "Bastard! Animal! I *hate* you!"

The loathing in her eyes is more than I can bear. I am filled with the blackest despair. Her bitter denunciations have brought back to memory a terrible truth that I had suppressed until now. In those dark hours after Golgotha, Mara Magdalene came to me just as Barbara did, hysterical with accusations, blaming me, reviling me. She said I was jealous of her and Jesus—that I deliberately plotted his death.

It was her hatred that drove me to the rope.

And now the rope draws me again.

January 1, 2001

Yes. I must once again destroy myself.

Or, rather, this grotesque, bestial body. I shall send it into oblivian.

It is fortunate indeed that I sealed Dr. Kosiba's notes into my memory, for the next epoch of mankind now depends entirely upon me. The wheel has turned; the awesome roles of history have changed. I have gone from the man behind the throne, to the throne itself. Dr. Kosiba was not the Messiah after all. He was, instead, my John the Baptist. His life prepared the way for mine, even as the Baptist's did Christ's. Was Christ at fault when John's head rolled to Salome and Herod? No. And I bear no blame either. Indeed, it is a heavy responsibility, but I will bear it gladly.

So now I go forward.

I see the rope of my swing, hanging very still. I will tear off the tire. It won't take long.

Now *I* am Christ, I am the Most High.

Follow me, and ye shall not surely die.

As a Still
Small Voice

MARCOS DONNELLY

AND YOU FEEL close to God?"

The darkness answered, a young voice, "Yes." Not an overly confident voice but at least a convinced one.

I wanted to probe, but not to push. I could be gentle. Often gentleness was the only force I had. "Do you feel close enough to Him to actually talk to Him?" I delivered the question well, I knew. Not condescending, not disbelieving, not even cold. A warm, factual question.

"Yes. That's praying, yes."

A good answer. I would have accepted it as complete from any other seminarian.

"And do you feel He answers when you talk to Him?"

A pause . . . Significant, and again I felt my hatred for confessionals. The darkness hid everything but the voice. I couldn't read his face and I couldn't see what his body was trying to tell me.

"God speaks to all of us in our hearts."

Shallow. He meant it to be shallow and he was controlling his voice a little better now. He was feeling more confident. Good.

"Danny, let's not talk circles around this. Do you hear God's voice in your head?"

"Yes, I do," and it was said that quickly. I felt foolish suddenly: a middle-aged priest whispering in a confessional to a college seminarian who claimed to talk with God. Ludicrous; not even worth serious confessional time. I should have suggested he discuss the matter with the staff psychologist and washed my hands of the problem.

But his voice—I listened to my heart, not in any metaphorical sense, my actual heartbeat throbbing dully in my ears at double pace, the way it would after hard exercise or a sudden shock—his voice sounded so *convinced*.

Twenty-two years as a priest, twenty-two years of praying and questioning and meditating and pleading, and I couldn't claim as much as a "Good morning" from the Almighty. This kid with less than a month of college under his belt was answering, "Yes, God does talk to me."

"Words, I mean, actual words?" It was an offer, a way out, in case Danny felt he had ventured too far. I leaned my head closer to the grill that separated us, squinting at the darkness to try to see even his outline, some movement or posture that would tell me more about how he felt saying it.

"Yes," Danny's voice answered, sounding a bit impatient now. "Words, full phrases, sometimes even long paragraphs. Look, you know this already, that's why you're asking. You just want me to confirm the rumors."

Fair enough. It was exactly why I was asking. I was a gentle, quiet rector, the sort who had a better opportunity to overhear what his seminarians said to one another, how the older boys explained the community to the newcomers. *Oh, and watch out for that Danny Gordon kid. A nice guy, real innocent, but he hears voices in his head. Says God speaks to him.*

The way I learned it, only canonized saints ever chatted with God, and most of them never talked about it much. There was an unwritten rule that said if you talk to God you should wait a century or two after your own death before discussing it with anybody. So I wanted to press him more, to learn how he could say such a thing so matter-of-factly, to learn how his saying it with such confidence could make my hands cold and my heart pound like it did.

"Father," Danny's voice said, "this is confession. Since I'm not asking forgiveness for talking with God, why are we even discussing this?"

Good point. I knew damn well that my only responsibilities in the confessional were to listen to a penitent's sin and offer absolution. That was one more frustrating thing about confessionals: they couldn't be used for any serious counseling.

"I know you must be frustrated, Father"—his voice soothing, reasonable—"and if you're interested in some serious counseling, we could do that some other time. For now, your only responsibilities are to hear my sins and offer absolution." Yes, he was right.

I realized why he was sounding so reasonable.

He was echoing my thoughts, almost word for word.

I gave him absolution; my hand was shaking when I made the sign of the cross.

In theory, a priest forgets what he hears in a confessional, protecting the sanctity and secrecy of the sacrament even from his own conscious mind.

I thought about Danny all afternoon. Late in the day, I went down to the game room, telling myself I was planning to mix with the boys but really looking for him. This time of the evening, almost all the boys gathered there, and he would be with them.

Thirty years ago, when I was a college seminarian here at Saint John Bosco, things were different. There was no game room; we couldn't drink or smoke; we wouldn't swear unless we were sure our rector was out of town, and even then we whispered.

"Goddammit," Bob Lembke was saying when I walked in the room, "that's six hands in a row!" He crushed out his cigar and threw his poker hand on the table as the other boys laughed.

Danny Gordon collected the pot.

Bob pulled two beer cans from a cooler next to the table. "Another?" he asked Danny, and set the beer in front of him without waiting for an answer. There were already two empties next to Danny.

"Hey, Father Lanning, jump in the game if you got any quarters," Bob said when he saw me. He shifted to the left, and dragged two other occupied chairs along with him to make room in the circle.

"Fine," I said, filling the space, "but it's only fair to warn you that among the diocesan priests I'm known as a fairly decent player." As I sat, I watched Danny fumble with the pull-tab on the beer can, spilling a bit when he finally managed to open it.

Bob was dealer; despite huge fingers, his shuffling was sharp and smooth. "Back in the Marine Corps, I was known as Five Aces Bobby." He grinned enormous teeth. "No reflection on my playing habits, of course."

"We're renaming him Bankrupt Bobby," one of the other boys said. "He's going to start having to take personal loans from Danny Gordon."

Bob scowled and dealt the cards. "Just twelve dollars. That's a fortune to you nickel-ante college boys, I know, but I've got enough saved to make that a petty loss."

I looked at Danny's winnings. He had at least twelve dollars in front of him. He anted his next quarter with a clumsy toss and held his cards in an awkward jumble.

"Have you been playing poker long, Danny?" I asked.

He nodded vigorously, boyish auburn curls bouncing across his forehead. "Two hours."

The others at the table chuckled. "I think he means before this game, Danny," one of them offered.

"Yes, I know," Danny said. He took a careful sip of beer, pursing his lips and slurping to be sure not to spill any more. "I've been playing since Bob taught me two hours ago. And I've won almost every hand. It's easy if you can just guess what everyone else is holding. Bob's a good teacher."

I was frowning, but kept my face lowered. It didn't sit well with me, someone as innocent as Danny learning the ropes in gambling and drinking from an ex-Marine. He had no use for tutelage of that sort, especially if he were a saint.

The thought froze me. A saint? When had I started thinking of him as a saint?

We picked up our cards. I kept two fours and threw out a ten, a three and a queen. I glanced at Danny; his eyes were circling the table, reading faces, until he sat back and smiled.

"Why did you leave the Marines?" one of the boys asked Bob as the replacement cards were dealt.

Bob shrugged, trying to concentrate on his hand. "I got what I needed out of it. They teach you how to be your own man."

Another boy laughed. "Bob," he said, "you're big enough to be your own man and somebody else's. Why a seminary? It's not the most common career change from the service."

"When I say being my own man, I'm not talking about this." Bob flexed a bicep about the size of a normal man's thigh. "I'm talking about up here." He tapped a finger to the side of his head. "Besides, the Marines aren't all that different from the Church. You've got your chain of command, your protocol." A wonderful thing for Danny to hear, I thought: the Church is like the Marines.

"The morals are a little different," I said coldly.

Bob wasn't the type to let that pass. "I figure with four years, Father, you'll find a way to turn me into a real nice guy." He swung his head around to glare at Danny. "We gonna sit here all day or are you gonna open bidding, hotshot?"

"I guess I'll start bidding at"—Danny shrugged—"five dollars."

Two of the seminarians folded immediately.

Bob was steaming. "He's bluffing. You're bluffing, aren't you?" He snorted with indecision, rocking uneasily in his chair. "Fine! Five dollars, And I'll raise you two. Father, you still in?"

I was looking at Danny. His smile was innocent, almost beatific, the sort of smile you would see on a statue of Saint Joseph or a portrait of Saint Francis. "Come on, Father," Bob urged impatiently. "He's bluffing."

I folded. Saint Francis wouldn't bluff.

After matching the raise, Danny showed a full house over Bob's two Kings. Bob pushed himself from the table—actually, he pushed the table from himself—and got up cursing. "That's it, I'm out. I can't sit through this anymore."

As Danny began gathering his winnings, I stared at him hard, and the whole situation began to feel strange, feel wrong. I was scared of him, I was drawn to him; all the years of working to gain some sort of proper, priestly control over my feelings became clouded as he grinned without any hint of malice, took another sip of the beer Bob had given him, and scooped dollar bills and quarters into his palms.

He suddenly seemed to me like a Samuel: young Samuel who could hear the voice of God yet couldn't understand what to do with it; Samuel who came to the old priest

Eli to learn how to deal with the voice. Eli who, despite his own shortcomings and probably against his own doubts and fears of a young boy who could hear God's voice, was still able to show Samuel the correct way to respond.

Hear God's voice. It wasn't even . . . rational.

"Danny," I said gently, my voice free of the shaking my mind was insisting it should have, "give him back his money."

Danny's face rounded to the pout of a scolded child, his large, brown eyes showing innocent incomprehension and hurt. Bob stopped in the doorway and simply looked puzzled.

"Father, no," Bob said, lifting his hands in resignation. "He won fair and square. Just because I show my temper . . ."

"Give it to him," I said, and Danny, still pouting, began counting out Bob's share of the money.

"Now hold it," Bob said, putting his fists on his hips and swelling his chest. "The kid won the money and I'm not taking it back. You let him keep it." He stared at me, dared me to argue.

Danny stood up between the two of us. "Look, everyone, there's no reason to get upset. Father doesn't want me to keep the money, so I'll put it in a charity box as a donation. Then there's no problem, right?" He was anxious, looking back and forth between us and pleading for a compromise to diffuse the tension.

"That would be fine, Danny," I said. "It's the right thing to do." I looked at him steadily, holding his eyes to avoid meeting Bob's. "It's important always to remember the right thing to do."

Bob kept glaring at me.

I was on the phone when Jerry bustled into my office at two forty-seven for the two o'clock appointment we had arranged. "Jim, we have to talk," he announced, throwing his worn briefcase on one of the chairs and tossing three files on the edge of my desk. I waved my hand to hush him.

"Look, whoever it is, tell them you'll call back. This is important." Jerry pushed the files in front of me. They were labeled PSYCHOLOGICALS, and Danny Gordon's name was on the first.

"I'm sorry, Bishop," I said into the receiver while my

eyes shifted between the file and Jerry's anxious face, "what was that again?" Jerry rolled his eyes and began pacing impatiently in front of my desk. He ran his fingers nervously through his unkempt hair and tucked in a shirt tail.

"Excuse me, Bishop," I said trying to stay focused on the phone conversation, "but how are we supposed to run a college seminary program if you move us to an undeveloped piece of land eight miles from the college?" Jerry lit a cigarette, and I automatically pushed across the ashtray I kept on my desk for him.

"Discontinue the program?" I sat up straight now; Jerry stopped pacing. "But Bishop, Saint John Bosco Seminary has been an established part of the priest formation program for thirty-six years. . . . I see. . . . Then it isn't definite yet . . . ? How soon will we know . . . ? Fine. Thank you, Bishop." I returned the phone to its cradle and dropped my head to my hands. "The bastard is thinking of closing us down to cut a land deal with the college."

Jerry's expression hardened; he hid his real reactions behind a quiet, professional tone. "That would be an unpopular move. This place has a strong emotional history for every priest in the Diocese who started out here." He softened a bit. "And for a lot of us who aren't priests, too."

He walked around to my side of the desk. I flinched a little, but he was careful not to touch me. "Besides, I've just brought you a more immediate problem."

I was holding my breath as he reached to pull a psychological file from the stack of three. But it was Bob Lembke's, not Danny Gordon's.

"Now look." He pulled a chart from the file. "These are graphed results of the Multiphasic Personality Inventory. It was the long form I sent you with the true and false answers for your three new seminarians."

The chart was impressively neat, especially for Jerry. "You guys at the clinic got a computer? Does this mean it'll be more expensive to contract you from now on?"

"Jim, pay attention." He always called me Jim, never Father Lanning, and in a strange way it made me feel a little more human. With most people I was always "Father," a bit of generic dough cut from some priestly cookie cutter. But Jerry and I had shared far too many years to reduce each other to titles. I never called him Doctor.

"Going across the page horizontally, you've got nine psychological categories. Hysteria, hypochondriasis, all that stuff. The black line across the middle of the page is the standardized mean of normalcy. And this little red line that goes above and below the center black line shows how far the test-taker's scores deviate from normalcy."

Bob's red line crossed the graph like a seismograph reading. "So this one's the problem?" I asked, sounding a little more relieved than I should have.

"No, not him. I'm showing you this one so you can see how the graph works. Now this kid, Robert Lembke—"

"Not really a kid, Jerry," I said, uncomfortable thinking again about last week's confrontation. "He did a tour of military duty before entering seminary. Marines."

"Good, then some of his deviations will make a little more sense." Jerry was nodding, looking closer at the graph.

"He's a deviate?"

"It's just a term for variation from a standard norm. We all have deviations."

I tried to catch his eye when he said that, but he was careful to stay fixed on the graph.

"Take a look," he said. "On Scale Five, Lembke's red line arcs above the black mean line quite a bit. It's a masculinity/femininity scale, and it means that on the test he tends toward an overly masculine view of himself and the world. Not surprising for a former military man, but it could indicate a need to develop more sensitivity for ministry. Now Scale Seven is a psychasthenia scale. He dips below the black mean, the normalcy line. It shows a tendency toward impulsive action, a disregard for ritual. Not an extreme problem according to the scale, but something to watch."

Impulsive action. Confrontation. Jerry's little graph knew its stuff.

"Now *this* is the graph that bothers me."

It was Danny's.

There was no red line.

"Jerry, it's a blank graph. Is this supposed to mean he has no personality?"

Jerry was frowning. "Look at the black normalcy line. Do you see the red superimposed over it?"

Yes, I could. A faint trace of red ink showed around the edges of the black line. It was perfectly straight.

"So that means he's normal?" Obscurely, I felt relieved.

Jerry was becoming annoyed. He snatched the graph from my hand and began to pace the room again. "Don't be naive, Jim. It means a hell of a lot more than that. It's a nearly impossible reading. Everyone has deviations." When he said it this time he stared right into my eyes, daring me to say it wasn't so. "The Multiphasic Personality Inventory has five hundred and sixty-four true-false statements that are scored according to nine different scales. There's even a tenth scale that adjusts all the other scores according to how much the test-taker is trying to put himself into a better light or how much he seems to be lying. All the scales overlap. An answer of 'true' to one question could help your score on two scales while it hurts you on three others." He stopped pacing and waited for me to register some sort of reaction. I kept my face from showing anything. Ignore conflicting emotions; priestly control.

If Danny's personality review showed problems, Jerry would ask for counseling sessions with him. In a counseling session, Danny would say he talked to God regularly. That would be recorded on his permanent file, and even in the Church—especially in the Church—that wouldn't be viewed as a psychologically sound state of mind.

Even if he really was talking to God. Even if he were a saint.

"Jim," Jerry said, tired of waiting for me to react, "this Daniel Gordon kid has somehow beaten the most complex standardized testing instrument in my profession, and I want to know how."

I was careful not to answer him.

What would I have said?

On Saturdays, I took the seminarians on service projects downtown. Sometimes we would serve on one of the food lines, sometimes we would visit nursing homes, those sorts of things that develop discipline and proper behavior. This particular Saturday we were working to clean up the church grounds of Our Lady of the Immaculate Conception, a parish in one of the poorer areas of town. The boys had rakes and shovels and sweat. So did I. It was good for us.

I watched Danny and Bob working on the far edge of the grounds, cleaning along the length of a chain link fence. Bob would grab the bottom of the links and strain to lift them as high as his waist; Danny would scurry under with his rake and clear the papers and broken glass from the weeds. They looked like David and Goliath practicing teamwork.

I started walking across the field in their direction. The two had been almost inseparable for the past month; I took every opportunity to interrupt Bob's amoral influence.

I was still too far away to hear what they were saying, but Bob was talking with great animation, waving his enormous arms to add emphasis to his stories. Danny listened with wide eyes. When Bob leaned over to whisper some bawdy point, Danny blushed angelically and laughed along with him. The chuckling subsided, and Bob reached out and gently set his massive hand on Danny's shoulder.

I froze in midstep.

Thirty years ago, Jerry and I stood laughing in the garden around the back of the seminary. There was a statue there of Saint John Bosco himself, and we were laughing about the stupid expression the sculptor had chiseled for the saint's face. It didn't seem an appropriate face for a saint; it was the face of a lout. Jerry and I were in our first year of seminary.

"The rector says John Bosco is the patron saint of seminarians."

"Looks more like the patron saint of idiots."

"Same thing as far as the rector is concerned."

We laughed. Back then it was still uproariously daring to say treasonous things about your rector. In fact, it was plain treason just for seminarians to associate in pairs. We were supposed to travel in groups of no less than three at all times. We were forbidden to enter one another's rooms.

"The rector was telling a story about Saint John Bosco at dinner the other night."

"Jimmy, Jimmy," Jerry said, putting his hand on my shoulder with mock sternness. "I'm getting a little concerned about this habit of quoting the rector every few sentences or so."

I was uncomfortable about the hand on my shoulder, and casually brushed it away. "No, listen, Jer. He said John

Bosco was one of the worst students in his seminary class, a real dolt when it came to studies. So one of the priests called him in and told him, 'Mr. Bosco, you are a complete ass.' And without missing a beat, Bosco answered, 'Father, considering what Samson did with just the jawbone of an ass, imagine what God can do with a complete one like me!' "

Jerry was surprised. "The rector said 'ass' right in front of you?"

"Twice! I'm not lying, he did!"

"I believe you," he said. "It's just this priesthood thing looks less pious every day. Rectors saying 'ass' and saints with lousy report cards. Hey, do you think we could pull it off? Going home and saying, 'Don't worry about the grades, folks, I'm going to be a saint one day.' "

He laughed; I dropped my eyes and moved away from him. I didn't feel as if I would cry, but I turned my back just in case. I wasn't sure if I could control my emotions that well.

Jerry realized the mistake immediately. "Oh, God, Jimmy . . . Look, I wasn't thinking. That was stupid to say." He put his hand on my shoulder again. I pushed it off, forcefully this time.

He could change so quickly from being cold to being gentle.

"I'm sorry, Jimmy. Hey, I'm an ass."

I smiled. He could even make me smile when I felt hurt. He had that gift with people. "A complete ass?" I asked.

"Agreed." He stood there without saying anything else. Even his silence could affect me.

"I don't know, Jerry. It's not your fault, it's just me. It's been more than a year since they died." I hugged my arms around myself. It wasn't cold, but I felt like it was. "A normal person would be over it by now. I can't get over feeling lost. I've got no control. Sometimes I'm even angry at . . . at God. It would be nice just to have a reason why they had to die."

Jerry listened. He always listened well when he thought that was what you needed.

He was really hurt when they expelled him from seminary the following month. He would have been a good priest, a listening priest. A homosexual priest, however, wasn't something the system was ready to tolerate. It was *the cardinal deviation. The rector, the dean and the psychologist certified his expulsion, sealed his file and gave him bus fare home.*

Bob had taken his hand off Danny's shoulder. It was innocent, I thought. It was.

A group of six Hispanic teenagers had rounded the corner of the church parking lot. They were all boys; they wore jackets with identical designs.

"Hey, check this, they got *gringos* cleaning our turf for us!"

I hurried the rest of the way over. I knew how impulsive Bob was. And Danny . . .

When I reached them, Bob was just smiling at the gang. "Our pleasure," he said.

I stood beside Danny and whispered, "You stay back from this." When he had moved away a foot or two, I turned toward the gang. "Good afternoon, gentlemen," I said. "May I help you?" Hispanics, even young ones, are a religious and superstitious people. The presence of a priest can have a very tranquilizing effect on them.

The tallest of the boys looked me over slowly from head to foot. "You the boss-man, Anglo?" he said. "Then you make sure they scrub it nice and clean, you hear?"

I realized I was dressed in blue jeans and a sweaty tank top. How were they supposed to know I was a priest? I'm a complete ass, I thought.

Bob was still smiling. He said nothing and returned to work. He's got it under control, I told myself. I looked around the grounds for the other seminarians. There were about twenty of us, but we were spread out, and none of the others noticed the exchange.

The tall Hispanic boy smashed a bottle against an area of the fence where Bob and Danny had finished raking. "Clean up that, too, while you're at it, okay, *hueros?*"

Bob ignored him. It was Danny who reacted. He walked forward and said, "God doesn't want you to aggravate us while we're doing a good deed. He says He wants you to leave now." Then he stood there, waiting for them to leave.

The Hispanic who had broken the bottle took a step forward but said nothing. He apparently had no immediate comebacks for words from God.

I moved to stand in front of Danny, but Bob was there ahead of me. Sometime during the last exchange he had lost his smile. "If the kid says God wants you to leave, then you leave."

The Hispanic bared his yellowed teeth in a snarl. "You gonna protect your little *maricón?*" It was the wrong thing to say.

"Hijo de puta," Bob answered. It was the wrong response.

"Bob!" Danny yelled. "He's got a switchblade in his back pocket! He's about to make a grab for it!" The Hispanic was, in fact, halfway through the motion of drawing a switchblade from his back pocket, but Bob knocked it from his hand before it was even open.

I grabbed Danny by the shoulders and tried to pull him back from the scuffle. He pushed my hands away forcefully, planted his feet, and closed his eyes.

"The kid to the left," Danny shouted, "he's got a knife in his boot!" The teenager to the left looked startled, as if just remembering he really did have a knife in his boot. When he bent over to release it, Danny cried, "His right shoulder is bad from an accident! It's his weakest point!"

Bob brought a fist down on the boy's right shoulder. I could hear the crack.

"The three in back are too confused to attack. The one you hit is trying not to cry. The first one wants to hit you, but he's scared without his knife and he feels like he's going to wet himself. One of the ones in back is thinking, *'Vamos, vamos, es loco, es brujo.'* He wants to run and get his brother."

The fighting had stopped. All the Hispanics were staring at Danny in disbelief.

"His brother's name is Santiago."

I stared too.

"He's twenty-five years old."

The gang began to back away slowly, then turned and ran. Their friend with the shattered collarbone limped after them at an awkward trot.

Danny opened his eyes and smiled at Bob.

"He has a sister, too," he said. "But she's only twelve."

My office is on the third floor of the seminary. I chose the room because it has a window overlooking the back garden and the statue of Saint John Bosco with his comic face. In the darkness now, his outline was little more than a vague shadow.

Bosco's priest had told him he was a complete ass. He failed to see the seeds of sainthood in the young man, had tried to make himself a stumbling block to the boy's growth. I would not repeat that mistake.

The knock on my door, as expected. I chose the emotion I needed to use.

"Come in," I said, like ice.

"Hiya, Father," Bob said, as cheerful as I was cold. "You wanted to see me?"

I turned to face him but stayed across the room. Make him come to me. "I suppose you are in such high spirits, Robert, because you had the opportunity to assault a teenager this afternoon."

Bob's eyes dropped and his face flushed. He closed the office door gently.

"Father, you were there. It was self-defense." He raised his eyes again, and in them there was a genuine bit of remorse I wasn't expecting. "I'm a loud guy, I know. I express myself a little too much and a little too honestly. But I have no great love for violence. If I did, I would still be in the Marines, drinking in the bars and accepting challenges to fight with guys who are just drunk enough to wonder if they could take on somebody my size."

Dammit, it wasn't the reaction I needed from him. Of all times for Bob's impulsive temper to become undependable.

"At the moment, Robert, I don't really care about your attempts to control your outbursts. I'm more concerned with the influence you have on Danny Gordon."

Bob laughed, another reaction I didn't expect. "Well, with God calling the shots for our side of the fight, I guess none of us should feel guilty about what happened."

"God?" I felt cold inside. Had Danny confided that much in Bob?

"Of course," Bob said, his eyebrows sinking into a puzzled look. "Danny says God talks to him. He told you that." I said nothing, made no change in my face. Bob nodded and the eyebrows lifted. "Oh, he told you in confession so you're not free to discuss it. He told me that, I forgot. Okay, then I'm telling you now, outside the confessional, Danny says God talks to him."

I broke from my authoritative stance and began pacing the carpet; I must have looked as frustrated as Jerry had looked pacing in my office. "You say that, Robert, as if it were the most natural thing in the world. Perhaps it's common among drunken Marines to think that God talks in their heads, but here in Saint John Bosco Seminary we don't encounter that sort of thing too often." I had already lost this battle. I had wanted Bob to lose his temper and yell at me, maybe even threaten me, so I could have some solid grounds for disciplining him and beginning to document him for expulsion from the seminary. I wanted his influence far from Danny. Bob had been able to reverse the situation: he was calm, I was losing control.

"Father, I'm just telling you what Danny says. He's obviously some sort of psychic, yeah; he reads minds faster than I read comic books. It's impressive. But I'm not so stupid as to think he actually hears the voice of God."

I stopped pacing and looked at him.

His eyes widened. "You're kidding, right? You don't really believe—"

I cut him off. "What I believe, Mr. Lembke, is that Danny's gift, however you wish to explain it, won't be helped by a character like you. Your friendship with him will do nothing but retard his growth."

I thought I saw what I wanted, the faintest trace of anger in Bob's face. He caught himself, though, and forced it down.

"Do you see what you're doing?" he asked evenly. "You've given that kid a different set of standards. The rest of us in seminary, we can gamble, swear a little, drink every once in a while, and you say nothing. You let us grow up. For Danny, all your rules change. You single him out because he's different." Bob shook his head slowly in condescending disapproval. "I don't know what your reasons are for trying to make him perfect, but if you force him to play Church that way, you'll lose him." He paused and looked thoughtful for a moment. "Maybe that would be the best thing. To let him go before you suffocate him."

I wanted Bob's anger. I wanted him to lose control. "Interesting opinions, Robert," I said, "but considering their source, I regard them as little more than garbage."

He shrugged and reached for the door. "Danny says you've been under a lot of stress lately. He says that in the back of your mind you're constantly thinking about the bishop trying to close the seminary. I don't want to aggravate you." He smiled before leaving. "Kind of makes you feel naked, having a psychic around, doesn't it?"

Jerry was back again, pacing my carpet.

"Jim, you wouldn't believe it. This kid's answers are flawless. I've been up late for five weeks now working out the numbers by hand. Where the hell is it?" He dug through his briefcase looking for the paperwork on Danny. "Here. The standard scales all checked out perfectly again, so I started tossing in some psychological subscales, special scoring patterns that are hardly even used any more. I've run his numbers on an Ego-Strength Scale, a Caudality scale, even an obscure Anti-Semitic Prejudice Scale. Every scenario registers the same: perfect textbook normalcy rating across the graphs, never the slightest deviation from the societal mean." He was talking too fast. His eyes shone.

I had a headache. I hadn't felt like this—uncontrolled, chaotic—since my parents' deaths, since my first guilt-ridden years of seminary. My attempt to enrage Bob had failed; my attempts to influence Danny looked fruitless; my attempts to talk the bishop out of trading the seminary for undeveloped land were pointless.

Jerry's antics weren't helping my bad humor, either. "Look," I said, my body tense and my back aching from the taut muscles, "maybe the kid *is* a saint. Would that be so terrible?"

"No, not a saint," Jerry said through the smoke of the cigarette he was lighting. "A real saint or visionary would register as a lunatic on a Multiphasic Personality Inventory. What we have here is a record of the perfect answer code for this test, for every valid scale ever used to evaluate it and for every scale overlap known today."

His pacing had accelerated; he was walking in quick little circles. "*The* perfect answer code, never recorded by any human being who ever sat down and took the test."

"Goddammit, Jerry, stop it!" He came to a halt with his mouth hanging open. I had jumped from my chair. "Just stop it! I've listened to you go on about 'this kid's numbers,' 'this kid's scales,' 'this kid's scoring patterns.' You've never even talked with him. You wouldn't know him if you passed him in the hall." I slouched back down into my chair. "Goddammit, Jerry, you haven't even asked if you could meet him."

We were quiet for a while, both of us embarrassed. Then he smiled in a way I hadn't seen in years. "Goddammit?" He shook his head with mock sternness. "The rector said that? Twice! I don't know, Jimmy, this priesthood thing looks less pious every day. Rectors saying 'Goddammit' and little saints with perfect psychological report cards."

He walked over and put his hand on my shoulder, the first time in years he had made any physical contact.

My face was hidden in my hands.

"We've changed, Jerry. The whole world keeps changing and we don't know what to do or how to act to keep up with it." When I was sure I wouldn't cry, I lifted my head. "When you and I were seminarians here, the rules were clear. Life was black and white, we learned exactly what was correct and what was wrong."

He dropped his hand from my shoulder and walked slowly to the window. He had turned his face from me.

"An interesting way to phrase it," he said distantly, sounding like a psychologist. "They taught us what was correct and what was wrong. Do you suppose they ever meant to teach us what was right?" His face was pressed against the glass. "Sometimes that's completely different from what's correct."

I joined him at the window. It was late fall, the trees complementing the ivy-covered building and making the whole grounds seem tired, old and holy. In the garden, shadows flickered across the comic face of our sculpted patron saint. Everything looked as if it were quietly waiting to die.

"We've been friends since grade school, Jerry, and I've never asked you. What did you want from this place when we first came?"

Jerry shrugged. "I came because I needed to feel special. But once we got here, I don't know. I just wanted to be normal. Hell of a contradiction, isn't it?" He turned his face toward me, grinning ruefully. "And what about you? I've always assumed you came here for some kind of stability. After your parents died, you needed some sort of control, something permanent. And since the priesthood was what they always wanted for you, it was a way to soothe the guilt."

I was nodding; I said nothing.

"Do you still blame me?"

I felt my stomach tense. "Christ, Jerry, blame *you*? I still haven't gotten over blaming me." I sat down on the carpet and pulled my knees up under my chin. It was an undignified pose for a priest. "Why do we do that? Why does someone always have to be guilty?"

Jerry sat down next to me. He said nothing. After all these years, he still knew when it was best to say nothing.

"For years, I've knelt down by my bed and asked God why they had to die. For years. And I'd give my soul just to hear a single word of explanation from Him. Just one word. But I've never been enough of a saint to merit a single syllable."

For a moment, huddled there on the floor and talking from the heart, I felt like we were kids again.

Danny. Words from God.

"Saints and visionaries, Jerry. You said they would look like lunatics on a standardized psychological test. Why?"

Jerry was disoriented by the quick change of focus. "Well, uh, I guess I assume they'll answer the party line on all religious questions. It would knock them all over the graphs on the Dominance, Hysteria and Schizophrenia Scales. And a real visionary would be answering 'true' to statements like, 'I hear voices others can't hear,' and 'I believe God speaks through me,' things like that."

"Those statements are part of the test?" I stood up.

"Yeah, and dozens more like them. What are you getting at?"

I couldn't tell him. Since Danny had opened up to me in the secrecy of the confessional, I wasn't free.

What *had* Danny answered to those questions?

"Come back tomorrow at noon," I told him. "I've been avoiding this, but I guess you need to meet Danny."

All evening I looked for Danny to inform him of the noon meeting. I was finally able to get one of the seminarians to tell me that Bob Lembke had taken him out to one of the local bars.

I waited. Jerry had left me all the paperwork on Danny,

so I read the copy of the Multiphasic Personality Inventory. It was five hundred and sixty-four statements with Danny's responses clearly marked. The perfect answer key.

"I have had very peculiar and strange experiences," the test stated. Danny had responded, "False." False?

Perhaps in his mind, talking with God wasn't strange and peculiar.

"Most people will use somewhat unfair means to gain profit or an advantage rather than lose it." True, said Danny. Most bishops, too, I thought. At least Danny wasn't naive about human nature.

"I have certainly had more than my share of things to worry about lately." Danny said false. I felt uncomfortable. I was glad I wasn't the one taking the test.

We all have our deviations.

"I loved my mother." Danny had left it blank. I looked back at the directions for the booklet. The test allowed for occasional blanks.

"I feel profound guilt for terrible things I have done in the past." Danny said false. I closed the booklet.

I loved my mother. I loved my father, too. They had always wanted me to become a priest; we were a family with a strong Catholic heritage. The night they died, during my last year of high school, they were angry with me; but I still knew they loved me.

Jerry and I shared everything. He was my best friend. When he told me he liked boys, not girls, I thought it was strange; but I didn't hate him. We were still best friends.

One afternoon, he was talking about it. He always talked about it. I let him, not just because he was my friend but because it fascinated me, the whole idea seemed so backward. I let him talk about how he felt. What he thought was beautiful about boys. We were in my room, the door was closed.

He said, 'Take off your shirt, just so I can look at you.' I wanted to and I didn't want to, it seemed strange but it drew me. 'I won't touch you,' he said, and I knew he was telling the truth. I took off my shirt, he took off his. We kept going like that, piece by piece, until we both had taken all our clothes off and lain on the bed, just talking, nothing else. My Dad walked in.

There was yelling, screaming. Jerry was thrown out of the house. The yelling kept up all afternoon. But nothing happened, Dad! It's stupid, it was nothing! Dad, why are you so upset when nothing happened? I didn't touch him!

My father was still hysterical when he left the house with my mother later that evening. I told myself endlessly, you can't hold yourself responsible for fate. For acts of God. The car accident was not my fault.

So for years I had knelt in prayer before falling asleep and asked, "Please just tell me why." And the same silence kept me from an answer.

I looked at Danny's test again. There was a statement there, "I believe there is a God."

Danny had left it blank.

At two-thirty in the morning they stumbled in, hooting and laughing like two sailors back from shore leave.

Danny was the less rational of the two. "Bob's been training me," he slurred through drunken giggles. "I can look at girls in a bar and read what they're thinking." He dropped his voice to a whisper. "And I can know which ones are thinking about having sex." They glanced at each other and burst into laughter.

"Get in my office."

"No, no, Father, don't worry," Bob said, "we were just out for observation, strictly hands off."

"Get in my office. Now."

Bob took hold of Danny's shoulders and straightened him up. "Come on, buddy, we've gotta get sober. We're in the shit."

"Sit," I ordered when we were in the office, and they both sank in slow motion, making sure not to miss the chairs. After another exchange of glances, the laughing resumed.

"You gentlemen will compose yourselves. Even in your fogged states of mind it must be becoming clear that this situation is unacceptable." The first indications of remorse began to cross their faces.

"Father, look. Danny and I were just out for a good time. A little stress management, you know?"

"A good time?" I came nose to nose with him. "Robert, I fail to see anything good about encouraging this young man to peer into the minds of other people looking for dirty thoughts. Dammit, you can see he has a special gift. Neither of us understands it, but we both see it. Do you have any idea what you're doing by using him for selfish purposes?"

Bob's eyes changed then. I could feel the anger.

"You son of a bitch." He rose from the chair. "You pompous son of a bitch."

His fists were clenched, and I was suddenly aware of his size.

"Using him? *Using* him?"

"Robert, leave the office."

"And what will you people do with him? You think you'll leave him alone? You think your wonderful, God-almighty Church will let him be for one minute?"

"Robert, get out now!"

"Or maybe you won't tell the Church, Father. Maybe you'll keep him as your own little prophet, your personal sideshow freak."

Danny staggered to his feet, much more affected by the alcohol than Bob. "Please, stop it."

"What's wrong, Father, nothing to say? Did I hit a nerve?"

"Stop it," Danny pleaded with stumbling words. "Bob, he thinks you're going t' hit him. He's scared. I know ya won't hit 'im, but you're making 'im scared."

"Look at him!" Bob shouted at me. "Can't you see? He's already programmed to try to make everything work out for everybody. You say I'm using him? Jesus Christ, Father, I'm just trying to show him how to care about *himself* for once in his life."

Danny had been trying to stand between us, but had fallen to the floor, sobbing. I reached down for him, but Bob grabbed my arm and pulled me back.

"Don't you even see what he goes through, Father?" His breath was short, his grip like an iron clamp on my arm. "Can you imagine what hell it must be knowing what everyone thinks and dreams and not being able to do anything to help them? Goddammit, you don't even know him." He released me, turned and slammed the office door as he left.

Danny was still on the floor, crying. "Why is ever'one so upset? Why do you all have t' be so upset?"

I was shaking.

I picked him up from the floor. "Danny," I said, trying to lift his head. "Danny, I want to know about your test."

"Wha' test?" His eyes were clouded and his mouth gave an annoyed frown. I was losing him to the alcohol.

"The psychological test you took when you first came here. The long one."

He opened his eyes to slits and tried to focus on me. "The true/false thing? I didn't take it."

I shook him a little, trying to rouse him. "Danny, stay awake! You did take it, I have your answer sheet!"

He pulled out of my grip and yelled, "Stop bein' upset! Why're people always so upset?" He put his hands over his ears and started humming, as if trying to block out sounds that were too loud. "Father, you worry so much and all of it's a game, don't y'see?" He began humming louder, and pressed harder on his ears, his elbows jutting straight out from his shoulders. He spun in awkward little circles, not dropping his hands, not stopping the humming, looking like an epileptic in seizure.

I grabbed him again and tried to force his arms to his side. He grabbed my shirt and began to laugh. He looked at me strangely, his eyes wild like I had never seen them, his smile contorted. It was a comic face, a face I recognized but not really Danny's.

It was Saint John Bosco's face.

He leaned into me and whispered in a conspiratorial tone. "You win, can't you even see that? The bishop, he can't take this place away from you. He can't! Wha' time is it?" He stared at his wrist, saw he was wearing no watch, and burst into insane laughter. "Anyways, anyways," he was patting my shoulder like a father pats a good child, "you do a good job here, an' if it's after midnight you got no more worries. The bishop can't do anythin' after midnight, Father." Then he raised his hands in the air and began making little dancing motions with his fingers and singing like a little child, "It's a game, it's a game, oh yes it's all jus' a game." Then his expression became grave. "I promise. I promise. Stop being upset."

"Danny . . ."

"I'll be good. I'll do what you tell me. Jus' tell me. I'll do it."

I had to steady him again. I had to steady myself, too, seeing him like this. "The test, Danny. You took the test."

"No, I didn't." His head began to droop and his tone was apologetic. "I didn't. I wrote in the answers, but they weren't my answers. God told me."

"God told you the right answers for the test?"

"God said none of the answers were really right, so I asked Him to make me look normal. Thas all. I jus' wanted it to look normal. I didn't wanna lie, but He said I wasn't lying, I was jus' writing down His answers for Him."

He speech was almost completely inaudible now. His head was dangling limply across his chest. "It's God's test. His answers. I talk to God, you know."

He passed out. I lowered him gently to the chair and turned off the office light.

I sat on the floor beside him. The room seemed so quiet and empty, only his slow breathing and a bit of light filtering through the curtains from the illuminated courtyard where the statue of John Bosco stood. After a long time I had the courage to whisper to the darkness.

"Danny, why did my mother and father have to die?"

In the morning, the word of the bishop's sudden demise shocked the Diocese. Due to cardiac arrest, he had been taken in his sleep to the Eternal Peace of Our Lord and Savior Jesus Christ. We all deeply regretted his passing, and all understood that the Diocese would be in a state of transition until a new Shepherd could be appointed by the Holy See. We all committed ourselves to strive toward maintaining the status quo in those turbulent times.

My seminary would remain open.

Jerry arrived for the noon meeting at twelve thirty-five sharp. By that time, Danny Gordon had already requested dismissal from the college seminary program and I had accepted on the condition that he promise to continue his college education.

Let him go before you suffocate him.

"He's gone?" Jerry asked, his voice pitched high with disbelief. "How can he be gone overnight?"

"He's still in the building, but he's packing. He requested dismissal early this morning and I complied. I couldn't very well ask him to stay on a little longer just to chat with the shrink."

"Maybe he'll chat with the shrink anyway. Let me have his test."

I shook my head. "Sorry, Jerry. All the paperwork was part of his personal file, and the file's been sealed. Didn't you make a copy?"

Jerry eyes narrowed, a look both puzzled and suspicious. "Get off it, Jim. I score eight hundred of these tests a year. I don't have any reason or any time to make copies. Give me the kid's test and let me talk to him."

"Jerry, it wouldn't do you any good. I have reason to believe he had outside help on the test. They're not his answers. I'm afraid I can't tell you whose they are or even how I know because the situation was shared with me in the secrecy of the confessional. It's a dead end all around. You understand."

He sat on the edge of my desk. He was staring at me hard.

"You're protecting him, aren't you?"

I nodded.

"From me?"

"And from me. People like us."

He sat thinking about it for a moment. "You sure you know what you're doing?" His face was softening.

I shook my head. "Nope. I guess I don't need to be sure."

"Then I'm with you." He put his hand on my shoulder, and I let him.

To this day, Father Bob Lembke insists Danny Gordon, wherever he may be, is merely a reader of minds. I nod, agree and let him keep thinking so. But Danny had told me the future that night in my office before the bishop died.

Whose Mind did he read to learn that?

His file stays sealed in a locked drawer in my office. Occasionally, I'll take it out and hold it. It gives me hope that perhaps even deviates and complete asses can play some useful role in the game. But I've never broken the seal to closely read again the psychological test. It's enough for me to believe that maybe, there in my own hands, is the personality of God.

Then I Sleeps
and Dreams
of Rose

DEBORAH MILLION

HELL JUST AIN'T NO SURPRISE. Mamma warned me. Preacher warned me. Even Honey-Sue, she warned me. Turned on me at the end, just like Rose, my Rose. Turned on me and drowned me with that sticky sweet I-found-Jesus-don't-you-know, until I thought I would choke.

But they were right. Yes sir, demon sir, here I am. Jake Crowley. Busted flat and no parole. Snake-eyes and forever's a long time. Preacher ain't got nothin' on me now.

Yeah, here I am, standin' on this long wood platform, and I ain't wearin' nothin' but a dirty white T-shirt and my old prison jeans. Not even a pair of shoes. Just this platform and a three-day beard and a taste in my mouth that could eat a hole to China.

Like I said, ain't no surprises here. There's even a train standin' next to the platform, lookin' like old black-'n'-whites in a vid, smellin' like rotten eggs and two-month garbage back of the hole. Yeah, the air's New Kay Cee all the way and if I wasn't dead, I'd need my mask. But it all kind of merges into one skunk lump of a smell and makes me feel a little at home.

At least until I realizes I ain't alone. People all around, mostly hardliners—Hell's just like New Kay Cee—and dopeys and suits and even some spacers. They all look kind of mean, but they don't scare—not me—except there ain't no wall for my back. No buildin's, either. Just the platform and the train and the tracks goin' nowhere in two directions, and flat flat nothin'. No dirt, no trash, no holes. Just greasy gray nothin'.

"Hey, you. Get in line," Demon says, his face as ugly as dopeys' bad trips, his body smellin' like dead rats in the wall, his voice low and deadly like Jimmy Lee's. "Get in line."

Slasher pulls his knife and Demon, he pushes Slasher onto the tracks and the engine spits black smoke and the train moves just a little and the screams go on and on. Kind of nice. But what about me? I moves.

Jimmy Lee, he already crossed me and that's why I choked him. Ain't fair I gets the jib-jab again. Ain't fair. But life's a bitch, like the suits all say, and I grins, thinkin' about how money only kept the suits out of Hell in New Kay Cee and this is where it all evens out.

Ain't forgot about Jimmy Lee, though, and how he took over my scam and pumped my Rose while I was doin' time, and how he made his slasher do the jib-jab on me when I tried to get her back. No, I ain't forgot. So while I'm standin' in line, I looks around, wonderin' if Jimmy Lee is here.

When I don't see him, I starts thinkin'. Maybe Hell ain't too bad if you don't cross Demon. After all, Demon's just a warden. And without Jimmy Lee I can beat any system. No, this ain't too bad, and I'm already plannin' when the suit in front of me starts whimperin' like a hungry dog and slappin' at his neck and face. "What's with you?" I asks.

"Lice," he says, "giant lice." He points at the ground. "They're everywhere."

I stares, but I don't see nothin'. Only the boards of the platform. So I shakes my head and shrugs and moves down the line.

Now a woman's right behind me, nice tits and ass. Ain't bad lookin' either. I smiles and moves a little closer and says, "Hey, honey, what's your name?"

She doesn't answer. I asks again. And again. She looks right through me and holds out her arms and tears are runnin' down her cheeks and she says, "Please talk to me. Someone, please talk to me. Don't leave me here alone." Then the dopey behind her is screamin' and cowerin' and his hair is fallin' out like he's radsick, and there ain't nothin' or nobody even near him.

I backs away from the line and Demon, he starts walkin' toward me, and Slasher, he's still screamin' from under the train. I feels funny, like I'm six years old again and I'm waitin' outside the school. My stomach's so sick I knows I'll throw up if the doors don't open soon, because inside I'm safe. Outside, Uncle Sammie can see me.

Uncle Sammie, he comes in our house any time he wants. Mama screams and curses, but Uncle Sammie only laughs and kisses Mama and asks, "Is that any way to treat your brother?" Then he eats our food and takes money out of Mama's purse and slaps her until she cries and lets him rip off her clothes and yank her to the floor. Uncle Sammie likes for me to watch. He says I need to learn how to be a man so I can take care of myself.

Mama does the best she can, but she works and I have to walk to school by myself and there's no place to hide while I'm waitin'. Then the school bell rings and I thinks I'm safe until someone slaps the back of my head so hard I falls down. Uncle Sammie. He doesn't want me to go to school. He says that there are better things to learn, that I'm his boy and that I'm comin' with him. Teacher, she's afraid. She just watches as Uncle Sammie grabs my hair and yanks me back to the hole.

Yeah, that's how I feels right now. Like I'm waitin' for school and I'm goin' to throw up if the doors don't open soon.

Demon, he keeps starin' me, just like Uncle Sammie, and I wonders if there's a way to break out of hell. Then Demon turns his head and the train moves back and Slasher stands. Healed up, just like that. Slasher's tame now, his face real pale against his dyed black braid, even gives up his knife—never saw that before—and gets in line.

Hell's a real live place, all right, no dead. Hell, we're all dead. Eternity, right? And what comes next?

I takes my chance and runs. Quick quick quick, dodge

suits and straights, out out out, until nothin's all around, gray nothin', and time stretches. One . . . two . . . three hundred years. Four . . . five . . . six. Nothin' goin' on and on and on until Demon walks up and that's a relief, even when he grabs my hand and I knows it's jib-jab all over again. I clenches my teeth while the flesh burns and pops and fades away and bones turn red and black. Inside I'm screamin'—just like Slasher under the train—but I chews on my tongue and don't let out even a moan. Uncle Sammie taught me that.

Then I nods, yes sir, no sir, and follows Demon to the train. It ain't full, so I climbs on and wanders back. Demon follows, but I keeps movin', lookin' for an empty car.

No luck. Everyone's got at least three hardliners and I ain't trustin' no strange hardliners, not me. I keeps walkin', until Demon says, "Sit here."

I looks at my new healed hand, and I sits.

Across the aisle, a suit sleeps, his body flopped back against the cushions like a strangled slut. Then his eyes open wide, and he whimpers, like Rose when I beats her—I ain't sorry, Rose, I ain't—and he pries open the window and jumps. I shrugs. Ain't nothin' out there, but a hardliner minds his own business. Even in hell.

Demon, he stares me, big red eyes, they read my innards. I yawns and tries to stand, I ain't no fool. Too late.

I sleeps and dreams of Rose.

Sunday night. Rose still gone, hours. Hey slut, I'm goin' to say, hey slut. I just know she's doin' the cheatin' run. I feels it deep.

So will she, when she gets back. No slut makes a fool out of Jake Crowley.

I paces the hole and drinks. Nothin' else to do—vid's broke, got to steal another tomorrow—and it doesn't take long before the booze is all dry, and all that's left is one thin joint. Been savin' it.

Before I lights up, Rose walks in, smilin' and hummin' like she won the lottery. She's all prettied up, too, wearin' her best dress and the gold earrings I gave her when we got paired. "Slut!" I yells and slaps her down to the floor. "Who's the pumper?" I hits her again.

She just lays there on the carpet, her blue eyes starin' me. She doesn't even see the roach crawlin' over her hand.

No, she just lays there, starin', and that makes me mad. My Rose ain't no coward, not my Rose. "Who's the pumper?" I asks again. But she just keeps starin'. Guess she thinks that lyin' look can help her.

I hits her some more. Then she whispers, real low and I almost don't hear, "Forgive him, he can't help it."

That real cold feelin' burns behind my eyes, and it's like I ain't got no control, just anger, the kind that saves me on the streets. I closes up my fist and slams it into her left eye. I told her, I told her more than once. No churchin' in my hole. "Preacher never did anything for you," I says. "Never stole you food or a vid or money for a hole." No, Preacher, he never did anything. Never even saved Mama from Uncle Sammie.

Rose still doesn't speak, just lays there silent, lookin' at me with one eye, stubborn-like. I knows she ain't listenin'. She ain't listened for months, and I don't like it. I wants my Rose back. My Rose. the one from the rehab house, the one that lied to the socials and cheated them so we could hole up together.

This time, I swears, I'm goin' to beat the old Rose out, so I hits her again . . . and again . . . and again. Tryin' to make her cry, tryin' to make her fight, tryin' to make her dead.

I wakes and the train's still not movin'. Demon, he's right here, hand on my shoulder, his touch burnin' a hole. Don't care. I can feel the cold fire behind my eyes. Yeah, there's somethin' about killin'. Somethin' about standin' there and watchin' that last breath and seein' the body slump and knowin' you did it. Yeah, there's somethin' about killin'. And I likes it.

Demon lets go of my shoulder and grins like Uncle Sammie. I smiles back because I remembers how good that butcher knife looks, and how long and sharp the blade is, and how the handle fits in my hand just right, and how I feels when I slides that knife in Uncle Sammie. He doesn't even see because he's pumpin' my Mama and he doesn't worry about no twelve-year-old boy.

Mama does though and that's why she starts on the churchin'. Makes me so mad, sometimes I have to beat her. I don't want to, she just makes me so mad.

One day, Mama frowns at me and says, "You ain't no

different from Sammie." That cold fire starts up behind my
eyes and I grabs Mama by the shoulder. When she struggles, I slaps her and rips her shirt. Mama stands up tall and
stares me and says, "You gonna rape me, too?"

I steps back, feelin' all weak and shaky, like I'm gettin'
the flu, and I want to say I'm sorry, Mama, but I can't. I just
can't.

Real sudden, the train starts up, chuggin' and
screechin' like a billion straights have just been wiped out
by the big bomb. Faster and faster the train goes, until the
nothin' streams past and turns into desert. I looks through
the window. No plants, no animals, no rocks. Just sand and
sun, as far as I can see.

Now it's hot. Sweat runs down my neck and back, and
my tongue swells up, and my teeth feel like they're covered with slime, and my lips dry and crack and bleed.

The suit groans. I turns and there he is—right out of
nowhere—sittin' across the aisle. Sweat's drippin' down his
face, stainin' his three-piece and he looks even hotter than
me. Demon laughs when the suit asks for water. I keeps
my mouth shut, but somehow Demon knows. Still laughing, he plucks a glass out of the air and drinks in front of us.
Suit, he whines and begs, then tries to grab the water.
Demon snaps his fingers and a gang of slashers appears.

They ain't real slashers, though. Their faces have big
red eyes—just like Demon's—and their smiles make the
suit cower. Before I can move, they tie both of us to our
seats. Suit, he moans and curses, but I knows better. Slashers like their victims scared.

Demon, he's playin jib-jab again, like Jimmy Lee, and I
know he's lovin' it when Slasher makes his first cut down
the side of my face. I don't make any noise—not me, even
though the pain's worse than I ever felt, worse than anything Jimmy Lee did, worse than when the warden
strapped me down and threw the switch. But I don't let
them know. Not even when they cut off my fingers, one by
one. Not even when they stab out my left eye. Not even
when they chop out my heart and Demon eats it.

Finally they start on the suit, and Demon, he looks at
the blood runnin' down my ripped chest, and stares me
until those red, red eyes are all I can see.

Then I sleeps and dreams of Rose.

                        *   *   *

Sunday night. Rose still gone, hours. Hey slut, I'm goin to say, hey slut. I just know she's doin the cheatin' run. I feels it deep.

So will she, when she gets back. No slut makes a fool out of Jake Crowley.

I paces the hole and drinks until the booze is all dry and all that's left is one thin joint.

Before I lights up, Rose walks in—and suddenly I'm her and I'm happier than I've ever been in my life. Then he slaps me. I falls to the floor and he yells, "Hey, slut, who's the pumper?" Before I can say anything, he hits me again.

I just looks at him as my mouth is swellin' up. He's been drinkin', and I wonder why I stays with him. But I don't move. No, I just lays there, starin'. Should get up and hit him back—I knows it—but I can't because I loves him, and I've never loved anybody like I loves him.

When he asks again "Who's the pumper?" I wants to tell him no one, but I just keeps starin' because I knows he won't believe me.

He hits me some more. My face and chest and ribs ache, and I feels so bad down deep where his fists can't reach that I whispers real low—don't want him to hear—"Forgive him, he can't help it." I ain't even sure if I'm talkin' to God or myself. Maybe both.

But he does hear and I can see that cold, cold look on his face, like the time he killed Jimmy Lee. He glares at me as he closes up his fist and slams it into my left eye.

It hurts bad—he's never hit me so hard before—but not like it hurts when I know he's goin' to make me dead.

When I wake, Demon's right here, hand on my shoulder, his touch burnin' a hole. Slasher's gone, body's healed. Yet all I cares about is Demon's red stare and I whimpers a little as my eyes heavy up and I knows I have to do it all over again.

> Then I sleeps and dreams of Rose.
> Then I sleeps and dreams of Rose.
> Then I sleeps and dreams of Rose.
> Then I sleeps and dreams of Rose.

I wakes up screamin', standin' on this long wood platform with nothin' on but a dirty white T-shirt and my old prison jeans and a feelin' that I've been here before. But I'm wearin' a pair of shoes and that's somehow different.

Then it all comes back, all those dreams of me killin' Rose and me killin' me, and I runs into the nothin'. Out and out, until nothin's all around, gray peaceful nothin'.

But this time I ain't alone. Rose's body lays under each step, thousands, millions of them, rottin', stinkin' corpses with starin' blue eyes, and then no eyes, and then only holes in white skulls.

"Go away," I says. "Go away."

They start movin', crawlin' closer, surroundin' me, touchin' me. The smell's worse than anything I ever knew in the hole. I can't breathe. I can't get away. So I starts fightin' the bodies, pushin' and shovin', but more and more of them jump up until I can see those blue eyes starin' me everywhere.

"Go away! Go away!" I screams. "For god's sake, go away!"

They're gone and I'm kneeling on red sand like tiny pieces of glass that cuts my legs. I am cryin'.

As soon as I knows that, I wipes at my eyes. Hardliners never cry. No matter what I do, though, I can't stop thinkin' about all the times I hurt her and about how she still cared. I wonders if I will ever understand.

In the back of my head, I can hear Uncle Sammie laughin' and cursin'. He's saying over and over, "You're my boy. You like killin'." But deep down, I feels just like I did when Mama died, and I knows I have to choose.

Finally I says, "I'm sorry, Rose. Sorry."

When I looks up, I sees one piece of green near my left hand, green so real I reaches out and pricks my finger. A cactus.

Demon, he walks out of nowhere and grabs my hand. In a second, we're back on the train, and Suit, he's still sittin' across the aisle. When he looks at me, his eyes seem empty and I thinks of Rose and feels sorry for him. Demon stares me, eyes red, but smaller, just a little smaller. "Sit," he says.

I sits, all the time wondering about one green cactus and a pair of shoes, and what'll happen when the train finally stops. Demon, he nods.

Then my eyes heavy up, and I sleeps and dreams of Jimmy Lee.

A Plethora
of Angels

ROBERT SAMPSON

NO ONE AGREES why the angels came to Twin Tree. Some claim they were sent and find confirmation in Genesis or Revelation. Others, younger and infected by science, speak of an accidental opening rubbed between alternate worlds. Myself, sometimes I believe the angels were an expedition that went wrong. Sometimes I think that.

But what do I know? I'm guessing like everyone else. And I have an advantage: I was there at the beginning, watching the angels spill from that shimmery place near the cliff face.

Not from a hole. It was nothing like that. It was more a dim indentation of air close to the rock. That's a vague description, I grant you. How else could it be? When those angels poured out, all those hundreds of angels rustling like blown canvas, I never thought to look at their doorway.

Neither did Dad nor Uncle Win. We all stood unbelieving in that muddy road.

"A million butterflies," Uncle Win yelped.

"They're little women," Dad cried. He sounded shocked to his bones.

Both were wrong. The angels weren't either. To tell the truth, I don't know what they were. We called them angels, and they might have been. But at first, I thought they were doves.

Until one fluttered down not two feet from my eyes. Its wings pulsed air against my face. It peered at me with golden eyes. Its face was the size of my thumbnail, even-featured, with a minute round mouth. Clearly not a bird, or a woman, either.

This happened in Twin Tree, Alabama, my hometown, an undistinguished little place just south of the Tennessee line.

If it hadn't been for a week-long rain, I don't suppose Twin Tree would have come closer to angels than Christmas decorations.

For one solid week, cold gray water sheeted down. The creek shoved into our back fields, tumbling and rough, growling to itself. Trees slumped black and leafless and gloomy. When you went outside between rain spasms, ground water rose around your shoes.

This was a few years ago. Back then I was fresh out of the Army and inclined to spend my separation money on jeans and beer and seeing if the girls were still cute. Only I felt shaky about going back to college. I'd spent two years in Germany, defending the Free World against the Evil Empire. That was great for the Free World. But I wasn't sure the Army had left anything in my head except brown fuzz.

The university waited for me a month away, glowing with menace like a red-hot block. That scared me. I decided to hole up at home to get reacquainted with calculus.

Dad said only a wimp would get free of the military and start reading calculus. Probably he was right. Anyhow, I settled in with the book, the sky curdled, the rain roared down.

You might think that weather was perfect for studying. But I wasn't alone in the house. Mom and Dad were cooped in with me. Also Aunt Ellen and Uncle Win.

That's too many people in too few rooms, listening to the rain pouncing at the roof, and the air so wet you stuck to what you touched. After a week of it, we could barely stand to look at each other.

Finally, on Wednesday afternoon, the storm blew out. Dad tossed his cards down on the table and ducked outside. Said he wanted to check things. About an hour later,

he came tramping into the barn, where I was shoveling out
the horse stalls. I should have been at calculus, but stalls
were easier.

His pants hung black with water. Looking soaked and
cheerful, he said: "That rock face down by the creek, it's
got a crack in it big as the Mayor's mouth. Think we ought
to take some dynamite to it."

That dig was at Mayor Stevens of Twin Tree. When
Dad and his old friend, Sheriff Hock, get together over a
weekend, they keep mentioning the Mayor. He is a
crooked, rancid liar with the brains of a tick, according to
Dad, who doesn't often exaggerate.

I was tired of books and stalls, so I followed Dad to the
outbuilding where he keeps gas and dynamite and such
excitable stuff.

"Those rocks let go," Dad remarked, "they'll cripple up
some of those pet horses of yours. It's right by where they
water."

I knew that the cliff face is usually thirty feet uphill
from the creek. Any horse wanting to get hit by falling
rock would have to hike for the pleasure. Since Dad
sounded defensive, I figured he really wanted to hear the
bang. That's more entertaining than watching the trees
drip.

While he was fingering through the sawdust in the dynamite box for those yellow-brown sticks, I saw Uncle Win
picking his way toward us. He moved through the wet
grass as cautiously as a cat meeting company.

Sticking his head into the doorway, he said in his thin
voice: "By God, Sam, you take care now."

I saw Dad go a little tight around the mouth. Over the
past week, he'd heard a lot of advice from Uncle Win.

I said: "Dad's going to knock down some loose rock,
Win. Want to go watch?"

"Well, I was thinking of doing something else," Win
said. "But I guess I better go along. He might make some
fool mistake."

That was not the smartest thing to let out of his mouth.
That's why we slopped down to the creek in a haze of bad
feelings, the two of them biting off short sentences at each
other.

The fields stopped at a line of thin trees, tangled and
black. Beyond them bare rock angled down to a cut roar-

ing with water. Along the upper cliff ran a two-inch crack, deep and ugly, looking ready to drop by itself. I doubted that we needed dynamite. But this was entertainment, not business.

"Now," Dad said to me, "let's see if the Army learned you anything."

We fixed a couple of sticks with detonators and fuse. Dad eased them down into the crack, and I packed them good with mud and rock.

Win cleared his throat and edged toward the road. "Sam, you cut that fuse mighty short."

"Long enough," Dad growled. "No need to stand in the wet all day."

He bent to fire the fuse. As it spurted smoke, we stepped off down the road, Win well ahead of us. Dad ambled slowly behind, demonstrating that he knew exactly how long to cut a fuse.

We stopped in an angle of the road that gave a clear view of the cliff face. After a longish wait, there came a dull little thud, sounding like a sack of cement dropped off the tailgate. Vague gray mist hazed up. A section of rock shrugged loose and slumped leisurely into the creek, slapping up brown foam.

As the stonefall lolled into the water, a bray of thunder hit us. It was just one peal but violent enough to jar us good.

Uncle Win yelped like he'd been scalded. Bits of white swirled against the gray rock. A cloud of white spurted up, expanding, whirling, becoming huge, fluttering like confetti in the wind. White billowed and tumbled out over the creek, swelled above the trees. It sprayed all around us.

I heard Dad's breath suck in his mouth.

Wings shone all around us. I heard liquid chattering, musical and soft. The air smelled faintly of sunny flower beds.

"Look out!" yelled Uncle Win, throwing up his hands. "They'll bite!"

Out of the crazy whirl dropped an angel. It hung before me, balanced on slowly pulsing wings. It was a tiny lustrous thing, perhaps a foot between wing tips. The feathers were lovely soft white, edged by faint blue and transparent yellow. Gliding shades of white flowed like liquid across the inside of the wings.

Between the wings canted a slender body, long as your hand, the color of rich milk. It had golden eyes. Silver-white fuzz, like dandelion fluff, covered its head. It was completely beautiful.

Not that it was anything like a woman. It had no sex. Just a smooth, neat, dainty body. It smiled at me and uttered a single silver-tone.

The world around me became peculiar and far off. Only the angel seemed real. It was solid as crystal. Every detail of feathers, arms, face, shone clear and bright. Myself, I felt like a ghost shaking in the wind.

As if it understood my feelings, the angel cooed softly. Next thing I knew, it was perched on my shoulder, pressing up against my cheek.

The minute it touched me, I felt better. The shock faded out of me. The angel couldn't have weighed over a couple of ounces and it felt resilient and warm. It felt completely right sitting there.

"Comfortable?" I asked, turning my head.

Murmuring dainty sounds floated from it. One little hand touched my face. It didn't say words, then or later. The angels got along on musical sounds. And touches. Their touch explained more than words.

Dad was standing in the road, face an absolute blank. On each shoulder rode an angel. All around Win, angels wheeled, patting his bald head and trilling.

"Why, ain't these cute!" he yelped, reached out a hand. An angel swooped down on his fingers and let its bright wings trail.

By then, hundreds of angels swirled around us, reached out to touch, their golden eyes wide, as if we were something they had always heard about but never expected to see. Their wings made the sound of crushing tissue paper.

Sometime later, surrounded by angels, we splashed back to the house.

Mom was outside, pouring pellets into the dog dish. When she saw us, her mouth came open. She dropped the sack and grabbed for the door.

"Sam Williamson," she shouted, "don't you bring those things in here!"

Two or three angels swooped to pat her face and hair, and marvel at the way she talked, and cuddle on her shoulders.

"Why, aren't they dear?" she said. "Ellen! Ellen, come out here and look."

I saw Aunt Ellen glaring from inside the screen door. "Birds," she cried, her voice sharp with disgust. "Get in this house, Virginia Ann. They carry disease."

"They're not birds," Mom said. She opened the screen.

Ellen squealed once as the doorway turned white with wings. When her face reappeared, we could see the peevishness and fright leaving her.

"They're little people," she said. "Aren't they lovely?"

We all crowded into the kitchen. It was a busy place. Across the ceiling wheeled dozens of angels, darting, touching, staring, trilling. The five of us stared at each other.

"Where did these come from, Sam?" Mom asked.

So Dad had to tell about the rock wall and the dynamite.

By the look on Mom's face, she had strong feelings about dynamite and was inclined to talk about them. Before she got started, an angel pressed its minute fingers against her mouth.

Wide-eyed amazement caught Mom's face. Instead of scolding, she looked gently concerned, said: "Sam, you know that's dangerous."

"Now, honey," Dad said, "I didn't want to worry you."

They fell to hugging each other in a surprising way for mid-morning.

Uncle Win glanced sideways at them and cleared his throat. He said: "Lemme get the mop. I'll just clean me some mud off this floor."

I saw we'd brought a lot of field into the kitchen. So I slipped off my shoes, and collected Dad's and Win's, intending to scrape them off outside. I was at the door, when angels began bobbing and chiming, all excited, around the kitchen table. Their white arms waved toward the cards scattered there. They might have been pointing out snakes.

Dad stared from cards to angels. Finally he gave a big sigh. "Well, I guess . . ."

He tossed the cards into the wastebasket. That pleased the angels. They flocked all over him, cooing and flapping, caressing his hair.

I went outside and cleaned shoes. When I stepped back

into the kitchen, Uncle Win had finished mopping the floor. Dad was at the sink washing dishes, which I'd heard him swear he'd never do, no, sir, not ever in this life.

In the living room, Mom was on the telephone. Half a dozen angels sang at her. More glided around inspecting the room.

Mom said: "Reverend James. This is Mrs. Williamson. I want you to come right over. It's the most wonderful thing. . . ."

Aunt Ellen caught at my arm. "Now would you look at this," she said.

A wall of angels fluttered between us and the television. Their backs were to the tube; their little hands gestured us away. They made a nervous chittering sound, like hens watching a hawk.

"They don't like TV," Aunt Ellen said. "It's the *Spin for a Million* show, too."

"Change channels," I suggested.

"I did. They don't like anything."

She fretted, working her mouth. Finally she reached among the vibrating wings to punch the screen off. "I wouldn't want to upset the poor things."

The angels seemed delighted. After the menace of television ended, a swirl of them spun around her, making a sugary murmur. Others floated about the room, fingering the curtains and probing the ceiling corners. On the coffee table, a pair rustled through the magazines, shoving all the hunting issues onto the floor.

Along the wall, half a dozen angels inspected Mom's collection of family photographs. After a while, they broke into an indignant belling. Two of them got hold of Aunt Fay's photograph—the one where she looks so blond and racy—and twisted it to face the wall.

Aunt Ellen looked at me. "You know," she said, "I always wondered about Fay."

I thought we might get awful tired of angels in judgment. But I said: "Guess I might go try the calculus again."

"You just do that," Ellen said. She sounded vaguely elated. "Believe I'll just sew up some potholders for the church."

That overjoyed the angels. As they chirped around Ellen, I went in back and opened the book. Angels clustered around to see if they could help. After the second problem, they gave it up and sat around purring sympathetically.

Before I worked half a page, a car door slammed out front. Looking out the window, I saw the Reverend James of the United Holiness Congregation hurrying toward the house.

The Reverend was short and heavy. Fighting sin had dragged down the corners of his mouth and eyes and bent his head. He moved like a man carrying too many rocks.

His full voice said: "Sister Williamson, it's a joy and a blessing to see you—"

At the way his voice cut off, I judged he'd got a good look at the angels.

"What on earth?" he barked.

Mom said: "They're just angels, Reverend. You come right in."

I closed up the calculus and drifted out to the kitchen. It wasn't every day I could see a minister face to face with the stuff of sermons.

He stood in the kitchen, looking as edgy as a man with a snake in his pocket. "But they're tiny!" he boomed.

"I guess an angel can be any size it wants," Mom told him.

"Can't be angels." He jerked off his hat and waved it at them. That amused the angels. They flittered around his head, making tiny joyous sounds.

"The Holy Scriptures say—" he began, trying to shake himself and talk at the same time.

Whatever the Holy Scriptures had to say, it was lost as the angels' touch took effect. His face lightened and some of his deeper wrinkles smoothed out.

"God's mercy," he gasped. "It's a miracle."

"Aren't they sweet?" Mom asked.

"Under the circumstances," he said, "I think we might join together in prayer."

I caught an un-Christian flash in Dad's eyes. Reverend James' prayers were more like novels than short stories, and they tended to get louder as they got longer.

I grinned to myself. And the Reverend prayed.

All the angels settled down to listen, their wings folded respectfully, their little hands closed. Now and then a wing jerked to a more comfortable position. Their bare feet rubbed together.

The Reverend started with our family and he prayed for each of us until you wondered when we'd had time to get that sinful. Then he discussed the angels, the solar system, the mystery of the universe, and the Inscrutable Will. He didn't leave much out. Before he finished, I noticed a lot of wing folding and foot twisting. The angels seemed used to less comprehensive prayers.

When he finally thundered "Amen!" angels shot into the air to whirl crazily around the kitchen, belling and chiming, making a golden racket.

"Dare I hope," the Reverend said to Mom, "dare I hope that they will join us in church in demonstration of the Infinite Glory of God?"

"I should think so," she said.

As he drove off, a cloud of angels traveled with him, floating above his automobile. Even after he was out of sight, we could track the car by the flock dipping and wheeling and moving slowly off through the trees.

Dad laughed. "Gonna be some surprised people come Sunday."

As it worked out, some people were amazed before then.

Long before supper time, Mom got to worrying about what she could feed the angels.

"They eat manna," I said.

She said thoughtfully: "I should have asked Reverend James. I'm not that sure about manna."

"It looks like goldfish food," I said. "White and sort of thin and sweet."

"Maybe I can make some little cakes," she said, sidestepping as Dad slouched into the kitchen.

He was smiling as if a tooth hurt. One hand clutched his pipe and tobacco. On his shoulders rode a pair of angels, hiding their faces and making a dismal low moaning.

In a forced voice, he said: "Guess I think I'll give up smoking."

He banged open a drawer, slammed in pipe and tobacco, and whacked the drawer shut.

"I'm proud of you," Mom said. "You should of quit years ago."

"I suppose so," Dad said glumly. The angels took their faces out of their hands to make sparkling little sounds.

Mom said to me: "Jack, you better go down to the store. I need some good flour."

"I'll see if they got any manna," I said.

"Get me some chewing gum," Dad growled.

Which is why I walked into Doc Steeger's One Stop at five-thirty, wearing an angel on each shoulder.

To tell the truth, I wasn't that eager to walk in decorated with angels. It was sure to draw lip from Buddy, Doc's son. Buddy is a red-faced lump of fat with curly black hair and a mouth that never quits.

I figured that when I couldn't stand his cracks anymore, I'd lean over and quick bump him with my fist before the angels made me love him. But that wasn't necessary. Angels had arrived at the One Stop before me.

A swarm of them floated around that big old store, playing tag with the four-bladed ceiling fan. More fluttered along the top shelves, inspecting cereal boxes. In the hardware section, wings flashed among the churns and tin tubs.

Doc himself was busy taping a sheet of butcher paper across the beer coolers. On the paper he'd printed SECTION CLOSED. When he saw me, he called: "Don't sell beer no more, Jack," as if I never came in for anything else.

I told him no beer was needed and moved to the counter. Buddy slouched there, as greasy and sulky as ever. Angels loaded him down.

"You, too?" he asked, looking at my angels.

"Uh-huh."

"Well, I tell you this, Williamson," he snapped. He stopped, swallowed, glowered, said: "You and me, we've had our differences. But I want to tell you, I forgive you. I don't hold no hard feelings and hope you feel the same."

His eyes said he'd like to bend my neck.

I grinned into his fat face. "That's mighty Christian, Buddy. I'm glad you've quit being such a worthless, no-good pain—"

Three angels dropped between us, lamenting and fluttering pitifully. The angel on my left shoulder placed an arm over my mouth. It made a fading, weepy sound.

"Oh, shoot," I said. "I guess I feel the same way."

"It's no use," Buddy said. "I've tried. They don't let you be natural."

I decided not to tell him that when he was natural, he

was disgusting. Instead I gave him Mom's order. He waddled off, accompanied by a covey of angels, fluttering up and down the shelves. Their wings blew out an astonishing amount of dust.

While I was sitting on the counter, keeping quiet, the Mayor's wife, Amelia Stevens, trotted in. As usual, she wore a pound of powder and a ton of Indian jewelry. She was enjoying her share of angels, too.

Marching up to Doc, she asked: "You got any Bibles, Mr. Steeger?"

"Well, no," he said, coming away from the beer cooler. "I'm ordering a gross tomorrow."

"I need one tonight," she said. "It's for the Mayor."

I saw Doc's eyebrows reach for his hair. "The Mayor?"

"I guess we've misplaced our Bible," she said, looking as if she had borrowed someone else's smile. "The Mayor wants to read about angels."

I thought it more likely he wanted to check the description of Hell. But I had enough sense to keep quiet. I slipped off home with the groceries and told Dad that the Mayor couldn't find his Bible.

"Burn the fingers off him to touch it," Dad said.

That remark set the angels lamenting and looking sad. Dad swallowed and put on an unreal smile. "I tell you, Jack," he sighed, "this living a blameless life is hard."

He was right. Over the next few days, the effort to live blamelessly took a lot out of us. Some of us gave up beer. All of us gave up second helpings at dinner. The angels didn't eat that much, being content with five or six crumbs from Mom's cakes. I thought small flying creatures ate their own weight every day; but not these.

Since television upset the angels, we spent evenings sitting around in clean clothes, telling each other how good we felt, how glad we were to live in a state of grace.

The cards stayed in the wastebasket and the tobacco in the kitchen drawer. Uncle Win and Dad chewed about eleven packs of gum between them. I read calculus till I almost believed it. It was Sunday all week.

Now and then, when the silence grew terrible, the angels sang in chorus. They never sang anything that I knew. They favored slow chants, soft and remote, sounding like gold and silver sheets shimmering through each other. Bursts of trills fell across that sound like dashes of

rain. It was delicate, very lovely. But by the time you went
to bed, you felt you'd spent the whole night crying.

"You figure this is all they do in Heaven?" Uncle Win
asked. He had been slouched down in the chair for an
hour, staring at the backs of his hands.

I said: "I've been thinking about that. You know, when
it comes down to it, they don't have to be from Heaven.
They don't even have to be angels."

Dad rolled his eyes toward the kitchen. "Your mother
hear that, she'd set you straight in a hurry."

"I read something once," I said. "About parallel universes. If there gets to be a hole between them, you could
cross right over. See the angels could be from another
dimension. Maybe another star."

Dad sniffed. "You've been reading those magazines.
They make you think funny."

"Besides," I added, "the angels don't even understand
English. They just react to voice tones."

Uncle Win looked as blank as if he'd been erased and
Dad snorted and grinned. "Well, look here," I said, picking
up an angel. After making sure that Aunt Ellen and Mom
were in the kitchen, I addressed the angel in a loving,
respectful voice, using some of the words I'd learned while
defending the Free World. Given the right tone, they were
exactly the right words for describing officers or removing
scale from metal.

"Merciful salvation," Dad said sharply. "Sounds like
you were brought up behind a mule."

The angel, which had been playing contentedly with
my fingers, went stiff at the sound of his voice. It wailed
dolefully.

"Good grief," he said.

"See," I told him. "It's all in the voice."

"Well, I'll be damned," Uncle Win said, gentle-voiced.
When the angel didn't respond to that, Win grinned all
over. Lifting out of his chair, he hurried off to practice his
art on other angels.

Dad shook his head. "I don't want to hear such talk. I
brought you up better than that. Angels probably don't
speak English in Heaven. Old Testament, likely."

I was feeling ashamed that I had deceived the angel, so
I stroked its back with a finger, making it arc its wings in

pleasure. I said: "They may look like angels. But I bet they're extraterrestrials."

"You let the women hear you," Dad said, "and there'll be war."

But I noticed elation in his eyes. I suspect he was thinking more about his pipe than angelic origins.

The next morning, Saturday, Dad rose from the breakfast table and said: "I'm going to Twin Tree. Want to see about a fan belt."

"I'll come along and help," I said.

Fifteen or twenty angels seemed interested in fan belts, too. No sooner did they get outside, away from the choral society, than they exploded straight up into the sky. We stood watching them roll and tumble and spread their arms to plunge headlong through the sunlight. They were winged creatures, after all. And wings like to fly. Not sit in a narrow house, harmonizing in five sharps and two intervals.

"Happy," I said, squinting up at them.

"So'm I," Dad said.

I realized then that, for the first time in days, neither one of us had an angel perched on him.

"We get back home," Dad said, "I'm going to open me a beer, angels or not. Being good's dry work."

"We can get us a couple in town," I said.

If I were paid for predicting, I wouldn't have made a cent. The two taverns in town were shut tight, blinds drawn, lights out. On Saturday morning, yet.

The one place in town doing big business was the United Holiness Congregational church. Cars and trucks, all bright with polish, jammed the parking lot. From the open doors surged singing. It wasn't as sweet as angel music, but it was enthusiastic.

Dad listened without unusual excitement. "I always sort of liked Willie Nelson," he remarked. And didn't say a thing more till we parked at Blackwort's Transportation City.

Blackwort's huge sign that usually flashed CRAZY DEALS in three colors was dark. Dad vanished through the open door. I stayed outside, enjoying the sun.

The air smelled softly sweet, like washed leaves. The sky glowed transparent blue, smooth and rich as glaze. I felt light and mildly foolish. Off over the center of town, a flock of angels drifted in a sleepy shifting spiral.

As I sprawled against the truck, enjoying the feel of warm metal, an angel glided over Blackwort's roof and curved lazily toward me.

I jerked erect, scowling at it, wondering what would happen if I ducked when it tried to sit on me. But that I never found out. The angel paid no attention to me.

As it curved by, not ten feet away, I saw that it peered eagerly back toward Blackwort's roof. Its wings glowed bright pink in the sunshine. It was the first angel I'd seen with colored wings.

As it floated overhead, I got the second shock of the day.

It was a little woman, all right. No question about it. Firm little breasts rose from the smooth white chest. Her lips shone bright red.

As she angled smoothly away, another angel streaked past. He was a he, too. No mistake. Blue-tinted wings twitched just a fraction, flicking him above the truck.

Over the middle of the road, he caught up with pink wing. They linked arms. Silver sound spilled out of the air, like tiny laughing. They curved up past the telephone lines, out of sight.

When Dad came out, carrying his fan belt, I was still squinting open-mouthed at the sky.

He said: "That Blackwort's gone slap crazy. Know what he's about? He's in there writing refund checks. Said the angels made him realize how bad he's been overcharging his customers. Wants to make it up to them."

"Know what I just saw?" I cried, all excited.

"He's worked back through 1984," Dad said. "Now he's starting on 1983. What's the matter with you?"

I told him what I'd seem. He laughed till he dropped the fan belt. "Why, they've been around people too much," he yelled. "Stands to reason. Little women. Now I heard it all."

He leaned against the truck, ha-ha-ing till I got disgusted and offered to drive.

By rights we should have headed home. But I was curious to see more angels holding hands. So I drove toward the center of town.

It was quiet as the Intensive Care ward. Nobody was on

the streets. Half the stores were closed. Nothing moved except a dozen angels whizzing among the trees. One of them, the color of new grass, chased one a light lemon shade. I saw at least a dozen reds and blues, and a single gaudy purple fellow.

"Pull over there by the jail," Dad said. His eyes were swollen from laughing. "I'll just stop in and tell the Sheriff to do something about that undressed lady."

I trailed him into the jail, which was also the post office, police station, and court. It was a low brick building that had been painted gray before it was painted white. Both colors were flaking off. Inside it smelled like wax and old cigarettes.

Dad pushed open the door to the Sheriff's office. We stepped into a narrow room packed with desks and filing cabinets heaped with papers. A tall, thin lady, with a cigarette hanging out of her mouth, tapped at a computer keyboard. At her elbow sat an ashtray mounded with cigarette butts. Beside it sprawled an angel, head propped on one arm, watching her. The angel had blue wings and looked as if he needed a shave.

"Hey, Dottie," Dad said, looking sideways at the angel. "Where's the Sheriff?"

"In the jail," she said, not looking up.

"Good place for him," Dad said. "I want to see him."

"Can't," she said. "Not visiting hours."

She spurted smoke down over the angel. Instead of leaping to her shoulder and looking unhappy, he tipped back his head to suck in a long breath. It was a he and could have done with a pair of pants.

"What's visiting hours got to do with it?" Dad asked.

"You can't see prisoners except at visiting hours." Her voice would have curdled lemon juice.

"Sheriff Hock!"

"Put himself in jail yesterday. Said he was in with bootleggers and should be locked up." She snorted. "I think he's gone crazy. Been listening to too many angels. I'm the only one here and I don't have time to—"

The phone rang. She scooped it up and, in a voice like cut glass, said: "Sheriff's office." A pause. "OK, Mildred. I dunno what we can do. But I'll send somebody around."

Whacking down the phone, she punched the intercom. "Johnny. You there, Johnny? Damn that fool, he's never there when—Hello, Johnny. Listen, Mildred Panatokis just called. Said there's a bunch of angels acting dirty outside her house. Run over and calm her down, will you?"

She slapped off the intercom and attacked the computer again.

Dad cleared his throat loudly. "About the Sheriff . . ."

"Got the cell right next to the Mayor's," she said irritably. "Give me a break, Sam. I got to get this report out by twelve."

"What did the Mayor do?"

"Turned himself in," she snarled. "I had to listen to him confess half the night. If we arrested everybody he named, we'd put wire around the town and call it Twin Tree Concentration Camp."

The angel rolled over on his stomach and sniggered.

"What's all that color on his wings?" I asked.

She transferred her glare from Dad to me. "It's that dry pigment. Mix it with water and you get poster paint. It's a big fad with the angels. Now, please, for God's sake, close the door on your way out."

As I closed the door, the angel lifted a butt from the ash tray and took a long sniff.

I stamped to the truck, mad to my bones.

"What's the matter?" Dad asked.

"Nothing."

A purple feather drifted down the windshield and blew across the hood. Overhead, two angels, pink and purple, rolled over and over across the sky, tightly clenched.

Squinting up at them, Dad remarked: "They sure learned quick."

"I liked them better when they were white." My own violence surprised me. "They were pretty, white."

"Things change," he said after a while.

We drove home silently. Not an angel returned with us. All the way back, I felt waves of anger beating in me. I felt sorry for the angels, embarrassed for them. Every time I thought of the purple and pink angels clinging to each other, I got mad all over again.

This week, gaudy feathers. Bright lips. Sex characteristics. Next week, they'd be swilling beer and shortchanging friends.

We hadn't meant to contaminate them. It was completely accidental. That's what burned me. For some reason or the other, they came rushing into this world. Unwary, friendly, impressionable, vulnerable to our casual bad habits. I felt ashamed for the human race.

If I'd come across Buddy Steeger just then, I'd have smacked his fat face sideways.

As we drove up to our house, Aunt Ellen came scampering to meet us. She oozed happy malice. "Those angels are hugging each other," she called. "I call that scandalous."

Scandalous was the word. While we had been gone, there had been an influx of decadence. Pairs of brightly colored angels threshed along the ceiling, piping and exuberant. Little legs kicked. A feather tumbled down.

"It was just half an hour ago," Aunt Ellen said. "Came flying in here like they'd gone crazy. Now look." She waved fiercely at an intertwined couple at the top of the curtains. "Stop that! Shoo!"

On the coffee table sat an angel, wings rigidly outstretched. Two others brushed pink powder onto her feathers. A dozen others watched, jingling musically among themselves. Some wore lipstick and sat swelling out their tiny breasts.

Mom eyed us grimly. "I'm going to have to pass out nightgowns," she said. "I don't hold with all this nakedness."

"All over Twin Trees the same way," I said, ashamed to look at the angels.

Cool air puffed in the side door, bringing faint thunder.

A cluster of white angels huddled on a bookcase watched the proceedings with amazed golden eyes. They looked fascinated and scared. I stalked over to them, said:

"Do something. They're your friends, aren't they? Settle them down. Don't just sit there."

"They don't understand the language, Jack," Dad drawled.

They understood my tone, though. They wouldn't look at me. They pressed close together, gripping hands, all humped up and looking sick. Even their feathers looked miserable.

Hot flecks of anger swam in me. Turning on my heel, I said to the angel on the coffee table: "Now stop that. Stop messing yourself up. You look terrible. You like like a prize from the midway."

Pink wings fluttered, throwing off a faint cloud of powder. The angel tipped back her head, impertinence in every line. She spilled out crystal teasing tones and darted to the top of a window. She began to posture and prance.

Thunder muttered in the distance. At the sound, the white angels bobbed and twittered. They sounded like hysterical chickens.

"Comin' up rain," Dad said, cocking his head. "I do admit, Jack, they don't act like they came from Heaven."

"They're heavenly creatures," Mom said grimly. "Or they used to be."

"They should have better sense," he said.

"We're heavenly creatures," Mom said, "and look at us."

In the kitchen, a dozen angels pressed against the screen door, peering toward the thunder. I opened the door for them. One by one, they soared out, skimming across the grass, flashing up suddenly to curve smoothly away above the trees.

The sky was clear but that dull thunder pulsed to my left.

Dad came to stand beside me. "It thundered when they came," he said.

Wings flashed and a velvet touch crossed my hand. A white angel hovered near my face. It uttered a single melancholy syllable. As I reached out, the angel pressed its face against my finger. Then it rustled away through the open door.

That seemed so much like a goodbye that I stepped outside to watch its flight. It was gone. High across the cloudless sky hurried a disorderly stream of angels. Uneven lines of them undulated overhead, white and blue and red, like bits of a shattered rainbow.

Dad shaded his eyes. "They're coming down at the creek."

"Let's run down there and watch," I said.

Uncle Win joined us in the yard. He looked bright-eyed and tickled. "You should of seen that pink angel dance," he said. "Say, when I was in Philadelphia—I guess it was in 1943—I paid three dollars to watch a worse dance than that."

Another rush of angels pushed from the kitchen. Crying in their sweet voices, they sailed past, wings rattling as they angled into the air. Among them, I glimpsed the pink-winged angel. She spiraled above my head, laughing down, making a teasing face.

"Best we get moving," Dad said.

Thunder growled.

Above the creek, the air churned with angels, thousands of them. They angled in clusters from the sky, flocking over the fields, swirling among the trees. They spun like merging galaxies, suns flashing among suns. The air shivered with the beat of wings.

I felt the hard pulse of my heart; my breath came short.

Over the creek, the whirling fed into a thick stream of angels that rushed steeply toward the gray rock wall. No thunder now. Only the sound of wings, and a softer sighing sound, like shaken silk. As the angels plunged into the stream, their wings folded; arms and legs extended like divers, they swept straight toward the rock.

To vanish a few inches from the wall. Even then, I never thought to look hard at their doorway.

I felt stifled. Images swarmed through my head and twisting bits of words. I thought of angry gods and other worlds, punishment, wings. My brains had melted to soup.

High above us, at the edge of the stream, sun glowed on pink wings. I saw a little arm wave jauntily toward us. Pink Wing seemed merrily unconcerned. No shadow of retribution marred that airy gesture.

She plunged smoothly into the stream and was gone.

I saw with a shock that the stream of angels had thinned. A few stragglers shot past, minnows fleeing for shelter. Thunder growled over the creek. The sound of wings stopped.

That was all. No angels. No depression in the air. All gone. Leaving behind only the liquid purling of the creek, a sound coarse after the delicate crying of the angels. A sore emptiness opened in me.

"Well, that's done," Dad said.

We moved slowly to the lip of the rock wall, peering down at the rocks below and the creek sliding past. A few straggling redbud grew at the edge. Behind them, a long ugly hole had opened in the soil, as if a groundhog tunnel had collapsed there.

Uncle Win knelt at the edge and stared over. "What I want to know is where those angels got to? Stands to reason, they must of gone someplace."

He sniffed sharply. "Stinks here. You can still smell the dynamite."

Faint breeze rattled limbs. I saw shadows twitch across Win's back and slip across his neck.

I took a quick step back. Just for a second, I seemed to see movement down in that hole. Movement and a transient glitter like mica bits, bright as tiny eyes.

The breeze died and the shadows stopped moving and, for the life of me, I couldn't decide whether one had flowed down inside Win's collar or not.

"Uncle Win," I said. "That sure looks like a snake hole."

"Snakes," he yelped, bouncing up away from the hole. "Lord, I purely hate snakes."

I saw Dad staring hard at the hole. A startled expression was smoothing from his face. "We best get back," he said loudly.

"Lord, yes," Win said. "I tell you what I want right now. It just come over me that I need a bottle of beer and a good game of stud."

I whispered to Dad: "Did you see it too? In the hole?"

"Didn't see a thing," he told me. "Not a thing."

He may have been right at that. Still I wasn't sure. It seems reasonable to me that if you can have angels, you can also have whatever things are opposite to angels.

So after dark, I borrowed some dynamite and eased off down to the creek. I used plenty of fuse. I was sitting at the kitchen table, having a beer and watching the card game, when that distant thud finally came.

Dad looked up from his cards. His eyes jerked around to mine. But he didn't say anything. No need to explain. He knew that sound. And I saw by his expression that he'd been thinking about the hole near the redbuds.

There's just no point taking chances. Not when dynamite is so cheap.

Strange
Attractors

LORI ANN WHITE

H E MIGHT BE LOST in the Utah desert with a ruined compass, he might have a half-empty canteen and no shelter, but for Sid Porter, the last straw was his chocolate-coated jeweler's loupe. He wondered again how he could have been dumb enough to save the candy bars from his lunch as an afternoon snack. At least he would have no trouble backtracking to the garnet field where he'd spent a good part of the morning. He could follow all the chocolate smears both rear jeans pockets had left on the rocks where he had sat to rest.

The sun was mid-afternoon high, and not even the steep sides of the arroyo Sid was following offered any shade. He gave up and slung his field pack beside the nearest rock, then sat with an *oof*, like a seat cushion being beaten of dust. Squinting past tumbled boulders toward the next bend, Sid pictured the arroyo opening out onto the flat, dry bed of dead Sevier Lake, where the wulfenite assay camp was set up, with its battered trucks, dusty tents, and boiled, gritty water. But the vision failed to stir him. He made it a point not to get up for fantasies.

The thought of maps hung with him, though, maps everywhere in that camp. Including the map he had forgotten. Although Sid swore he'd slipped it in his pack just before Ginny came sprinting out of Bill's tent, stark naked, a scorpion clinging to her ass.

He grinned at the memory. The camp had been pretty chaotic for a while, and not just the normal "all Hell's broken loose" sort of chaos, but that new kind of chaos that was being written up in all the journals. What was that term in the *Scientific American* article Sid had just finished? "Strange attractors"? That was Ginny and Bill, all right.

Sid raised his canteen and sloshed it experimentally. Still over half full. He uncapped it and lifted it in a toast. To unlikely lovers? No, that sounded too much like him and Judy. He would drink to the Lady Molybdenum. Deceptively soft and easy to work with, but she was a tough old bitch, and a little bit of her went a long way. "To Molly Be Damned," Sid muttered. His lips cracked when he pulled them apart, and he winced. Best not to talk to himself anyway. Judy hated it when he talked to himself. She would say, "Hey, Sid. Look at me. Give the words to me." He would try, but talking to her felt exactly the same.

He squinted up at the sun, letting its light dazzle pictures of Judy away. Then he pulled out his compass. It was filled with sweet brown gook that had oozed through a crack in the crystal. He'd already wiped off the little crispy things. Sid gripped it tight, tighter, felt the crystal give again, and cocked his arm to throw. Let the ants and lizards discover the joys of a sugar high. Just give him one good flare and a gun to shoot it with.

"You're lost."

Sid spun about, trying to track the voice, and slid off the side of the rock, landing on his pack with a grunt. The compass dropped into his lap. Staring into the pure, hot sky, Sid saw the blocky silhouette of a woman wearing overblouse and tiered skirt, standing on the edge of the wash. The sun cutting over her left shoulder made his eyes tear. Cheap trick, thought Sid.

"I'm lost. No shit." Silence. Sid coughed, and it hurt. "I mean, yes, I'm lost. Can you help me get back to camp? Or at least point me toward the highway? I mean, I'm with the USGS assay team, but I got separated—"

"Your pattern," she interrupted him, her voice a low, smooth contralto. "Your pattern is so small and round and regular. Like little frozen rabbit turds. How sad."

"Pattern?" Sid blinked; sweat burned in his eyes and he closed them. He had no idea what she was talking about, but thought he should probably feel insulted.

"Pattern," the woman said, agreeably enough. "We each have a pattern. The patterns make our lives, like the patterns of the corn and the sheep." She spoke slowly and deliberately, and Sid, listening to her, felt the tired despair of one so close, yet so far. She wasn't going to lead him anywhere. Except perhaps some nut-filled religious commune.

"The corn grows every summer, but sometimes it grows thick, sometimes it is weak and dry. The sheep lamb every spring, but some die, some twins are born. The pattern changes, but remains the same. And they grow. As we grow. But some men do not grow. They do not change. Their patterns become frozen, like the patterns of a finely woven blanket. Beautiful to see, but never changing. Or a pattern shrinks away to nothing and vanishes, and the man is no more, though he walks among his friends."

"Just like death and taxes," muttered Sid. He squinted up at the sharp silhouette. "Who the hell are you?" he asked.

"You would ask that," she said, and disappeared.

"Whoa." Sid blinked again. He hoisted himself slowly up onto the rock and stretched out his legs, so he could think. The canteen sloshed at his side.

"Hell." Ray Bearchild. It must have been Ray. Ray, with some elixir of his ungodly mushrooms, in Sid's canteen. All the geologists had their reasons for putting up with fieldwork—Sid himself had found an incredible, third-of-a-carat, gem-quality sapphire when he should have been drilling for oil shale—but Ray's motive was legendary throughout the region. Ray went out in the field so he could take mushrooms in the desert night and stare up at the stars until his eyeballs dried out.

But Ray was the closest thing Sid had to a friend on the whole crew. Sid rested his forearms on his knees and let the sweat drip off his face. "Don't kid yourself," he said. Ray was the closest thing he had to a friend. They'd met at an auction of loose stones, both bidding determinedly for a piece of fine turquoise. Ray had gotten it, and Sid had almost turned on his heel and left right then, but instead he had gone to the display table to say good-bye to the piece. He'd gotten a closer look at Ray, at the silver and turquoise rings encrusting his fingers, the conches on his belt, the silver around his wrist. It was all very fine, and, although Sid didn't mount his stones—he never wore jewelry, and he never gave his stones away, so why bother— he admired good work. "You do this?" he'd asked. Ray had looked around, startled, then nodded once. "I'm glad you got the piece," Sid had said, and surprised himself by saying it. Ray had invited him to coffee, and they had talked stones ever since.

But he shouldn't kid himself about that, either. Judy was Ray's sister, and Ray, Sid recalled, had handed him his canteen as he fled the uproar that morning. Either that, or —eat your heart out, Carlos Castaneda.

No. The woman was a hallucination. Plain and simple. Not good. Not good at all.

Sid did not know which scared him more—the thought of being lost in the desert, or the thought of being lost in the drug. He managed a dry chuckle. No contest. The discomfort of western Utah was familiar, manageable. He knew the high plateau land, scrubby with sagebrush, rubbled with boulders, inhabited by scuttling lizards the same color as the gritty yellow dust that coated everything: hair, clothes, food, throat.

This he'd learned while finding the hidden stones: the feces-brown pebbles of garnet; the dull blue-green of malachite; the opal, trapped in its muddy matrix and awaiting a gentle tap of his hammer to split it open and let its rainbows flow. Apache tears, carnelian, agate, quartz. The sun was lover to all of them, and he owned the light born of the union. It paid for scrabbling in the dirt.

Hallucinations, visions—they would own him. Once Sid had dreamed about lying outside at night, in the middle of a vast, flat desert land, under a sky crowded with stars. He was naked, but not cold, and soon a warm, multicolored light began to drip onto him, as though all the stars were gems, and something was squeezing the gem juice from them. It flickered and splashed onto Sid, and where it touched he bubbled and sizzled like cheese on a pizza. "Help me, I'm melting!" he screamed, but no one heard, and Sid oozed down into the earth, past buried dinosaur bones and reservoirs of oil, into hot fire that swept him up like a river. He realized it would be a long, long time before his essence was compressed into diamond.

Sid would much rather be lost than on drugs. And to be both at once—

He closed his eyes, tried to calm his thoughts, tried to analyze what he felt, smelled, heard. Everything seemed normal enough. Perhaps a bit too bright and hard-edged, as though there was suddenly a greater distance between objects and their backgrounds. His sweaty kerchief chafed his neck. His stomach rumbled. No smelling colors, or tasting the feel of the grit that had worked its way into his boots. No tasting much of anything, with his dry, swollen tongue.

"What will you do when you have to drink again?"

He almost elbowed her in the eye as he spun to look at her. She sat next to him, silver conches braided into her black hair and decorating her thick, deep-blue velveteen blouse. Her skirt, a dark emerald green, fanned out across the baked mud in ripples of broomstick pleats. She wore a necklace of heavy round beads, turquoise, coral, jet, white shell. Sid ached to run his fingertips across the skin of her face; it was a rich, burnished red-brown, like a polished shard of red obsidian. Like Judy's skin. But with grit and a soft cloth, he knew he could make it smoother.

"Aren't you hot in that get-up?" he asked.

"No." She smiled; her teeth were large and white. Her hands, too, were abnormally large; clasped loosely, they lay in her lap like a grindstone. "And you? Are you hot? Are you thirsty? What will you do now?"

Anger flared, so intensely that Sid's hands began to shake. He took a deep breath before answering. "I'll sit. I'll wait. If I have to, I'll drink the rest of the water in my canteen. Even if it means talking to you for the rest of the day."

She nodded at that. "You asked me for help," she said. "Do you no longer need it?"

"Heck, no. Maybe you can just channel me right back to camp, huh?"

The woman laid a large hand on Sid's thigh. She felt real enough. The heat of her palm made his skin itch. "Have you even considered that you might not be drugged?"

"God damn it." Sid shoved her away and stood awkwardly, clinging to the rock for balance. "Who are you? What do you want from me?"

"I want you to ask the right questions," she said, and disappeared again.

"Jesus." Sid looked around for something to throw. "Bitch," he muttered. He hadn't thought he'd had enough experience with women to create such a realistic one. Just like Judy, always thinking he should be able to read her mind, not to mention remember every little detail: birthdays, anniversaries, the perfume she wore when they first met, the clothing he pulled off her when they first made love.

Maybe he should skip being rescued, just stay here in the desert, dig rocks, turn yellow in the dust. Except the desert could be just as demanding as any woman.

If he really wanted to stay alive.

Oh, bullshit. He had options. As much as Sid hated the thought, he would have to keep drinking the water. He was rapidly dehydrating. But, he didn't seem to be on too intense a trip (were they still called trips?) and before he drank again, he would gather a good pile of sagebrush and light a fire. Damn stuff was oily, and should smoke like hell. Next best thing to a flare. He couldn't have gone far from camp; there was a good chance someone would spot it. Then, he could drink up and chat with the weird woman until the others found him.

Climbing up the wall of the arroyo was more difficult than Sid had anticipated. It had been pounded smooth by every flash flood, as solid and forceful as a battering ram, for hundreds of years. He had to chip handholds with his rock hammer.

Once on the bank of the wash, Sid stopped to catch his breath. He was sweating even more freely now, though the heat and light of the sun seemed distant. Of more immediate concern were the little black dots clustering before his eyes. He dropped to his knees and took deep breaths until the dizziness passed. Then he looked around.

Any faint hope of seeing the camp from the plateau vanished. The camp and the flat, dry bed of Sevier Lake could be in any direction, obscured by the heat waves dancing up from the ground. He did see a rock large enough to cast a shadow, and he headed for it, ignoring the sharp crackles of little scuttling creatures in the brush around him.

Sid glanced at his watch. About four-thirty. Several hours of daylight left. It would be a long time before he was really missed, although they were all supposed to report back to Ryan, the project's chief geologist, by six, to compare and correlate the day's findings. Perhaps he would spot *their* smoke. Unfortunately, he expected to be higher than a kite by then.

"Sagebrush, sagebrush." Sid told himself to stand up and get busy. But crouching in the shade was so nice. Just being out of the direct heat of the sun seemed to lift a weight from the top of his head. Damn it all, couldn't a guy ever just relax? Did he always have to be pushing, pushing, pushing?

"In this case, yes," Sid told himself. He heaved himself to his feet and took a deep breath, knowing that as soon as he stepped into the heat, his breath would be sucked from him.

After clearing a small fire-pit, Sid scrounged for loose brush. Soon, he was reduced to hacking off branches with his rock chisel, and swearing in a quiet monotone with each stroke. He quit when he thought he heard the brush swear back. He was afraid it might try to bite him next.

When smoke was puffing satisfactorily up into the clear blue, Sid backed away from the sparks into shade. He no longer had to crouch, but collapsed gratefully against the rock anyway, reaching for his canteen. Damn Ray's drugs. The stuff had scarcely affected him, anyway. The dose in his water must have been just enough to bring on the weird woman.

"You may call me the Dine'h."

Sid stiffened. She was back, before he'd taken the first swig. The heat, this time. That was it. He drank, and the warm, gritty water had never soothed him so.

It was hard, but Sid forced himself to stop after a few swallows. He capped the canteen, and wiped his mouth on the back of his hand. Then, he looked at her. This time her hair was tied off her neck in a chongo, and her face was patterned in yellow cornmeal. "You are Navajo."

She did not answer.

"Aren't you a ways north of home?"

"My people roamed this entire basin long before your

kind herded us into a pen." She spat. "Not even sheep are penned."

Sid raised his hands. "That wasn't me," he said, then realized he had just spoken precisely the wrong words.

Dine'h looked at him, her eyes narrowing. Otherwise her broad face remained impassive. "No, you are correct. It was not you," she said. "You do nothing."

"Well, shit. What do you want me to do? I do my job, I take care of myself, I stay out of people's way. What's wrong with that?" Now it was Sid's turn to glare, though he wasn't quite sure why her words upset him.

"Nothing. I want you to do nothing."

"Well, then, what do you do, besides appearing to poor schmucks who really just want a good canteen of water and a way home? Besides spouting crap, I mean."

"I change."

Sid watched her for a moment. Then he stood and threw more brush on the fire. Almost six by his watch. They should start looking for him soon. But the sun would not set until after eight. And the air would not start to cool until some time after that. He returned to his seat. "That simple, huh?"

"They won't come for you, Sid."

He looked at her suspiciously.

"There's been a storm in the mountains, and your camp is in danger from flash flooding. They must move to a safe place. They will wait for you as long as they are able, then leave. They will return for you in the morning."

Despite himself, Sid almost believed her. She sounded so calm, so reasoned. "I can last," he said. "I've got some water. No food, but hell, if I can't be rich, at least I can be thin."

"Desert nights are cold."

"Stop it." Sid leaned his head back against the rock and closed his eyes. "Just stop it, please." He'd had no idea he was such a pessimist. "I'll rest now, and stay up tonight to feed the fire." When he opened his eyes to look at her, she was gone.

Six o'clock came and went, followed by seven, then eight. The sun ballooned as it sank, turning into a huge, red, rippling ball. A sunset breeze kicked up, drying the sweat on Sid's face, making him shiver. He continued to feed the fire and chop more brush. He'd considered taking a nap, but was filled with the restless, nervous energy that sometimes accompanies exhaustion. The Dine'h's words kept playing over in his mind. Patterns that weren't patterns. Growth, stagnation, death. She changed. He did nothing.

He stood and paced around his fire. She was describing attractors. Strange attractors again. Patterns that described the actions of complex systems. Like weather, and drifting smoke, and the beating of his heart. The patterns looked like skewed spirograph designs that never repeated themselves exactly.

Sid trickled some water in his mouth and waited for the Dine'h to reappear. She did not. He sloshed the canteen experimentally. About a quarter left. "Plenty," he whispered. "Plenty."

No one came. Sid even managed to rouse himself during a magical half hour when the shadows of the rocks looked like portals into night and the whole land was drenched in rose and gold. But the short, beautiful time did not last, and then he had to rouse himself again, as darkness came and the temperature began to drop.

He scooted closer to fire, until he reached a delicate equilibrium between being warm and being able to breathe through the thick smoke. But warm was not warm enough. The sage brush did not burn hotly.

Night sounds closed around him and Sid retreated into his own misery. He dared not drink enough to really relieve his thirst, and his hunger had grown to a sharp pain in his stomach and head. His skin, coated with dirt and the salt of dried sweat, itched. He tried to settle himself on the hard ground and wrapped his arms about his knees. He coughed and leaned away from the smoke. For a moment, he was face into a stiff breeze blowing down from the Confusion Mountains. He thought it smelled sweet and charged, like rain. Had the Dine'h been correct about the rain?

What else had she talked about? It was obvious to Sid where the woman and her words came from: all the bits and pieces and misinformation cluttering his own mind. Stories from Ray about his childhood, glimpses of Judy that he got too seldom, articles that he'd read in a magazine. That he could combine them in such an imaginative way surprised him, and he struggled to recall her words. "Or the pattern shrinks away into nothing and the man is no more, though he walks among his friends."

What had she meant by that?

Sid struggled to remember what he'd read in the article. Perhaps the Dine'h had a point. These attractors described energy systems. What was each separate, living creature but a discrete energy system? Perhaps it could be defined by its own specific pattern. In that case, what would happen when the creature died? Could the pattern continue? Or would it decay into a repeating pattern, and then into the spiral of ultimate entropy and death?

What happened if a pattern decayed while the creature was still living?

"You do nothing," she had said. "I change."

"This is bullshit," Sid whispered. "Sheer, utter bullshit."

One more phrase popped into his head. "Have you considered that you are not drugged?"

Sid drank again, defiantly, and waited for the gem juice.

He almost hoped the Dine'h came back instead. There was one question Sid wanted to ask her.

"Hey!" he yelled. "Hey! Why did Ray do this?" Sid could usually ignore what other people did to him. But he could no longer ignore the question of Ray and the drugs. From everything Sid had ever heard, friends did not do such things. Friendships were like a nice piece of amber: tough, and glowing, and sometimes more interesting for the bugs trapped within. But this was not a bug. This was a knife in the back.

The Dine'h touched his shoulder, and Sid stiffened, although he didn't turn around. He must be getting used to her popping in like this. She said again, in a voice so warm with sympathy Sid wanted to hold up his hands to it, "You are lost."

"I thought we'd already decided that."

"No. I have decided you are lost. You have decided you cannot find your camp." Sid turned to look at her. She sat next to him, smiling. The fire stained her silver jewelry a ruddy hue, and her eyes were lost in the smoke and darkness. "Perhaps your friend is your friend, and is concerned that someday you will no longer walk with him."

"That's no excuse for spiking my canteen." What happens if I die out here? Sid thought, but he was not yet ready to say those words aloud.

"You are already dying," said the Dine'h calmly. "And when you die your family will gather about your coffin and scatter your stones upon you, and they will break your bones and sink through your flesh." Sid froze, his mind blank. A dark wave washed through him and he raised a hand, turned to strike her. And stopped.

"My children no longer have their own world in which to grow, but they will learn and thrive. They wear your clothes, eat your food, sleep in your houses, take your jobs. And they will live." She disappeared.

"Damn," Sid whispered. "Damn, damn, damn." It wasn't his world. She just didn't realize it wasn't his world. His world was what he tried to make with his stones. A beautiful world. He had tried other ways, too. Judy. He didn't know if he loved her or not, he wanted to see how his friendship with Ray progressed, but he knew he liked to watch the way she moved when she brushed her hair, and he liked to see her smile, and he liked to listen to her soft words.

But she'd given him an ultimatum: stop spending all his time in the field, or stop expecting her to be there when he got back. Fine. He would expect nothing from her.

And Ray—

Sid shook his head, rocked back and forth with his arms wrapped around his knees. He had his stones. He was so certain of them, it was hard to step away toward something else. He reached for the soft chamois bag holding the garnets he'd found that day, and patted at his waist until he remembered that this time he hadn't tied the bag to his belt. This time he'd left it in his field pack.

And his field pack was at the bottom of the arroyo, abandoned as too much of a bother to carry up.

Sid slumped down, coughing weakly at a lungful of acrid smoke.

Damn. This whole ordeal would be for nothing if he had lost those garnets. They'd been too dirty to really determine their quality, but they'd all been a good size, the largest of them as big as the last joint of his thumb.

He wanted his garnets back.

Sid stood, letting the cold wind catch him. Now that the moon was up, he felt certain that he would be able to find

the section of bank he'd notched handholds in and be able
to climb right down, scoop up the pack, and climb right
back.

Sid peered over the edge into the arroyo. He'd been
right; he could see the handholds. The first three, anyway.
Farther down, they were lost in shadow. His eyes would
adjust. Sid sat down, then turned himself carefully about
until he was balanced on the edge, hard dirt and rock
pressing against his rib cage, his arms trembling as they
tried to take his weight. But he was weak now. For one
panicked instant, Sid realized that he would have to find
those notches. He could no longer hoist himself out using
just his arms. The toe of one boot caught, and he tested it
gingerly. It would bear his weight. Sid climbed down.

He paused to rest, forehead against cool dirt. He should
wait until morning. But nothing had gone his way the
whole damn day. He wanted his stones.

Step after step, he fumbled his way down. Damn, he
didn't remember it being so far to the bottom. The shadow
sliced into his legs, then across his waist, then finally split
the earth above his head, and Sid paused to let his night
vision sharpen. He looked up. The stars sprang at him. He
thought again of his dream, and gem juice. He chuckled,
and wished he could free one hand to take a drink of water.

Three more steps, a misstep, and Sid slid down the rest
of the way, scraping his shins and landing heavily on his
knees while pebbles and clods of dirt rained down. He
coughed, waved the dirt away. Just as well. He'd probably
have to feel for his pouch on hands and knees anyway.
Perhaps he should just spend the rest of the night down
here, Sid thought. Away from the wind he wasn't too cold.
And it would beat trying to climb back up.

Legs wobbly, Sid dropped onto hands and knees and
turned toward where he thought he'd left his pack. A
surge of adrenaline had cleared his thoughts, though his
heart was now beating far too quickly. He felt alert, but
weak. He closed his eyes to speed his night vision and
crawled forward.

After a few minutes, Sid decided that he had crawled in
the wrong direction. He also noticed that his arms and legs
were shaking badly, and if he didn't find the pack soon, he
would either have to leave it or spend the night at the
bottom of the wash. He opened his eyes. The pack must

look like one more rock among the tumbled mess. That one to the left looked familiar, though, and he took a deep breath and stood, wanting a different perspective. He lurched and stumbled to his knees again, realizing that his arms and legs weren't shaking. The ground was.

The Dine'h had been right. Flash flood. Sid bit his lip, trying to keep his breathing slow, his heartbeat calm. His first thought was to get out of the wash, and he almost backed toward the wall, but he was too close to the pack to leave now. Stubborn, stubborn, he thought, but he wanted his stones. They were all he had. They would be so beautiful when he finished with them—

His hand brushed something that ran away. Sid almost screamed. Get out, he told himself. Now. He could hear nothing, but the trembling in the ground shook him like holding a chain saw, and around him the rocks were beginning to settle. He closed his eyes more tightly than before and crawled, patting the ground as he went.

He'd given Judy a star garnet once, a glorious six-point star he'd found and polished himself. "Oh," she'd said. "Oh." And that was all. But Sid had known what was wrong. It wasn't turquoise in silver to hang around her neck and drag her toward the earth, or clear and faceted and set in a ring, given while he ground his knees into some hard pavement and declared his undying love. He'd given her what he could, and it hadn't been enough. The next day, he'd brought a rough but clear quartz crystal and tossed it to her. She'd held it to the light and asked if it was a diamond.

No, what he had with Judy wasn't very beautiful. Nor with the other geologists on the team. Nor, it seemed, with Ray. And certainly not with his dad and sister. His grandmother didn't count anymore; she was dead.

He wanted his stones.

But Sid could hear the water now. A dull rumble, just at the edge of sound, that made his jaw hurt. He crawled forward again.

And his hand came down on the pack.

Sid cried out. He gathered it up carefully in both hands, unzipped it, scrabbled inside until he felt smooth chamois and stones within, shifting and playing over each other. He pulled out the bag and let his pack drop, then staggered to his feet, trying to keep his balance.

Sid had never been in an earthquake before. Eastern Washington was not known as earthquake country. But the ground now was giving a good imitation. He stumbled toward the ladder notched into the side of the wash, tripping once and landing heavily on his forearms. He would not let go of the pouch.

A wind had kicked up inside the arroyo, made of air forced before a rushing wall of water, and it dragged at Sid's shirt, whipped his hair about his face. Sid looped the pouch's leather thong about his neck, felt the comforting weight of the stones bump gently against his chest, and fumbled outward for the ladder. He couldn't feel it. He'd crawled to one side or the other while he was searching, and now could not find the notches.

A powerful gust caught him and flung him against the hard-packed dirt. The water was no more than a minute or two away, and he could hear it clearly now: a huge, still growing roar that drowned out his own voice as he screamed. Sid looked up.

There. To the right, he could see the notches he'd cut in the dirt as black pockmarks caught in the light of the moon. *Quick* warred with *careful* in Sid's mind, and he stumbled down the arroyo, running his hands over the wall. His fingertips slid into the first notch.

Sid hoisted himself up. But his arms were so weak; they trembled already, and he was afraid he would have to pause and rest between each rung. He had no time. He reached for the next rung, and pulled.

Now the shuddering of the arroyo wall was threatening to dislodge his hands. All this for a bag of rocks, Sid thought wildly, as he reached and pulled. His head popped up into the moonlight, but Sid knew he would have to make it all the way to the top and over the side before he would be safe.

Maybe he should just let go. Just relax, for once relax and drop back into the coming water. It would be fast, this death, instead of the slow chipping and grinding of the death he lived every day.

A cascade of pebbles rained down on his head, and Sid looked up.

The Dine'h's head jutted out past the edge of the bank above him. She was crouched on the bank watching. Simply watching.

The wall bucked under him, but he clung to it. The wind tore at him, and he flattened himself against the dirt. More pebbles fell. She was still there. Damn persistent for an illusion. For a moment he saw patterns, patterns in stone, never changing except to fade and disappear. Like monuments, carvings, gravestones. He thought again of letting go, of taking the first step toward becoming stone, but somehow he couldn't do that with her watching. He had questions, and they angered him.

What did she want from him? What did Ray, or Judy, or anyone want from him?

The first waves swept past Sid's feet, and he could hear the sticks and small rocks tumble and crash, like the agates he tumbled at home. He could hang here until the water plucked him from the side and tumbled him away, or he could—what?

Ask an illusion for help?

"But you're not real," Sid yelled. Spray splashed him. He could trust his friend Ray.

Sid looked down the arroyo. The water was coming, gleaming in the moonlight, as high as his shoulders, at least. He thrust a hand up. "Help me!" he yelled.

Her clasp was warm and strong. Sid felt the spray sting his cheeks and arms as he was pulled up and over the edge.

"Oh, Jesus, oh, Jesus," he whispered, and curled up in a ball on the bank. Dine'h dragged him farther from the edge. He began to shiver. She wrapped herself around him, but Sid could not get warm.

"Not to worry, little one," she whispered in his ear. The words meant something, Sid knew they did, but he could not decide what. "You are cold. I will warm you. I will change."

And suddenly Sid was surrounded by thick, coarse, acrid, wonderfully warm fur. He unfolded into it, stroked it, buried himself in it. After a time, he slept.

Sid was still sleeping when Ray found him about noon the next day. He rolled groggily to his knees and blinked up into the sun. Then he looked about. The desert had bloomed.

"Are you all right, Sid?" Ray asked. "Jesus, I'm sorry we didn't get out a search party until this morning. But first it rained in the mountains, then it rained this morning over the lake, and—"

"I'm fine," said Sid. He blinked again, and let Ray help him to his feet, took the canteen and candy bar his friend offered. "Really, I'm okay. It was quite an adventure."

Ray stared, and Sid realized he must be wondering why Sid hadn't started screaming invectives and threats to sue. Maybe later. Desert flowers were certainly beautiful, Sid thought. He'd slept right through the rain.

Ray sucked in his breath and shifted uncertainly. Sid looked at him, and noticed the fine red lines streaking Ray's eyes, the sweat stains already blossoming on his shirt. They probably weren't all from the heat. "Really," Sid said again, "I'm fine." He didn't know how to speak of forgiveness. He only hoped Ray understood.

Ray grinned. He pointed toward the ground, at a patch of drying mud with a paw print pressed deeply into it. Sid saw more, in a circle about where he'd slept. They seemed to make a pattern, but one he knew would never repeat.

"Bear?" he asked Ray, who nodded. Sid bit the inside of his cheek, considering, then grinned, too.

"Will Josh fix me an omelet?" he asked. "I'm starved."

"I expect so. Then we have to get you to a phone. Judy is worried sick."

"She is?" Sid took a deep breath. The next phase of his pattern would take some getting used to.

"She is." Ray took his arm and helped him toward the jeep, leading him carefully through an opening left in the circle of paw prints. Sid looked forward to the shower he would take after talking to Judy.

"By the way," he said to Ray, "I got some great garnets yesterday. Help me clean them and you can pick whichever one you want."

Barbara Hutton
Toujours

GAY PARTINGTON TERRY

SAD. EMPTY. HEAVYHEARTED. Even though you watch everyone around you die, you never quite get used to it, even when omens tell you to prepare for it and you spend your teenage years in the city morgue studying bodies under pretext of looking for a runaway cousin, even when you steel yourself for loneliness. First one goes, then another: mother, friend, father, your only uncle and finally, the man you married in order to escape that loneliness. It never gets any easier." Alice wadded up the postcard and dropped it into the wastebasket; it didn't help to write out her feelings and there was no one to send a postcard to anyway.

Marty, her husband, had been very fond of insurance, which left her reasonably well fixed in at least one aspect. At forty-two, she thought she might go back to school and become a librarian or research assistant, anything solitary and all-consuming. Instead, on a whim, she took a long trip. She sought solitude and peace in the museums of Europe but never quite shook the feeling of restless agitation.

London was a pleasant town but hard on the sinuses; Paris was entirely too intrusive. Rome was glorious with its excellent food and Roman shadows, but the innocent warmth of its inhabitants made it difficult to remain anonymous. Athens frightened her: its ruins so sterile and precise, its population so viscous. Spain's obsession with relics and ritual only served to make her more depressed.

The truth was, with all of this, she hadn't learned to accept death. Not for herself. And not for anyone else. She kept thinking that she saw someone in a crowd: Marty, her mother. She would run after them but, of course, it was never them. Sometimes she would lose them and then believe that it had really been the person she thought it was. Because of this, she had convinced herself that the dead, or some of them, still walk among us and just don't allow themselves to be found. That those souls possessed of aspiring attachments have established parallel lives and persist among the living.

She had begun to think of school again and dusty, seclusive research projects, when she was accosted by a gaggle of American tourists at her Malaga hotel—a situation she'd successfully avoided throughout the trip.

"For god's sake don't go to Tangier," they said.

"The stench!"

"The obscene people!"

"Not safe in Arab countries, you know. Especially for women traveling alone."

Not only did she go immediately, but she took the Algeciras ferry. She did, however, book first class, a regrettable decision since she spent the entire voyage standing at the door that separated the classes, watching veiled women and dark men holding chicken and goats. The gamy smells and murmur of voices beyond that door invigorated her as much as any great museum. They captured her entire attention except for several minutes when she was drawn to the great Rock of Gibraltar which thrust itself up from the water and was only partially claimed by man. Just as the rock had ruptured the province that belonged to water, so the tenuous margin between real and unreal had been weakened beyond that door. It seemed an excellent context to conceal the deception of Death.

The landing was chaos: shimmering heat, dark smells, and heavily draped people. Frightened tourists being accosted by potential guides who were illiterate in eight languages.

"Hashish? Kif?" they called.

"Everyone comes to Tangier seeking something. What is it you seek?"

What indeed, Alice thought. Peace of mind? Peace of spirit? Eradication of the self-imposed myths that give me hope? Release from the ghosts who follow me? No, they were all ghosts now, friends and family; it was fitting that she keep them with her. Maybe she just needed a reason to shave her legs again or wear makeup, or just get up in the morning.

Two smarmy Arabs fought over her luggage and Alice was barely able to escape into a cab and get to her hotel. The Hotel Toujours was run by Arabs, and not Frenchmen as she'd feared, but it had a French menu as well as Arab and what they called International, the names of which were as obscure to Alice as the Arab specialities. The food, however, was seductive in taste and smell, and the cool, tiled corridors a delightful maze. The hotel was central and although the front overlooked the busy city and entrance to the Medina, the back looked out onto a lush garden with a splendid azure pool. Alice took her mint tea on the back terrace after dinner with vicarious contentment.

"Excuse, Madam," a young waiter bowed.

"Yes, I should love to have a pastry." Alice smiled at the African moon.

"Certainly."

The boy was back in a flash with a silver tray.

"This one, please." She watched as he ceremoniously lifted it onto a clean dish and placed it in front of her.

"Has Madam secured a guide yet?"

Alice thought of the two men fighting over her luggage and the twenty or so other dirty hucksters who had accosted her at the ferry landing.

"No. Is it really necessary?"

"Not if one knows the streets, and can bargain in Arabic, and can protect one's self from the unsavory characters who prey upon tourists."

"Oh." Alice surprised herself by having the first easy conversation with anyone since she'd begun the trip. Surely it signified the end of her reluctance to go home, an unhappy thought in this exotic place, but convenient since she had less than three days left. Later, she would not remember this misread omen.

"If it please, Madam, I have a small brother, knowledgeable of the streets and history of the city, trustworthy as the Prophet's word. He is needing money to enter the University, and free for several days."

Alice could not bear to take even a small forkful of her pastry in front of the boy and give evidence of American bad manners, nor could she bear to dismiss him for some reason.

"Very well, but I sleep very badly and I don't know when I will be taking breakfast in the morning or when I shall be about."

"No matter, he will wait at the entrance of the hotel. Many thanks, Madam." And the boy backed into the hotel.

Alice was relieved at the chance to finally take a bite of the delightful pastry in front of her. She was not disappointed in the flavor, which was thick with coconut and honey, nuts and . . . Was that ginger?

The waiter appeared once more with a plate of macaroons. "Try these, Madam. Barbara Hutton says that our cook makes the best *ghoriba* in all of Morocco. She orders thousands for her parties."

Alice smiled and took one. How odd. She was sure that Barbara Hutton was dead. So, I am not the only one who carries around the ghosts of dead acquaintances, she thought as the young waiter disappeared into the kitchen.

Drat, she thought, I forgot to discuss money. Never mind, I'll hash it out with the child in the morning. Her sense of well-being in this mysterious place made her smile despite the complications.

Alice's nights had become ritual. Ritual cleansing, methodical arrangement of time and possessions, order that was meant to tranquilize but never quite did. The book had to be in a certain spot so that when she woke up in the middle of the night, she could evade her own thoughts. Tissues. Slippers. Extra blankets. Sometimes it took several to stop the tremors. The dreams were disconnected, unresolved. But each had its own sad song, a song she would hum to herself through the following day.

She rose late and felt no need of hurrying her breakfast for she did not really expect the "small brother" to be waiting for her. As she was not the type to seek company anyway, she was relieved to face the prospect of exploring the city alone. She was dressed in a brown and turquoise rayon skirt and beige cotton sweater, her "travel suit," because, from what she'd seen on the way to the hotel, she could tell that the Moslems were very proper and well mannered. Her figure, once considered "sturdy," had compressed itself with grief.

She stepped out of the hotel and into the clutter of Arab mid-morning. For a moment she panicked despite herself, then a dark, bone-thin boy of about fifteen or sixteen broke away from a huddle of boys across the street and ran up to her. He was wearing a Grateful Dead T-shirt and trousers that barely reached his ankles.

"I am Mohmud, brother to Rashid."

"The waiter?" Alice asked, and he nodded his head.

Below them by the entrance to the Medina, Alice could see a group of men and women wrapped in bright colors.

"Who are they?" she asked.

"Bedouins. Nomads from the desert. Come to trade."

Perhaps it would be well to have a guide, she thought, to lead her through the peculiarities of this place.

"Where do you wish to go?" His English was quite good and he had an unintrusive smile. When he spoke, he looked away.

"I don't know," said Alice. "Where is there?"

"The Medina, the Grand Socco, the palace of Sidi Hosini which was owned by Barbara Hutton, the Kasbah? Perhaps Madam is looking for something special? I am acquainted with many fine merchants."

"No, nothing special. I would just like to walk, to see the old city."

"Ah, the Medina," and he led her through the arches, down through dark, narrow, pungent streets. The heat was confining but not oppressive. The buildings reminded her of adobe houses built by Indians, only more ancient, more enclosed. What color was adobe? She couldn't remember; certainly not the somber ash-gray of these structures.

They stopped to listen to children chanting behind an uneven cloth that hung at the opening of one building.

"It is Koran School," said Mohmud.

People hurried by, most wearing traditional robes.

"Haiks, jalabahs, baboush," Mohmud instructed.

Many women wore veils, and all were covered from head to foot. When she considered them, it made Alice self-conscious to have her legs sticking out. Mostly she felt detached, a feeling that was becoming less and less unusual. Instead of her mind wandering to her dead friends and family, in this place it wandered nowhere—everywhere. Things were no longer what they once had been, but a universe of swirling colors, the scent of cinnamon and jasmine, the tinkle of camel bells. In the background there were Egyptian singers whose pinched voices came out of transistor radios. In Europe, remote feelings in breathtaking surroundings were a dilemma. Here, alienation seemed to enfold her and mark her place in the ethereal setting. It seemed fitting, this combination of fervent, fascinating, and intangible.

Mohmud kept up a running dialogue which she tuned in and out of. He kept away beggars and hawkers, and did not intrude upon her thoughts. He pointed out the mosque's fine minaret and kept her from being run over by school boys with their books wrapped in prayer rugs. He commented upon the anonymous checks which had rained down during the stay of Barbara Hutton to alleviate the suffering of the poor.

The mention of Barbara Hutton attracted her. The Arabs of Tangier spoke of her often, as if she were still alive. She'd always thought of Barbara Hutton as a woman of obsessions and delusions, but the Moroccans thought of her as a distinguished celebrity, a generous lady, and a visionary with the means and fortitude to transform reality. Certainly, the components for such a transformation were here. Past, present, and future intermingled and left only a primeval unity of feeling. The rules of logic did not seem to apply.

At the market place he pointed out cosmetic powders and incense, dates and rice, precious stones, and household goods; caravan goods that became a sensory tumult in Alice's head. The ghosts that filled her life and caused her great agitation seemed to float quietly around her, silenced by the exotic clatter and the scent of freshly baked *khobz*.

"What is that?" she asked of a sound that caught her interest late in the afternoon.

"It is the muezzin's summons to prayer," Mohmud answered.

"Do you wish to stop and pray?"

"It is not necessary. I am not so devout."

She almost told him how she was searching for her own truth and seemed to drift further and further from reality, but thought better of it and only nodded understanding.

This abrupt transition to the reality of communication, however, made Alice realize that it was already late afternoon. They ducked into a cafe for couscous and mint tea. Old men smoked hashish in the corner. Mohmud chattered on about school and his sisters—Alice barely noticed —then excused himself to talk to friends at another table, all the time keeping an eye on her, shooing away the riffraff.

Alice's thoughts in the cafe were not thoughts at all but feelings; she drifted from one memory to another. It was strange to be with someone and not be with him, to be here and not here. Mohmud didn't seem to notice or care, or perhaps he understood her need for solitude and respected it; it didn't seem to offend him as it did Americans and Europeans. Perhaps everyone was marginal in this strange milieu. Alice wondered if she could drift along this way for the rest of her life, without connections to anyone. She'd nursed too many sick people, eaten in too many hospital cafeterias, sat in the front row of too many funerals. She no longer hoped for the best or breathed easy after a crisis; for after one crisis, one only had to wait for the next.

"Do you wish to see the Kasbah now?"

"No, not today. I'm too tired. I must go back to my hotel and rest."

"Tomorrow, then? I will wait for Madam."

"Yes, tomorrow."

They walked back silently. For a moment Alice thought she should be frightened, alone with a strange Arab boy, lost in the maze of the Medina, the sun due to go down any time now. But she wasn't. And she was amazed that Mohmud found his way back to the arches and the Bedouins, who were no longer there. What an odd thought —had they become a part of her catalog of missing faces?

"What shall I pay you?" She dreaded bargaining and the Arabs seemed so fond of it.

"Pay me tomorrow."

She knew she should settle now, but didn't have the strength to argue and so, saying good-bye, went up to her room and had a long bath with soap that smelled of some magical desert flower.

Dinner was pigeon and *harira;* she drank a traditional French wine and finished with another succulent pastry. An Englishman at the next table tried to speak to her; his dinner smelled of peppers and fennel, lemon and saffron. He smelled of tobacco. She only shook her head and drifted back to her room. Her eyes closed with a vision of infinity that was a whorl of dancing arabesques in gold wash upon a sunwashed wall and had the first good night's sleep she'd had in ages.

She took breakfast on the terrace under a serene blue sky. Oh, Marty, if only you had lived to see this! And my dear friend Joya, wrapped around a tree in your new Audi. What a waste of talent and happiness. Would you, Marty, have spent all those long hours in the cleaning store, building up business if you had known about the cancer incubating in your cells? Would you, had you known there was such a sky in another part of the world? She put on her sunglasses to hide oncoming tears.

An emaciated old European woman was speaking to the cook just below. She was wearing a vintage Chanel suit and a bit too much makeup. Alice had been unconsciously staring at her and when she put on the sunglasses, the woman made a sympathetic gesture. Alice thought she looked familiar but fearing another ghostly illusion, buried herself in her newspaper.

The *Herald Tribune* described Shiite assassinations but could not really hold her attention. Tomorrow she must return home. To what? A small house that would be too big for her to rattle around in alone? A street full of people who felt sorry for her? Wasn't it bad enough that she felt sorry for herself? Civilization and telephones. God, how she hated telephones, a piece of equipment which, in her experience, was used mainly to spread the news of Death.

Morose thoughts. They had returned because she was lingering over breakfast. She must go. No matter that Mohmud would never expect her to be out this early. She would find the Kasbah on her own.

But Mohmud was waiting outside the hotel, just as if he'd never left. Waiting. "Like Death," she thought. The other guides hadn't arrived yet and he was reading. He stuffed the small book into his back pocket when he saw her.

"Where to, Madam?"

"The Kasbah, Mohmud. Let's see this Kasbah of yours."

Down through the network of the Medina they plunged, both lost in their own thoughts.

"Who are those men with rifles?" Alice asked.

"Mercenaries. Just walk quickly. They are not crazy, Tangier is dependent upon its tourists." She wondered if this were true; but could anyone who smelled of sucre and pistachio be dangerous?

Soon they began climbing out of the shadows of the Medina and into the sunlit nimbus of the great palace. They stood on the threshold of a world of harems and dancing girls.

"Do you see the dervish over there?" Mohmud pointed.

"Dervish?"

"The strange man sitting by that door."

"Yes."

"That is the apartment of Barbara Hutton."

"Oh, yes, the heiress." Occasionally the Moroccans mentioned the names of other celebrities who had resided here—Jimi Hendrix, Brian Jones—but never with the reverence granted the name of Barbara Hutton.

"Before that it was the palace of Sidi Hosini. Barbara Hutton outbid Generalissimo Franco for it. My father remembers her quite well. All of Tangier remembers her parties." He studied her face for a moment. "It is customary to bring your friends to a party in Morocco."

Could he see her ghosts as well as his own? There was something about this boy.

As they stared at the protective stone walls of the tall, whitewashed structure, the dervish stood and waved at them.

"*Taqabbil Allah,*" he called.

"May God accept your prayer," Mohmud translated.

Did she have a prayer? Alice could not take her eyes off the strange man and yet, could not see him clearly. It was as if he were a heat mirage from the desert. How safe it must be behind those walls. She could well understand Barbara Hutton's need for a refuge from the curiosity and judgments, the pity. She had read in a book she'd found in an alcove of the hotel that Barbara Hutton had taken great pains to transform reality into a continuous fantasy. Perhaps this was why the Arabs revered her. Perhaps it was why she, Alice, felt comfortable in this enchanted milieu. This was the only place she'd found where she could live undisturbed in her cocoon of thoughts.

"Come inside." Mohmud guided her into the Kasbah. "Soon he will come begging." Mohmud's hand brushed her elbow, warm and alive, the first human contact that wasn't an indication of pity in— Oh, how long? Perhaps he had lost someone too.

Inside, a few tourists huddled in corners with their guides, Mohmud murmured tales of the history of the palace, but Alice did not hear; it was the voice of the genie instructing the infidel. Often, he mentioned Barbara Hutton as if she were the patron saint of the city—if Moslems had such a thing. She trailed her hand along the cool tiles and studied the graceful writing, a never-ending dance of prayers and praise to Allah. She noticed very little else; it was as if she were searching for something, some cipher which would connect her to the living.

It was not to be.

"Many tourists find Tangier oppressive. It is a matter of temperament. Others, like Barbara Hutton, seem to have it in their blood," he was saying. For a moment she thought of the poisonous things that were in Marty's blood but was lulled back by a vision of fig trees in a courtyard below. What a luxury to have your painful memories tempered by mythical environment.

Finally, they stepped out onto a mosaic balcony overlooking the sea. Again the perfect blue of Allah's heaven astounded her and she must have stood watching the sea crash onto rocks for a long while. Perhaps this was the place she'd looked for, perhaps it was in her blood. Mohmud was silent. She smiled at him, thankful for his patience.

Two mercenaries appeared on the terrace; they murmured prayers and turned to her.

"Unworthy foreigner. Infidel pig—you defile our homeland! *Allah akbar!*" They raised their rifles but Alice felt no fear about joining her friends and family. It all seemed so natural, inherent in the hypnotic situation. She watched their nicotine-stained fingers tighten on the trigger. Certainly not religious fanatics, she thought. She knew that if she closed her eyes, she would see Joya's face as the car slid uncontrollably toward that tree; it was the only thing that scared her.

"No!" Mohmud leaped toward her just as the men opened fire.

In a moment they were gone, the sounds of a chase following them through the palace. People, police, screaming, hysteria. Mohmud was the calm in the center of chaos. He was lying in a pool of seeping blood, eyes open, but no longer seeing this world. Alice knelt above him, the sound of the sea momentarily drowned out by the ghostly echo of gunshots, footsteps, and screams. It had happened so fast; now you see him, now you don't. The familiar smell of Death was in the air.

"Another one," she sighed. The world around her swirled in pastel colors and wails. "You didn't have to do that." What would she tell his brother? She could remember a time when the death of a bird would have affected her. Now grief was her prevailing emotion; one more seemed to make little difference. A voice from deep inside her spoke: the spirit of the dead is the same as that of the living; only the appearance has changed.

Why so calm this time? Was it shock? Was it the general inertia of Tangier that had penetrated her soul? Or something even more devious?

She could easily have done an entire funeral service, she was that familiar with death. Perhaps she should throw him off the balcony into the care of the sea, but no, instead she put her hand to her temple and felt the warm ooze of blood. She'd been hit. Little droplets splashed into the larger pool that came from Mohmud.

Slowly she stood. "Come with me," she whispered to the spirit of the dead boy. It is customary to bring friends. . . ."

Her shoes tap-tap-tapped through the tiled corridors. Outside of the palace, clouds swirled in front of the sun, diminishing its angry glare. The sky had changed to a more sober color, the gray of obelisks and tombstones.

She stumbled through the shadowed streets of the Medina. Mohmud, Marty, Uncle Hal, Joya. Mother, father. Nothing to go home to. Businesses dead, whole towns gone

with the coal companies. Steel mills collapsing, rivers loi-
tering to a trickle. People looked at her but she was not
embarrassed today, she'd worn pants and a long-sleeved
shirt, even a scarf tied about her hair. She was well covered. Where was the hotel? Must get out of the gloom.

Finally, a patch of sunlight. The rue Ben-Raisul; she'd
never paid attention to street names before—what made
her think she recognized this one? Hawks circled above
her. Was she back at the Kasbah, or was this the entrance to
the hotel? Her eyes were starting to play tricks on her,
perhaps it was stress or hallucinations caused by the varie-
gation of light and shadow. Perhaps it was the spell of
Tangier that confused real with unreal. She felt faint. Was
that the dervish in front of the door to Barbara Hutton's
apartments, or the hotel porter? He was motioning to her.
She was out of breath.

"Toujours?" she managed to whisper. "Is this
Toujours?"

"As-salaam alaykum." The man smiled and bowed as
he opened the door.

Inside was cool. Not the hotel but endless corridors
with arabesques and mosaic patterns multiplied forever.
Oriental carpets, gold candelabras, cushions, flowers,
splashing fountains. The scent of rosewater and pastilles,
aloes and ambergris. She put her hand to her head. The
small wound had apparently stopped bleeding.

A handsome young man approached. He was carrying a
very thin woman with thick dark eyebrows. She was smoking a cigarette and wearing an astrologer's robe and an
emerald and diamond tiara.

"Meet the Queen of the Medina," the young man said,
and he placed her upon a large throne-like chair.

"It's the librarian. We're so pleased you've come," the
woman said. "Many of your friends are here already.
There are so many to catalog. But you must rest first." She
clapped her hands. "Mohmud will show you to your room
where you may wash and perform your devotions."

"Mohmud?" Alice's eyes would not focus.

"Oh, yes," said the woman. "They're all called
Mohmud or Hassan here. Take this ointment for your in-
jury."

She pressed a small brass bowl in Alice's hands. In it was
fiery water.

"Thank you."

"Life is whole here. Undivided and undiminished, continuous. There is no hierarchy, no barriers between different spheres."

"I understand."

"Good. Now rest. The fleet is in tonight and we've prepared an entertainment."

She was so frail and delicate, but the light in her eyes made Alice confident that this woman was quite capable of rearranging the elements of reality, of combining all of nature into one great society of life; past, present, and future, all one.

A strong hand led Alice through corridors, up and down staircases. The liquid in her bowl turned luminous in the dark. She was so tired. Each room had a clock and many had smiling people lounging with books or drinks in their hands.

"Was that Barb—" She was really too exhausted to speak.

"Muhammad, himself, was an orphan," said the voice behind the hand that led her. It was as gentle as the breeze from the terrace.

Alice felt a great relief. She had grown so used to being alone with her thoughts; now, strangely, she was thankful for company. She was thankful to be within someone else's fantasy. Her eyes strayed to the chambers as she passed. Was that Marty on the terrace with a bowl of walnuts? Was it Joya grinding limouns in the kitchen?

The Gamemaker

CAROLYN IVES GILMAN

Y U VANG BENT OVER THE DISHPAN to perform a divination.

First drop, the world.

As it fell upon the surface of the water, the soap drop blossomed into a film. Opalescent petals spread to the edge of the basin. Yu Vang's thin face followed the swirling colors intently. The divination was working.

Second drop, the will.

The patterns changed as the next drop hit the surface. Entranced, Yu nearly lost track of his purpose. With an effort he pulled back: he was observer this time, not participant.

He studied the patterns that formed in the film: the snail, the lotus, the saber. All good. All confirmed the promise he had read in the night sky. His freedom was enfolded in the shifting chances of the night ahead.

A gust blew from the open kitchen window, rippling the water, destroying the fragile foretelling. Yu Vang rinsed out the basin and turned to the greasy cookware stacked on the counter. But his mind was on the night before him.

It was the first chance fate had given him to seize control. In the months since coming to America, he had been the pawn of everyone else's decisions: the INS, the Welfare people, the social workers, the job placement agency. They meant well, but they did not understand his *charmon*. His desires were summed up in the only word of English he had known at first: "California." But when he said it they shook their heads. Instead, they had sent him to this place so cold people said the tires froze to the ground in winter and not even cockroaches could survive.

He would need all his cleverness, all his poise, tonight. If the divination were true, he would escape from this house where the social workers had assigned him. He would leave his employer's family, their cold land and their cold ways, and be on the road west by morning.

With a brisk shake of her head, Gloria Callander declined the drink her new Laotian hired hand had brought her on a tray. She set down her empty glass and leaned back in the creaking wicker chair, absently smoothing the lavender scarf that set off her silver hair. One drink was enough tonight, she decided. On other nights, a second gin and tonic soothed her before the drive into town to visit the chapel she had built to hold her husband's remains. But she would have no time for chats with the pastor this night. She would be playing a game which, unlike life, she might have a chance of winning.

Two of the other players had already arrived. With dinner past, they had gathered on the porch of Gloria's rambling summer cabin, the same knotty pine porch where President Coolidge had once relaxed during his visits to Great-Grandfather Callander. It was mid-July, but here in the old forests on the south shore of Lake Superior the nights were always cool. As twilight gathered, the small-paned windows gleamed benignly out onto the well-made coverlet of the lawn. Beyond the pines, the lake glowed salmon in the sunset.

Gloria disapproved of her guests just enough to make their company pleasant. David and Adriane had driven up from the city together, as usual. It sometimes irked Gloria to think they had met in her house. They seemed so mismatched. It didn't matter that Adriane was fifteen years younger than David—she was still too old for him. Adriane had been born world-worn. She was not the type to appeal to an aggressively youthful college professor like David; yet here they were. They had a grown-together look, like

two unrelated trees that had accidentally sprouted too
close to one another.

The Laotian gave the guests their drinks, then departed with the shuffling gait of a person used to wearing
sandals. Adriane watched him go, milking a cinnamon cigarette with short, quick breaths. Bright ceramic earrings
peeked from the slits of her blond hair like cats' eyes,
watching.

"I think we should tell her, David," she said.

A moment ago, David had been joking tenaciously
about his attempts to teach Business Ethics to a class of
engineers. He had fallen silent, as if his own satire had
bitten him. Now, staring out at the lake, his rough-hewn,
intellectual profile momentarily betrayed its age. They
hadn't yet left the city behind, Gloria thought. There was
still some of the brittleness of glass and pavement about
them.

"What is it you have to tell me?" Gloria asked.

"I wanted to wait until Erin got here," David said.

"Well, you can't leave me in suspense now."

David ran a hand through his unruly blond hair. Gloria
wondered briefly what he used to keep it from going gray.

"Gerhard's not coming tonight," he said.

Gloria clicked her tongue in surprise. It was rare for
one of them to miss a Dreamgame. And tonight in particular—they were so close to winning. Gloria felt an ungra-
cious elation that Gerhard would be out of the running.

"I'm sorry to hear that," she said. "I was looking forward to seeing him."

It meant she would only have to contend with David,
Adriane, and her son Erin. Gloria felt a momentary flash of
confidence. She knew her guests' weaknesses intimately.
David played with an almost frantic flamboyance; Adriane
inched along with the same hypercritical cautiousness that
kept her endlessly revising her computer graphics. Neither of them deserves to win, Gloria thought. They play
only to escape. They don't play from the heart as I do.

She and her son's friends had been playing the Dreamgame on summer weekends for three years now, since just
before her husband had died. David had discovered the
game on a trip to San Francisco. They played in a dream
realm as rich and real as their hired Gamemaker could
create. And their Gamemaker was the best.

"It leaves us with a problem," David was saying. "If the Gamemaker has only four of us to keep track of, he'll be able to create devilish problems for us. We need to think of something to distract him."

"Is that fair?" Gloria asked.

"His contract says five players, doesn't it? Why should we give him a break?"

They were interrupted by a crash of crockery from the dining room, where the hired hand was clearing the table. Gloria rose to protect her grandmother's Wedgwood but Adriane, who sat by the door, waved her down again. "Nothing broken," she said.

Gloria settled back, not quite trusting an artist who collected Fiesta Ware to understand Wedgwood.

"Who is that?" Adriane nodded toward the dining room.

"Oh, one of Erin's projects," Gloria said. "A Hroob refugee I'm paying to help around the house. He was supposed to be some sort of philosopher, but it turns out he was more like the village shaman's apprentice. I think he wants to leave, but he won't say so. Frankly, I wish he would."

"Hroob. Are they the ones who do those sweet embroideries?"

"No," David said. "The Hroob are ethnic Tibetans. Listen, I've got an idea. Why don't we have Confucius there stand in for Gerry? That would give the Gamemaker something to think about."

"Oh no, David," Gloria protested. "Yu scarcely speaks a word of English."

"What does that matter? We don't need Shakespeare in the Dreamgame."

"I don't think Erin would let us."

For several minutes, the hum of a motor had been creeping toward them across the still lake. Now, a ketch nosed its way toward the Callanders' pier, sails furled.

"Expecting visitors, Gloria?" David asked.

She shook her head, frowning at the intrusion. Whoever it was, they had chosen a bad time to drop in.

When a slim figure in jeans and windbreaker leaped from the boat's deck to the pier, mooring line in hand, Adriane gave a surprised exclamation. "It's Erin!" she said. "I didn't know he sailed."

"Neither did I," Gloria murmured.

The yellow yard light went on as Erin came down the dock, and the elderly caretaker appeared. The two met on the path and exchanged some sports talk before the old man turned to look over the boat. Erin bounded up the fieldstone steps onto the porch.

"Since when did you take up yachting?" David asked as Erin pecked his mother's cheek and threw himself wearily onto a wicker loveseat.

Erin laughed and took the sailor's hat off his dark, tousled hair. He glanced at his watch. "Since three hours ago. I rented the boat at Superior."

"And sailed it here alone?" Adriane stared.

"You've got to be joking!" Erin grinned. "I don't know a winch from a winding sheet."

"You mean a shroud," David corrected drily.

"Do I? I'd swear the man at the marina said something about sheets. Yes, I know he did, because I thought he meant the sails. Well, they *look* like sheets, don't they?"

"Then did you motor the whole way?" Adriane asked.

"No, I pointed it east and blew hard. I thought it would be good practice for when I go to the Andaman Islands."

Calmly, Gloria passed a bowl of nuts. "You're going to the Andaman Islands?" she asked.

"Yes, next week. It's all about a legal fund for nuclear waste victims." Erin sprang to his feet again. "Is there any beer in the house? I'm parched." As he prowled off into the kitchen, the others exchanged a look of tolerant commiseration.

"You should have put a governor on him, Gloria," David said.

"You were the one who taught him ethics."

David didn't respond. He didn't like to be reminded that Erin had been his student. He preferred to think of his students as peers, himself as eternal undergraduate.

"Nuclear waste victims," Adriane mused. "He was battling information monopolies the last I heard."

"That was a long time ago," Gloria said. "He's been into water politics since then."

Adriane tossed her hair back from her face like a lasso artist flicking his rope. "Why doesn't he try something hopeless?"

"Your Hroob Buddhist would say it was charmon," David said, expertly aspirating the *ch*. "It's the same root as karma: the life-pattern each of us is fated to follow. Erin's charmon decrees that practicality will never tyrannize over him—"

Adriane's snort cut him off like an ax. "What do the Buddhists know? They say a tree's only a tree because we think it's a tree."

Erin returned to the porch with a beer bottle in one hand and a fistful of macadamia nuts in the other. "Say Adriane, I saw Les Cleaver, the art dealer, at lunch the other day. He's looking for graphic artists for a new show. I mentioned you."

Adriane laughed tensely. "I don't think he'd like my work."

"How do you know?"

"He's a dealer. That means he's after things that go well over the fireplace in the downtown condo. Nothing thought-provoking, nothing that might upset the spaniel." She paused. "Besides, I don't have anything ready."

No one said anything. In the two years since Adriane had turned passionately professional, none of them had seen anything but sketches.

"Well, think about it," Erin said.

"I guess it's not my charmon to be a darling of the art dealers," Adriane said with a glance at David.

"Is the Gamemaker here yet?" Erin asked suddenly.

Gloria looked at her watch. "It's past nine. He should be."

"Then we've got a problem to solve fast. Did you hear that Gerhard's not going to make it?"

The others nodded. "David wants to let your Buddhist shaman play in his place," Adriane said.

"David, that's a fantastic idea!" Erin exclaimed. "The Gamemaker won't know what hit him. Brilliant!"

"Bot ov corze," David replied, feigning a French accent.

"Let's get on with it, then," Adriane said, rising. "I've been waiting all day."

The Callanders' game room lay on the third floor of the house, under the log-beamed eaves. The dormer windows normally looked out over the lake, but now the thick curtains were drawn. There was no furniture; instead, a thick Ladakhi yak-wool carpet covered the board floor, and cushions were heaped everywhere. In the center of the room, on a small hearth of bricks, stood a hibachi and a bag of camphra. On the west wall was the door into the adjoining room, where the Gamemaker waited out of sight.

The surroundings were comfortable, the camphra was the best; but it was their Gamemaker that made their Dreamgame unique. His art was like that of the carpet weaver; but his threads were dreams, and his shuttles the will of the players. He had elevated the Dreamgame from a primitive, chance-ruled contest to a pastime of exquisite originality. Over the years that the friends had competed, he had twined their fantasies into a shared dream realm almost as vast and complex as the world outside.

Much as they owed him, none of Gloria's guests had ever met the Gamemaker. He preferred it that way. Like many geniuses, he was eccentric. He took their cash, wove their game, then left before morning. The caretaker claimed that a midnight-blue van waited for him all night by the highway. Though they grumbled, Gloria's guests rather enjoyed the mystery of the Gamemaker's behavior. He acted like a visitor from some cloak-and-dagger fantasy of his own.

When they entered the room, the contestants moved automatically to the places they always occupied. Gloria placed the large manila envelope containing the Gamemaker's payment by the western door, while Erin lit the hibachi. When the charcoal was aglow, he set a copper bowl of water on the grill and settled back, waiting for the water to boil.

The Laotian still hovered by the door, uncertain why he had been brought along. "What's his name?" Erin asked Gloria in an undertone.

"Yu Vang."

"Yu, come here," Erin said. As he approached hesitantly, Erin held up the plastic bag of camphra. "I bet you know what this is."

The man's eyes widened at the sight, and everyone laughed. "A universal language," David observed.

Pulling on Yu Vang's arm, Erin got him to sit on a pillow. "We are going to share our camphra with you," Erin explained slowly, with broad gestures. "We're going to let you play in our game." Yu's eyes never left the bag that held the drug.

The water was almost boiling, so Erin cast a handful of the crushed root on the water. It instantly filled the room with a gingery smell. The others gathered close.

Yu Vang closed his eyes, his mind rebelling. All he could think of was the small pack of belongings he had hidden behind the kitchen door in preparation for his departure. The omens had been so good. He had been sure tonight was the night to seize control. Yet here he was again, thwarted by someone else's whim. Everyone seemed to get a chance to guide Yu Vang's life but Yu Vang himself.

When he smelled the familiar scent of the boiling camphra, he longed to protest. What did these strange Americans know about the camphra trance, and why did they want him to be part of it? It frightened him that there was no Master near, no one to guide them into the realms inside reality. As he felt unwillingly the first slipping of his mind's hold on the world, he quickly summoned his half-forgotten training. *Wash the mind clean,* his tutor had once said. *Enter the self as if it were a temple, and you the humblest worshiper.*

The scented steam rose from the copper bowl. The players gathered close to breathe it in. Its first effect was to clear the sinuses like menthol, so that every breath was piercing and vivid. Then the cold tingling at fingertips and toes began, followed by a numbness moving up the limbs to the heart and mind. They continued to lean over the brazier until the moment before consciousness was snuffed out; then they settled back one by one onto the pillows as the pungent steam filled the room.

They all woke in the same instant. The dim light that filtered through the tiny window high on the sweating wall showed them lying in a tumbled pile, just as they had fallen, on the chill stone floor. The drip of water sounded loud in the echoing cavern.

The players did not stir at first. They lay for a while, accustoming themselves to their new surroundings. The stone was rough and unrelenting; the chilly air smelled of seeping alkali. When they began to stir, the small rustles and scrapes bounded eerily against the walls. It was touches like that which set their Gamemaker above the rest.

The play always started here in the Gamemaker's dungeon. Their first challenge, long ago, had been to learn the secret escape route. After that, they had spent days threading their way through the mazy corridors and treasure rooms of their captor's castle, pursued by implacable guardians. In one dramatic turn, they had set fire to part of the castle and escaped down a drainpipe into the town below the castle crag. In a seamy riverside inn they had divided the treasure and tools acquired in their foray. From there they had split up, each to pursue his or her way to freedom alone.

As the players roused, they began to disappear one by one, like extinguished lights. Gloria, who had wakened near Yu Vang, saw him stare as people winked out of existence around him. He turned to her, eyes wide in his dark face. "What has happened to them?" he asked. To her surprise, Gloria understood perfectly, though she had an impression he had not spoken English.

"They are going to take up the game where they left off last time," Gloria said. "In the first choosement we can go anywhere we have been before. You, of course, will have to find your own way out. Be careful. The Gamemaker will try to keep you prisoner; you must outwit him to be free."

"Who is the Gamemaker?" Yu Vang asked softly.

Gloria gestured to encompass everything around them. "The creator of all this. The umpire of the Dreamgame. Our adversary."

She thought of giving him a few hints, but decided against it. It was his own game; he would have to play it as he chose. So she closed her eyes and made the choice to resume her own game where she had left it.

Light exploded around her. Wind roared past her ears; the saddle jolted her breath away. She grasped desperately at the pommel as her left foot slipped out of the stirrup. For a moment she saw the grass whipping by beneath the horse's hooves and thought she would fall. She wrenched back into control and caught the rhythm of her mount's gallop.

Glancing behind, she saw that the Gamemaker's horsemen were no longer pursuing. She eased the horse to a walk, patting its sweating neck. Around her on every side, the rolling prairie shouldered up to the sky. Constellations of daisies spangled the grass. Gloria paused to savor the gentle, heather-scented breeze, wondering whose mind had held the makings of this beautiful, illusory landscape. Did she herself create the setting, as in any normal dream? Had this summer morning been lying dormant in her memories for years? Or was the Gamemaker responsible?

It didn't matter. Glad for the sun, she threw her head back and laughed—then stopped, startled in spite of herself at the deep baritone of her voice. For she was no longer Gloria Callander, unassuming widow and gracious hostess. She was Torquin Vangelist, the commanding character she had devised.

Torquin was tall and silver-haired, as her husband John had been. Like him, Torquin had a booming laugh and a marksman's eagle eye. They both strode the world with authority. Gloria had not consciously modeled him on her dead husband, but she had come to recognize the resemblance—and to enjoy it in a furtive way. For she could not help but notice that she was as good at being John Callander as he had been himself. Better, in some ways. For Torquin was John without the stubbornness, without the teasing insensitivity, without his doubt about the fitness of others.

But merely being John and being good at it was not enough. She had a driving need to win—to make it to the edge of the Gamemaker's realm before any of the others could. So she urged her horse into a canter, turning all her attention to the task of being Torquin.

It was about noon when Torquin Vangelist came upon a dirt cart-track leading southwest. He debated whether to follow it, since the Gamemaker had obviously put it there for a purpose. But the grassland had become monotonous, so he turned onto the road. Soon he saw a village ahead, an eccentric collection of wooden structures whose steep, ridged roofs looked too large for the buildings beneath. A crowd of shaggy ponies and forlorn donkeys before one building marked the local tavern.

The adventurer walked boldly through the bright red inn door. In the semidarkness, five men were gambling at a wooden table. They quickly hid the stakes when they saw the stranger.

After ordering a pot of ale, Torquin scanned the room for tools, treasure, or signs of danger. There were none. Finally he broke the silence that had lasted since his entry.

"Tell me, friends," he said in his most easygoing way, "is this the road to Oiser?"

The ill-shaven yokels exchanged looks. One suppressed a snicker. At last the oldest drawled, "Aye, and the road to fairyland as well." The others roared with laughter.

With an effort, Torquin held his temper. "I am a traveler, seeking the land beyond this realm. They told me its name was Oiser."

"Aye," the old man said again. "But I don't see your wings, or the magic wand to take you there."

Torquin did not like being mocked. His sword seared out of its scabbard, glinting in the dull air. "This is all the magic I need," he said. The spokesman's chapped skin turned pale beneath the red. "Now will you tell me the way to Oiser?" Torquin asked slowly.

"There is no Oiser, stranger," the man said roughly. "It's a fable. There is nothing beyond this realm. See for yourself. Follow the road south for a mile; you'll come to the boundary. Nothing lies beyond."

Not for a moment did Torquin believe it. The Gamemaker was crafty, but not unfair. There had to be a way to win the game. Perhaps not for these rustics who didn't even know they were figments of someone's imagination. But Torquin Vangelist was real. For him there would be a way.

Torquin's horse was reluctant to turn south. Its eyes rolled and its flanks quivered nervously. Torquin, expecting the Gamemaker to try to stop him, scanned the landscape with a keen and critical eye.

But no danger appeared. The daisy-strewn hills hid no spells, the road was empty of pursuit. Torquin pressed forward, anxious for victory.

After a mile, a chilly breeze began to blow from the south, like a draft through a door that stood ajar. Ahead, two humped hills stood like gatehouses astride the road. Torquin swung to the ground. The moment his foot hit the grass a gust of wind made the horse rear in panic. The reins jerked from his grip as the horse bolted back along the road.

Torquin did not try to pursue; he was too close to his goal. Drawing his sword, he passed resolutely forward between the guardian hills.

On the other side, the road stopped. So did the land. Torquin stood staring, the tip of his sword drooping in the gravel.

Before him lay a precipice as sheer as if some angry god had split the land with a cleaver. Columns of black basalt dropped into a chasm whose bottom not even the sunlight could reach. Hundreds of feet below, clouds boiled on the chill updrafts rising from whatever unimaginable land lay at the foundation of the cleft. The other edge of the chasm was hidden by gray mist.

So this was the Gamemaker's last puzzle. Somehow, Torquin needed to devise a way of crossing the chasm. He did not doubt there was another side, even though it lay hidden. But the chasm was wider than any log would reach. Perhaps a rope tied to an arrow might make it across, but there would be no way of securing it to hold a man's weight.

He picked up a rock and hurled it across. It disappeared soundlessly into the mist, giving no hint of how far the other side was. Torquin sat on a stone to think.

There were rumors of giant rocs in the western mountains; perhaps they could be tamed to carry a man across. Even better, a glider could ride the wind to freedom and the realm of Oiser.

But Torquin did not know how to make a glider. He was impatient to solve the puzzle right away. He stared across the abyss to where freedom waited, close enough to taste. Why could he not simply spread his arms and fly across in one giant leap? After all, this was only a dream, where anything was possible. Better yet, it was a camphra dream, where the dreamer was not the prisoner of the random subconscious, but an active participant. Camphra left the will unimpaired. Why not exercise free choice now, by choosing to negate physical law?

Torquin stood on the edge of the precipice, poised to fling himself into the air. But in the instant before he acted, a small voice of doubt spoke in him, and suddenly he was no longer Torquin Vangelist, adventurer; he was just Gloria again, and Gloria did not believe she could fly.

She blamed herself for weakness. The reasoning was not faulty; she ought to be able to change the rules, since the rules came ultimately from her mind. If only she could believe utterly in her power to do it.

But her doubt was instinctive. Looking down, she knew exactly what would happen. If she let Torquin throw himself from the brink he would plummet like a stone and die. And she could not bear the thought of losing him as she had lost John.

Backing away from the edge, she spied a large boulder and decided on an experiment where the stakes would not be quite so high. She scrambled atop the boulder and stood, trying to compose her mind. Fiercely she concentrated on winging to a patch of shrubbery twenty feet away. Then she jumped.

She fell straight to the grass. Picking herself up, she brushed off her knees. She felt a little foolish, but the experiment had proved her point. She said a mental "I told you so" to the Torquin inside her. Trying to quell his anger and frustration, she made him turn away from the precipice. Oiser might be on the other side, but Gloria needed better guarantees. Wearily grasping his sword hilt, Torquin started the long walk back to the village.

Dwilimi of Cortscham crouched in the willow bushes along the River Whey, clutching her spellstones. They were all she had left. She had bargained away all her treasures, tools, and weapons for magical power. Now the bargain was about to pay off. As she arranged the stones on the ground in a pentacle and spoke the sleep-spell words, the crew of the riverboat moored nearby began to yawn mightily as they went about their evening chores. Soon they would be sound asleep.

The other players would have recognized Dwilimi as Adriane; but they would have been only partly right. Dwilimi was a barbarian sorceress, unpolished and not overly encumbered with intelligence. Adriane's seven years of graduate school and art training were lost on Dwilimi.

When the players had split up, Dwilimi had decided to follow the river. Since then, she had been stowaway, passenger, crew, and even prisoner on every type of river craft between the Gamemaker's capital and the sea. She was very close to her goal now. In the previous turn she had reached the delta, and might have made it to the mouth if she had only kept better guard against the pirates who had attacked her felucca in the night. Now she needed a new boat—fast. She wanted badly to beat the others to the land beyond the Gamemaker's control. Then she would turn back and beat him at his own game.

The harmonica that one of the river men had been playing fell silent. Soon there was no sound but lapping water. Dwilimi broke from cover and sprinted to the boat. She untied the mooring and leaped aboard. Not a shout followed her. As the current tugged at the hull, she seized the limp body of the helmsman by the feet. Adriane might have squeamishly let him live; but Dwilimi heaved the man into the water. Then she went below to take care of the cook. As she slit his throat, the blood spurted out onto her face. Stomach turning, she raced back on deck to wash herself off.

The river swept her fast downstream. She took her place at the helm, her spellstones laid out before her, ready for the Gamemaker's opposition. He had a way of finding old, half-forgotten nightmares buried in her brain. She felt her skin prickle as she remembered the time a horde of spiders had dropped on her boat from the trees, forcing her to dive into the leech-infested water. Only barbarian callousness had saved her then. This time she was determined not to let the Gamemaker use her fears to defeat her.

The river branched ahead, and Dwilimi studied the choices with narrowed eyes. One of the channels was sure to hide a trap. The right-hand channel was wooded, with vines drooping from the bending trees; the left was covered with blooming water lilies. She waited till the very last minute before pulling the rudder hard to right. Sweat trickled down her temple as she realized she could not go back.

Before long the channel separated again into three equal parts. She gripped the tiller with white knuckles, trying to decide which way to go. Desperately she wanted more time to think; but the current swept inexorably on. At last she steered into the middle course, which looked deepest.

After that the wide stream began to split into tiny veins and the veins into tangled capillaries. Channels veered off only to redouble on themselves. Adriane realized she had plunged into a maze without a guide. Bitterly she regretted having left the helmsman behind.

The current slowed as she was driven deeper and deeper. Hovering insects made ripples on the stagnant water, and frogs sang monotonously in the clogging reeds. Sweat dripped down Adriane's face as she thought of ending her journey in a deadwater pool with nothing but miles of humid, breeding marsh around. She hated every choice. She had always followed the river because it was a path already chosen for her; the land demanded too many decisions. Yet here she was, surrounded by a nightmare of proliferating options, entangling her like a decision tree gone wild.

It seemed to last forever. Ten times she narrowly missed turning into the entrapping jaws of a backwater where she would be imprisoned forever. Exhausted and near tears, she happened into a channel where the current flowed a little stronger. Soon other arteries began to join hers. Weak with hope, she noticed the whine of frogs was dying away behind, and another sound was taking its place. She did not recognize the sound until the trees ended and she looked out across sand flats where the sea roared.

Swiftly now the river swept her toward the spot where the current met the breakers. But the sweat did not dry on her face. There was another trap ahead. The sea lay flat and empty as far as the eye could see. The wide horizon was featureless, devoid of coastline or even a rainbow to mark the way to the mythic island of Oiser. Which way was she to turn?

She chewed on her thumbnail, a habit she thought she had left behind in the waking world. This was worse than the delta; here were not just a thousand choices, but a literal infinity. And any one might be wrong.

The Gamemaker had stopped playing fair. He had abandoned her without so much as a buoy to lead her to the promised land.

Angrily she jerked the tiller toward land. The boat responded more quickly than she had expected, and ended up broadside in the channel. She saw the breaker coming and desperately tried to right the craft; but it was too late. The water hit the starboard side and foamed over the rail. The deck tilted and she slipped, clutching for a handhold.

When the port rail went underwater she knew the boat was swamped. She leaped into the surging water.

The undertow pulled as if to tempt her out to sea; but she was a strong swimmer, and the beach was near. When she staggered onto the sand, she turned to watch the boat capsize with a gurgle. It was no great loss; she was not about to risk setting forth into a saltwater desert where every direction was the same, where she would be caught in an eternity of decisions.

She glared at the sea for a moment, then turned to trudge back inland on foot.

Erin sat under a lone globe tree, chewing a stalk of grass and watching the long train of his followers snake toward him across the meadow. There were easily two hundred of them by now. They moved by every conceivable vehicle: charette, travois, donkey, wain, and horse. Grandmothers walked, bent over their canes, and children tottered through the tall grass. They had slowed his progress nearly to a crawl.

But he could not leave them. He had liberated each one from the Gamemaker's cruel tyranny, and now they followed him with trust and devotion. They came from a score of towns he had passed in his pilgrimage toward freedom and the land of Oiser. Wherever he had seen poverty, injustice, and oppression he had shared the story of his quest. He had seen hope crack the walls of indifference. He had been their salvation; now they were his responsibility.

"How much farther, Reisen?" a weatherworn cobbler asked as he drew near. They had begun calling Erin "Reisen" recently, after the prophet their legends foretold. Erin had not stopped them. Who knew? Perhaps he *was* their Reisen.

"Not far," Erin said. "The map says the boundary lies just beyond this orchard."

The word passed swiftly back along the line, and the pace quickened in anticipation. They all longed for a sight of Oiser.

As Erin rose to continue on, the pilgrims started up one of their lilting folk songs. The tune seemed vaguely familiar, the way things often did in this land. The refrain kept recurring:

We'll be free this day,
Far away,
Over the hills in Oiser.

Erin fingered the map in his pocket, hoping it was trustworthy. He had paid dearly for it back in the Gamemaker's
castle. For such a price, it ought to be right.

"Tell us about Oiser again, Reisen," a girl beside him
said. She had brown braids, a fresh face, and the expression
of a girl in love. Erin laughed and put his arm around her
shoulder.

"I don't know what Oiser is like now, Tani. But when
we get there, we'll establish a cooperative community
where all the decisions will be made by consensus. There
will be no power structure, no privilege, no private property. We'll grow strong by helping one another." The people nearby fell silent to listen. The words came fast and
easy. He had laid his plans carefully. He was not going to
conquer the Gamemaker by violence, but by good example. Under Erin's rule, Oiser would become a beacon to
the serfs of the Gamemaker's realm. Tyranny could not last
once the road to justice had been blazed.

The children cavorted among the globe trees, whose
transparent fruit caught the sunlight like liquid in a glistening cup. Silver leaves rustled like tinsel in the breeze. It
was like being in a forest of Christmas trees, Erin thought,
all decorated and waiting for the presents.

It was noon when they reached the wall. The singers
fell silent when they saw it rising black and sheer above
the treetops. As far as the eye could see, east to west, it cut
across the gaily colored fabric of the land. It could not have
been built by normal means, for it was not formed of
blocks, but was all one piece. Its face was slick as obsidian.

All eyes turned to Erin. But he was equal to the puzzle.
"We will form a human pyramid to see what's on the other
side!" he announced.

Good-naturedly, some of the strongest men knelt on
hands and knees beside the wall, and others clambered on
their backs. Soon an irregular human stair teetered thirty
feet high against the wall. Erin climbed over the backs of
his followers and pulled himself up to peer over the edge.

At first he felt a mild disappointment. The other side
was a multicolored, rolling farmland, similar to the realm

at his back. There were patches of woods and orchard, fields of tassling maize and sweet alfalfa. A wagon road wound down toward a river, on the other side of which lay a town, and on the crag above the town—

Erin's heart almost stopped. In a panic he dropped down onto the back of the person below. Whipping the map from his pocket, he studied it feverishly. He could not be *that* wrong. Not unless the map had lied. Not unless he had gotten turned around, as he always did on the Interstate. He almost groaned out loud as his disbelief turned into a terrible certainty. It was true. The castle beyond the wall was the Gamemaker's stronghold.

The rest of the people were waiting below, but Erin could not face them. He could not bear to tell them. It was an honest mistake; he had merely led them south instead of north, back to where he had started. But prophets weren't supposed to look at maps upside down.

His face was grave when he reached the ground and called the people around him. "The Gamemaker is trying to trick us," he said. "This wall is an illusion he has thrown up to keep us from gaining our freedom. We can't pass into Oiser this way, or he will catch us. We are going to have to find another way."

They believed him. They turned back disappointed, but with a sort of fatalistic cheerfulness. He told himself that they were only figments of his imagination, but it did no good. With every step back into the mocking Christmas-tree orchard he could feel them behind him, like a ball and chain on his leg.

David stood at the edge of the haunted pass that pierced the Barrier Range on the western bounds of the Gamemaker's kingdom. Dressed in sheepskins, he nevertheless shivered uncomfortably at the sight of the misty gap ahead. Sullen stains of grimy snow smeared the hills on either hand. Behind him, the stamp and jingle of horses told where his men waited. They were members of the brigand troop with whom he had swept like a marauding whirlwind across the Gamemaker's realm. They were brave and loyal; but they were superstitious to a man. And the haunted mist ahead was said to steal men's souls like bleach stole the color from a garment, leaving it bland and pale as water.

The men knew David as Flavin Connaster. Here in the Dreamgame he was young again, with dark, curly hair and a carefree, vivid smile. In fact, he had grown to look more and more like Erin as the turns had passed. Whether it was his own decision or the Gamemaker's, he was not quite sure.

Lately he had begun to wonder a lot where his own decisions ended and the Gamemaker's began. More and more frequently he felt manipulated. As he came closer to freedom, the game's choices increasingly had only one acceptable solution. It was as if the Gamemaker thought David had only a limited repertoire of responses, and was trying to play on that advantage.

David wished he were more like Erin. He would then be free of convention, free of responsibility, free of the nagging restraints of his own personality. Perhaps it would all come true, once he crossed the pass into Oiser.

Behind him, two of his men were talking softly. As he turned, a shaggy horse stamped and shook its head up and down, snorting a cloud of steam into the pale air. None of the men would look at him; they were afraid, and ashamed of their fear.

"Establish a camp in the meadow below us, and wait for me," David said. "I will go on alone."

Already, he knew, his cleverness and bravery were the subject of campfire tales among his men; this challenge of the haunted pass would make him mythic. Conscious of their eyes on him, he turned to take the steep path on foot. He felt buoyed up by their admiration, and he neither paused nor wavered as he reached the edge of the mist that shrouded the pass.

He could tell he had entered the mist only by the diminished light and the slight chill against his face. But as he climbed, the edges of the rocks on either side began to blur and take on a uniform, monotonous gray. He could hear with amazing clarity sounds from far back down the mountain: the cry of a hawk, the jingle of a harness, the crack of a dry branch. But as he pressed ahead even those faded and silence closed around him.

Gradually, visibility shrank. He pressed on, impervious to the fears of falling or losing his way which would surely have stopped him if he had had a life to lose instead of a game. He knew he must be near the pass's summit; soon the path would turn downward and the mist would clear to reveal the realm of Oiser. He peered ahead into the grayness for a glimpse of snowy spires.

But the mist was so thick he could no longer see his feet, nor his hands, nor anything but universal grayness. He was wondering how to keep from stumbling when he realized he was no longer walking on rock. He was no longer walking on anything.

He strained on, ordering feet he could no longer feel to keep moving. He felt strangely detached from his body. No, not just from his body—from his brain as well. He was dissolving, as if his being had been dropped into a strong solvent. A flash of light pierced him and he recoiled in panic—back into his mind, back into his body, back onto the mountainside, shutting himself into a box within a box within a box in horror at the terrible unbeing he had touched.

He was racing panic-stricken back down the mountainside, his heart leaping in his rib cage. Nearing the edge of the fog, he saw a rock he recognized and forced himself to stop, breathing heavily. His superstitious comrades had been right about the haunted pass. The mist *did* steal men's souls. That was the price of Oiser.

But the price was too high. David could not give up his own self, not even for the sake of freedom. His individuality, eccentric and tormented as it was, was the only thing he was sure of.

Filled with rage, he pounded a clenched fist against the rock. The Dreamgame had always been his liberator from the anxieties and failures of real life. Now it was just another prison. And yet he knew he had come close. In that one terrifying instant of not being he had glimpsed a light as of shining glaciers below him. He had seen the mountaintops of Oiser. For a moment, he had encompassed the world below him, and his mind had touched the mind of All. He had tasted, for the first time in his life, true and utter freedom.

Turning, he glared uphill into the mist, then gave the finger to the land of Oiser.

Yu Vang did not move for a long time after the others left. The dungeon was still except for a dank draft. He stared at the rusty grating that penned him in, bitterly blaming the divination that had promised him freedom. All the signs had lied. Now he was caught in a prison within a prison. As if daily life had not been enough, charmon had woven yet another trap from the phantoms of his faithless senses. He was penned inside nested boxes of worlds, each one as self-consistent as the next.

He flinched as a rat scuttled through the dripping darkness toward a pit in the center of the room. Queasily Yu Vang rose to his feet. He had not liked rats since his days in the refugee camp. He thrust the unwelcome memory from his mind and started to prowl his jail.

In the back corner, where a deep shadow fell across the wall, he spied a spot where the masonry seemed uneven. Squatting down, he ran his fingers along the wall. One of the large stones was loose. Brushing away the crumbled mortar, he worked his fingers into the crack and lifted. The stone grated, shifting. Patiently Yu Vang worked at it until the stone fell out, revealing a dark tunnel just wide enough for a man to squirm through.

Head first, Yu Vang crawled into the tunnel, feeling his way with his hands. His body blocked off even the dim light from the dungeon, and the air was close and stale. He wriggled stubbornly forward, refusing to let himself think of getting stuck.

A dim patch of light lay ahead. As he crawled eagerly toward it, he felt his knee hit a lever, and suddenly the floor collapsed beneath him. Unable to catch himself, he plummeted down a chute. The rough stone scraped his hands and tore at his trousers as he tried to break his fall. He landed with a breath-jarring thump in another prison cell identical to the first.

The fall knocked a sense of reality into him. He sat with his knees drawn up and his arms around his legs, nursing his bruised shin. He understood what was happening now. Whatever he did, he would only be playing into his captor's hands. The creator of this world needed only one thing to control his players: their belief in the reality of the things around them. But Yu Vang did not want to play. He was here unwillingly; he had no stake in believing. And doing *anything* simply entangled him further. The only sensible thing was to sit and wait out the dream.

At first nothing happened. Soon a rat emerged from the pit in the center of the floor, whiskers twitching. Yu Vang ignored it. It was not, after all, a real rat. Before long a second one appeared. Yu Vang stilled his breathing and centered his mind, intent upon transcending the rats. A wriggling, many-legged thing dropped upon his shoulder. He refused to believe in it.

The rattle of keys sounded in a faraway lock. Footsteps approached down a long corridor. Yu Vang smiled to himself at how quickly the Gamemaker had grown tired of this inaction.

The guard who came to a halt at Yu Vang's cell was the incarnation of all the hoodlum fighters he had known in his flight from his homeland: a fanatic, a child-man with nothing to worship but the weapon that gave him power. Death was his religion, cruelty his government. In a rage, the guard started shouting threats at Yu Vang, brandishing his handgun.

But Yu Vang no longer felt the visceral fear he should have. "You are not real," he told the guard serenely. "You are within my dream, and the dream is within my mind, so you also must be within my mind. But I choose not to remember you." With a tremendous effort, he shut out the sound of the soldier's tirade, blocked off sight of the cell, and concentrated on nothing. Clearly, the Gamemaker was drawing challenges from his prisoner's own mind. If Yu Vang could make his mind transparent, the Gamemaker would have no weapons.

He suddenly realized that he was no longer sitting on stone. He shifted, and a cushion yielded beneath him. Warily, he allowed himself to look. Before him, a dying wisp of steam rose from the bowl on the hibachi. Sprawled on the thick carpet lay the people with whom he had entered the trance. He watched their faces, tense and troubled even under the drug. Then he raised his eyes to the exit.

He was back in his own world, miraculously unaffected by the camphra. It was late at night; not a soul would be watching. He could escape now, and no one would be able to tell the social worker when or where he had gone.

But as he was about to rise, his eyes turned to the closed door at the western end of the room. It did not move, but somehow he knew that the Gamemaker waited beyond. Then Yu Vang saw the trick. Unable to trap him in one dream, the Gamemaker had put him into another in hopes of making him mistake it for reality.

But what if it *was* reality? Yu Vang's heart pounded with the stress of indecision. If it was reality, he would miss his chance to act, to continue the flight that seemed to stretch back across his life as far as he could see behind him. He would miss his chance to go to California, to become entangled in yet another reality, perhaps another dream.

Suddenly Yu Vang laughed aloud. How little he had to lose! Closing his eyes, he stubbornly refused to believe in what lay around him. It was a trick, a delusion. Whatever Gamemaker had spun it, he had power only so long as Yu Vang let himself be hoodwinked. The smell of the camphra, the softness of the cushions, the distant rumble of thunder from across the lake—all were meant to distract him, perhaps to amuse him for a time, but to delude him in the end.

One by one the things around him faded from his mind. His thoughts fell in step until they came to rest, like a spinning top, at a point of equilibrium. He seemed very far away from his body, far from all sensation. Deeper and deeper into reality he sank, away from the imprisoning dream.

He had crossed effortlessly into the realm beyond the Gamemaker's control before pausing to wonder whether he ought to turn back. He could see his body sitting in the carpeted room in the house by the great lake, no doubt still convinced of its own reality. The scene was like a board game left half finished by a petulant child. Turning, he beheld the heavens spinning above him in pinwheel radiance, concentric shells upon an axis of purest light. He did not turn back.

The players lay silently as the camphra trance released them. Rain was beginning to drum loudly on the board roof, and lightning flickered behind the curtains. For a while they sat gazing at the ceiling, at the floor, at anything but each other.

David was first to speak. "What do you pay him, Gloria?" No one had to ask who.

"Two hundred dollars," Gloria said.

"Are you kidding? Only two hundred?"

Gloria sounded embarrassed. "It was John who hired him and made all the arrangements. He's never asked for more."

"No sacrificial virgins or the blood of your firstborn?" David's smile was sardonic.

Gloria frowned, wishing David could resist being flip.

"Well, I don't think he even earned two hundred tonight," Adriane said positively. The others all looked at her. She shook her hair out, ceramic earrings flying. "He wasn't playing fair. He manipulated me. He fixed it so I couldn't possibly win. That's not in the contract. I think I'm going to tell him so."

Before anyone could stop her she was on her feet and making toward the closed door. Erin and David both shouted for her to stop. The Gamemaker had made it clear that no one was to intrude upon him. But Adriane paid no attention. Angrily, she flung open the door.

The room was empty. She stared into it for a few moments, fists on her hips, then stooped to pick up the manila envelope by the door. The money was gone. "He got away," she said.

"Idiot!" David scowled. "If you'd offended him, he might never have come back."

"So what?" Adriane said. "I don't want to play with someone who stacks the deck. The whole damn game has been a big shaggy-dog story. For two years we've been trying to escape. Now I don't think there's a way to escape. There is no Oiser."

"Yes, there is. There has to be!" Gloria said earnestly.

"Have you seen it?"

"Almost," Gloria said. "I know it's there. How else can we get free?"

"Does it matter?" David said.

The others stared at him.

"Don't be ridiculous!" Erin scoffed. "Of course it matters. You have to be able to win."

"Really?" David persisted. "Think about it. If we won, we'd become like Gamemakers ourselves. And that means we'd be responsible for what happened. Not for me, thanks. That's no game. That's real life."

"So you think we should just stop trying?" Adriane eyed him speculatively.

"If we want the game to go on. There's a lot of things I

haven't seen yet, adventures I haven't had. That whole world was created for our amusement. I want my money's worth before we pack it in."

Slowly, Erin said, "That makes a lot of sense. I'll stop trying to win if you will."

Wordlessly, the others nodded.

"That leaves Gerhard," Erin said. "We'll have to tell him."

Now that someone had mentioned the fifth player, they noticed that Yu Vang had not yet moved. "He should be coming to by now," Gloria frowned. Erin, who was closest, leaned over to look. He gave a low exclamation.

"What is it?" Gloria asked.

Wordlessly, Erin felt the man's wrist for a pulse. When he let the hand drop it fell limply to the floor. "He's dead," Erin said.

With one exclamation, they rose to crowd around.

"Oh my God," Adriane said in a small voice, "what if it was the camphra?"

"The camphra was all right," Gloria answered. "We would have noticed something by now if it were poisoned."

"It's SUNDS—the Sudden Unexplained Nocturnal Death Syndrome," Erin said positively. "It affects Asian immigrants. They die in their sleep. Of nightmares, they say."

"Must be some nightmares." Adriane's voice was shaky.

But David knew better. The expression on the dead man's face had nothing to do with nightmares. It was a look of joyful realization—just such an expression, David thought, as might have been on his own face when in a piercing instant he had beheld the radiant land of Oiser. Clenching his fists violently, he turned away from the sight, deeply and irrationally ashamed of himself.

The occupants of Gloria Callander's summer house stood watching in the early morning rain as the paramedics wheeled out the gurney with the sheet-covered body. Adriane, wrapped in a blanket and sipping some hot coffee, tried to catch David's eye; but he had an angry, preoccupied expression.

At the kitchen door the caretaker and his wife stood watching. They were not terribly upset. They had never gotten to know Yu Vang well, and had rather resented his diligence. As the ambulance motor roared to life the man reached into the pocket of his overalls to finger the two hundred dollars they had secretly taken, as they always did, from the manila envelope Gloria left by the spare room door.

An Excerpt from
The Confession of the Alchemist Edward Dee,
Who Was Burnt in the City of Findias
on the Planet Paracelsus,
1437 PIC
(*Post Imperial Colonial Period*)

MICHAELA ROESSNER

ALTHOUGH you gentlemen and gooddames have broken my body and will soon separate it from what you term my "soul," I cannot admit to what you term my "crimes." Not from the evil stubbornness you assign me, and only in part for what I might foolishly call my own "faith" and "integrity," so different from your own. But mainly because in these dark, chaotic times I no longer understand human events, and why my own and others' studies would be called Satanic. Satanic! If not for my pain I would laugh that in the end human imagination is so limited that you must fall back on that old bugaboo.

I have gleaned a grain of hope of late in the very savagery and confusion which destroys myself and others. I sought knowledge as I could, trying to understand, but perhaps the solution was this instead: the breakdown of everything we brought to this planet, so that the power of this world could finally emerge and begin its transformation upon us.

When I was young, our presence on this planet was young, and Science still reigned as God. I knew Science as a blind God, stumbling about the hidden reality of this place, so I did not mourn its eventual dethronement. Ahh, the irony—for in the course of my studies I fell back time and again, at least in method, on that Science I belittled and sneered at; and the "enlightened superstition" I'd hoped would replace it turned out to be a mindless beast. No offense meant, of course, to your "gentle" selves. For all my studies and searching, all I've truly discovered is that the secret of human existence, the heart of human existence, is fear.

So I have this to say to the charges you've leveled against me: I do not understand them.

But I do have one confession to make, for my own conscience. It is the only crime I am guilty of. Yet even in this I am bemused, for did I inadvertently do something truly horrible, or was I the unwitting instrument of an act of miraculous beneficence? Whichever, it was this deed which has been the burden of my life, and which started me on the road leading to this time and place and these circumstances.

During my childhood there lived close to my home another family with a boy my own age, both of us second generation born on this world. I was (and still would be, if not for the current fractured state of my bones and joints) typical of the type that colonized this planet: tall and thin, narrow-boned, with pale, sharp features.

My parents shared these characteristics too, as did the mother and father of my neighbor, Danny. Danny, however, was another sort altogether: shorter, stockily-built, with a broadly planed face. When we played together in the sun, his skin stained quickly to a gilded chestnut color, while mine reddened for days before eventually darkening.

Danny, in short, was one of those "sports" we are all familiar with. I've often thought that it is as if this planet were displeased with the homogenous stock that colonized it, and decided to assert its own mark on a few of our children in protest.

Just as he was physically of that "sort," so Danny was in all other ways as well.

His type has always been laughed at and called "simple," as if they lacked intellectual faculties, or possessed weak memories. This is untrue. At school they learn as quickly, perhaps more so, than normal children, and never give up a piece of information once absorbed.

But in short order other children discover their extreme gullibility, and from then on these unfortunates are marked as fools. They learn anything that is told them and believe it with all of their trusting hearts. With the cruelty common to the young, the other children make them the butt of all practical jokes. Time after time they are exposed to ridicule. Yet they never lose their disposition of faith: I believe cynicism is an emotion alien to their nature. And so they lack the self-protective guards necessary to any real survival in a human world.

Danny was not only such a child—he epitomized the breed.

We lived on the fringes of Alban Arthan Township, in a neighborhood isolated by its newness. Beyond the houses, the terraforming lay like a bare veneer over the terrain. The planet's original structure still poked through in places like old bones under the thin, worn-velveteen hide of a starving dog.

No other children near our age lived in the immediate area, so Danny was not ridiculed and I was not drawn, through peer pressure, into ranks against him. Thus we grew up together as friends.

Beyond the edges of our neighborhood we explored the tame fringes of terraformed forests and the wild, sterile spaces—part of the little that remained of Paracelsus' original, lifeless form. The barren spaces were our favorites. Their bleakness formed a blank canvas for our creativity. When we were still very young my innocence and ability to believe matched Danny's.

And if we sometimes experienced unusual but muted sensations—as if the ghosts of fish swam in the ghost of a river right past our faces—and if we sometimes thought we almost glimpsed unseeable things, we simply thought them part of our concocted adventures, or natural phenomenon that adults would someday explain to us.

In a few years we were packed off to the local first-school. I made new friends. Danny did not. Looking back, I'm tempted to feel a wistful admiration for myself as a child. I can see now that, all unconscious, I possessed a balance and sociability rare for that age. I kept my friendship with Danny. Indeed, at times I became his protector.

Yet I managed to avoid sharing his taint of ridicule. I was accepted and liked by the other children. It is true that Danny and I didn't spend as much time together, and I wasn't always able to keep the others from taunting or playing pranks on him. But I never joined in, and when I felt it safe, would defend him.

Other than looking lonely and a little hurt at times, Danny accepted the situation with equanimity, as if he had been born knowing how things would be. In the time we still spent together after classes, he seemed just as happy. After school and on the holidays we spent our idle hours much as before, in exploration and imagined derring-do.

In the passing years the tenor of our games gradually changed. Instead of unreal adventure, we played at the sort of edgeless competition boys that age enjoy: racing against each other, seeing who could skip a pebble across the Stone Sea, comparing our strength in lifting feats. Whoever won, the other rejoiced in his prowess. We goaded and supported each other to greater heights.

Even that finally had to change. At the age of fourteen we were sent to mid-school; a single, larger institution in the heart of town.

Matriculating from small first-schools sprinkled around the township, the entering students arrived in a state of shock. We were all overwhelmed by the school's size, the patronizing and razzing of the older students, and the physical onslaught of adolescence itself.

Separated by different classes, new circles of acquaintances (at least for me), and the greater burden of schoolwork, Danny and I drifted apart. I didn't mean to desert him. Those circumstances were beyond my own or any child's control. Without even thinking about it, I gave up trying to protect him. I was having a hard enough time protecting myself from the predations of the older students. And I think I assumed that he would naturally gravitate into friendships with the few others like him.

On weekdays and holidays we still occasionally managed to go off together, although ever more rarely. Besides a heavier load of studies, I'd made new friends from other parts of the township, friends with whom I experienced real, rather than imaginary, adventures.

One afternoon—as it turned out, one of the last times we would spend together—Danny and I found ourselves clambering over the ring of boulders that edged the plateau of the Sea of Stones.

The Sea of Stones. I don't believe it exists anymore. If my memory serves, a number of years ago the tumorousness of the township spread over it, converting it into a subterranean layer supporting the elevated homes of the rich.

In my youth it lay untouched, an artifact of the original planet. It was a vast plain of stones, all mysteriously sculpted into a soft-looking roundness. Danny and I had spent hours, days, weeks there in contests pitching the smaller pebbles. Danny, more muscular, always threw farther, while I consistently won in accuracy.

On this day we threw no stones. I knew I'd come to an age where competition was no longer edgeless: where resentment, not rejoicing, met another's success.

So instead we strolled, talking of aimless matters. Already the Sea of Stones looked smaller, diminished by my own growth—shrunken simply by the fact that I now looked down at it from a different angle and a greater height.

Danny was immersed in his own reverie. He picked up stones and rolled them between his hands, studying them, then let them drop. Lost in our thoughts, we lapsed into silence; two boys entirely separate, walking side by side as if by coincidence.

Danny emerged first and spoke, startling me from my thoughts. "Why are these stones like this?" he asked. The rock he held was smooth, with a soft contoured hole worn through the middle.

"What?"

"Why are these stones like this?" he repeated. "In science class the teacher said shapes like this are made by water. But even back in first-school they told us there wasn't any water before terraforming."

I took the stone from him and hefted it in my hand. Only its shape was smooth. Its surface felt granular against my palm. It had a pleasing weight.

"Maybe the wind shaped them, over millions of years," I told him.

"Could the wind make a hole like that?" he asked.

"Sure, with enough time. If some grains of sand got

caught on the stone's surface. The wind would keep grinding them in till they ground through," I replied.

Danny looked content with my explanation.

Then, God forgive me, I had a thought. The idea for an innocent jest, or so I thought, crossed my mind. If only I had never spoken!

"Of course, there's another possible explanation," I said casually.

Danny looked up with interest.

"My mother told me that old legends from the first world, Terra, have it that these kinds of stones are fairy stones. If you look through the hole and the conditions are just right, you catch a glimpse of the fairy land."

I expected Danny to look momentarily confused.

But instead his eyes widened with belief, not disbelief. "Really?" he said.

I pushed the joke farther. "Well, maybe," I said. "We can see, can't we?" I held the stone's hole up to my eye. "Nah, there's nothing. But wait a minute, maybe if I get it at just the right angle, in just the right light . . ." I made a huge show of shifting the stone, cocking it this way and that. "Danny! Danny! I *do* see something. Not clearly . . . just a glimmer. Something silvery and shimmery. Danny, it's true!" I pulled the stone away, trying to set my features in the lines of pure wonder I'd seen so often on Danny's face.

Danny hopped from foot to foot with excitement. "Really? Really?" he kept saying. "Can I see too?"

"Here. See for yourself." I tossed the stone back to him.

He snatched it up and looked. "I don't see anything," he complained. He mimicked my movements of shifting the angle of the stone against the sunlight. I clutched my sides, trying to hold in my laughter. Danny lowered the stone, looking disappointed and bewildered. A twinge of shame disrupted my merriment. I started to think of words that would gently explain my prank to Danny.

Before I could speak, I saw a thought cross his easily read face. "Of course," he said to himself. "I did it wrong." He lifted the stone again and turned it around, so that he looked through the hole from the other side. A huge, happy sigh escaped him. "That was it," he murmured, still to himself. "It really is there. It's so beautiful." He stood, absorbed, for a long time.

I froze. Doubt and then suspicion seized me. Completely against his nature, had Danny turned the tables on me? I would have been relieved, absolved somewhat of my guilt if that had been the case. I knew that I deserved it.

But when he at last lowered the stone and slipped it into his pocket, no trace of guile shadowed his face. His features glowed, transfixed. For the first time I saw, different as he was from everyone else I knew, his incredible beauty. Radiant, he looked at me with a sense of shared wonder. "It really is there," he breathed. "All these years we've played here and we never thought to look." Another thought occurred to him. "We're the only ones who've seen it, aren't we? Otherwise there would be people everywhere, looking for stones like this for themselves. Thank you. Thank you!" Danny launched himself, grabbing me in a bear hug.

I endured his embrace, squirming deep inside myself, embarrassed by my adolescence at this sort of contact with another boy, miserable in my guilt, and angry that his gullibility forced me to continue the joke.

I felt shabby, a counterfeit friend. I knew myself at last to be no better than all the other children that had tormented Danny. In those moments I lost a cherished illusion of myself. With adult vision I saw how naturally I'd slipped into the easy cruelty I'd looked down on in others.

As we walked home, my perception of Danny also changed. He not only believed the tale I'd told him, but his brain and eyes had conjured up a vision so he could convince himself of its truth. This made him more than merely gullible. He really was a fool.

I began to separate from him and our childhood together. We walked back as strangers, though Danny didn't know that yet. He thought we shared a brotherhood even closer than before, as mutual guardians of the wonderful secret. After that day, I consciously avoided Danny.

But soon, something happened anyway to drive that afternoon completely from my mind.

Within the space of a single day, or perhaps even hours, I discovered (or I should say, my body and senses discovered) girls. Before, female classmates had been the same as boys, only a little different. Overnight they metamorphosized, and became enticing, exasperating, frustrating, alluring, irritating. They mysteriously attracted me, as if they could provide something I lacked and could satiate a hunger that plagued every part of my body. Their presence made me nervous and hostile. I clung for refuge and comfort to packs of other equally shaken boys. At the same time I wanted to touch these girls, stroke their silky hair, laugh and joke with them with unstumbling words.

So my first sexual awakenings were normal, consisting of confused and unrelieved torment, afflicting my adolescent life with itching, physical anguish.

When Danny came to me a few weeks after my transformation, I hardly remembered our last outing.

He approached me shyly in the hall. "Hey, Edward, I haven't seen you much lately."

"I've been busy, Danny," I said. "You know, schoolwork and stuff."

He nodded. "Yeah, I figured. Look, I've got this great idea. Can you go up with me to the Sea after school today?"

Our walk came back to me. I shifted my stance in discomfort. "I'd like to Danny, really. But I'm staying in the library to study." I'd been stalking a group of girls I was beglamoured by, not sure if I was the hunter or the prey. Earlier I'd heard them mention the library, so I was staying afterward to study—them.

Danny stared at me, struggling to understand. Looking at that transparent, honest face, I knew his thoughts. He was trying to comprehend my supposed devotion to school when I could be investigating the wonders he thought we'd seen together. He couldn't understand, but as always, in the end, he believed me.

"All right," he said, defeated. "Maybe you can come out and help me some other time."

I looked at him closely. His clear, open face seemed untouched by the pubescent torment afflicting the rest of us.

"Sure, Danny, but it'll be a while. I'm way behind in my schoolwork."

Danny's eyes saddened at my evasive desertion. "Maybe you can come look, then, when I'm done," he said.

"Course I will. Just let me know."

I didn't see Danny for months after that. Life was full enough as my hormones and social skills slowly began to balance each other out. When I emerged from the haze I found that I indeed lagged in my studies. I threw myself into catching up.

Finally one day Danny approached me again. "I'm all done," he said. "I finished a couple of weeks ago."

I looked at him without comprehension.

"Out at the Sea of Stones . . . What I've been building," he explained patiently. "I'm done. You said you'd come see."

I started to make excuses.

"You said you'd come," he persisted with uncharacteristic stubbornness.

He looked so hurt and sounded so like a child that my protectiveness toward him resurfaced. "All right," I agreed. "We'll go this afternoon."

How can I describe to you that last hike up to the Sea of Stones? My feelings fluxed between boredom and a pompous nostalgia. I reviewed with condescending fondness the happy, childish times we'd spent there.

At last we scrambled up onto the plateau. Something had changed. A lumpish shape grew out of the middle of the Sea.

Danny danced with glee at my surprise. "I made it," he crowed. "It took me a long time, all by myself. But I did it, and it's perfect. Come look at it, Edward."

The structure was a small hut, not quite as tall as myself, constructed of hundreds of stones of varying sizes, each with a hole bored through it.

"It took me a long time to find that many fairy stones," Danny said with pride. "There are so many more of the other sort, the kind without holes. When I tried to put them together, they kept falling in on each other. That's when I thought of setting them in the frames."

Danny had dragged lengths of wood up and crudely nailed them together in irregular shapes. The stones were wedged tautly into the frames.

"See how I fit the frames together, bound them with rope?"

"But why, Danny?"

"So it would all fit and stand up without falling in."

"But what did you build it for?"

"So I'd capture the place," he beamed. "Well, not capture it, exactly, but make a space to find it in."

Seeing the bafflement on my face, he explained patiently, as though I were the childlike one. "Look, if I can look through and see the place through the hole, then it must be on the other side, right?"

I nodded numbly.

"But it isn't, of course," he continued. "There's just the other side of the stone, and all this." He gestured at the sky, the rocky plain, the world. "So I figured that to get at it I had to surround it, contain it, make a space that's nothing *but* the other side of the hole. Holes," he corrected himself, looking at his creation.

"Go in," he invited me. "It's wonderful inside. I've wanted so badly to show you."

The greater his eagerness, the stronger my reluctance. The whole situation struck me as eerie, a descent into madness. I walked around the hut. "How?" I asked. "It's all sealed up."

"This is the door." Danny dragged away a single large stone, propped between supporting frames. Its removal left a space barely big enough to shimmy through. With dread I crawled in. Inside, to sit, I had to curl my knees up to my chest to fit. I looked about. Not only were the irregular walls constructed of the fairy stones, but Danny had paved the ground with them as well.

"I'm going to close it up now," Danny said. "That's when it becomes the other place."

I wanted to cry out in fear not to shut the door. With boyish hubris I forced myself to stay quiet. Even in the middle of my panic I knew my fear meant that in some still-young spot deep within, I believed that Danny was right. I would not give in to that. The stone grated against the frame as Danny shut me in.

My heart pounded. I closed my eyes and held my breath, waiting for something to happen. I heard and felt nothing. Slowly I opened my eyes. The sun spackled light through the hundreds of holes, dimly illuminating the small space. My haunches rested uncomfortably on the hard irregular seat provided by the stones of the flooring. It was very peaceful but stuffy in there. I let out my breath, quietly. Danny called out to me. "I can see you in there. Isn't it wonderful, Edward? Isn't it beautiful?"

I followed the sound of his voice. His eye peered at me through one of the holes.

I felt a tremendous grief for him, and a sensation as if we were being carried off away from each other, away from our marvelous childhood, at the speed of light. "Yes, Danny. It's really something. I'm ready to come out now."

He pulled aside the door-stone. "That was fast," he said. I squirmed out. "It's my turn now." He clambered in. "Every time I go in a little further and stay a little longer," he confided, as if I understood what he meant. I started to help wedge the door in place.

"No, that's all right," he said. "I'm used to doing it by myself."

I sat and waited for him a while, the stones outside no more comfortable to sit on than those inside the structure. From time to time I heard Danny laughing and singing. After a bit I decided it was time to get him out. Standing up beside the hut to call to him, I peered in to see how he was amusing himself.

Instead of Danny sitting cramped and alone on the ground, I saw something that after seventy years of pondering and reliving I still cannot describe.

Lights and undiscovered colors swirled within. Except that it wasn't a "within." Luminous chaos extended to infinity. Abstract images of unimaginable beauty shot across my field of vision, changing and shifting as they went. There was nothing inside of any recognizable shape, height, or depth.

"Danny!" I shrieked.

"I guess I've been in here a long time," his voice floated from the bewitching riot. "I lose track, you know. I'll come out pretty soon."

As it appeared to me, Danny didn't exist as a single entity any more. His words percolated up from a myriad of sparkling, shimmering bits, some of which were disappearing at great speed into a horizonless distance.

Wonderful odors drifted up to me. They smelled completely unfamiliar, yet punched strong emotional messages directly into my brain. I recalled how I felt when I smelled fresh-baked bread, the first freesias of spring, and the maddening, clean-scrubbed wholesome smell of the girls at school.

It was more than just scent. Whatever Danny had become, floated, was immersed in, a sea of tactile sensuousness. All the painful longings I'd suffered of late: the answer to them lay before me in an undiluted form far more complete, pure, and true than the awkwardness of girls.

I scrambled around to the door, yanked it aside, and plunged my head in. Only the quiet, light-speckled stones greeted me. The space was empty of Danny. I screamed.

I started to tremble. Sweat flooded my pores. I shook my head frantically, trying to clear it. Danny had said the space didn't work unless it was all closed up. I slithered back in. As I awkwardly dragged the door closed from the inside, I wondered if Danny would emerge beside me, our two forms overcrowding the space to bursting, or if I would join him in that disembodied wonderland. I remained there alone. "Danny?" I finally whispered. There was no answer. I climbed out one last time and resealed the door.

I looked in again from the outside. The wild and beautiful place was there again, still as captivating, its allure so powerful I wished I were water so that I could wash through the holes in the stone to join it. "Danny, are you in there?" I called hopelessly.

"I want to stay a while longer," his voice came to me, ever more distant. He was leaving me behind. "You don't have to wait for me."

I can't explain what I did next, even to my own satisfaction. Was I trying to retrieve Danny, or rescue him? Or did I lose control of myself in a frenzy to get in and join him? I started tearing at the hut; pulling the stones from the frames, punching them out, then ripping the frames themselves out. About a third of the way down I came to myself, stopped, and looked in. Stones littered the bottom of the hut. Open to the sky, it was now flooded rather than dappled by the harsh light of the sun. There was no sign of my friend.

"Danny?" my voice quavered.

This time he did not answer. He never answered again.

I tore the whole structure down to hide my deed. I scattered the ropes and fragments of wood from the frame, dispersed the stones. When it became evident that Danny was missing, a search was instigated. Constables questioned me, but in spite of my fears, not at great length. Danny's mother knew I'd been shunning him for months.

She hadn't known we'd gone off together that day. No one looked for him in the Sea of Stones. That had always been one of our secret places.

Eventually people assumed he'd gone the way of many of his kind—led away by someone through his gullibility, or simply wandered off in his loneliness.

I returned to the Sea of Stones weeks later, when I'd recovered from the events enough to think more clearly and be haunted by guilt. I rummaged over the ground, trying to find all the rocks Danny had used in his construction. It was futile. Realizing I couldn't duplicate his efforts, I settled for building a smaller, rougher structure, hoping it might provide a way back for him and a way in for me. It took me months to build. Each day that I worked I thought of Danny spending the same kind of day with his hope, rather than my despair, in his heart. I left my hut standing for a long time, but he never came back.

Finally I remembered the day I'd first teased him, how he'd turned the stone around to find the right side. Not gifted with his sight, I realized I had no way of knowing which way all those hundreds of stones should face. I dismantled the hut.

Over the years I was able to stop worrying about Danny, although I never lost my guilt. I could not know whether he'd found another way out or whether he's still "inside," frightened and lost, or happily at home in that strange place. From what I glimpsed of that wonderful land that was not a land, I would guess the latter. It is I who for seventy years have been tortured and haunted by what I saw and could not reach, not he.

Decades of study have led me nowhere, except to those experiments which you, in your ignorance and fear, have called my crimes. I did develop a theory, which I believe as much as anything else. It is this: Paracelsus was dead and barren when our kind discovered it. I think it has never experienced "life" as we understand it. But what we see and know of Paracelsus is a sort of facade, or "outer" structure. Somewhere deep within or through its substance, it leads an existence richer, more wonderful than any we can imagine. I believe, too, that its spirit is leaching through to change a few of us, like Danny, who can be counted the lucky ones, if they by chance find the way, as he did.

One last thing torments me. It is what Danny said to me

as I sat in his hut and he looked in on me. He asked me if didn't I think it was wonderful. Did I look to him as he shortly afterward looked to me? Was I floating, surrounded and fragmented by wonder, just as he was, but couldn't see it?

The Doorkeeper
of Khaat

PATRICIA A. McKILLIP

THERE WERE KHAATI EVERYWHERE in Theore, those days, refugees from the war on the other side of the planet. There were Meri in the city also, but Meri had been moving into Tatia for a hundred and fifty years. There were Datu, but the land the Tatians had civilized had been theirs once, anyway. Now they ran restaurants in one side of the city, and in the other, they stole transport parts or painted huge bright murals on tenement walls and called themselves artists. There had always been Tatians in Theore but not as many now, Kel noticed, as there used to be. As the Khaati and the Meri moved into the city, Tatians moved out to the country, to the northern cities, to the sea-colonies if they could afford it. For a while, before he decided to become a poet, Kel had lived in one of the tiny, white domed spaces in a sea-colony. His father had bought the space for him as a reward for finishing his engineering studies. Kel spent afternoons swathed in light, swaying gently to the movements of tide, listening to words well up from some shadowy, unnamed river running through his brain, fit themselves together as neatly as molecules. One day he left the sea-colony full of golden faces like his own and went to live on the oldest street in the oldest city in Tatia.

A hundred years ago, the street had been famous for its

passionate, impoverished poets. Now it was populated mostly by Khaati. Kel, intoxicated by the past, saw their pale, aqua-eyed faces so constantly that he forgot his own was different. The odd singsong language he heard on the street formed an undistracting background for his thoughts. He drank their alcoholic teas, bought steaming, spicy fish from their shops, nibbled it as he walked down the street in the evenings. From behind paper curtains, he heard their odd, tuneless, meandering music that told of places no boat could sail to, of thresholds no shod foot could cross.

There were rules on that street. He couldn't remember learning them, he just knew them: rules his poet's eye had observed while he himself was doing nothing much. Do not look their maidens in the eye, the rules said. Do not compliment the babies or lay a hand on the young children's heads. Never step on the shadows of the elderly. Do not whistle in their shops. Never point at anyone, you could lose a finger. Be careful what small amusing tourist trinket, pin, or jacket you buy—you might find yourself wearing the emblem of the latest street gang, and unlike Tatians, they did not discriminate. And don't call them gangs. Clans, they were. Clans.

He lived from hand to mouth there, from moment to moment, as a poet should live. Or at least as he understood them to have lived on that street in Theore a hundred years before. He tracked down their forgotten poems, read voraciously, and tried to imitate them in his writings. They had written of everything, they valued every word, for each word, each experience, was equally sacred, equally profane. His Tatian lover, who had come with him from the sea-colonies, bore with his obsession for a couple of months. Then she realized that he was absurdly content in that neighborhood among the Khaati, that he had no inclination to take a job from his father, live in the great light-filled high-rises mid-city that strove like gargantuan plants toward the sun. She left him, disappeared into the Tatian heart of the city. The shock of her leaving and for such reasons fueled much articulate and bitter poetry. Sometimes, sobering up and rereading his work, Kel felt almost grateful to her for the experience of pain.

Around the time that brooding over his lost love was

becoming habitual rather than unavoidable, Kel met Aika. He sat down beside her in a Khaati bar one afternoon. The scent of her mildly intoxicating tea wafted toward Kel as he chewed over his loss. Sometime during the next couple of hours, he found talking to Aika more interesting than getting drunk. She neither laughed nor sighed when he said he was a poet. She raised a thin white eyebrow and told him she was going to Khaat.

"Khaat," Kel said blankly. He had been wondering why her eyes—the same light, clear blue as every other Khaati he had ever seen—were so astonishingly beautiful. Then he blinked. "Khaat?"

"Yes."

"Khaat is not a place. Khaat is a war."

"I was born in Khaat." She sipped tea delicately; her fingers were long, tapering, ringed. "My parents escaped just after I was born. So I have lived in Tatia all my life. I know two languages, I have a Tatian education. But Khaat is still my country, even at war with itself. My heritage."

"Your heritage—the best of it—is on this street," he argued. "There can't be much left in Khaat. It's been tearing itself apart for so long nobody remembers who's fighting who or why."

She smiled after a moment, a thin-lipped, amused smile. "Just Blues fighting Blues in one of their interminable clan wars."

"No. Clan wars I understand. But Khaat seems intent on destroying itself. What do you think you'll find there but a dying country with nothing left of it but a name?"

Her level gaze did not falter at his glib bluntness, but her eyes seemed to grow enormous, luminous. She only said dryly, "You want to be a poet. Read Coru."

He sat up until dawn reading Aika's copy of Coru's poems, while she slept beside him. The poet-shaman had lived two thousand years before in a Khaat that Kel had not realized was so old. Coru had spent his life wandering down farm roads, through jungles, into villages, bringing both practical and mystical remedies for everything from hangnails to impotence. He wrote of everything: fish soup, morning dew, sex, starving children, clan battles, and white tigers. Words kept the world orderly, he believed, kept the past from vanishing.

Soul, like butterfly, has no language.
We who walk from moment to moment,
Must say where we have been
Moment to moment,
Or we disappear.
So, like rice pickers,
We harvest words out of our mouths,
To feed ourselves.

Aika made an irritated movement in her sleep at Kel's
voice. He stopped reading, blinked gritty eyes at the dawn.
Strange images prowled in his head like ghosts of somebody else's relatives: the white tiger that appeared sometimes ahead of the poet to lead him to a place where he
was needed; monkeys and teal-eyed birds screaming at
one another in different languages; noon sun on a chalk-
white road; the stout, broad-faced, sweaty farmer's widow
whose lovemaking Coru compared to every natural disaster he could think of; the Doorkeeper, the mysterious,
many-faced woman who carried the keys to the Doorway
of Death on her belt.

"Yes, but," Kel, his eyes closed, heard himself say, "that
was two thousand years ago. The shelf-life of a country's
soul is two generations after the revolution that formed it."

Aika, waking, snorted sleepily. "You Tatians. How
would you know? Everyone knows you are born lacking
souls."

"Maybe. But whatever soul Khaat has, it's tearing into
bloody pieces now."

"Maybe," she said softly, turning away from him,
"that's why I want to go."

If he didn't talk about it, he figured later, maybe she
would forget. He began to know her, the way her pale hair
fell across her brows to snag her eyelashes, the way he
could change her habitually brisk, humorless expression,
the way her eyes caught light sometimes and turned so
clear they held only the memory of color. Her white skin
smelled of almonds; the perfume she sometimes wore
smelled of apricots. She had a lovely laugh, like water
running in a forest on a hot day, like distant bells of some
unknown metal. He loved to hear her laugh. But no matter
what he did to distract her, the thoughtful distant look

would return to her eyes, and at those times she would not hear him say her name.

"But why?" he asked helplessly. "It would be like going into a burning house when it's simply too late to rescue anything."

She sighed. "If there was a child in the burning house?"

"If it's too dangerous even for that?"

"Suppose this happened in Tatia—you had such a civil war. At what moment would Tatia no longer be Tatia? And you no longer be Tatian?"

"That's diffcrent. You want to go back and rescue something that might have existed in a poem. Tatia can be rebuilt. Tatians grow anywhere, like grass or mold. They don't worry about carrying their souls with them."

She propped her chin on her hand, sighing. "Do you know what the Khaati word for Tatian is?"

"I can guess."

"Cloud."

"What?"

"You are cloud people, we reach right through you. You have no past."

"Sure we do," he protested. "Everyone does."

"You have no gods, no magic. No myths, no shadows."

"We had myths. We never liked shadows."

"You don't like secrets. You don't like anything you can't take apart, put back together. You explore everything, try to know everything. If you know everything, where is the shadow to rest in?"

"What shadow?"

"The shadow you need crossing the desert of knowing everything. The shadow behind the language." But she was laughing at herself, now, or at whatever he had been doing to her.

"I know enough," he said, "to get along."

But her words clung to him; he considered them at odd moments. Past was only a way of getting to the present, myth and magic were a pair of shoes too small to walk in any longer. Learning everything was a busy-minded civilization's way to survive. It was a road that increased in proportion to its traveled part. Still, he wondered, what in Tatian culture made its people seem like clouds? Insubstantial, always changing form . . . They were thinkers, creators, they built roads across deserts, they did not waste time sitting under shadows. They pushed back the night; it was busy with artificial lights blazing against the background of stars. They even counted stars, they were so busy. They counted everything: people, nuclear particles, cold viruses, board feet, time.

You have no past.

Sure we do, he thought, and it's as bloody as everyone else's.

The shadow behind the language . . .

Aika left him finally, as he knew she would. She did not ask him to come with her.

He missed her sorely. He watched endless news-holos of the distant war, hoping and fearing for a glimpse of her face on some schoolteacher, soldier, nurse. Gradually the ache lessened, became bearable. He pursued his fragmented, kaleidoscope existence; he cooked soya-chili at a restaurant, tended bar at another; he cleaned floors at the Aquarium at night and saw how the brooding octopus never slept. He drank wine sitting on the curbs with wizened Khaati grandmothers, who needed to get away from their bustling families. They taught him a few Khaati words, he taught them a little Tatian.

Then he received an order from his father: Come home.

Home was a city in the north full of Tatians, a structure of glass and steel and light, light everywhere, always. We landed in the desert, Kel thought, confused, as he stepped off the air-shuttle. But it was only the Tatian preference for sun in the chilly north. The golden, hairless faces, his own face, after a street filled with Khaati, startled him.

"I'm dying," his father said abruptly, when they were settled in the vast apartment overlooking out of all sides most of the north end of a continent. Kel took a large gulp of brandy, opened his mouth; his father continued without letting him speak. "It's a congenital virus. My mother had one of the first known cases of it. There's no cure yet, it hasn't been around long enough. You show no signs of it in your system, I had them check. They would have found the virus in you by now, if you were going to get it."

"I—" Kel said, and coughed on brandy fumes.

"Let me talk. You have this thing about being a poet."

"I—"

"So you go and live on a street full of Khaati. I don't

know you too well, but you're one of three people I trust, and the other two don't have your connections. One's dead anyway," he added surprisedly. "There's a drug the Khaati make. It's lethal, but in my case it doesn't matter. It will kill the pain, which does matter. They give it to their old people when they don't want to live anymore. I want you to get me some. Will you?"

Kel was still swallowing brandy fumes. "You want me—" His head finally cleared, along with his throat. "You want me to give it to you because you don't want to live anymore."

"I do want to," his father said. There was no expression in his big, stolid, golden face. None in his voice. All in his words. "I do," he said again. "But I won't. And this will give me some hours, days maybe, without pain. Then pouf. Finish." He added, with a shade of amusement in his voice, "Anything else I take they can cure me of. But not this. That's why it's illegal. Do it for me? You can write a poem about it afterward, I don't mind."

"If I don't wind up in jail," Kel said. He was regaining control; his hands were trembling but he kept them locked around the brandy glass. "How'd you know about that stuff anyway?"

"Dr. Crena told me," his father said. His face seemed more peaceful, less implacable, now that he knew Kel wouldn't fuss, need things from him. He smiled slightly at Kel's expression. "He's known me since I first swore at him coming out of the womb. He has a right to advise me how to go back in. He knew I'd never betray him. And I know you won't."

"I'm just surprised," Kel said, and swallowed more brandy. "How does he know about it?"

"It's no secret, it's just illegal. It's not a street drug or a party drug, it's what you take to die. There's no popular demand for it."

Kel shifted. He felt, suddenly, intensely uncomfortable, as if his head were the wrong size, or his bones were trying to outgrow his skin. It was an idea forcing itself into him, he realized; he had to chew and swallow and make it part of himself. It was like trying to eat a stone.

"How can you be so calm?" he burst out finally, furiously. Again the expressionless, tawny gaze, reticent, impersonal.

"Don't shout," his father said mildly. "Doesn't do any good. I know. I've told you what will help me. Will you help me?"

Kel stared back at him. He could feel it then: the shadow between his bones and his skin that had been there since the day he was born. "All right," he said, thinking of clans, the Khaati grandmothers, the thin, thin secret paper walls. "All right."

Bu. That was what the drug was called. Just that. *"Bu?"* he said to one of the grandmothers or great-grandmothers who had come out in the night to get a moment's peace, look up at the three stars showing above the city, smoke a cigarette smelling like ginger. She said nothing, stared at him as she drew in smoke, her cheeks hollowed. Her blue eyes looked sunken, pale. He repeated the word; the cigarette was replaced by a very old finger pressed against her lips. "For my father," he explained. *"Na babas."* But she was gone, she was a trail of smoke and a shadow, motionless, inside the open door.

The next evening, as he walked late through the quiet streets after sweeping the Aquarium, he was jumped.

He hit the pavement on his back, too surprised for a moment to realize what had happened. Then he saw the silver sun, looking like a demented sunflower, dangling from a chain in front of his nose. He saw the Khaati face above it. He felt the hard street pushing at his back, his skull.

"You want Bu, Tatian?" the young man murmured. He had a drooping white mustache and a tic near one eye. Kel remembered seeing him pulling down the awnings at one of the shops. He slid one hand around the back of Kel's neck, tightened his fingers. Stars, more than were ever seen in the night sky above the city, roared down around Kel. He tried to see, tried to scream, could do neither. Someone said something; the stars dulled, a thick night faded away like fog.

"Aika knew him," he heard. The name echoed: Aika, Aika. He could finally see. The fingers were still there, feather-light. The blood sang in his ears. Behind the Khaati bending over him, he saw others: one watching, smoking, one with three suns in one ear, one smiling a thin, crooked smile.

"That's the poet," he heard and someone laughed. Poet, poet. He tried to speak; a thumb licked his throat slowly and the words froze.

"Aika said he reads Coru."

"Who is Coru?"

"Ignorant Sun. You dumb kid." There was a brief dance, flashes of knife-light, a good-natured laugh. Someone else said:

"Why does he read a Khaati poet?"

"Ask him."

"Why, Tatian?"

"Why do you read poetry?"

"Why do you want Bu?"

"For my father," he said through the ice-floe in his throat. There was silence. His head thudded back on the pavement; he closed his eyes, seeing stars again. "For my father," he whispered. Then the silence became empty; he opened his eyes and saw no one.

He tried to write a poem about that: about the dancing suns and the wild stars and the hard, cold hand of the world against the back of his head. But the memories kept intruding between him and the words. I saw the dead-end of time, he thought. I nearly died. On an empty street in a Khaati neighborhood. Died of not being able to speak. I would have been a body and a stack of poetry. They would have put the body in the ground and the poetry in the garbage. That's it. End. Finis. Poof. He couldn't sit still, he was too aware of his body, the amazing, continuous beating of his heart despite all odds against it. I should be able to write this, he thought. But he couldn't.

Poet, poet.

Give it up, he thought the next morning. You don't have to get Bu. You don't have to kill your father.

But that evening, as he walked home from a bar, a woman stepped out of a doorway and beckoned to him. She was back-lit, a sketch of a woman, a seduction of familiar lines: long, long hair, no face, a lithe body stylized as a cave drawing, to be recognized until the end of time. She lifted a slender hand; rings flashed. He turned mid-step, followed her. He heard the silken whisper of the traditional tight-fitting sheath that covered her from throat to ankle. Birds flew across it, spiraled around her body to hide within her hair. When she finally turned, he was startled at how old she was.

She smiled slightly, young-old, knowing. They were in a small room behind a restaurant; he smelled spices, heard plates clatter, meat sizzling. Her face was very delicate, paper-pale, a country of small, secret roads. Her eyes were outlined in black, her hollowed cheeks flushed with pink powder. She smelled of ginger cigarettes and the perfume Aika wore. The perfume and her graceful, tapering fingers confused him. She was Aika, she was not Aika. She was young, she was old. Birds circled her. Her hair was dead-white, her eyes were beginning to sink a little into her head. Her body looked supple as a child's. He wanted her, he did not.

The smile-lines deepened under her eyes, beside her mouth. "Do you know," she asked him, "how much death costs?"

"No." He had to say it twice before he could hear himself. "No."

"It is not cheap."

"No," he agreed, though privately he considered death the cheapest thing in the universe. Hell, it was free. It handed itself out to anybody, anywhere. He cleared his throat again. "How much—" He thought of his meager salaries and shook his head. "I mean, it doesn't matter. My father will pay. There's nothing else he wants to buy."

"He wants it? Or you want it for him?"

He stared at her, then realized what she was asking. "Do I want to murder my father, you mean? Not, not really. Do you want me to bring you a note from him?" He felt himself trembling and wished he could sit. But it was like sitting in front of a goddess. The goddess pulled a battered chair out from the table and gestured. She sat across from him and lit a cigarette. She narrowed her eyes at her smoke, or at something she saw in the smoke. She no longer smiled.

"This is business," she said. Her voice was low, slightly grainy from the smoke; if he closed his eyes she would be the faceless woman in the doorway, eternally young, beckoning with her voice.

"Would they have killed me?" he asked abruptly. She looked at him, a face without an answer anywhere in it. "Khaati have customs, as you do. We, perhaps, are more practical. You regard death as an end. We see it as a doorway. If someone wishes to enter that doorway, we are not so reluctant, so terrified to let them. You Tatians do anything to avoid entering that doorway. You see only a wall. So. Things that are illegal for you may be overlooked for us. As long as we keep certain rules. As long as we do not provide death for the wrong reason. Once that happens, once we have that reputation, of selling death for the wrong reason, we will be subject to your rules. We must be very careful. Especially of Tatians. They do not buy death for good reasons. I must know that you are buying death for a good reason. Your father is rich?"

He nodded, mute.

"You live among us, not among wealthy Tatians. You eat our food, read our poets. Perhaps your father will not share his wealth with you now. If he dies you will be very rich."

He blinked. "Not very rich. Rich."

"Then you will no longer have to live among the poor, eating our food, listening to our music."

He shrugged, not answering. He smelled the perfume again, but he did not want the woman who said those things. She only wanted to be safe; she could never understand. He said finally, "I chose to live here. I could kill my father and be rich, yes. But then I would not have my father." He was silent again, while she watched him. His mouth shook; he lifted his hand, hid it. "He is dying, anyway."

"That can be cured by Tatian ways. They always want to cure the dying."

"And they always die. This can't be cured. It's a recent, very rare virus. He will die in pain."

She said, "Ah," very softly.

"So his doctor told him about the— About death Khaati death. And he asked me to get it for him. He'll pay. Whatever you ask, he'll pay. If you want to get rich yourself."

Something flickered in her eyes; she smiled fully then, showing blackened, broken teeth. "Money cannot buy death from me."

He drew breath, suddenly bewildered, depressed. "He'll die anyway," he said, more to himself than to her. "I don't have to do this. But he asked me to. He asked me. I can't remember the last time he asked me for anything.

He always tried to give me things. A job, a trip, my own private air-shuttle. He never asked me before for anything that I might be able to give him. And now he asks this. So." He looked at her wearily. "It's not important how much."

Her terrible smile had gone; she watched him from behind her smoke. She put out her cigarette slowly, in an ashtray full of butts. She was looking beyond him again, her face thoughtful, absent; looking at her past, he realized, as he saw the ghost of her youth fly out of her face.

"I gave Bu to my mother," she said softly. "You are Tatian and I tell you that. A moment of peace, a dream, a doorway—that is what you will buy from me for your father. Not a wall, a doorway. You are Tatian, but you have found your way to me. You may have what you want."

"Thank you," he whispered.

"For my price."

"What is your price?"

She told him.

He flew north three days later, carrying a very old, very expensive bottle of brandy for his father. His father met his flight. He looked shrunken, and very tired, though he moved and spoke as stolidly as always. His vigor required more effort; his face glistened constantly with a sheen of sweat.

"I brought you brandy," Kel said when they were safely in the apartment.

"Thanks," his father said, and Kel gave him the box. He seemed to sense something, holding it. His eyes went to Kel abruptly, wide, and with more expression in them than Kel had seen in a long time. He lifted the bottle out of the box; both hands closed around it. He sighed, his eyes closing, opening again, and Kel's throat burned at the relief in them. "Thanks, Son."

"You can take a few days to drink it. It won't make you drunk right away."

"It's all right," his father said. "This place is private as a tomb. You can say what you want."

"They just—" He stopped again, rubbing his eyes. "I'm used to talking about it that way. They said you'll have three or four days free of pain. Then you go through the doorway."

"Through the doorway."

"That's what they say. It's not a wall but a doorway. Not an end. Just a path through to someplace else."

His father grunted. "They say where?"

"No."

He smiled. He put his arm around Kel's shoulders. "I never read any of your poetry. Send me some."

"I will. When—how long—"

"Dr. Crena says I'll need to go into the hospital soon. He says I won't come back out. I'd rather not go in."

"So—" He was breathing shallowly, not finding air. "So—"

"So you should go back home."

"No." He drew breath with his mouth open, finally found air. "You shouldn't drink this alone. I want to stay with you."

"You do?"

"Keep you company. Is that all right?"

"Oh, yes," his father sighed. Kel moved closer to him, just to feel his big, sagging body, his breathing, his hold. "I didn't want to ask you. I'd never have asked. I've done a lot in my life, but I never cared much for the thought of dying alone." Kel's face turned, burrowed against his shoulder a moment. Then he straightened, thinking: a doorway. That's all it is, a doorway. "One thing I learned about life," his father added, patting him awkwardly. "It wins all the arguments. Sit down, I'll get a couple of glasses." He loosed Kel, turned to a cupboard. "You didn't say what this is costing me."

"Not much," Kel said. His father turned to look at him then, with the direct, opaque look that he used like a microscope to examine things he was given and wasn't sure he liked. Kel met his gaze, shrouding himself with visions of rain forests, white tigers, old woman with long white hair and beckoning hands. When he was sure of his voice, sure of tranquillity, he continued, "What do you care, anyway? You're opening the door and leaving me the rest. Unless you've written me out of your will. What kind of poet am I going to be, surrounded by all this?"

"Ah." His father waved a less costly bottle of brandy, reassured. "You'll get used to it." He handed Kel the bottle and a glass. He touched Kel's glass very gently with the bottle Kel had brought. "Cheers."

* * *

Two weeks later, Kel sat on a shuttle heading east. A book of Coru's poems lay open in his hands. But he no longer had to read it. He was about to travel into those words: into Coru's land of dusty roads and green rivers, children hungry for rice, for souls.

Find Aika, the old woman had said. Find Aika and bring her back. For your father I open the door. For Aika I close it. She is my daughter. Bring her back.

That is my price.

He waited, his blood singing in terror, to enter Aika's land, where the children cried as they had never cried in Coru's time, and where poems awaited him, and everywhere every door was open.

Dogs Die

MICHAEL KALLENBERGER

IT WOULD BE EASIER if I still hated them. But hatred comes from not understanding, and maybe, just maybe, I've begun to understand my crewmates. Though I can never appreciate their black-and-white values, their petty rivalries, their diligence in pursuit of mediocrity, I've recognized that my own—well, foibles—may make them equally uncomfortable. Kind of ironic that this should happen now, isn't it?

Stop this. This won't help you cope. Condescending to them won't make their murders any easier than hating them would have. Face it. You love them, you hate them, they must die. And it must be by your hand.

Runyeager stubbed out his cigarette. Long anglo view of the lone biochemist in his darkened lab: leaning back, one foot propped on an open drawer of the credenza, head framed by the fractional distillation apparatus. Fluids of miraculous colors should have been percolating from its bank of tubes, but none of the equipment had operated for days. The samples gathered on the surface of 57-Klein IV remained in their synthetic environments. Lately Runyeager had been passing his time in other pursuits.

The *John F. Kennedy*'s antenna was parabolic in cross-section, of course, so that when the ship was in stellar space all the rays of an incoming communication's laser beam were directed toward the focal point. Everyone aboard knew of the theorem that asserted this. Except that, several days earlier, Runyeager had found his thought processes catching on that phrase *everyone knew;* how did they know? He couldn't remember when he'd been told about parabolas and their properties, but he was pretty certain he'd never seen a geometric proof of this. And if *he'd* never bothered to question it, certainly none of his crewmates would have. How did they know they hadn't been lied to?

So Runyeager had gotten out a pad of paper, and after several false starts he'd sketched out a pair of axes, a parabola, and all the necessary line segments. After forty-five minutes of struggling to resurrect his trigonometry, he proved to himself that the antenna would indeed work as claimed.

He'd spent the days since then convincing himself that no conspiracies had been perpetrated regarding other geometric theorems he'd previously accepted without proof.

Runyeager was willing to expend so much time in this pursuit for several reasons, not the least of which was that it seemed *important.* A second reason: he was certain that the report on the Klein samples he was supposed to be analyzing would never reach Earth anyway. A third reason: it gave him something to think about other than the murders he was carefully planning.

The door sounds, and opens at a command from me. Emily Graf, our geologist, enters.

"Come for a chat?" I joke; Emily seldom has time for small talk, at least with me. But in addition to biochemistry my duties on board ship include those of medical officer, and it's in the latter role that my crewmates usually see me.

" 'fraid not, Gene." As she says this a smile dusts her lips, and her gaze turns downward, her eyelids like lifting gull wings. It's nobody's business but her own, though it makes me a little sad that Emily doesn't seem to like me. How else to interpret this spurning of even the small intimacy of eye contact—*her gaze turns downward*—and her smirk of superiority—*a smile dusts her lips?*

I like that phrase. *A smile dusts her lips, and her gaze*

turns downward, her eyelids like lifting gull wings. I should be a writer. I think I'd like to give it a try some day. I already know what my first story would be—a fictionalized account of this voyage. Except, of course, that nobody will ever be able to read it. That doesn't bother me.

Popularity has never been something I've courted, but lately it seems that some people can't even get comfortable around me. I've given up on most of them, with no hard feelings; I should add Emily to that list, though I doubt I ever will.

I adjust my features to their best diagnostic set. "Anything wrong?"

She cants her head. "No, no. Volse just wants to see everyone. Right away."

"Old Volse the Vice-Jaw is calling another officers' meeting? The Voice of Volse?"

Turning to leave: "That's the one." She doesn't know what else to say.

We are the last arrivals at the meeting room. Captain Adam Volse, who'd been standing at the head of the table with his hands clasped in the small of his back, fingers his pipe and nods in greeting. He joins the four of us at the table.

Mahogany-smudge reflection of Volse in the tabletop. Pan up to forearms leaning atop inverted forearm smear; shoulders; head with back-combed wavy hair.

"Angus?" The captain looked to the blond, sharp-cheeked youngster on his left.

Angus Petersby put down the pen he'd been absently twirling between the fingers of both hands, and pressed his shoulder blades against the chair's cushioned back. To the group he said, "I just told the captain that the damaged lens array is beyond internal repair."

"One of us will have to go outside to fix it," Volse hurriedly interjected. "Sorry, Angus, but I got the feeling you were about to volunteer." Gripping the stem of his pipe with the bowl protruding between ring finger and pinky, he nodded toward Petersby's right hand, embedded in a cast.

Runyeager raised his hand almost distractedly.

"Yes? Gene?"

"I'm volun*teer*ing."

Volse was clearly resisting the urge to raise his eyebrows; Mariana Alciforo, the social sciences generalist, not only didn't bother to resist, she snorted her skepticism quite audibly. Runyeager's apparent lack of emotional involvement with the mission had hardly gone undiscussed by the rest of the crew.

"Excellent." Volse broke into his off-center grin. "I'm glad to hear that, Gene, very glad. Angus?"

"I . . . It's fine with me. We'll go over what has to be done."

"How much time do we have?" Emily Graf asked.

"It's three days until the next scheduled jump," he responded with a glance toward Runyeager, who was looking at the wall. "I can show Gene what needs to be done in . . . oh, less than an hour. Two at most."

"All right, what about the rest of you? Anything to report? Let's get the long-winded one out of the way first. Mariana?"

Petersby laughed as Alciforo, scowling, hurled a wad of paper at the captain. The crew of the *Kennedy* had found only microorganisms on this voyage; no aliens more complex than rabbits had ever been found. They all knew how intensely she longed to be the first sociologist to practice her science on an exploratory mission. Their teasing, they supposed, helped dispel her tension. They weren't entirely correct.

"Gene?"

"I've been plugging away at all the standard stuff. Nothing particularly interesting to report."

Volse looked dubious about the second statement, but he turned to Petersby. "Angus?"

Muffled clatter. Graf, startled: "Gene! What is it?"

The biochemist had kicked his chair back, and was standing doubled over. "I . . . I . . . Oh, Christ."

Before she could get to his side he was standing, taking his breath in slow, measured rasps. "Some . . . Some indigestion lately, I don't know. Problems with my gut. I'll . . . take care of it." And he was out of the room.

Graf looked plaintively to Captain Volse, who seemed to be appraising Runyeager's after-image through narrowed eyes. Petersby and Alciforo exchanged glances.

* * *

The door to my lab whisks closed behind me and, gasping for breath, I prop my fingertips and rear end against its reassuring bulk. One hand combing a spray of hair just off my forehead, I step to the physiometer and lay my arm in the harness. The needle pierces my forearm and seconds letter a magnified view of my blood appears in near-perfect resolution on the wall screen.

They're not there.

The blood appears perfectly normal. There's no trace of the blue-green, vaguely hexagonal structures that had pervaded the screen the last time I'd looked.

Somehow, somewhere on 57-Klein IV we picked up these alien microorganisms. Under guise of routine examination I'd found them in the blood of two of my crewmates. Three days later, all four of them were infected.

Don't ask me how it's possible—how they got past the decontamination, the multiply-redundant procedures, the exhaustive checks and re-checks. But they were there.

And now they're not.

What the hell does it mean?

And then a notion forms—a notion I resist, because it's terrifying, because it's absurd. But it's the only explanation.

The green hexes must be intelligent—intelligent enough to be devious, to learn that I've discovered them and to respond by hiding.

I extricate my arm, automatically swabbed and bandaged, and sit back, frowning, in the chair. My gaze never wavers from the screen. Pick a white blood cell, focus on it, watch its movements—there. Was that an edge of green momentarily showing from behind it?

If there were ever any question about my duty, the answer's been provided. The green hexes are not only contagious, they have the resourcefulness to lay claim to metabolism after metabolism. The others must not find out —they don't have the courage to do what I must do. They would stop me, lock me up, call me crazy.

The *John F. Kennedy* must be prevented from reaching Earth—prevented from becoming the instrument of an alien invasion.

* * *

View from 45 degrees above horizontal: the hooded lamp, capping a lighted cone of solitude in the black frame. Pan down to find Mariana Alciforo, wearing gray cotton shorts and a baggy T-shirt, sitting cross-legged atop the bunk with a book spread across her lap.

"Well, Gene, what an unexpected surprise."

Runyeager stepped into the portal she'd just opened by remote. The overt tentativeness of his manner was perhaps just a bit contrived, though Alciforo guessed that the feeling itself was sincere enough.

The door closed behind him. "I came to see you . . . in your capacity as psychologist." He sat in the desk chair, next to the bunk.

Her eyebrows arched. "Practicing our Mr. Spock impression, are we?" His lack of response chastened her. "Well, sure, I mean . . . we can get right down to it if you want . . ."

"I'm sorry. But you have to admit, your hello wasn't exactly free of sarcasm."

He was clearly a man who needed to unburden himself. Seeing this, she licked her lips, and said "You're right. I'm sorry, too. Let's talk." She reached for the remote.

"Don't . . . turn on the lights. This is fine."

It was almost pitch dark outside the cone projected by the lamp. "Gene . . ." She gave the room lights a gentle nudge upward. "How's that? Okay?"

"Good." He bent his head so that his forehead came to rest within the fingertips of his right hand. Looking up again, he inhaled like a man about to dive off a high cliff. "Good. When I got out of college, when I first got my bachelor's—I worked at the shipyards. The big ones, out past Pluto. I was a welder. School hadn't been a pleasant experience for me—up to that point, at least. Lots of bloated egos, and— well, anyway. I took off, half intent on making welding in the yards my career."

Alciforo pushed her book aside, leaning her body ever so imperceptibly toward him in a gesture of empathy that at first puzzled herself. For Runyeager to open up to any of them was unheard of. Her instincts to see the vulnerable side of all men, long-suppressed in her relationship with the biochemist, now rose readily to the surface. And there *was* a certain pride that he'd chosen her to open up to, though as he'd pointed out, she was, of course, their psychologist.

"I wasn't the best welder there. Oh, I was more than good enough, but it was just like school in a way—short attention span. I tried to do my best, always, but . . . well. You know how most of the time you don't think about being *you*, you're just there, interacting with everyone and everything around you, but other times you kind of, you know, retreat into yourself, you see yourself as . . . as a point of consciousness, looking out at the world from inside your body? When I was working in the yards it was that way all the time. It was like . . . the essence of me had sort of been drawn inward from my skin, had been distilled down to a pea-sized thing in my head, looking out through my eye sockets at my hands doing the welding.

"Only sometimes I wondered if the real me *was* those hands, guiding the torch, feeling the pressure of it against my bones—I *was* my body, and the pea-sized thing that controlled my body was something else, some*one* else guiding me from inside. But mostly *I* was the pea-thing, inside looking out."

She said "I know what you mean."

"Good. I thought you might. Well, anyway, sometimes I'd start a weld, and the pea-thing would kind of take over, and I'd just . . . just start *thinking*, you know, about a lot of different things. And when my hands would get done with the weld, the pea-thing would start paying attention again, and damned if I didn't even know I'd been working. But I'd check the weld, and it was always good."

"Everyone daydreams while they work, Gene."

He met her gaze with a half-grin. "Even you? Like right now?"

She was taken by his loss of his usual stilted manner, and grinned in spite of herself. "You'd never know if I did. But I wouldn't. Go on."

"Sometimes I wouldn't be able to sleep at night, because I'd start worrying about what I was doing. Sure, the welds I checked always looked good, but suppose the pea-thing hadn't given my body—"

"Gene, by this pea-thing stuff you do mean *you*, right . . . ? Daydreaming?"

"Right, right. Suppose I'd gone through more than one weld that way? Maybe more than two, even—like ten or twenty. I was working on a line, I had no way to go back and check anything other than the weld I was working on at the moment. It scared me."

"And does it still scare you now? Looking back?"

"No."

"Why do you think it bothered you so much then?"

"I don't have to *worry* now that it might have happened—because it *did* happen. We had a ship blow up—a liner." He was whispering now. "The *Ganymede*. On a down-Sol run. They never investigated."

"Gene . . ."

"You're right, I know what you're going to say, you're right. I don't know that I was responsible! There were hundreds of us working on those ships, thousands. And inspectors, too. But don't you see? That's the worst part, not knowing. If I'd pulled out a gun and shot them, it would have been better! Damn, damn, damn, damn!" Teeth gritted, cords bulged from the side of his neck for just a moment as he inhaled sharply. He dropped his face into his hands. "I used to think when I was a stupid kid that I'd made my peace with dying. It wasn't so bad if you did it right! You had a long life, you prepared yourself, you went out knowing you'd made the best of your eighty or ninety years. That's how people should die, knowing, knowing, with dignity, understanding what's happening to them. When you're alive one second and dead the next, not knowing, with no chance to reconcile your life in your own mind, that's how dogs die! Like dogs by the side of the road, run over by cars, not knowing, not understanding, that's how they died! Don't you see?"

She did see, she thought, all too well. And because by the end of his tale she'd long since stepped outside her seldom-used role of psychologist, she pulled herself up to the edge of the bed next to his chair and rested her hand on his shoulder. "Gene, Gene . . ." she whispered, and she smelled his sweat.

Angus Petersby's pride is spread open on the conference table: a three-ring binder, filled with a ream of the *John F. Kennedy's* specs, each page encased in a plastic sheath. He tells me he prefers the solidity of such a manual to the electronic variety. In a way it *is* primitively handsome.

Petersby is our chief engineer, and yet in just over an hour of poring over these diagrams he's told me nothing I hadn't already been aware of. The depth of my knowledge, however, must remain a secret. My feigned eagerness seems to be working; if he even suspected my boredom, he would react in anger. Our lives, he believes, are riding on what I learn today.

Ships like the *Kennedy* traverse the galaxy in a series of "jumps" through null-space. The process is often described with the fanciful though inaccurate metaphor of a stone skipping over the surface of a pond. Null-space literally has no dimensions. Yet it's not appropriate to think of it as a point, since it can be accessed from anywhere within our own three-dimensional space. When the *Kennedy* enters null-space, in a very real sense we're everywhere and nowhere.

Returning to a given set of coordinates in normal space from null-space isn't an exact science. It's not even close. Twenty percent of all returns wind up more or less on target, that is, the ship emerges traveling on the same vector it'd been using when it left normal space, although significantly farther along the path. Errors of all magnitudes are possible, though larger errors have correspondingly smaller probabilities. Jumps three-quarters of the way across the galaxy from the target have been recorded.

Perhaps, Mr. Einstein, God does play dice with the universe. The macroverse as well as the microverse. Of course, wiser minds than my own insist that we merely do not have sufficient navigational technology to aim more accurately.

The lens array that I've been selected to repair performs the function of determining our location once we return to normal space, so that we can get properly oriented for our next jump. Without it, we would be helplessly, hopelessly lost.

Petersby lights a cigarette as he leans back. "You seem to have it down pretty well. I'm not worried—about the repair. I'm more worried about the EVA."

"Hmm?"

"How long has it been since you trained?"

A shrug. "Maybe sixteen years."

"That's a long lay-off. Walking on a spinning hull can be pretty disorienting. It's like working upside-down."

"I'll be okay."

Today's study completed, we leave the room, and with no further comment I quickly put Petersby behind me. I make my way to the navigational library, making sure no one sees me enter, and latch the door.

The green glow of the holotank is the room's only illumination. I call up a map showing our current course in yellow, with glowing red points marking our departure from normal space and our targeted point of return.

On the flat screen overhead I call up a simulated view of space as seen from the second red point; the cylindrical view assembled from the rotating lens array is unrolled and displayed as a rectangle. I adjust the arrangement by an arbitrary factor of 5%, and key to record it on a magnetic pin.

I repeat the procedure with each of the targeted return points along our route. Pressing a plastic tab causes the pin to pop out into my waiting palm.

Nobody sees me leave, either.

Emily Graf was listening to ethereal music of the sort trans-Jovian cultures pointed to when they wanted to make a case for Earth's infatuation with the past. Graf, however, had never lived inside the asteroid belt.

Mariana Alciforo stepped into this environment tentatively, pausing before she gestured for the door to close behind her. Even the photograph of Olympus Mons was somehow off-putting, a symbol of an older culture.

After some small talk that flowed less than freely despite the best efforts of both women, Alciforo said, "Emily, I need to talk to you about Gene."

"Gene?"

"You've always been close to him. Well, not close, but you've always . . . Hell, you've defended him where no one else would, sometimes."

"He's just different, that's all. I understand that."

"That's why I came to you. How well do you know him, really?"

Graf paused as if rejecting a lie. "Not very well."

"I'm having problems saying this. I think Gene is . . . a very troubled man."

"Has he come to see you? Professionally, I mean?"

Alciforo held her breath for a moment. "Yes. I shouldn't

be telling you that, but there wouldn't be much point in lying right now. I absolutely can't tell you what we talked about, though."

By this point Graf's features made her seem very upset. "Did he tell you about the shipyards?"

"Shipyards?"

Resignation crossed her features. "About how he used to daydream? How he blames himself for a ship that blew up?"

"Well . . . yes."

"I see."

"Then there's no point in not telling you the rest. After we talked I checked Gene's file, to see if I could find anything that might be useful in dealing with his problem. Emily, he never worked at the shipyards. At Pluto, or anywhere else."

"Wh— What are you saying?"

"I'm saying his records show that he went to college right out of high school, went straight through without interruption to his Ph.D., and worked summers as a bookkeeper for his father. He went from college to the exploration program."

Graf shook her head. "No . . ."

"A very middle-class life, Emily. Just the type that would see manual labor in the trans-Plutonian shipyards as something romantic."

"Why would he lie?"

"The whole story is really pretty romantic, don't you think? The compulsive loner, struggling to maintain his integrity despite the burden of his guilt? Gene has never made friends easily, Emily, and this story provides a rationalization for that, in a sense."

"You're saying he believes this himself, aren't you? You think he's . . . sick."

"It's . . . It's a possibility. That's why I came to you. As psychology goes, what I'm proposing may not be very appropriate. But frankly, our lives are going to be put in Gene's hands. We need to find out. We need to know just how . . . Well, how stable he is. There's no point in pretending it's not a concern."

Her gaze became distant. "The bastard . . ."

"Really, Emily, he may not have believed he was lying." But Alciforo feared it was obvious that she repeated this only to postpone the other's pain.

Graf only shook her head, her eyes focused on something within. And Alciforo realized that the geologist's anger did not have its source in lies; she was upset because she was not, after all, the only person with whom Runyeager had chosen to share his lies.

My blood is thick with the blue-green hexagons, surrounded by withered red corpuscles. It's difficult to find a functioning cell amid the devastation. The invaders taunt me by letting me glimpse them from time to time, but always they return to hiding. I've seen them.

I don't dare test my crewmates again for fear of arousing their suspicions, but is there really any point? The exact count is academic now; nothing will stay me from my intent.

Tools and electronic components are spread over the operating table in sick bay. My attention is currently occupied by a chip no bigger than a thumbnail, which is actually a fairly sophisticated computer. To this I must connect the magnetic pin I prepared in the navigation library.

"Gene?"

Startled, my instrument hand jerks away from the table. Then it sinks in that the voice has the vague hollowness of the intercom; no one has been spying on me.

"Yeah?"

"Gene, it's Volse. Would you report to my office, please?"

I scowl and purse my lips. "Can't it wait?"

A pause. "I'd really rather we did this now."

The materials and tools carefully swept into a drawer tray, I lock the cupboard, and the sick bay door behind me as well. By the time I'm standing outside the captain's office I'm regretting having given in so readily.

Inside, Volse is half-reclining in his plush chair, one elbow propped atop the desk and his fingertips alongside his temple. He flops closed a magazine and tosses it atop a stack of papers.

He nods me into a chair, his ever-present pipe momentarily in his hand. I comply.

Without straightening up: "Angus says you're ready to repair the damaged equipment."

"I am." Involuntarily I pull my head back ever so slightly, appraising him.

"When was the last time you EVA'ed?"

"Training."

"Sixteen years ago?"

I nod. "You checked."

He chuckles around the pipe stem. "I did. Any concern about the long lay-off?"

"No."

"I've got to be honest, Gene, I've got some concern. You're a brilliant scientist. When you entered the program, leading academics were practically lining up to recommend you. But your scores on the physical tests were barely passable in some cases."

"But the point is, they were passing grades."

Volse nods to concede the point. "No pulling punches, here, Gene. You're a career academic. You've never done anything else. You're not the best choice for this repair work."

"What do you want me to tell you?"

His desktop intercom buzzes. He looks momentarily annoyed, then leans forward and keys to accept. "Yes?"

"It's Emily, Captain. Do you have a minute?"

Volse opens his mouth, hesitates, then glances apologetically at me; he invites Emily in "as long as it's only a minute." There's a certain rehearsed tone to all this.

"Oh—hello, Gene."

The captain says, "Gene and I were just discussing the repair work. You wouldn't by any chance have any recent EVA experience, would you, Emily?"

"No. No, I don't." As she says this to him a smile dusts her lips, and her gaze turns downward, her eyelids like lifting gull wings. Her self-consciousness, her transparent affectations of modesty around Volse are compelling; her suppressed desire for him is obvious.

I say nothing, watching and waiting only.

"I just wish someone around here had some practical experience working with their hands under weightless conditions."

The pregnancy of the stillness is almost laughable.

Emily turns toward me expectantly. "Gene . . . ?"

"What?"

"What about the yards at Pluto? Didn't you . . . Didn't you tell the captain about that?"

So that's what this meeting is all about! Volse isn't worried about my ability to make the repair. Somehow, he's become aware of Emily's bizarre fantasy that I once worked in the shipyards. He's testing me to see if I'm as deluded as she is.

I lean forward, forearms draped over my thighs. "What are you talking about?"

Volse acts surprised. "Yes, that sounds like a good question. What *are* you talking about, Emily?"

"Gene used to work as a welder in the trans-Plutonian shipyards. He told me all about it."

"What? You must be thinking of someone else. I never told you that."

She only looks at me as though she doesn't know whether to feel pity or hatred. Such is her contempt for people who work with their hands. That's probably the source of her delusion; she's rationalizing her contempt for me.

"No arguments?" I wonder aloud, perhaps too smugly.

Her gaze intent upon me, she shakes her head as if in disbelief, then without sound says "Liar." She's convinced herself; I'd have to say she seems genuinely hurt, though not startled, by what has transpired.

Volse reaches toward her. "Emily . . ." He swallows, forces himself to remain seated. "Emily, I think we can discuss your problem later. Gene and I were in the middle of something. I'm sorry."

I stand, and Volse suppresses a protest. "No, no, that's all right. Captain, the only person who might be better qualified for that repair is Angus, but not with a broken wrist. I intend to proceed as we've planned, unless your orders are otherwise . . . ?"

He shakes his head in dismissal, and I leave. I hope I didn't spoil their little playlet.

"Mariana?" Volse pressed the rewind button.

Alciforo tapped her index finger against her pursed lips. "He's an asshole. A born liar right out of Machiavelli. But I see no reason to believe he's not mentally competent."

"You're convinced?"

"That's my professional opinion. Does that mean I'm convinced?"

"I only wish we hadn't dragged poor Emily through this."

"Emily's a grown woman. It was the best way to get at what's in Runyeager's head."

Palms out defensively, Volse nodded. "Agreed, agreed. I deferred to your judgment, didn't I?"

Alciforo looked at the frozen image of Runyeager in the tank. Her defiant body language said *I refuse to be fooled again.* "Asshole," she muttered. "But then, we've always known that."

Naked save for form-fitting trunks. A tube the size of a billy club is strapped to my inner thigh, the thinner plastic hose held in place along my torso and throat by simple tape. They insert the tip into my mouth while I make sure to keep my tongue very still; they don't notice the bulge of the capsule I've hidden underneath it. A shield-shaped visor is fitted over my face, heavily cushioned around the perimeter. Boots with soles as thick as dictionaries are nestled over my feet. I step into the stall, pulling the door closed between myself and my spectators. The nozzles move into position, and the film is sprayed over my body. The milky fluid instantly dries and knits itself into a taut, transparent disposable spacesuit, capable of protecting me for up to thirty hours in space.

I run my tongue around the nipple, moistening my lips behind the cushioned flange, and shift the capsule to my cheek. They open the stall, and my shoulders stiffen; I don't like being on display for the others this way. But I regulate my breathing, I force myself to relax. My full attention must be on the task at hand, for if I fail, this ship will reach Earth intact, infecting and killing untold billions.

Petersby hands me the shoulder bag containing tools and the replacement lens array. As I walk with long, uncomfortable strides toward the airlock, Volse, Petersby, the others move too, uncertain as to whether they're accompanying me or merely following. Before entering, I turn, separated from them by microns of plastic and by light-years of something else.

Volse spans my shoulders with his arm, claps me heart-

ily. Petersby says something encouraging. Graf and Alciforo nod good luck. I don't want this. Muttering
something akin to thanks, I turn my back on them and
cycle through the lock.

Then: the hull. Very cautiously raising myself to my full
height. I inhale sharply with a trace of coriolis-induced
vertigo. Our "gravity" within the ship is provided by
centrifugal inertia, better known by the misnomer
centrifugal force. The wheel-like ship's spin is, of course,
undetectable to me as such; walking on the hull with magnetic boots is very much like dangling from a ceiling.

My equilibrium tentatively restored, I relax my arms
and open my eyes. Wet, sparkling jewels line the papery
night: the stars, as I have never seen them, as I will never
see them again; and for that I know a trace of regret. With
the ship's rotation they flow overhead. To be immersed in
their gentle stream like this is to know beauty and power
by name.

They will die like dogs, unknowing and unprepared.

Cautious steps. The magnets respond to the pressure in
my soles. Something somersaults in my stomach. Not sick,
just a strange feeling.

The lens arrangement comes into view over the great
wheel's curvature; four round-tipped glassy cones each the
size of a fist, mounted in a cluster on a metal board set flush
with the hull. Standing astride it like a colossus astride a
city, something within me starts to wonder how I came to
be here, at this place, at this moment. I push those
thoughts aside.

I crouch too quickly; fists of blood pound against my
right ear, and my stomach curls in on itself. Vomit rises in
my throat, subsides. The taste lingers. Eyes closed, breathing steady, steady, steady. Heart thrumming like a piston.

Press on. Fingers fumbling at my shoulder bag's seal, I
have to close my eyes again, but I keep working. Various
objects spill upward, including the replacement lens array,
moored by utility straps to the bottom of the bag. Unclip a
tool. *What combination of circumstances put me here?*
Removing the fasteners on the lens board, one by one.

There's the hole, almost invisible. When the *Kennedy*
was still in orbit around 57-Klein IV I made sure I had a
solo run in the shuttle. Before docking with the ship, I

made a pass by this section of the hull, and punctured the lens array with a single computer-aimed laser pulse.

The third fastener is jammed, but I work at it with the tool. Sinus pressure squeezing my head. Upside-down. Chest pounding. *Circumstances* . . . Suddenly, the lens board is a light-year distant, my awareness flees to the back of my eye-tunnels, coalesces, draws in on itself. . . .

Detached from my mind thus, still my hands labor on. The third fastener comes loose and my fingers start to work on the last one. Awareness focused in a kernel the size of a pea. Look down the eye-tunnels. Hard to concentrate, head, vertigo. But my hands know what to do.

The last fastener gone, I pry loose the board supporting the damaged lens array. Clip it to a free utility strap. *Not circumstances. Action. Courage to do what is necessary.* Hands know what to do. *Still, don't let the pea-thing steal your attention away.* . . .

But I am the pea-thing. It is my awareness, me.

I inhale, exhale slowly, blink away these vertigo-induced distractions. There are two wires tucked into a slot along the side of the replacement board. Without unclipping it, I use the tool to pry some slack into these. It takes a few minutes to scrape away some of the insulation, exposing bare copper, at two points along each wire.

Now my concentration will be crucial. I remove a roll of emergency suit-repair strips and a tiny scalpel from the bag. I draw air deeply into my lungs, exhale, draw air even more deeply with the second intake, and hold it. Gathering my courage, I run the scalpel along the juncture between my faceplate and the rubbery suit. I have no more than eight seconds; tilting the mask away from my lower face, I spit the hidden capsule into my palm; my skin ripples at the exposure to vacuum; hastily, I press the faceplate closed, trembling fingers smoothing a series of patches along the lesion. *Stick, damn you, stick!*

I test my breathing; the seal is not perfect. Air is escaping. I must work quickly. Splitting the capsule in two, I remove the pin-and-chip arrangement. I take the four leads from this and wrap them around the four exposed spots on the new lens board's wires. My fingers tremble, but I work through it. *Could've done this in advance if that damned Petersby hadn't insisted on testing the replacement array right up until the end!* Taping the splices secure, I sever each wire at a point between the two connections, and cap the loose ends.

We make our own circumstances. . . .

Like dogs.

No. Chance, fate. No! Murderer! And only I will die like a human being . . . I don't merit the dignity.

Dignity? You love them, you hate them, they must die. Courage . . .

Dangling in space. Another wave of vertigo washes over me. Fight it back, breathe deeply. But the answering inrush of fresh air isn't there; it's thin, diluted with vacuum. *The pea-thing, me/awareness/eye-tunnels.* Head throbbing. Facial skin prickling. Air going. Move quickly!

Unclip the new lens array, push it into the bare spot on the hull. Tamp down the corners, re-fasten them.

The next time we make a jump and re-emerge into normal space, the lens array will feed an image of the surrounding stars to the computer. But the pin-and-chip will intercept the signal, instead sending to the navigational system one of the canned views of space that I've recorded (with arbitrary error factors, to avoid suspicious degrees of accuracy); the computer will respond with only minor adjustments, no matter how far off course we may be. In all likelihood, before long we will be outside the Milky Way galaxy itself.

I've spliced in pictures that lie—I've spliced in death for all of us—but I've spliced in life for the rest of the human race. . . .

We make our own circumstances. . . . Does that make me a hero . . . ? The burden . . .

Perhaps it's better to die like dogs. . . .

Take a step forward. Moving in syrup. One foot, then the other. Hurl me off the hull. The magnets will hold, the magnets will hold. Air going. . . .

But maybe they won't have to die unprepared. Maybe when the fuel is sufficiently depleted, I can tell them. They'll have the opportunity to reconcile themselves, to draw their thoughts and memories together in an act of completion. Of course, in all likelihood they will not thank me; they don't have the courage. They may even rise up and kill me in their anger.

I hate them, I love them, why am I murdering them? It would only be what I deserve, to die suddenly like that. Like a dog. That would be just. Perhaps it would be my redemption.

Redemption? But mine is an act of courage. . . .

Another step. Air . . . Awareness fading, pea-thing dissolving, me dissolving. Don't remember entering the lock. Closed, cycling through. Air! Inside. Are they cheering? What are they saying? More sweet, delicious air. . . .

Emily . . .

A smile dusts her lips, and her gaze turns downward, her eyelids like lifting gull wings.

I've killed four innocent people. Four innocent people. We've beaten the green hexagons. But four innocents . . . We make our own circumstances. I'm the one that deserves to die. They've never done anything, take me, take me. . . .

Adam Volse entered the sick bay and found Angus Petersby hovering nervously over the recuperation capsule. With a narrowing of his eyes and a cant of his head the captain said much: you're doting, we've done everything we can, come take a break.

In a husky whisper he said, "Anything new?"

Petersby glanced back. "He can't hear us. He may be in a coma for a long time. Ran out of oxygen somehow."

Volse nodded, as he always did. "Emily's trying to figure out how his suit ruptured. Ah . . . does his lack of oxygen mean . . . ?"

"Brain damage? It's possible, but I don't know. After all, Gene's the doctor. But he did make it to the lock, so he must've had air right up until then. Signs of exposure to vacuum are minimal—probably no more than a few seconds with no oxygen at all. Certainly less than a minute." He swallowed, looked down at his feet. "Come over here, Captain. I want to show you something."

They stepped to the operating table, on which Petersby had spread the components of the damaged lens array. He picked up one of the glassy cones and pointed to a speck on the side. "Puncture. Looks like it was probably a micro-meteor." He shook his head. "A one-in-a-million shot. Maybe a billion. I'll examine it more closely later. Something else has me more curious."

He picked up the board and turned it over. "Look at this."

Volse removed his pipe and craned his neck forward. His expression became puzzled. "Some kind of splice?"

"Yeah. It doesn't make sense. . . ."

"Maybe Gene tried to repair the old unit before replacing it."

"In the middle of a tricky EVA?"

Volse gingerly touched something hanging by the ragged wires.

"It's a computer chip with an auxiliary memory pin," Petersby said. "Crushed. We'll never be able to read it."

Unasked questions seemed to hover in the momentary silence. Finally, Volse said "What do you suppose Gene was trying to do?"

"Chips like this can be used to enhance a signal, but look at the lens—it's ruined. There wouldn't have been any incoming signal to enhance."

The captain cleared his throat. "Damn. Do you suppose he could've gotten confused, and started attaching this thing to the wrong lens?"

"Maybe." Petersby sucked his lower lip for a moment. "I think this EVA was even tougher on him than we imagined. Maybe you're right—for some goofy reason, he thought it would help to enhance the signal, but he spliced this thing into the punctured lens by mistake. But why the hell wouldn't he tell us what he was planning?"

"That's just Gene, I guess."

"Shit—just Gene? The bastard could've killed us playing engineer!"

Puffing on the pipe again, Volse said, "But he didn't, Angus, just remember that. He saved our lives. And very nearly lost his own in the bargain."

Petersby swallowed, seemed to consider this, and visibly calmed himself under his captain's even gaze. For the sake of something to say: "Is the new lens array still working smoothly?"

Volse smiled as if proud of Runyeager's performance. "We came out of the jump with a deviation from course of over 1000%, so we adjusted and re-jumped immediately. Came back only 12% off course, and adjusted again. Next jump in two days, as scheduled. We're doing fine. Gene did fine."

The pea-thing/awareness/me . . .

But the hands are me too. Hands know what to do. . . .

As if by unconscious agreement they turned to look at Runyeager again, though they moved no closer to him. Petersby sighed. "I'll have to take back a lot of things I've said about him." With a forced chuckle: "Of course, there're a lot of shitty things I've called him that still hold."

Volse said, "It may sound foolish to say this about a man in a coma, but he looks so peaceful. What do you suppose would be going through his mind?"

No, not circumstances. Murdered . . . like dogs. . . .

Petersby shook his head. "If anything, I'd say he was feeling like a hero. And justifiably so."

Rain, Steam
and Speed

STEVEN POPKES

THE SQUARE was blurred by mist, darkened by night, and highlighted by the streetlamp. Gossic leaned drunkenly against the lamp, watching. The rain-slicked brick was rainbow-colored, jeweled, and layered by water. He could smell bananas, apples, the archaic aroma of Greek sausage, tobacco smoke, car exhaust. The quiet was spattered by the staccato of Spanish, slurred English, and Chinese echoing inside itself like bells.

He drank some more wine, holding onto the lamppost. He wanted to sing. He saw brush strokes moving, pigment drawing what he saw into substance from the moment time. He didn't paint, he thought. No. It was more like applying turpentine or thinner to the pigment and the colors blended, ran and fell away. From beneath the paint came the picture. A paring away rather than a putting down. His cheeks hurt from grinning. He lurched away from the lamppost toward the subway. Briefly, he thought of burnt out and bombed Berlin—and moved deliberately away from that thought.

Home now, he ran up to his apartment two steps at a time. Inside, he threw down his jacket and grabbed a blank canvas, settling it on the easel. A fear entered him; he ignored it. Above him, the high ceilings were dim. Shadowy drawings and prints of paintings hung on the dark

walls. All the images looked alike: different views of one
city. All save two: a sketch of a woman's face and a print of
a painting of the same city as the others, but filled with
light.

He turned to the blank canvas, as broad as the world.
Berlin? he thought. Elaine? He glanced toward the sketch
of the woman and away. Darkness settled within him. He
started to block in the framework of the painting, tried to
capture what he had felt. The pigment became mere pigment: oil and solvent mixed with metal ores. He put the
palette down and picked up the bottle of wine, moved to
the window. He could feel Elaine's eyes upon him. He
looked down and watched the few people walking along
the street. The rain gutters were choked thick with mud
and dissolved mortar. He finished the wine and stared out
the window for a long time, listening to the night music.
Nachtmusik, he thought sarcastically.

Gossic sat on a bench outside of the Museum School
absorbing the rare March sun like a supplicant.

"There you are!"

Gossic frowned, refused to open his eyes. "Why are you
bothering me, Dilmar? Can't you do your curating somewhere else?"

Dilmar sat down next to him and laughed. "Of course.
But you bother other people; I must bother you. Equity is
thus conserved."

Gossic grunted and felt irritated. This was, however, a
common feeling to him and he ignored it.

Dilmar was silent a few more minutes. "We are sending
Unter den Linden Strasse to Centaurus."

His stomach twisted. Gossic couldn't breathe a moment. Elaine? Berlin in flames painted itself on the insides
of his eyelids. After a moment he shrugged. "I've done
better."

"Not recently. It was chosen for the show."

"What show?"

"Oh," Dilmar sighed expansively, "an exhibition of
some science, some poetry, some drama: enough to im-
press the Centaurans but not enough to embarrass us later.
All of the drama and poetry will be of a, ah, certain patriotic nature."

Gossic laughed softly. "And the art? Will it too be of a 'certain patriotic nature'?"

Dilmar sounded shocked. "Of course not! The Whore—excuse me, your beloved director—is on our side after all."

Gossic leaned back and relaxed. "You're taking *Linden Strasse*. Interesting."

"It will be good for the school, funding and all that. It will be even better if you go too."

Excitement, a churning in the gut, a sudden feeling as if the heart had stopped, the glands working overtime. *I wonder what they're like. . . .*

Fear following close behind.

"I don't travel anymore," he said thickly.

"That's true," said Dilmar nodding. "This much sense you have," he snapped his fingers. "No more, no less. You need to do something interesting—you used to do such things. I didn't drag you here from Berlin after the war just to watch you rot."

Bless you, Guillermo, he thought around the hard knot of fear and anger. "I don't travel anymore," he said.

"Just so," said Dilmar resignedly.

Gossic felt uncomfortable at the party. It was absurd that he'd been invited, crazy that he had come. The party was held in the grand ballroom of the museum and the guest of honor was the collection being sent to Centaurus. Gossic had been sent an invitation. He had refused. He had been sent a memo to the effect that the school always required funds and needed his association at this event. He had a reputation. He had a name. He refused again. Muscle had come to his studio in the form of Director Melinda Mael. She had fixed him with her eyes and said in precise, Mandarin-inflected English: "If you cannot help us by going, help us by attending the reception."

And so he stood there, drink in hand, punchbowl nearby, raging. I should be painting, he said to himself. Painting what? came the answer. Skylines of Berlin?

"That's true," he whispered slowly, suddenly feeling depressed.

Dilmar was talking animatedly to his lover, a Captain Heimholtz. The director was making a contributor feel welcome, and more generous. Across the room, he saw a woman watching him. He glanced away, embarrassed. She was tall, with blond hair and wide, pale blue eyes.

He moved away from the party and out the door into the darkened halls and galleries. Obelisks from China and Egypt looked down on him. He walked beneath the plump women of Rubens, the dancing colors of Renoir, past a gallery of Rodin sculpture. He did not have to think where he was going: his feet knew the way.

The museum had only a few Turners—most were in collections of Europe. Three were on loan here: *The Harbor of Dieppe, Babylon* and his favorite, *Rain, Steam, and Speed.* He stood in front of *Dieppe* first, drinking slowly and watching the delicate buildings reflected in the gentle water. The details were everywhere but in the sky. There, vague ambivalence reigned and left only the light and warmth of the sun. Next to *Dieppe* was *Babylon.* He remembered Ruskin on Turner: ". . . impatient shadow of a darker spirit, seeking rest and finding none." He thought of Berlin.

"I wondered where you would stop."

He turned to the voice. It was the woman he had seen in the ballroom.

"I'm Olathe Copi," she said.

He liked her voice, low, warm. She smiled and he smiled back. "François Gossic. Turner's a weakness of mine."

"Oh."

He looked at her sharply for a moment, then away. There was an interest in her voice, a warmth. *You can talk,* it seemed to say. Or not. See? he said to his own continuous dialogue, you can stop now.

It didn't.

She moved past him to stand in front of *Rain, Steam, and Speed.* "The first two I understand. A harbor. A legendary city. This one escapes me. What is interesting about a railroad?"

Gossic felt vaguely jealous and irritated with her. What's the matter? Thousands of people every day stare at these paintings. They're *art.*

He shrugged. "When Turner was born, men were limited to the speed of horses. Some scientist proved a person couldn't breathe moving much faster."

" 'Proved'?"

He had to smile. "Scientists are always proving something. When the railways were first built there was an exhibitory ride and Turner was invited. It was a day like this." He pointed to the painting. "Blurry, wet, cold. All of the windows were up. Turner shared his seat with an old woman. An old matron, I imagine. I don't know. When the train reached top speed, Turner rolled down the window and stuck his head out. From that experience came the painting."

Her eyes were blank.

He shook his head. "It wasn't enough to hear about it. It wasn't enough to read about it in a journal somewhere. He had to see for himself. Nothing less would do. And if it killed him, that was the price he was willing to pay."

"It couldn't have, though."

"*He* didn't know that. The greatest minds of his day said it might. Such courage."

Gossic realized he was nearly shouting and stopped. He looked at the ground then back at the painting. Such courage. And what was he, François Gossic, doing?

He noticed she was watching him. There was no contempt or even embarrassment on her face. A small smile played on her lips but it was a fascinated smile. He had her whole attention.

"Turner is, as I said, a weakness of mine."

"It doesn't seem to be a weakness at all." She laughed and took his arm.

They left, *The Harbor* and *Babylon* and moved toward the rotunda. "Why are you here?" he asked and immediately felt clumsy. Blunt, Dilmar called him. Tactless. Haven't you proved this sufficiently tonight?

She seemed not to notice. "I'm the pilot."

He digested that. He was unsure what a pilot of a starship did. "You're the captain, then? Like Heimholtz?"

"God, no. I'm the *pilot.*" She looked at him and laughed. "I actually fly the thing. Or move it, anyway."

There was a look in her eyes, a glint of knowledge he wanted to know. It seemed private to him, a thing shared by experience and not by words. He began to feel thawed, warmed by her as by sunshine. Smiling, they wandered randomly through the galleries, from period to period, from abstraction to expressionism, from Goya to Mondrian. A moment came when he knew she wanted him and he wanted her as well.

They returned to the party and separated. For a time, he watched her and saw her at times glance up at him. Later, he left and went home when she was looking elsewhere.

He could make no sense of the article at all.

The magazine had said on the cover: "Starspace: What Really Happens?" It spoke of "interfaces" and "n-space," and "apparent velocity" and "fictional environments." He knew nothing of them and the article didn't bother to explain. Fictional environments? "From any point in n-space, any other point has an equal probability of existence." What the hell did that mean? The world was based on a whim? At times, the article seemed to think a starship moved through space, at others that space moved around it, and at others that the ship was recreated in its new location. "The universe," the article concluded, "is much more malleable than was ever thought possible."

He threw the magazine across the room.

Outside the window, he could see the students walking the streets. He had been thinking of Olathe when he bought the magazine. He had been thinking of Olathe a great deal. What does a pilot do? he thought. What lay behind her smile?

He paced around the apartment again. Sketches of Berlin hung just above eye level. He looked up toward Elaine over the window. To her right was a print of *Unter den Linden Strasse:* Berlin filled with light. He sighed, said to the sketch as he had said hundreds of times before in the years since he had left Berlin: "Elaine, I think I killed you."

The canvas in the center of the room was still blank.

He lit a cigarette, inhaled, coughed, inhaled again. Goddammit, didn't Monet smoke cigarettes? Maybe so, but you haven't for twenty years.

Twenty years? Has it been that long?

Christ.

He looked up at *Linden Strasse.* When Berlin was liberated during the War of the Beasts, the great biological weapons patterned after *T. Rex* had thundered down that street in parade. The city had smelled burnt, leveled, dusty. The *T. Rexes* had smelled sour and pungent. Above, clouds had built up over themselves like broken mountains. He had wept watching and his fingers had twitched and ached until he set them to work at the easel. Oh, that day! The cracked buildings, the smell of gunpowder and hot steel and saurian. The ragged people, the triumph, the joy, the relief. He felt a trembling inside as he looked up at the painting. That feeling— Damn! that feeling: a kind of nauseous excitement. *Oh, my God. This is a live one.*

When he came downstairs, the apartment had been wrecked and Elaine was gone.

The phone rang.

"Yes?"

"Dilmar. I missed you at Her Majesty's Wake. Are you alive?"

Gossic smiled slightly. "Maybe."

"A woman asked about you."

"Oh?"

"You must be moving up in the world. She's the pilot."

"What does a pilot do? Heimholtz ought to know."

Dilmar was quiet a moment. "That's an interesting question. I asked that of your pilot . . ."

"She's not my pilot."

". . . and she said something strange. It goes:

> Away! Away!
> The spell of arms and voices,
> the white arms of roads,
> their promise of close embraces.
> The black arms of tall ships
> that stand against the moon,
> their tale of distant nations,
> they are held out to say,
> We are alone,
> Come.

"I wouldn't have remembered it, but Heimholtz did. It seems they all say that at one time or another."

The excitement flared again in Gossic. "I want to talk to Heimholtz." Fictional realities? Malleable space?

Pause. "I didn't realize you were interested in men."

"I'm not. I just want to talk to him."

Dilmar sounded hesitant. "All right. I'll set something up."

* * *

They met at Lilly's on the waterfront. Heimholtz was a short, portly man who moved little and spoke softly. He was waiting for Gossic when he arrived.

"I'm glad you could come," said Gossic slowly.

"It is a favor for Guillermo I will enjoy doing."

Gossic was quiet a moment, not sure what to ask. A starship captain must be a formidable person, he thought. He felt foolish. "Have you made the voyage to Centaurus?"

Heimholtz chuckled. "You get on a starship, you get off. There is no time to speak of in the trip. It is not what I would call a voyage, but a visit. I have visited Centaurus five times."

Gossic shook his head. "But to go there and back takes a week. I saw the schedules at the party."

"No time is taken on the trip," said Heimholtz, "however, the trip takes time. Confusing, no?"

"Absolutely."

"Getting away from the planet takes time. Landing takes time. Some time is lost matching the comings and goings of the various ships coming into port. The interface takes only the time the pilot wishes."

Interface: one of the words in the article.

"What's it like?"

Heimholtz shrugged. "I have no idea. You should ask a pilot."

"Have you asked one?"

"Of course."

"And?"

Smile. " 'Away! Away . . .' "

" 'The tall white arms of ships.' Dilmar told me." Gossic rubbed his face. Outside, he could hear a light rain begin to fall. "Why only the pilots? Why no one else?"

Heimholtz leaned back in his chair and looked wistful. "We sleep, my friend. We sit down in the plush, soft chairs, and the pilots sing to us a lullaby. Then, they take us home, or away from home. We trust them to chart strange waters we do not know."

"But why?"

He shrugged. "In the early days, the pilots were not alone. And we lost them, every one. No ship came back. Then, Olathe returned."

"Olathe? Olathe Copi?"

"Your pilot." He smiled sadly. "Only one can go through the interface, she told us. And that one must take the rest along, building the way there. She was backed up by the licensing board and they were backed by the Customs Commission. The rule: only the pilot is to go through n-space conscious. The crew and passengers were anesthetized and no more ships were lost."

Gossic sat back and thought. He felt Berlin loom about him with Elaine's dead face watching.

The article made only a little more sense now. The term, "fictional environments," kept coming back to haunt him. A malleable reality. He leaned back and let his mind wander. It led him through his abortive painting attempt two nights ago, past the party, through Lilly's. It lingered thinking about Olathe. He felt as an old lock or a door must feel to finally be turned or opened. As always, his mind returned to Berlin.

It was toward the end of the war, when its riotous starving underground excitement was winding to a close. He lived in the upper floor of a half bombed-out building. Daily, he struggled through the downtown streets, around what remained of the markets and across the ruined parks, shivering, returning to his apartment gaunt, feverish, ready to paint. The city had been occupied early in the war and he made his living by painting the portraits of generals and colonels of the occupation forces. The portraits were sent back home to lovers and wives. Elaine ate at the same small cafe he did. He helped her clear out the downstairs apartment beneath his shortly after they became lovers. Not long, not long at all before the end of the war.

He had painted *Unter den Linden Strasse* in an afternoon, lost in a creative haze. As he painted, someone had forced their way into the house, taken Elaine and destroyed the apartment. They hadn't known the upstairs apartment was his.

He had found her several blocks away, shot, never knowing why.

He felt of her face and knew he was crying.

The doorbell rang.

"You should open this door immediately. I bring gifts."

Dilmar pounded on the door.

He had brought cheap champagne. "If you aren't going to follow your painting, I'm not going to waste good liquor on you. Watch it!" The cork bounced from the ceiling and struck the blank canvas. "Good shot," said Dilmar idly.

"To the Impressionists," said Gossic.

"Damn the Impressionists!"

Through the window they watched the Boston skyline in silence. The old brick and bronze buildings made a broken jumble of pipes, walls, antennas, and corners. The city roared under its breath. A siren called like a cat in heat.

"You're stupid not to go," said Dilmar suddenly, with no pretense but a controlled, quiet anger.

Gossic looked up in surprise, then back out the window. "Maybe."

"I found you babbling in the rubble. You were so sick you couldn't see. 'Who is he?' I asked. No one knew. I almost left you. There were thousands of people worse off than you." He sipped the champagne. "An old man grabbed me, a tailor. 'That's François Gossic, the painter.'" Dilmar barked a short laugh. "Before the war I'd been buying your paintings for the museum. Take him home, I thought. Get him away from here so he can heal." He drained the cup and put it gently down on the windowsill. "You crawled from Berlin directly into a box. I wish I'd never brought you here."

"I didn't crawl anywhere."

"An attractively furnished, well-upholstered box with fitted plumbing and a stylish view. It's pleasant." He shrugged. "Lord, I know that. I live in it myself. I *like* boxes. I was *built* to live in boxes."

"I didn't hear them," said Gossic absently.

Dilmar turned away from the window. "Who?"

"I don't know. Whoever took Elaine."

"Elaine is dead."

"I know. I killed her."

"You weren't there."

"That's why." Gossic sat down next to the window. Night had fallen now. The low sunlight painted the old stone buildings a deep red, and they in turn were reflected in the newer, glass ones. The symmetry almost took Gossic's breath away. The sounds of the city seemed sharper, more defined. *Nachtmusik,* he thought. "The bottom floor was all torn apart, so she must have struggled. They dragged her three blocks away."

"You were painting."

"Yes. I was." Gossic tried to remember how long he had known her. One month? Two? Long enough to be lovers. Enough time to feel something special growing. There had been a feeling of waking up, of stepping out of sleep. That thought nagged at him a moment until he gave it up. Berlin fell and so did Elaine.

"That's impressive," said Dilmar quietly, looking up at the print of *Linden Strasse*. "Damned impressive."

Gossic shook his head.

"Everything you've done since has been crap."

It hurt to hear that. "What?"

Dilmar held him, both hands on his cheeks, looked him in the eyes. "Crap. Do you hear me? Crap. Garbage. You were as good as Degas or Goya. There was *Rain on Titan*, *Fujiyama*, *Canyon Dancer*, and *Unter den Linden Strasse*. And nothing. *Nothing* but this other crap since." He nodded to the walls.

Gossic pulled Dilmar's hands from his face.

Dilmar leaned against the windowsill. "You were a lot like Turner. I think of him on that old stuffy British railroad, head out the window, wet, half-blind, not knowing if the speed of a stray branch would kill him. Out of that came *Rain, Steam and Speed*. You were like that. Go, for God's sake!"

Gossic was silent for a while. "What's a 'fictional environment,' Guillermo?"

Dilmar sighed. "I acquiesce. I cannot penetrate that concrete nodule you call a brain. Did Heimholtz mention that? It's got something to do with pilots. Heimholtz tried to explain it to me once. Since all things in n-space have an equal probability of happening, all realities have an equal probability of being perceived. Or something like that. I'm not entirely certain."

Things could be different, he said to himself. I could change it. "That makes it more clear. I'll go."

Dilmar stared at him warily. "Why? Why *not*?"

"Your eminent persuasive ability has swayed my opinion."

"Crap."

Gossic breathed deeply. "My reasons are my own. I think it's important."

"It's important because it gets you out of the *box!*"

A voice within Gossic he had never listened to before cried back to Dilmar: I want *out!* He laughed and it eased the tightness in his chest. Was it only fear? Excitement? There were flutterings and tremblings all through him. "This is cheap champagne."

"Only the best for you, my dear François. Only the best. To the Impressionists."

"Damn the Impressionists!"

He watched the exhibition ship *Divers Arts* from the viewing salon. Heimholtz had given him a letter of introduction and he fingered it in his pocket as he watched the ship approach. The salon was dark and he was alone. The other passengers had left it to prepare to disembark. Only he had remained to watch.

Night, he thought. One's perception of outer space was determined by how one felt about night. The slow creakings and quick snappings of the ship became *nachtmusik.* Turner should have lived now.

"I think we have similar tastes," came a familiar voice.

He was startled but not surprised. Without turning to her, he answered, "I suspect you are right. Why aren't you on the ship?"

Olathe stood next to him, only barely visible in the starlight. "I fly here. That's enough." She looked at him. "I thought you weren't coming."

He nodded. "I had a change of heart." Long pause. "Will I see you on Centaurus?"

"Are you going to run away again?"

A wan smile. "I don't think so. Not any more."

"All right, then." She smiled and he could feel the warmth in the darkness. "I'll see you there."

She left him and he watched the ship come nearer. *Nachtmusik,* he thought.

The captain's name was Praihm. The letter of introduction brought him as far as the crew's lounge, where the captain was talking slowly and methodically to the bartender. The bartender listened not at all. Praihm read the letter and leaned against the bar. "Okay. What do you want?"

"You are in charge of the ship—"

Praihm laughed and interrupted him. "We shuttle from one civilized fleshpot to another. I am not in charge. I go to sleep with the rest of you and I wake up at the same time."

"Are you not in charge until we actually leave?" Gossic placed a hundred-credit note on the bar.

Praihm watched him more closely. "In theory, yes. The captain is a legal office rather than an actual one. I take legal responsibility for the *Divers Arts.*"

Gossic covered the first note with a second. "Then you have no power at all."

"Some."

A third note appeared. "The ship has several boxes and containers attached to it. What are they?"

"Freight, mostly. Special equipment. A few animals and passengers in cold storage." Praihm did not look directly at the money.

"How do they make the trip? Do they have devices aboard them to bring them along with the ship?"

Praihm was silent until another bill joined the first three. "No. Anything attached to the ship is brought into the field. There's a radar mapping done just prior to entry and the field is defined by contact."

"I want something out there."

"What?"

"Me."

Praihm laughed. "That's crazy."

"Probably." Gossic held a thousand-credit note in his hand. Praihm's gaze was reluctantly dragged to it. "You'd need a space suit," he said slowly.

"Can that be arranged?"

Praihm shrugged. A second thousand-credit note turned that to a nod.

"And you'll have to be drugged."

"No."

Praihm shook his head. "If you came out crazy or dead I'd be in trouble."

Three more thousand-credit notes appeared in Gossic's hand.

* * *

Gossic found the suit just inside the airlock. He waited there with it in his hands until he heard last call. Now, he knew from talking with Praihm, passengers were sitting or lying down on the couches waiting for sleep to overcome them. Gossic donned the suit easily, remembering when he had painted *Rain on Titan*. Outside, he attached the safety line to the ring by the hatch. He felt a familiar nausea and suppressed it.

He pushed himself gently away from the ship, paid out the hundred or so feet of line and snubbed himself to a stop. Around him were stars. He could see Saturn and Jupiter, but not earth. He relaxed, waiting. Peace filled him. If, in n-space, all things are equal, then are all acts and desires equal as well? Was it enough to come out here ready to try to change what had occurred already? Was it necessary to actually *do* it? Questions spun inside him. Part of him said, yes: it is enough to be willing to try. A second part argued, no. The thought was not enough. The act, the attempt is what is important. He watched the night around him and decided both were correct. He could return to the ship right now, free. But his freedom was not sufficient. Elaine was dead and he had not helped her. The will had been there, had he known what was happening, but the attempt had never been made. Now, it would be.

There was a new sensation of falling, different from the feeling of weightlessness.

Annoyed, Gossic looked around him. The feeling of falling became more intense. It made him afraid. He started to pull himself in, made himself let go of the line. He looked back toward the sun. It was surrounded by a rainbow halo. Around him, things began to look scratchy and vague, as in an old, brittle photograph. Reflexes buried in his hindbrain and spinal cord took over and he thrashed on the end of the line. Terror held him and he screamed and fell, faster and faster, through a wash of vision toward an unimaginable impact. He was *falling*.

He hit and felt himself splatter.

He was in pieces, spread everywhere. He was split, broken, shattered: a Jackson Pollock, flowing. Downhill? Drawn as if by gravity. Like a river, he was and he flowed. Down? Down. Coalescing, touching himself and rubbing himself. He funneled together. Down, down—

He was sitting next to a tiller in the stern of a sailboat. The sun was hot and tropical and the ocean opalescent. Islands in the distance were an incredible green. For a long time, he just watched, not thinking. He felt a touch on his arm and looked toward it reflexively.

Olathe was watching him, pale blue eyes and a crooked smile.

"I almost didn't find you."

He shook his head and his mind caught. "Find me? Where was I?"

"Everywhere. Nowhere." She smiled again. He watched her steer the boat downwind. For a long time there was silence between them.

"Are you crazy?" she said at last.

He thought for a moment. "I don't think so."

Olathe watched him a moment, then the sails. "You might have never made it back and just wandered, spread out over all creation."

"Where am I now?"

"My world. I felt you as soon as we hit the interface. I decided to bring you here. My world. I made it."

"Who's crazy?"

She laughed. "You know what I mean. You're going to try it yourself."

"How do you know that?"

Silence again. "This place is mine. There's not much in it I don't know."

"Will you help me?" he asked after a time.

"You'd make a bad pilot." She drank some water. "You have too much imagination."

"That's the first time I've ever heard it was a liability."

"You're an artist. You change. That's how creativity works. That's your business. That's *you.*" She stopped at the look of confusion on his face, stood up and lifted one of the deck seats. Underneath was a compact electronic device. Gossic had no idea what it was. "It's a monitor," she said. "I brought it with me. I *chose* to do that. It measures how I change so I can figure that in when I find my way back. I'm a good pilot because I don't change much." She stopped again, sighed. "Look, you're a product of the universe. Everything that occurs, all of the moments making it up, all of the events, time, movements, leave their mark on you. You are also, then, its source. N-space is the source of *everything*, including you. Or me. When I decide to go back, I'll know how to recreate the universe to fit me. The ship will be in its berth. The passengers will wake up. I'll be there."

"I still don't understand."

She said gently: "You don't change things. You change yourself. You build everything else from scratch each moment, bit by bit, whisper by whisper."

"Will you help me?" He bent his head, not wanting to watch her.

"All right," he heard her say. "But tomorrow."

And though they stood on a boat in the sunlight, it was the night in the gallery when he knew he wanted her and she wanted him. She was an incredible lover. She would be, here, he thought with awe. It was her world.

They sailed away from the islands into the open sea the next day. Two days passed, then a week. The sea changed color from the beautiful opalescence that had enchanted Gossic to a dusky blue, to a choked gray. The sun faded into mist. Well into the second week, they were enshrouded in fog.

"Is this the dark side of your nature?" chuckled Gossic nervously.

Olathe was unsmiling. "We'll come shortly to the limits of my world. After that, you're on your own."

Gossic nodded.

The sea turned a gray-green and oily. The fog closed thick and cold. The foredeck could not be seen from the stern.

"Okay," said Olathe quietly. "We're here."

"How do you know?"

"This is still my world, mostly. It's the border. I still make *some* of the rules."

Out of the sea and the fog came a low, shadowy boat. It was black and empty. There were no oars and no mast.

Gossic didn't like it. "This is awfully symbolic."

"It's yours. I didn't bring it." She stared at it, then looked at him. "Get in."

Gossic did so and sat in the stern looking at Olathe. His fingers clenched the railing, were white like bleached bones.

"You make your own rules from here on." She steered

her boat around and moved away into the fog. Soon, she was gone.

Darkness gathered about him. He felt Berlin, and Elaine, coming at him in a dead run.

"All right," he said slowly, trying to feel his way clear, "all right."

Berlin? The smell of broken and burnt buildings, the feeling of masonry dust in the air, settling on your skin. Berlin? The smell of pigment and the sharp, acid smell of saurian.

Berlin!

He was in his studio. In the center was the half-finished *Linden Strasse*.

Elaine was downstairs. Was it now? Here? He picked up a knife in fury and slashed the painting. From the cut oozed blood. He stared at it blankly. This is my world, he thought, I make the rules.

He ran down the stairs. Now, he would know who. Now, he would know why.

She was sitting and reading in the living room. She looked up, wide face and a crooked smile and pale blue eyes. He shook his head, confused for a moment.

"Is it finished?" She stood up, excitement in her voice. "Can I see it?"

Outside, he heard voices shouting. Many voices. He looked out the window. There were hundreds of people shouting his name, her name. They carried torches, guns, farm implements. "A mob," he breathed.

He pulled away from the window just as the door exploded inward. Forty, fifty, a hundred people swarmed into the small room. His arms were held back behind him. Elaine was pinned against the wall. Somebody swung a pick into his abdomen, jerked it up. He danced on the pain like a fish on a hook. They ripped off Elaine's clothes and a man picked up a sledgehammer and brought it down on her legs. Gossic screamed.

He stood trembling in the studio; his hands covered his face. Gradually, he brought down his hands and looked around. It was quiet. He felt of his stomach. It was intact.

There was no mob. There had *never* been a mob. A struggle, a fight, a murder, but by a small group or one person. Never a mob. His imagination had gotten in the way. He smiled grimly at himself. He probably *would* be a bad pilot.

The painting was still in the center of the room. Idly, he picked up a knife and slashed it. The edges of the cut burned and blackened. The pigment curled and melted, smoldering. In seconds, the painting was entirely charred.

Downstairs, Elain was reading in the living room.

"Is it finished?" She stood up.

There was a knock at the door.

Control, Gossic thought. Let things come. He was still carrying the knife. He opened the door.

The man there was small, effete. "Excuse me, Monsieur Gossic. I have come many miles to speak with you."

Elaine touched Gossic on the shoulder. Gossic growled and held out the knife. The small man paled. "François," said Elaine, "let him in. It's cold outside."

Gossic moved reluctantly out of the way. "He's a killer."

"François!"

"He *is!*"

The little man edged around them. "Close the door, please." He had a sudden hardness in his voice. "You have been cooperating with the enemy."

The little man pulled out a gun. Gossic leaped toward him. The man didn't even blink. He shot Gossic down in mid-air, then shot Elaine.

"Death," said the man quietly, "to the traitors."

Gossic crawled over to Elaine but she was already dead.

He lay on the floor of his studio. It was quiet. Below, he could hear Elaine sighing softly. The evening air was wet with spring and smelled of saurian. Outside, it was raining.

He stood, looked at the half-finished painting.

Now, he knew why she had been killed. Painting? Consorting with the enemy? He thought of the words but could not absorb them. They had come for him and had killed Elaine because he had not been there. Had he known this? He had never thought of it before. Still, it felt familiar. There was no little man, of that he was sure. He did not have to invent anyone. Olathe had said it herself. Everything leaves its mark. He felt the box closing in on him even now. Deep inside, he shouted: I want *out!*

No price was too great.

He looked at the painting. No, he thought, you are not appropriate. Elaine died for you. He closed his eyes and opened them on blank canvas. This is my world. I make the rules. He carried nothing downstairs.

Elaine stood up. "Is it finished?"

He looked at her. God, she was young. How could she ever have been that young?

There was a knock on the door.

He opened it. Outside, there were three, no, four men in dark raincoats. "Monsieur Gossic?" said a tall one. He looked tiredly and significantly at Elaine. "We would like you to come with us."

Gossic nodded and took up his jacket. He smiled and waved to Elaine. "I'll be back shortly."

They took him down the street toward a nearby park. He could smell early spring maples and elms. This is how it should have béen, he thought. It was me they wanted all along.

"You have cooperated with the enemy," said the tall man.

"I painted paintings. That's what an artist does."

"Not for *them!*" He spat and jerked his head toward the east.

"I paint for myself." It was true then—now—but not for years. It would be true again.

The tall man waved that aside. "We are cleaning up the remnants of the traitors. You are one of the last."

Gossic nodded. They had probably already shaved the heads of the prostitutes and hung the policemen.

The tall man continued. "Have you anything further to say?"

Gossic watched him, felt the rain drizzle down his back and from his hair into his eyes. He shook his head.

They stopped in an alleyway. He was leaned against the wall. One of the others pulled out a gun. This was, Gossic thought and smiled, exactly the way it should have been. They fired and Gossic crumpled to the ground.

Gossic sat in the boat for a long time, at home in the darkness. There were no stars and the fog was as warm as steam, not cold at all. He was alone. The darkness is my own, he thought, my *nachtmusik*.

In a world bounded only by infinity, Elaine lived and lived not. He had made a world for her, but it was not *his* world. He was tired of abstractions, tired of guilt. He wanted to go home. He stood in the boat and looked around. The sky cleared and the stars came out. He reached up and touched them and they became scratchy and vague, receding from him, becoming a part of the background for boxes and containers surrounding him. All things were haloed by rainbows. Saturn was gone and the sun was in a different piece of the sky. The breath he breathed smelled of iron and his vision was circumscribed by the bubble of his helmet.

He drew himself back into the airlock. Inside, he left the suit and returned to the bar. He waved to Praihm, who looked relieved, and went on to find his baggage.

His paintings were delivered to the exhibition hall. Around him as he took a public walkway he saw Centaurans. They looked to him like medieval death images. They watched him in return. He shrugged. He would find out about them later.

At the hall, he found a blank canvas and his paints. He whistled to himself and became unconscious of anything around him. He and the painting were once more their own world.

An hour before the exhibition opened he finished. The painting looked deep into a well. The sides were black and white, gradually including color as the well was plumbed by the eye. Far away, toward the end of where the eye could see, there was a bright flickering light, alive with possibility. He had no idea what to title it. Watching it, he felt as if he were falling. His stomach trembled.

He placed the painting and waited for the doors to open.

By noon, the hall was filled. He watched the Centaurans stand and stare at his paintings, linger over the new one. He felt a touch on his shoulder, turned and saw Olathe.

"That's a new one, isn't it?" she asked him, pointing. "I think I recognize it."

He chuckled. "Only you would."

"What's it called?"

He started to say it had no title, stopped. *"Rain, Steam and Speed."*

She looked at him quizzically. "An odd title."

"There are two stories behind it, one you know and one you don't. I'll tell you later if you like. Over dinner. Drinks. Mutual explorations."

She laughed.

"Tell me," he said teasingly, "are you as great a lover in the real world?"

She watched him for a long minute. "Honey," she said so softly only he could hear. "I thought you knew. I *am* the real world."

Close to Light

CHARLES OBERNDORF

K ATHRINE FELT LIKE the rumor must have blue-shifted through the United Nations lunar colony. She could tell that her husband Gregory already knew; whenever he looked at her his gaze was as cold as the lunar surface. Someone must have told him while he was skating their four-year-old daughter Gunnel home from the Academy. Now he knew, and it lay waste to her whole afternoon: skipping write-ups on several patients, coming home early, buying four bottles of Eastwing beer, and rehearsing all the ways that she could explain to him that Project Barnard was being reactivated, that she was being asked to join the crew, that she didn't know what decision to make. For the past three months, when the initial rumors were as weightless and as full of intangible light as a dream, Kathrine had assured him that nothing would come of it, that Gregory had no need to worry, that, yes, she'd go to Seattle with him.

Now those words had been consumed by an older desire, and Kathrine felt like she'd begun to conspire behind his back. Meanwhile, little Gunnel had removed her skates and had reached up to switch the window to a scene from Oz. Kathrine stared at the yellow brick road winding past Munchkin fields of grain and vegetables while Gunnel, a perpetual motion machine, went into action, grabbing all the cushions and pillows she could find in order to rebuild the sofa into a tan and white Emerald City. Kathrine knew she should join Gunnel; one-sixth G and limited floor space made the furniture a series of minor hazards for a (literally) bouncing four-year-old. But Kathrine found it difficult to move; for the second time since she'd left home, Kathrine felt helpless.

During dinner she stared at the rice and beans Gregory had prepared. Silence was like an invisible field that held the three of them, and Gunnel, who usually went on endlessly about the day's fingerpainting or holofilms with different Earth animals, cast her eyes downward, as if she'd done something wrong. She occasionally glanced up at her mother, seeking approval. For a moment Kathrine was struck by the feeling that Gunnel already knew, and that the guilt on her daughter's face was a foreshadowing of how Gunnel would feel if her mother decided to leave.

However, the look and Kathrine's premonition faded once Gunnel began to beg for a later bedtime. Kathrine bathed her in the ultrasonics, laid out her stuffed animals (the teddy bears, the lions, the frog, the dog, and the cat, plus the old mangled horse that had belonged to Kathrine when she was a child), and read her a chapter from *The Wizard of Oz*. Never one to be put to bed quickly, Gunnel came up with new versions of old questions: why couldn't Oz be on some planet that the starship will visit?—someone told Daddy that they're putting it back together. Kathrine firmly kissed her daughter goodnight and told Gunnel that she loved her, but the tone of Kathrine's voice sounded like her father's, all ritual, no meaning.

As a child, Kathrine had loved the rain. Her father would complain that the gray skies over Seattle were just too depressing, but Kathrine secretly loved them. She loved running as naked as her mother would allow out into the summer rains. She loved stomping in the puddles on sidewalks, splashing her hands in the waterlogged grass. She imagined the front yard's giant puddle—a mini-pond, or even a lake—to be full of amphibious people with different ways of doing things. She found her father's wanderlust became hers, but it propelled her imagination rather than her feet.

When she was thirteen, her father was traveling

through Africa without itinerary or address and her brother died of toxic-induced cancer. The gray skies of Kathrine's adolescence filled her with a certain angst that led her wanderlust to search for escape. First, there was Baum's Oz, all fourteen books. Then she returned to her front yard puddle when she discovered James Blish's miniaturized men, engineered to live in a puddle on a water world orbiting Tau Ceti. And she no longer needed an imaginary Oz; something real waited above Seattle's gray skies. She began to read all the space fiction she could find. She became Blish's Jack Loftus, communicating with energy creatures living in space. She was a crew member on Poul Anderson's out-of-control Bussard ramjet, living beyond the death and rebirth of the galaxy. She was Abraham Hecht's Gunnel Ordahl, establishing new planetary colonies, directing the building of new cultures.

All that had mattered, all that she had desired, was to travel to the stars.

Six years ago it had almost come true.

"When were you going to tell me?"

Kathrine was lying in bed, naked under the covers, wondering the same thing herself. His question had sounded more like an accusation, and Kathrine had to force herself to relax.

Gregory was standing up, occupying the rest of the space in their small cubicle bedroom. He was changing from his clothes into his pajamas, another statement made in gestures. "I knew this would happen," he said. He looked almost caged standing there. He was the Colony's historian, a professor of Economics and Social History, and Kathrine could sense his need to pace out this discussion. "I knew that once the visas were cleared and the job at the University of Washington was for real, that something would happen. For the past three months the U.S. has talked about rejoining the United Nations. For three months I told you the money would be back. I told you they'd start the project all over again."

"I didn't know they'd ask me," Kathrine said.

"They'd've been stupid not to."

"Look, I'm thirty-five, not twenty-nine. Hell, I'm not even in shape to go to Seattle in two months, with this lunar layer." She automatically patted her belly. "Don't look at me that way. I didn't expect it to happen like this. We didn't go back to the U.S. when they pulled out; until your Seattle job, we were *persona non grata*. The most I'd expected was to be taken on in some kind of advisory capacity. I'd help them set up their mental health maintenance program."

"You're too valuable for that." His gaze dared her to argue the point: a Ph.D. in Closed Environmental Psychology, a B.S. in Physics, a B.S. in Mechanical Engineering—an overachiever who'd specialized in all the right areas.

"Do you want me to turn it down?"

"Would you if I asked you to?"

Kathrine found it impossible to say yes. She swallowed hard and forced herself to nod.

Gregory stood as if stunned, as if whatever script he'd prepared for this encounter had gone astray. He sat down beside her and reached out to touch her leg with his hand; the blanket divided palm and knee. "I can't ask that. I want you to stay because your love for Gunnel and me is at least equal to your need to be on that ship."

"It's not a competition," she said softly.

He was looking down at his hand, or perhaps imagining her bare leg beneath the blanket. "You know, if you'd absolutely needed to stay, I wouldn't have taken the Seattle job. Gunnel and you have always come first."

Kathrine wanted to feel tender. She wanted Gregory and Gunnel to come first, but she felt as if something unspoken was being left out of the equation. She couldn't bring it up though; he looked so fragile now—as if all his efforts to be cold and distant, the soft scientist trying to adapt to the emotional facade of his hard scientist neighbors, had drained him. She did so want to feel tender toward him, so she pulled his head toward hers, brought lips to touch lips: the marital resolution to all moments without resolution. He found his way under the blankets, and he hastily embraced her as if she might change her mind. The Gregory she wanted at that moment would have been gentle, understanding: let's share this moment of love as communion, a mingling of kisses, an exploration of surfaces, a reaching within for lights flashed behind mutually closed eyes. Instead, however, she found herself embracing a Gregory who kissed her desperately, who worked his way atop her, who pulled down his pajama bottoms, who slid penis into vagina, only seeking release within her. When his back shuddered, when she could feel his body loosen as if all its energy had been released with the barely felt one, two, three twitch of ejaculation, Kathrine realized she had been wrong. He whispered in her ear how much he truly loved her, and she knew she was projecting onto him a selfish Gregory rather than a tormented, confused one. "Please, don't go," he said, and she locked her arms around him, trying to pull him into her, for once wishing that she had Earth's full gravity to give his mass greater substance, to help it press down more firmly upon her body, to hold her there so she would not feel, even while she was under him, that she had floated away from this embrace, miles away, light-years.

Later that night her period started. It figured.

All the space fiction Kathrine had read in high school were dreams coming true. Corporations—Chinese, Japanese, North American—were building orbital factories, mining asteroids, turning the moon into an interplanetary hub of exploitation and commerce. She began to study physics; the knowledge of movement, the laws of interaction, she felt, would open the window, give her the proper trajectory. The disastrous breakup of a space station, the meltdown of a planetary probe's reactor, convinced Kathrine to add engineering to her studies when she entered the University of Washington. She joined the Air Force ROTC for good measure, even though it meant transferring to California and living away from her mother.

It all changed when her mother, who was oh so careful about whom she slept with, finally hit the lucky number and waited patiently while cancer and pneumonia morbidly competed toward her death. Her father, who'd been everywhere and had slept (most likely) with almost anyone, didn't even show up for the funeral. At that point, Kathrine began to count just how many friends she had, how little courting (sex was out of the question) she had done. It was then she'd taken up psychology, and quickly found herself fascinated by studies of the effects of closed environments on human behavior.

Her education, her perseverance, and (she admitted) sheer luck got her into the recently announced Project

Barnard. She was going to outdo her father—travel farther, with a distinct, humane goal. Lunar telescopes, seeing with a clarity that was impossible through Earth's atmosphere, had detected planets orbiting Barnard's Star —there were now other worlds, fresh chances to start anew.

The next morning, Gunnel remembered what was always at the back of Kathrine's mind. It was day fourteen, and the sun would be rising an hour before it was time to be at the Academy. Gregory, who was doing his best to treat Kathrine as kindly as a new lover, offered to take Gunnel, even though it was Kathrine's turn this week. A fist was clenching Kathrine's uterus, and she didn't want to take Gunnel nor did she want Gregory to be friendly. She sipped her coffee, muttered that she'd take Gunnel. For a brief moment Gregory looked frightened: he knew what was visible from the Observation Deck. Kathrine almost changed her mind.

Gregory helped Gunnel put on her skates (breaking one of his own rules that Gunnel should do as much for herself as possible, like any Lune). Kathrine let Gunnel, flushed with excitement at seeing the sunrise, lead the way. Gunnel soon got tired of trying to be first, and let her mother catch up. She then launched into more questions. Which animals were faster: the dog? the lion? the horse? on Earth? on the moon? in space? She hunched her shoulders forward and smiled impishly. She knew animals couldn't run in space. She liked being silly, and, right now, Kathrine, who had never discouraged her flights of fancy, hated her daughter's silliness.

When the elevator doors opened, Gunnel darted ahead to the eastward side of the Deck and pressed her face up against the thick glass. All she wanted to see was the starship. Kathrine stood behind Gunnel, her right hand resting atop her daughter's head, surprised that sunrise could create such awe that her daughter would hold still for more than a moment or two. To their right, the elevator doors opened and shut, adding new voices, the smells of different colognes and soaps as new people emerged: an African couple she knew with their eight-year-old son, an Asian engineer and a Chilean doctor, young couples, children without adults, some faces she didn't recognize,

maybe tourists. They all crowded against the thick glass of
the oval bubble. Curving away from them was the smooth
gray of the lunar surface, several meters of it smoothly laid
atop the curves of the colony's concrete domes. The lunar
regolith protected the colonists from the sun's hard radiation just as the tinted, thick glass of the Deck tried to do.

The sun was already breaking away from the horizon.
"There it is," the Chilean doctor said, and kissed her lover.
Gunnel's face was tilted down, eyes focusing on the dark
edge of the crater. Kathrine watched in the distance—
without a terrestrial atmosphere everything was so clear
and obvious. The line dividing day from night was as solid
as any border on a color-coded map. Light seemed to push
at dark, and the line of darkness glided toward the crater,
light inexorably following. New shadows were cast within
no distant craters, upon nearby mountains: the darkness of
shadows, the brightness of lunar gray. The line dipped into
the crater, and seemed to tumble in slow motion with the
moon's lighter gravity.

"There it is, Mommy!" Gunnel shrieked as she pointed.
"There's the starship!"

Lying where tractors had flattened the surface, near
where the crater wall rose, was the *Poul Anderson,* separated into sections, looking more like the remains of a giant
toy model that some child had tired of and forgotten to
assemble. Gray moondust, whipped around in different
patterns each time ships landed or departed from the Colony, gave the sections a dull, patterned sheen. It had been
vivisected like some dead animal six months after the U.S.
had pulled out of the United Nations, when it became
obvious that the U.S. would not declassify the necessary
information to finish the electromagnetic scoop, when
China and Japan were not willing to increase their share of
the funding. It was when they'd finally brought it down,
laid it to rest, that Gamel Hjaij—the *Poul Anderson*'s general engineer and Kathrine's lover—told her that he was
going to return to New Palestine, to his extended family
that lived in East Jerusalem. Gamel had told Kathrine over
dinner. Her right hand had clenched into a fist, and the
wineglass in her hand shattered, the white wine exploding
outward like a special effects explosion in a space movie.
She hadn't felt the shards of glass that had cut into her
palm until later.

"Is the starship really faster than the horse?" Gunnel asked.

"The horse would be faster right now," Kathrine said, finding the question easy to answer because asking questions was almost like a game for Gunnel. "But when the starship is put back together it will be the fastest thing ever." Except for the speed of light, she thought.

"When are they going to put it together?"

Kathrine used to say, I don't know, honey. "Maybe within a year. By the time you're six, it will leave."

"Can kids go?"

"Not this time." Kathrine had the sensation that the Chilean doctor, or perhaps the African couple, had heard the rumors and had started to listen in. She tried to ignore the feeling. She wanted to look over her shoulder, see if anyone would quickly glance away as if they truly weren't paying attention, but she fought the temptation. "This time they'll just take grown-ups. They want to make sure the trip is safe. Maybe next time they'll take grown-ups and their children."

"Will I be seven then?"

"Remember, I told you that it's a much longer trip."

"Longer than our trip to Earth?"

"Much longer. By the time the ship comes back, you'll have graduated from college." And I'll be over fifty, too old to be asked again on such a voyage.

"Oh." Gunnel said, digesting the impossible to imagine years ahead—four times her present lifetime.

Gunnel knew that her mother had been on the first crew—They stopped the mission so your daddy and I could have you, Kathrine had once told her. Gunnel was bright enough to ask if Mommy would go this time. Kathrine prepared herself, tried to think of some answer, or better yet, some way to put it off so she wouldn't have to tell her in front of all these people. What would they think, the Chilean doctor and her Asian engineer, the African couple with their own child? There's Dr. Geist, leaving her daughter for the stars. No: that was too much like her mother's friends talking about her errant father. A Lune's thought would be something much different: there's Dr. Geist, who sacrificed the comfort of living with a family to be one of the first to go to the stars. Would Gunnel, graduating from college when the *Poul Anderson* returned (if it hadn't been destroyed during the voyage), be able to think of her mother's departure in such a noble fashion? What would she think, with all of her four years, if she asked this moment and I found a way to answer?

By now the the line separating dark from light had slid across the crater, past the Colony. The Observation Deck was bathed in light. Gunnel didn't ask, and Kathrine still had no answers.

When Kathrine had arrived on the moon as part of the *Poul Anderson* crew, she was twenty-eight, eager to participate in the one-year training, and immediately in love with the lunar colony. It seemed clean, shiny, and wondrous—the stuff of dreams, an Emerald City where every ornament served a function. The Colony was free of disease, everyone tested before entry. Crime seemed absent, at least the kind of crime accompanied with an open knife or a leveled gun.

The Colony was oriented around Central Park: grass, rocks, flowing expensive water: all for games, relaxation, couples, fliers. Surrounding the Park—back then, before the days of overexpansion—were the various living sectors that took on the flavor of neighborhoods as like attracted like, either by profession or by culture. Residents shared shifts in the stores, established tearooms, cafés, pubs; opened mosques, churches, temples.

It wasn't sterile at all. It was rich and textured. Nothing seemed to stagnate. The Colony was ever-expanding as new ways were developed to exploit the resources of the moon, of the asteroids, of close-passing comets; there was always new construction, new specialists, new plans.

It was everything Earth could once have been, and Kathrine felt that she was part of the vessel that would carry the best of humanity outward. The cool burning of her studies—the perpetually controlled chain reaction—now made her radiant. For once, she felt open and secure. She risked her first kiss, made love for the first time, the lunar gravity freeing motion, Gamel's large form resting firm within her embrace, not at all the heavy and oppressive weight she had imagined. It astonished her, after everything she'd grown up with, that such clear, sweet pleasure could exist.

It ended all at once—the terse official announcement,

the dissection of the *Poul Anderson,* Gamel's reluctant announcement of his departure, and the shattering of glass in her hand—and only then did Kathrine notice a different aspect of everything she'd previously romanticized. There were no gangs, no drug or video addictions, no muggings, no homeless or beggars, but there was the invisible shifting of money, the projects that never led anywhere and somehow cost more than they were worth, the assignments of duties based on deals rather than qualifications. There was a richness with peoples of so many lands, but there was also the bickering between Africans of different tribal heritages, the tension between Arabs and Anglos, the envious resentment of Asians, the veiled attacks on Jews. The hard scientist berated the soft scientists, all scientists complained about administrators, and neither group mixed well with the maintenance crews.

When the U.S. had declared that all its citizens must withdraw from United Nations-sponsored activities and return home, or risk losing citizenship, Kathrine decided to stay with the Colony. If nothing else, it was better than Earth.

The enjoyment of routine, the daily order providing form for exploring deeper content, Kathrine felt, was a quality needed for someone taking an extended voyage in an elaborate, high-tech tin can pulling itself through the void. Kathrine loved healthy routines, the rituals of daily life: seeing her patients, exercising, lunch, research, playing turnabout or softestball, dinner at home, putting Gunnel to bed, sitting up to talk with Gregory when he wasn't overworking to meet the deadline on his book.

Gunnel's unspoken question, caught in the hard glare of the new day's sun, made the routine crowd in on her, surround her in some indefinable way: the way the void surrounds a starship, always present, never touching, and the pinpoint of light, the destination, incomprehensible in the dark vastness.

Kathrine found it hard to be patient with two Water Efficiency researchers who refused to get along. The North American felt the German was being secretive because he *always* had to keep his office door closed. The German felt the North American was prying, *always* wanting to see what was going on. Both refused to understand that the arguments' roots were cultural: Germans and North Americans used doors differently. They bickered and yelled and found something else wrong each with the other and Kathrine wanted to send them both home. Of course, until the amnesty was declared, the Northamerican had no native country to return to.

She liked and sympathized with thirteen-year-old Roberto, but today he seemed like a spoiled child. He'd been caught shoplifting twice. A week ago he'd been flying over the Park when he decided to dive-bomb several children, strafing them with urine. He didn't want to be on the moon; he wanted to be back in Argentina; his parents were too important to send home, and Roberto was too young to eject from the Colony. He didn't want to cooperate with her, either.

Kathrine wasn't sure if she was relieved or not when Gregory called. "I'm really fed up with the book," he said. On the vid' he looked tired. "I thought we could both use a break."

"Sorry, hon. I'm busy until this evening."

"I know. So am I. What I was thinking was that Gunnel keeps asking to visit Petra, so maybe we could leave her for the night with the Osheroffs and have the evening to ourselves."

"Remember, my period started."

"It doesn't have to be that kind of evening. The last few months or so, with me trying to get this book done, haven't been so great. I just want, well, you know, a good evening."

"Sure," she said, even though she didn't like the idea of Gunnel being away for the night. "It sounds like a good idea." After breaking the connection, she wished she'd been honest with him. He wanted a good moment with her, to remind her of all his wondrous qualities: his sensitivity, his intelligence, his charm, his devotion. He acted as if he were competing with another lover, or as if all this could really be was a career choice, just as continuing on the Colony's resident historian or teaching at the University of Washington was a career choice.

But that wasn't the way it worked. This wasn't: do I act as Closed Environment psychologist for the United Nations or for some private firm? This wasn't private advancement: do I settle for Smalltown, U.S.A., or do I make it big in Beijing? This wasn't Ego versus Family. This was

Columbus seeking the Indies. This was Balboa feeling the
salt air and spray of the Pacific. This was Jesuits bringing
their Truth to the Natives; this was Buddhists coming to
China. This was Armstrong stepping upon the moon, Kim
Luc stepping upon Mars. This would be the first humans
traveling in a ship that approached light speed; this would
be the first humans exploring a sun other than Sol. And
there were worlds orbiting Barnard's Star: new knowledge, new hope. Who, in their right mind, could say no to
that?

Exercise was the penance Kathrine paid to be one step
closer to the stars. The lifting of weights, the submaxima
aerobic flowing of blood, reduced stress and prevented the
deterioration of musculature in lower gravity, the increasing brittleness of bones. However, Kathrine, who didn't
like leg and arm curls to begin with, disliked the doubled
regimen she now had to follow to prepare her body for the
full force of Earth's gravity when they finally went to Seattle. She forced herself to admit that she would willingly,
though unenthusiastically, have tripled her regimen if it
were necessary to prepare for the one G acceleration of
interstellar travel.

She walked over to a mirror and studied herself. She
examined her face, and except for the way her face went
slack when she was tired, she could find no traces of her
emotional hypocrisy, nor of the way her uterus seemed to
betray her. Disliking the image for lying as equally well as
her face, she turned away. A young Arab man doing bench
presses had been watching her; he smiled. She found herself smiling, shyly, wishing that she didn't look so bulky in
her warm-up suit, or in any suit for that matter. His face
reminded her of Gamel's.

She left before he could get up and say anything to her.

When she arrived home, after writing hasty, third rate
summaries of her morning sessions, reshuffling her research notes, playing group turnabout in the Park, she
found that Gregory had spent the last part of his afternoon
preparing for the evening. Gregory, who was normally
careful with budgeting the month's resources, had purchased a white tablecloth, candles, and a bottle of imported Californian Reserve Wine. He had made a liquidy

lentil soup, the way Kathrine liked it, and was frying imported lamb chops. The mint jelly was probably not domestic either. On the window was a view of city and surrounding fields as seen from one of the towers of Emerald City; everything was tinted green so that even the sun seemed to shine green rays.

The dinner was almost a reenactment of the night they had first made love, but then Gregory hadn't known her tastes and had made pasta. The view from seventeenth-century Boston Harbor had been on the window: pale blue sky, the Doppler-shifting screeches of gulls diving toward the sea, the scent of salt water and brine, the gentle motion of an approaching ship. Gregory had invited her to dinner after they'd known each other for a month. They'd met after the Project was canceled, after Gamel had gone home to New Palestine. Gregory, writing a comparative history of colonial and interplanetary commerce for scholars, was also writing a popular account of Project Barnard and the possibilities of interstellar expansion. What had begun as a series of interviews ended as mornings following nights of heated debate over the future of human expansion. Kathrine wove tapestries of words about the wisest and most courageous carrying humanity forward, about how interaction with different environments, with other sentient races, would diversify and enrich the human race. Gregory, almost self-righteously, argued that history showed the exact opposite: Europe's contact with the many cultures of their world subtly changed Europeans but did little to enrich their humanity, or diversify their beliefs and their cultures. Besides, such economic networks of the colonial experience would be impossible to maintain across the vast distances of interstellar space.

The tension of their conversations masked—or rather, embellished—another delicious tension building between them. Kathrine looked forward to a relationship with someone who didn't talk about stars, hydrogen reactors, and moonbase engineering. She found herself longing to be with someone who traveled with his mind, worked with his thoughts.

His behavior the night she came to his quarters for dinner still surprised her. Accustomed to Gamel's self-assurance, Kathrine didn't know how to react to Gregory's awkwardness when he was robbed of words, when he couldn't control the situation by directing the topic at hand. They'd kissed for hours because Gregory was afraid that she didn't really want to make love.

Seated now, while Gregory ladled out the soup, Kathrine tried to draw those old emotions back into her, fuse them together, warm her heart. It seemed as if she could only force smiles when her uterus tightened.

She had once felt that their lovemaking had been another form of conversation, another means of sharing, that in the early days of their relationship talking led to an embrace as readily as the lull after orgasm opened up the moment for talking. Sipping wine, watching Gregory eat, she tried to remember when was the last time they'd consumed an evening with such warmth and energy. She found it hard to stop sipping the wine. Maybe it would ease the cramps. Maybe it would wash over everything she was thinking: perhaps their conversation, like their lovemaking, had been routine since Gunnel's birth. Talk and sex were necessary rituals, performed without embellishment, as if nothing was left to be discovered. Whole evenings and nights of talking, debating, wooing, being silly, and sounding poetic; whole hours of skin touching skin, the yearning for warmth; all was nothing more than the setting of patterns so they could comfortably move around each other as they tended the needs of a growing child.

From somewhere, she heard her father bellow out at her mother. She couldn't remember the words, but she could hear the shout. It snapped her to attention, made her realize that she didn't want to think about any of this.

"The food's good," she said to Gregory.

"I'm glad you like it."

The silence settled in like dust upon the moon: it seemed it would stay forever. The first time her father had left her she'd been six. He'd left after she'd gone to bed, and she woke up the next morning expecting to see him at dinnertime when he came home from work.

"You know," Gregory said, "I'd been expecting us to talk a lot. I thought the wine and the food would make us comfortable."

"After five years of being together, silence can be something relaxing."

"It can be. When the air's clear. I was just hoping . . ."

"I know, honey. And I appreciate that I

haven't made a decision. When they asked me to be on the crew, I didn't lift up my thumb and say where do I press."

"You didn't say no, either." His voice was tremulous. He poured himself more wine, sipped too much of it.

Kathrine found herself feeling warm and maternal. Gregory seemed weak, insecure, the one who needed to have things carefully explained so his heart wouldn't be broken. "You haven't tried to understand me at all. Ever since I can remember I've wanted to be on a ship like the *Poul Anderson*. Think of everyone who's ever wanted to travel to the stars, and only forty are given the opportunity. Everything I've done until I met you was done so I could be on that ship. Fifteen years of my life are fighting with the other five."

He put the wineglass down and seemed to stare at the motion of the surface, perhaps comparing the steep arc of wine sliding against glass with the gentler motion under Earth's full gravity. Perhaps he was weighing the numbers she'd just offered him.

Kathrine reached out with her right hand. Gregory released the glass and touched her fingertips, raising the hand into the air, drawing it toward him, palm turned upward. With the index finger of his other hand he traced the scars on her palm. Her skin, where his finger touched, began to tingle, and the sensation traveled up nerves to her elbow. Instinctively, her hand closed around his, elbow bent, and she drew his hand to her lips. "Let's go to bed."

"We don't have to," he said, his way of saying yes when he felt he shouldn't. "Especially if your cramps are bothering you."

"I feel fine."

She led him into the tiny bedroom, and the lunar gravity arc of their motion gave her the sense that they were dancing. She undressed and cleaned up in the bathroom, preferring water to ultrasonics. The lights were out when she came to bed, and she remembered how he used to like to watch her when she was naked. He greeted her under the covers with a kiss and an embrace.

"We don't have to do anything," he said, but his erection made the offer sound foolish.

She kissed him again. She found the cream in the bedside drawer and tenderly applied it. His sigh reminded her that sex was a way of not talking. She rolled onto her side,

pulled her knees up and stared off through the open door
into the living room. She could see the edge of the window,
the distant green-tinted fields of Oz. He snuggled up behind her, and she tried to recall the stirrings of warmth,
mingled with a trace of sexual desire, whenever they'd
done this before. It would seem to complete their relationship: her vulnerability paralleled by her sense of control as
she gave him pleasure; his capacity to hurt and the aphro-
disiac of extreme tenderness. Like always, he applied
cream to her, before touching up against her so carefully.
Like petals of flowers, he'd said the first time, looking,
touching softly, his voice hoarse, the words made poetic by
the sweet tension. Now, like always, he slid in carefully,
never sliding back and forth, just slowly moving in until he
could embrace her completely, chest against shoulder
blades, knees cupped by back of knees. And Kathrine felt
as if she were in the distant green fields she could see
through the bedroom door, and she didn't want to feel that
far away. She wanted to be here, up against his body, and
she wanted to feel something toward Gregory. She didn't
know what, but she wanted to feel *something* and she
could hear herself say, "Move," and she rocked her hips,
creating a rhythm while telling him to press harder, hold
onto her tightly, and the back and forth of penis against
sphincter blossomed in pain, the pain reminding her that
Gregory was truly there and that his desire could hurt her.
"Harder," she whispered, her voice fierce and not her
own. His cheek was pressed against her ear, and his breathing sounded obscene. He pulled back—pain shot through
her body with the strength of a climax—and he thrust
against her once, pressing into her, his arms tight around
her. His breath spasmed, and his body shook, and she could
only imagine the semen filling her. She could only imagine
the person behind her. The pain was everything; the pain
was hatred. She forced his arms apart, grabbed the edge of
the bed, and pulled herself away. The still erect penis
pulled at her, then was out, the pain causing her to stumble, and she caught herself at the doorjamb.

   She could hear Gregory roll across the bed, place his
feet on the floor, take the two steps over to her. He placed
his hands on her shoulders. "Are you okay?" he whispered.
She shrugged forcefully, tugging shoulder blades down
away from his hands.

"Leave me alone," she said.

"I got carried away. I'm sorry."

"Just leave me alone, you and your goddamned penis."

"Kathrine, you're acting like I meant to hurt you."

"You have no idea what I'm feeling right now. Just, please, leave me alone."

"I don't understand what just happened."

"Of course you don't. You don't understand anything. Everything is books for you. If it isn't in a book, it's not true."

"What the hell are you talking about? Are you talking about yelling 'harder, harder' or are you talking about my books because I don't believe in all that Columbus and Balboa bullshit you like to spout off?"

She wheeled around, hating the fact that she stood naked in front of him, and shoved him with her hand. He stumbled backward. She walked around him and collapsed in bed. She pulled the blanket up to her chin, and wrapped it around her as she curled up into a ball. "Just leave me alone," she whispered.

"Fine. If that's what you want. But while you're lying there, you better psychoanalyze yourself for a change. Just think about what you're doing. For the past three months, I haven't been able to do a single thing right. Ever since we heard the U.S. might be back with a little money for our favorite project. Just think about why you don't want to love me anymore. Think about why you don't want me to love you. And if you want it to work, think about your dad."

Kathrine found herself covering her ears, even though she could still hear perfectly. She said, tautly: "Get out of here."

"And tomorrow, I want you to tell Gunnel everything."

Pleading: "Leave me alone."

"I want her to know what decision you have to make. Because you're going to have to leave her, too."

Vehemently: "Get. Out. Of. Here!"

At first, Kathrine had not been sure why she wanted a child. It will change your life, friends with children had warned her. It will cut down on your options, Gregory had said. None of the advice seemed important. Everything grew and fell into place naturally.

She loved everything about having a child. She loved holding Gunnel to her breast, looking at her face, mother's eyes meeting daughter's eyes. She found changing diapers less of a chore, more of a pleasure. She relished the slow process of introducing Gunnel to the bath, was amused rather than irritated by Gunnel's loud complaints when she had to go under the ultrasonics rather than into the water.

Gregory took care of Gunnel in the morning, and Kathrine did in the evening. During the afternoon, when her daughter was kept in child care, Kathrine could not help but think of Gunnel as being in storage. Kathrine and Gregory both enjoyed sharing the child, and it didn't seem to matter that when the time came for sleep, they were both too tired to do anything but sleep.

As Gunnel grew, Kathrine grew dissatisfied with the Colony's design. Her Emerald City, she realized, was built as a pleasure palace for hard-working adults. There were no places in public restrooms for changing diapers. In neighborhoods where the people were culturally more modest, there was no private place for nursing a child. The floor space restrictions seemed to restrict the space a baby in one-sixth G needed to roll about without parental fear of a knocked head. There was too much furniture in too little space for a baby to stand up and collapse and stand up again.

While Kathrine worked with other parents for legislation to expand family quarters, to divert some of the profits and put them back into the Colony, she began to realize something else as one day passed after another, fourteen earth days leading to another sunrise or sunset. She wasn't going anywhere. Her love of ritual, which was to have maintained her in the sixteen-year journey, maintained her now, and gave a great sense of security to a growing, changing child. The day was a ritual in itself, centered around the repetitions and incremental changes of a young life. It was a balancing of forces. It was the moon, month after month, circling the Earth; the Earth year after year, circling the sun, the sun revolving around the center of the galaxy, the galaxy speeding outward: Kathrine, Gregory, and Gunnel reliving each day within each other's orbits, all three changing, moving forward, and if there was ever a goal or a destination, it was provided only by the mind, never by nature.

Kathrine was always amazed that she was never bored.

Sometime in the middle of the night, Kathrine walked into the living room. The view from an Emerald City tower was still on the window, and the light from the fields cast a green pall on Gregory's face. She touched his face, spoke his name. Gregory opened his eyes, and in the reflected light looked confused.

"Come to bed," Kathrine whispered, as if Gunnel were in the next room.

"I'm okay here."

"We shouldn't sleep apart. Not after what happened earlier."

"It doesn't matter."

"It does. Come to bed."

Kathrine turned off the window and groped her way through the dark back to bed. She held her body stiffly and fought back the confusion. Some time later—it seemed like hours—Gregory came to bed. Kathrine felt she should stretch her arm out, slide over and cuddle up with him. Neither moved. She imagined him lying there in the darkness, just like her, staring at the high invisible ceiling. She listened to him breathe until she fell asleep.

She woke up the next morning before Gregory did. Calculating each gesture so as to be as quiet as possible, Kathrine made her way to the bathroom and showered with water longer than their monthly ration permitted. She wanted to feel hot water cascade over her head, down her hair; she needed the relaxation that comes with water pounding into shoulder blades, the heat loosening taut muscles. She felt unclean—not grungy from her period or last night's sex, but unclean. Her profession allowed her to know too much about herself: she wanted the ties between herself and Gregory severed, she wanted nothing as invisible as gravity to pull her away from the *Poul Anderson* and its voyage. But how could she ever make herself want to leave Gunnel? If she truly loved her daughter, then she shouldn't go. She shouldn't wait for some classmate of Gunnel's to inform her of her mother's decision; she shouldn't kiss her daughter good-bye, tell her she loved her, and then disappear for sixteen years. It wasn't right.

When Kathrine was seventeen, insecure and self-righteous like many adolescents, she had become fed up with her mother's need for some sort of gratitude. "Just because you're my parent doesn't mean I owe you my life," Kathrine had blurted out. "I would have hoped," her mother had somehow said firmly even though she was on the verge of tears, "that staying with you and your brother when your father took off would have counted for something." Her words made Kathrine feel like her mother would have been happier elsewhere, leading some other kind of life.

So how could Kathrine let her own daughter destroy the one dream that had guided her entire life?

A certain dread held Kathrine as she skated to Little Israel and the Osheroffs' quarters. She planned to find some way to tell Gunnel, but what if Petra already had? Or even the Osheroffs, who could be rather self-righteous at times? How would Gunnel look at her mother then?

But Gunnel only looked surprised that her mother had come to pick her up at the Osheroffs; she said she wanted to skate to school with Petra.

"I came early," Kathrine said, "because I wanted to show you something."

"Can we see the starship again?"

"Sort of. I want you to see what it will look like when it flies."

"Can Petra come?"

Kathrine looked up from Gunnel to Petra's parents. Petra's mother patted Gunnel on the head. "Why don't you go with your mom? Petra still has to clean up before she's ready for school."

Gunnel liked the Colony History Museum, but she always made it clear that she liked the Art Museum better. She liked all the colors and she liked to guess what the people in the paintings or the statues were doing. Bottles lined up behind a bar were filled with juice or soda. Running lovers were playing tag. Suns talked with mountains. Boxers were two squabbling brothers. Lots of people were naked; why did she have to wear clothes all the time?

In the History Museum, Gunnel liked the holographic images of all the spaceships, but Gregory wouldn't let her think that the spacesuited figures were playing rather than working. And she'd dealt with enough machines to know that most of them didn't talk, nor did she want them to. It was animals, who were cuddly, who should be talking. And, as of yet, animals were not part of lunar history.

So Gunnel walked around with her mother, pointed at ships or scenes she could identify. "That's a tanker." She pointed, and smiled when Kathrine told her she was right. "That's a Sixteen Legger." Kathrine nodded. "That's a pooper scooper." She smiled mischievously, hunching her shoulders forward, looking like a little imp.

Kathrine felt like static electricity was spilling out of her elbows, filling her forearms. It was the way she had felt when she came home from school to find the house empty, and sensed something wrong before she'd found her father's three-sentence note on her pillow, before she'd torn the note into confetti and tossed it all over her room. It was the same nervous energy she had felt when she'd sat down to dinner with Gamel and sensed what he would tell her, long before the glass shattered in her hand. It was as if she was feeling the dread that Gunnel was too young to feel for herself.

Kathrine didn't know anymore how she was going to lead her daughter to the holograph of the *Poul Anderson*. If she didn't have the courage to explain herself, how could she claim to be part of the new humanity moving outward? Yet all she could imagine was Gunnel pointing at the holograph, saying, "There's the starship," and waiting for the approval before walking on.

"Let's go over there," Kathrine said.

"Are we going to see the starship?"

Kathrine nodded, searched for words. If I looked at her as a patient, maybe I could explain it. But how could a four-year-old understand a life decision? Four-year-olds in the Academy were learning how to play with others, how to share, how to think about what their words mean.

The holograph projector, three lenses mounted at different angles, protruded from the pedestal at a level even with Gunnel's eyes. Kathrine watched her daughter crane her neck, look up at the substantial image of light.

The front section of the *Poul Anderson* looked like little

more than an elaborate thimble, plenty of wide decks for the crew to inhabit during one gravity acceleration and deceleration, plus plenty of shielding. Extending from that was a cylinder that branched out around the ship's giant reactor. Alone, the ship was ugly, if one did not look at it with the eyes of an engineer, who could see all the wonders of mathematics that would hold this ship together as the gigantic nuclear thrust accelerated it forward. The beauty came with the electromagnetic scoop that would stretch out hundreds of meters. The holograph gave it color, and it looked like an intricate, symmetrical spiderweb, its lines flowing out into the void as if reaching for contact. Flowing in were spots of light, representing invisible hydrogen, drawn into the web, funneled into the reactor at increasing velocity.

"It's beautiful, isn't it?" Kathrine said. Her voice sounded tentative.

"I like the real one better," said Gunnel. "Can we see that, too?"

Kathrine averted her eyes from the image and looked at her daughter. Now or never: this is when I should start telling her.

"Can we look at something else now?"

Kathrine turned to the *Poul Anderson.* The image flowed through space without moving. The holoprojector was as silent as the vacuum of space. Kathrine bit her lower lip. There's something Mommy has to tell you, she heard the words in her head. They sounded flat. I want to be part of history. Your daddy loves you very much, and he doesn't really need me. History; the Stars; it all sounded out of place.

"Mommy?"

Kathrine tasted blood, and realized how hard she'd been biting. She couldn't stop herself: the blood, the stinging in her lip felt right. Words had failed her. They all sounded clichéd—or cornball: her father's words for anything that had lost its wonder. She could feel her hands shake, the static electricity within her taking over, and she knew that all she had to do was turn away, lead her daughter to school. But how could she surrender that easily? She'd wanted to help create a new world, where options weren't mutually exclusive, where decisions like this wouldn't have to be made. The starship shone brightly, drawing in specks of light. It remained stationary, but the real one would be assembled, would be departing, and Gregory, Gunnel, everything she cared about seemed to send the electricity throughout her body, charging her with energy, making the inertia insupportable.

Her hand swung out, hit one of the projectors. The image wavered; she heard herself shout out in pain.

"Mommy!"

Her hand lashed back again, and she watched her arm strike the three projectors, watched them slapped out of position, and somehow knew that a decision was being made. Plastic snapped. Metal rattled and skidded against the concrete floor. Before she knew it, before she could hear Gunnel's crying or feel the blood running down from her hand and across her forearm, the *Poul Anderson*—a gathering of light—had shattered and disappeared.

Twelve days later Kathrine went to the Observation Deck. While others faced westward to watch the sunset, she watched the lines separating pursuing dark from pursued light slide into the crater, glide across the surface. The dark cast a shroud over everything and rendered the *Poul Anderson* invisible. Within fourteen days, the light would pursue dark, and the dissected starship would be visible again. Within a year, the sections would be reassembled in orbit, then the starship would be gone.

Kathrine swore to herself that she'd never hold it against her daughter, but deep within her, where her mother resided, she knew that it was a lie.

Shiva

JAMES KILLUS

I DESTROYED ANOTHER UNIVERSE today. Probably more than one, actually. One is an irreducible minimum according to the sub-quantum transfer functions. I am incapable of calculating the maximum likelihood destruction coefficient. The metric is reduced, is all. What does that mean? What does it matter? Seen one universe, seen them all.

This is how I do it. After I've spent a certain amount of time rattling around in the house, pretending that I'm going to go out that day, trying to pick up the clutter, but never doing anything more than shifting it around, since to really clean up would require throwing something away, something that reminds me of Dorothy and— Well anyway, after a suitable period of time, I go down into the basement. And I stare at it for a while. The sub-quantum toroid. Sometimes it seems to shimmer, but maybe that's just the basement light. Or maybe it's some reaction to its activation in one of the other universes that it resides in. No matter. After a while longer I turn on the power.

Then the toroid glows for real. It's only a plasma effect, but it's theatrical. I open the hatch and climb inside.

It's bigger inside than out. That's a little joke, really. It is impossible to describe how much bigger it is inside than out. Inside the toroid, probabilities are mapped into a non-euclidean spatial metric. The distance between two universes which differ by only a single quantum event is too small to measure. Distances which humans can travel amount to differences that matter to us, macroscopic events. That seems fair. If anything is really fair, that is.

Multiply zero by infinity. No answer.

Or every answer.

Inside it's seamless gray and every direction is uphill. There are bumps and hillocks and in some directions steep cliffs. Time is a spatial dimension in here as well. Professor Jameson and I once calculated that a three-mile climb up one of the cliffs could actually put one about a picosecond back in the past.

The other directions lead to other realities. Might-have-beens. Not everything you could want or imagine, since we can imagine things that are not at all possible. But a lot, nevertheless. Somewhere off in the distance Kennedy, Hendrix, and Lennon are still alive. Somewhere there's an American continent where everyone speaks French, somewhere the Indians aren't named Indians because the Europeans never arrived, having died in some nameless doom. Somewhere the Earth is inhabited by beings with organic molecules optically reversed from ours. Somewhere there is no Earth at all.

But I can't get to any of those. My travels are constrained by the dimensions of the quantum toroid and the energy requirements of lateral transfer. I can freely move anywhere within the light cone of the initial construction of the toroid, all possible realities generated within the last twelve years. Anything else, well, I might as well try to go to the moon on a bicycle.

Any energy expended in the toroid shrinks the metric.

I walk for about ten minutes, not in a straight line. I've been in most of the straight-line realities, I think. The path used determines what reality one exits into. I'm only about five hundred meters from my beginning point when I reach down and pull up on the door lever for an exit. The floor drops away and I squirm my way out of the toroid.

I haven't made much noise, but it's enough. I only have to wait a couple of minutes before he comes down to investigate.

They are always a bit shocked to see me. That's only

proper. What would you do if you went down to investigate a basement noise and found yourself there already?

But he's quick on the uptake. "What are you doing here?" he demands.

Sometimes I say nothing and climb back into the toroid. His presence here is proof of another failure. Sometimes I say something about it being a mistake (though that is not true) and leave quickly. But tonight I am lonely. Tonight I feel the need to talk.

A voice comes down from upstairs. It is Dorothy. His Dorothy. "Is everything all right, dear?"

He looks at me carefully. I shrug. He calls out to her, "Yes, you go on up to bed. I just realized something that needed fixing down here. I'll be up in a little while."

She says all right and the upstairs door closes. He is still looking at me. I say, "You probably want an explanation."

He nods and says, "Yes. Theodore and I agreed that the toroid should not be used. We weren't sure of the possible physical interpretations of the equations and some of the possibilities looked risky."

Strange. He calls Professor Jameson by his first name. I used to do that too, I realize. He was my father-in-law, after all. I must have stopped thinking of him that way after—

I say, "You deserve an explanation, but I can't really explain. You won't understand, not really."

He says, "Try me."

I say, "One becomes less concerned with risks when one has little to lose."

He seems about ready to say speak again, but I say, "Remember Mrs. Feldman?" Whatever he was about to say, he does not say it. He remembers.

Mrs. Feldman was the aunt of someone I knew in college (someone *we* knew, we used to be the same person, not so many months ago). A gloomy and depressing woman. She had lost all of her immediate family in World War II, some to the Nazis, some to the Russian labor camps, some to the last Polish pogrom after the end of the war. She came to the United States, made a new life for herself, only to lose her husband and two children in a fire that also destroyed her house and left her destitute. She still had scars on her arms and back from the fire, still had a tattoo from the Nazis.

So Mrs. Feldman carried her gloom around like a personal climate that we could never change, merely endure. Some of us tried to change her, to cheer her up or draw her out, but it was useless. She was not interested in consolation or commiseration. Certainly not from us.

Maybe she was wrong. Maybe she could have overcome that much grief twice. Maybe she shouldn't have inflicted her attitude on the rest of the world. But my feeling at the time was that none of us had lived through enough to give us the right to judge, to give advice, to tell her how to think or feel. Maybe she was a hero just for living, for not pulling the plug.

I glance toward the upstairs. "My Dorothy is dead," I say.

His face clouds. The full enormity cannot sink in, but enough does for pity, for the standard condolences. "I'm sorry," he says, as if to a stranger. "How . . . ?"

"It was an unlikely accident," I tell him. "Driving in the rain, a drunk driver from the other direction jumped the divider. I have only found four other realities where it occurred. In two of them we both died."

He thinks for a moment. "But why are you doing this? Why use the toroid? You can't bring her back."

In that moment I hate the bastard, because he has what I've lost and because he doesn't understand, can't understand. I want to kill him, to strangle away his smug condescension.

Instead I say, "I'm looking for a reality where I died and Dorothy survived."

I can tell that I have shocked him. He begins "But you can't—" then he stops.

He says, "If Dorothy died . . ." It sinks in a bit more, but not enough, never enough.

Dorothy was Theodore Jameson's daughter. She had been the only woman I ever loved. The only woman I ever wanted. And she was dead. My Dorothy dead. Of all the uncountable numbers, why was mine the one to die?

How was I supposed to go on living as if living mattered? When there was a chance that she still lived somewhere, and needed me? Or so I tell myself.

"I have to keep looking," I tell him. "I have no choice."

I turn to the toroid. It glows again, awaiting my reentry. Rosinante, my quantum-mechanical steed.

"But wait," he says. "You have used it many times. What does it mean? The metric shrinks, how does that change the world?"

"Who can say?" I tell him. The pity I see in his eyes grows too great to bear. "The workings of God are strange and subtle. I think that in this case, nothing of any real note is lost. Each person contains his own universe, you see."

"That sounds like solipsism," he says. "Or insanity."

"Perhaps," I tell him. "Or just remorse. I wish we had stayed at home that night." I climb into the toroid and pull it shut behind me.

The trip home is always easy, downhill all the way. I leave the toroid drained and depleted. It is always thus.

In some other universe I clutch my wife with all the love that I so seldom show her, because a ghost has shown me the brevity of life. In yet another world I pull together the pieces of my life and set out to try to make whatever I can, in spite of the tragedy that has come to me. In still another place I am dead, unable to live with the guilt, because in that world, I was the drunken driver and her death is on my hands.

In another universe I told my other self the plain and simple truth, that the sub-quantum toroid changes time and possibility into energy and distance, that shrinking the metric merely means that time spent chasing might-have-beens is time not used in creating your own future. The topography within the toroid changes and in this way are universes destroyed.

But I did not tell him these things. That would be too much human contact. That would interfere with my own and only fate. I take my death in piecework, each day another little suicide. I conspire with the past and present to murder the future and each moment not lived leaves its futures unborn, destroyed.

So I will shrink my private metric one futile day after another. I will grow old this way, I think. Perhaps I already have.

It's all just a matter of viewpoint, actually.

Just a lonely old man, mad with grief, spends all his time talking to himself.

Sleepside
Story

GREG BEAR

OLIVER JONES differed from his brothers as wheat from chaff. He didn't grudge them their blind wildness; he loaned them money until he had none, and regretted it, but not deeply. His needs were not simple, but they did not hang on the sharp signs of dollars. He worked at the jobs of youth without complaining, knowing there was something better waiting for him. Sometimes it seemed he was the only one in the family able to take cares away from his momma, now that Poppa was gone and she was lonely even with the two babies sitting on her lap, and his younger sister Yolanda gabbing about the neighbors.

The city was a puzzle to him. His older brothers Denver and Reggie believed it was a place to be conquered, but Oliver did not share their philosophy. He wanted to make the city part of him, sucked in with his breath, built into bones and brains. If he could dance with the city's music, he'd have it made, even though Denver and Reggie said the city was wide and cruel and had no end; that its four quarters ate young men alive, and spat back old people. Look at Poppa, they said; he was forty-three and he went to the fifth quarter. Darkside, a bag of wearied bones; they said, take what you can get while you can get it.

This was not what Oliver saw, though he knew the city was cruel and hungry.

His brothers and even Yolanda kidded him about his faith. It was more than just going to church that made them rag him, because they went to church, too, sitting superior beside Momma. Reggie and Denver knew there was advantage in being seen at devotions. It wasn't his music that made them laugh, for he could play the piano hard and fast as well as soft and tender, and they all liked to dance, even Momma sometimes. It was his damned sweetness. It was his taste in girls, quiet and studious; and his honesty.

On the last day of school, before Christmas vacation, Oliver made his way home in a fall of light snow, stopping in the old St. John's churchyard for a moment's reflection by his father's grave. Surrounded by the crisp, ancient slate gravestones and the newer white marble, worn by the city's acid tears, he thought he might now be considered grown up, might have to support all of his family. He left the churchyard in a somber mood and walked between the tall brick and brownstone tenements, along the dirty, wet black streets, his shadow lost in Sleepside's greater shade, eyes on the sidewalk.

Denver and Reggie could not bring in good money, money that Momma would accept; Yolanda was too young and not likely to get a job anytime soon, and that left him, the only one who would finish school. He might take in more piano students, but he'd have to move out to do that, and how could he find another place to live without losing all he made to rent? Sleepside was crowded.

Oliver heard the noise in the flat from half a block down the street. He ran up the five dark, trash-littered flights of stairs and pulled out his key to open the three locks on the door. Swinging the door wide, he stood with hand pressed to a wall, lungs too greedy to let him speak.

The flat was in an uproar. Yolanda, rail-skinny, stood in the kitchen doorway, wringing her big hands and wailing. The two babies lurched down the hall, diapers drooping and fists stuck in their mouths. The neighbor widow Mrs. Diamond Freeland bustled back and forth in a useless dither. Something was terribly wrong.

"What is it?" he asked Yolanda with his first free breath. She just moaned and shook her head. "Where's Reggie and Denver?" She shook her head less vigorously, meaning they weren't home. "Where's Momma?" This sent Yolanda into hysterics. She bumped back against the wall and clenched her fists to her mouth, tears flying. "Something happen to Momma?"

"Your momma went uptown," Mrs. Diamond Freeland said, standing flatfooted before Oliver, her flower print dress distended over her generous stomach. "What are you going to do? You're her son."

"Where uptown?" Oliver asked, trying to control his quavering voice. He wanted to slap everybody in the apartment. He was scared and they weren't being any help at all.

"She we-went sh-sh-shopping!" Yolanda wailed. "She got her check today and it's Christmas and she went to get the babies new clothes and some food."

Oliver's hands clenched. Momma had asked him what he wanted for Christmas, and he had said, "Nothing, Momma. Not really." She had chided him, saying all would be well when the check came, and what good was Christmas if she couldn't find a little something special for each of her children? "All right," he had said. "I'd like sheet music. Something I've never played before."

"She must of taken the wrong stop," Mrs. Diamond Freeland said, staring at Oliver from the corners of her wide eyes. "That's all I can figure."

"What happened?"

Yolanda pulled a letter out of her blouse and handed it to him, a fancy purple paper with a delicate flower design on the borders, the message handwritten very prettily in gold ink fountain pen and signed. He read it carefully, then read it again.

To the Joneses.

Your momma is uptown in My care. She came here lost and I tried to help her but she stole something very valuable to Me she shouldn't have. She says you'll come and get her. By you she means her youngest son Oliver Jones and if not him then Yolanda Jones her eldest daughter. I will keep one or the other here in exchange for your momma and one or the other must stay here and work for Me.

Miss Belle Parkhurst
969 33rd Street

"Who's she, and why does she have Momma?" Oliver asked.

"I'm not going!" Yolanda screamed.

"Hush up," said Mrs. Diamond Freeland. "She's that whoor. She's that uptown whoor used to run the biggest cathouse."

Oliver looked from face to face in disbelief.

"Your momma must of taken the wrong stop and got lost," Mrs. Diamond Freeland reiterated. "That's all I can figure. She went to that whoor's house and she got in trouble."

"I'm not going!" Yolanda said. She avoided Oliver's eyes. "You know what she'd make me do."

"Yeah," Oliver said softly. "But what'll she make *me* do?"

Reggie and Denver, he learned from Mrs. Diamond Freeland, had come home before the message had been received, leaving just as the messenger came whistling up the outside hall. Oliver sighed. His brothers were almost never home; they thought they'd pulled the wool over Momma's eyes, but they hadn't. Momma knew who would be home and come for her when she was in trouble.

Reggie and Denver fancied themselves the hottest dudes on the street. They claimed they had women all over Sleepside and Snowside; Oliver was almost too shy to ask a woman out. He was small, slender, and almost pretty, but very strong for his size. Reggie and Denver were cowards. Oliver had never run from a true and worthwhile fight in his life, but neither had he started one.

The thought of going to Miss Belle Parkhurst's establishment scared him, but he remembered what his father had told him just a week before dying. "Oliver, when I'm gone—that's soon now, you know it—Yolanda's flaky as a bowl of cereal and your brothers . . . well, I'll be kind and just say your momma, she's going to need you. You got to turn out right so as she can lean on you."

The babies hadn't been born then.

"Which train did she take?"

"Down to Snowside," Mrs. Diamond Freeland said. "But she must of gotten off in Sunside. That's near Thirty-third."

"It's getting night," Oliver said.

Yolanda sniffed and wiped her eyes. Off the hook. "You going?"

"Have to," Oliver said. "It's Momma."

Said Mrs. Diamond Freeland, "I think that whoor got something on her mind."

On the line between dusk and dark, down underground where it shouldn't have mattered, the Metro emptied of all the day's passengers and filled with the night's.

Sometimes day folks went in tight-packed groups on the Night Metro, but not if they could avoid it. Night Metro was for carrying the lost or human garbage. Everyone ashamed or afraid to come out during the day came out at night. Night Metro also carried the zeroes—people who lived their lives and when they died no one could look back and say they remembered them. Night Metro—especially late—was not a good way to travel, but for Oliver it was the quickest way to get from Sleepside to Sunside; he had to go as soon as possible to get Momma.

Oliver descended the four flights of concrete steps, grinding his teeth at the thought of the danger he was in. He halted at the bottom, grimacing at the frightened knots of muscle and nerves in his back, repeating over and over again, "It's Momma. It's Momma. No one can save her but me." He dropped his bronze cat-head token into the turnstile, clunk-chunking through, and crossed the empty platform. Only two indistinct figures waited trackside, heavy-coated though it was a warm evening. Oliver kept an eye on them and walked back and forth in a figure eight on the grimy foot-scrubbed concrete, peering nervously down at the wet and soot under the rails. Behind him, on the station's smudged white tile walls hung a gold mosaic trumpet and the number 7, the trumpet for folks who couldn't read to know when to get off. All Sleepside stations had musical instruments.

The Night Metro was run by a different crew than the Day Metro. His train came up, clean and silver-sleek, without a spot of graffiti or a stain of tarnish. Oliver caught a glimpse of the driver under the SLEEPSIDE/CHASTE RIVER/SUNSIDE-46TH destination sign. The driver wore or had a bull's head and carried a prominent pair of long gleaming silver scissors on his Sam Browne belt. Oliver entered the open doors and took a smooth handgrip even though the

seats were mostly empty. Somebody standing was somebody quicker to run.

There were four people on his car: two women—one
young, vacant, and not pretty or even very alive-looking,
the other old and muddy-eyed with a plastic daisy-flow-
ered shopping bag—and two men, both sunny blond and
chunky, wearing shiny-elbowed business suits. Nobody
looked at anybody else. The doors shut and the train grumbled on, gathering speed until the noise of its wheels on the
tracks drowned out all other sound and almost all thought.

There were more dead stations than live and lighted
ones. Night Metro made only a few stops congruent with
Day Metro. Most stations were turned off, and the only
people left standing there didn't show in bright lights.
Oliver tried not to look, to keep his eyes on the few in the
car with him, but every so often he couldn't help peering
out. Beyond I-beams and barricades, single orange lamps
and broken tiled walls rushed by, platforms populated by
slow smudges of shadow.

Some said the dead used the Night Metro, and that
after midnight it went all the way to Darkside. Oliver
didn't know what to believe. As the train slowed for his
station, he pulled the collar of his dark green nylon windbreaker up around his neck and rubbed his nose with one
finger. Reggie and Denver would never have made it even
this far. They valued their skins too much.

The train did not move on after he disembarked. He
stood by the open doors for a moment, then walked past
the lead car on his way to the stairs. Over his shoulder, he
saw the driver standing at the head of the train in his little
cabin of fluorescent coldness, the eyes in the bull's head
sunk deep in shade. Oliver felt rather than saw the starlike
pricks in the sockets, watching him. The driver's left hand
tugged on the blades of the silver shears.

"What do you care, man?" Oliver asked softly, stopping
for an instant to return the hidden stare. "Go on about
your work. We all got stuff to do."

The bull's nose pointed a mere twitch away from Oliver, and the hand left the shears to return to its switch. The
train doors closed. The silver side panels and windows and
lights picked up speed and the train squealed around a
curve into darkness. He climbed the two flights of stairs to
Sunside Station.

Summer night lay heavy and warm on the lush trees and grass of a broad park. Oliver stood at the head of the Metro entrance and listened to the crickets and katydids and cicadas sing songs unheard in Sleepside, where trees and grass were sparse. All around the park rose dark-windowed walls of high marble and brick and gray stone hotels and fancy apartment buildings with gable roofs.

Oliver looked around for directions, a map, anything. Above the Night Metro, it was even possible ordinary people might be out strolling, and he could ask them if he dared. He walked toward the street and thought of Momma getting this far and of her being afraid. He loved Momma very much. Sometimes she seemed to be the only decent thing in his life, though more and more often young women distracted him as the years passed, and he experienced more and more secret fixations.

"Oliver Jones?"

A long white limousine waited by the curb. A young, slender woman in violet chauffeur's livery, with a jaunty black and silver cap sitting atop exuberant hair, cocked her head coyly, smiled at him, and beckoned with a white-leather-gloved finger. "Are you Oliver Jones, come to rescue your momma?"

He walked slowly toward the white limousine. It was bigger and more beautiful than anything he had ever seen before, with long ribbed chrome pipes snaking out from under the hood and through the fenders, stand-alone golden headlights, and a white tonneau roof made of real leather. "My name's Oliver," he affirmed.

"Then you're my man. Please get in." She winked and held the door open.

When the door closed, the woman's arm—all he could see of her through the smoky window glass—vanished. The driver's door did not open. She did not get in. The limousine drove off by itself. Oliver fell back into the lush suede and velvet interior. An electronic wet bar gleamed silver and gold and black above a cool white-lit panel on which sat a single crystal glass filled with ice cubes. A spigot rotated around and waited for instructions. When none came, it gushed fragrant gin over the ice and rotated back into place.

Oliver did not touch the glass.

Below the wet bar, the television set turned itself on.

Passion and delight sang from the small, precise speakers.
"No," he said. "No!"

The television shut off.

He edged closer to the smoky glass and saw dim street
lights and cab headlights moving past. A huge black building trimmed with gold ornaments, windows outlined with
red, loomed on the corner, all but three of its windows
dark. The limousine turned smoothly and descended into a
dark underground garage. Lights throwing huge golden
cat's eyes, tires squealing on shiny concrete, it snaked
around a slalom of walls and pillars and dusty limousines
and came to a quick stop. The door opened.

Oliver stepped out. The chauffeur stood holding the
door, grinning, and doffed her cap. "My pleasure," she
said.

The car had parked beside a big wooden door set into
hewn stone. Fossil bones and teeth were clearly visible in
the matrix of each block in the walls. Glistening ferns in
dark ponds flanked the door. Oliver heard the car drive
away and turned to look, but he did not see whether the
chauffeur drove this time or not.

He walked across a wood plank bridge and tried the
black iron handle on the door. The door swung open at the
suggestion of his fingers. Beyond, a narrow red-carpeted
staircase with rose-bush carved maple banisters ascended
to the upper floor.

The place smelled of cloves and mint and, somehow, of
what Oliver imagined dogs or horses must smell like—a
musty old rug sitting on a floor grate. (He had never owned
a dog and never seen a horse without a policeman on it,
and never so close he could smell it.) Nobody had been
through here in a long time, he thought. But everybody
knew about Miss Belle Parkhurst and her place. And the
chauffeur had been young. He wrinkled his nose; he did
not like this place.

The dark wood door at the top of the stairs swung open
silently. Nobody stood there waiting; it might have opened
by itself. Oliver tried to speak, but his throat itched and
closed. He coughed into his fist and shrugged his shoulders
in a spasm. Then, eyes damp and hot with anger and fear
and something more, he moved his lips and croaked, "I'm
Oliver Jones. I'm here to get my momma."

The door remained unattended. He looked back into

the parking garage, dark and quiet as a cave; nothing for him there. Then he ascended quickly to get it over with and passed through the door into the ill-reputed house of Miss Belle Parkhurst.

The city extends to the far horizon, divided into quarters by roads or canals or even train tracks, above or underground; and sometimes you know those divisions and know better than to cross them, and sometimes you don't. The city is broader than any man's life, and it is worth more than your life not to understand why you are where you are and must stay there. The city encourages ignorance because it must eat.

The four quarters of the city are Snowside, Cokeside where few sane people go, Sleepside, and Sunside. Sunside is bright and rich and hazardous because that is where the swell folks live. Swell folks don't tolerate intruders. Not even the police go into Sunside without an escort. Toward the center of the city is uptown, and in the middle of uptown is where all four quarters meet at the Pillar of the Unknown Mayor. Outward is the downtown and scattered islands of suburbs, and no one knows where it ends.

The Joneses live in downtown Sleepside. The light there even at noon is not very bright, but neither is it burning harsh as in Cokeside where it can fry your skull. Sleepside is tolerable. There are many good people in Sleepside and Snowside, and though confused, the general run is not vicious. Oliver grew up there and carries it in his bones and meat. No doubt the Night Metro driver smelled his origins and knew here was a young man crossing a border going uptown. No doubt Oliver was still alive because Miss Belle Parkhurst had protected him. That meant Miss Parkhurst had protected Momma, and perhaps lured her, as well.

The hallway was lighted by rows of candles held in gold eagle claws along each wall. At the end of the hall, Oliver stepped into a broad wood-paneled room set here and there with lush green ferns in brass spittoons. The oriental carpet revealed a stylized oriental garden in cream and black and red. Five empty black velvet-upholstered couches stood unoccupied, expectant, like a line of languorous women amongst the ferns. Along the walls, chairs covered by white sheets asserted their heavy wooden arms. Oliver stood, jaw open, not used to such luxury. He needed a long moment to take it all in.

Miss Belle Parkhurst was obviously a very rich woman, and not your ordinary whore. From what he had seen so far, she had power as well as money, power over cars and maybe over men and women. Maybe over Momma. "Momma?"

A tall, tenuous white-haired man in a cream-colored suit walked across the room, paying Oliver scant attention. He said nothing. Oliver watched him sit on a sheet-covered chair. He did not disturb the sheets, but sat through them. He leaned his head back reflectively, elevating a cigarette holder without a cigarette. He blew out clear air, or perhaps nothing at all, and then smiled at something just to Oliver's right. Oliver turned. They were alone. When he looked back, the man in the cream-colored suit was gone.

Oliver's arms tingled. He was in for more than he had bargained for, and he had bargained for a lot.

"This way," said a woman's deep voice, operatic, dignified, easy and friendly at once. He could not see her, but he squinted at the doorway, and she stepped between two fluted green onyx columns. He did not know at first that she was addressing him; there might be other gentlemen, or girls, equally as tenuous as the man in the cream-colored suit. But this small, imposing woman with upheld hands, dressed in gold and peach silk that clung to her smooth and silent, was watching only him with her large dark eyes. She smiled richly and warmly, but Oliver thought there was a hidden flaw in that smile, in her assurance. She was ill at ease from the instant their eyes met, though she might have been at ease before then, *thinking* of meeting him. She had had all things planned until that moment.

If he unnerved her slightly, this woman positively terrified him. She was beautiful and smooth-skinned, and he could smell the sweet roses and camellias and magnolia blossoms surrounding her like a crowd of familiar friends.

"This way," she repeated, gesturing through the doors.

"I'm looking for my momma. I'm supposed to meet Miss Belle Parkhurst."

"I'm Belle Parkhurst. You're Oliver Jones . . . aren't you?"

He nodded, face solemn, eyes wide. He nodded again and swallowed.

"I sent your momma on her way home. She'll be fine."

He looked back at the hallway. "She'll be on the Night Metro," he said.

"I sent her back in my car. Nothing will happen to her."

Oliver believed her. There was a long, silent moment. He realized he was twisting and wringing his hands before his crotch and he stopped this, embarrassed.

"Your momma's fine. Don't worry about her."

"All right," he said, drawing his shoulders up. "You wanted to talk to me?"

"Yes," she said. "And more."

His nostrils flared and he jerked his eyes hard right, his torso and then his hips and legs twisting that way as he broke into a scrambling rabbit-run for the hallway. The golden eagle claws on each side dropped their candles as he passed and reached out to hook him with their talons. The vast house around him seemed suddenly alert, and he knew even before one claw grabbed his collar that he did not have a chance.

He dangled helpless from the armpits of his jacket at the very end of the hall. In the far door appeared the whore, angry, fingers dripping small beads of fire onto the wooden floor. The floor smoked and sizzled.

"I've let your momma go," Belle Parkhurst said, voice deeper than a grave, face terrible and smoothly beautiful and very old, very experienced. "That was my agreement. You leave, and you break that agreement, and that means I take your sister, or I take back your momma."

She cocked an elegant, painted eyebrow at him and leaned her head to one side in query. He nodded as best he could with his chin jammed against the teeth of his jacket's zipper.

"Good. There's food waiting. I'd enjoy your company."

The dining room was small, no larger than his bedroom at home, occupied by two chairs and an intimate round table covered in white linen and a gold eagle claw candelabrum. Miss Parkhurst preceded Oliver, her long dress rustling softly at her heels. Other things rustled in the room as well; the floor might have been ankle-deep in wind-blown leaves by the sound, but it was spotless, a rich round red and cream Oriental rug centered beneath the table; and beneath that, smooth old oak flooring. Oliver looked up from his sneaker-clad feet. Miss Parkhurst waited expectantly a step back from her chair.

"Your momma teach you no manners?" she asked softly.

He approached the table reluctantly. There were empty gold plates and tableware on the linen now that had not been there before. Napkins seemed to drop from thin fog and folded themselves on the plates. Oliver stopped, his nostrils flaring.

"Don't you mind that," Miss Parkhurst said. "I live alone here. Good help is hard to find."

Oliver stepped behind the chair and lifted it by its maple headpiece, pulling it out for her. She sat and he helped her move closer to the table. Not once did he touch her; his skin crawled at the thought.

"The food here is very good," Miss Parkhurst said as he sat across from her.

"I'm not hungry," Oliver said.

She smiled warmly at him. It was a powerful thing, her smile. "I won't bite," she said. "Except supper. *That* I'll bite."

Oliver smelled wonderful spices and sweet vinegar. A napkin had been draped across his lap, and before him was a salad on a fine china plate. He was very hungry and he enjoyed salads, seeing fresh greens so seldom in Sleepside.

"That's it," Miss Parkhurst said soothingly, smiling as he ate. She lifted her fork in turn and speared a fold of olive-oiled butter lettuce, bringing it to her red lips.

The rest of the dinner proceeded in like fashion, but with no further conversation. She watched him frankly, appraising, and he avoided her eyes.

Down a corridor with tall windows set in an east wall, dawn gray and pink around their faint silhouettes on the west wall, Miss Parkhurst led Oliver to his room. "It's the quietest place in the mansion," she said.

"You're keeping me," he said. "You're never going to let me go?"

"Please allow me to indulge myself. I'm not just alone. I'm lonely. Here, you can have anything you want . . . almost . . ."

A door at the corridor's far end opened by itself.

Within, a fire burned brightly within a small fireplace, and a wide bed waited with covers turned down. Exquisitely detailed murals of forests and fields covered the walls; the ceiling was rich deep blue, flecked with gold and silver and jeweled stars. Books filled a case in one corner, and in another corner stood the most beautiful ebony grand piano he had even seen. Miss Parkhurst did not approach the door too closely. There were no candles; within this room, all lamps were electric.

"This is your room. I won't come in," she said. "And after tonight, you don't ever come out after dark. We'll talk and see each other during the day, but never at night. The door isn't locked. I'll have to trust you."

"I can go any time I want?"

She smiled. Even though she meant her smile to be nothing more than enigmatic, it shook him. She was deadly beautiful, the kind of woman his brothers dreamed about. Her smile said she might eat him alive, all of him that counted. Oliver could imagine his mother's reaction to Miss Belle Parkhurst.

He entered the room and swung the door shut, trembling. There were a dozen things he wanted to say; angry, bitter, frustrated, pleading things. He leaned against the door, swallowing them all back, keeping his hand from going to the gold and crystal knob.

Behind the door, her skirts rustled as she retired along the corridor. After a moment, he pushed off from the door and walked with an exaggerated swagger to the bookcase, mumbling. Miss Parkhurst would never have taken Oliver's sister Yolanda; that wasn't what she wanted. She wanted young boy flesh, he thought. She wanted to burn him down to his sneakers, smiling like that.

The books on the shelves were books he had heard about but had never found in the Sleepside library, books he wanted to read, that the librarians said only people from Sunside and the suburbs cared to read. His fingers lingered on the tops of their spines, tugging gently.

He decided to sleep instead. If she was going to pester him during the day, he didn't have much time. She'd be a late riser, he thought; a night person.

Then he realized: whatever she did at night, she had not done this night. This night had been set aside for him. He shivered again, thinking of the food and napkins and the eagle claws. Was this room haunted, too? Would things keep watch over him?

Oliver lay back on the bed, still clothed. His mind clouded with thoughts of living sheets feeling up his bare skin. Tired, almost dead out.

The dreams that came were sweet and pleasant and she did not walk in them. This really was his time.

At ten o'clock by the brass and gold and crystal clock on the bookcase, Oliver kicked his legs out, rubbed his face into the pillows and started up, back arched, smelling bacon and eggs and coffee. A covered tray waited on a polished brass cart beside the bed. A vase of roses on one corner of the cart scented the room. A folded piece of fine ivory paper leaned against the vase. Oliver sat on the edge of the bed and read the note, once again written in golden ink in a delicate hand.

I'm waiting for you in the gymnasium. Meet me after you've eaten. Got something to give to you.

He had no idea where the gymnasium was. When he had finished breakfast, he put on a plush robe, opened the heavy door to his room—both relieved and irritated that it did not open by itself—and looked down the corridor. A golden arc clung to the base of each tall window. It was at least noon. Sunside time. She had given him plenty of time to rest.

A pair of new black jeans and a white silk shirt waited for him on the bed, which had been carefully made in the time it had taken him to glance down the hall. Cautiously, but less frightened now, he removed the robe, put on these clothes and the deerskin moccasins by the foot of the bed, and stood in the doorway, leaning as casually as he could manage against the frame.

A silk handkerchief hung in the air several yards away. It fluttered like a pigeon's ghost to attract his attention, then drifted slowly along the hall. He followed.

The house seemed to go on forever, empty and magnificent. Each public room had its own decor, filled with antique furniture, potted palms, plush couches and chairs, and love seats. Several times he thought he saw wisps of dinner jackets, top hats, eager, strained faces, in foyers, corridors, on staircases as he followed the handkerchief. The house smelled of perfume and dust, faint cigars, spilled wine, and old sweat.

He had climbed three flights of stairs before he stood at the tall ivory-white double door of the gymnasium. The handkerchief vanished with a flip. The doors opened.

Miss Parkhurst stood at the opposite end of a wide black-tile dance floor, before a band riser covered with music stands and instruments. Oliver eyed the low half-circle stage with narrowed eyes. Would she demand he dance with her, while all the instruments played by themselves?

"Good morning," she said. She wore a green dress the color of fresh wet grass, high at the neck and down to her calves. Beneath the dress she wore white boots and white gloves, and a white feather curled around her black hair.

"Good morning," he replied softly, politely.

"Did you sleep well? Eat hearty?"

Oliver nodded, fear and shyness returning. What could she possibly want to give him? Herself? His face grew hot.

"It's a shame this house is empty during the day," she said. *And at night?* he thought. "I could fill this room with exercise equipment," she continued. "Weight benches, even a track around the outside." She smiled. The smile seemed less ferocious now, even wistful; younger.

He rubbed a fold of his shirt between two fingers. "I enjoyed the food, and your house is real fine, but I'd like to go home," he said.

She half-turned and walked slowly from the stand. "You could have this house and all my wealth. I'd like you to have it."

"Why? I haven't done anything for you."

"Or to me, either," she said, facing him again. "You know how I've made all this money?"

"Yes, ma'am," he said after a moment's pause. "I'm not a fool."

"You've heard about me. That I'm a whore."

"Yes, ma'am. Mrs. Diamond Freeland says you are."

"And what is a whore?"

"You let men do it to you for money," Oliver said, feeling bolder, but with his face hot all the same.

Miss Parkhurst nodded. "I've got part of them all here with me," she said. "My bookkeeping. I know every name, every face. They all keep me company now that business is slow."

"All of them?" Oliver asked.

Miss Parkhurst's faint smile was part pride, part sadness, her eyes distant and moist. "They gave me all the things I have here."

"I don't think it would be worth it," Oliver said.

"I'd be dead if I wasn't a whore," Miss Parkhurst said, eyes suddenly sharp on him, flashing anger. "I'd have starved to death." She relaxed her clenched hands. "We got plenty of time to talk about my life, so let's hold it here for a while. I got something you need, if you're going to inherit this place."

"I don't want it, ma'am," Oliver said.

"If you don't take it, somebody who doesn't need it and deserves it a lot less will. I want you to have it. Please, be kind to me this once."

"Why me?" Oliver asked. He simply wanted out; this was completely off the planned track of his life. He was less afraid of Miss Parkhurst now, though her anger raised hairs on his neck; he felt he could be bolder and perhaps even demanding. There was a weakness in her: he was her weakness, and he wasn't above taking some advantage of that, considering how desperate his situation might be.

"You're kind," she said. "You care. And you've never had a woman, not all the way."

Oliver's face warmed again. "Please let me go," he said quietly, hoping it didn't sound as if he was pleading.

Miss Parkhurst folded her arms. "I can't," she said.

While Oliver spent his first day in Miss Parkhurst's mansion, across the city, beyond the borders of Sunside, Denver and Reggie Jones had returned home to find the apartment blanketed in gloom. Reggie, tall and gangly, long of neck and short of head, with a prominent nose, stood with back slumped in the front hall, mouth open in surprise. "He just took off and left you all here?" Reggie asked. Denver returned from the kitchen, shorter and stockier than his brother, dressed in black vinyl jacket and pants.

Yolanda's face was puffy from constant crying. She now enjoyed the tears she spilled, and had scheduled them at two hour intervals, to her momma's sorrowful irritation.

She herded the two babies into their momma's bedroom and closed a rickety gate behind them, then brushed her hands on the breast of her ragged blouse.

"You don't *get* it," she said, facing them and dropping her arms dramatically. "That whore took Momma, and Oliver traded himself for her."

"That whore," said Reggie, "is a rich old witch."

"Rich old bitch witch," Denver said, pleased with himself.

"That whore is opportunity knocking," Reggie continued, chewing reflectively. "I hear she lives alone."

"That's why she took Oliver," Yolanda said. The babies cooed and chirped behind the gate.

"Why him and not one of us?" Reggie asked.

Momma gently pushed the babies aside, swung open the gate, and marched down the hall, dressed in her best wool skirt and print blouse, wrapped in her overcoat against the gathering dark and cold outside. "Where you going?" Yolanda asked her as she brushed past.

"Time to talk to the police," she said, glowering at Reggie. Denver backed into the bedroom he shared with his brother, out of her way. He shook his head condescendingly, grinning: Momma at it again.

"Them dogheads?" Reggie said. "They got no say in Sunside."

Momma turned at the front door and glared at them. "How are you going to help your brother? He's the best of you all, you know, and you just stand there, flatfooted and jawboning yourselves."

"Momma's upset," Denver informed his brother solemnly.

"She should be," Reggie said sympathetically. "She was held prisoner by that witch bitch whore. We should go get Oliver and bring him home. We could pretend we was customers."

"She don't have customers any more," Denver said. "She's too old. She's worn out." He glanced at his crotch and leaned his head to one side, glaring for emphasis. His glare faded into an amiable grin.

"How do you know?" Reggie asked.

"That's what I hear."

Momma snorted and pulled back the bars and bolts on the front door. Reggie calmly walked up behind her and stopped her. "Police don't do anybody any good, Momma," he said. "We'll go. We'll bring Oliver back."

Denver's face slowly fell at the thought. "We got to plan it out," he said. "We got to be careful."

"We'll be careful," Reggie said. "For Momma's sake."

With his hand blocking her exit, Momma snorted again, then let her shoulders fall and her face sag. She looked more and more like an old woman now, though she was only in her late thirties.

Yolanda stood aside to let her pass into the living room. "Poor Momma," she said, eyes welling up.

"What you going to do for your brother?" Reggie asked his sister pointedly as he in turn walked by her. She craned her neck and stuck out her chin resentfully. "Go trade places with him, work in *her* house?" he taunted.

"She's rich," Denver said to himself, cupping his chin in his hand. "We could make a whole lot of money, saving our brother."

"We start thinking about it now," Reggie mandated, falling into the chair that used to be their father's, leaning his head back against the lace covers Momma had made.

Momma, face ashen, stood by the couch staring at a family portrait hung on the wall in a cheap wooden frame. "He did it for me. I was so stupid, getting off there, letting her help me. Should of known," she murmured, clutching her wrist. Her face ashen, her ankle wobbled under her and she pirouetted, hands spread out like a dancer, and collapsed face down on the couch.

The gift, the thing that Oliver needed to inherit Miss Parkhurst's mansion, was a small gold box with three buttons, like a garage door opener. She finally presented it to him in the dining room as they finished dinner.

Miss Parkhurst was nice to talk to, something Oliver had not expected, but which he should have. Whores did more than lie with a man to keep him coming back and spending his money; that should have been obvious. The day had not been the agony he expected. He had even stopped asking her to let him go. Oliver thought it would be best to bide his time, and when something distracted her, make his escape. Until then, she was not treating him badly or expecting anything he could not freely give.

"It'll be dark soon," she said as the plates cleared themselves away. He was even getting used to the ghostly service. "I have to go soon, and you got to be in your room. Take this with you, and keep it there." She removed a tray cover to reveal a white silk bag. Unstringing the bag, she removed the golden opener and shyly presented it to him. "This was given to me a long time ago. I don't need it now. But if you want to run this place, you got to have it. You can't lose it, or let anyone take it from you."

Oliver's hands went to the opener involuntarily. It seemed very desirable, as if there were something of Miss Parkhurst in it; warm, powerful, a little frightening. It fit his hand perfectly, familiar to his skin; he might have owned it for as long as she had.

He tightened his lips and returned it to her. "I'm sorry," he said. "It's not for me."

"You remember what I told you," she said. "If you don't take it, somebody else will, and it won't do anybody any good then. I want it to do some good now, when I'm done with it."

"Who gave it to you?" Oliver asked.

"A pimp, a long time ago. When I was a girl."

Oliver's eyes betrayed no judgment or disgust. She took a deep breath.

"He made you do it . . . ?" Oliver asked.

"No. I was young, but already a whore. I had an old, kind pimp, at least he seemed old to me, I wasn't much more than a girl. He died, he was killed, so this new pimp came, and he was powerful. He had the magic. But he couldn't tame me. So he says . . ."

Miss Parkhurst raised her hands to her face. "He cut me up. I was almost dead. He says, 'You shame me, whore. You do this to me, make me lose control, you're the only one ever did this to me. So I curse you. You'll be the greatest whore ever was.' He gave me the opener then, and he put my face and body back together so I'd be pretty. Then he left town, and I was in charge. I've been here ever since, but all the girls have gone, it's been so long, died or left or I told them to go. I wanted this place closed, but I couldn't close it all at once."

Oliver nodded slowly, eyes wide.

"He gave me most of his magic, too. I didn't have any choice. One thing he didn't give me was a way out. Except . . ." This time, she was the one with the pleading expression.

Oliver raised an eyebrow.

"What I need has to be freely given. Now take this." She stood and thrust the opener into his hands. "Use it to find your way all around the house. But don't leave your room after dark."

She swept out of the dining room, leaving a scent of musk and flowers and something bittersweet. Oliver put the opener in his pocket and walked back to his room, finding his way without hesitation, without thought. He shut the door and went to the bookcase, sad and troubled and exultant all at once.

She had told him her secret. He could leave now if he wanted. She had given him the power to leave.

Sipping from a glass of sherry on the nightstand beside the bed, reading from a book of composers' lives, he decided to wait until morning.

Yet after a few hours, nothing could keep his mind away from Miss Parkhurst's prohibition—not the piano, the books, or the snacks delivered almost before he thought about them, appearing on the tray when he wasn't watching. Oliver sat with hands folded in the plush chair, blinking at the room's dark corners. He thought he had Miss Parkhurst pegged. She was an old woman tired of her life, a beautifully preserved old woman to be sure, very strong . . . But she was sweet on him, keeping him like some unused gigolo. Still, he couldn't help but admire her, and he couldn't help but want to be home, near Momma and Yolanda and the babies, keeping his brothers out of trouble —not that they appreciated his efforts.

The longer he sat, the angrier and more anxious he became. He felt sure something was wrong at home. Pacing around the room did nothing to calm him. He examined the opener time and again in the firelight, brow wrinkled, wondering what powers it gave him. She had said he could go anywhere in the house and know his way, just as he had found his room without her help.

He moaned, shaking his fists at the air. "She can't keep me here! She just *can't!*"

At midnight, he couldn't control himself any longer. He stood before the door. "Let me out, dammit!" he cried, and the door opened with a sad whisper. He ran down the corridor, scattering moonlight on the floor like dust, tears shining on his cheeks.

Through the sitting rooms, the long halls of empty bedrooms—now with their doors closed, shades of sound sifting from behind—through the vast deserted kitchen, with its rows of polished copper kettles and huge black coal cookstoves, through a courtyard surrounded by five stories of the mansion on all sides and open to the golden-starred night sky, past a tiled fountain guarded by three huge white porcelain lions, ears and empty eyes following him as he ran by, Oliver searched for Miss Parkhurst, to tell her he must leave.

For a moment, he caught his breath in an upstairs gallery. He saw faint lights under doors, heard more suggestive sounds. No time to pause, even with his heart pounding and his lungs burning. If he waited in one place long enough, he thought the ghosts might become real and make him join their revelry. This was Miss Parkhurst's past, hoary and indecent, more than he could bear contemplating. How could anyone have lived this kind of life, even if they were cursed?

Yet the temptation to stop, to listen, to give in and join in was almost stronger than he could resist. He kept losing track of what he was doing, what his ultimate goal was.

"Where are you?" he shouted, throwing open double doors to a game room, empty but for more startled ghosts, more of Miss Parkhurst's eternity of bookkeeping. Pale forms rose from the billiard tables, translucent breasts shining with an inner light, their pale lovers rolling slowly to one side, fat bellies prominent, ghost eyes black and startled. "Miss Parkhurst!"

Oliver brushed through hundreds of girls, no more substantial than curtains of rain drops. His new clothes became wet with their tears. *She* had presided over this eternity of sad lust. *She* had orchestrated the debaucheries, catered to what he felt inside him: the whims and deepest desires unspoken.

Thin antique laughter followed him.

He slid on a splash of sour-smelling champagne and came up abruptly against a heavy wooden door, a room he did not know. The golden opener told him nothing about what waited beyond.

"Open!" he shouted, but he was ignored. The door was

not locked, but it resisted his entry as if it weighed tons. He pushed with both hands and then laid his shoulder on the paneling, bracing his sneakers against the thick wool pile of a champagne-soaked runner. The door swung inward with a deep iron and wood grumble, and Oliver stumbled past, saving himself at the last minute from falling on his face. Legs sprawled, down on both hands, he looked up from the wooden floor and saw where he was.

The room was narrow, but stretched on for what might have been miles, lined on one side with an endless row of plain double beds, and on the other with an endless row of free-standing cheval mirrors. An old man, the oldest he had ever seen, naked, white as talcum, rose stiffly from the bed, mumbling. Beneath him, red and warm as a pile of glowing coals, Miss Parkhurst lay with legs spread, incense of musk and sweat thick about her. She raised her head and shoulders, eyes fixed on Oliver's, and pulled a black peignoir over her nakedness. In the gloom of the room's extremities, other men, old and young, stood by their beds, smoking cigarettes or cigars or drinking champagne or whisky, all observing Oliver. Some grinned in speculation.

Miss Parkhurst's face wrinkled in agony like an old apple and she threw back her head to scream. The old man on the bed grabbed clumsily for a robe and his clothes.

Her shriek echoed from the ceiling and the walls, driving Oliver back through the door, down the halls and stairways. The wind of his flight chilled him to the bone in his tear-soaked clothing. Somehow he made his way through the sudden darkness and emptiness, and shut himself in his room, where the fire still burned warm and cheery yellow. Shivering uncontrollably, face slick with his own tears, Oliver removed his wet new clothes and called for his own in a high-pitched, frantic voice. But the invisible servants did not deliver what he requested.

He fell into the bed and pulled the covers tight about him, eyes closed. He prayed that she would not come after him, not come into his room with her peignoir slipping aside, revealing her furnace body; he prayed her smell would not follow him the rest of his life.

The door to his room did not open. Outside, all was quiet. In time, as dawn fired the roofs and then the walls and finally the streets of Sunside, Oliver slept.

* * *

"You came out of your room last night," Miss Parkhurst said over the late breakfast. Oliver stopped chewing for a moment, glanced at her through bloodshot eyes, then shrugged.

"Did you see what you expected?"

Oliver didn't answer. Miss Parkhurst sighed like a young girl.

"It's my life. This is the way I've lived for a long time."

"None of my business," Oliver said, breaking a roll in half and buttering it.

"Do I disgust you?"

Again no reply. Miss Parkhurst stood in the middle of his silence and walked to the dining room door. She looked over her shoulder at him, eyes moist. "You're not afraid of me now," she said. "You think you know what I am."

Oliver saw that his silence and uncaring attitude hurt her, and relished for a moment this power. When she remained standing in the doorway, he looked up with a purposefully harsh expression—copied from Reggie, sarcastic and angry at once—and saw tears flowing steadily down her cheeks. She seemed younger than ever now, not dangerous, just very sad. His expression faded. She turned away and closed the door behind her.

Oliver slammed half the roll into his plate of eggs and pushed his chair back from the table. "I'm not even full-grown!" he shouted at the door. "I'm not even a man! What do you want from me?" He stood up and kicked the chair away with his heel, then stuffed his hands in his pockets and paced around the small room. He felt bottled up, and yet she had said he could go any time he wished.

Go *where?* Home?

He stared at the goldenware and the plates heaped with excellent food. Nothing like this at home. Home was a place he sometimes thought he'd have to fight to get away from; he couldn't protect Momma forever from the rest of the family, he couldn't be a breadwinner for five extra mouths for the rest of his life . . .

And if he stayed here, knowing what Miss Parkhurst did each night? Could he eat breakfast each morning, knowing how the food was earned, and all his clothes and books and the piano, too? He really would be a gigolo then.

Sunside. He was here, maybe he could live here, find work, get away from Sleepside for good.

The mere thought gave him a twinge. He sat down and buried his face in his hands, rubbing his eyes with the tips of his fingers, pulling at his lids to make a face, staring at himself reflected in the golden carafe, big-nosed, eyes monstrously bleared. He had to talk to Momma. Even talking to Yolanda might help.

But Miss Parkhurst was nowhere to be found. Oliver searched the mansion until dusk, then ate alone in the small dining room. He retired to his room as dark closed in, spreading through the halls like ink through water. To banish the night, and all that might be happening in it, Oliver played the piano loudly.

When he finally stumbled to his bed, he saw a single yellow rose on the pillow, delicate and sweet. He placed it by the lamp on the nightstand and pulled the covers over himself, clothes and all.

In the early hours of the morning, he dreamed that Miss Parkhurst had fled the mansion, leaving it for him to tend to. The ghosts and old men crowded around, asking why he was so righteous. "She never had a Momma like you," said one decrepit dude dressed in black velvet nightrobes. "She's lived times you can't imagine. Now you just blew her right out of this house. Where will she go?"

Oliver came awake long enough to remember the dream, and then returned to a light, difficult sleep.

Mrs. Diamond Freeland scowled at Yolanda's hand-wringing and mumbling. "You can't help your momma acting that way," she said.

"I'm no doctor," Yolanda complained.

"No doctor's going to help her," Mrs. Freeland said, eyeing the door to Momma's bedroom.

Denver and Reggie lounged uneasily in the parlor.

"You two louts going to look for your brother?"

"We don't have to look for him," Denver said. "We know where he is. We got a plan to get him back."

"Then why don't you do it?" Mrs. Freeland asked.

"When the time's right," Reggie said decisively.

"Your momma's pining for Oliver," Mrs. Freeland told them, not for the first time. "It's churning her insides thinking he's with that witch and what she might be doing to him."

Reggie tried unsuccessfully to hide a grin.

"What's funny?" Mrs. Freeland asked sternly.

"Nothing. Maybe our little brother needs some of what she's got."

Mrs. Freeland glared at them. "Yolanda," she said, rolling her eyes to the ceiling in disgust. "The babies. They dry?"

"No, ma'am," Yolanda said. She backed away from Mrs. Freeland's severe look. "I'll change them."

"Then you take them into your momma."

"Yes ma'am."

The breakfast went as if nothing had happened. Miss Parkhurst sat across from him, eating and smiling. Oliver tried to be more polite, working his way around to asking a favor. When the breakfast was over, the time seemed right.

"I'd like to see how Momma's doing," he said.

Miss Parkhurst considered for a moment. "There'll be a TV in your room this evening," she said, folding her napkin and placing it beside her plate. "You can use it to see how everybody is."

That seemed fair enough. Until then, however, he'd be spending the entire day with Miss Parkhurst; it was time, he decided, to be civil. Then he might actually test his freedom.

"You say I can go," Oliver said, trying to sound friendly.

Miss Parkhurst nodded. "Any time. I won't keep you."

"If I go, can I come back?"

She smiled ever so slightly. There was the girl in that smile again, and she seemed very vulnerable. "The opener takes you anywhere across town."

"Nobody messes with me?"

"Nobody touches anyone I protect," Miss Parkhurst said.

Oliver absorbed that thoughtfully, steepling his hands below his chin. "You're pretty good to me," he said. "Even when I cross you, you don't hurt me. Why?"

"You're my last chance," Miss Parkhurst said, dark eyes on him. "I've lived a long time, and nobody like you's come along. I don't think there'll be another for even longer. I can't wait that long. I've lived this way so many years, I don't know another, but I don't want any more of it."

Oliver couldn't think of a better way to put his next question. "Do you like being a whore?"

Miss Parkhurst's face hardened. "It has its moments," she said stiffly.

Oliver screwed up his courage enough to say what was on his mind, but not to look at her while doing it. "You enjoy lying down with any man who has the money?"

"It's work. It's something I'm good at."

"Even ugly men?"

"Ugly men need their pleasures, too."

"Bad man? Letting them touch you when they've hurt people, maybe killed people?"

"What kind of work have you done?" she asked.

"Clerked a grocery store. Taught music."

"Did you wait on bad men in the grocery store?"

"If I did," Oliver said swiftly, "I didn't know about it."

"Neither did I," Miss Parkhurst said. Then, more quietly, "Most of the time."

"All those girls you've made whore for you . . ."

"You have some things to learn," she interrupted. "It's not the work that's so awful. It's what you have to be to do it. The way people expect you to be when you do it. Should be, in a good world, a whore's like a doctor or a saint, she doesn't mind getting her hands dirty any more than they do. She gives pleasure and smiles. But in the city, people won't let it happen that way. Here, a whore's always got some empty place inside her, a place you've filled with self-respect, maybe. A whore's got respect, but not for herself. She loses that whenever anybody looks at her. She can be worth a million dollars on the outside, but inside, she knows. That's what makes her a whore. That's the curse. It's beat into you sometimes, everybody taking advantage, like you're dirt. Pretty soon you think you're dirt, too, and who cares what happens to dirt? Pretty soon you're just sliding along, trying to keep from getting hurt or maybe dead, but who cares?"

"You're rich," Oliver said.

"Can't buy everything," Miss Parkhurst commented dryly.

"You've got magic."

"I've got magic because I'm here, and to stay here, I have to be a whore."

"Why can't you leave?"

She sighed, her fingers working nervously along the edge of the tablecloth.

"What stops you from just leaving?"

"If you're going to take this place," she said, and he thought at first she was avoiding his question, "you've got to know all about it. All about me. We're the same, almost, this place and I. A whore's no more than what's in her purse, every pimp knows that. You know how many times I've been married?"

Oliver shook his head.

"Seventeen times. Sometimes they left me, once or twice they stayed. Never any good. But then, maybe I didn't deserve any better. Those who left me, they came back when they were old, asking me to save them from Darkside. I couldn't. But I kept them here anyway. Come on."

She stood and Oliver followed her down the halls, down the stairs, below the garage level, deep beneath the mansion's clutter-filled basement. The air was ageless, deep-earth cool, and smelled of old city rain. A few eternal clear light bulbs cast feeble yellow crescents in the dismal murk. They walked on boards over an old muddy patch, Miss Parkhurst lifting her skirts a few inches to clear the mire. Oliver saw her slim ankles and swallowed back the tightness in his throat.

Ahead, laid out in a row on moss-patched concrete biers, were fifteen black iron cylinders, each seven feet long and slightly flattened on top. They looked like big blockbuster bombs in storage. The first was wedged into a dark corner. Miss Parkhurst stood by its foot, running her hand along its rust-streaked surface.

"Two didn't come back. Maybe they were the best of the lot," she said. "I was no judge. I couldn't know. You judge men by what's inside you, and if you're hollow, they get lost in there, you can't know what you're seeing."

Oliver stepped closer to the last cylinder and saw a clear glass plate mounted at the head. Reluctant but fascinated, he wiped the dusty glass with two fingers and peered past a single cornered bubble. The coffin was filled with clear liquid. Afloat within, a face the color of green olives in a martini looked back at him, blind eyes murky, lips set in a loose line. The liquid and death had smoothed the face's wrinkles, but Oliver could tell nonetheless, this dude had been old, old.

"They all die," she said. "All but me. I keep them all, every john, every husband, no forgetting, no letting them go. We've always got this tie between us. That's the curse."

Oliver pulled back from the coffin, holding his breath, heart thumping with eager horror. Which was worse, this, or old men in the night? Old dead lusts laid to rest or lively ghosts? Wrapped in gloom at the far end of the line of bottle-coffins, Miss Parkhurst seemed for a moment to glow with the same furnace power he had felt when he first saw her.

"I miss some of these guys," she said, her voice so soft the power just vanished, a thing in his mind. "We had some good times together."

Oliver tried to imagine what Miss Parkhurst had lived through, the good times and otherwise. "You have any children?" he asked, his voice as thin as the buzz of a fly in a bottle. He jumped back as one of the coffins resonated with his shaky words.

Miss Parkhurst's shoulders slumped. "Lots," she said. "All dead before they were born."

At first his shock was conventional, orchestrated by his Sundays in church. Then the colossal organic waste of effort came down on him like a pile of stones. All that motion, all that wanting, and nothing good from it, just these iron bottles and vivid lists of ghosts.

"What good is a whore's baby?" Miss Parkhurst asked. "Especially if the mother's going to stay a whore."

"Was your mother . . . ?" It didn't seem right to use the word in connection with anyone's mother.

"She was, and her mother before her. I have no daddies, or lots of daddies."

Oliver remembered the old man chastising him in his dream. Before he could even sort out his words, wishing to give her some solace, some sign he wasn't completely unsympathetic, he said, "It can't be all bad, being a whore."

"Maybe not," she said. Miss Parkhurst hardly made a blot in the larger shadows. She might just fly away to dust if he turned his head.

"You said being a whore is being empty inside. Not everybody who's empty inside is a whore."

"Oh?" she replied, light as a cobweb. He was being

pushed into an uncharacteristic posture, but Oliver was damned if he'd give in just yet, however much a fool he made of himself. His mixed feelings were betraying him.

"You've *lived*," he said. "You got memories nobody else has. You could write books. They'd make movies about you."

Her smile was a dull lamp in the shadows. "I've had important people visit me," she said. "Powerful men, even mayors. I had something they needed. Sometimes they opened up and talked about how hard it was not being little boys any more. Sometimes, when we were relaxing, they'd cry on my shoulder, just like I was their momma. But then they'd go away and try to forget about me. If they remembered at all, they were scared of me, because of what I knew about them. Now, they know I'm getting weak," she said. "I don't give a damn about books or movies. I won't tell what I know, and besides, lots of those men are dead. If they aren't, they're waiting for me to die, so they can sleep easy."

"What do you mean, getting weak?"

"I got two days, maybe three, then I die a whore. My time is up. The curse is almost finished."

Oliver gaped. When he had first seen her, she had seemed as powerful as a diesel locomotive, as if she might live forever.

"And if I take over?"

"You get the mansion, the money."

"How much power?"

She didn't answer.

"You can't give me any power, can you?"

"No," faint as the breeze from her eyelashes.

"The opener won't be any good."

"No."

"You lied to me."

"I'll leave you all that's left."

"That's not why you made me come here. You took Momma—"

"She stole from me."

"My momma never stole anything!" Oliver shouted. The iron coffins buzzed.

"She took something after I had given her all my hospitality."

"What could she take from you? She was no thief."

"She took a sheet of music."

Oliver's face screwed up in sudden pain. He looked away, fists clenched. They had almost no money for his music. More often than not since his father died, he made up music, having no new scores to play. "Why'd you bring me here?" he croaked.

"I don't mind dying. But I don't want to die a whore."

Oliver turned back, angry again, this time for his momma as well as himself. He approached the insubstantial shadow. Miss Parkhurst shimmered like a curtain. "What do you want from me?"

"I need someone who loves me. Loves me for no reason."

For an instant, he saw standing before him a scrawny girl in a red shimmy, eyes wide. "How could that help you? Can that make you something else?"

"Just love," she said. "Just letting me forget all these," she pointed to the coffins, "and all those," pointing up.

Oliver's body lost its charge of anger and accusation with an exhaled breath. "I can't love you," he said. "I don't even know what love is." Was this true? Upstairs, she had burned in his mind, and he *had* wanted her, though it upset him to remember how much. What *could* he feel for her? "Let's go back now. I have to look in on Momma."

Miss Parkhurst emerged from the shadows and walked past him silently, not even her skirts rustling. She gestured with a finger for him to follow.

She left him at the door to his room, saying, "I'll wait in the main parlor." Oliver saw a small television set on the nightstand by his bed and rushed to turn it on. The screen filled with static and unresolved images. He saw fragments of faces, patches of color and texture passing so quickly he couldn't make them out. The entire city might be on the screen at once, but he could not see any of it clearly. He twisted the channel knob and got more static. Then he saw the label past channel 13 on the dial: HOME, in small golden letters. He twisted the knob to that position and the screen cleared.

Momma lay in bed, legs drawn tightly up, hair mussed. She didn't look good. Her hand, stretched out across the bed, trembled. Her breathing was hard and rough. In the background, Oliver heard Yolanda fussing with the babies, finally screaming at her older brothers in frustration.

Why don't you help with the babies? his sister demanded in a tinny, distant voice.

Momma told you, Denver replied.

She did not. She told us all. You could help.

Reggie laughed. *We got plans to make.*

Oliver pulled back from the TV. Momma was sick, and for all his brothers and sister and the babies could do, she might die. He could guess why she was sick, too; with worry for him. He had to go to her and tell her he was all right. A phone call wouldn't be enough.

Again, however, he was reluctant to leave the mansion and Miss Parkhurst. Something beyond her waning magic was at work here; he wanted to listen to her and to experience more of that fascinated horror. He wanted to watch her again, absorb her smooth, ancient beauty. In a way, she needed him as much as Momma did. Miss Parkhurst outraged everything in him that was lawful and orderly, but he finally had to admit, as he thought of going back to Momma, that he enjoyed the outrage.

He clutched the gold opener and ran from his room to the parlor. She waited for him there in a red velvet chair, hands gripping two lions at the end of the armrests. The lions' wooden faces grinned beneath her caresses. "I got to go," he said. "Momma's sick for missing me."

She nodded. "I'm not holding you," she said.

He stared at her. "I wish I could help you," he said.

She smiled hopefully, pitifully. "Then promise you'll come back."

Oliver wavered. How long would Momma need him? What if he gave his promise and returned and Miss Parkhurst was already dead?

"I promise."

"Don't be too long," she said.

"Won't," he mumbled.

The limousine waited for him in the garage, white and beautiful, languid and sleek and fast all at once. No chauffeur waited for him this time. The door opened by itself and he climbed in; the door closed behind him, and he leaned back stiffly on the leather seats, gold opener in hand. "Take me home," he said. The glass partition and the windows all around darkened to an opaque smoky gold. He felt a sensation of smooth motion. *What would it be like to have this kind of power all the time?*

But the power wasn't hers to give.

Oliver arrived before the apartment building in a blizzard of swirling snow. Snow packed up over the curbs and coated the sidewalks a foot deep; Sleepside was heavy with winter. Oliver stepped from the limousine and climbed the icy steps, the cold hardly touching him even in his light clothing. He was surrounded by Miss Parkhurst's magic.

Denver was frying a pan of navy beans in the kitchen when Oliver burst through the door, the locks flinging themselves open before him. Oliver paused in the entrance to the kitchen. Denver stared at him, face slack, too surprised to speak.

"Where's Momma?"

Yolanda heard his voice in the living room and screamed.

Reggie met him in the hallway, arms open wide, smiling broadly. "Goddamn, little brother! You got away?"

"Where's Momma?"

"She's in her room. She's feeling low."

"She's sick," Oliver said, pushing past his brother. Yolanda stood before Momma's door as if to keep Oliver out. She sucked her lower lip between her teeth. She looked scared.

"Let me by, Yolanda," Oliver said. He almost pointed the opener at her, and then pulled back, fearful of what might happen.

"You made Momma si-ick," Yolanda squeaked, but she stepped aside. Oliver pushed through the door to Momma's room. She sat up in bed, face drawn and thin, but her eyes danced with joy. "My boy!" she sighed. "My beautiful boy."

Oliver sat beside her and they hugged fiercely. "Please don't leave me again," Momma said, voice muffled by his shoulder. Oliver set the opener on her flimsy nightstand and cried against her neck.

The day after Oliver's return, Denver stood lank-legged by the window, hands in frayed pants pockets, staring at the snow with heavy-lidded eyes. "It's too cold to go anywheres now," he mused.

Reggie sat in their father's chair, face screwed in

thought. "I listened to what he told Momma," he said. "That whore sent our little brother back here in a limo. A big white limo. See it out there?"

Denver peered down at the street. A white limousine waited at the curb, not even dusted by snow. A tiny vanishing curl of white rose from its tailpipe. "It's still there," he said.

"Did you see what he had when he came in?" Reggie asked. Denver shook his head. "A gold box. *She* must have given that to him. I bet whoever has that gold box can visit Miss Belle Parkhurst. Want to bet?"

Denver grinned and shook his head again.

"Wouldn't be too cold if we had that limo, would it?" Reggie asked.

Oliver brought his momma chicken soup and a half-rotten, carefully trimmed orange. He plumped her pillow for her, shushing her, telling her not to talk until she had eaten. She smiled weakly, beatific, and let him minister to her. When she had eaten, she lay back and closed her eyes, tears pooling in their hollows before slipping down her cheeks. "I was so afraid for you," she said. "I didn't know what she would do. She seemed so nice at first. I didn't see her. Just her voice, inviting me in over the security buzzer, letting me sit and rest my feet. I knew where I was . . . was it bad of me, to stay there, knowing?"

"You were tired, Momma," Oliver said. "Besides, Miss Parkhurst isn't that bad."

Momma looked at him dubiously. "I saw her piano. There was a shelf next to it with the most beautiful sheet music you ever saw, even big books of it. I looked at some. Oh, Oliver, I've never taken anything in my life . . ." She cried freely now, sapping what little strength the lunch had given her.

"Don't you worry, Momma. She used you. She *wanted* me to come." As an afterthought, she added, not sure why he lied, "Or Yolanda."

Momma absorbed that while her eyes examined his face in tiny, caressing glances. "You won't go back," she said, "will you?"

Oliver looked down at the sheets folded under her arms. "I promised. She'll die if I don't," he said.

"That woman is a liar," Momma stated unequivocally. "If she wants you, she'll do anything to get you."

"I don't think she's lying, Momma."

She looked away from him, a feverish anger flushing her cheeks. "Why did you promise her?"

"She's not that bad, Momma," he said again. He had thought that coming home would clear his mind, but Miss Parkhurst's face, her plea, stayed with him as if she were only a room away. The mansion seemed just a fading dream, unimportant; but Belle Parkhurst stuck. "She needs help. She wants to change."

Momma puffed out her cheeks and blew through her lips like a horse. She had often done that to his father, never before to him. "She'll always be a whore," she said.

Oliver's eyes narrowed. He saw a spitefulness and bitterness in Momma he hadn't noticed before. Not that spite was unwarranted; Miss Parkhurst had treated Momma roughly. Yet . . .

Denver stood in the doorway. "Reggie and I got to talk to Momma," he said. "About you." He jerked his thumb back over his shoulder. "Alone." Reggie stood grinning behind his brother. Oliver took the tray of dishes and sidled past them, going into the kitchen.

In the kitchen, he washed the last few days' plates methodically, letting the lukewarm water slide over his hands, eyes focused on the faucet's dull gleam. He had almost lost track of time when he heard the front door slam. Jerking his head up, he wiped the last plate and put it away, then went to Momma's room. She looked back at him guiltily. Something was wrong. He searched the room with his eyes, but nothing was out of place. Nothing that was normally present . . .

The opener.

His brothers had taken the gold opener.

"Momma!" he said.

"They're going to pay her a visit," she said, the bitterness plain now. "They don't like their momma mistreated."

It was getting dark and the snow was thick. He had hoped to return this evening. If Miss Parkhurst hadn't lied, she would be very weak by now, perhaps dead tomorrow. His lungs seemed to shrink within him, and he had a hard time taking a breath.

"I've got to go," he said. "She might *kill* them, Momma!" But that wasn't what worried him. He put on his heavy coat, then his father's old cracked rubber boots with the snow tread soles. Yolanda came out of the room she shared with the babies. She didn't ask any questions, just watched him dress for the cold, her eyes dull.

"They got that gold box," she said as he flipped the last metal clasp on the boots. "Probably worth a lot."

Oliver hesitated in the hallway, then grabbed Yolanda's shoulders and shook her vigorously. "You take care of Momma, you hear?"

She shut her jaw with a clack and shoved free. Oliver was out the door before she could speak.

Day's last light filled the sky with a deep peachy glow tinged with cold gray. Snow fell golden above the buildings and smudgy brown within their shadow. The wind swirled around him mournfully, sending gust-fingers through his coat for any warmth that might be stolen. For a nauseating moment, all his resolve was sucked away by a vacuous pit of misery. The streets were empty; he briefly wondered what night this was, and then remembered it was the twenty-third of December, but too cold for whatever stray shoppers Sleepside might send out. *Why go? To save two worthless idiots?* Not that so much, although that would have been enough, since their loss would hurt Momma, and they *were* his brothers; not that so much as his promise. And something else.

He was afraid for Belle Parkhurst.

He buttoned his coat collar and leaned into the wind. He hadn't put on a hat. The heat flew from his scalp, and in a few moments he felt drained and exhausted. But he made it to the subway entrance and staggered down the steps, into the warmer heart of the city, where it was always sixty-four degrees.

Locked behind her thick glass and metal booth, wrinkled eyes weary with night's wisdom, the fluorescent-lighted token seller took his money and dropped cat's head tokens into the steel tray with separate, distinct *chinks*. Oliver glanced at her face and saw the whore's printed there instead; this middle-aged woman did not spread her legs for money, but had sold her youth and life away sitting in this cavern. Whose emptiness was more profound?

"Be careful," she warned vacantly through the speaker grill. "Night Metro any minute now."

He dropped a token into the turnstile and pushed through, then stood shivering on the platform, waiting for the Sunside train. It seemed to take forever to arrive, and when it did, he was not particularly relieved. The driver's pit-eyes winked green, bull's head turning as the train slid to a halt beside the platform. The doors opened with an oiled groan, and Oliver stepped aboard, into the hard, cold, and unforgiving glare of the train's interior.

At first, Oliver thought the car was empty. He did not sit down, however. The hair on his neck and arm bristled. Hand gripping a stainless steel handle, he leaned into the train's acceleration and took a deep, half-hiccup breath.

He first consciously noticed the other passengers as their faces gleamed in silhouette against the passing dim lights of ghost stations. They sat almost invisible, crowding the car; they stood beside him, less substantial than a breath of air. They watched him intently, bearing no ill will for the moment, perhaps not yet aware that he was alive and they were not. They carried no overt signs of their wounds, but how they had come to be here was obvious to his animal instincts.

This train carried holiday suicides: men, women, teenagers, even a few children, delicate as expensive crystal in a shop window. Maybe the bull's head driver collected them, culling them out and caging them as they stumbled randomly aboard his train. Maybe he controlled them.

Oliver tried to sink away in his coat. He felt guilty, being alive and healthy, enveloped in strong emotions; they were so flimsy, with so little hold on this reality.

He muttered a prayer, stopping as they all turned toward him, showing glassy disapproval at this reverse blasphemy. Silently, he prayed again, but even that seemed to irritate his fellow passengers, and they squeaked among themselves in voices that only a dog or a bat might hear.

The stations passed one by one, mosaic symbols and names flashing in pools of light. When the Sunside station approached and the train slowed, Oliver moved quickly to the door. It opened with oily grace. He stepped onto the platform, turned, and bumped up against the tall, dark uniform of the bull's head driver. The air around him stank of grease and electricity and something sweeter, perhaps blood. He stood a bad foot and a half taller than Oliver, and in one outstretched, black-nailed, leathery hand he held his long silver shears, points spread wide, briefly suggesting Belle Parkhurst's horizontal position among the old men.

"You're in the wrong place, at the wrong time," the driver warned in a voice deeper than the train motors. "Down here, I can cut your cord." He closed the shears with a slick, singing whisper.

"I'm going to Miss Parkhurst's," Oliver said, voice quavering.

"Who?" the driver asked.

"I'm leaving now," Oliver said, backing away. The driver followed, slowly hunching over him. The shears sang open, angled toward his eyes. The crystal dead within the train passed through the open door and glided around them. Gluey waves of cold shivered the air.

"You're a bold little bastard," the driver said, voice managing to descend off any human scale and still be heard. The white tile walls vibrated. "All I have to do is cut your cord, right in front of your face," he snicked the shears inches from Oliver's nose, "and you'll never find your way home."

The driver backed him up against a cold barrier of suicides. Oliver's fear could not shut out curiosity. Was the bull's head real, or was there a man under the horns and hide and bone? The eyes in their sunken orbits glowed ice-blue. The scissors crossed before Oliver's face again, even closer; mere hairs away from his nose.

"You're mine," the driver whispered, and the scissors closed on something tough and invisible. Oliver's head exploded with pain. He flailed back through the dead, dragging the driver after him by the pinch of the shears on that something unseen and very important. Roaring, the driver applied both hands to the shears' grips. Oliver felt as if his head were being ripped away. Suddenly, he kicked out with all his strength between the driver's black-uniformed legs. His foot hit flesh and bone as unyielding as rock and his agony doubled. But the shears hung for a moment in air before Oliver's face, ungrasped, and the driver slowly curled over.

Oliver grabbed the shears, opened them, released whatever cord he had between himself and his past, his home, and pushed through the dead. The scissors reflected elongated gleams over the astonished, watery faces of the suicides. Suddenly, seeing a chance to escape, they spread out along the platform, some of the station's stairs, some to both sides. Oliver ran through them up the steps and stood on the warm evening sidewalk of Sunside. All he sensed from the station's entrance was a sour breath of oil and blood and a faint chill of fading hands as the dead evaporated in the balmy night air.

A quiet crowd had gathered at the front entrance to Miss Parkhurst's mansion. They stood vigil, waiting for something, their faces shining with a greedy sweat.

He did not see the limousine. His brothers must have arrived by now; they were inside, then.

Catching his breath as he ran, he skirted the old brownstone and looked for the entrance to the underground garage. On the south side, he found the ramp and descended to slam his hands against the corrugated metal door. Echoes replied. "It's me!" he shouted. "Let me in!"

A middle-aged man regarded him dispassionately from the higher ground of the sidewalk. "What do you want in there, young man?" he asked.

Oliver glared back over his shoulder. "None of your business," he said.

"Maybe it is, if you want in," the man said. "There's a way any man can get into that house. It never turns gold away."

Oliver pulled back from the door a moment, stunned. The man shrugged and walked on.

He still grasped the driver's shears. They weren't gold, they were silver, but they had to be worth something. "Let me in!" he said. Then, upping the ante, he dug in his pocket and produced the remaining cat's head token "I'll pay!"

The door grumbled up. The garage's lights were off, but in the soft yellow glow of the street lights, he saw an eagle's claw thrust out from the brick wall just within the door's frame, supporting a golden cup. Token in one hand, shears in another, Oliver's eyes narrowed. To pay Belle's mansion now was no honorable deed; he dropped the token into the cup, but kept the shears as he ran into the darkness.

A faint crack of light showed beneath the stairwell

door. Around the door, the bones of ancient city dwellers glowed in their compacted stone, teeth, and knuckles bright as fireflies. Oliver tried the door; it was locked. Inserting the point of the shears between the door and catchplate, he pried until the lock was sprung.

The quiet parlor was illuminated only by a few guttering candles clutched in drooping gold eagle's claws. The air was thick with the blunt smells of long-extinguished cigars and cigarettes. Oliver stopped for a moment, closing his eyes and listening. There was a room he had never seen in the time he had spent in Belle Parkhurst's house. She had never even shown him the door, but he knew it had to exist, and that was where she would be, alive or dead. Where his brothers were, he couldn't tell; for the moment he didn't care. He doubted they were in any mortal danger. Belle's power was as weak as the scattered candles.

Oliver crept along the dark halls, holding the gleaming shears before him as a warning to whatever might try to stop him. He climbed two more flights of stairs, and on the third floor, found an uncarpeted hallway, walls bare, that he had not seen before. The dry floorboards creaked beneath him. The air was cool and still. He could smell a ghost of Belle's rose perfume. At the end of the hall was a plain panel door with a tarnished brass knob.

This door was also unlocked. He sucked in a breath for courage and opened it.

This was Belle's room, and she was indeed in it. She hung suspended above her plain iron-frame bed in a weave of flowing threads. For a moment, he drew back, thinking she was a spider, but it immediately became clear she was more like a spider's prey. The threads reached to all corners of the room, transparent, binding her tightly, but to him as insubstantial as the air.

Belle turned to face him, weak, eyes clouded, skin like paper towels. "Why'd you wait so long?" she asked.

From across the mansion, he heard the echoes of Reggie's delighted laughter.

Oliver stepped forward. Only the blades of the shears plucked at the threads; he passed through unhindered. Arm straining at the silver instrument, he realized what the threads were; they were the cords binding Belle to the mansion, connecting her to all her customers. Belle had not one cord to her past, but thousands. Every place she had been touched, she was held by a strand. Thick twining ropes of the past shot from her lips and breasts and from between her legs; not even the toes of her feet were free.

Without thinking, Oliver lifted the driver's silver shears and began methodically snipping the cords. One by one, or in ropy clusters, he cut them away. With each meeting of the blades, they vanished. He did not ask himself which was her first cord, linking her to her childhood, to the few years she had lived before she became a whore; there was no time to waste worrying about such niceties.

"Your brothers are in my vault," she said. "They found my gold and jewels. I crawled here to get away."

"Don't talk," Oliver said between clenched teeth. The strands became tougher, more like wire the closer he came to her thin gray body. His arm muscles knotted and cold sweat soaked his clothes. She dropped inches closer to the bed.

"I never brought any men here," she said.

"Shh."

"This was my place, the only place I had."

There were hundreds of strands left now, instead of thousands. He worked for long minutes, watching her grow more and more pale, watching her one-time furnace heat dull to less than a single candle, her eyes lose their feverish glitter. For a horrified moment, he thought cutting the cords might actually weaken her; but he hacked and swung at the cords, regardless. They were even tougher now, more resilient.

Far off in the mansion, Denver and Reggie laughed together, and there was a heavy clinking sound. The floor shuddered.

Dozens of cords remained. He had been working at them for an eternity, and now each cord took a concentrated effort, all the strength left in his arms and hands. He thought he might faint or throw up. Belle's eyes had closed. Her breathing was undetectable.

Five strands left. He cut through one, then another. As he applied the shears to the third, a tall man appeared on the opposite side of her bed, dressed in pale gray with a wide-brimmed gray hat. His fingers were covered with gold rings. A gold eagle's claw pinned his white silk tie.

"I was her third," the man said. "She came to me and she cheated me."

Oliver held back his shears, eyes stinging with rage. "Who are you?" he demanded, nearly doubled over by his exertion. He stared up at the gray man through beads of sweat on his eyebrows.

"That other old man, he hardly worked her at all. I put her to work right here, but she cheated me."

"You're her *pimp*," Oliver spat out the word.

The gray man grinned.

"Cut that cord, and she's nothing."

"She's nothing now. Your curse is over and she's dying."

"She shouldn't have messed with me," the pimp said. "I was a strong man, lots of connections. What do you want with an old drained-out whore, boy?"

Oliver didn't answer. He struggled to cut the third cord but it writhed like a snake between the shears.

"She would have been a whore even without me," the pimp said. "She was a whore from the day she was born."

"That's a lie," Oliver said.

"Why do you want to get at her? She give you a pox and you want to finish her off?"

Oliver's lips curled and he flung his head back, not looking as he brought the shears together with all his remaining strength, boosted by a killing anger. The third cord parted and the shears snapped, one blade singing across the room and sticking in the wall with a spray of plaster chips. The gray man vanished like a double-blown puff of cigarette smoke, leaving a scent of onions and stale beer.

Belle hung awkwardly by two cords now. Swinging the single blade like a knife, he parted them swiftly and fell over her, lying across her, feeling her cool body for the first time. She could not arouse lust now. She might be dead.

"Miss Parkhurst," he said. He examined her face, almost as white as the bed sheets, high cheekbones pressing through waxy flesh. "I don't want anything from you," Oliver said. "I just want you to be all right." He lowered his lips to hers, kissed her lightly, dripping sweat on her closed eyes.

Far away, Denver and Reggie cackled with glee.

The house grew quiet. All the ghosts, all accounts received, had fled, had been freed.

The single candle in the room guttered out, and they

lay in the dark alone. Oliver fell against his will into an exhausted slumber.

Cool, rose-scented fingers lightly touched his forehead. He opened his eyes and saw a girl in a white nightgown leaning over him, barely his age. Her eyes were very big and her lips bowed into a smile beneath high, full cheek-bones. "Where are we?" she asked. "How long we been here?"

Late morning sun filled the small, dusty room with warmth. He glanced around the bed, looking for Belle, and then turned back to the girl. She vaguely resembled the chauffeur who had brought him to the mansion that first night, though younger, her face more bland and simple.

"You don't remember?" he asked.

"Honey," the girl said sweetly, hands on hips, "I don't remember much of anything. Except that you kissed me. You want to kiss me again?"

Momma did not approve of the strange young woman he brought home, and wanted to know where Reggie and Denver were. Oliver did not have the heart to tell her. They lay cold as ice in a room filled with mounds of cat's head subway tokens, bound by the pimp's magic. They had dressed themselves in white, with broad white hats; dressed themselves as pimps. But the mansion was empty, stripped during that night of all its valuables by the greedy crowds.

They were pimps in a whorehouse without whores. As the young girl observed, with a tantalizing touch of wisdom beyond her apparent years, there was nothing much lower than that.

"Where'd you find that girl? She's hiding something, Oliver. You mark my words."

Oliver ignored his mother's misgivings, having enough of his own. The girl agreed she needed a different name now, and chose Lorelei, a name she said "Just sings right."

He saved money, lacking brothers to borrow and never repay, and soon rented a cheap studio on the sixth floor of the same building. The girl came to him sweetly in his bed, her mind no more full—for the most part—than that of any young girl. In his way, he loved her—and feared her, though less and less as days passed.

She played the piano almost as well as he, and they planned to give lessons. They had brought a trunk full of old sheet music and books with them from the mansion. The crowds had left them at least that much.

Momma did not visit for two weeks after they moved in. But visit she did, and eventually the girl won her over.

"She's got a good hand in the kitchen," Momma said. "You do right by her, now."

Yolanda made friends with the girl quickly and easily, and Oliver saw more substance in his younger sister than he had before. Lorelei helped Yolanda with the babies. She seemed a natural.

Sometimes, at night, he examined her while she slept, wondering if there still weren't stories, and perhaps skills, hidden behind her sweet, peaceful face. Had she forgotten everything?

In time, they were married.

And they lived—

Well enough.

They lived.

Frankenstein Goes Home

ALAN RODGERS

THE MONSTER COUGHED, and he tasted blood—the same blood he always tasted when the force of air in his throat was too great. The seams that bound the membranes of his lungs to his larynx weren't strong enough to cope with coughing, or even hard breathing. Like most of the seams that bound the disparate portions of his body together, they'd never healed well enough to truly fuse.

The Monster was going home.

Home as he remembered it, anyway. He wasn't sure that home existed anymore; wasn't even sure that it ever *had* existed.

This forest, at least, was as he remembered it. He could remember hunting deer in this forest a lifetime ago . . . or maybe it was longer ago than that. When he looked at them too closely his memories became hard to sort from each other.

There were voices, children's voices, somewhere on the far side of the hill.

The Monster didn't pay them any mind. He'd fallen into the old trap again, his own special trap that he'd been hiding from for years, and needed every bit of heart and spirit he had to keep from being swallowed by his own self-pity. Years ago he'd decided that he needed his self-respect too much to let himself indulge in self-pity. As long as you had your self-respect, he thought, you were human.

Even if you did think of yourself as a Monster.

Even if the doctor liked to call him Frankenstein.

He wasn't Frankenstein. It wasn't his name, and it never had been. Neither had it ever been Dr. Thompson's name, though when he was of a mood he liked to say that he was Dr. Frankenstein. The Monster wasn't certain whether, at these moments, the madman was indulging or deluding himself. Not that it made any difference. "I am Doctor Frankenstein," Thompson would say, "and you are my Frankenstein Monster." For that matter the doctor wasn't a doctor at all: he had a Ph.D. in molecular biology, and he was crazy enough to have been in and out of the state mental hospital half a dozen times in the last ten years. The man was too unstable to hold down a university position, much less one in industrial research. If it weren't for family money the doctor wouldn't have been able to maintain an apartment, let alone the ersatz castle where the Monster had spent the five years of his new life.

The children were closer, now. Soon they would see him. Would they scream? Or would they assume that he wore some bizarre costume—the sort of costume the Monster had seen so many times on television?

The Monster was unsure that he wanted to learn. He turned so that his path bore more to the left, hoping to avoid them.

The first time the Monster woke he was in a dingy room full of strange equipment. He'd felt confused even before he'd had a chance to realize the strangeness of his body. Partly that confusion came from the strangeness of the surroundings; partly it was the result of the fact that the disparate parts of his self had not yet begun to fuse.

But the source of his confusion was also the monster's strength; at the moment he woke to life the world was already a familiar place. The vague biochemical ghosts of the people he'd been had lived . . . lifetimes. Between them all he'd had more than his fill of the world of men.

The Mad Doctor explained that to him, after a fashion, only a few seconds after he opened his eyes. "Take it easy," the Doctor said. "Not too fast." He cackled as he spoke in a peculiar fashion that the Monster later learned meant that the mad scientist was pleased with his own wit—though the Monster had never been able to see that wit himself. "I bet you're all shook up. Must be. Three-quarters of a dozen people all sailing at half mast inside your head, and none of them even know about each other yet. Worse yet, they all think they're one person. Well, they will be, sooner or later. Later or sooner, heh heh. You'll be fine. You have to be—I'm so proud of you. My crowning creation. My shining glory! Ha!"

The Monster looked up at him and blinked, trying to clear his head. And suddenly the madman's voice became very serious.

"It's the RNA. It gives you memory; it's everywhere inside you. Most of the body's ribonucleic acid is the brain, so much of it that the rest isn't important. But I treated your brain with an enzyme, an RNAase. It's part of the experiment. I need to see . . . how you come back together."

Not much of that sunk through to the Monster. He was too caught up in seeing his body for the first time, examining the mad scientist's crude stitchwork. Seeing the blood that still seeped from seam-wounds that would never heal completely.

But later, much later, he heard the Doctor's words echo in his ears, almost as though they'd been a baptism.

He looked back up at Doctor Frankenstein. "I'm—" he said. And then the words jammed up in his throat, and nothing came out at all.

"You're beautiful," the madman said. He smiled in a way that tried to be proud and loving, but only came out sick and warped.

"I'm a monster." And as he heard the words he knew that it was absolutely true, true and undeniable as his phlegmy breath. After he'd said those words he'd never been able to think of himself by any other name.

"Yes. A monster of greatness, of magnitude. A testament to life!"

It wasn't any use trying to avoid the children. When the Monster saw them running across the hill and down toward him, he almost thought—for just a moment, mind, just a moment; he'd spent too long living with a madman not to be mindful of his own paranoia—the Monster almost thought that the children knew about him and had come to follow him. Scented him, like hounds.

He didn't want to see those children. Seeing them, he knew, would bring home to him the corruptness of his physical nature, rub his nose in his own unnaturalness in the worst possible way. Worse, he didn't want them to see him. In his imagination he could already hear them, innocent little children screaming at the sight of him.

And they did see him. Their path led straight past the gnarled oak he tried to hide behind. If they'd just kept going, maybe none of them would have seen him. But they didn't just keep going; as the first of them ran by the child stumbled on one of the old oak's roots, tumbled head-over-heels and again through the leafy forest floor. When the boy looked up he was staring straight into the Monster's eyes.

No, the Monster thought. *Please, God: No.*

It was just bad luck. The Monster tried to tell himself that, but hard as he tried he couldn't make himself believe it. He probably couldn't have convinced himself of anything, then: he was too busy bracing himself for the sound of the child's scream, for the screams he was sure would come an instant later from the others a footstep behind.

The Monster was so intent on steeling himself for the horror of it that at first it didn't even register that the boy wasn't screaming. The child didn't even look afraid, in fact —just curious, or maybe mystified.

"You're . . ." the boy began, but then his voice just trailed off to silence.

The Monster let the words hang there in the air for all the time he could bear to leave them there, but finally he had to speak.

"A monster. I'm a monster."

The boy shook his head. "No. Not a monster. Something wonderful, something strange—I don't know. But not a monster."

And the Monster felt as though all the blood had drained from him at once, and small hairs rose and stood stiffly erect all over his body, and he wanted to scream but he didn't dare because he couldn't do that, couldn't scream with his bloody-raw throat in front of the children. So he ran, he turned and ran from the children as far and as fast and as hard as he could.

He didn't run in fear or in horror. He ran because there was something in what the boy had said that he could not bear to face.

He kept running, too, for most of the twenty minutes it took to get to the edge of the town.

When the mad scientist was gone, the Monster closed his eyes and tried to sort his thoughts. Even more, to sort his memories; everything the Monster knew about himself was confused and addled and made no sense at all. He was a man, he knew that—but just as certainly he knew that he was a woman, a thirty-five-year-old spinster. Or maybe someone younger—a freckled, red-haired girl just past her teens. And he remembered going to work yesterday, to the job in the big city that he commuted to by car. And remembered waking up earlier that morning in the hospital where he'd gone to die of leukemia six weeks before.

No. None of that was even possible. It was all too contradictory. He needed to focus himself, to trace his steps backward and sort the false memories from the true ones.

He remembered waking, here in this room, not more than an hour ago. That was clear and distinct. Nothing about that memory was impossible or contradictory. But where had he been before then? He had no memory of this place whatever, confused or otherwise. He calmed himself, quieted himself, tried to concentrate.

He could remember . . . being in a car. Yes. There was a harmony about that car, an extra realness. That made it, he was sure, truer than all those other possibilities in his past. And in the car right there beside him was his sister-in-law. They were in the car, and he was driving, and they were on the highway going toward the city. The train station. His wife was there—or she would be, soon. She'd been away for most of a week, down by the shore, taking the holiday they'd meant to take together but that he hadn't been able to get away for. He felt guilty about that. Even now, in the center of all this confusion, he felt guilty about it.

It wasn't the only thing he felt guilty about, either. He tried not to glance at his sister-in-law as he felt himself blush. He hadn't wanted another woman in all the time since he and his wife had married—honestly hadn't felt the first pang of desire. And now, in the week that his wife had been away, her sister had stopped by every night to cook for him, to fuss about the house . . . and that was all she'd done. All *they'd* done. But there was a curve about her waist he'd never noticed before, and her lips always seemed full, and moist, and when the sun was going down it would cast the most incredible sheen across her full, black hair. And . . . damn it, he didn't want to feel the need for her. He didn't want to think the things about her that he did. But he did think them, he did, and he could see from the guilty light in her eyes that she felt all of it as strongly as he did, and maybe more strongly.

Bad enough to find himself wanting another woman—at his age, yet. But his wife's sister . . . ? There was something sick about it, something demented. He clenched his jaw, and shook his head, and turned to steal a glance at the object of his desire. And found her *looking* at him, staring at him, almost. That was more than he could cope with right then, and in the time it would have taken to snap his fingers he lost himself, completely lost track of who he was and what he was and where he was and the fact that he had the car moving along the highway at eighty-five miles an hour. And that time, that tiny smidgen of time—that was all the time it took.

Because of that tiny moment, staring onto the eyes of a woman he couldn't dare to love, he didn't see the BMW swerve into his lane and cut him off. Nor did he see when that car had to brake very suddenly in the traffic that was heavier than it ever ought to have been on a Saturday afternoon. If he'd even managed not to panic when he felt his bumper crunching into the BMW's hood, he could have come out of the accident alive.

But he did panic. He felt the shock of impact through his feet and his hands and his belly digging its way into the steering wheel, and without even thinking he tried to yank the steering wheel around, to pull himself and the car out of a sequence of events from which the laws of physics would allow no escape. And instead of just rear-ending some fool in an expensive German car, he caused his own car to go spinning around and around and around on the fast, crowded highway. At least five times as the car spun he felt it slam into other vehicles. The sixth hit—or maybe it was the seventh—brought his right rear fender into the grill of a moving van. Then, instead of spinning round, the car was turning over—rolling off the road like a log that had been pushed out of the way. He felt the impact of the car's roof pounding itself onto the grassy shoulder of the highway, felt it through his skull and his neck and—

—the memory shifted. And he realized, with a touch of horror, why the memory had such harmony, such resonance for him. For her. For the Monster. The Monster didn't want to think of himself as an it, but for the moment he was tempted to—because the sister-in-law was as much a part of him as the husband was. The Monster remembered the twisted wreckage of her brother-in-law's car, remembered seeing it from inside the wreck, through her own eyes.

The Monster was upside down, and her neck was twisted at a strange angle—an angle that she knew was farther to the right than any neck ever ought to be able to bend, which meant that her neck was broken and she was going to die soon. She tried to raise her hand to her face and brush away the blood that was leaking into her eye, coming from either her nose or her mouth, she wasn't sure. But when she tried to move her hand it was like there wasn't any hand there at all. And she wasn't breathing anymore, either. That meant that her neck wasn't just broken; the cords inside it were already torn loose. And even though she was still alive, watching the crushed, bright-red corpse of her sister's husband, even if she was still alive she was already dead. Her body hadn't completely caught on to the trick of dying yet, but she was on to it.

It occurred to her that she ought to pray, or see her life scroll before her eyes, or make her peace, or something. But she didn't have it in her to do any of those things. Instead she spent the moment she had left thinking about the man who'd spent the last week leering at her. Or, she thought, be fair: trying not to leer. But she'd seen it, watched it all week, and she knew that he was to blame. It was all his fault that she was dead, and even now, remembering, the Monster resented himself for it. Never mind that she had been thinking about him *that* way a long time before. It didn't show when she felt that way—she'd been alive for a good long while and she knew that it couldn't show. It was his fault and he was tempting her and even if she was tempted that was her secret and it was none of his damned business. And the last thing she thought, as the world began to fade to grey all around her, was that she hated that man, hated him, hated his disgusting body—

And then the Monster had awoken, here in this strange place where a madman drooled and sputtered and talked nonsense at him.

And all those shadow memories that writhed and sputtered and shimmered in his head—and lied to him, *lied* to him, telling him impossible things about where he'd been and what he'd done on days that had to be the same—all of those memories were just as real as anything else about him.

And none of them were real at all.

Because none of them were *his*. They were the memories of other people, dead people who lived inside his body like parasites. Or maybe they were him—maybe he was all of those people. When he thought about it it was hard to tell which was the case, or whether they both were true—or whether neither was.

The door of the white-white room creaked open slowly, and the crazy man stepped in. He let the door swing closed behind him, crossed the room, and looked the Monster carefully in the eye.

"How are you feeling?" he asked. There was a slight spray from his lips as he asked the question; the Monster felt tiny droplets of spittle landing on his cheeks. He tried to ignore them, to be polite, but it was hard.

"I'm okay," he said. He looked away, down toward the floor, trying to avoid the spray. "Why are you asking? Are you keeping notes, recording me like an experiment—the way you'd keep track of some frog you were dissecting on the laboratory table?"

He'd expected that to anger the man. Maybe it was foolish to play with the temper of a man who was already half unhinged, but right then the Monster resented the fact of his own being, and it didn't concern him that the crazy man might do something out-of-hand.

But instead of the angry words or shouting that he'd expected, there was only silence—quiet so still and sad that it left the Monster shaken. He looked up and saw that hurt painted all over the madman's face, and he knew he'd said something wrong—and not just wrong, but mean.

"No. I wouldn't probe you that way, not without telling you. Not you. You aren't just an experiment to me—you're important, the way a son would be important. Or a daughter." Dr. Frankenstein sniffled, and rubbed his nose across his sleeve. The Monster pictured himself, for a moment, as a child to the madman, and the idea of it made him feel ill, even if he was also feeling a little sympathy for him. "But it's more than that. Much more. I didn't create you just to satisfy my own needs, but the needs of a world: It's your perspective that's precious. Your very nature. . . . I have a theory. A very interesting theory, one that created the need in me to create you."

Dr. Frankenstein paused, long and hard, as though he was prompting the Monster to press him for the theory's details. But the Monster didn't think he wanted to hear a theory that had made his existence necessary—he wasn't sure, in fact, that he wanted to hear any of the madman's theories. So he let the pause stretch on, and finally Dr. Frankenstein filled it himself.

"I believe," he said, "that all of science's greatest discoveries, all our greatest inventions—all our truest insights!—have come from the hearts of men. Those amazing revelations that we find in the nature of the universe can only be found in those who have those wonders already in their hearts. And is not invention always the product of the bent of the inventor? And insight anchored to the eye of the seer? You, my friend, my child, my wonder, are born of the fusion of hearts. And in that fugueing fire is the truest vision this world will ever behold!"

Getting back to the town was an eerie experience for the Monster. He remembered it clearly, down to the smallest detail. Remembered it through at least five different sets of eyes. And yet he knew that he'd never been to the place in his life.

The town had grown more worn in the years since he'd died so many times. But it hadn't changed, not in any substantial way. He didn't see any changes that weren't just wear and tear until he turned off the town's main road, and passed a house that had once been his.

The door to that house was boarded shut; its windows were bricked over, and the mortar between the bricks was mossy.

The Monster hurried away. There was nothing in the house that drew him; that life was over and done with. That part of him had left behind no unfinished business, no unrighted wrongs. It had left no one behind, in fact—no relatives, no friends. Sometimes the Monster would melancholy over the emptiness of that life. But at other times he was grateful that there was nothing in that part of his past that still called to him.

The way, for instance, the house at the far end of this road called to him—it called to him because the woman who lived inside it was the one who had been both his sister and his wife. Or, at least, she'd been those things to parts of him. He'd been away for so long that there was no way to know that she was still there in that house where they'd lived together for years. But even if there wasn't any way to be sure, the Monster was certain she'd be there. He'd known her for two lifetimes, and that was long enough, he thought, to know things about her that he could never be sure of. And what he knew was that she'd be waiting for him. Not waiting for him the way she'd hold dinner on those evenings that he'd come home late; she'd have gone on with her life. Waiting, maybe, the way she'd wait for the missing final chapter of a novel.

When he got home he didn't go right in. That wouldn't have been right, not now, not after all this time. But he couldn't just walk up to the house and knock on the door, either; the house was home. He'd lived in it for years, visited it for years—owned it for the best years of a lifetime. So the Monster walked around it for a few minutes, trying to figure out what he should do, or whether he should do anything at all.

That was why he saw his wife and sister for the first time in his life through the kitchen window. She was washing dishes, or maybe drying them. She gave a start when she saw him, and he was expecting that. He was a horror, and he knew it, and he expected the people he knew and loved to jump half out of their skins at the sight of him. But she was important to him, and he watched her carefully, and he saw that she wasn't screaming or terrified. Just startled, surprised the way anyone would be to see a stranger staring in through a window.

Even a stranger who wasn't a stranger at all. Especially so.

When her start was over she set down the dish she'd been drying and frowned at him, as though she recognized him but couldn't quite place him. Finally she shook her head and moved away from the window. A moment later she was coming out the back door of their house, still staring at him, watching him intently, as though he were one of the great mysteries of life come to roost on her doorstep.

She walked toward him until she was close enough that the Monster could smell the quiet scent of her perfume, close enough to reach out and touch him. She did that, too, she raised her hand to his face, and her fingertips on his skin—partly probing, partly caressing—were strange and powerfully electric. He wanted to tell her something, but he didn't know what it was he had to say, and when he moved his lips a bloody-scratchy sound came from his throat.

Then she said the name, one of the two names that hurt so desperately to see her, and that was wonderful and beautiful and the most horrible thing that had ever happened to him in any life he'd ever lived, because the name she'd said was the sister's name. And the sister loved her, and needed her, and missed her, but the husband was there, too, and the husband loved his wife as he loved nothing else in the world, and he'd looked at her and tried to speak to her and she'd seen someone else in his eyes. And all of that was there on his face, and he knew it: joy and recognition and response, and the husband's wound that would never heal—a wound so bad that he wanted to curl up and die right then, *right then.*

And she saw all of that, the woman who was his sister and his wife did. When she saw her sister's joy flicker on the Monster's face she looked for a moment both puzzled and amazed, as though she were witness to a peculiar miracle. But then she saw her husband's devastation painted on his same features, and the muscles of her jaw went slack, and she said the *other* name, the husband's name. And the Monster, all broken and unhinged inside, nodded to answer her before he had a chance to give the act a moment's thought.

That was the worst thing he could have done. When she'd recognized him, he knew, she'd been off-balance and only guessing that there was someone she knew inside him. And because she was only asking questions in the dark it couldn't have sunk through to her that her husband and her sister both stood before her in one body.

She screamed, then. The Monster knew that woman well—maybe better than he'd ever known another soul—and because he knew her so well he could tell that she wasn't screaming at the horribleness of his nature but at the horror that that nature meant to her. It still hurt him powerfully to see the terror on her face, and the sound of her scream hurt him too. When she raised her fists and started pounding out her anger on his chest it hurt him worst of all, though the blows themselves didn't do his body any damage.

He stood through it all, in spite of the pain, because he felt he had an obligation to. He did his best to honor that obligation; it wasn't until she broke down sobbing, ran back into the house, and slammed the door behind her that he even let himself cry. When she was finally gone he wandered away from the house, wailing like a banshee.

He managed to keep himself going until he reached the small playground at the far edge of the town. He sat himself on a bench in that playground, and he stayed there—staring into the dirt and not moving a muscle that he didn't need to breathe—for hours.

Dr. Frankenstein had been right—the Monster *did* have a special insight. During the five years that he'd spent in the castle, the madman had heaped whole libraries full of books in front of the Monster, and because there was no other thing that could demand the Monster's attention, he'd taken the reading of those books to heart. The remarkable part was that even though the Monster was in essence only a student, often as he read—very often—he would strike on solutions to the problems that the books posed. Solutions that the authors had never intended, nor even conceived of. The Monster knew, as that happened to him again and again, that there was something to Dr. Frankenstein's "theory"; that there had to be some special magic in his segmented heart. He knew, certainly, that he wasn't any true genius; his mind was certainly no better than it had ever been in any of his lives. Only different.

And bothered.

The real reason he kept himself buried in books wasn't

boredom or the need to learn or any of those things. He felt bad for the madman. Sometimes he felt ashamed for him, or even embarrassed. But he wouldn't have pressed himself into study just because he'd been told to. No. He read because he had to, because there was something from his past that haunted him. And when he concentrated hard enough on the work in front of him, his heart was easier to ignore.

He was reading that afternoon when Dr. Frankenstein finally said the thing that pushed the Monster out of his five-year daze—sitting in the sun in a lounge chair on one of the castle's terraces, reading a fat, heavy book on the nature of germ plasm. The madman stepped out onto the balcony through the open doorway, and then he stopped. For a long while he just stood there on the grey, sunny stone, staring at the Monster, not saying a word. The Monster could feel the weight in the air from whatever it was the man wanted to say, and he didn't like the touch of it; he kept reading, and let the man hold his peace. He stood there for five minutes, at least, before he managed to screw up the nerve to get the words through his lips.

"Monster," he said. It'd taken the man a long while to get used to the idea that the Monster could think of himself by no other name, but once he'd understood he'd respected the Monster's wishes, and called him by the name he'd chosen for himself. "I love you, Monster, you know that. Don't you?"

The Monster knew it, all right. But he'd never had to deal with the idea out loud before, and it made him uncomfortable as sin. He nodded, partly to avoid having to say the words himself, partly to answer the question. Nodding only made him more uncomfortable; he tried to imagine that he was someplace else, anywhere, any where else in the world but right there and right then.

"Well, what I need to know is, is this: do you love me, Monster?" A thin line of saliva descended toward his lapel from the corner of his mouth. "I mean: do *you* love *me*?"

The Monster tried to make himself quiet inside. He really did. But inside his head there was rushing and roaring and horrible things, and he was afraid—he was a Monster and he knew it and he was afraid—that he'd do something monstrous, something monstrous and horrible and violent and evil.

He didn't know the answer to the madman's question. And he didn't know why the question did to him what it had. He didn't think he wanted to know either one of those things.

So he set his book, gently as he could, on the lounge table beside him. And got up. And walked away, and hid himself in the deepest, darkest dungeon that the castle had.

He stayed holed up in the dungeon all morning and into the early afternoon, licking wounds he didn't understand—and licking wounds he didn't even truly know he had. As he sat there, curled up in the dusty corner of an ersatz cell, his mind wandered. Wandered, for the first time in his five years, around and toward . . . not Dr. Frankenstein, or his sad, drooling love, but toward those pieces of the Monster's past that for all of those five years he'd been avoiding. And the thing he thought about most of all was that woman he loved twice over. The woman who'd been wife to one piece of him, and sister to another.

He loved that woman. Loved her like . . . like the whole damned world, and every star and every other thing he could imagine, all together at once. Loved her, and missed her, and needed her, and. . . .

But just as he thought those things, felt those things, he knew that she was a person and a life that was behind him. A love of another life; *the* lover of another life. And he knew that even if he could find her, tell her who he was and love her—if she *could* love a monster—all he'd be doing would be denying himself and what he'd become. A monster couldn't love a woman, not as a sister or as a wife, and if he could it wouldn't be right, anyway. And too: he wasn't the man who'd loved her. Nor the woman. Not even if he held all that was left of their lives inside him. His heart knew that the worst thing he could do to himself was pretend that he was somebody else.

Or, at least, that's what he tried to tell himself as he crept out of the dungeon, into the forest. Toward town. And he knew, as he hiked, that all of his reservations were founded. Tellingly so. Still: even though he tried with all his heart to turn away, back toward the castle, all he could do was continue. In his mind's eye he saw Dr. Frankenstein, drooling at him brokenly, and his heart told him that he was betraying the one real love he had in this life. But that didn't stop him, either.

The road that the playground was on was the town's main thoroughfare, and though it was empty because it was unpopular with the town's children, it was in plain sight of what traffic the town had. All that afternoon as the Monster sat staring at the grass, the people who passed on foot and in car *saw* him, and they *watched* him. Twice police cars cruised by him slowly. The Monster's appearance was a suspicious thing to the police, but there was no crime that the Monster committed by sitting on a bench and staring at the grass, and therefore there was no reason that the police could or would do anything to or about him. The Monster was too deep in the fog of grieving to notice any of them.

But as the hours went by that fog grew thinner and thinner, and eventually it burned away altogether. The grief itself was still full and brimming in his heart, but the world, just as the world always does, brought itself back to him. On toward early evening a crowd gathered on the sidewalk that ran between the playground and the street, and the mass of them—it looked to the Monster's eye as though half the town were there—stood there for a long time, just watching him quietly.

The Monster didn't ignore them, exactly, because that would have been rude, but he didn't pay the crowd a whole lot of attention, either. It occurred to him that they might be like the lynch mobs of villagers from the Frankenstein movies, gathering to destroy him. But he didn't have the heart to cope with that thought, not even if it was true. He needed quiet to cope with his grief, and he made that quiet for himself, in spite of the fact that he felt like some animal in a zoo.

Half an hour after the sun had finished setting, the woman who'd been the Monster's sister and his wife pushed her way through the crowd, walked across the playground, and sat down on the bench beside him. When she'd been there for a while she reached over and took his hand, and held it in her warm, soft fingers.

"I heard on the radio that you were here," she said.

The Monster nodded. It didn't please him that news of his whereabouts was on the radio, but it didn't surprise him, exactly, either. Either way, he didn't have much to say about it.

They sat there that way for half an hour, with everybody and his brother watching them, and finally she stood up, still holding his hand, and asked him to come home with her.

The Monster nodded, and he followed her. When they got to the edge of the park the crowd parted for them like a Biblical sea, and she led him back to the house where they'd lived for years as man and wife. Once they were home she fixed a rich dinner of stewed lamb and potatoes and onions. And that night they slept together—though sleeping was all they did, because even though they'd spent lifetimes together they were still at the same time very new to each other.

And that could have been the end of it, right there. If they'd put their hearts and minds to it they could have lived happily together forever afterward. But even if that would have been wonderful, it wouldn't have been right, or true, or even honest. The Monster realized that as he dreamed that night, lying next to her, warm and comfortable under the clean, smooth sheets.

The clearness of the vision was still in the Monster's mind when he woke that morning, half an hour before dawn. He still felt hollow inside from what the dream pressed home to him: how he *wasn't* the man who had loved this woman for all of his adult life. Nor was he the woman who had loved her sister as dearly as any woman has ever loved another. He was another person altogether —his own life, his own wants and hopes and needs. His own mark to make on the face of the world, no matter that he was made from bits and pieces of the lives of others. As he sat there, staring out at the cool blue-grey morning sky with the warm body of a woman he loved beside him, he knew that he couldn't stay. Not if he was ever to have any hope of being true to himself. No matter how wonderful it would be.

She was awake beside him, now—not yet upright, but wide awake. He looked over at her, and he started to speak, but then he saw in her eyes that she already knew what he was planning.

"I shouldn't have come back," he said. It wasn't what he'd meant to say. "I shouldn't be here."

She smiled at him, a little sad. "But you did that," she said. "You are." She took his hand and she squeezed it.

"It isn't me who loves you." The Monster winced and shook his head; that wasn't the right thing to say, and when he heard the words out loud they sounded cruel and mean. "I love you, but . . . I wasn't the one you loved. It wasn't me. It isn't." And winced again, because he felt as though he'd lied.

She squeezed his hand, and lifted herself up off the bed to kiss his cheek. "It doesn't matter who you are," she told him. "That's really not the point."

The Monster didn't know what to say to that; he couldn't parse the sense of it. So he nodded and he said he had to go, and she smiled at him understandingly. Then he got up and left that house forever, to return to the castle and the madman and his destiny. The madman welcomed him home with open arms and fat tears in his eyes, and the Monster hugged him back, and his heart knew that he loved that man, and that he'd missed him—and he told Dr. Frankenstein so.

But nowadays, when it's quiet and all the problems that lie at hand are solved (which is more often than is comfortable), the Monster sometimes thinks of that woman. Not painfully, these days. A little sad maybe—and not comprehending at all. He doesn't know that back in that house, in that town, she waits for him to this day. Her life goes on, pleasantly and well, but in her way, she waits. Eventually, though, when the moments get long enough, the Monster will realize that she does.

The Edge
of the World

MICHAEL SWANWICK

THE DAY that Donna and Piggy and Russ went to see the Edge of the World was a hot one. They were sitting on the curb by the gas station that noontime, sharing a Coke and watching the big Starlifters lumber up into the air, one by one, out of Toldenarba AFB. The sky rumbled with their passing. There'd been an incident in the Persian Gulf, and half the American forces in the Twilight Emirates were on alert.

"My old man says when the Big One goes up, the base will be the first to go," Piggy said speculatively. "Treaties won't allow us to defend it. One bomber comes in high and *whaboom*"—he made soft nuclear explosion noises—"it's all gone." He was wearing camouflage pants and a khaki T-shirt with an iron-on reading: KILL 'EM ALL AND LET GOD SORT 'EM OUT. Donna watched as he took off his glasses to polish them on his shirt. His face went slack and vacant, then livened as he put them back on again, as if he were playing with a mask.

"You should be so lucky," Donna said. "Mrs. Khashoggi is still going to want that paper done on Monday morning, Armageddon or not."

"Yeah, can you believe her?" Piggy said. "That weird accent! And all that memorization! Cut me some slack. I mean, who cares whether Ackronnion was part of the Mezentian Dynasty?"

"You ought to care, dipshit," Russ said. "Local history's the only decent class the school's got." Russ was the smartest boy Donna had ever met, never mind the fact that he was flunking out. He had soulful eyes and a radical haircut, short on the sides with a dyed-blond punklock down the back of his neck. "Man, I opened the *Excerpts from Epics* text that first night, thinking it was going to be the same old bullshit, and I stayed up 'til dawn. Got to school without a wink of sleep, but I'd managed to read every last word. This is one weird part of the world; its history is full of dragons and magic and all kinds of weird monsters. Do you realize that in the eighteenth century three members of the British legation were eaten by demons? That's in the historical record!"

Russ was an enigma to Donna. The first time they'd met, hanging with the misfits at an American School dance, he'd tried to put a hand down her pants, and she'd slugged him good, almost breaking his nose. She could still hear his surprised laughter as blood ran down his chin. They'd been friends ever since. Only there were limits to friendship, and now she was waiting for him to make his move and hoping he'd get down to it before her father was rotated out.

In Japan she'd known a girl who had taken a razor blade and carved her boyfriend's name in the palm of her hand. How could she do that, Donna had wanted to know? Her friend had shrugged, said, "As long as it gets me noticed." It wasn't until Russ that Donna understood.

"Strange country," Russ said dreamily. "The sky beyond the Edge is supposed to be full of demons and serpents and shit. They say that if you stare into it long enough, you'll go mad."

They all three looked at one another.

"Well, hell," Piggy said. "What are we waiting for?"

The Edge of the World lay beyond the railroad tracks. They bicycled through the American enclave into the old native quarter. The streets were narrow here, the sideyards crammed with broken trucks, rusted-out buses, even yachts up in cradles with staved-in sides. Garage doors were black mouths hissing and spitting welding sparks, throbbing to the hammered sound of worked metal. They hid their bikes in a patch of scrub apricot trees where the railroad crossed the industrial canal and hiked across.

Time had altered the character of the city where it bordered the Edge. Gone were the archers in their towers, vigilant against a threat that never came. Gone were the rose quartz palaces with their thousand windows, not a one of which overlooked the Edge. The battlements where blind musicians once piped up the dawn now survived only in Mrs. Khashoggi's texts. Where they had been was now a drear line of weary factory buildings, their lower windows cinderblocked or bricked up and those beyond reach of vandals' stones painted over in patchwork squares of gray and faded blue.

A steam whistle sounded and lines of factory workers shambled back inside, brown men in chinos and white shirts, Syrian and Lebanese laborers imported to do work no native Toldenarban would touch. A shredded net waved forlornly from a basketball hoop set up by the loading dock.

There was a section of hurricane fence down. They scrambled through.

As they cut across the grounds, a loud whine arose from within the factory building. Down the way another plant lifted its voice in a solid wham-wham-wham as rhythmic and unrelenting as a headache. One by one the factories shook themselves from their midday drowse and went back to work. "Why do they locate these things along the Edge?" Donna asked.

"It's so they can dump their chemical waste over the Edge," Russ explained. "These were all erected before the Emir nationalized the culverts that the Russian Protectorate built."

Behind the factory was a chest-high concrete wall, rough-edged and pebbly with the slow erosion of cement. Weeds grew in clumps at its foot. Beyond was nothing but sky.

Piggy ran ahead and spat over the Edge. "Hey, remember what Nixon said when he came here? *It is indeed a long way down.* What a guy!"

Donna leaned against the wall. A film of haze tinted the sky gray, intensifying at the focal point to dirty brown, as if

a dead spot were burned into the center of her vision.
When she looked down, her eyes kept grabbing for ground
and finding more sky. There were a few wispy clouds in
the distance and nothing more. No serpents coiled in
the air. She should have felt disappointed but, really, she
hadn't expected better. This was of a piece with all the
natural wonders she had ever seen, the waterfalls, geysers
and scenic vistas that inevitably included power lines, railings and parking lots absent from the postcards. Russ was
staring intently ahead, hawklike, frowning. His jaw
worked slightly, and she wondered what he saw.

"Hey, look what I found!" Piggy whooped. "It's a stairway!"

They joined him at the top of an institutional-looking
concrete and iron stairway. It zigzagged down the cliff
toward an infinitely distant and nonexistent Below, dwindling into hazy blue. Quietly, as if he'd impressed himself,
Piggy said, "What do you suppose is down there?"

"Only one way to find out, isn't there?" Russ said.

Russ went first, then Piggy, then Donna, the steps ringing dully under their feet. Graffiti covered the rocks, worn
spraypaint letters in yellow and black and red scrawled
one over the other and faded by time and weather into
mutual unreadability, and on the iron railings, words and
arrows and triangles had been markered onto or dug into
the paint with knife or nail: JURGEN BIN SCHEISSKOPF.
MOTLEY CRUE. DEATH TO SATAN AMERICA IMPERIALIST.
Seventeen steps down, the first landing was filthy with
broken brown glass, bits of crumbled concrete, cigarette
butts, soggy, half-melted cardboard. The stairway folded
back on itself and they followed it down.

"You ever had *fugu*?" Piggy asked. Without waiting for
an answer, he said, "It's Japanese poisonous blowfish. It has
to be prepared very carefully—they license the chefs—
and even so, several people die every year. It's considered
a great delicacy."

"Nothing tastes that good," Russ said.

"It's not the flavor," Piggy said enthusiastically. "It's
the poison. Properly prepared, see, there's a very small
amount left in the sashimi and you get a threshold dose.
Your lips and the tips of your fingers turn cold. Numb.

That's how you know you're having the real thing. That's how you know you're living right on the edge."

"I'm already living on the edge," Russ said. He looked startled when Piggy laughed.

A fat moon floated in the sky, pale as a disk of ice melting in blue water. It bounced after them as they descended, kicking aside loose soda bottles in styrofoam sleeves, crushed Marlboro boxes, a scattering of carbonized spark plugs. On one landing they found a crumpled shopping cart, and Piggy had to muscle it over the railing and watch it fall. "Sure is a lot of crap here," he observed. The landing smelled faintly of urine.

"It'll get better farther down," Russ said. "We're still near the top, where people can come to get drunk after work." He pushed on down. Far to one side they could see the brown flow from the industrial canal where it spilled into space, widening and then slowly dispersing into rainbowed mist, distance glamoring it beauty.

"How far are we planning to go?" Donna asked apprehensively.

"Don't be a weak sister," Piggy sneered. Russ said nothing.

The deeper they went, the shabbier the stairway grew, and the spottier its maintenance. Pipes were missing from the railing. Where patches of paint had fallen away the bolts anchoring the stair to the rock were walnut-sized lumps of rust.

Needle-clawed marsupials chittered warningly from niches in the rock as they passed. Tufts of grass and moth-white gentians grew in the loess-filled cracks.

Hours passed. Donna's feet and calves and the small of her back grew increasingly sore, but she refused to be the one to complain. By degrees she stopped looking over the side and out into the sky, and stared instead at her feet flashing in and out of sight while one hand went slap-grab-tug on the rail. She felt sweaty and miserable.

Back home she had a half-finished paper on the Three Days Incident of March, 1810, when the French Occupation, by order of Napoleon himself, had fired cannonade after cannonade over the Edge into nothingness. They had hoped to make rainstorms of devastating force that would lash and destroy their enemies, and created instead only a gunpowder haze, history's first great failure in weather control. This descent was equally futile, Donna thought, an endless and wearying exercise in nothing. Just the same as the rest of her life. Every time her father was reposted, she had resolved to change, to be somebody different this time around, whatever the price, even if—no, especially if—it meant playacting something she was not. Last year in Germany when she'd gone out with that local boy with the Alfa Romeo and instead of jerking him off had used her mouth, she had thought: Everything's going to be different now. But no.

Nothing ever changed.

"Heads up!" Russ said. "There's some steps missing here!" He leaped, and the landing gonged hollowly under his sneakers. Then again as Piggy jumped after.

Donna hesitated. There were five steps gone and a drop of twenty feet before the stairway cut back beneath itself. The cliff bulged outward here, and if she slipped she'd probably miss the stairs altogether.

She felt the rock draw away from her to either side, and was suddenly aware that she was connected to the world by the merest speck of matter, barely enough to anchor her feet. The sky wrapped itself about her, extending to infinity, depthless and absolute. She could extend her arms and fall into it forever. What would happen to her then, she wondered. Would she die of thirst and starvation, or would the speed of her fall grow so great that the oxygen would be sucked from her lungs, leaving her to strangle in a sea of air? "Come on Donna!" Piggy shouted up at her. "Don't be a pussy!"

"Russ—" she said quaveringly.

But Russ wasn't looking her way. He was frowning downward, anxious to be going. "Don't push the lady," he said. "We can go on by ourselves."

Donna choked with anger and hurt and desperation all at once. She took a deep breath and, heart scudding, leaped. Sky and rock wheeled over her head. For an instant she was floating, falling, totally lost and filled with a panicky awareness that she was about to die. Then she crashed onto the landing. It hurt like hell, and at first she feared she'd pulled an ankle. Piggy grabbed her shoulders and rubbed the side of her head with his knuckles. "I knew you could do it, you wimp."

Donna knocked away his arm. "Okay, wise-ass. How are you expecting to get us back up?"

The smile disappeared from Piggy's face. His mouth opened, closed. His head jerked fearfully upward. An acrobat could leap across, grab the step and flip up without any trouble at all. "I— I mean, I—"

"Don't worry about it," Russ said impatiently. "We'll think of something." He started down again.

It wasn't natural, Donna realized, his attitude. There was something obsessive about his desire to descend the stairway. It was like the time he'd brought his father's revolver to school along with a story about playing Russian roulette that morning before breakfast. "Three times!" he'd said proudly.

He'd had that same crazy look on him, and she hadn't the slightest notion then or now how she could help him.

Russ walked like an automaton, wordlessly, tirelessly, never hurrying up or slowing down. Donna followed in concerned silence, while Piggy scurried between them, chattering like somebody's pet Pekingese. This struck Donna as so apt as to be almost allegorical: the two of them together yet alone, the distance between filled with noise. She thought of this distance, this silence, as the sun passed behind the cliff and the afternoon heat lost its edge.

The stairs changed to cement-jacketed brick with small buttresses cut into the rock. There was a pile of stems and cherry pits on one landing, and the railing above them was white with bird droppings. Piggy leaned over the rail and said, "Hey, I can see seagulls down there. Flying around."

"Where?" Russ leaned over the railing, then said scornfully, "Those are pigeons. The Ghazoddis used to release them for rifle practice."

As Piggy turned to follow Russ down again, Donna caught a glimpse into his eyes, liquid and trembling with helplessness and despair. She'd seen that fear in him only once before, months ago when she'd stopped by his house on the way to school, just after the Emir's assassination.

The living room windows were draped and the room seemed unnaturally gloomy after being out in the morning sun. Blue television light flickered over shelves of shadowy ceramic figurines: Dresden milkmaids, Chantilly Chinamen, Meissen pug-dogs connected by a gold chain held in their champed jaws, naked Delft nymphs dancing.

Piggy's mother sat in a limp dressing gown, hair unbrushed, watching the funeral. She held a cup of oily-looking coffee in one hand. Donna was surprised to see her up so early. Everyone said that she had a bad problem with alcohol, that even by service wife standards she was out of control.

"Look at them," Piggy's mother said. On the screen were solemn processions of camels and Cadillacs, sheikhs in jellaba, keffigeh and mirrorshades, European dignitaries with wives in tasteful gray Parisian fashions. "They've got their nerve."

"Where did you put my lunch?" Piggy said loudly from the kitchen.

"Making fun of the Kennedys like that!" The Emir's youngest son, no more than four years old, salaamed his father's casket as it passed before him. "That kid's bad enough, but you should see the mother, crying as if her heart were broken. It's enough to turn your stomach. If I were Jackie, I'd—"

Donna and Piggy and Russ had gone bowling the night the Emir was shot. This was out in the ruck of cheap joints that surrounded the base, catering almost exclusively to servicemen. When the Muzak piped through overhead speakers was interrupted for the news bulletin, everyone had stood up and cheered. *Up we go,* someone had begun singing, and the rest had joined in, *into the wild blue yonder.* . . . Donna had felt so sick with fear and disgust she had thrown up in the parking lot. "I don't think they're making fun of anyone," Donna said. "They're just—"

"Don't talk to her!" The refrigerator door slammed shut. A cupboard door slammed open.

Piggy's mother smiled bitterly. "This is exactly what you'd expect from these ragheads. Pretending they're white people, deliberately mocking their betters. Filthy brown animals."

"*Mother!* Where is my fucking lunch?"

She looked at him then, jaw tightening. "Don't you use that kind of language on me, young man."

"All right!" Piggy shouted. "All right, I'm going to school without lunch! Shows how much you care!"

He turned to Donna and in the instant before he

grabbed her wrist and dragged her out of the house, Donna could no longer hear the words, could only see that universe of baffled futility haunting Piggy's eyes. That same look she glimpsed today.

The railings were wooden now, half the posts rotting at their bases, with an occasional plank missing, wrenched off and thrown over the side by previous visitors. Donna's knees buckled and she stumbled, almost lurching into the rock. "I have to stop," she said, hating herself for it. "I cannot go one more step."

Piggy immediately collapsed on the landing. Russ hesitated, then climbed up to join them. They three sat staring out into nothing, legs over the Edge, arms clutching the rail.

Piggy found a Pepsi can, logo in flowing Arabic, among the rubble. He held it in his left hand and began sticking holes in it with his butterfly knife, again and again, cackling like a demented sex criminal. "Exterminate the brutes!" he said happily. Then, with absolutely no transition he asked, "How are we ever going to get back up?" so dolorously Donna had to bite back her laughter.

"Look, I just want to go on down a little bit more," Russ said.

"Why?" Piggy sounded petulant.

"So I can get down enough to get away from this garbage." He gestured at the cigarette butts, the broken brown glass, sparser than above but still there. "Just a little further, okay guys?" There was an edge to his voice, and under that the faintest hint of a plea. Donna felt helpless before those eyes. She wished they were alone, so she could ask him what was wrong.

Donna doubted that Russ himself knew what he expected to find down below. Did he think that if he went down far enough, he'd never have to climb back? She remembered the time in Mr. Herriman's algebra class when a sudden tension in the air had made her glance across the room at Russ, and he was, with great concentration, tearing the pages out of his math text and dropping them one by one on the floor. He'd taken a five-day suspension for that, and Donna had never found out what it was all about. But there was a kind of glorious arrogance to the act; Russ had been born out of time. He really should have been a medieval prince, a Medici or one of the Sabakan pretenders.

"Okay," Donna said, and Piggy of course had to go along.

Seven flights farther down the modern stairs came to an end. The wooden railing of the last short, septambic flight had been torn off entire, and laid across the steps. They had to step carefully between the uprights and the rails. But when they stood at the absolute bottom, they saw that there were stairs beyond the final landing, steps that had been cut into the stone itself. They were curving sway-backed things that millennia of rain and foot traffic had worn so uneven they were almost unpassable.

Piggy groaned. "Man, you *can't* expect us to go down that thing."

"Nobody's asking you," Russ said.

They descended the old stairway backwards and on all fours. The wind breezed up, hitting them with the force of an expected shove first to one side and then the other. There were times when Donna was so frightened she thought she was going to freeze up and never move again. But at last the stone broadened and became a wide, even ledge, with caves leading back into the rock.

The cliff face here was green-white with lichen, and had in ancient times been laboriously smoothed and carved. Between each cave (their mouths alone left in a natural state, unaltered) were heavy-thighed women— goddesses, perhaps, or demons or sacred dancers—their breasts and faces chipped away by the image-hating fol- lowers of the Prophet at a time when Mohammed yet lived. Their hands held loops of vines in which were entan- gled moons, cycling from new through waxing quarter and gibbous to full and then back through gibbous and waning quarter to dark. Piggy was gasping, his face bright with sweat, but he kept up his blustery front. "What the fuck is all this shit, man?"

"It was a monastery," Russ said. He walked along the ledge dazedly, a wondering half smile on his lips. "I read about this." He stopped at a turquoise automobile door someone had flung over the Edge to be caught and tossed by fluke winds, the only piece of trash that had made it down this far. "Give me a hand."

He and Piggy lifted the door, swung it back and forth three times to build up momentum, then lofted it over the lip of the rock. They all three lay down on their stomachs to watch it fall away, turning end over end and seeming finally to flicker as it dwindled smaller and smaller, still falling. At last it shrank below the threshold of visibility and became one of a number of shifting motes in the downbelow, part of the slow, mazy movement of dead blood cells in the eyes' vitreous humors. Donna turned over on her back, drew her head back from the rim, stared upward. The cliff seemed to be slowly tumbling forward, all the world inexorably, dizzyingly leaning down to crush her.

"Let's go explore the caves," Piggy suggested.

They were empty. The interiors of the caves extended no more than thirty feet into the rock, but they had all been elaborately worked, arched ceilings carved with thousands of *faux tesserae*, walls adorned with bas-relief pillars. Between the pillars the walls were taken up with long shelves carved into the stone. No artifacts remained, not so much as a potsherd or a splinter of bone. Piggy shone his pocket flash into every shadowy niche. "Somebody's been here before us and taken everything," he said.

"The Historic Registry people, probably." Russ ran a hand over one shelf. It was the perfect depth and height for a line of three-pound coffee cans. "This is where they stowed the skulls. When a monk grew so spiritually developed he no longer needed the crutch of physical existence, his fellows would render the flesh from his bones and enshrine his skull. They poured wax in the sockets, then pushed in opals while it was still warm. They slept beneath the faintly gleaming eyes of their superiors."

When they emerged it was twilight, the first stars appearing from behind a sky fading from blue to purple. Donna looked down on the moon. It was as big as a plate, full and bright. The rilles, dry seas, and mountain chains were preternaturally distinct. Somewhere in the middle was Tranquility Base, where Neil Armstrong had planted the American flag.

"Jeez, it's late," Donna said. "If we don't start home soon, my mom is going to have a cow."

"We still haven't figured a way to get back up," Piggy reminded her. Then, "We'll probably have to stay here.

Learn to eat owls and grow crops sideways on the cliff face. Start our own civilization. Our only serious problem is the imbalance of sexes, but even that's not insurmountable." He put an arm around Donna's shoulders, grabbed at her breast. "You'd pull the train for us, wouldn't you, Donna?"

Angrily she pushed him away and said, "You keep a clean mouth! I'm so tired of your juvenile talk and behavior."

"Hey, calm down, it's cool." That panicky look was back in his eyes, the forced knowledge that he was not in control, could never be in control, that there was no such thing as control. He smiled weakly, placatingly.

"No, it is not. It is most emphatically not 'cool.'" Suddenly she was white and shaking with fury. Piggy was a spoiler. His simple presence ruined any chance she might have had to talk with Russ, find out just what was bugging him, get him to finally, really notice her. "I am sick of having to deal with your immaturity, your filthy language, and your crude behavior."

Piggy turned pink and began stuttering.

Russ reached a hand into his pocket, pulled out a chunk of foil-wrapped hash, and a native tin pipe with a carved coral bowl. The kind of thing the local beggar kids sold for twenty-nine cents. "Anybody want to get stoned?" he asked suavely.

"You bastard!" Piggy laughed. "You told me you were out!"

Russ shrugged. "I lied." He lit the pipe carefully, drew in, passed it to Donna. She took it from his fingers, felt how cold they were to her touch, looked up over the pipe and saw his face, thin and ascetic, eyelids closed, pale and Christlike through the blue smoke. She loved him intensely in that instant and wished she could sacrifice herself for his happiness. The pipe's stem was overwarm, almost hot, between her lips. She drew in deep.

The smoke was raspy in her throat, then tight and swirling in her lungs. It shot up into her head, filled it with buzzing harmonics: the air, the sky, the rock behind her back all buzzing, ballooning her skull outward in a visionary rush that forced wide-open first her eyes and then her mouth. She choked and spasmodically coughed. More smoke than she could imagine possibly holding in her lungs gushed out into the universe.

"Hey, watch that pipe!" Piggy snatched it from her distant fingers. They tingled with pinpricks of pain like tiny stars in the darkness of her flesh. "You were spilling the hash!" The evening light was abuzz with energy, the sky swarming up into her eyes. Staring out into the darkening air, the moon rising below her and the stars as close and friendly as those in a children's book illustration, she felt at peace, detached from worldly cares. "Tell us about the monastery, Russ," she said, in the same voice she might have used a decade before to ask her father for a story.

"Yeah, tell us about the monastery, Uncle Russ," Piggy said, but with jeering undertones. Piggy was always sucking up to Russ, but there was tension there too, and his sarcastic little challenges were far from rare. It was classic beta male jealousy, straight out of Primate Psychology 101.

"It's very old," Russ said. "Before the Sufis, before Mohammed, even before the Zoroastrians crossed the gulf, the native mystics would renounce the world and go to live in cliffs on the Edge of the World. They cut the steps down, and once down, they never went back up again."

"How did they eat then?" Piggy asked skeptically.

"They wished their food into existence. No, really! It was all in their creation myth: In the beginning all was Chaos and Desire. The world was brought out of Chaos—by which they meant unformed matter—by Desire, or Will. It gets a little inconsistent after that, because it wasn't really a religion, but more like a system of magic. They believed that the world wasn't complete yet, that for some complicated reason it could never be complete. So there's still traces of the old Chaos lingering just beyond the Edge, and it can be tapped by those who desire it strongly enough, if they have distanced themselves from the things of the world. These mystics used to come down here to meditate against the moon and work miracles.

"This wasn't sophisticated stuff like the Tantric monks in Tibet or anything, remember. It was like a primitive form of animism, a way to force the universe to give you what you wanted. So the holy men would come down here and they'd wish for . . . like riches, you know? Filigreed silver goblets with rubies, mounds of moonstones, elfinbone daggers sharper than Damascene steel. Only once they got them they weren't supposed to want them. They'd just throw them over the Edge. There were these monasteries all along the cliffs. The farther from the world they were, the more spiritually advanced."

"So what happened to the monks?"

"There was a king— Althazar? I forget his name. He was this real greedhead, started sending his tax collectors down to gather up everything the monks brought into existence. Must've figured, hey, the monks weren't using them. Which as it turned out was like a real major blasphemy, and the monks got pissed. The boss mystics, all the real spiritual heavies, got together for this big confab. Nobody knows how. There's one of the classics claims they could run sideways on the cliff just like it was the ground, but I don't know. Doesn't matter. So one night they all of them, every monk in the world, meditated at the same time. They chanted together, saying, it is not enough that Althazar should die, for he has blasphemed. He must suffer a doom such as has been visited on no man before. He must be unmade, uncreated, reduced to less than has ever been. And they prayed that there be no such king as Althazar, that his life and history be unmade, so that there never had been such king as Althazar.

"And he was no more.

"But so great was their yearning for oblivion that when Althazar ceased to be, his history and family as well, they were left feeling embittered and did not know why. And not knowing why, their hatred turned upon themselves, and their wish for destruction, and they too all of a single night, ceased to be." He fell silent.

At last Piggy said, "You believe that crap?" Then, when there was no answer, "It's none of it true, man! Got that? There's no magic, and there never was." Donna could see that he was really angry, threatened on some primal level by the possibility that someone he respected could even begin to believe in magic. His face got pink, the way it always did when he lost control.

"No, it's all bullshit," Russ said bitterly. "Like everything else."

They passed the pipe around again. Then Donna leaned back, stared straight out, and said, "If I could wish for anything, you know what I'd wish for?"

"Bigger tits?"

She was so weary now, so pleasantly washed out, that it

was easy to ignore Piggy. "I'd wish I knew what the situation was."

"What situation?" Piggy asked. Donna was feeling langorous, not at all eager to explain herself, and she waved away the question. But he persisted. "What situation?"

"Any situation. I mean, all the time, I find myself talking with people and I don't know what's really going on. What games they're playing. Why they're acting the way they are. I wish I knew what the situation was."

The moon floated before her, big and fat and round as a griffin's egg, shining with power. She could feel that power washing through her, the background radiation of decayed chaos spread across the sky at a uniform three degrees Kelvin. Even now, spent and respent, a coin fingered and thinned to the worn edge of nonexistence, there was power out there, enough to flatten planets.

Staring out at that great fat boojum snark of a moon, she felt the flow of potential worlds, and within the cold silver disk of that jester's skull, rank with magic, sensed the invisible presence of Russ's primitive monks, men whose minds were nowhere near comprehensible to her, yet vibrated with power, existing as matrices of patterned stress, no more actual than Donald Duck, but no less powerful either. She was caught in a waking fantasy, in which the sky was full of power and all of it accessible to her. Monks sat empty-handed over their wishing bowls, separated from her by the least fictions of time and reality. For an eternal instant all possibilities fanned out to either side, equally valid, no one more real than any other. Then the world turned under her, and her brain shifted back to realtime.

"Mo," Piggy said, "I just wish I knew how to get back up the stairs."

They were silent for a moment. Then it occurred to Donna that here was the perfect opportunity to find out what was bugging Russ. If she asked cautiously enough, if the question hit him just right, if she were just plain lucky, he might tell her everything. She cleared her throat. "Russ? What do you wish?"

In the bleakest voice imaginable, Russ said, "I wish I'd never been born."

She turned to ask him why, and he wasn't there.

"Hey," Donna said. "Where'd Russ go?"

Piggy looked at her oddly. "Who's Russ?"

It was a long trip back up. They carried the length of wooden railing between them, and every now and then Piggy said, "Hey, wasn't this a great idea of mine? This'll make a swell ladder."

"Yeah, great," Donna would say, because he got mad when she didn't respond. He got mad, too, whenever she started to cry, but there wasn't anything she could do about that. She couldn't even explain why she was crying, because in all the world—of all his friends, acquaintances, teachers, even his parents—she was the only one who remembered that Russ had ever existed.

The horrible thing was that she had no specific memories of him, only a vague feeling of what his presence had been like, and a lingering sense of longing and frustration.

She no longer even remembered his face.

"Do you want to go first or last?" Piggy had asked her.

When she'd replied, "Last. If I go first, you'll stare at my ass all the way up," he'd actually blushed. Without Russ to show off in front of, Piggy was a completely different person, quiet and not at all abusive. He even kept his language clean. But that didn't help, for just being in his presence was enough to force understanding on her: that his bravado was fueled by his insecurities and aspirations, that he masturbated nightly and with self-loathing, that he despised his parents and longed in vain for the least sign of love from them. That the way he treated her was the sum and total of all of this and more.

She knew exactly what the situation was.

Dear God, she prayed, let it be that I won't have this kind of understanding when I reach the top. Or else make it so that situations won't be so painful up there, that knowledge won't hurt like this, that horrible secrets won't lie under the most innocent word.

They carried their wooden burden upward, back toward the world.

The Part of Us
That Loves

KIM STANLEY ROBINSON

WHEN THEY CAME and told him of John's death he crumpled onto the packed earth of the marketplace and rocked back and forth in a fetal ball, howling. He was a small wiry man, dressed in a caftan the color of sand. His feet and hands and head were big for his size, long feet dirty in old sandals, hands immense and strange looking, head a mass of tangled unkempt black hair. Face thin under the wild hair, dominated by intent brown eyes which now stared off at nothing, or at his own death, so much like John's and now so much closer.

The autistic rocking ceased and in a staccato voice he asked how it had happened. Peter told him what they had heard and with a fierce roar he beat the ground, leaped to his feet and shouted furiously. Cheap, disgusting, meaningless, foul! His band drew back, afraid of him as they so often were. He darted through the growing crowd and ran out of the miserable fishing village to the hills, to deal alone with his fury and grief.

His little crew straggled after him, looking confused, appalled, sick. No telling what he might do next. He might disappear never to be seen again, he might return and lash them all with his fierce tongue, or with an actual flail, who could say? Or at the first sight of him they might be re-immersed in the flood of his exuberant love. So they followed.

And the inhabitants of the village hurried out after them, carrying their sick and paralyzed, careless of their homes and possessions, fearful that if they waited even an instant they might lose him forever, and life return to the agony it had been before he came. No one could stand the thought of it. An hour after he had run away the entire population of the village was on foot and after him, straggling into the baked brown hills.

Naomi woke as the bus hissed to a halt. She put her pocket Bible into her daypack, grabbed her clarinet case and hopped out the door just as it was closing. Some boys were laughing at her, and haughtily she tossed her short hair and took off across Shiloh Park, skirting the long pond on her way to the church.

She remembered what she had read on the bus and forgot the boys, feeling disturbed. The Bible was so strange. People outside the church acted like reading it made you an innocent, completely out of it, and yet here it was filled with blood and gore and sex and perversion—all the world's evil, wrestling the good with devilish vigor. Chopping John's head off like that! And all because he had told Herod to stop messing around with Herod's brother's wife. And that wife, and her disgusting daughter who did the dance! It made Naomi shiver. She couldn't help trying to imagine just what sort of dancing could inspire a man to such evil. Naked, no doubt. Like the strippers in Las Vegas or *Penthouse,* or like Jeanette Thompson in the showers after workout, arms overhead and spinning under the spray. Except in this case under the eye of a dirty old man. Who went along with a slut like that even when she wanted a saint's head chopped off. And to bring the head in on a platter with her still walking around the room naked, no doubt! Oh, it was perverted all right; it made her feel queasy just to imagine it. No wonder Jesus had gotten so upset and run off into the mountains. Naomi had visited Colorado Springs, she knew what a comfort the mountains could be, how they lifted you above it all and made you feel the world was holy. Jesus needed such places; after all, he knew all along what was going to happen to him. At this time he had only a couple years left. Horrible to know like that. No wonder he led the disciples on such a rollercoaster of feeling. Every day must have seemed like a year, especially the long days, like this one beginning with the news of John's death. Filled with wonder and pain. Days all four of the Gospel writers remembered, years later when they were writing it all down.

Green park on a muggy summer morning. She came to the church complex and walked into the band room. All the band members not at work—mostly younger ones—were arriving for an early rehearsal. Putting together instruments, warming up, talking. Naomi sat next to Penney and put her clarinet together. A whole gang of boys barged in together, including Tom Osborn. Surreptitiously Naomi watched Tom go to his seat, four down from hers. She was first clarinet and he was the first and only oboe, but the band was arranged with the other first clarinets between them. Tom put his oboe together and talked to the boys in the trumpet section behind him. He looked down the row and saw Naomi, waved and said hi, went back to talking with his friends. His movements were abrupt and uncontrolled; he had grown about four inches in the last year, on the way to becoming a tall, lanky redhead. He stumbled a lot. And his laugh was a kind of boisterous honk that burst out of him before he even knew he was amused. Only his long fingers showed any sort of coordination, and that only when he was playing. Of course it took a lot of coordination to play the oboe's double reed, but that was in the mouth and no one could see it. The other girls thought he was weird for choosing the oboe in the first place. But he was interesting.

Their conductor shuffled slowly into the room. Several people greeted him. "Morning, Dave." He looked up briefly, smiled, stepped carefully onto his podium, each foot placed securely before he moved the next.

The bandmaster was old. Conductor of the Zion Band for many decades now, he was in his eighties, and suffered from a disease of the nerves that made him shake. Probably Parkinson's, although one couldn't say for sure, as he and his wife still followed the teaching of the town founder, Dr. Alexander Dowie, who had held that doctors were unnecessary and that the only true healing was accomplished by Christ, through the word of God. In any case Dave had trouble moving, and his hands and mouth shook. Sometimes Naomi was amazed that he could still

conduct the band. But obviously the act itself was a restor-
ative. Like this morning; first he talked to them softly
about this evening's concert. They were playing in the
park's band shell for the residents of several local nursing
homes, to celebrate the hundredth birthdays of two of the
old folks. Also for whomever else came to listen. Quietly
Dave named the tunes they would play, listing them with a
weak smile. He seemed hesitant, drained, incapable of
lifting his arms. But then it was time to rehearse, and he
stepped forward to his music stand, and it was as if (as she
had heard Tom say) he had a socket in the bottom of one
shoe and had just stepped onto a plug, connecting him to
some powerful electric source. He conducted clearly and
vigorously, with a strong four-four beat, head tilted up and
to one side as he listened. If you made a mistake a wrinkle
would form between his eyebrows; if you played a hard
part with accuracy and expression he would look your way
and smile—just a glance, but you knew he heard everything. He smiled at Tom's playing frequently; Tom and
Andrew on the baritone were the real musicians in the
current band, Naomi thought, and she could tell Dave
agreed. How he enjoyed listening to them!

That's why we're here, she thought, here on a sunny
summer morning: because Dave was a man who loved
what he did. He would say, I've been lucky my play has
been my work and not many can say that, and all his life he
had been ready at any moment to sit down and make
music, to speak through it, which speaking filled him with
joy. And seeing that people were drawn to it. It's like that
with some bands, some choirs; the conductor has a presence, spreads a joy, and the band or choir gets larger and
larger, prospers even in times when fewer people know
how to play or sing. Because of Dave it had been like that
in Zion for almost fifty years.

Then rehearsal was over, and it was time to get to the
other side of the complex for the weekly Bible class. Dave
was teaching that as well this year, so there was no need for
Naomi to hurry; he would be a while.

As she left the room Tom Osborn rushed up, banged
into the closing door, said brightly, "Hey Naomi, are you
on your way to class?" She nodded. "Good, I'll walk over
there with you!"

"Sure," she said, pulse quickening.

So when he came out of the hills and down the broad
sandy wash, winding between shrubs and humming a random tune, he came on them all at once. The whole mangy
lot of them. For a moment anger drove its iron spike
through him—never to be left alone! Then he saw the
looks on their faces: fear, hope, sudden release at the sight
of him, deep relief. They wore all the clothes they owned:
a caftan, a shirt, a tunic, wrapped skirts, threadbare with a
thousand washings, sewn up, dusty, torn. Under that, ribs,
scars, open sores. Distended bellies of malnourished children, gaunt musculature of malnourished adults. This was
his constituency—he would never have any other—people
so poor that the slightest drought might kill them, every
day spent thinking about the next meal—where it would
come from, how they might ration it—going without so
their children could eat, falling asleep at night feeling that
pinch in the gut, that pain. With disease permanent, unex-
plainable, unavoidable. Like a curse. And he understood
suddenly that he was their only chance to escape lives that
were like the lives of their beasts, grinding in poverty and
pain, sudden death touching down among them like
soundless heat lightning on a black summer night. Their
only chance. Except you have souls it is no more than this,
he said to himself, looking at the desperation in their faces,
the desperation that had brought, my God, the whole village after him.

So he sat them down, using his little band as messen-
gers, spokesmen scurrying anxiously around saying he'll be
here in just a moment, sit down and he'll come. And all the
while thinking of John's fierce pure devotion, he walked
among them. And they watched him and waited for his
approach. An ordinary little man with a tangle of hair and
a dancer's stop—how he drew the eye! They felt the compulsion to watch him, they felt the awful contradiction of a
man who seemed relaxed, calm, soft-spoken, and yet at the
same time stuffed with energy, a violent internal spin revealed in every gesture he made. Squatting elbows on
knees, talking to each of them in turn with that direct gaze
pinning them, brown eyes under the stray lock of hair
steady and searching right to the bottom of their selves,
understanding all he saw and loving them nevertheless.
While he talked his strange oversized hands were always
moving, fingers pointing, shaping ideas, touching his lis-

teners—making a cap for a boy's head, wrapping around a twig-like leg, rimming an open sore or laid flat on a patch of leprosy that no one else would dare touch, and as he did so there was an almost audible tension in the air, a tension such that his low musical voice could be clearly heard all the way across the wash, humorous tones bouncing like his visible image in the heatwaves rising from their alluvial ampitheater, sounding as if spoken right into the ear, clear in the palpable silence of their ensemble breathing. And here a paralyzed arm would quiver and clench at him, a skeletal woman would swell like a wineskin and rise and ask for water, and everyone would sigh under the burning sun and sleeping children smile with contentment. And always the voice floating through the baking air, saying you are more than animals, you are human beings, God's own children, God's mirror and message, with spirits that transcend the flesh and all the flesh's meager explanations. Spirits that never die. And we prove this by the way we behave toward each other, by our compassion and love given not just to family, which after all even animals do, but to all creation and especially to other human beings, your brothers and sisters all over the world. And they could feel in their marrow it was true, because of this little man spinning among them with his big hands and his quick laugh (head thrown back to the sun, teeth white in his black beard) and his quick brown eyes and his quick musical voice—because of his *presence*.

Naomi jerked and sat up. Bible class again. A bit dull. Even with Tom sitting next to her. There were only eight students there, all of them in the summer before their junior year of high school, most known to each other since childhood, and many of them restive at this class, which was mostly taken because parents commanded it. Jeanette glancing into her makeup mirror, the boys on the other side of Tom fidgeting, Martha nearly asleep, and Dave sometimes seeming not much more awake himself. Teaching this class did not transform him as conducting did, and mostly he just asked them in turn to read aloud from the Gospels, reading different versions of the same events from the four books, then reading a companion study guide, or a modern language version, to clarify any obscurities. And to the nearly infinite host of questions plaguing Naomi, all the whys and wherefores and what exactly does this *mean*, he had only his slight inward smile and a manner like that she had heard psychotherapists used. Well, what do you think it means? he would answer her. Why do you ask? What troubles you about that? And so on, until he would ask someone else to read on, and listen with a very faint, abstracted look of pleasure, enjoying it as if it were some quiet form of his beloved music. Leaving Naomi to her own devices, all the questions still snapping away inside her. Her puzzle to solve, without the help of anything on earth.

By the time he had finished wandering through the crowd the sun was low in the sky, it was cooling down marginally and they could finally feel the sweat on their skin. His band gathered around him and Philip said You'd better send them home now, they've got nothing to eat and they've been here all day. He looked at his men with the exuberant spin still clear in his gaze and laughed. How will we feed all these people, Philip? Where will we get the bread? Feeling the urge that so often struck him, to tease or even taunt these brothers of his, the men he knew best in all the world, who despite all still followed him around gnawing one worry or another, as frail and lovable as simpletons, which some of them in fact were. Philip, who was constantly trying to keep them from going broke, spluttered about how much it would cost to buy that much bread—a couple hundred pennies' worth at least—only he could make such a quick estimate of something like that—meanwhile the women of the village were walking up from a spring with the water jugs full on their heads, still in balance over their graceful swaying. They were expecting a supper of water; it wouldn't be the first time or the last. He laughed again and, returning Thomas's truculent gaze, said You feed them. Feeling mischievousness like a fountain in him, a response to the women's beauty. Who could stem it? Serious Andrew went to their bags and said slowly, We've got five loaves of bread. Oh, and two fish. Dense big loaves of brown barley bread, each would feed several men. Two smoked lake trout, bony and short, staring up with a round-eyed expression just like Peter's. He laughed again. Fine, he said. Have them move into groups of about fifty.

And they went off to do it, Thomas rolling his eyes, the rest looking puzzled and frightened almost to tears. As they arranged things he emptied out their baskets and moved onto a pebbly rise at the upper end of the wash, where everyone could see him. Certainly their eyes were all on him. He put the five loaves and the two fishes into one basket, and for a long time he stared into the setting sun, becoming still as the rock under him. He could feel the world breathing, the movement of the stars, the gaze of the people sitting in the sand around him. His long fingers twisted the first loaf of barley and tore off a chunk. He dropped pieces of bread into an empty basket, then used a fingernail to tear flesh from the fish, careful not to include bones. Thank you, lake trout. By the time his men had re-gathered around him he had filled two baskets. He was still just beginning on the first loaf. Peter did his fish imitation. He laughed as they scurried off with the baskets.

Watching him frightened them. His hands moved like a tailor's, quick and precise, tearing away mouthfuls of bread from loaves that never seemed to get smaller, so that it seemed barley bread and chunks of smoked fish were pouring out of his palms. It was enough to make them run away with their full baskets, running to the hungry eyes that watched it all intently, people silent as boulders scattered on the wash, focusing their concentration on the little man at their center. They ate without taking their eyes from him. And it went on like that until the red oblate sun touched the hills to the west, and the air was thick with apricot light and the smell of sweat and smoked fish. Every visit to him was more confounding; same thing happening, hands tearing quickly, his gaze direct and sardonic, challenging, a laugh playing under his moustache. So that it was actually a relief to stumble away from him with yet another full basket. This was the central fact of the experience, every time they stepped out into the luminous realm of the miraculous: it was frightening to see it! There was a lot of terror in awe.

When he was done producing food out of the five loaves and the two fishes he stood and stretched like a cat. He took up a handful of the bread, regarded it curiously, ate it piece by piece, chewing slowly. When he was done he said to the twelve Take your baskets out and collect the scraps they haven't eaten. They did it wearily, and came back humping full baskets, every one of them. Staring open-mouthed. He laughed. We can have leftovers tomorrow, he said, and looking out at his people he felt the surge of affection coming from them; he turned it back out on them, the mirror of their capacity for love.

Tom tapped Naomi on the knee, startling her. He leaned over so he could whisper in her ear. "Matter replicator," he said softly; she could hear that he was smiling as he spoke. "Alien visitor from a planet with a higher technology. It's obvious, don't you think?"

Blushing, and fearful that Dave had heard him, Naomi shook her head. And Dave cocked his. "Tom?"

"Oh, uh—nothing, Dave." Tom straightened in his seat, buried his nose studiously in his Bible.

Dave looked at him dubiously. "Jeanette, would you continue?"

Naomi groaned inside. Jeanette read in a smarmy, over-expressive voice, relentlessly marking each sentence by emphasizing words or phrases chosen at random. That to her was drama. And apparently Dave liked it, or at least had no objection. Tom shifted restlessly, rolling his eyes at Jeanette's melodramatics and surreptitiously flipping through his Bible, looking for who knew what. Jeanette was reading from John, while Tom was looking through Mark. Naomi, at first pleased to sit next to Tom after their walk around the complex, now began to get annoyed. He definitely made it harder to concentrate.

"Then those men, when they had seen the *miracle* that Jesus did, said, This is of a *truth* that prophet that *should* come into the world. When Jesus *therefore* perceived that they would come and *take him by force*, to make him a *king*, he departed again *into a mountain* himself alone."

How disappointing, how terrible it must have been, to have had a day like that, filled with wonder and the tight sense of community that participation in one of his miracles always brought with it—and then suddenly to have them rise up and rush toward him shouting Be king! with their faces transfigured. Lead us! Be king! With his twelve men going right along with it as usual, jumping up and down in the front row.

To come out of that state of still spinning in which such things happened: shock, confusion, incomprehension. Then he understood; if he could make food from nothing, and if he became their king, then maybe it would happen every day. Free food, no work, security—return to infancy and sweet mother's breast. Or, to be more charitable, an end to the threat of starvation. Steep plummet of disappointment, empty despair, followed immediately as he was jostled by that old spike of anger. Shout wordlessly at them, strike at his doggy disciples and blast through them like Moses parting the sea, so he could run stumbling up the wash, to spend the night in the hills alone.

Leaving the twelve and the five thousand standing there confused, staring at baskets of bread and fish scraps. The twelve looked at each other and sighed. Done it again. They couldn't predict him; they didn't understand him, and they knew it.

John and Mark took charge and sent the villagers back, with the contents of the twelve baskets. After that they were left on the caked shore of the Sea of Galilee, with no shelter and no food, only a plan to go next to Capernaum, across the sea. And no sign of him. Doubtless gone for the night.

Irritably John suggested they precede him over the sea to have a roof for the night, and the others agreed; they convinced a fisherman who had witnessed the day to lend them a boat, and they got in and started rowing.

Night fell, the wind picked up and came right in over the bow. Low dark clouds, steep short waves falling over in white lines, in a roar of wind and water mixed, until they had to shift toward the stern so the bow would clear the waves, and they were tossed about, elbows bashing ribs and heads in the dark, the rowers crying for room and everyone getting scared; it would be difficult if not impossible to turn back without swamping the boat.

Then Matthew cried out, and when they saw what caused his shout they were terrified: there was a figure in white walking on the sea, gliding smoothly in a little pocket of stillness—

"Ah ha HA!" Boisterous horselaugh, from Tom of course. Startled, Naomi drew back and stared at him. He had a hand clapped over his mouth, but was still laughing; obviously he had been helpless to stem the outburst. Those gangly awkward arms. Everyone was staring at him. Embarrassed for him, Naomi looked down at her lap. The red lines of Christ's speech jumped off the page of black print.

"Well, Tom?" Dave said with his wrong-note frown.

"I'm sorry," Tom said, "I really am. It's just that in Mark

it says, wait, here—'he cometh unto them, walking upon
the sea, and would have passed by them.' I mean"—he
stopped, suppressed another laugh with difficulty—"it sort
of sounds like he went out there to help them, and then
just forgot about it on the way—spaced out and would
have strolled right on by, if they hadn't yelled for him!"

Several members of the class tittered at this interpretation, and Tom grinned widely. Dave frowned, but didn't
offer a counter-explanation. He looked around at the others. "What do you think?"

"It was pitch black and storming!" Naomi said, surprising herself. She looked at Tom. "He went out there to save
them, but once out there it would have been really hard to
see anything." Her conception of the night on the sea was
altering as she spoke. "He just lost sight of them is all."

Dave was nodding. "Jeanette, would you please continue?" Even though she'd already read most of the chapter. "Yes, let's stay with the Book of John for the moment."

Jeanette recommenced her mangling of the text, but
Tom, still tensed, on the edge of a new guffaw, scribbled
something on his Pee-Chee folder and slid it over onto
Naomi's leg. Curious despite herself, she read it: *Walking
on water—Anti-Gravity Device! See what I mean?*

She took out her ballpoint and quickly penned under
his message: *Don't forget Peter did it too, then fell in when
scared. It took BELIEF.*

Tom scowled, grinned, wrote: *Unless he stepped outside the field.*

Then Dave cleared his throat, and they were both nose-
deep in Bibles.

It was, to put it simply, a scramble. The ferocity of
concentration necessary to stay on the surface of the water
was challenged by the steep tumbling waves, and eventually he was reduced to every kind of acrobatic maneuver:
hopping over broken whitecaps, skidding down the backsides and sinking ankle-deep as he bottomed out in the
troughs, occasionally going to hands and knees, or jumping
from crest to crest and treading deep in the mush—sweeping wet hair out of eyes, pausing legs spread wide to look
for the foundering boat . . . So that by the time he
neared them he was sopping wet, glissading down the
backsides of waves, broadjumping up the frontsides, surf-
ing on his feet to close the cross-distance, crawling in

places, slipping around like a drunk on greased glass, up and down, up and down.

Then they saw him and shrieked in fear, so that he relocated them off to one side. A ghost, a ghost! He had to laugh. They never learned. Be of good cheer! he shouted, laughing crazily as he sideslipped down a swell, balancing perfectly. It's me! Be not afraid!

And Peter, bold as the child he was, said if it's you, Lord, bid me come to you on the water!

Come then, he said, riding up and down and concentrating on Peter's bulk, his low center of gravity, his childlike mind. It made him smile with affection to see Peter step right over the transom onto the water, which held him like thick mud. Peter took five or six steps before a wave jostled him; he went to hands and knees and looked at what was under him—black water right under his nose —and yelped. Help, Lord! Save me! And then it was a real struggle, he had to skid over the waves and reach down under the surface and grab him by the arms and lift him up bodily, balanced on the swells all the while. He threw Peter over an oarlock and followed him with a neat step onto the mid-bench. They were both soaked, they couldn't have gotten any wetter. He cleared hair from his eyes and laughed. Oh man of little faith, he said to Peter, why did you doubt? But then again, to take that first step out of the boat . . . He gave the bedraggled and shamefaced child a hug, then threw his mind against the wind. Spirit versus spirit. Father help me. The wind calmed, the whitecaps disappeared.

"Then they *willingly* received him into the ship: and *immediately* the ship was at the land whither they went."

Tom's eyes bugged out and with a jerk he scribbled on his Pee-Chee, poked it so that Naomi would look. *TELE-PORTATION!!!!!*

Naomi pressed her lips together to keep from smiling, rolled her eyes, poked him hard in the ribs.

When class was over they put their things in their daypacks without looking at each other. Then as they walked out into the humid sunshine he rushed up to her side and almost tripped. "Hey, are you going to eat lunch now?"

Naomi nodded.

"Me too. You want to— I mean . . ."

"I've got a sack lunch, I'm going to eat in the park."

"Me too! Want to eat together?"

"Sure."

A laugh burst out of him. "Ha! And so they broke bread together. What a class!"

She snorted. "Just call you Doubting Thomas."

"Well, I can see his point. I mean, a little proof—I wouldn't mind some of that myself."

She shook her head. "You have to have more faith."

"Faith," he said, testing the word, weighing the sound of it. He shrugged. "Maybe I do."

They sat on the grassy rise at the north end of the park, and got out their lunches. Tom's was just three peanut butter and jelly sandwiches, and a Snickers bar; his family didn't have much money. He worked several nights a week at the Jack in the Box, which no doubt didn't help his complexion any. Too bad he wasn't on the swim team. Or working at Sears, like she did.

She traded a baloney and cheese sandwich for one of his, and they ate. As they ate Tom gestured at the town around them. "We live in a strange place, you know? One of a kind."

Naomi swallowed. "I know." Zion, Illinois. Founded by the Australian faith healer Dr. J. Alexander Dowie, who set up a tent outside the Chicago World's Fair at the turn of the century, and urged visitors to avoid the iniquity of the fair and live a pure life. Many people responded. His plan had been to set up Zions outside all the major cities of the world, but the town fronting Lake Michigan on marshy land north of Chicago was the only one they succeeded in building. Even that had been a close thing, at first. Now it stood there like any other Midwestern town—only different. The north-south streets were named after characters in the Bible, in alphabetical order starting at the lake and moving inland, with a peculiar emphasis on the letter E: Edina, Elizabeth, Elam, Emeus, Enoch, Eschel, Ezekiel, Ezra . . . They must have had plans for a big town. Bethel and Shiloh Boulevards crossed at the central church complex, and there were diagonal streets crossing there as well, and a circular street around it. The park to one side. A city dedicated to God, the way they were all supposed to be.

"It was a kind of utopia," Tom said thoughtfully, blinking as he looked across the park in the direction of Dr. Dowie's big house, now a museum. "One of the last of the religious utopias started in America in the 1800s. One of the last started and one of the last still going. At least within the confines of the Christian Catholic Church of Zion, Illinois."

"Don't make fun."

"I'm not! It was a real accomplishment! In fact they had to break the laws separating church and state to do it. No drinking, no smoking, no gambling or card-playing . . . I even read a book that said they passed a law against jazz in the Twenties. But when I asked Dave about that, he got mad and said there had never been any such thing."

"I'm sure Dave knows more about music in Zion than any book."

"Me too. In the band for over seventy years!" He laughed with delight at the thought, spitting out white bits of chewed bread. "Incredible. I think"—he stopped, swallowed, looked serious—"I think Dave's the real heart of Zion. Not old Dowie." He waved a skinny arm at the museum.

"I don't see why you're so down on Dr. Dowie. He was a famous man, he did a lot to spread the word of God."

"Famous, anyway. The reincarnation of Elijah, as he decided—he certainly should be famous! He's even in Joyce's *Ulysses*, did you know that? I was looking through that book trying to read it when I came across him. I couldn't believe it!"

"So why don't you like him?"

"Well, have you seen those pictures of his church in Chicago? The walls are covered with the crutches of people he healed. Covered with them."

"So? He was a faith healer."

Tom shook his head violently. "Come on, Naomi. You know that faith healing is just what it says—a matter of faith. It's like Peter walking on the water. During the actual ceremony everyone's excited and crippled people really want to be healed, they believe it's happening and they're all pumped up and other people are standing, and so they channel every bit of strength into it, and everyone's encouraging them and so they stand and walk around a little, and everyone says they're healed. But the next day!" He blew out his cheeks. "Then it's like when

Peter begins to doubt, and sinks like a stone. I'll bet you a whole bunch of those cripples woke up the next day and found they needed their crutches again, and where were they? Decorating the walls of Dr. Dowie's church! Trophies nailed up to show what a great healer he was! Pah!" He waved the big house away with both hands. "I don't like it."

"But Tom," Naomi said, troubled by this vision of the town founder. "Some people are healed by faith. I mean, Jesus did it all the time."

"Yes, I know. Healed the sick and everything else."

"But Tom! Don't you believe in Jesus?"

"Well . . . I don't know." He looked uncomfortable, troubled by the question, which Naomi could tell he had asked himself before.

"What do you believe in?" she asked, shocked.

"Well . . ." His left hand gathered up twigs, tossed them aside as if throwing coins in a toll booth hopper. "I guess what I think is . . ." He bogged down, looked at her tentatively. "I guess what I think now is, that when we talk about God, we're talking about a part of ourselves. God is inside us, right? We say that. And what I think is, there's a part of us that is better than our usual self—the animal selfishness and cruelty and all the rest. And we recognize that part in us, we know it's different, and we call it God. So that when we talk about Christ, what we mean is the part of us that loves, the part of us that helps to feed the poor and heal the sick and all like that, even if they're strangers. The part that says everyone on the planet is family."

Nodding, Naomi said "But there's more to it than that. I mean Christ was a man who lived in Israel. He really did all those things."

Tom waggled a hand.

"You don't think so?"

"Well, he certainly did some things, sure. But which ones, exactly? You know how the commentaries Dave had us read said that the first three gospels were written about the same time, and then John wrote his a long time later. Now look at the differences in John's version! All the other three say that Christ walked over the water to the boat, and when he got in the winds died and they went on their way. But John! In John, Christ gets in the boat and they're instantaneously in the other town! I mean, am I supposed to believe that? It's teleportation! If it happened, why didn't the others mention it?"

"Maybe they forgot," Naomi said, wanting time to think.

"It sure isn't something I'd forget if it happened to me! It would've blown my mind! No, it's the kind of thing you write down forty years later, after a lifetime's remembering has heightened things a little. And then you read the rest of John and you see he was a real mystic, a space cadet in fact. I mean, have you read *Revelation?*"

"Yes I have."

Another uncontrollable horselaugh, apparently at the expression on her face. "It's crazy, you know it is! I mean the man was spaced! So how much am I supposed to believe? How much was embellished later?"

Naomi shook her head, bore down on the main point. "Dave says we should believe it all, and chalk up discrepancies to the problems people have in seeing and remembering complex and unusual events. It's true, you know—one time Mr. Delany arranged for some people to jump into class and tussle with him and run out, and afterwards when people told what they had seen, it was all different! He said that's why the police have such trouble with eyewitnesses. Everyone sees something slightly different, especially when something incongruous happens. Besides"—she poked the grass next to his restless hand—"all four of them reported a lot of the miracles, like feeding the five thousand or walking on water. They all reported it the same! How do you explain that?"

Tom shrugged, sighed. Naomi felt herself trembling, and she could see by Tom's hands that he was excited too, color high, thinking fast, really into it, and with a little quiver she thought, without articulating it to herself, finally someone as smart as me, finally someone to really talk to!

Tom said, "Maybe he was an alien, like I said. Member of an advanced race, come to teach us to live better. Impressing us with high tech."

Naomi shook her head decisively. "It's more than high tech. We're talking basic laws of physics here—time, gravity, matter coming from nothing—what kind of aliens are you talking about?"

"God-like aliens," he said, and laughed a little.

Naomi shook her head. "Either those men were walking around for three years hallucinating frequently, or else there was a being there outside the laws of nature—able to bend them at will! That's why John was so spacy, Tom, I mean think about it—he spent three years of his life following a guy around who was constantly performing miracles, healing the sick, feeding people, raising the dead! Why, one time John went out to talk to him at night in the garden and he and his clothes and everything around him were a pure glowing white! Three years of that kind of thing is bound to make you a little mystical, you have to be fair to him. I mean he saw Jesus come back from the dead, talked to him after the crucifixion! And all those miracles—"

"Yes I know."

"Well? They were one of the main reasons people were so impressed by Jesus. He was a supernatural being. God, in fact. He said so all the time. Jesus Christ was God, the creator of the universe."

Tom frowned, shifted uncomfortably.

"Who else, if not God?"

The question stopped him; it seemed to fill the air, reverberating around the park. She could see that he was really thinking about it, and not just shunting it aside the way people did, to avoid the radical problem it presented. She liked that.

But he was troubled. Eventually he said, as if to push the whole thing away again, "Look, to be alien is to be *alien*. It might very well look supernatural to us, it might very well *be* supernatural, how can we say if our four dimensions are all there are? Time, space, gravity—there's no way to be sure those things can't be manipulated."

Naomi pinned him with a look. "Manipulated by God, sure! It's God you're talking about! You just use all that sci-fi stuff to skip the crux of the thing, the real question of do you believe or don't you. Come on, get serious!"

He was looking upset. "Well," he said querulously, "he disappeared from age eighteen to age thirty—maybe he went to India like they say and learned a bunch of yogi tricks."

"Yogis can't do what he did."

"They can walk on fire, that's kind of like—"

"They can do that because when you step on the coals

you crush down a little layer that's nowhere near as hot as their middles, and then they hurry fast as they can."

"Maybe it's the same with water, you know, hotfoot to wetfoot."

"Stop joking!"

"I'm not joking," he cried, distressed. "I'm serious, I never joke!" Hoping to slide out of it with yet another one.

"I believe it," Naomi said sharply. "But it still comes out sounding like jokes. Which I find very sad indeed."

His mouth twisted, and suddenly, awkwardly, he grabbed his daypack and lurched to his feet, then stalked away.

Speechlessly Naomi watched him leave. Oh shoot, she thought, I've hurt his feelings. She found she was trembling hard, and her lunch felt heavy and lumpy in her stomach.

She was furious at herself for hurting his feelings; but she was excited as well. To have a real conversation with someone, to really go all out and argue about important things without holding back as she always had to do with her teachers who would think her insolent, her parents who would think her rebellious, her friends who would think her conceited—it was exciting! Oh, if only she could make it up with him, and go on talking! Argue him back into belief, even. Or just be friends. Close friends. Close friends. Oh, she would have to make it up! She felt like she could. Like anything was possible.

She packed her things and walked downtown to the shops on Shoreline Drive, to do some desultory shopping for her father's birthday. Gang of mothers in Rooks's for coffee and gossip. Zion was still alive all right. Little nineteenth-century religious experiment . . . But not entirely, not any more. Zion was being inundated by greater Chicago, and signs of it were everywhere: crowds thick downtown, graffiti scrawled on the walls, more police, locked bicycles, evidence of vandalism, tales of theft, drug dealing, all the rest. A lot of cheap apartments had been thrown up in the last ten years, filled by the tide of people from the big city, many of them black, most of them poor, and Zion was changing. The little utopia, such as it was, retaken by the real world. Dikes broken. Islet in the flood. She walked on, looking in the windows. Could be just an ordinary American town now, Anywhere U.S.A. With all the emptiness that implied.

Then it was time for workout. Miz Hollins, their high school coach, ran summer workouts three afternoons a week, and everyone serious about being on the team had to come. Besides, it was fun. To clip the clear blue water and glide through that first lap without any effort at all, in a smooth rhythmic freestyle; it was one of the best moments of the day, and certainly one of the coolest.

Naomi's speciality was long-distance freestyle, mostly the 1,000 meters and the 1,500, unless they visited a twenty-five yard pool in which case she did the 1,650. So after a warm-up of sprints and IM work, she and Martha and Sandy were given pull buoys and put in the wall lane to grind out 2,500 meters, timing themselves every 500. Miz Hollins, a short, compact woman who had won a bronze medal in the breaststroke two Olympics before, gave them their instructions quickly and then went over to work with her real love, the sprinters. Barb, Simone, Jeanette: a loud lane. Jeanette was fast all right, but had no endurance at all. Anything over two hundred meters and Naomi had her beat. Tortoise and the hare.

As she swam the five hundreds she fell into the thoughtless trance-like state that was one of the reasons she enjoyed swimming. Glide along watching the bottom thinking slow, lazy thoughts. Thinking nothing. The fifty-meter pool was perfect for that; she stroked insulated in her own water world for so long that the appearance of the wall was a perpetual surprise, she had to remember how to do flip turns. Then it was off again. Remembering the day. The talk with Tom. Crutches on a wall. Hands with a rapid, neat movement (like the catch at the beginning of the pull), tearing brown bread. And the loaf never got smaller. Moving from group to group, stuffed to buzzing stillness with energy, atoms of his hands barely held together by the skin. Flip turn. The eye had to follow him. She imagined the process: God the Father and the Holy Ghost, trying to stuff Christ's spirit into a little human body, like fitting a water balloon into a small shoe. Push, heave, grunt, catch that spurt back out, finally the Ghost holds the child and the Father is jumping up and down to compress that last bit into his mouth, strain, heave, get all the pressures right and Pop! it's in there at last. And ever after he

walks around fit to burst with it! A compression of everything: love, compassion, calm, indignation, anger, amusement, pride, energy. All human qualities intensified,
concentrated in the red sentences among the black. Except the really bad ones. Evil not a natural part of us. If you
read just the red sentences, Tom joked. Different book?

In the last 500 she was tired, arms like wood, and as her
hands caught and pulled slowly down the midline she felt
the water like butter or jello about to set, something so
thick and tangible that it was hard to believe it was clear.
Such resistance—*of course* it might be possible to walk on
it! Water was solid stuff; just increase the surface tension
the slightest bit and crawl on up. . . . Feeling the thick-
ness of the water and the lightness of her body, she felt she
could almost do it herself. Belief. Or some sort of device.
Magnetic fields. The nuclear power station down by the
lake.

Afterwards Miz Hollins said, "Good pacing, Naomi—
that last one was your fastest."

That's why they call it the crawl, coach.

Then in the changing room the IMers were talking
about the latest Michael the Fox movie, and Jeanette and
her clique were talking about a hot party in Waukegan, big
deal, when Martha said to her, "Hey Nome, I think Tom
Osborn is about to make his move on you."

Jeanette heard her and laughed. "Tom Osborn! He's
such a nerd."

"He's not a nerd," Naomi said sharply. "He's just
smart."

They all laughed at this, at the weakness of the defense,
and what it said about how Naomi felt. Jeanette began to
comb out her hair.

"Anyone smart in this town gets called a nerd," Naomi
said bitterly.

Jeanette just laughed again, and the others joined her.

Simone said, "In that case Jeanette is in no danger of
her boys being called nerds, hey Jeannie?"

The other girls laughed, but this time at Jeanette; her
latest was Frank Martin, the high school team's quarter-
back, who was a cutie and could throw a football a mile,
but was notoriously stupid. It was said he could only remember four plays. Jeanette gave Simone a poisonous look
and said, "True no matter how you define it. At least I only

have one boyfriend at a time." But Simone walked off to the showers with a laugh, impervious, saying over her shoulder, "The more fool you." She was a cheerleader the same as Jeanette, and had more natural authority, being black and a little bit scary. The rest of the girls followed her lead and abandoned support for Jeanette's taunting.

In the showers Naomi gave Simone a grateful look and Simone smiled, scrubbed soap into her wirebrush hair. No one could be prejudiced against Simone, she was too confident, too direct, too accomplished. We're prejudiced against black people, Naomi thought suddenly, because they are more beautiful than us. They have more presence. Black skin gleaming like some sort of fantastic wood . . . Naomi and Simone had almost the same figure, but inside black skin it looked a lot better—more muscular, fuller. Seeing Simone made Naomi feel better about herself.

After that (busy day), it was back to the band room for the dress rehearsal with the whole band, the adults coming from work in office suits and dresses, or construction-site overalls, chattering and filling up the seats. A hundred members, Dave always told reporters, from twelve to eighty-six years old. Actually there were about seventy playing at any one time.

Naomi sat down and saw Tom walk in. He avoided looking in her direction and once in his seat he twisted to start up a conversation with the guys behind him, making them laugh. Naomi sighed, worried. This might turn out to be more difficult that she had thought.

Stragglers were still arriving, and the room was loud. Naomi put together her clarinet, thinking hard. She looked up and was surprised to see Dave, shuffling between music stands to her. He smiled briefly. "I want you to be sitting next to the oboe instead of the first flute tonight," he said, "so you and Tom can hear each other on the duet in 'American Eagle.' Here, just flip-flop the first clarinets."

So Naomi stood and awkwardly shifted between the row of cheap folding chairs and black metal stands, trading places with Bob Caspar. Penny and Doris switched the two inner seats, giggling as they bumped into each other. It occurred to Naomi that she had a duet with the first flute in "Holy, Holy, Holy" as well. She sat next to Tom. The room was quieting down, but Dave was discussing something with the percussion section, so they weren't going to start immediately. She turned to Tom and put a hand briefly on his thigh.

"I'm sorry about what I said at lunch," she said in a quick low voice. "It was stupid."

Tom looked surprised, pleased. You could read his face like a billboard.

She said, "I was . . ." and squinched up her mouth.

"That's okay," Tom said. "I was being stupid myself."

"I mean, I believe. . . ."

He nodded. "Sometimes I just talk, you know? Whatever occurs to me—"

"I like that," Naomi interjected.

"I shouldn't have walked off, that was dumb."

Naomi shook her head.

Tom grinned, obviously pleased by the turn of events. He flipped open the music to "American Eagle." "Shall we go over our part? It looks like Dave'll be a while yet."

They played the passage pianissimo, instruments slanted in together. Well, Naomi was thinking. What do you know. And all because of Dave moving me. Could he have known? She missed a sharp, concentrated. Have to play a bit louder than Tom in concert, to compensate for the oboe's penetrating timbre. Fun to play together. Music was . . . like swimming.

After rehearsal the whole band went to Rooks's to have dinner together. Naomi and Tom sat in a group of friends at one of the long tables, and joined in the chatter and horseplay. They said little to each other, but Naomi was constantly aware of his presence beside her. Occasionally their elbows or knees would bump; Tom was a gawky eater, and restless in his seat, shifting to find a more comfortable position or jerking back to splutter with sudden mirth, often at a joke that only he perceived. When they bumped he paid no attention to it, as if this were ordinary and not to be noted. Naomi talked to Martha and Doris and Penny about the swim team and Martha's upcoming trip to Door County and the Upper Peninsula, feeling a general glow. She saw Dave drifting between tables and talking to people. He didn't like to eat in public anymore, as he had trouble controlling his mouth. Besides it would have taken time away from the socializing. Naomi waved when he was looking their way, and ten minutes later he stopped behind them and talked for a bit. He smiled as he surveyed the crowded tables, and he seemed to glow with the contentment he always exhibited when the band was together. This was his life, right here, extending all through the town and back through the years—a four-dimensional creature, as Tom would say. The past alive in him like a lamp. All those bands, players, concerts.

The way he talked about tonight's concert was cute: "The old folks really love these things, the nurses say it's their best medicine." As if many of the people they would entertain weren't actually younger than he was. But they had lost something he was still suffused with. He really did seem to glow, his old skin was spotted and sort of waxy and no doubt caught the light in a peculiar way, but she was sure she could see it. "A hundredth birthday, can you imagine! I'll bet they're proud tonight, those two. It's quite an accomplishment."

They talked of the two centenarians, both of whom had been born on exactly this day a hundred years before. All the papers had written up such a coincidence. "That means when they were your age it was still the 1800s," David said. "Horse and buggy to spaceships and moon landings, all in one life." He smiled at the thought. "We'll send them into their second century with a good concert."

They walked back across the park in a large straggling group. It was cooling off at last, and the late evening sun buttered the leaves on the tall trees. "Zion's only skyscrapers," Dave muttered as he shuffled beside Naomi, looking up at them with a pleased expression. Across the pond a crowd was gathering before the bandshell. It looked like a lot of them were in the middle of picnic dinners. The crickets were starting up in force, and frogs by the pond and mosquitoes around their ears added to the song of the Illinois summer evening.

When the front of the band reached the bandroom door there was a small commotion. "Hey!" someone said loudly. Then there was a rush inside and more cries. Dave tilted his head to the side curiously, and without discussing it he put a hand onto Naomi's offered forearm so he could walk faster.

By the time they entered the room the cries of alarm and outrage had mostly died away, and the members of the band were standing around in shock, looking fearfully at Dave. The room was a shambles, the floor covered with torn sheet music and tipped-over music stands, the drums punched through, the Sousaphones dented by kicks; and all the cubbyholes on the far wall were empty. Their instruments were gone.

Dave shuffled into the room, looking befuddled. He stopped to lay a trembling hand on the rim of the bass drum, his mouth turned down, his eyes searching the floor. Mr. Stevens the band manager approached him, face scarlet. "They've stolen all the smaller instruments," he said in a tight, angry voice. "And wrecked these."

Somebody was crying. Hands clenched at mouth. People stood stunned, staring at Dave sick with worry at how he might react.

"What will we do?" Mrs. Jackson said.

Dave stepped over to his podium. "Everyone sit down and start sorting out the sheet music," he said absently.

"All the music stores in Waukegan will be closed by now," Mr. Stevens said. Dave himself had owned a music store once—it would have come in handy now, but he had closed it years ago. "Besides, we don't have time. We'll have to postpone—"

"We won't postpone!" Dave said sharply. He was a gentle man these days, but oldtime members of the band said that when he was younger he had had quite a temper— you didn't want to make him angry with you. Now Naomi saw what they were talking about, just in the sound of his voice, the expression on his face. "It's those folks' one hundredth birthday today, you can't postpone that. We'll just have to make do. Sit down and get the music sorted out. Come on." A single imperious gesture.

So they sorted as he shuffled through the wreckage, inspecting the Sousaphones, poking his head in cubbyholes, pausing in corners, looking distant, pensive. People watched him anxiously. When the sheet music was all picked up and sorted Mrs. Saunders, the pastor's wife, suggested they pray. Dave nodded impatiently and bowed his head, and they all did the same. "Dear Lord," he muttered, "hear us in an hour of need. Forgive the foolish vandals who did this, and help us find a way. For Jesus' sake amen." He raised his head, opened his eyes slowly, looked around. "Okay, what have we got left?"

They added it up: three of the five Sousaphones were still playable. Jack had had his trumpet with him. A piccolo in its tiny case had been overlooked, at the back of a cubbyhole. And two clarinets had been left in one of the practice rooms.

At the end of this wan reckoning Naomi saw Tom slowly straighten from a crouch on the far side of the room. He looked around the room for her, and when their gazes met he smiled sardonically. She shrugged, uncomfortable with the joke he was making.

Dave was nodding in an absentminded way. He fumbled in his pocket, got out his keys. "Alan, would you go in my office? The Christmas instruments are in there."

Tom caught Naomi's gaze again, rolled his eyes at the ceiling. But she noticed his hand was clenched hard over a music stand; and it seemed to her the air was becoming chill.

Dave said, "First let's change one of the Sousaphones into something more like a baritone, for Andrew." Keeping his best musicians equipped. "Here, everyone sit down in their proper places. We only have a little time. Jack, have you got two mouthpieces for your trumpet?"

"Four," Jack said.

"Good. Some of you check the practice rooms again, will you? Mouthpieces, parts, anything. And some of you should start moving the piano out to the bandshell, we're going to need it. I'll get Gloria out of the audience to play."

They brought him the least damaged Sousaphone, and he directed them to take off the last part of the bell, and replace the mouthpiece with a trumpet mouthpiece. "It fits if you tighten these here. I learned this down at the Orange Parade when we lost the baritones. Try that, Andrew. No, you have to blow hard to get it up an octave. Really hard. There you go."

Alan and Terry came out of Dave's office carrying the Christmas instruments: a tambourine, maracas, a big heavy set of jingle bells, a grinder that spun on a stick, polished coconut shells to make the sound of horses' hooves, a small glockenspiel, and some plastic slide whistles. Also some New Year's Eve instruments, in the form of a dozen kazoos and noisemakers.

Dave inspected these, handed back his keys. "Out in the trunk of my car is a case of instruments I use when I visit the elementary schools. Mostly toys, I'm afraid, but that's okay." It was amazing he was still allowed to drive, Naomi thought. He went fast, too. Frowning with concentration, he said, "Kathy, Linda, Jerry, get scissors and rubber bands out of my desk drawer and cut pieces from the bass drumheads. You should be able to re-head a snare drum at least, and you can rubber-band other pieces around the end of valve tubes, they'll be like bass kazoos." There were worried faces everywhere now, a kind of basic confusion, as people contemplated the bizarre instruments Dave was proposing; they were afraid of making fools of themselves. Naomi and Tom worked side by side feeling an entirely different sort of fear, afraid to look at each other, afraid to look up at Dave. It was cold . . .

Dave wandered, threading the bustle slowly. He sat at his podium and showed them how pieces of the drumheads could be wrapped over valve tubes from the Sousaphones, and when the extra mouthpieces were stuck in them, they could indeed be played like big kazoos. They laughed shakily as he demonstrated. "Dave, how do you know how to make these?"

"All kinds of things will make music. Here, try that."

And then the trombone players came in from the church in a rush, waving long thick plastic tubes they had found in a back room. No one had ever seen these tubes before, nor was it clear what they were for. Blowing in them made a deep hoot. Dave nodded. "Blow into the drums, it'll make them louder." It did; they sounded like foghorns.

Dave stood again, wandered around as they figured out what sounded like what, and who would play what, and worked on the drums. Then he stopped suddenly and said, "Alan, Terry, did you look in my bottom drawer?"

"They're still out at your car, Dave."

"Oh yes." He shuffled into his office, came back out with an armful of wooden recorders of all sizes, nodding to himself. "Naomi, you and Penny take the clarinets, and the rest of the clarinets and saxes take these. Tom, you take this one." He gave Tom the longest recorder.

Naomi and Tom's eyes met again, very briefly. Tom was shaking; he took the recorder reluctantly and then held it between two fingers at arm's length, as if it might burn him like dry ice. Where . . . Naomi could feel herself lift-

ing up, it seemed to her the light in the room had changed
and was coming from all directions at once, somehow.
Something . . . It was cold! Did only Tom and she notice?
People went a section at a time into the uniform rooms to
suit up. She couldn't take a smile off her face, couldn't
move the corners of her mouth back in. She had to bite the
reed of her mouthpiece to manage it. Honks, thumps, the
tinkling of the glockenspiel. "Jack," Dave said, "you'll have
to mute your trumpet or we won't be able to hear anyone
else." Then blinked, looked confused, smiled. "We used to
say that to my brother Bob, years ago, as a joke." He and
four of his brothers had formed a saxaphone quintet, one
each for bass, baritone, tenor, alto and soprano; Bob had
played baritone until killed in a car accident, decades ago.
"His sax is still around here somewhere. . . ." He started
looking through the cupboards under the cubbyholes,
helped by the whole sax section. They found it deep in the
back of a cupboard, and again Naomi looked at Tom, saw
him looking for her, saw his wild eye and a crazy startled
grin fixed on his face. *Where?* Frightened, exhilarated, she
thought *No more, please.* She and Tom sat down together
and tried the duet from "American Eagle," shaking in the
cold so that they could hardly play. "I've never played a
recorder in my life," Tom babbled, staring at the small
wooden thing in his hands, squeezing it. "Simple fingering,
I'll say that." He ran up and down a scale.

"Let's try to tune," Dave said. "One at a time. We'll use
the glockenspiel's C. Come on, sit down, we don't have
much time. First the regular instruments."

They tuned themselves to the *bing* of the glockenspiel,
with difficulty, alternating between fits of laughter and
anxiety. Alan and Terry returned with the case of children's instruments. The drummers pounded happily at a
repaired drum, improvised cymbals and a triangle. Finally
Dave had then all play their tuning note. Weird blatting
Huhmmmmm . . . He shook his head, frowned, smiled
his slight inward smile. "Well," he said, "it'll be different."

They trailed out to the bandshell in the silence of collective fright, clutching their new instruments and staying
close to each other. Not a peep. Dave led them, glowing in
his white conductor's uniform with the flat-topped cap,
stepping high as he did in the Labor Day parade every
year. Surge of adrenaline temporarily shoring up those

damaged old nerves. Up the back steps and into the bandshell. A Midwestern bandshell in the summer dusk, the park around them a furry crickety black, fireflies scoring the distant trees, the stars all smeary, the faces of the audience lit by the light of the shell, pale blobs uplifted and attentive. The old folks in the front row looked unaware that anything was wrong, all clustered around the two wheelchaired centenarians whose laps were heaped with bouquets, all looking happy and expectant. Behind them the rest of the audience had pressed in closer; no doubt they had heard somehow, the word spreading quickly through them as they sat on the cooling grass waiting. Now their faces had the look you see on people listening to a young performer in a first recital, encouraging and anxious. Naomi looked up at the white half-dome overhead. They would need the shell's amplification tonight. Half near and white, half distant and black. Naomi shut her eyes. Calm spinning in a restless crowd, the touch of a hand. Dave ticked his baton on the music stand.

Inevitably the first march, "Atlantic Seaboard," was ragged and out of tune, their sound weaker and rougher than usual, and just plain strange. Naomi felt her cheeks burn and her heart pump and she thought We can't keep on like this! But then Dave raised his other hand and began conducting two-handed, as if drawing attention to himself. He had a stern expression on his face, and his eyes darted from player to player, commanding them to watch him. He gestured for more volume from each of the players who still had a real instrument, including Naomi; he looked her eye-to-eye for a moment and she felt a little jerk, and played on at double-forte even though her music said mezzo-forte. And over to the side Dave's daughter Gloria was pounding away with all ten fingers on the piano, she had backed up all kinds of lame church ensembles in her time and knew what to do to fill in gaps. Lot of experience between those two, hundreds of concerts played and little could shake them anymore. Naomi played louder still. Then it was over and the band sat back in their seats with a collective gulp. The applause from out in the dark was loud, warm, supportive. Dave gave them no time to think, but went immediately into "Onward Christian Soldiers," smiling his little inward smile, hand bobbing in the clear vigorous 1-2-3-4 motion. The people playing the slide whistles began to get a gauge on the little plungers. Dave gestured for the row of trombone players, troublemakers to a man, to blow louder into their bizarre assortment of plastic tubes and valve slides; they thumped in behind Andrew on his alto Sousaphone, and Naomi could see their eyes grinning as they heard themselves provide the bass line. Fear shifting into something akin to it, but different.

After that they did "Semper Fidelis" and Dave had Jack uncork his trumpet for the solo, and then Naomi and Penney led the piccolo and penny-whistles through the high addition, and lastly the trombone boys joined in and powered through the bass addition, and they all marched through the last chorus and the coda in fine spirits, and they were off at last. All of them focused on Dave, which was only normal with a band and its conductor, but now it was his pleasure they needed to see, that they relied on. The way he enjoyed it, the way it was his whole life! After all there were his trembling hands suddenly as steady as a magician's, and if he could do that why should these new strange instruments be any obstruction to them? Most only took singing or humming the tune anyway, and as for the rest, a kind of heightened ability to concentrate flowed from the look on Dave's face: watching him Naomi thought she could feel what a redemption music was from ordinary existence, how much singing was like praying. Same thing, mother. And then they were in "American Eagle," and playing the duet with Tom she noticed that he was not playing the written music at all, but an improvised part of his own, higher and more penetrating. He continued to do it after the duet was over, and in "Holy, Holy, Holy," where in their marching band arrangement the oboe had a prominent high harmony, he kept doing it, exploring the upper limits of his new recorder. Dave smiled to hear it, and then suddenly in the last great chorus of the hymn Tom was off and floating above the rest of them, in a pure clear descant. It was the reverse of the usual sound of the orchestra, Naomi thought, usually the orchestra as a whole had a clear sound, and the oboe cut through that with its double-reeded buzz; now with half the orchestra playing kazoos or honking into plastic tubes, it was the orchestra that had a furry, buzzing, bagpipey timbre, and Tom with his little recorder who had the clear tone, a pure sweet sound that he was discovering as he played above them. Dave had them do "Amazing Grace" out of order because it too had a high floating harmony for oboe, and he shushed the orchestra and looked to Tom to play up a bit, and Tom took off in a flying clear peaceful melody, and Naomi glanced sideways at Tom's face and saw he was staring amazed at Dave, as round-eyed as if he had his fingers knuckle-deep in the holes in Christ's palms.

And then they played "The Yellow Rose of Texas" and "When Johnnie Comes Marching Home Again," and "The Stars and Stripes Forever," in which Sheila Matthews played the piccolo solo perfectly for the first time in her life, without a trace of the fright that usually marred her performance; it was enough to make Dave go over after the song and shake her hand and have her stand for an extra round of applause from the cheering audience. And they played "Washington Post," and "Columbia, the Gem of the Ocean," and "The New Colonial," and "The Battle Hymn of the Republic," and lastly "America the Beautiful," and over the sound of the band, which in any case was not all that loud, Naomi could hear the audience singing along, and with the faint sound of the words and Tom playing an octave up and the look on Dave's face, she thought it was the most beautiful thing she had ever heard in her life. She could feel her cheeks flush with it.

And then the concert was over and the band was standing and walking around hugging each other and hugging Dave, and shaking Tom's hand and Sheila's too, and the trombone section was doing their part from "Semper Fidelis" as an impromptu encore, laughing and swinging their tubes back and forth in unison. Then off the stage and out of the shell, to mingle with the crowd, which was mostly friends, family, acquaintances. Part of a community. One of the centenarians stood up and declared it was certainly the finest birthday she had ever had, as far as she could remember. Dave walked around overlooking it all with the same small smile of contentment he always wore after a concert. The trombone section marched through the crowd in Preservation Hall style, playing "Hold That Tiger."

Naomi and Tom returned to the stage and sat in their chairs, leaned back exhausted. Under her stiff uniform jacket Naomi could feel the sweat running over her ribs. "You see?" she said to him under the din. "A miracle."

"True," he said, nodding easily. Then, more serious: "That was my kind of miracle, though—we made it happen ourselves, you see?"

"Dave made it happen."

"Sure," he said, nodding again. She had never seen him look so relaxed and happy, it was as if he would agree to anything she said. "Dave made us believe we could do it. Faith, like you say."

"Faith in God, too."

He assented easily. "Faith in God. But, you know—nothing really . . . supernatural."

"What! What about those recorders?"

He frowned, stared at the instrument still held loosely in his right hand. "Well . . . they must have come from somewhere, surely."

"Have you ever seen them before tonight?" she demanded.

"No, can't say I have." He grinned broadly, stared cross-eyed at the recorder. "Maybe I better keep this!"

She had to laugh. And he threw back his head and honked like the trombone players. "Whatever!" he said. "Whatever happened, it's ours."

And later they walked down to the shore of the pond together, still in their band uniforms. In the close warm dark summer night, cricketsong creaking underfoot. And in one pause, very awkwardly, Tom leaned down to give her a kiss, and she was quick enough to meet him halfway. Brief touch of the lips, the warmth of the other. After that they held hands, and walked the pond's edge away from the darkened bandstand.

Tom laughed softly. "That was so great. I mean, we really sounded good."

"After the first couple, anyway."

"Oh yeah. That first one . . ." They laughed. "Horrible!"

"I didn't think we were going to be able to get through."

"But later!" Tom disengaged his hand to wave it around, jerking with excitement. "I couldn't even believe it."

"It was a miracle," Naomi said, mostly to herself. She gave herself a shivery hug.

They stopped at the pond's end and looked back down the length of the park. Over black trees rose a sickle moon. For a second she felt a cold touch of premonition; she knew this too would end, time would pass, and she saw snatches in her mind's eye: of saying good-bye as they left for different colleges; of the trembling stilled at last, struggling against darkness on the afternoon of a Christmas concert until hearing a voice saying it's all right, Dave, the band's all right. . . . These things would come. But at that moment, standing side by side in the close summer night, the memory of the music fresh in their bodies, still *felt*—she knew that it was all worth it, that music and community and love redeemed all the trembling and pain and grief there were. To lift off and soar like that! A miracle in Zion. Big hands moving quickly, neatly, tearing away chunks of brown bread, filling a basket with a frayed upper rim and a hole in one side, the laughing eyes meeting yours in the baking sun, the loaf getting smaller but not getting smaller, still there, still spongy and brown under those deft hands that moved so deliberately despite their speed, no trick possible, nothing to it: but the hungry were fed, the sick were healed, the lame could walk and the blind see. Ah God, yes, please! If it happened once . . .

God's grace. Or a dream we once had, a shared dream, to help those who need it. To heal the sick. The best part of our selves. Naomi looked up at Tom's horsey face, took his hand. No need to decide, tonight. Hands breaking bread, moving quickly, neatly. Giving. A miracle in Zion. Go you and do likewise.

"And when they were come out of the ship, straightaway they knew *him*, and ran through that whole *region* round about, and began to carry about *in beds* those that were sick, where they heard he was.

"And whithersoever he entered, into villages, or cities, or country, they laid the sick in the streets, and besought him that they might touch if it were but the border of his garment: and as many as touched him were made whole."

ABOUT THE CONTRIBUTORS

GREG BEAR has been a major contributor to the science fiction and fantasy fields throughout the '80s. His novels include *Eon, Blood Music, Eternity*, and *The Infinity Concerto*. He has won two Hugo Awards and three Nebula Awards. He has recently published a collection of stories, *Tangents*. His newest novel is *Queen of Angels*.

DAVID BRIN was recently voted "Favorite Author of the Eighties" by the readers of *Locus* magazine. He has won many science fiction awards for his novels, *Startide Rising* (Nebula, Hugo and Locus), *The Postman* (John W. Campbell Memorial and Locus), and *The Uplift War* (Hugo and Locus), along with a Hugo for his short story, "The Crystal Spheres." "The Giving Plague," which was first published in the U.K., was nominated for a 1989 Hugo Award. His new novel, *Earth*, will be published in the summer of 1990.

EDWARD BRYANT is one of the leading critics in the science fiction and fantasy field as well as an accomplished short story writer. His fiction has been nominated numerous times for major awards and his stories "Stone" and "giAnts" won the Nebula.

DAVID IRA CLEARY is a graduate of the Clarion Workshop. "All Our Sins Forgotten" was his first published story.

MARCOS DONNELLY made his first professional sale with "As a Still Small Voice." He is married to novelist Nancy Kress.

JOSEPH GANGEMI was the youngest graduate ever from the Clarion Workshop. "The Painted Man" was his first published story.

CAROLYN IVES GILMAN has published short fiction in a variety of places, including *Writers of the Future, Volume III*.

KAREN HABER has published stories in several science fiction magazines. Her first novel, *The Mutant Season*, written with her husband Robert Silverberg, was recently published. Its sequel will be published in late 1990. She is also co-editor with Robert Silverberg of the new *Universe* original anthology series.

ELIZABETH HAND has published fiction in *Twilight Zone* and book reviews and criticism in the *Washington Post Book World* and *Science Fiction Eye*. Her first novel, *Winterlong*, will be published later in 1990.

MICHAEL KALLENBERGER made his first professional sale with "Dogs Die."

JAMES KILLUS has been publishing science fiction for several years and has received special attention for his short stories.

JACK MCDEVITT has published two novels, *The Hercules Text* (winner of the Philip K. Dick Special Award and the Locus Award for Best First Novel) and *A Talent for War*. His story "The Fort Moxie Branch" (published in the first *Full Spectrum*) was a Nebula Award finalist.

VONDA N. MCINTYRE is currently in her second decade as a major contributor to science fiction literature. Her novel, *Dreamsnake*, won both the Hugo and Nebula Awards and she also won the Nebula for her story "Of Mist, and Grass, and Sand." She has been nominated for other major awards several times. Her newest novel, *Transition*, (sequel to *Starfarers*) will be published in late 1990.

PATRICIA A. MCKILLIP has written many noted novels, including the fantasy works comprising *The Riddlemaster Trilogy*, the science fiction novel *Fools Run*, and the contemporary novel *Stepping from the Shadows*. "The Doorkeeper of Khaat" is her first science fiction short story.

MIKE MCQUAY is the author of many acclaimed science fiction novels, including *Memories* (winner of the Philip K. Dick Special Award), *The Nexus* and *Jitterbug*. He is currently working on a novel of contemporary American politics, *Puppetmaster*.

DEBORAH MILLION is a graduate of the Clarion Workshop and was a finalist in the Writers of the Future contest.

CHARLES OBERNDORF is a graduate of the Clarion Workshop. His story "Mannequins" appeared in the first *Full Spectrum* anthology. He is currently nearing completion of his first novel, *Sheltered Lives*.

KIM STANLEY ROBINSON has published four novels, *The Wild Shore, Icehenge, The Memory of Whiteness* and *The Gold Coast*, along with a collection of stories, *The Planet on the Table*. His novella "Black Air" won the World Fantasy Award in 1984 and his novella "The Blind Geometer" won the Nebula Award in 1988.

ALAN RODGERS won the Bram Stoker Award for his story "The Boy Who Came Back From the Dead." His first novel, *Blood of the Children*, was published earlier in 1990 and his newest, (*Fire*), will be published in the summer of 1990.

MICHAELA ROESSNER is the author of the novel *Walkabout Woman*, which was recently voted runner-up for the Locus Award for Best First Novel.

JAMES SALLIS has been publishing since the late sixties. He was editor for more than a year of the groundbreaking British SF publication *New Worlds* and has contributed stories and poetry to such publications as *The Bloomsbury Review, The Georgia Review, American Poetry Review* and *The Magazine of Fantasy and Science Fiction*.

ROBERT SAMPSON writes both science fiction and mysteries and won an Edgar Award for short fiction. He also contributed "A Gift of the People" to the first *Full Spectrum* anthology.

STEVEN SPRUILL has published several novels, the most recent of which is *The Paradox Planet*. He is currently at work on a medical thriller.

MICHAEL SWANWICK has been nominated for the Nebula Award for his stories "Ginungagap," "The Feast of Saint Janis," "Trojan Horse," "Marrow Death," "The Gods of Mars" (which he wrote with Gardner Dozois and Jack Dann), and "Godfight" (which he wrote with William Gibson). "Dogfight was also nominated for a Hugo award and another story, "The Man Who Met Picasso," was nominated for the World Fantasy Award. He has published two novels, *In the Drift* and *Vacuum Flowers*.

GAY PARTINGTON TERRY has published short fiction in *Twilight Zone* and wrote the screen play for "Toxic Avenger II."

LORI ANN WHITE is a graduate of the Clarion Workshop. Her short fiction has appeared in several publications, including *Writers of the Future, Volume III*.

The
Spectra Special Editions
Sampler

Here's a special introduction to this exciting program of fantastic fiction by many of todays most visionary writers. On the following pages you can read a brief sample of each Special Editions title currently in print, available wherever Bantam Spectra paperbacks are sold.

THE NEXUS
by Mike McQuay

After Mike McQuay won the Philip K. Dick Special Award for **Memories,** *he followed up with* **The Nexus.** *It is the story of Denny Stiller, a cynical reporter, and Amy Kyle, a young autistic girl who can literally work miracles. Roger Zelazny called it "McQuay's best book to date."*

The man stood, staring down in disbelief at himself. The leg that had a moment before caused anguished cries because of its ugliness was perfectly formed, perfectly normal. Hargrave turned to stare at the camera, an image Denny would never forget as the man's face lit up with a mixture of fright and overwhelming joy in the presence of something beyond belief or understanding.

Not a sound could be heard in the arena as people stared in shocked disbelief, faith rewarded beyond reason, beyond even their dreams or desires.

Denny, still in shock, turned and stared at the camera. What in the name of God had he captured on tape?

He zoomed in on the little girl. She was rocking back and forth, totally oblivious to the excitement around her.

OUT ON BLUE SIX
by Ian McDonald

"Ian McDonald peers at the world from a very strange perspective indeed, one that allows him to create settings and characters unlike those of any other writer," says Science Fiction Chronicle. **Out on Blue Six** *is set hundreds of years in the future when the world is "perfect." Courtney Hall, however, is a fugitive. Her only escape is to drop through a manhole into a strange underground of discontent, a labyrinth of nests and tunnels beneath the surging metropolis.*

She was not alone.

Sometimes the thought terrified her; cold, hostile hands reaching into the cozy little womb she had woven into the underpinnings of New Paris Community Mall. At other times the presence of others/brothers sharing her runways and conduits was almost welcome. The solitude at the bottom of Shaft Twelve was absolute and unbroken. She had drawn one hundred and seventy-four Wee Wendy Waifs on her walls, smiling down like Botticelli angels. For company. They only deepened her sense of isolation. She had always been a solitary creature. The Compassionate Society had made her that way. But there was a world of difference between being solitary and being alone. Before there had always been the possibility of company: the Dario Sanduccis, the Marcus Fordes, and his four and twenty cushioncats. Down in Shaft Twelve there was only herself. And the dream.

PHASES OF GRAVITY
by Dan Simmons

Dan Simmons burst on the scene in 1986 when his first novel, Song of Kali, *won the World Fantasy Award. He has since proved an equal facility for horror (*Carrion Comfort*) and world-building science fiction (*Hyperion *and* The Fall of Hyperion*). Phases of Gravity marks yet another level of Simmons's writing skill. In it an ex-astronaut goes on a personal odyssey looking for something—anything—to equal the experience of standing on the Moon.*

Richard M. Baedecker Day dawned warm and clear. The skies were so blue that cornstalks in the fields visible beyond the new houses seemed brittle with light. Outside, the midmorning heat was already reflecting up from the sidewalks and beginning to soften the asphalt of the highway. Baedecker blinked and tugged his aviator sunglasses out of his shirt pocket. He was wearing the white linen safari shirt, tan cotton slacks, and desert boots he had worn in Calcutta a few weeks earlier. He found it hard to believe that this world of scalded blue sky, flat white storefronts, and empty highway could coexist with the monsoon mud, endless slums, and crowded insanity of India.

The city park was much smaller than he remembered. In Baedecker's mind the bandstand had been an elaborate Victorian gazebo, but all that stood there now was a flat-topped slab of concrete raised on cinder blocks. He doubted if the gazebo had ever existed.

Baedecker sat down on a park bench. His shoulders ached with the weight of things. He closed his eyes again and tried to summon the often-retrieved sensation of bouncing across a glaring, pockmarked plain, the light throwing a corona around Dave's white suit and PLS pack, gravity a lessened foe, each movement as fluid and effortless as moving tiptoe across the bottom of a sunlit lagoon.

The lightness did not come. Baedecker opened his eyes and squinted at the polarized clarity of things.

STRANGE TOYS
by Patricia Geary

Patricia Geary's Philip K. Dick Award-winning novel,
Strange Toys, *carries one young woman named Pat on a
difficult and dangerous journey in a stunningly original novel, blending the real and the unreal in a story of
love, power, and the occult.*

At bedtime, while I was waiting for Linwood to
come kiss me good-night, I opened up my cigar box, the
one that my friend Gaylin had gotten from her father
for me. All my special stuff was stored in the box. When I
opened the lid, the world was made of delicious, endless
possibility.

Sitting there with those things, I had the strangest
feeling . . . I almost wanted to pray to them, but *pray*
wasn't exactly right. Contained in their box, faint aroma
of cigar, they exuded energy, real energy.

And the energy was only for me.

But the weirdest part was, I had this sudden, intense
feeling that somehow, someway these objects were with
me for life. It was as if they had *attached* themselves to
whatever it was that made me *me*. Plus, there was something that could be done with them—what?—as if they
could be made into a kind of machine, a generator to
manufacture . . . what?

UNICORN MOUNTAIN
by Michael Bishop

Michael Bishop has many accomplished novels to his credit, including the Nebula Award-winning No Enemy But Time. Unicorn Mountain *is the story of four fragile human beings who encounter a species of unicorn as beautiful and mysterious as it is vulnerable to a deadly plague. Together the four seek to save the magical beings, and the magic in themselves, from total extinction. Greg Bear called it "a courageous book. Bishop is at the top of his form."*

What was Libby going to do with the herd of stupid unicorns in her pockets? What had made her swipe them? She went down to the gas station at the crossing and asked a burly man in greasy coveralls for a key to the rest room.

Inside, she began pulling glass and pewter unicorns from her coat pockets. She lined them up on the rear of the sink, on the upper edge of the urinal, on the chipped porcelain top of the commode. Beneath the rest room's naked 60-watt bulb, the unicorns either glinted or sparkled. Surveying them in their ranks, Libby congratulated herself on her decorating skills. This was exactly where they belonged.

She pulled a paper towel from another dispenser, found a pen in her shirt pocket, and wrote in block letters on the towel:

THESE AREN'T UNICORNS—THEY'RE COMMERCIAL STEREOTYPES. REDEEM THEM WITH OUR ATTENDANT FOR A FREE GALLON OF GAS OR A STRONG DOSE OF REALITY. ONE TO A CUSTOMER, PLEASE.

MEMORIES
by Mike McQuay

This Philip K. Dick Special Award-winning novel is the story of David Wolf, an embittered psychiatrist, and Silv, a woman from one hundred decades in the future who takes him on an extraordinary odyssey through time. Locus *magazine called it "cause for great celebration.* Memories *stands with a small handful of science fiction novels that successfully convey the pain and wonder of being alive."*

There was a voice and a vision.

The voice tried to reason with him, to calm him down. But the vision was everything. Crystal clear it was, and fraught with understanding. It showed him the history of the world, his world, and beyond. There were no bombs in this world. There was only the gradual deterioration of self-indulgence. It was the inevitability that wore him down, the monster of selfishness that waits to destroy everything. The visions crammed out everything else. Poisons in the land, in the water, in the air, in the populations—a world worn out, unable to support itself. Life in the dark, underground, far underground. The vision was bleak with despair, without hope, like his dreams. But he knew, really knew, the vision was real. There was no hope. There was no future.

Davy Wolf was twelve years old, and hope was his mainstay.

He closed in. He couldn't even hear himself screaming, even after they had come and taken him away.

STRANGE INVASION
by Michael Kandel

Until recently, Michael Kandel was known strictly for his superlative translations of Stanislaw Lem's work, for which he was nominated twice for the National Book Award. With his first novel, Strange Invasion, he has become an author in his own right. Before the Washington Post Book World *proclaimed the novel "A winner," authors in the field had already declared him one of their own. Hugo and Nebula Award-winner George Alec Effinger said "[Kandel's] work is wholly original and dangerously twisted, in just the way that science fiction needs to be twisted every once in a while."*

I opened the letter. It read:

Mr. Griffith:
　　We feel that one who every day must cope—and who copes successfully—with an exotic neurological disorder that causes him to suffer alarming hallucinations regularly, yet who notwithstanding this affliction remains on a tolerant, even friendly footing with his mind—we feel that such a person is eminently suited to fill the difficult position of guardian against the Öht.

"The Öht?" I asked.
The phone rang.
"They are, you might say, tourists," a voice began conversationally when I picked up the receiver. "'Tourist' may not sound threatening, but consider what tourists are and what they do."
"Who is this?"
"Tourists," the voice went on, "show no respect. They track mud in a museum, eat potato chips in a temple. With their chewing gum and transistor radios they demoralize the natives."
It took a lot, these days, to make me scream. . . .

NO ENEMY BUT TIME
by Michael Bishop

We're proud to be able to include not one but two of Michael Bishop's novels in the Spectra Special Editions line. No Enemy But Time *is Bishop's Nebula Award-winning novel about a man who, because of his unique abilities, is chosen to travel back through time to the Pleistocene era. Greg Bear called it "a courageous book. Bishop is at the top of his form."*

The ground is only a body length below me. For the present, though, I gaze upward into a column of space furnished with the arcane equipment that has helped me make this transfer. The rest of the omnibus—the tire, the chassis, the body—is utterly invisible, for it exists in material fact only in the final fifth of the twentieth century. Briefings and simulations have not prepared me for the *weirdness* of this effect, and I peer into this hovering hole in the Pleistocene sky like a fretful Alice regretting her introduction to Wonderland.

GYPSIES
by Robert Charles Wilson

"Grounded in our deepest longings, the premise of **Gypsies** *fascinates," says the* New York Times Book Review *of Robert Charles Wilson's third engrossing novel, a tense flight through alternate worlds. "A blend of science fiction, mystery, and thriller . . . spellbinding," said* Publishers Weekly.

"Divorce" wasn't the only unmentionable word around Michael's house. Deeper and more disturbing was this business of the Gray Man.

Michael had seen him for the first time when he was ten years old. They were driving cross-country and they had stopped at a gas station along the highway somewhere out in Alberta. A hot day, car windows down, nothing but blank space and blue horizon and this shanty filling station, some old guy pumping gas, and in the shade of the plankboard souvenir store, obscure amidst all this clutter and dust: the Gray Man. The Gray Man peered out from under a gray slouch hat with a fixed, attentive look Michael remembered, too vividly, from his dreams.

Terrified, Michael looked to his mother, but his mother had seen the Gray Man at the same time and she was terrified, too. He could tell by the way she was breathing, tight little gulps of air. Dad was paying the pump jockey, attention focused on his credit card as it ratcheted through the stamper in the old man's hand, worlds away. Michael opened his mouth to speak but his mother laid a warning hand on his arm. Like a message: *Your father won't understand.* And it was true. He knew it without thinking about it. This was something he shared with his mother, and only with his mother. This fear. This mystery.

A HIDDEN PLACE
by Robert Charles Wilson

Robert Charles Wilson gained immediate recognition with this, his first novel. The San Francisco Chronicle *praised him as "clearly a writer to watch"; the* Ottawa Citizen *called* **A Hidden Place** *"an astonishing debut." It's the story of two young lovers, a beautiful, haunted woman from another world, and the mysterious stranger who shares her awesome secret.*

It was strong, he thought, this thing that was special about her—stronger the closer he got to her. Touching her, it seemed as if she had come somehow to embody everything connected with the female sex, was not so much a single woman as an aggregation of femininity. He stroked her perfect cheek, and she trembled.

"Anna?"

Her eyes were still closed. The tremor in her grew stronger.

She twitched in his arms, then convulsed.

Abruptly he was frightened. "Anna? *Anna!*"

She was shaking now, rivers of mysterious energy pouring through her. Her eyes came open suddenly—

And Travis gazed into them.

It was a mistake. In that moment she was not Anna Blaise. She was not even a woman.

Not human.

THE CITY, NOT LONG AFTER
by Pat Murphy

Only eight science fiction and fantasy titles published in 1989 are recommended as "Notable Books of the Year" by the New York Times Book Review. *Pat Murphy's latest novel is among them. Set in San Francisco after a plague has wiped out most life on earth, it is a powerful follow-up to her Nebula Award-winning* **The Falling Woman.**

Dawn broke in the city: gray light shone on the gray stone buildings that surrounded the Civic Center Plaza. The statues on the facade of the public library showed signs of neglect. Over the years, pigeons had adorned the statues' heads with streaks of white and had deposited a clutter of feathers and broken nests at their feet.

In a tree that grew in the Plaza, a gray-muzzled monkey, one of the oldest of the troop that lived in the city, dreamed of the Himalayas. Icicles hanging from the eaves of a temple roof melted in the morning sun. Drops of falling water struck a bell, and the metal rang with a musical note. The water trickled away, whispering and crackling softly as it melted a path through the snow. The monkey stirred in its sleep. Changes were coming.

MEMORY WIRE
by Robert Charles Wilson

Called "profound and beautiful . . . a tense thriller" by Orson Scott Card, **Memory Wire** *is the story of a man who chooses to give up his past and his future to become an Eye, an all-seeing, unfeeling human video recorder. But when he meets a beautiful and haunted young artist in terrible trouble, he must struggle to overcome these changes.*

Keller knew it was dangerous surgery. The Army did it a dozen times daily, but still it was dangerous. It could not be otherwise, messing with your brain.

"It's hard work," the medics warned him. "It's not a free ride. If you're an Angel there's an attitude you have to cultivate. *Wu-nien.* You know what that means, Mr. Keller? It means you're a machine. You don't think, you look. You don't look where you want, you look where it matters. You *are* a camera. You're not there to *do* the work. You *are* the work.

Keller understood perfectly. Byron had already taught him a little Angel Zen. *To see without desire. The perfect mirror.*

"You won't be Raymond Keller anymore. What you want, what you care about, you have to learn to leave it all behind. You're a pair of eyes, a pair of ears. That's all.

Keller thought it sounded pretty good.

RUMORS OF SPRING
by Richard Grant

Richard Grant has published three novels to date, in-cluding the Philip K. Dick Special Award-winning Sara-band of Lost Time *and* Views from the Oldest House. Rumors of Spring *was his second novel. The* San Fran-cisco Examiner *called it "wry, hilarious, human . . . a joy." The* Los Angeles Daily News *called it "a rare and marvelous tale." It is set during a time in our future when much of the world has gone cold and when a group of Crusaders venture into the heart of the one forest which continues to grow.*

If a change occurs in a forest when no one is around, who will understand it?

Early in the third century, as though driven by some new spirit akin to wanderlust, the forest began climbing the edges of its glacier-scooped bed. By yards and then by miles it extended itself onto mountainsides that had lately been held by ice. For a decade at a time, it would pause, thickening its trunks along the high frontier, be-fore again hurling pine-cone grenades against ramparts of stone and resuming its slow advance. Finally—five hundred years after that summer of heat and death—it unfurled its green banners on the mountaintop. Its ad-vance guard of eagles soared into the skies of an unac-customed world.

Unlike the other great forests in that world, the Car-bon Bank Forest had found a way to survive. But like the rest of them, it had become something remarkably different.

ABOUT THE EDITORS

LOU ARONICA is the Publisher of Mass Market Paperbacks at Bantam Books. He lives in Connecticut with his wife, Barbara and their daughter, Molly.

SHAWNA MCCARTHY has edited several previous anthologies and was the editor of *Isaac Asimov's Science Fiction Magazine* for several years and was a Senior Editor at Bantam Books. She won the Hugo Award for Best Professional Editor in 1984. She lives in Manhattan with her husband Wayne Barlowe, and their daughter, Cayley.

AMY STOUT is an Executive Editor at Bantam Books and previously worked at *Issac Asimov's Science Fiction Magazine*. She lives in Manhattan with her husband, Alan Rodgers.

PATRICK LOBRUTTO was a Senior Editor at Doubleday Books. He lives in New Jersey with his wife, Kathy, and their daughter, Jennifer.